Other Books by Author

The Crystals of Syre:

Book 1: Awakening

Book 2: Revelation

Book 3: Ancestry (in the works)

Book 4: Restitution (planned)

A Colorado Cowboy Romance Story:

My Texas Streak

Call Me Home

Forever Love (planned)

Assassins' Guild of Obseen:

Vision of a Torn Land (Prequel Book)

Book 1: The Cost of Redemption

Secrets of the Past (in the works)

The Crystals of Syre

Book Two: Revelation

By Lindsey Cowherd

ISBN: 978-1-7345691-0-0
Self-Published by Lindsey Cowherd
Cover art by SelfPubBookCovers.com/riafritz

"For things to reveal themselves to us, we need to be ready to abandon our views about them." — Thích Nhât Hanh

The Kingdoms of Syre

(Note: this list only includes characters from each kingdom that are mentioned in this book. Other characters will continue into Book 3.)

"**Six Companions**" refers to: Anibus Farryl, Patrick Kins, Jacen Novano, Rio Ravesbend, Merchant Roland Seagold, and apprentice Sage Cooper (deceased)

Crystal:

Royal Household:
King Lanar Starkindler;
wife: Queen Lestial
Children:
Heir: Prince Lance Starkindler
Second son: Page Starkindler
Third son: Zeek Starkindler
Daughter: Zeera Starkindler

Crystine Cavalry:

Commander Matar (aka: *Khataum*)
Second-in-Command: Wix
Lieutenant: Madden
Second: Cole Hayden

Staria:

Royal Household:
King Merretham Maushelik
Wife: Selene (deceased; former Duchess of Port Al-Harrad)
Heir: Prince Al'den Reddiar Maushelik

Military:

First Guardsman: Meeg Thorson
Captain: Sean Woodman, Starian cavalry
Lieutenant-Commander: Terrance

Starian Court (mentioned):

Lord William and Lady Rosetta Greyson
Lady Diane Levine
Lady Selena Durrow
Lady Kaitlin Lepree
Lady Rosa Quartlett
Zale Herth

Sheev'anee:

Sheev'arid:
Shi'alam: Sheev'arid
Son: Terrik Sheev'arid
Daughter: Zyanthena Sheev'arid
Khapta to Terrik: Decond (former farrier from Crystal)
Nephew: Kor'mauk Siv'arid
Niece: Shaul'auna Siv'arid
Cousin: En'ril Savam'eed
His *khapta*: J'iya Tav'eem

Other clansmen:
Siv'arid cousins: Kor'ar and Kor'moon
Scout: Re'shaird Aerrisson
Retainer: Shy'tin

All'ani:
Cum'ar All'ani
Sister: Lan'esha All'ani
Cousin: Kei'shkï Siv'ala

Others:
"Three Kala": Shík Savam'eed, Shík Cum'eri, Shík All'aum
Oracle

Kavahad:

Lord-Governor Darshel Shekmann
Friend: Viscount Markus LaPoint

Cousin: Jeremy Freedman
Advisor: Abrus

Kavahadian Cavalry:
Commander Raic (deceased)
Second Commander: Gordon
Lieutenant Dawson

Rubia:
Royal Household:
King Corbin Chível
Heir: Prince Derek Chível;
(his heir: Miguel)
Other:
Lord Protector: Yory Selèv

Mertinean (Military):
Commander Ethan Kins
Son: Patrick Kins
Commander Tyk: Raven's Den
Commander Grant: Raven's Den
Lieutenant-Commander Curtis Marx
(under Comm. Kins)
Commander Dane Price (palace guards)

Sunrise:
Royal Household:
King Raymond Sunrise
Wife: Queen Sylvia
Children:
Heir: Rowin Sunrise
Second Son: Connel Sunrise
Other:
Lord Protectors: Rio
Ravesbend, Elis Thorpson (deceased)

Sunarian Army:
Commander Loris Ravesbend
Second-in-Command Bradon
Thane Cornell

Blue Haven:
Royal Household:
King Jarod Eldon
Wife: Queen Elise Eldon-Tomino
Children:
Heir: Prince Jace Eldon
Princess Éleen Eldon-Tomino
Two daughters (not mentioned)
Cousin: Jessi Clayton

Others:
Lord Nexlé of Zircon
Son: Carrod Nexlé (Lord Protector to
Princess Éleen)
Personal Advisor: Camu Doln

Soldiers: First Guardsman Jauken
Lautvine
Commander Hartford
Captain John Corbus, Ensign Danver

Golden:
Royal Household:
King Gregory Argetlem; wife (deceased)
Children:
Heir: Prince Kent Argetlem
Other:
Lord Protector: Lieutenant-Commander
Eric Sloane (deceased)

Golden Military:
Lord-commander Nicól Ivance (Sardon,
capital)
Lord Aeronson (royal advisor; former
lord-commander)
Commander Charles Hadley; Colonel
Jared Deed (archers)
Officer Keatten (archers)

Sealand:

Royal Household:
King William Fantill;
Wife: Queen Kesnia
Children:
Heir: Par Fantill
Daughter: Celeste
Other:
Lord Protector: Lord Gordar Farrylin
Cousin: Priest Anibus Farryl

Landarian Court (Mentioned):

Duke and Duchess Limonté
Daughter: Yvonne

Others:

Swordmaker: Ferris Galandrés
Eminary: Paulrē Esquire
Nuns: Nadine, Cādene, Sari, Giselle, Catlene
Girl: Rosemary Myler

Sealand Militia

Commander Averron
Lieutenants Marcus and Tennet

Crystalynian:

Royal House:
King Trev'shel Xraxrain
Queen: Kestral (both deceased)
Children:
Heir: Verrin
Daughter: Arrez

Bil'cordys Militia:

General Curtis Mooreland
Commander Paget
Commander Corbin
Lieutenant-Commander Berg
Lieutenant-Commander Newman
Colonel Perry
Duke Merrymount of Westview

Wolves of Crystanian:

Alpha: Swift Hunter;
Mate: Moon Ember
Others: Long Scar, Howler, Autumn, Too Soon, Tiny, Sky Walker, Rowdy, Far Tracker, Quiet Stalker, Silent (aka "talks-too-much")

Maunstorz (People of Xercon):

Xercon'vlr: Zephthaniel
Seka'vlr: Mansocan
First: Rokell
Second: Silvarron
Third: Chornauk
Fourth: Nan'an
Fifth: Chaenyeu

Stones of Syre:

Bellor; jade (Blue Haven)
Ravel; diamond (Rubia)
Amun; citrine (Staria)
Kevel; ruby (Sunrise)
Sevén; pearl (Golden)
Vauldin; obsidian (Crystalynian)
Serein; sapphire (Sealand)

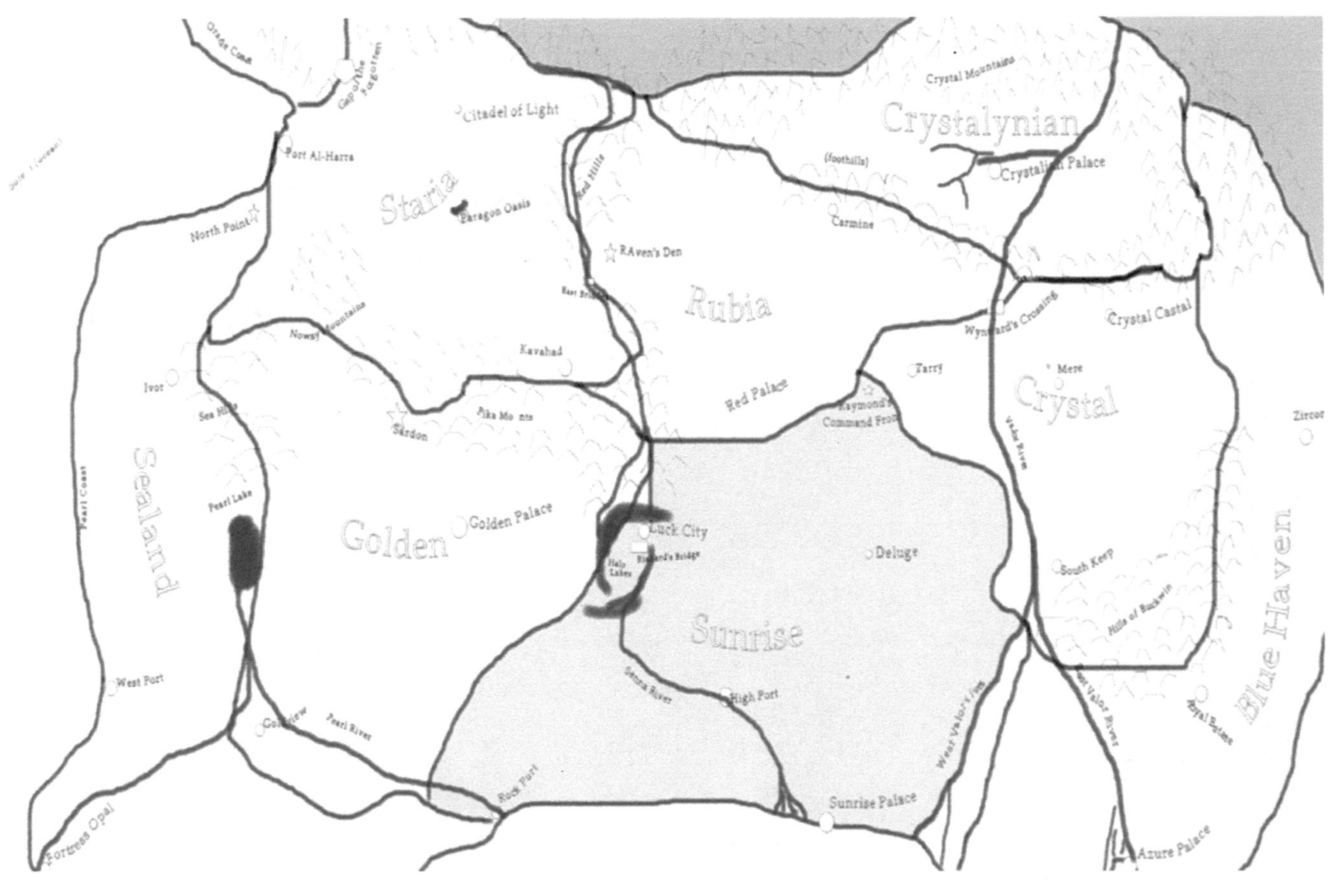

Orade Coast
Cap of the Forgotten
Citadel of Light
Port Al-Harra
Staria
Paragon Oasis
North Point
Crystal Mountains
Crystalynian
Crystalian Palace
(foothills)
Carmine
Red Hills
RAven's Den
Rubia
Kavahad
Nowsy Mountains
Ivor
Sea Hills
Sardon
Red Palace
Raymond's Command Post
Tarry
Wynward's Crossing
Crystal Castal
Mere
Crystal
Zircon
Valor River
Sealand
Pearl Coast
Pearl Lake
Golden
Golden Palace
Luck City
Halo Lakes
Deluge
South Keep
Hills of Buckwin
Blue Haven
Sunrise
West Port
High Port
Senna River
Pearl River
Rock Port
Sunrise Palace
West Valor River
Royal Estate
Fortress Opal
Azure Palace

Prologue

§

Crystalynian
(88 SC, Storage and Gathering Time)

I

"Majesties! Majesties!" The servant came scampering into the billiard room with no decorum. He startled the two kings, who were waiting anxiously with their brandies by the fireplace. King Trev'shel Xraxrain, ruler of Crystalynian, and his friend, King Richard of Sunrise, looked up from their conversation in anticipation.

"Is it time?" King Trev'shel asked, setting his drink, already forgotten, on the mantle.

"Sire—sires." The man bowed. "It is, Majesty. The baby comes!"

The two kings beamed at each other and clasped hands. It was hard to tell which of them was happier. "Take us to them," the Crystalynian ruler bade his man. The servant was quick to comply, leading the two warrior-kings up the west landing to the queen's chambers.

The midwife was already leaving the room as they arrived. She looked pleased but exhausted. "Your Majesty," she bowed, beaming. "You have a beautiful daughter. A little fighter, that she is. And strong lungs in that one."

"Thank you, Margareet." The king clasped her hands. "Your assistance with the birth was greatly appreciated."

"Of course, Your Majesty. I'll get to say I was at the little princess's birthing. I will remember the honor as long as I live. Now, if you will excuse me, I have need of a little refreshment for myself."

"Go. I will stay with my wife for as long as you need."

The midwife and the servant, both of whom looked in great need of food and rest, left the two kings. Continuing to the bedchamber, the kings saw the little girl for the first time, and saw her mother, whom both men loved dearly.

"Welcome, darling husband and dearest friend. I promise our little girl will be the sweetest sight you've ever seen." Queen Kestral lifted a hand to them while she cradled the swaddled babe in the other. Though the queen's long, raven hair was drenched in sweat, the warrioress and stone-bearer of Crystalynian looked proud and glowing over her accomplishment of bringing the baby into the world. Her prompting brought the men closer. "Take her," Kestral bade Trev'shel. Her radiant smile turned teasing as the great king took the babe overcautiously.

"It's been so long since I've held a child," Trev'shel said to explain his nervousness. Indeed, their son and heir, Verrin, was a young man; seventeen years had passed since his birthing.

"Ah, it'll come back quickly enough," King Richard said as he peeked around the baby's blanket to the little one's face. "She's got her mother's eyes."

"And her father's temperament," Kestral added. "You should have seen her those first few moments. She'll be a feisty one. I can tell already."

"Good. Feisty like her parents." Richard squeezed the queen's fingers and leaned over the bed to give her a kiss on the cheek. "You did well, *Kest'auleen*," he said, giving the queen her Keshic nickname of "desert bird."

"Oh, you flatter me," she teased back. "'Shel, give him the child before he hurts himself on compliments."

The two men laughed, and Trev'shel passed the little princess to the man they had decided would be the girl's godfather and guardian. The decision had been anonymously agreed upon by everyone. Seeing the Sunarian king holding the little babe in his arms, they knew the choice had been right; King Richard Sunrise was already wrapped around the little one's finger. *"Aerrezín,"* the Sunarian whispered to the child in Keshic. *"Aerrezín ĕshaum,"* he called her, meaning "precious one to me."

"Hm," Trev'shel murmured. "Yes, that would be her name—but perhaps it is too hard for the Crystani people to say?"

"Then, Arrez," Queen Kestral provided.

"My gem," King Richard murmured and nodded. "I think that is true. This girl is the jewel of Crystalynian, far more precious than even Vauldin himself."

"Yes." Kestral had reached up to the obsidian stone around her neck. "She is and will always be. The line of the Xraxrain matriarchs has always produced strong-blooded women of valor and esteem. I feel little Arrez will be just as great."

"Getting ahead of ourselves, aren't we?" Trev'shel teased as he leaned in to give his wife a kiss.

"Never, my king."

Richard chuckled and cooed to the babe as he gently bounced her. "I think this little gem will be every bit as esteemed as her parents. No child born of Crystani and Sheev'anee blood could be anything less. I can't wait to see her grow and learn to ride horses and wield swords."

"Now who's ahead of it?" the Crystalynian king said to his wife as he sat beside her. "Our daughter's guardian is already weaving plans to bring up the next warrioress of Crystalynian."

"Oh, she'll be taught in your people's ways," Kestral agreed. "She has Sheev'anee blood in her veins. Arrez will have the same desire to fight and lead as her father." Her husband was a tenth-level *she-koum-o* practitioner, only one of twelve Tashek to hold such an honor. His clan name, Tamar'in, had been dropped when he agreed to marry into the Xraxrains; however, he was still a notable Guardian to the second Shík of the Sheev'anee.

Queen Kestral had fancied the desert nomads' culture since she was a young child, especially with one blood relative able to trace her line back to the Sheev'arid clan of Staria. Because of her interest, the second princess of Crystalynian had been a frequent guest to the House of Staria and its nomadic kinsmen. Her ascension to queen, after her elder sister's death during childbirth, had not diminished her desire to incorporate Sheev'anee fighting and horse husbandry techniques into Crystalynian's own programs—no matter the opposition from the Crystani court.

"Or maybe she'll be genteel, like Aunt Corinthina was. You shouldn't be trying to mold my little sister's future so soon after her arrival into our world."

The three rulers looked up to greet Prince Verrin and his betrothed, Princess Marínna Chível, third princess of the Rubian crown, as they entered the chamber to greet the new baby. A fine young man, Prince Verrin looked very much like his father, with Tashek traits of light copper skin and dark features. Steady and centered, he was the calming storm opposing Trev'shel's domineering nature. Together, father and son made an imposing command on the battlefield.

"May I see her?" Princess Marínna asked, holding out her arms to King Richard. As soft and delicate as a pale flower, she was smitten with any little one she could lay a hand upon; Princess Arrez was in good hands with her soon-to-be sister-in-law.

"Gently, gently," Richard fretted as he passed the babe over.

"You worry like a first-time mother," Marínna teased as she took Arrez. "And here I thought you've already dealt with a baby boy?" King Sunrise had a five-year-old son, Rowin, back in his home kingdom.

"Boys, as far as I've seen, are far less delicate."

Marínna tsked. "Not a Crystani girl." She rocked Arrez and cooed to her softly. "You'll see, this little one will be strong and independent." The princess brought the bundled babe over to her brother so the two could become acquainted. Prince Verrin looked awkward to be confronted with something so small. "She'll be taken with you, big brother."

"Oh, I don't know about that," Verrin replied, though he did reach out a finger to his new sister. "She and I are so distant in age. I'll be more like another father figure to her than a brother."

"Not that I'll allow," Marínna countered and grinned as Arrez took hold of her brother's available finger and pulled it close to suck. Verrin seemed stupefied by the action.

"Enough taking up my little gem's time." Richard came over to collect the babe once more. "She's my little gem, and I'm calling rights on holding her the most."

The child's parents shared a laugh, happy to see their dearest friend and paramour being so possessive of the child. It had been their entire reasoning for naming him Arrez's guardian. "Just so, our dearest." Kestral smiled. "Makes sure 'Shel get his own turn."

"He'll have plenty of it soon enough. Now that Arrez has arrived, I'll have no more reason to stay away from Sunrise and my court. I've stayed two weeks too long as it is."

"Indeed," Trev'shel agreed, though he was saddened by the fact. Neither he nor Kestral got to see their friend as much as they liked. Being king, Richard could not call off from his duties often and only visited periodically throughout the seasons. It meant their short times together were spent with as much love and companionship as possible, but they left all feeling doleful at the last. Still, the arrangement kept their paramour relationship secret from all but a select few who knew the truth. It seemed a connection worth fighting for.

"Speaking of," Prince Verrin cut in, "I came to say that a Starian report has come from our western outposts."

Kestral frowned at her son. "Verrin, I told you I've no wish to hear of such matters on this day."

"Oh, I know, Mother, but this missive is important. It seems—"

"We will hear of this outside," Trev'shel interrupted and asked that the three men be excused so as to not sully the birthing room with wartime matters. He gave one last kiss to baby Arrez's head before Richard passed the babe back to her mother. Reluctantly, the two kings pulled themselves away from the loves of their lives. Shutting the door, Trev'shel turned a sour frown on his son. "What news dictates ruining such an occasion?"

Verrin bowed and extended the missive. "My apologies, Father. King Merretham sends word of enemy skirmishes increasing in number all along northern Staria. His men report more battles moving eastward and find their numbers alarming. Speculation of influxes into the woods north of Rubia make them think something could be brewing with these maunstorz."

The term *maunstorz* was still new to the people of Syre; the Mausheliks had begun to use the name found in ancient texts left from Syre's Second Age. The Ancestors had written accounts of these maunstorz—the old Syrean spelling for creatures of nightmare—near the end of the Golden Age. They were cursed things, with red eyes white hair, that spoke a guttural tongue. The enemies that had appeared in this Third Age certainly fit the description of the Ancients' maunstorz.

"It's rather close to First Snows to be seeing such activity," Richard said as he viewed the missive over Trev'shel's shoulder.

"Exactly King Merretham's point," Verrin agreed. "He requests that a council be called for the eight stone-bearers."

Trev'shel's eyes narrowed in concern at everything the missive contained. "A council will take five weeks to call—sooner if a horse can reach Prince Lanar Starkindler. Anything later will be hindered by the snows."

"These occurrences seem more in need of generals and commanders than the Stones of Power," Richard voiced. He himself was the heir to Kevel, the ruby stone of Sunrise, but he still preferred traditional methods over those of majik (the ancient Syrean word for magic).

"Only armies of Rubia, Staria, and here could move to a call so close to First Snows, but I doubt we could feed them all. But I do prefer Merretham's idea of using magical means to handle this foe. Eight stone-bearers are much easier to assemble."

"That's assuming First Prince Jarod Éldon or King Gregory Argetlem would come to such a call." Given that King Gregory had been just newly crowned that Snow Thaw, it seemed far from likely. "And Prince William Fantill hates to be away from Sealand for longer than one month."

"Then we'll enlist Prince Lanar to teleport everyone here."

Richard sighed. "Wearing him out just to get everyone assembled in a timely manner seems selfish."

"We have always come to everyone else's requests," Trev'shel countered. "They can return the favor."

"But you wouldn't ask Marínna to fight, would you?" Verrin sounded alarmed. His betrothed was Sheveth's new stone-bearer, but she was untried in anything beyond simple spells.

"No, of course not, my son." Trev'shel put a hand on his shoulder. "Marínna would help heal the wounded and construct barricades. The real battles would be left to the wielders who can fight."

Richard frowned. "The numbers Merretham writes of are more than we can expect majik to deal with. Real soldiers need to be called."

"Then I'll request the Sheev'anee and Starian forces."

"We need mertinean and Crystine too," said Richard. "I will request them of Prince Lanar."

"And I'll go with you," Verrin elected. "My ties with Rubia will be a great help on enlisting mertinean."

Trev'shel seemed reluctant, but the other king was quick to agree. "That would be best for all involved. We shan't create a political gaffe by asking too much. I trust in your negotiating skills with King Corbin Chível. You, at least, have a rapport."

"Thank you, Father."

Richard nodded. "Prepare to leave in the morning, then. We'll ride at the fastest pace the horses can handle. I'll leave it to you to pick out our escort."

"Right. Thank you, sire!" Prince Verrin saluted the Sunarian king and turned heel to get their trip arranged.

Trev'shel was frowning as his son left. "You will take care of my son," he said. "Verrin looks up to you as one of the greatest leaders of our time. I'm afraid that adulation could make him reckless on the field."

"Don't worry, my friend. I would not let harm befall him. It's my promise to you, *paramouré*." Richard squeezed his arm in reassurance.

"Now, however, I need to pick out a horse. I was thinking that young black one that Kestral was training. He looked robust and capable."

"The black one? Oh, you mean our queen's pride and joy: Veiled Darkness, colt of her own Ruelle of the Valley. I'm not sure she'd let you take him."

There was a gleam in Richard's eyes. "Oh? Just watch me." He grinned a challenge and went to ask the queen for the colt. He returned to the hallway shortly, gloating his victory. "*Kest'auleen* loves me. She says the colt is mine to fly the winds with—if he accepts me."

Trev'shel tsked in pseudo-indignation. "I see. When our paramour is around, only he gets all the favors."

"And her husband gets all her love all the times besides," Richard teased back. "Come, show me to Veiled Darkness. We're to get acquainted before the morrow."

"I'm not sure the colt the best choice for a trip south," Trev'shel cautioned.

"On the contrary, I'll bet the colt has the endurance of his sire. He'll be the focus of Crystanian's eyes as I ride to the castle."

"You just like making a grand entrance."

"A king's allowed his frivolities."

They made their way to the royal stables on the western side of the palace. The horse-master greeted the kings with bows and directed them to the outmost pens, where the black colt in question was. The horse-master turned away to procure tack while the kings headed outside.

Veiled Darkness was a stunning young stallion, black as midnight and with a temperament of fire. Among the other horses of Crystalynian, he was a king in his own right.

"He's a lot of horse," King Trev'shel voiced again. "Most of the staff avoids him, and only Kestral can control his fury. He would not be my choice for a mount."

"I'm not looking to control him," the Sunarian said. "An animal like that needs only to know you are in command—with good reason. Forcing him will do no good."

Richard stepped to the gate. Already, horse and man were in a stare-down. Without taking his eyes from the colt, the king collected up the halter and let himself into the pen. Staying calm but confident, Richard strode deeper into the colt's lair. He halted about twenty paces from the snorty black. "How would you like to get out of this confinement and run with the winds?" he asked the fiery horse.

Veiled Darkness looked every part of his war courser breeding. With long limbs, a strong bone structure, and muscles that were more profound than a sculpture, the colt looked built for a long campaign at war. It was the proud look in his eyes that spoke of his demanding nature to be respected to the utmost. The Sunarian king enjoyed that trait. Here was a horse fit only for the greatest of men.

"So, what will it be, young one?" he asked, and held out a hand in invitation. In this game, Richard knew he should not step further into the colt's domain until invited.

Veiled Darkness stood at attention, his nostrils flaring at the stranger who threatened his space; however, the man did not approach or retreat further, which seemed to ease the tension thrumming through the horse's body. For a breath count of three minutes, it seemed as if neither king nor colt would yield, but then, the black became curious at the lack of advance. Cautiously, the colt took one step and then another toward the stranger, staying wary of any threat. It was only when his velvety nose stretched out to smell the king's offered hand that it seemed there was progress to be had.

"That's it," Richard murmured and reached out to pet the black's neck. The colt skittered back at the touch but stopped a few feet away. "There's no need for that," the Sunarian said, and stepped in an arc around the horse until the black yielded his hindquarters to him. Veiled Darkness turned so that his head was back near the stranger's shoulder and in a position to be haltered. "So, shall we go?"

The king stepped a little closer to Veiled Darkness's left shoulder. He slipped a section of the halter around the black's neck and nudged the colt to bend his head around him. Understanding, the colt bobbed his head toward the open noseband of the halter and pushed into it. After that, haltering the rest of the way was easy. "That's it." Richard smiled and stroked the colt's shoulder. "We'll get along just fine, won't we?"

Trev'shel was shaking his head as the pair returned to the gate. "I swear you've got horse whisperer in your veins. You speak to him almost as well as Kestral."

Richard patted the black. "Yes, well, I've got nothing on our lady with the ability of animal-speak, but I can learn a few things."

"Veiled Darkness is very selective. Most people, he'd rather trample and intimidate."

"And it would be all bluff. But I won't let him get one past me."

"Well, shall we tack up and ride to Bil'cordys?"

Richard nodded and led Veiled Darkness through the gate his paramour opened, and then the kings headed back up the lane to the stables.

Waving away assistance from the stable hands, the two men tacked up their mounts and headed away. King Trev'shel's horse, a dark grey of Keshic descent, seemed small in comparison to the tall black; however, the desert mount proved more than an adversary as the two kings let the chargers go in a game of who's-the-fastest. In the end, Veiled Darkness got a slight lead as the sight of Bil'cordys, one mile north of Crystanian, came into view. The war chargers were pulled up to a cooling walk as they entered the town's outer limits.

Bil'cordys was the post of the kingdom's army. Hosting three thousand soldiers and their families, it was dedicated to the arts of war: training of the regiments in weaponry and strategy, as well as the practice of battlefield medicines. Not a city for commerce, it was dedicated solely to the protection of Crystalynian.

The two kings continued through the town until they came to the central command building. Dismounting and hitching their horses at the front, they entered the long, two-story structure and headed for the main general's office. General Curtis Mooreland was King Trev'shel's eyes and ears on affairs away from the capital. He would know best the situation on their western front.

A young officer was at the receiving desk. He was quick to attention and saluted the arrival of the two rulers. "Majesties!"

"At ease, man," Trev'shel bade. "I'm here for General Mooreland. Is he about?"

"Aye, sire. I will notify him of your arrival immediately."

"Thank you, officer."

To the lad's credit, he was quick to get the kings in to see the general, and Mooreland knew better than to ignore the king at his door. "Come in, Majesty… Majesties. Sit. May I pour some brandy?"

"Please, General, and thank you," the Crystalynian king agreed politely and waited for the drinks to be served before continuing.

"General, I received word from King Merretham of enemies amassing to our west. Have you heard of this?"

"Majesty, yes," Mooreland began as he settled himself in his chair. "There have been various reports from towns on the western border, new sightings of these... cursed men of Starian myth."

"Maunstorz of white hair, red eyes, and guttural speech?"

"Yes, sire. There seem to be more accounts of their camps seen in the wilds of the west. Though much of those forests are uncharted, town watches have reported campfires seen in the distance at night. Their numbers grow."

"As Merretham said," Richard agreed. "Do you have an estimate of their numbers?"

"It is uncertain, Majesty. Sightings are scattered, so reports estimate as little as one hundred enemies, all the way to the thousands."

"That's rather significant, that difference," the Sunarian complained.

"Yes, sire. It is."

"Quite concerning," Trev'shel agreed, finding the tallies too varied. "I, being a cautious man, opt for believing the worst."

"As do I." Richard rose from his chair to walk off the anxiety from hearing such news. "Such numbers make me desire immediate correspondence to Crystal and Rubia."

"Indeed, my friend." The other king waved for calm. "But you travel for that need on the morrow, so be less pressed. As for us," Trev'shel asked of General Mooreland, "do we have more troops ready to march to the west's aid?"

"Yes, sire. I've alerted five regiments to leave in three days, and a cavalry commander has voiced his desire to head out immediately, once supplies are packed."

"I grant them all leave to do so. Is it Commander Paget who is champing at the bit to go?" The man was known for his haste.

"Yes. Paget is the man."

"Always so reliable. You can tell him I appreciate that quality."

"Aye, Majesty, I will pass that along."

"Good, my thanks. And the other units?"

"Ah." Mooreland searched his docket. "Commander Corbin, Lieutenant-Commanders Berg and Newman, Colonel Perry, and Duke Merrymount of Westview."

"Good men all." Trev'shel approved of the list. Each man had a proven battle record. Of all in Bil'cordys, they were the most veteran of the different divisions. "Give them everything they need. I trust in your wisdom to know where each will be of the most use."

"I thank you, Majesty." Mooreland bowed from his waist.

"That is not idle breath, my good general. You've served me well all these years. Having you at the helm gives me relief." King Trev'shel finished his drink and stood. "Now, let's have a look at those maps…"

Looking over the Syrean maps took nearly an hour. General Mooreland pointed out the various sightings of the enemy, as well as how all the forces were positioned—including those he knew of from Staria and Rubia. All their forces looked ready to act against any unusual activity from the maunstorz.

By the time their meeting was concluded, it was nearing noon. The two kings left the general to his duties and headed away to the local mess hall and bakehouse, a large building in the center of town committed to feeding all the soldiers. Gossip from the men would be easy to hear over a hearty meal of mashed potatoes, pork, and root vegetables with bread and soup. The army of Crystalynian was well fed to keep the soldiers healthy through their vigorous training and deployments.

Afterward, their business took them to the smithy, where Trev'shel had ordered a fighting sword to be fashioned for Prince Lanar Starkindler. "Soon to be coronated, if rumors are correct." He winked at Richard. "I was hoping this beauty could help soothe negotiations with Crystal."

"Prince Lanar has never needed bribes," Richard berated gently, but he took up the broadsword fashioned for the Crystani royal.

"Ah, but a gift can help. This is Sorengraand, sword of the brave."

The broadsword was well tempered. Its double-edged blade gleamed in burnished silver, and the crystals in its hilt were polished to a glassy mirror. The scabbard was made of the toughest of black leather and etched in lovely scrollwork fit for a king.

"Well, I'll admit, I do like the looks of this sword. But if I didn't know better, it's grander than my own you commissioned for my last Berneisse."

"Oh, posh! Your Tengrand, sword of kings, is mightier in bite and weight—just as you like. Don't be telling me it is less worthy."

"I jest, of course," Richard assured and sheathed Sorengraand. "The Starkindler prince will love it."

"He'd better," Trev'shel joked back. "It's worth nearly a dreite."

"A hundred gold bars? Stars, 'Shel, no sword should be worth that!"

"Only one fit for a king. Yours was worth two, by the way."

Richard rolled his eyes. "Never tell the price of a gift, my friend, lest you undervalue yourself."

"O-oh! Now you're getting rank. I think it's the last gift I will ever give you."

"No matter, my *paramouré*. Kestral will give me all that you do not."

"Now you're pushing it." Trev'shel shoved his friend out the door to their horses and took Sorengraand back. "I might be relieved of your leaving this time. At least then Kestral will give me all her love and attention."

"Arrez will take up all of that from now on," Richard reminded him, sounding wistful. Leaving Crystanian and all his dearest people behind was sobering. Even with a wife and son to return to in Sunrise, the taste of that relationship compared this one with the Xraxrains was as different as bitter medicine to rock sugar.

The kings fell silent as they mounted, and Richard waved them southward. "Back to Crystanian?"

Trev'shel nodded. "I've taken you away for too long today as it is. The rest of your time should be all for Arrez and Kestral."

"Indeed, it shall," Richard agreed. "Tomorrow will come too early, and I'm in need of seeing little *Aerrezín* as long as I can."

§ §

"And how was my mighty black?" Kestral asked as the two kings walked in to find her suckling the babe.

"Veiled Darkness was indeed a whirlwind, my lady," Richard said as he leaned over to kiss the queen woman on her forehead. "But we got along."

"The colt tried to buck him off twice," Trev'shel tattled. "But our *Jusoreen* lived up to his reputation." He used their term of endearment for their paramour, which was a keshic phrase for "a brave man or a man of great conviction".

The queen tsked. "I say, Richard, you do have a way of omitting the truth. To think my colt wanted to unseat you! I thought him over that."

"I'm sure he just wanted to try to see where we stood. Tomorrow, he'll be over the trial and behave perfectly."

"Now that I doubt. I'll make sure to have a talk with him."

"*You* should be worried about resting." Her husband mothered his wife and took Arrez as the milk-sated infant began to doze.

"And I should be worrying," Kestral countered. "We can't rightly send the king of Sunrise home with a broken arm—or worse!"

"I can manage," Richard assured. "You recover from giving birth to our beloved gem."

"I am loath to rest anymore." The queen had been on bedrest for nearly a month before labor, by order of the royal physician, and the fiery woman had become stir-crazy. "Other women are back to work right after, so why not me?"

"Valiant of you, *Kest'auleen*, but not fit behavior for a queen." Richard kissed her forehead again as he came to sit with her on the bed. "Your only duty is to rest."

Kestral scoffed but snuggled into the other's chest and sighed at the comfort of his spicy scent and the slight cling of sweat and horse.

"Our paramour is right, my sweet," Trev'shel agreed as he bobbed their infant to sleep. "Rest is your order of the day. Later, after you've healed from her birthing, you can take up your sword once more and lead with your iron fist."

"He makes me sound tyrannical," Kestral whined to Richard, who chuckled and stroked her raven hair. The queen of Crystalynian did have a reputation for her passionate disposition. Having a baby hadn't dampened it much. She continued. "And I've been too long in this bed already. I am ready to see more of my palace than these few rooms."

The kings' eyes met knowingly, and Richard said for them both, "You used Vauldin to heal yourself, didn't you?" She had to have used magic to be so robust after giving birth.

"Of course. My womb refused to stop bleeding. The midwife was in a panic, so I solved the problem."

"Then you should be resting all the more," her husband berated. "Majik-casting just after…" Trev'shel cut himself off with a shake of his head. Here was an argument he would never win. While he had always been of the belief that majik should be used sparingly, his wife was usually of the opposite view. Kestral used Vauldin as easily as breathing—and that worried the king the most.

"I am fine, my dear husband. And Arrez is fine. Stop your clucking and bring her here. I would rest better with all my loves by my side."

Trev'shel relented, though he was still frowning, and came to his wife's other side to set Arrez between them. He lay down beside the little bundle and kept his eyes on her as the baby dozed. After some time, Trev'shel said, "Our *Aerrezín* is much calmer than I remember Verrin as a babe. He'd fuss at any provocation!"

"It's still early," Kestral warned, starting to sound sleepy herself. "The delivery should have shocked her. Arrez may not be so docile as her days begin."

"Ssh, don't jinx her," Richard murmured into Kestral's hair as he too began to sink into a nice afternoon lull. "I say she'll be an easy babe, only turning fiery when she's older."

"No spell-casting," Trev'shel warned.

"Just a blessing on her, my friend, and nothing more. Trust me, having our gem stay sweet will keep your disposition more pleasant."

Kestral said, "You two and your stones."

The Sunarian chuckled softly. "It's what you get for courting two stone-bearers…" Whatever Trev'shel said in reply was lost to the other two royals, as both had fallen asleep. Shaking his head at them, the Tashek man relaxed into his own pillows and let all the dozing about him pull him under.

Without their room, the day slowly waned into evening, and the staff prepared the palace for the coming chill of the fall night.

§ §

Dawn came soft and warm. Soaking in its first rays, King Richard Sunrise sat on the staircase leading out to the balcony from the queen's chambers. Alone in the quiet, he took in the last vestiges of his time in Crystanian while knowing he should already be horseback. The Sunarian was stalling for time to allow the king and queen of Crystalynian to wake. And, oh, how he longed for a proper goodbye! However, time was pressing for his to ride to the Crystal Castle and then to his long-neglected Sunarian duties of state.

On that thought, waiting just a little longer seemed best.

"My friend."

Richard turned and waved to the other man. "'Shel, good morning."

"Yes, I dare say it is," Trev'shel said as he sat beside the other king. "The warmth of morning. Ah, a thing of delight it is!"

"Is Kestral…?"

"Still asleep, of course." Trev'shel grinned. "She was all talk yesterday. Even with majik, a lot of effort was expended."

"Let her sleep, then."

They lapsed into silence for a time. Then: "Have you eaten?"

"Of course. I was well up before the sun to check everything. Verrin has everything ready, though, so there was little for me to do."

"He's a good lad, my son."

"And I will take care of him, *paramouré*."

"I know you will. You make a greater shield than any known to man."

Richard nodded his thanks and then let the morning calm come between them. After some minutes, he rose—albeit reluctantly. "I've tarried too long, my friend."

"Yes. And you have much to do." Trev'shel stood too. "I will walk with you."

They returned to the bedroom, where Richard kissed the queen and babe a soft goodbye. Then, they headed away to the stable yard. The party was there, waiting for the Sunarian king to arrive. Richard thanked Prince Verrin for his work and took up Veiled Darkness's reins to do a final check of his tack. With nothing left to do, Richard turned back to the king of Crystalynian. "'Shel—"

"May the grace of the Stars go with you, my friend," Trev'shel interrupted to give a Keshic blessing.

"And may their light guide you always."

The two kings stood a moment longer, their eyes saying all that words could not. Finally, Richard stepped close to offer an embrace. "If all goes well, I will be back before the next Season."

"I know. Take care until we meet again."

The Sunarian pulled away at last and mounted the black colt. His face slowly formed into a resolved mask. He was returning to duties long overdue. What mess was at Sunrise's capital was only his guess, but usually there was plenty. Hardening himself for life beyond the quiet lull of Crystanian, King Richard Sunrise gave a last good-bye to King Trev'shel Xraxrain and called the party away.

II

"This is ridiculous! Do we really have to wait for those two to come? It's been over a week since the agreed-upon meeting time."

"Ah, you're just bored, cousin."

Prince Jarod Eldon, first son and heir to the Blue Haven crown, gave a sour frown. "I'm not bored, I'll have you know. I just don't like waiting around this palace while there's good hunting to be had."

"You *lads* can hunt whenever you like."

The voice alerted the two men to another visitor to the billiard room. Prince Jarod and his cousin, Jessi Clayton, rose to a proper seat on the chairs they'd been lounging in. There was a faint blush to their faces at being caught loafing by two other royal guests: newly crowned King Gregory Argetlem of the Golden Kingdom and Prince William Fantill of Sealand. It had been the latter who had berated them, albeit kindly—as was the man's nature.

"Majesty." The two Haveners had the sense to properly address the one man above their station, though, "Highness," sounded like an afterthought.

"Prince Jarod," King Gregory returned, raising his brandy tumbler. Coming closer, he indicated they play a round of billiards, which all agreed to. "For this time of the year, when much is being done in preparation for the snow seasons, this 'retreat' of ours gives us time to bring home wild game from the Crystal Mountains back to our courts."

"We know our cover story," Jarod Eldon replied as he picked up a cue stick.

"Just so, you've had three weeks now to enjoy the forests of Crystalynian."

"We've caught many elk and deer," Jessi Clayton said. "And smoked the biggest trout I've ever seen."

"Still," Prince Jarod continued, "we came at King Trev'shel's call that the stone-bearers needed our biannual meeting. Now, however, he has asked us to wait overly long—as Prince Lanar and King Richard have yet to show."

"It is unusual for King Richard to be late," Prince William said in the man's defense.

"Exactly," said Prince Jarod. "So, why should we wait on him?"

King Gregory started their game, breaking the balls and claiming a solid as his own. He sank another before missing and then allowed the two cousins to take their turns. "We wait, I suspect, because of the news King Trev'shel has for us this year. It is different from usual."

"Oh?" The Haveners did like a juicy rumor. They eyed the king expectantly, though neither asked aloud the question.

King Gregory's eyes flickered at them over his brandy glass as he considered if he should answer. It was William, being a closer friend to the two royals in question, who responded instead. "My assumption is that the North has reports of those...*creatures* they've been fighting in the forests bordering the unknown regions. The tallies I've heard have grown substantially since the few sightings from Planting Time. Certainly, I would like to know what our brethren know on this matter—unusual as it all is."

"I don't see how that would involve the South," Jessi said, a bit untactfully. "Those abominations haven't ventured much beyond the northern borders, and it sounds as if the Mausheliks and Xraxrains have it under control."

"We are all Syre!" Prince William objected. "What affects one kingdom affects the rest. What is in the North can affect the South. We need to stay on top of this situation."

"Easy, my friends," King Gregory bid them, sensing a Havener-Sealander clash was in the offing. "Let us finish our game and speak of better things. Any musing on the matters that called us here should wait until the assembly."

The two princes made faces but settled themselves enough to continue their turns at billiards. Complying with the king's wishes, they took up a conversation on hunting, boasting to each other about their catches. They managed to finish the game without delving into the reasons for their journeys to Crystanian—if "journeying" was even a word for being *teleported* by Prince Lanar Starkindler's crystal stone, Ravel. Traveling hundreds of miles in only a breath was rather like cheating. The royals finished with their game and cleaned up. Then, discussions on lunch had them leaving the room and heading for the great dining hall.

On their way through the palace, the men ran into Prince Verrin Xraxrain, recently returned from Rubia with some mertinean and King Corbin Chível's blessing. The dark-featured prince was practicing with his longbow from the portico. He was in a competition with his friend, a courtesan's son, as they tried to hit objects in the back garden. As usual, the talented prince was winning.

"You're a good shot, Highness," Prince Jarod said as he slunk onto the portico from the open double doors. "Quite impressive."

"Thank you, Highness." Prince Verrin bowed respectfully to the other prince, who was thirteen years his senior.

"Our prince is the best marksman on the estate," Verrin's friend boasted for him.

"My, that is an honor," Jarod replied and asked if he could study Verrin's longbow. Verrin handed over the weapon with some reluctance. "Hm, this craftsmanship is exquisite. Crystani bows seem far slenderer than our own, but I see their reach is longer."

"Their full range is over two hundred and fifty yards, though it's most effective around one hundred and eighty or less."

"Amazing!" Prince William stepped out of the palace hallway, intrigued by the prince's words. "Even our traditional longbows do not have such a range."

"Fascinating." Jarod held the bow up and noticed a peculiarity. "I see the lower limb is shorter than the upper."

"Yes. If it was the same length, it'd drag on the floor," Verrin said, pointing out the difference.

"But still, the balance seems perfect."

"Yes. It's the soft wood and binding techniques we use. Light, extra flexible, and long. Adjusting the bows this way has made the difference."

The prince of Blue Haven had a look in his eye that was too calculating, like he was considering stealing such a prized bow and dissecting it. Luckily, they were all saved from rescuing the Crystani weapon by King Gregory, who finally stepped forward and extended his hands to see it himself. "I have heard of the superior craftsmanship of Crystani weaponry. I see it is indeed ingenious. May I have a go with your weapon, Highness?"

"Indeed, sire. Please do." Prince Verrin looked relieved to have his bow out of the Havener's clutches. He stepped aside to give the king room to shoot while his friend handed over an arrow. They all watched as the Golden royal raised the bow in perfect form and loosed a shot—only to have it fly completely off target. The king guffawed amid laughter. Verrin politely contained his own laugh as he took pity on the man and explained the difference in technique for firing the Crystani bow. After he was talked through the process, King Gregory's next arrow flew true.

"I don't know how you do it so well, Prince Verrin," King Gregory said, "but it is a sight to watch. I hope you choose to enter in Syrean contests in Golden sometime. You'd make a good marksman." He handed back the weapon. "Thank you for letting me try it out."

"Of course, Majesty."

"Good lad." Gregory clasped Verrin's shoulder and squeezed. "Now, we are all on our way for some lunch. Would you both care to join us?"

Verrin's friend looked wide-eyed at the invitation to be among such esteemed guests; however, the prince was quite accustomed to such company. He agreed politely for them both and waved his friend to help hurry and pack their bows. Once the bows were properly stored, they trailed the other four men the rest of the way to the hall.

Their timing proved fortuitous, as the rulers of Crystalynian had been ready to call them for lunch in any case. Seating the guests at their high table, away from the rest of the court, gave them all some privacy. While talking around the servants passing out food and filling glasses, the guests and rulers kept up casual chatter about their visit or accounts from their own kingdoms. It was well into the meal before Prince Jarod let slip his discontent over waiting for the last of the stone-bearers to arrive.

It was over an accounting of Crystalynian's Harvest-Gathering festival, a week away, that the Havanese royal let it slip out that, certainly, he and the others would be returned home right after that event. After all, First Snows was upon them, and travel in wintertime that far north would be unreasonable.

"Yes," King Trev'shel agreed, holding in a sigh in an attempt to stay diplomatic. "It would be best to send you off by that time."

"Prince Lanar will be available by then, correct?"

"Yes, that was the agreement." Still, there was tension to the Crystani king's jaw. Trev'shel was concerned for Prince Lanar and King Richard, now two weeks overdue—and six weeks since Richard had left Crystanian. It was not like either man to be late.

"Relax, husband." Queen Kestral squeezed her king's hand before setting her keen, brandy-colored eyes on their guests. Her look boded ill for any who dared question her authority. "You have all been gracious to come north for our meeting of the stone-bearers. Your patience will not be without reward. King Merretham has given report that he is a day's ride from us. King Richard and Prince Lanar will likely be right behind his arrival."

"So, you've had word?" King Gregory asked, taking advantage of his station to gain an answer.

Kestral's eyes narrowed and flashed warning of the need for caution when addressing her; no quarter would be given for countering her words. "You, out of all of us, King Gregory, would know best where our wielders of Kevel and Ravel are. Or have you yet to scry them?"

Unfazed, King Gregory said in reply, "I know they are not near, Queen Kestral, but I would seek out their signatures, if that would be best?" The raven-haired woman gave the barest of nods, the closest she would come to asking such a favor. However, King Gregory understood the gesture. "I will seek out your library after dinner and see what I can discover."

"Thank you," Kestral returned.

By then, the rest of the table had gone silent as the two rulers vied with each other; though no cross words had been spoken, the mood at the table had made them all aware to tread carefully. It had been some time since a disagreement between stone-bearers had occurred—thankfully—but it was always best to keep tempers in check. One slip into magic and the results could be electrifying. Literally.

"That would be welcome. Thank you, Gregory," King Trev'shel spoke into the silence. He kept his tone and mannerisms light, so as to ease his wife's disposition; she had been prickly since Richard's departure. "Ah, here it is!" He changed the subject as a platter of venison and elk was placed before them. "This was yesterday's catch. You won't find much fresher."

The meat, though lean as many animals from the high mountain grasses were, was sweet and juicy. The entire lot of steaks were grabbed up in a moment. Relieved at the distraction, King Trev'shel led their conversation away from matters of importance until they were all back to bantering gaily about festivals, family members, and the occasional joke.

It was right about the time for sweet delights when a scattered-looking page came bursting into the dining hall, startling everyone. "Majesties!" the boy cried out, ignoring the whispers about his lack of decorum. "Majesties," the lad panted again as he made it to their table.

"What is it?" Queen Kestral sensed the young man's distress and tried to keep her own emotions in check.

"At the Southern gates, Majesty…the guards say…King Richard and…Prince Lanar have arrived… They are not…not well."

The queen was on her feet in an instant, her husband right behind her. "You stay here, lad, and catch your breath. Verrin, keep to our guests' needs. Your father and I will be back soon."

"Yes, Mother."

It took no more prompting than that. The two rulers of Crystalynian were out of the dining hall and on their way to the stables, then horseback, off to see the king and prince at their gates as quickly as possible. Their worries were laid bare for all to see: something had indeed been wrong. Just how bad, they had yet to know.

§ §

To hasten their departure, Queen Kestral had foregone guards. Instead, she called out to the palace's true guardians: the wolf pack of Crystanian. The ten enormous shapes, serving as the rulers' eyes and ears in the dark, dogged their two mounts as they rode through the woods. The wolves did not sense a need for a battle regiment, for the report was that there were only the usual number of guards at the South Gate, and two more men besides. Kestral believed the pack's words and followed their lead through the Forbidding Forest southward toward the guardhouse.

They came upon the southern gates half a mile south of Crystanian and slowed the horses so their arrival would not spook the guards. Under muted lamplight, the two rulers dismounted and hurried to the small guardhouse. The men there had split their ranks: one group to help the two royals, the rest to continue their watch. The men still on duty were relieved to have the queen's wolfpack join them on point, as no man's senses could compare to those of a wolf. They promised due diligence as their leaders passed inside.

"Richard, Lanar!"

"They are here, my queen." The head guard called their attention to the back of the guardhouse, where two cots were supplied for wearied watchers.

The king and queen hurried to the small back room. The two men were there, resting on the cots. Prince Lanar was sitting up, while King Richard lay face up on a cot. The Crystal-born prince looked exhausted but beyond that seemed little worse for wear; the Sunarian king, however, looked beat to shit.

"Lanar!" Queen Kestral was ashen with shock as she turned her eyes from Richard to their other friend for details on what happened to the Sunarian king.

The prince raised a hand to ask for quiet. With the head guard's help, he stood and hobbled to the front room. "His Majesty has finally found sleep. It'll be best to not wake him."

"What happened? He looks as if he was attacked."

Prince Lanar's face was crestfallen. "King Richard was imprisoned and tortured by Raymond, his own brother. There was a coup at the capital. I didn't get to see him upon my arrival at the Sunlight Palace. For nearly a week, I was stalled. After, well, I had to strategize a plan to teleport into the king's cell and then away. The effort has cost me greatly."

"And Kevel?"

"Still with His Majesty, else I would have had to break into the cells by force. However, the ruby is suppressed. Thank the Stars, or I'm not sure I could have moved him. It's still glowing but otherwise isn't reacting to me or anyone else. I assume the Sunarians were wary of removing Kevel while the king was awake. Yet, once he passed out from his injuries, the stone created a barrier of protection around its master. I was barely able to approach him as it was."

"This makes no sense," King Trev'shel murmured, anger making his voice crack. "Richard was a beloved ruler these past three years. A coup? Against him?"

"Prince Raymond must have sown discord," said Lanar. "Worse, I was witness to Queen Sylvia's backing of the removal of her king. The queen still sits the throne. I heard rumors that she has vowed Prince

Rowin's protection and preservation of his succession, despite everything."

"What? That's even more unprecedented. Prince Rowin threatens Raymond's position more than Richard does. To keep the young prince at the palace..."

Lanar shrugged. "It's all I could make sense of. I was more concerned His Majesty would lose his head if I delayed any longer. As a stone-bearer and guest, I did not feel welcome in Sunrise."

The king and queen, disturbed by this recent occurrence, shared an uneasy glance. The Sunrise Kingdom was nine hundred miles to the south, and trade and treaties would become strained without Richard on the throne. Richard's brother had been loath to make pacts with the other kingdoms of Syre, spouting predominance to Sunrise over diplomacy. It boded ill for future dealings with Sunrise.

"And what of Richard's injuries?" Kestral asked, trying to keep to the here and now.

"Extensive. I've done what I can, but only Sevén may be able to heal him."

"King Gregory is still here," Trev'shel assured the prince. "He promised to wait until all the stone-bearers were present."

"Stars' grace to that." Prince Lanar looked exhausted. It was doubtful he had another jump in him to retrieve another stone bearer. Thank the stars, King Gregory had the forbearance to wait so Lanar didn't have to attempt a jump to bring him back.

"Can we move him?" *Really*, Kestral thought, *did they dare?*

Lanar looked in the direction of the back room. "He's stood his injuries this long. Another half hour is tolerable. King Richard is a tough soul."

"Then carefully," King Trev'shel said, taking charge, "Pass him up to me on my horse. I'll hold him in front of me in the saddle."

They began the process of getting the injured ruler from the cot to Trev'shel's mount. King Trev'shel stepped up into the saddle and then slipped behind its cantle—there was no way both grown men would fit otherwise. He helped the men haul the unconscious Sunarian up onto his horse and then held him tightly to his chest. Prince Lanar then clambered up behind Queen Kestral on her horse, and the royals started the journey back to Crystanian.

It took over thirty breath counts, almost half-an-hour, to make the journey back, but they arrived with no problems. Staff helped to move Richard to a comfortable sofa in the nearest sitting room, and a message was sent for King Gregory. The Goldener arrived with Prince Verrin in tow. Gregory looked ready to face the worst. "What am I in need of doing?" he asked without preamble, knowing that being called meant the healing powers of his pearl were needed. Lanar gave his report before stepping away so that Sevén's wielder could assess the Sunarian king.

Gregory Argetlem knelt by King Richard's side and looked over his body with critical eyes before bending closer to assess the man's breathing and temperature. He made a scan of the king's injuries, hovering a hand over his body from head to toe. Using Sevén's magic, he learned of the trauma to the other ruler. He finished by sitting back on his heels and opening his eyes to take in the audience, whose silent expressions asked how bad the prognosis was.

Reluctantly, King Gregory told them what Sevén had revealed. "He was tortured, as you said, and barely fed. If his people wanted him dead, they came close." The news was sobering. "Eight ribs are fractured, there's an injury to his spleen, a broken collar bone and jaw, smashed knees. His fingers were dislocated, his nails pulled off, and I sense an infection in his gut, hence the fever."

"So much!" Kestral sucked in a breath. "Can you save him?"

"Yes. Sevén has shown the way, but Richard will need many months to fully recover."

"He'll be well taken care of here," Trev'shel vowed.

"Then I will begin. Have beer and bread ready for me when I'm done. I'll need the sustenance."

Closing his eyes once more, King Gregory reached into Sevén's powers and sent them through his hands into Richard. A pale, green light poured forth and soaked into Richard's body. Sevén dictated how and when each piece should be healed, starting from the direst of injuries and working to the least troublesome. Nearly three hours later, Gregory made his final adjustments and sat back in utter exhaustion.

"How did it go?" Kestral whispered as she passed over the requested food items. She had stayed by Richard's side the entire time, holding on to her hope.

King Gregory gave a wan smile, as much as he could muster. "I have healed all I can. The rest will be up to time and what nature can allow. But—he will live."

"Thank you, Gregory."

He nodded and patted the queen's hands before rising and stretching. A groan escaped his lips. "Stars, that was an ordeal! I'll be to bed, m'lady, and will see you all in the morning."

The Xraxrains thanked the Goldener profusely before having an attendant help him to bed. After his departure, they all crowded around the sofa, where Richard still lay, and waited for his revival. It took nearly another hour, but the royal's striking eyes finally fluttered open.

"Oh!" Kestral let out a cry and took Richard's hand in hers. "Thank the Stars, my beloved, you have awoken!"

King Richard was groggy—he thought himself still dreaming for some moments—but when he realized he was back in Crystalynian, he shed his own tears. "*Kest'auleen*, 'Shel, Prince Verrin…"

"Ssh, no need to talk right now. Prince Lanar brought you to us. When you'd been so late…" Kestral choked on the words. "But it matters not. You are here now and safe. King Gregory has healed your injuries."

The memories of what had been done to his body were still reflected in his eyes, but Richard trusted his other stone-bearers and his paramours. The knowledge that he was away from the Sunlight Palace and the Sunrise royals' machinations kept him from panic. Slowly, he tested his body and found he could make it to a sitting position. The king and queen came to sit beside him and held him in their arms while their son filled a cup with rock sugar and tea. They all stayed unobtrusive as Richard took the first sips of liquid he'd had in days.

"*Jusoreen…*" Trev'shel began.

Richard cut him off. "I'd like to speak of Sunrise later."

"Of course, *paramouré*."

"You can come lie with us and hold little Arrez," Kestral suggested. "She's grown so much since you were here last."

"I would like that," Richard agreed and let his paramours help him to standing. The effort was great to walk up to the king's quarters—with its larger bed—but they all managed. Holding Arrez at last, the Richard felt his eyes well up with tears as emotion over everything he had lost claimed him. His two paramours came beside him and held Richard as he cried. Their beloved was no longer the king of the Sunrise Kingdom, yet neither was he alone. Without words, they knew Richard was now a man of Crystalynian.

§ §

A day and night passed before Gregory and Richard were fit enough to join the council of stone-bearers. While they healed, the others convened to discuss developments in Staria, as King Merretham had arrived with news. His reports of these strange enemies beginning to concentrate north of Rubia were disturbing to all but Prince Jarod—who continued to hold the view that northern Syre was not his problem. Still, their council concluded that the maunstorz's numbers were not too overwhelming for the great desert king's forces to handle. With backup from Rubia and Crystalynian, all could be managed.

Queen Kestral passed along the council's discussion to Richard and Gregory that evening, in her garden. They were sitting near the ancient obelisk that graced its center. Kestral, as usual, had gone to its towering height to caress the Syrean symbols upon its obsidian surface. The language of the Ancestors was barely understood by modern-day Syreans, but the queen had a fascination with the ruins and thus was an astute scholar of the relic. Because of her preoccupation, her focus had to be pulled back to her audience at times as they spoke.

"*Kest'auleen*, Merretham said he was assured of their continued victory?" asked Richard.

"Yes," she replied and pulled away from the stone pillar to at last come sit by Richard's side. "He says the enemy has an aversion to horses. It's given his forces an advantage. The particular use of the Sheev'anee seems of the greatest affect."

"Merretham overextends himself," said Gregory. "It will be a disadvantage eventually."

"I think he knows that, Gregory, hence his reasons for coming all the way to Crystanian instead of sending a proxy. We will stand with him," said Richard.

"You do have the forces for a long campaign," Gregory agreed.

"And the snows are near upon us," Richard continued. "It will deter attacks. Even the enemy cannot campaign without adequate shelter and food."

"Nor can we. I will not send any of my men north until the snows have thawed. I'm sorry, but on that I must be clear."

"We know," the Crystani queen assured the Goldener. "We've been given support from Rubia." She waved to a group of mertinean soldiers who kept their distance from the three royals. At her gesture, they came near. "These men and their troops have volunteered to stay in Crystalynian for as long as we've a need." *Or until King Corbin Chível calls them back, which seems more likely*, she thought, but left that unspoken. "May I introduce you to Commander Darius Corranth of Carmine, his major, Sean Lanthian, and…" Kestral paused, realizing she had yet to be introduced to the last man. "I apologize, solider."

"No problem, Your Majesty." The red-haired lieutenant stepped forward and extended a hand to the king, an unusual protocol. "I am Lieutenant Ethan Kins from Dublain, north of Raven's Den."

The Rubian's charming smile dismissed any disgruntlement his lack of etiquette might have caused. Richard Sunrise in particular seemed to approve of the man's forthright character. He rose to make a proper handshake, ignoring protests from the Rubian commander and major that he was too high a station to greet the lieutenant in such a familiar way. "We are grateful for your assistance and willingness to come so far north."

"Not at all, Your Majesty," Commander Corranth said. "It is our honor to fight alongside the great king of Sunrise."

Richard's face pinched at the reminder of the title he had lost; however, he was quick to train the expression away. There would be time later to announce the change of his status. With these men, who were eager to please a man of his reputation, he knew better than to call attention to it. "Thank you, Commander, Major, Lieutenant. I look forward to having you and your men in our campaign against these maunstorz. We know what you've given up to come here. We will not forget such valor."

The men saluted the Sunarian for his words. It was obvious whose command these mertinean would follow. Richard Sunrise would have their forces to call upon in lieu of the Sunarian regiments that were no longer his own.

"We can have you all better acquainted over dinner," Queen Kestral suggested. "Then, it's to bed." She left out *for the two of you*, so as not be dismissive of Richard's and Gregory's status.

"That is an offer I'm ready for." King Gregory stood. "And we will have our full council tomorrow, m'lady?"

"Yes."

He nodded in return. "Good. For I must leave by late afternoon on the morrow." He had overstayed his trip as it was, so the queen knew he spoke the truth. All the stone-bearers had duties to return to at their respective homes.

The group of royals and mertinean turned in, then, to dinner and rest—though the latter came many hours later for Richard Sunrise. He was captured by tales told by the mertinean men until well into the evening. However, waking tired and bedraggled for the Stones of Power meeting in the morning showed the Sunarian that he could regret such overextended actions. The former king of Sunrise took his customary seat to the Southeast section of the table and pinched himself awake.

The others all sat according to the positions of their stones: Prince Jarod Eldon of Blue Haven in the North, Princess Marínna Chível of Rubia in the Northeast, King Merretham Maushelik of Staria in the East, Richard of Sunrise in the Southeast, Prince Lanar Starkindler of Crystal in the South, King Gregory Argetlem of Golden in the Southwest, Queen Kestral Xraxrain in the West, and Prince William Fantill of Sealand in the Northwest. Before them on the table they set their Stones of Power, lest heated discussions activate their magic by accident.

King Merretham started things off. "You've had a night to think about this new enemy at our borders. What say you on protecting our northern front?"

"We are with you," Queen Kestral voiced. "King Corbin sends his agreeance, as well." It was normal for Crystalynian and Rubia to assist Staria in such matters.

"And Crystal will send some forces," Prince Lanar added. "Though our movements will have to wait until Snow Thaw." Even as Ravel's wielder, Prince Lanar found that his talent for moving people and objects was limited to handfuls. Although the texts spoke of the crystal's abilities to move great scores of men, he had been unable to do so without great expense to his person.

"That is reasonable," Merretham agreed before turning critical eyes to the bearers from the south.

"I cannot ask my men for such a march north," King Gregory said. "However, Golden can support your forces with food shipped up the

Senna River. If more aid is needed, I have a young commander who is eager to join the boats."

"This would be Colonel Ivance, would it not?"

"Yes. He is newly commissioned to my royal guards. He hails from Sardon and is itching for action against these maunstorz you've written about. My Lord-Commander Aeronson says this man would be of some use to your men."

"We will take his assistance, if you so grant it."

"I will think upon it."

The interplay between the two rulers brought the tension up in the room until Richard Sunrise intervened. "And Prince Jarod, could Blue Haven not send such supplies up the Valor River? I am sure Prince Lanar and his people could assist in manning the barges."

Prince Jarod frowned at the attention cast his way. "I would have to speak with my father about such a matter," he said, squirming under the direct stare the Sunarian cast his way. "Though, I am sure something can be arranged. But what of Sunrise?"

"I have added four hundred dreites to the commission of equipment for all the forces," said Richard. The exorbitant amount had the royal Havener shutting his mouth. Four thousand gold bars were nothing to sneer at. Richard continued: "As for men…"

"Your gracious commission is more than adequate," King Gregory made sure to fill in. The change of the Sunarian kings was a matter better left for time to spread rumors throughout the kingdoms of Syre. "Besides, the brave king of Sunrise will bolster the forces' morale more than any Sunarian troops could. As for the use of our stones…"

"Yes, that is my reason for calling you all here to Crystanian," Queen Kestral Xraxrain stepped in smoothly. "With the Stones of Power, I believe we can take down this enemy with much less loss to our forces and supplies. Do I have your guarantees of coming to our support with your powers?"

"Of course, Majesty," Princess Chível was quick to reply. She was echoed by Prince Lanar and King Merretham—and, of course, Richard Sunrise, who was already committed. However, there was hesitation from two men in particular…

"I ask for Your Majesty's understanding," King Gregory began. "I have always had reservations on using such powers to assist battles. It seems excessive, as well as derisive to men giving their life on the field."

Queen Kestral replied, "I know, Majesty, I do. I thought that perhaps your Sevén could be of use in saving lives, not taking them." The pearl was a healing stone, after all.

"On that," King Gregory finally conceded, "I would be happy to assist the fighters in battle."

"Thank you." The queen's brandy-colored eyes flickered to the other silent ruler in the room.

Prince Jarod jumped as if she had kicked him from under the table. "I—I would need some concession for assisting your kingdom so."

Queen Kestral's eyes were flat. Of course, the Havanese snake would say something like that. "As if we, in turn, would ask such of another stone-bearer?"

Jarod lifted his chin in defiance. "I feel justified in the asking. It's not as if using our powers is free. We all suffer costs. Thus, I want compensation for my services."

She hated to ask but did anyway. "And what compensation would *Your Highness* like this time?"

"Our northern borders extended into Crystalynian. It's not as if there's much in the way of life in your eastern mountains."

Queen Kestral's face darkened considerably, like a storm cloud building up for a downpour. Yes, most of eastern Crystalynian was high mountains; however, there were some citizens eking out a living in those forests. The question of giving away such territory on a Havanese whim was infuriating.

"That is not a price worth a few spells, Prince Jarod," Richard Sunrise berated, keeping his own anger in check. "Nor should you ask a sitting queen for such a boon. I say a whelp like you should stay home in his blue palace if he is to display such rudeness to another kingdom."

"*Jusoreen*." Kestral waved him down, but she was grateful for her beloved's words; Prince Jarod looked decently cowed at the reprimand. "The Crystani crown denies you such a concession, Prince Jarod. If you cannot think of a more appropriate payment, we will forego having your Bellor in our arsenal against the maunstorz. With Kevel, Amun, and Vauldin, we may not need yours anyway."

Queen Kestral looked away dismissively to ask Prince William Fantill for his own assistance—of which the Sealander was more forthcoming. They ended the meeting soon after and bid travels to those not using Ravel's powers of teleportation.

Alone in the war room afterward, Richard came to Kestral to hold her and voice his concerns. "Blue Haven has always been hard to deal with, but Prince Jarod's behavior bodes ill for more to come."

"Indeed." Kestral rubbed her temples. "And it will be worse when the pompous lad becomes king."

"Let us pray to the Stars that he does not for some time yet."

"Or never," Kestral muttered under her breath.

Richard laughed. "That would be a glorious relief." Yet he sobered quickly. "But we will have to keep an eye on Blue Haven more closely after this." Crystalynian and Blue Haven did share a border, after all. A conflict arise with the other kingdom would affect the Crystani citizens closest to its lands.

"Let us hope it doesn't come to that," Kestral agreed. "I would be opposed to a battle against them, not with another enemy at our doorstep. But—I will send some forces eastward to protect my people from that possibility."

"And divide your forces so?"

"Yes, as we must. I cannot trust Blue Haven to not try for a seizure."

"Then 'Shel and I will discuss the matter with General Mooreland. He will know who best to send."

"I'm sorry, Richard, for dragging you into all this. You've enough to deal with after all that's happened."

"My lady." Richard gave her a smile. "I am happy to be by your and 'Shel's side. Though I suffer, I am freer than I've been. Perhaps I was not a dutiful king, always more suited for the life of a soldier. Maybe this is the Stars' decree for how my life should be lived."

"So, you will not fight to get back your throne?"

"No." Richard pulled Kestral in close. "I stay here among the only people who truly love me. For that, I am the richest man in the world." He kissed her forehead. "And I'll see little Arrez grow up and become as strong as her mother. I can have no regrets living like that."

"Just so, our beloved…" Kestral almost argued more, but she surrendered when Richard gave her a look. "Then I will let it be and pray for good fortune to follow you from now on. May you be blessed by the Stars, my great King of Sunrise."

III

Fall came to Crystalynian, with its vibrant golds and reds, and then the snows came soon after to blanket all the north in a cold, white mass. The kingdom lost touch with the outside world, separated as it was by the natural barrier. Nights grew long, and the populace snuggled in by fires to keep warm. The deep snows finally began to ease as Snow Thaw drew near. With it came the anticipated slow openings of the southern passes. Trade would soon be possible again in Syre's northernmost kingdom—but so would war.

The anticipated enemy attacks did come; however, they came sooner than expected and in greater number. The warning of their arrival came from a Starian falcon—and almost too late to muster a counter.

King Merretham's eastern post commander noticed increased maunstorz activity through his scope nearly a fortnight before the missives reached Rubia and Crystalynian. By then, forces on Crystalynian's western border were reporting failed attempts to stop an enemy route through the Snow Eagle Pass, an area of the Crystal Mountains north of Carmine, in Rubia, that was among the first to lose its deep snows, though still a passage considered impossible to traverse until later in the year. Yet the maunstorz had gone for this passage instead of the easier foothills to the east. The Crystani forces lost sight of the enemy as they traveled afoot over the pass, only to reemerge in the small town of Clover, just on the other side. The enemy's attack left none alive in Clover, and the maunstorz vanished into the Forbidding Forests and did not take any of the established roads deeper into the Crystal Kingdom, choosing instead to rough the wilds.

All of these reports reached Crystalynian just as the first day of Planting Time was approaching. The capital was in the throes of a spring festival when the aviary keeper brought the messages to the royal family. King Trev'shel and Queen Kestral were presiding over the midday feasting when the man approached the Xraxrain table. Not wishing to interrupt, the keeper passed the missives to Prince Verrin and Richard Sunrise and backed away.

The prince and the Sunarian leaned close to read the messages without calling attention from the queen's speech; however, their expressions of shock were enough to make Kestral cut short her blessings of their soon-to-be planted fields. Without acting overly rushed, she skipped to the final prayers of thanksgiving and hope, blessing the bounty before them. King Trev'shel ended the blessing by calling all to be merry and to enjoy the celebration as they saw fit.

Turning away from the released crowd, the king and queen settled into their chairs and kept their expressions cheerful while asking for the news in a hushed breath. Prince Verrin, closest to them at his father's right, said, "Reports from Colonel Perry. Says there was an attack on Clover. Enemies came over the Snow Eagle Pass and annihilated the town. No sign of them has been seen since. Commander Corbin has scouts looking for them. Tracks lead into unmarked parts of the forest."

King Trev'shel couldn't hide his frown. "How many?" To take down a town like Clover, with a population of a few thousand people, he expected a few regiments.

"They stated nearly six hundred—estimated."

The king's jaw clenched. That was an unusually concentrated number for the maunstorz.

"Another force was seen by King Merretham's men. They took another pass: Quartzmine, I think," Richard murmured around the prince.

"Quartzmine! That's impossible this time of year," Queen Kestral hissed back.

Richard shrugged. "It's what's written." He began skimming the Starian missive again.

"More reports matching these are coming in from all over our western front," Verrin continued. "I count six, separate missives here. The enemy's made it past our outer defenses as if they were nothing."

"This kind of route is impossible," Trev'shel muttered. No army—especially one on foot—could have made it so deep into Crystalynian without losing to the elements or duking it out with their forces. It was almost as if the enemy had magic on their side; though, to Syreans' knowledge, only the eight Stones of Power contained any known supernatural abilities.

"It may not be as outlandish as that," Richard cautioned. "The enemy may have ingenious military leaders at their command."

"You assume they are human, these maunstorz."

The former king nodded to Trev'shel. "Until I see otherwise, I refuse to give them more power than that."

"Then, what does the wielder of Kevel say to all this?"

Richard said, "I say keep it hidden from the capital's citizens for now while readying our forces at Bil'cordys for an attack. Even at running speed, the enemy cannot reach us for at least a fortnight at the soonest. Give the people the last vestiges of peace before their world shatters."

Queen Kestral had kept her features neutral until his last sentence; however, her second-beloved's colorful words had the lines on her face tightening. "I have always counted on your mind for war tactics, *Jusoreen*, but this—"

"Six separate commands of maunstorz could very well be coming here, my queen. That's thirty-six hundred men if these reports are accurate. And let us hope they are. Crystanian could hold off that number, but barely. More than that, and we'd need the forces deployed to our eastern and western borders—but they would not reach us in time."

"Then we get the stone-bearers."

He nodded solemnly. "And hope we can last while using up all our majik on one or two big efforts. If we cannot, Crystalynian loses its last major defense."

§ §

And so, in the following days, the rulers of Crystalynian kept up a strong front to their people while their forces gathered about the capital. Watchers were posted, looking day and night for signs of the enemy forces in the forest. The palace had one great strength: its sides were defended by fierce rivers on two sides and on a third side by a waterfall that dropped into a deep gorge. It was the north, then, that was the most vulnerable—hence, why Bil'cordys had been built a mile northward. Such natural barriers meant most armies would not attack Crystanian head on—but, then, most armies were not these mysterious warriors who had haunted northern Syre all summer.

The twelfth day of Planting Time drew near, and the Xraxrains became tense. They finally told their citizens what they suspected and showed them to prepared carts that would take them eastward to meet up with forces defending that area from Blue Haven. Only a single cavalry was sent as escort for the people's safety; sending more meant their flank could fall too easily. Queen Kestral sent all who wished to leave to seek shelter with the high mountain people of the east. Those who stayed helped prepare for a siege. In another day, only those with the strength to fight remained. The capital had never seemed so empty.

"You should have sent Arrez with her nursemaid," Richard said to his paramours.

Kestral disagreed. "I've made different plans for our little gem." She motioned for her scribe to show Richard the letter. "Prince Lanar's wife, Lestial, has lost her baby—stillborn. They've agreed to nurse *Aerrezín* and keep her safe at the Crystal Palace. Lanar comes today to take her to Lestial."

It was the first Richard Sunrise had heard of it. "But she should be with her people!"

"She should be where she is safest, *paramouré*," Trev'shel reasoned. "And we would be honored if you would continue to be her guardian." To emphasize the point, he waved their scribe to bring over a pinewood case, which contained an item the king and queen had commissioned.

Kestral continued, "You vowed to us once that *Aerrezín* was the light of your life, and so we've written your words on this gold bracelet, just as you spoke them." The three-banded bracelet was written in the three languages the rulers shared and used as their secret code: Sunarian, Keshic, and ancient Syrean. The words were etched in a flowing script and trimmed by three suns. The design was breathtaking. "Will you continue this vow, my beloved?"

Their friend and lover was speechless, caught between duties: to fight and to protect. His reply was strangled. "And leave you both to face the maunstorz alone?"

"No. No, our dear." Queen Kestral came forward to hold him. "Lanar will take Arrez and then return to fight. He's vowed to jump you away from here if the fighting turns ill. Promise us you will go, to be Arrez's guardian, if you must."

"You noose me around many promises, my paramours." Indeed, Richard looked trapped by all his good intentions. "But I will protect your heart until she can be reunited with you."

"It's all we ask, *paramouré*." Trev'shel joined their embrace. "And let us pray you will not need to make such a choice in the first place. I would have you fight at my side any minute, any hour, or any day and not have you leave my back cold."

Richard understood the Keshic phrase: that of a warrior to his closest comrade. He grasped Trev'shel's hand and squeezed it tight, for no words could be as true as that touch. The three paramours stayed close until an attendant interrupted to say that Prince Lanar Starkindler had arrived. They broke their embrace to bid Arrez good-bye.

§ §

By the time night fell, Prince Lanar jumped with Arrez back to the Crystal Castle. He returned on midmorning the next day, bringing with him King Gregory Argetlem and Prince William Fantill. The extra jumps made Ravel's wielder look haggard. Queen Kestral berated him for such an expenditure—even if it was useful—and bade him to eat a hearty meal and get to bed. With the other two stone-bearers in tow, the Crystani queen then proceeded to check the capital's defenses and update Sevén's and Serein's wielders on reports.

"All has been readied as can be," Kestral said to Prince William and King Gregory. "Our main forces amass just south of Bil'cordys, and watchers are at every tower to our eight cardinal directions. Princess Marínna has constructed barricades along our open ground to the north and northwest. Medical stations are at the town center and here in our northern courtyard. We've readied tarred arrows and oiled trenches all about our outermost lines to the palace."

The two men noted all the changes to the usually serene countryside. King Gregory seemed disturbed. "You act as though a great force is coming here, and yet your numbers say a few thousand?"

"It's all speculation," King Trev'shel replied, coming to meet them with Richard Sunrise and Prince Verrin at his side. "Numbers have varied by reports, so we're unclear on exactly how many enemies there are. The maunstorz have kept hidden from most of my forces on their march here, and sightings are all over the map," he said, pointing out marked locations on the Crystani map spread before the wall of the northern bastion. "I've assigned Starian cavalry to cover the distance between all our checkpoints. King Merretham and the Shi'alam of the Sheev'anee have granted me all the Tem'arid horses. With our own, that's six hundred mounts."

"And we've three regiments of mertinean," Richard continued, and showed the two men where they were stationed, just to the northeast. "I will be leading them alongside Commander Corranth and his subcommanders."

King Trev'shel added, "King Merretham and his forces continue to track into Crystalynian from the west. His last missive places them just this side of the Crystal Mountains. They continue to scour the forest for maunstorz."

"So, you're asking for support from us—where?" King Gregory asked.

"Sevén should be at Bil'cordys," Kestral said. "The main medical tents will be there. Princess Marínna will assist you."

"And I?" asked Prince William.

"Will be here at Crystanian." She smiled. "I thought you would do best with Serein around all our water defenses."

"Yes, I can do that."

"And how long until you estimate an attack?" King Gregory asked.

"Any day, any hour," Trev'shel replied honestly. "Be prepared to take up arms at a moment's notice."

"Quite the optimist, aren't you?" King Gregory teased hollowly. "Well, then. Let's get to our respective positions and acquaint ourselves."

"We thank you for coming to our call," King Trev'shel said before they parted.

"Thank me afterward. Battles can go any way."

§ §

[Day 14 of Planting Time, 89 SC]

Drums in the predawn darkness sounded out, catching the watchers by surprise.

"To the north!" a man called to rouse the others. The cry scattered the forces at Bil'cordys into action, taking battle positions. They cast glances in the dim light for sign of the enemy, and then they froze when first one torch and then another was lit in enemy hands. Ten, fifty, one hundred… another line deep beyond the first and then more.

"Stars preserve us!" a solider whispered to King Gregory's right as the men stood on the command center's roof to survey the battlefield. The expression seemed understated; before the town, an estimated five thousand torches made the forest seem alight in a blanket of fireflies.

"Colonel," the King Gregory called to the soldier General Mooreland had assigned him, "get your men to send word to our other ranks. Our men at town center will be overrun without backup." He stated the order with a calmness that he did not feel, but the Crystani soldier was quick to hop to it.

Returning his attention to the field, King Gregory sent up a silent prayer to the Stars for their help and protection. Only their grace could help Crystalynian now.

§ §

At the front of the Crystani army, King Trev'shel Xraxrain and his son, their stomachs in their throats, stared into the mass of enemies converging on their armies. The king tightly gripped his *kora* sword and tried to muster his courage to lead his people against the maunstorz before them. Calling out a command to hold and be strong, Trev'shel raised his sword high to flash silver at the glowering, red-eyed maunstorz. Yelling out an order to attack, the ruler of Crystalynian led his fierce cavalry and foot soldiers into a direct assault against the oncoming convergence. In a moment, the two forces clashed, and the Crystani cavalry bore deeply into the enemy mass. The great warrior-king on his silver steed and Prince Verrin on his bay were swallowed up in the writhing mass of steel and flesh.

§ §

"They attack! The enemy attacks!"

Richard Sunrise strode from his makeshift tent, fully armored, to intercept the runner and find out the news. "Full report, soldier," he demanded, taking the man's mount in hand to keep him from running off.

"Majesty, the maunstorz attack north of Bil'cordys. Their number is larger than estimated."

"How much more?"

"Five thousand, they say."

Richard cursed. "Run through the tents and rally the men. We will go to meet them."

"Sir!" The rider turned his horse to comply with the order; however, no sooner was he off than another runner, one of the mertinean, came to the Sunarian in a panic. "A maunstorz force comes from the west, sire!"

"What?!"

"A full regiment, sire, or more. Commander Corranth bides us to make a stand. All men are called to our west."

Richard let the man pass by to continue yelling the order. Shocked at the numbers, he leapt aboard Veiled Darkness and urged the colt to the mertinean frontline. He came upon them just as the maunstorz force emerged from the trees. The enemies' blood-encrusted bodies, riddled with scars and fresh wounds alike, made the former king pull up the black. He suspected the worst: this contingent of maunstorz may have just come from slaughtering the escaping townspeople, or they had butchered the western watchers in a savage fury.

"Commander!" he bellowed as he reached the mertinean line.

"Richard, sir, you should stay back. We will take the first wave."

"No!" Richard argued back. "The force at Bil'cordys reports facing five thousand maunstorz." The mertinean man blanched at the overwhelming number. "We must not fail here. I will take on this line. You, ready the men for a march north."

"But—?"

The Sunarian wheeled Veiled Darkness away, not taking the time to explain. There was no time! All Richard Sunrise could think was that the mertinean forces could not fall there. Bil'cordys needed their reinforcement. Kneeing the black colt to the fore, Richard centered himself and reached his thoughts into the deep reservoir of power he had contained in Kevel.

In a mighty display of majik, he called forth the Stone of Blood and War's ultimate defense. An enormous, impenetrable shield formed between the enemy force and mertinean, glowing red and translucent. In a decisive blow against the oncoming fighters, Richard directed Kevel's power to ram into the running mass with all the force he could muster. The great wall of red slammed into the maunstorz and mowed them down in an instant.

§ §

At Crystanian, Queen Kestral and Prince William sensed the subtle use of magic. Sharing a glance, they rushed to the northern bastion to see what was happening. The red glow of Kevel's lingering magic-shield drew their eye to the northeast.

"There, Richard has unleashed Kevel!" Prince William pointed. The effects of the powerful assault tingled in the air and raised the hair on their bodies.

"But why did he resort to majik so soon?" Kestral wondered aloud. Richard had always been one to preach moderation with the Stones of Power.

"There, a rider comes from the north," Prince William pointed out. "He'll have news."

They hurried to the courtyard and hailed the man, calling him away from his report to General Mooreland. While the great general of the armies was busy recalculating how their forces stood, the messenger told the two royals what he knew. The words were enough to make them go cold.

"And King Trev'shel?" Prince William asked, as Kestral looked on, unable to speak.

"He was at the fore, Highness. He and Prince Verrin led the cavalry charge straight in."

"Stars!" the queen choked out. "William, we must—"

Before the queen could say that they needed to teleport to the battle, shouts at the eastern bastion called their attention to a new problem. "Maunstorz are climbing the cliffs!"

The near-impossible words had the three leaders scrambling to the eastern side to see. Leaning over the walls beside the ever-firing archers, they looked down into the mighty spray of water to see where the enemy was climbing.

William pointed. "There, to the left." The enemy had made it three-quarters up the cliffs of the deep gorge. They seemed to be attaching rope to metal clamps already set in the high walls—but how had they gotten that far up without discovery?

Queen Kestral chilled at the sight and shared a glance with the general. "They prepared all of this ahead of time," she said. But for how long, that could only be guessed at. The cliffs were a difficult climb, wet and dangerous. The work to clamp its face would have taken days… and all without Crystanian knowing?

The whistle of arrows being released at climbing maunstorz called their attention back. General Mooreland called for arrows to be aimed carefully and for other men to ready themselves for skirmishes. However, as dawn began to break against the cliffs, it revealed the sheer size of enemy forces; there were about three hundred at the cliff's base, ready to climb up behind their comrades. Even that number would overwhelm the soldiers at the palace.

"William!" Kestral started to say.

"I'm already on it."

The wielder of Serein closed his eyes and began to murmur words of power. He called out Serein's song of the oceans and rivers and cast it toward the waterfall of Crystanian. The magic took hold of the mighty falls and slowly rerouted the water's veil outward, like a curtain floating in the breeze. Wafting it left, Prince William directed it to crash onto the maunstorz force. In a mighty whoosh, the water slammed down to crush the climbers and continued onward to the precarious island the enemy had made a stand on. In a moment, the enemies were washed away, and then the waterfall returned to normal.

The Crystani forces in observance were shocked speechless.

Kestral laid a hand on the prince's back. He looked on the verge of collapse.

"My queen," Prince William Fantill could only whisper. "I'm sorry, but I cannot go with you to Bil'cordys at the moment. I've exhausted myself."

"Then rest. I will ride with Mooreland."

"Maybe Prince Lanar—"

"Is likely as fatigued as you," Kestral interrupted. "Rest, Prince William. I will take it from here."

§ §

Smoke trailed in the air; the city was afire. Maunstorz torches had touched enough buildings to set the town aflame. The deadly blockade forced the Crystani armies into the waiting enemy; there was nowhere to go but north.

Most of the cavalry was still on horseback—their one saving grace to the whole mess. King Trev'shel led the charges and kept his foot soldiers as protected as possible. The walls of horseflesh were still the greatest deterrent to the maunstorz—the mighty steeds' flying hooves and gnashing teeth were as great a success as swords and spears. "Keep them back!" King Trev'shel ordered over and over. As long as the cavalry was the first line of defense, the Crystani army would hold.

Across the field, Prince Verrin had been separated from his father. Now afoot, his destrier dead, the heir of Crystalynian was fighting in close quarters with his father's best soldiers at his side. Their swords continued to hammer away against the enemy's jagged blades, axes, and hammers; however, after five hours of intense fighting, the prince's movements were sluggish. A misaimed swing allowed an enemy sword through his defenses. The blade bit deeply into the royal's side. Verrin cried out as the toothy weapon pierced armor and flesh. It burned as the enemy tore it from him.

"Highness!" The soldiers rallied to beat back the maunstorz enough to pull their prince deeper into the Crystani forces. One man who had assisted the prince found a place safe enough to lay Verrin down for inspection. The wound was deep and nasty. "You must get to our medics immediately, Highness," said the soldier.

Though Verrin was the verge of passing out, he said bravely, "I will not leave you men."

"Nonsense, Highness!" The soldier gingerly backhanded the prince to check his coherence. "He's fading!" he yelled to the two others who guarded their backs.

"Get him to the medics. We will cover you."

Together, the three men began to drag and defend their prince as they headed for the capital's center.

§ §

"Majesty, princess! You must evacuate." A guard said to King Gregory and Princess Marínna as they were stooped over Crystani fighters, healing them. Though their work was tiring and ever-increasing, they had kept pace with the medical team. Now, however, it was becoming clear that the town's center would soon in flames.

"We need to get these men out of here," King Gregory ordered.

"Yes, Majesty. We've brought carts to the back door and are loading the wounded as we speak."

King Gregory looked about their little hospital, disturbed at the number of bodies still occupying it. "We will not leave until every last man has been removed."

"But, sire!"

"The more air you waste on me, the less time we have. Put it to use."

The man saluted and stopped arguing to lend a hand transporting the wounded. They worked diligently until the room was clear. By then, the smoke from the fires was seeping into the hospital.

"Now we go," King Gregory said and helped Princess Marínna walk around the mess they had made of the room. They hurried to the back, where the last of the carts were being loaded with men. Stepping out onto the street showed how close the fires were; soon it would be too smoky to see or breathe.

And out of the smoke, a trio of soldiers came, carrying a body.

Princess Chível cried out at the sight of her betrothed and rushed to his side. "Verrin!"

"Highness." The lead soldier bowed his head. "He was wounded on the side."

Marínna was already bending to inspect the injury, but tears blurred her sight. Gregory came near and took her hands. "Let me."

The same attendant as before said, "It is not safe to heal him here. We must flee south."

King Gregory frowned at being hurried, but he could not deny the fire and smoke headed their way. "Can you carry him farther, soldiers?" he asked the loyal men who had dragged the prince from the field.

"Aye, Majesty."

King Gregory held in a sigh. "Then, let's go. Marínna, hold your hands to Verrin's wound. We must slow his bleeding."

"Yes," the Rubian princess replied. However, *agreeing* and *doing* ended up being two very different tasks. By the time they had made the long, agonizing trek to the northern walls of Crystanian, Marínna's hands were painted in blood and Prince Verrin was pale, clammy, and unconscious. Worse, he wasn't the only one. Before King Gregory and Princess Marínna was a field of dying solders—and even magic could only do so much.

§ §

The complete annihilation of the maunstorz on the eastern field had stunned the mertinean. Floored, they gaped at the scene before them until Lieutenant Ethan Kins—the first to recover—rushed out to where the great warrior had fallen from his horse. "King Richard!"

Richard groaned at the bone-deep aches of his body—the effects of pouring so much majik out all at once. "Lieutenant," he managed to say as his vision cleared enough to see who spoke. "I am all right."

"Stars, sire, I'd believe anything right now! You completely decimated the enemy with—with…"

"Majik, Lieutenant. Majik." He pulled out his Stone of Power to show the mertinean. "A gift from the Stars."

Ethan Kins looked oddly at the king, skepticism and belief warring on his features. "I'll take your word for it, sire."

"Our men?"

"All unharmed, if not still shocked out of their minds."

"They need to get to King Trev'shel's forces."

"Commander Corranth is on it, Majesty," Kins assured him.

"Then I must…" Richard tried to stand so he could join them. Instead, he flopped back to the ground, his legs useless.

"I don't think you should join the fighting yet, Majesty." Ethan said, "But I'll get your horse." The mertinean jogged away to retrieve Veiled Darkness.

When he had left, Richard beat the ground with his fist, angered at his body's incompetence. Still, he could see that Commander Corranth had taken the opening to move the mertinean northward. At least that was something.

"Got him, Majesty." Ethan Kins returned with the snorty black colt. "He hadn't run too far, luckily."

Richard accepted help to stand and then slumped against the great war charger. "If I can't fight, I should, at the least go to Crystanian to tell them of Bil'cordys."

"Right, sire," the lieutenant agreed but then hesitated. "But how will you fare riding?"

"Poorly, I suppose."

The mertinean took up Veiled Darkness's reins. "Then I will ride with you. You can hold on to me while I guide."

It seemed a waste of breath to argue with the man—correct as he was in his reasoning—so Richard agreed and struggled to mount while Ethan Kins held his horse. He managed to get behind the cantle so Kins could join him. Then, they headed south at a jog, heading for the palace.

They made the gates by the time the sun rose. The guards let them in quickly. Upon arrival, however, Richard learned of more disturbing news.

"Kestral went to Bil'cordys," Prince William said after greeting them. "She saw your magic and needed to see for herself."

"Damn it, Fantill! You should have kept her from it."

"You know I can't win an argument with her," Prince William said defensively. "General Mooreland went with her. They took half the forces. As for us…" The Sealander waved a hand about wearily.

Richard finally recognized the movement for what it was: the aftereffects of majik use. "Crystanian was attacked."

"Right up the cliffside. The stubborn bastards found a way up by sheer determination."

Richard insisted seeing their route. He shook his head at the evidence of their efforts. "That had to be planned in advance. It would have taken days."

"That was our thought too. They had to be scoping out Crystanian for weeks."

"This all seems rather elaborate," Lieutenant Kins said, voicing his own opinion. "These enemies studied Crystalynian and made the most of their plans. It is as if they have a grudge with your kingdom and came to bring it to ruin." The words sounded ominous.

Richard Sunrise frowned. "Then they knew how many forces we had and that our confidence in our defenses would make us blind to their movements."

"Crystanian is done for if we don't get a better defense," Prince William said.

"Yes, but all our forces are on the field," Ethan Kins continued.

"There is one we have yet to call…" Richard mused, thinking over all their options. "William, where is Prince Lanar?"

"Oh, no! You don't think he's still abed? He was exhausted after using so much magic yesterday."

It seemed odd for a warrior-prince to still be abed with all the commotion, but then again, the prince had teleported five times in less than twelve hours. They all hurried to the prince's guest quarters to find them empty. Cursing, they rushed to ask the few remaining palace staff for any news of his whereabouts. The queen's scribe was able to tell them something. "He was stumbling for the foyer, Majesty. I believe he was heading for the northern bastion. Quite unsteady, he was."

Running back outside, they came across the Starkindler prince as he was coming back from the bastion, having sensed two stone-bearers nearby.

"By the Stars, there you are, man!" Richard berated, fatigued yet further by all the back-and-forth.

"I could say the same of all of you. All this majik in the air woke me. By then, I had missed half of the morning's events! I was filled in by a guard at the northern bastion."

"So, you know the extent of our troubles?" Prince William asked.

"Seeing your faces, I can guess it's bad," said Prince Lanar.

"We need to get to King Merretham," Richard said without further preamble. "We need his cavalry to support the Crystani forces. And we need Amun."

"I know what you want, but I warn against the use of teleportation," said Lanar. "I have one good jump left in me without better rest. It should be saved for the last opportunity."

"So, we ride to him," Lieutenant Kins reasoned.

"No, they are still two days' ride from here. We 'd reach them too late."

"Prince—"

Lanar shook his head at Richard's request. "No jumping, but we could ask King Gregory to send a message. That'd be faster than anything."

Going to Bil'cordys sounded like the next best thing. "Fine," Richard agreed. "And when we arrive, be prepared to go all out with whatever powers you've got left."

§ §

Queen Kestral's entourage battled their way into the town limits. Her men were becoming accustomed to her powerful onslaught of crackling, lightning-like attacks, which were all more frequent because of her concern and fury. Though it was rare for the Crystani ruler to show her subjects the gifts of her Stone of Power, the moment's dire need took over her inclination to keep things under wraps. With Vauldin's awesome powers, they cut a deep swath in the enemy forces.

"Mooreland, get me to Trev'shel!"

"Aye, my queen." The general angled their men to make an arc around the burning town to where their forces were still fighting at its northern edge. They reached the battlefield by late afternoon.

The sight was appalling.

Bloated corpses, beginning to decay in the sun's heat, littered the green field. The stench and flies only worsened the scene. A mount only too familiar was standing, head-down and injured leg cocked, at the edge of the rest the field. Around the war charger were more Crystani cavalry mounts, many dead.

"Trev'shel!" Kestral choked and reined her horse to a halt near her husband's beloved Tashek mount. The king was nowhere to be found.

"He must be afoot, heading up the battle, my queen."

Kestrel knew Trev'shel would never compromise his mighty Silverwind once the steed was injured. "Yes," she breathed and held on to her hope that General Mooreland was right. "Let's go." Kestral released Silverwind's bridle and climbed back onto her own horse. "Mooreland, from here you must give me berth. I plan to unleash Vauldin's powers on our enemy. Let them taste my wrath."

The general's face whitened; however, he had seen how effective the obsidian stone was. "As you order, Majesty."

Kestral nodded, her face resolved. "To battle!"

§ §

As they reached the outer walls, they came upon the medical team. The sight of all the wounded stopped the four men in their tracks.

"Majesty!" Richard picked out King Gregory from the crowd and cued Veiled Darkness around the mass of injured.

"Sunrise," the Golden king greeted back. It sounded hollow.

"Bil'cordys?"

"Is burning to the ground. We evacuated who we could. The battle has turned against us. It is too dangerous by the field."

Richard understood the need for the medics to stay safe; without them, more would die. Still, to walk nearly a half mile to the first walls? Then, he saw the prince. "Verrin!"

Gregory stood aside for Richard to make his way to Verrin's side. Princess Marínna was beside herself, completely incompetent as she sat beside her beloved. "King Richard…" she began but faltered. Richard squeezed her hand.

"Verrin?" he asked quietly. The youth was too still.

King Gregory came up behind them. "I should have tried to heal him sooner."

Marínna shook her head, "We'd have been burned at the medical camp."

Richard held back tears as he bent forward over his paramours' son. The boy's body was becoming cold, and rigor mortis was setting in. "'Shel and Kestral?" he choked out.

"At the battle, I suspect." King Gregory looked north. In the very distance, they could sense the electrical charge of the queen's stone.

Richard stayed hunched over Prince Verrin for another breath count before tearing himself away. "Lanar, William?"

"We'll go," they promised, still by their horses.

Richard came back to them and took the black's reins from Lieutenant Kins. They all mounted. "Gregory," he said to the Golden ruler, "we'll be back. You're in charge until our return. Keep these walls strong."

King Gregory nodded, though he knew this meant he could no longer act as a healer but as the army's commander instead. "They won't fall. On my word."

§ §

The Crystani forces were overwhelmed. There were pockets of resistance throughout, but the scattered groups were not as effective. Still, the men hung on bravely. King Trev'shel was in the thick of it, his *kora* blade singing out right and left to wound the enemies. Fighting the maunstorz was exhausting, calling Trev'shel to utilize all his *she-koum-o* skills. Yet he blocked and attacked as quickly as he could; a loss of cadence would alert his foe to his tiring.

Afternoon was leaning toward evening, and Trev'shel knew they would be at a total loss if they fought into the night. He called to his men to stay strong—even as more were whittled away. Soon, something would have to give…

Unusual shrieks came from their field to the west, making all the fighting pause for just a moment. Through the thicket of bodies, King Trev'shel thought he saw riders coming his way. The first, intense strikes of electricity sent into the maunstorz near him confirmed what he suspected: his wife had taken to the field.

"Kestral! Kestral, here!" he yelled, though it was hard to know if the queen heard over the din. The tide turned, then, and the king and queen of Crystalynian met each other's eyes. Trev'shel started to smile…

…when a lance pierced through his chest.

"No!" Kestral screamed over and over as her forces continued to hack through the maunstorz toward the king. They made the location in a few more minutes, and the queen was off her horse before it was safe. "'Shel! 'Shel!"

"Protect them!" Mooreland ordered and had their horses form a defensive ring around the rulers. "Majesty, you must collect him and go. We cannot hold here for long."

There was still life in the king, Kestral could see that, but her grief was overpowering. It took some moments for the queen to collect herself enough to break the long shaft of the lance, leaving only the section that still penetrated his chest alone, and then try and hoist Trev'shel atop her horse. Unable, she cursed out until strong arms from two soldiers took the king's weight.

"Get ahorse, my queen," a soldier directed as they set King Trev'shel upon her horse's withers. To the queen's credit, she obeyed immediately. Clutching her husband to her, Queen Kestral took back her mount's reins and forced herself to focus on getting them out of their predicament.

"Charge east!" Mooreland ordered, seeing fewer enemies on that side.

Bringing her horse to a gallop, Queen Kestral forced her mount to the fore. "After me!" she screamed and unleashed her full fury on the maunstorz. Whips of lightning licked out from her extended palm, directing Vauldin's magic to clear their way. She pushed their forces eastward through charcoaled, unrecognizable bodies. By the time they broke free of the fighting, Kestral was swooning in her saddle.

"My queen." General Mooreland reached out to steady her.

"General, take us south," Kestral forced out through her fatigue.

"Aye, Majesty." He turned away to issue orders to protect their flank. "Be sharp, men! We must get our rulers home."

§ §

As circumstance would have it, Richard, Princes William and Lanar, and Lieutenant Kins came upon the queen's group as they left the field. Richard Sunrise was aghast at learning of Trev'shel's injuries, but he was quick to see a bigger problem: their forces were faltering under the maunstorz's onslaught.

"General Mooreland!"

The leader saluted. "We have the king and queen."

"Yes." Richard locked eyes with Kestral and shared a pained smile. "But if we don't help our forces retreat, this will be for naught. We'll go sound the retreat. Be ready to close the northern gates and man our walls. The trenches can be set afire once our men are across."

The general nodded. "Agreed, but you—"

"We'll manage. You just keep our exit open."

"Yes, sire!"

The man collected up their courage. This next task seemed daunting.

"What do you suggest?" Prince William said as they hurried forward.

"We have one try at this," said Richard.

"And a need not to overextend ourselves and pass out," Prince Lanar reminded.

Richard nodded and took stock of the battle before them. "The men to our southwest...you see it?" He pointed to where the Crystani forces were most concentrated. "We'll direct the forces to retreat from there. William, can you use Serein to amplify my voice to the men?"

"Not amplify, but she will carry it."

"That'll have to be enough. Lanar, use what you can of Ravel to throw up earthen walls behind our men's retreat. They don't need to be strong, just enough to slow the maunstorz."

"I can do that."

Richard glanced at them all. "Oh, and lieutenant, you'll need to take our horses if we pass out." Ethan Kins gulped but nodded solemnly. "All right, men. Now!"

Using the water in the air, Prince William carried Richard's "voice of command" across the battlefield: "Crystani, retreat to the northern walls. Retreat now!" The words reached across the entire field, startling all the fighters. Yet it was enough to set the men in motion.

Trusting the familiar voice, the Crystani forces began to make their way to where Richard Sunrise directed. When he yelled, "Run now!" the Crystani forces did as they were told.

The maunstorz howled their anger at the retreating backs and mobilized to head them off, but suddenly the ground sprang up in barriers to block them from the Crystani forces. The walls stayed up long enough for the men to be well away from the enemy.

Exhausted, Prince William slumped over his horse. "It's all I can do."

"It's enough," Prince Lanar assured him. "And I'll let my spirit animal take down what enemies it can," The Starkindler prince called forth his magnificent snow leopard from his crystal.

"That'll do," Richard agreed. "Let's race south to be with our forces. We should make it to the gates before the enemy reaches us." Pushing their horses to a gallop, they hurried to catch up with the Crystani soldiers fleeing to safety. The entire force made the northern walls just as the sun began to sink below the horizon.

§ §

Between the oily smoke of the trenches and the distant fire from Bil'cordys, manning the northern walls was a disagreeable job, made worse by the cries of the injured men and the stink of the dead. All of it made the situation seem hopeless. Crystanian stood, but its forces were at a loss.

In the northern courtyard, King Trev'shel had been laid as comfortably as he could be; his queen was crying over him.

"Majesty, we've found King Gregory. He's on his way." A captain informed his ruler.

Queen Kestral didn't seem to register the words. She was holding Trev'shel as delicately as she could while trying to avoid the remaining piece of the lance still poking through her husband. Without it the king would surely have bleed to death before they'd reached the courtyard.

Richard Sunrise, who had followed the attendant, motioned the man away and came to his paramours. "*Kest'auleen*, my love."

"Richard," she breathed and turned to fall into her second's arms. In his embrace, she wailed out her pain, and he let her. When she had exhausted her tears, Kestral managed to say, "'Shel…he's…"

"I know." Richard could see that the lance had pierced a lung and was close to the heart. That it had somehow missed the vital organ was the only reason he still clung to life. "Gregory is on his way, but he will warn you that there's little hope of even Sevén healing such a wound. He's been working all day to heal—"

"He has to save him!" Kestral hissed. "Of everyone, Trev'shel must be saved!"

Richard choked back words. He knew grief was making his beloved desperate. To add to it, Kestral hadn't yet heard about Verrin. Her heart would surely break.

"Majesty!" Another man came running. "The maunstorz—"

Richard shook his head for quiet. Queen Kestral would be in no state to help direct what remained of their armies. "I will find Gregory," he promised and sat Kestral upright. He kissed her forehead before standing and pulling the soldier with him. He directed another man to assist the queen before giving the soldier his attention. "Speak. What about the enemy?"

"They have prepared siege towers. They've pulled them from the forest."

Richard was too tired to be properly alarmed. This enemy had been ahead of them the entire fight. "And how long until they reach us?"

"They're working through the second line of trenches—at least, when I headed this way."

One line to go. "And how many can still fight?"

"A mark over five hundred, sire. Some of the injured swear they can stand with us."

"No. Adding bodies will not give us enough advantage. Order the wounded back to the courtyard. I want men to start evacuating down the gorge." Rappelling baskets and boats would take some time, but he hoped it could save lives.

"We're abandoning Crystanian?"

The words made Richard angry. "Use your head, man! A palace is just walls, not the heart-blood of its people. As long as we live, it will remain. Now, get orders out! We need to regroup downstream. I'm getting a message to King Merretham to direct his forces to us."

"Y—yes, sir!" The man hurried away.

Alone, Richard Sunrise let himself take a moment to feel the full weight of his grief and sorrow. Too many had been lost that day, too many precious souls stolen too soon. And King Trev'shel was likely to join his son before too long. After years of experience on the battlefield, Richard could tell. There were some injuries even the pearl Sevén could not heal…

Remembering the Stone of Power had him turning heel to find King Gregory. As much as Richard wanted to rush him to Trev'shel's side, a message had to be sent to Amun before the Golden wielder became too exhausted to try to reach King Merretham.

§ §

The siege towers reached the northern walls by midnight. From there, close combat was once again par for the course.

Richard Sunrise stood atop the leftmost end of the wall with Lieutenant Kins, who had become Richard's newly elected subordinate. To the center, General Mooreland had pulled together the freshest of the men and vowed to hold their position to the end. On the far right, Prince Lanar Starkindler and Prince William Fantill directed the rest of the forces. All the stone-wielders promised to avoid all but simplest of magics unless absolutely necessary. The walls would be fortified by sheer will only.

Fighting in the burning night gave a new element to the nightmarish enemy. The fire's glow made their red eyes and white hair seem more apparition-like. Terrifying and haunting, the sight of the maunstorz made some of the men go mad, and these men fought like berserkers, as much a threat to their comrades as the enemy. More than one man had to be put down by his kinsmen. Still, the Crystani forces managed to hold out the night and kept the maunstorz from breaching the northern wall.

Morning came, and a runner returned from the waterfall with news for Richard Sunrise: all of the wounded had made it safely to the bottom of the gorge. Princess Marínna—with Prince Verrin's body—and King Gregory were among them.

"And Queen Kestral?"

"I heard the queen would not leave Crystanian…yet. She has her scribe recording things."

"And the king?" He didn't want to know.

"Is still alive, as far as I've heard."

Richard was pleasantly surprised. There was hope then… "Thank you, soldier." He surveyed the field. The maunstorz had pulled back at dawn to regroup—and strategize, he assumed. "We'll take this opportunity to get more men to the gorge. Inform Mooreland. He'll know how best to give us retreat."

"Yes, sir!"

§ §

The two princes met back up with Richard Sunrise. Though exhausted and bloody, they looked better than they claimed they felt. Taking advantage of the lull, the princes, Richard, and Kins shared crude pork sandwiches as breakfast. They were all joking—as much as men forced into war could do—and gulping down food and water when the ground began to shake.

"Wha—?!"

Shocked, they were to their feet in an instant. When standing, it was apparent that the earth was moving, and it was getting stronger.

"Earthquake?" Lieutenant Kins asked, though such a natural disaster was unusual for the high mountains.

The three wielders shared a glance before looking southward to Crystanian. "No," Richard murmured, sensing the growing majik.

"It's Vauldin," Prince William said.

"What is Kestral doing!" Prince Lanar demanded; however, no sooner were the words out of his mouth than the shaking grew more violent. They watched in horror as Crystanian began to break apart. Worse, the entire vicinity of the palace was also being swept up in the obsidian stone's magic.

Down the line, the northern wall began to shake apart underneath the men's feet. They heard screams as men fell. "Grab on to each other!" Prince Lanar yelled. As soon as they were clinging to another, he activated his stone's power of teleportation. In a breath, they were on a hillock overlooking the palace far below; the other wielders recognized it as one of the spots he would disappear to when he wanted to contemplate life.

The shaking, cracking, and rumbling continued, though the sound was muted at that distance. The four men turned, aghast, as they looked back on Crystanian and its lands. In a final, violent collapse, the entirety of the royal grounds fell into the earth, shattered to ruins.

The concussion of the powerful blast radiated outward, like an echo, finally reaching the men. It shuddered out further, going beyond the castle grounds proper to alert the rest of the kingdom to its destruction.

The four observers stood stupefied at the extent of its ruination.

§ §

When the earth began to shake and boulders fell from above, King Gregory yelled for all the boats to clear the landing. Paddling hard, they managed to get deeper into the gorge as Crystanian was pulled apart by magic. Gasps and shouts rang out as the party of wounded men watched their capital fall into ruins.

Sitting in stunned silence, King Gregory and Princess Marínna shared a glance. They had sensed Vauldin's powers and knew the queen had unleashed something deadly.

"She…" Marínna started and tried again. "Gone. It's all gone. And the men!"

"Kestral!" King Gregory felt anger grow as he took in everything. "That queen was always a bit rash, but this…"

The princess was trying to keep herself together, but there had been so much loss. "I… I wish a Stone of Power had never come to me. Look at how little I could do, but Kestral—"

"But nothing! That woman just destroyed everything, not counting the cost."

"I know," she admitted quietly. Her hand went to hold her lost prince's cold arm. "Let's get away from here. I wish to lay Verrin in a tomb not of his ancestors'. I'd like to go the Rubia…"

The king looked around at all the weary faces and nodded. "Men!" he called out. "We need to get to calmer waters. Take us south!"

§ §

After some time, the princes, Richard, and Lieutenant Kins could finally move.

"Lanar, can you take is to the palace?"

The prince nodded to Richard's question. "I think I can manage." Really, he was feeling at his limits, but he wanted to see Crystanian for himself. It took some effort, but they teleported back to the inner courtyard.

It was difficult, at first, to tell where anything was in the ruins; however, Richard Sunrise was the most well versed in the palace's layout. He found a way deeper into the ruins, to the area on the main floor that would have been under the queen's chambers. His intuition was correct. They found Queen Kestral and King Trev'shel's bodies in the rubble where they'd fallen. Richard held back his cry of pain and went to his two beloveds.

"*Kest'auleen*. 'Shel." Their bodies were battered and broken, but the former king did not care. He picked them up and rocked them in his arms.

The others let their companion have his time to mourn. Only when he seemed to come out of it did they come closer. Prince Lanar set a hand on his shoulder.

"You feel it, don't you?" Richard asked his two other stone-bearers. "Kestral tried to use a forbidden majik to bring her husband back."

"Yes," Prince William admitted. He had reached out with Serein to grasp the memories still floating around the queen's body, saw the afterimages.

Lieutenant Kins was wide-eyed at the destruction. "By the Stars above, this was from majik, you're saying?"

"Indeed, Lieutenant. A kind of magic that should not be attempted." William's blue eyes cast about the aftermath of the spell. "I'd say Vauldin had something to say on that. He didn't agree with it."

"She thought she knew better," Richard said. He had laid his paramours down and was propping them comfortably side by side. His hands paused over the king's hand. Bending closer, he saw words written on his skin in Keshic coal: *The oracle knew*. His heart froze. Kestral and Trev'shel had had arguments about the oracle of the Sheev'anee in times past, an argument of some Fate. If Kestral had seen the message, he knew, it could have triggered her daring to counter a Tide of Fate with Vauldin's magic. "We need to leave," he said, surprising the others. Richard took the obsidian stone from his lover's neck and stood.

"But?"

"The maunstorz may have survived the earthquake. It's not safe here without a full army."

Prince Lanar nodded. "That's true, but are you sure you're ready?"

"Yes." He stepped up to the Crystal prince and handed Vauldin over. "The stone must go only to the only blood heir of Crystalynian." Richard headed outside before the other men could mount an objection.

Leading the way, Richard Sunrise got them clear of the ruins to a section of the property least damaged. There, they found six horses still alive and unharmed. Veiled Darkness was one of them. All were still tacked up.

"Well, that'll beat walking," Prince William said, relieved as they managed to catch the horses despite their skittishness. The men decided to head south to where the boats—if any were intact—would find landing on safe shores. They started away from the ruins of Crystanian.

§ §

By evening, all the scattered forces managed to meet up at what would have been the town of Piking—only the town was burned. King Merretham's cavalry had reached the location first and put out all the fires by the time the others arrived. Only a handful of residents had managed to survive, hiding in a nearby mine to wait out the maunstorz attack. Everyone, soldiers and common folk alike, looked exhausted.

In a Tashek tent that served as the main command post, King Merretham met with the other stone-bearers. He had news little better than what the others said of Crystanian. "I hate to tell you, but all the towns we came across in the maunstorz's path were burned to the ground. There's stragglers here and there, but not more than a handful of the population survived."

"The enemy's attack was total," King Gregory assessed, studying the results on the map. "They wanted Crystalynian annihilated—and they accomplished that."

"And all those men at Crystanian…" Prince Lanar beat a fist on the table. "Queen Kestral handed them a victory by using Vauldin. She killed so many—and for what?"

Prince Fantill agreed: "She was selfish. I am sorry to say."

Richard Sunrise, raw in his grief, had let the others have their say; however, the prince's apology had him shaking his head. "No, you're right.

Kestral could have done anything with the powers she was given. Instead, she brought down the kingdom in a dangerous gamble with majik better left alone."

"You're sure it was death majik?" King Merretham asked. "Kestral abhorred using it in the past."

"There was no doubt."

"That is grievous, then, that she was so consumed by loss to resort to such a thing."

They were quiet, processing the king's words, before Gregory said, "Well, what's done is done. Now, we have to pick up the pieces. I'm headed to Rubia with Princess Marínna. Any Crystani who wish refuge have been granted it by the Rubian crown."

"I'm sure there'll be plenty," Richard agreed. "The princess wishes to bring Verrin with her?"

"Yes. She wants to give him a royal burial. You have our word that the greatest respects will be shown him."

"I never doubted that." Richard's words made the rest pause in silence.

"So, then…we will rest tonight and head our separate ways in the morning?" Prince William asked.

"Yes. I think that is best for all considered. You've been through an ordeal," King Merretham said. "My forces will take point tonight. Get what sleep you all can. Tomorrow, we'll divide supplies and decide on the best ways to head home. Good night, men."

§ §

Morning broke over their camp in a subdued silence. Already, boats provisioned as well as could be mustered were loaded down with survivors. In short order, King Gregory's command headed downriver to find other towns better able to provide a way to Rubia. After his parting with the majority of the camp, the place looked empty.

Richard Sunrise walked out from the Tashek camp, leading Veiled Darkness. He stopped the colt before Prince Lanar Starkindler, who was refreshed enough to jump back to the Crystal Castle. A handful of men were ready to leave with him. "Highness," he greeted. "I want you to take Veiled Darkness. The colt should be the princess's."

Prince Lanar looked shocked. "But he's yours!"

"On loan from Kestral," Richard corrected. He patted the black, satiny neck. "And as much as I get along with him, I will not risk such a long journey on such a young horse."

"So, you aren't coming back to Crystal with me."

"No. I have some things to clear up first. After…I'll return to be Arrez's guardian."

"And here I thought the princess took priority over everything else."

"She does," the Sunarian assured. "But I have loose ends to tie up."

"One being your throne?"

Richard shook his head. "No. Stones of Power business. King Gregory wants nothing more to do with Sevén, so I'm taking the pearl somewhere safe."

"In Staria?"

"In Staria."

"Promise me you'll come back."

They shook hands as Richard said, "I have yet to break a promise, prince of Crystal. I don't intend on starting now. Until we meet again, my friend."

"May the Stars watch over you. Safe journeys to wherever your road goes."

IV

In the next days, the Stones of Power became dormant, one by one. However, before they were rendered useless, a final magic altered the face of Syre.

In her grief, Princess Marínna used her powers over her diamond, Sheveth, during Prince Verrin Xraxrain's funeral to induce a wish of illusion over the kingdoms. She prayed, with hope and power alike, for Syreans to forget the trauma brought on by the mysterious invaders, the maunstorz, and that the populace could move beyond a time of reliance on the Stones of Power. Sheveth's magic cast the strongest of spells she had ever woven. With it, those who wished to forget the recent war did, and those who needed the scars of war healed, be they physical, mental, or emotional wounds, found them gone in a night. Only the people who held firmly to their beliefs in the Stones had any memories after the spell's conclusion. From that one wish, the Stones of Power became only myth and legend to the people of Syre.

As for the stones themselves, once they were dormant, each was treated differently. Amun, Ravel, and Serein were promised as heirlooms to the firstborn of each royal household. Vauldin, of course, was promised to be kept safe by Prince Lanar Starkindler until little Arrez grew old enough to claim her birthright. Sheveth, it was claimed, was laid with Prince Verrin, in the tomb where Princess Marínna buried him. As for Bellor, well, none knew quite what Prince Jarod had done with it. When it became dormant and useless, he could have tossed it aside; however, it was known that in his anger over losing its powers, the prince blamed Kestral Xraxrain. In recompense for his loss, he took the eastern part of Crystalynian as his own, saying the rulerless subjects needed a master.

Lastly, Sevén and Kevel were given to the Sheev'anee of Staria, King Trev'shel's people, known as the "Keepers of the Truth." However, it was unknown what happened to the deposed king Richard Sunrise after he gave up the stones. The Xraxrains' paramour and guardian of their daughter, Arrez, was lost to the winds in Staria, and only rumors remained of the great warrior.

With Crystalynian vanquished, Syre was left adrift to fight the enemy of the Ancients' myths. The maunstorz had shown themselves quite capable of taking them on, with fangs sharp and hungry for the rest of the kingdoms' ruin. Without the high seat at Crystanian and the Stones of Power, the alliances of the Northern and Southern kingdoms became fragile.

And it wasn't until two riders from Staria, Lord Shekmann of Kavahad and Zyanthena Sheev'arid of the Sheev'anee, were pushed into the ruins of Crystanian by maunstorz pursuers that the Stones of Power came back into play. Twenty-one years and four seasons to the day, Vauldin was returned to the site of its slumber. The obsidian stone awoke with a roar, quaking the kingdom to its bones—just as it had before. Vauldin had come home and so, too, had its heir. Magic began to stir in Syre once more…

For every stone, an animal fare,
to protect and guide the stone-bearer.

A hawk for far-vision to Amun of the Sun.
A wolf for sense to Vauldin of the Night.
A fox for cunning and disguise to Kevel of Rubies.
And a stag for speed and grace to Sevén of Grains.

A snow leopard for stealth to Ravel of Earth.
A snake for transformation and shape to Bellor of the Air.
A phoenix to carry Sheveth to flaming heights,
And a sea serpent of the deep for Serein of the water.

Each of these, a majik of Earth and Stars
to carry the prayers of the Stones of Power.

Part I

§

(Year 110 SC, Levies and Storage Time)

Chapter One
§
Remembering

Deep, unnatural snows fell over most of Syre, blanketing even the mountainous regions of the southern kingdoms. It came too early, too thick and cold, leaving many unprepared. Panic ran high as the common folk feared starvation or freezing to death.

High to the north, the old obsidian walls of Crystanian stood cold and erect as they once had a quarter of a century ago. Their sudden resurrection had shaken the foundations of the kingdom of Crystalynian as, stone by shattered stone, the entire structure of the palace and its surrounding buildings came together in one powerful movement. The event had then shuddered out from the epicenter to all corners of Syre, its roar proclaiming the awakening of the great stone Vauldin.

Soon after, the snows had come—the alarmed reaction of a distant enemy concerned by what it meant for the obsidian stone to flare to life so suddenly and violently. Ravel, the other stone, was focused to make the snows fall deepest at Crystalynian, as if to wall off the new danger from the rest of the world. The effort was in vain, for tucked warmly in the renewed walls of the palace, the few inhabitants there were quite unaware of events in the rest of Syre.

The lone figure of Lord Darshel Shekmann of Kavahad—tall, chiseled, and aristocratic—could be seen pacing the spacious landing of the balcony to the king's chambers. It had become a regular chore of his of the past three weeks. The Shekmann would pace until he felt he could sit another turn. He would then go back inside the room to sit by Zyanthena Sheev'arid's bedside. On occasion, the lord-governor would speak to the two grey wolves that guarded the unconscious Tashek; other times, he would make his way to the kitchens and try to make a meal of the miraculously filled cellars; sometimes, he would succumb to fatigue and sleep. Yet, mostly, the Kavahadian worried over the still-comatose form of his companion.

Zyanthena Sheev'arid had seemed dead when Lord Darshel found her in the ruins of Crystanian, having taken a fall from her black stallion's back onto a pile of flagstone rubble. However, the pack of wolves that stood guard over the ancient place had forced the Shekmann to move her still body to a site deep in the heart of the ruins. When he had done so, the black stone around the desert warrioress's neck had flared to life, lifting her body from the lord's arms. In all the bright light and loud rumbling that followed, Lord Darshel had been unable to see what happened. It wasn't until the stone's powers settled that the Shekmann had found Zyanthena laying naked in the center of a newly formed Great Hall.

That had been twenty-two days ago. Zyanthena had not woken, and Lord Darshel's hopes had fallen. Only the wolves' constant vigilance had prevented him from calling the Tashek lost, which staved off his contemplations that he would inevitably be burying her in the frozen ground outside the palace walls—should death finally come to collect.

He didn't think that this day, which had dawned in a steady sprinkling of snowflakes, would be any different from the others, but the alpha wolf and his mate were unusually restless around Zyanthena's bed. Lord Darshel crossed to her side and slipped his hands around her left hand as he sank to a knee. His emerald eyes searched her lovely face, looking for some sign of awareness.

At first, he thought it was false hope that had him imagining the slight fluttering of her eyelids—yet, after five breath-counts, it became clear that, indeed, the desert woman was not just in a dream state. She was finally coming to! "Zyen?! Zyanthena, are you…?" Darshel's voice choked on the words as relief overwhelmed him. Silent tears, held in from his constant worrying, slid down his chiseled cheeks to drop onto his hands. He felt her react to the wetness on her skin. "Oh, Stars," he laughed, "you are awake! You were out so long, I thought you never would… Oh!" He laughed again and brushed away the tears on his face. "Damn, woman, you've gotten me to be quite the sorry sap!"

Zyanthena murmured in her dry throat, and her eyes opened wider, only to close again.

"Here. Here's some water. Sorry, you're probably parched." Carefully, Darshel dribbled some of the nourishing liquid onto the lovely woman's lips. He was pleased to see her attempt to suck it in. "That's it. That should be better."

It took a while for Zyanthena to wake up fully, but to Lord Darshel, the time meant nothing compared to the hours he had spent looking after her still form. He was so elated to see her brandy eyes looking at him—even if they lacked their normal sharpness. She cleared her throat and murmured again. A wispy word came from her lips. "'Shel?" She moaned slightly and tried again. "Darshel. Lordship." Her voice was hoarse from lack of use, but the words came out clear enough.

"Zyanthena." The Shekmann smiled and brought her hand to his chest, "You've been out nearly the full of the month. I thought you'd never wake."

Zyanthena felt well enough to give Darshel a confused look. Then, her eyes shifted around the room, taking in the roaring fire, the marble-and-obsidian stonework, and—lastly—the grey wolves. A sharp certainty came to her eyes as comprehension lit in them. "Crystanian. Vauldin."

Darshel was shocked at her accuracy. "Yes. We are in the palace of Crystalynian, or what is now the palace…" He glanced around warily, still not quite trusting his eyes at finding the palace rebuilt by magical means. He turned back to find Zyanthena pushing herself to a sitting position. "Zy'ena, stop! You need to rest after being in a coma for so long."

Sharp eyes, slightly accusing, refocused on the tall, dark-haired lord. "My clothes, Lord Darshel?"

So, she had realized she was still naked beneath his cotton shirt. "You have none. Whatever happened during that…blast of light…event—or whatever it was—ruined them. That's all I had for you."

The warrioress stared at him calculatingly; she certainly had come back around if she could do so this easily. Yet, Darshel was used to her looks and no longer felt unnerved by them.

Finding the Kavahadian lord-governor not easily cowed, Zyanthena relaxed her frown, no longer accusing him of untoward actions. "Is there anything to eat? I'm feeling unusually famished."

Lord Darshel chuckled. "I'm sure you are. I will go get some broth ready. It will be easiest on your stomach." She gave a silent nod in consent.

A short while later, Darshel returned with warm broth and another cup of water. He found Zyanthena still awake, snuggled next to the alpha's mate, with the alpha wolf lying guard-like at her feet. "They certainly like you," he commented as he set down the water and perched himself next to Zyanthena's other side. "I'm not sure they like me so much."

"They like you well enough," Zyanthena said as she grasped the spoon he offered.

Zyanthena's first attempt at eating, however, made her beautiful face fold into a frown. Her hand shook too much to get the broth to her lips. "Here. You rest," Darshel commanded, taking the bowl and spoon back before they dropped in her lap. "It's normal for the body to take time to adjust after being in a coma for so long."

"You sound like you know."

"Well"—Darshel dodged the subject—"I do. Here, eat." He carefully ladled the broth into her mouth. "You know, this palace is quite unbelievable. The entire kitchens are well stocked—as is the barn—and most of the rooms are full of furniture and the like. I feel like I've fallen into a dream."

"It's just as it was the day Crystalynian fell."

Zyanthena's comment took him off guard. "Well, I'm not sure how that could be, but then none of this makes much sense to me."

"It is," Zyanthena insisted, her voice certain. She took another sip and looked around again. "If I have only been out for three weeks, then why is there deep snow outside?"

"Leave it to you to be so observant. *That* came down mere hours after all of this came up. It's been falling since."

"It's quite soon…not normal for this season."

"No, it is not," Lord Darshel agreed. "Nothing has been. Come on, you need to eat. It will get your strength up."

Zyanthena chuckled at that, somewhat amused at the lord-governor's mothering. She continued eating as prompted. Once the bowl was finished, Zy'ena yawned and sank back into the thick down pillows. "I will sleep some more now, I think. Thank you, My Lordship."

"Darshel, please."

"Lord Darshel," she conceded.

The Shekmann had to content himself with that. "I will take these back to the kitchens and then get some sleep myself. There are other chambers across the way, but I can stay here if you think you'd have need of me? I've gotten quite used to sleeping propped-up next to the bedside," he joked, wanting to make it clear he had not taken advantage of Zyanthena's unconscious state in any way.

"I will be fine with you there. A bed will suit your body better than the stone floor—even if it does have a rug."

Lord Darshel laughed at her own show at humor. "Sleep well, Zy'ena."

§ §

Darshel awoke sometime later and found the sun sinking to late afternoon. Surprised he had slept so long, he jumped up from the bed and raced across the hall to the king's chambers to check on Zyanthena's condition. To his vexation, the desert woman was not abed, and neither she nor the two wolves were to be found. He cursed and went back to retrieve his boots and outer jacket and began a hurried search of the palace. Lord Darshel had to ask himself, *How far can a woman go right after waking from a coma?* But the answer was obvious after some minutes of searching: very far. She was not in any of the upper or lower halls, nor in the Great Hall, kitchens, or banquet hall. Lord Darshel was running out of places he knew to look—and he was getting worried.

He must have been making sounds of distress, however, because he came upon the alpha male waiting for him at the exit of another room. The huge grey wolf eyed him boredly and stood from his seated pose to stalk down the hallway. Darshel sighed at the wolf's usual manner toward him and followed obediently, like a pup being led home. He was surprised to be shown to the great library—a room he had yet to explore. Awed, Lord Darshel paused at the entrance to stare about the enormous space.

Crystanian's library had, at the time of the Xraxrain reign, been famous for its great collections of history, art, music, and lore. Thousands upon thousands of leather-bound compendiums about Syre stretched three levels upward and fourteen shelves deep. Lord Darshel had never seen such a large amassment of books. Slowly, he stepped deeper into the room, only to stop once more at another sight. The largest map ever made of Syre stretched across the main floor of the library. Its details were etched in a shimmery paint the lord-governor was not familiar with. It seemed to change and dance in the soft light coming in from the ceiling windows. The sight of it drew his eyes about the map, trying to catch every nuance.

"You should see it from here." Zyanthena's voice floated down from the second-story balcony. Darshel looked up to see her leaning over the railing, watching him with her keen brandy-colored eyes. He followed her wave to the steps and joined her on the next landing.

"You have a way of distressing people, running hither and yon with no warning."

"I have a way of distressing *you*, you mean," Zyanthena teased and eased herself back into the chair she had occupied. Lord Darshel noted she had found an elegant winter dress of thick, rich brown brocade from somewhere. Yet, before he could ask about it, she continued, "I could not sleep. Being in a coma for so long must have robbed me of it. So, I took my time coming here. I needed to find answers."

"Answers to?" Darshel asked as he slid into the opening she had left him by the railing. He tried to occupy himself with admiring the map below—which really was more marvelous from that height—and not give away his anxieties.

"Myself, and all the new insights swimming around in my head."

Lord Darshel turned to look at her, confusion on his face.

Zyanthena's features softened into a teasing smile. "Your expressions of late have been quite different from what I remember."

"Yes, well…" The Shekmann came closer and took a seat next to the desert woman. "I think the recent ordeal has aged me some. I was afraid I was going to be alone with the wolves for the winter."

There was a softness to Zyanthena's look then—unusual and fleeting as it was—as if she sympathized with his trial. "But you are not. I too am happy with this outcome. It's much better than being dead." She turned to finger the page of a codex she had spread open before her. "And I seem to have answers now to the questions I've had over these past eight summers. Even as incredible as they are, I am grateful to know this now."

"Know what, perchance?"

Zyanthena took a deep breath, as if preparing herself for the information she was about to impart, and then she began. "Whatever powers Vauldin possesses, it gave me back my memories, as well as an understanding of my birthright. I…I was raised as Princess Zerra Starkindler of the Crystal Kingdom." She huffed at the craziness of it. "I remember being her. All those years in the castle, being with my brothers, riding Veiled Darkness… I see *that attack* on the castle, the one when the maunstorz killed the queen—my mother—and forced the rest of the family across Syre. I remember the heat of the Aras as it beat down upon me, snuffing out my life—and awakening with none of these memories, in front of the Shi'alam…" Her brandy eyes looked distant as an old lifetime, long left behind, still played within them. She became still and let the silence become a deafening proclamation to the revelation. Finally, Zyanthena stirred and averted her gaze to the book. "A part of me wishes my memories were false—but they feel so real, so right! And yet, even if I am *that* Zerra Starkindler, I have to be more, too. Vauldin belongs to the heirs of Crystalynian and wakes only for them."

"Just how hard did you hit your head? I think the fall and the coma have addled your mind."

A wan smile answered Lord Darshel's denial of the truth. It startled the Shekmann to see the hurt look in the liquid-brown shine of her eyes. "Wanting to deny the truth seems so easy when you say it is impossible, but I cannot deny it." Zyanthena tapped on the page opened before her. "Here are the last pages written by the royal scribe for Queen Kestral Xraxrain. Written are all the events leading up to Crystalynian's fall. Read it."

Lord Darshel didn't really want to look at the text. Doing so would open his eyes to the truths he would rather keep denying. He realized that the fear stemmed from another truth: his affection for Zyanthena Sheev'arid...even being a Tashek (and thus an enemy of the Shekmann family) had not made her less desirable. For her to be someone other than a Tashek of Staria seemed preposterous—but the sad look she gave him made the Shekmann take the book and start reading where she pointed.

> *It is the fifteenth day of Planting Time 89 S.C., King Trev'shel and his heir, Prince Verrin, have been mortally wounded in battle; they may not live the night... Queen Kestral has ordered her baby daughter, Arrez, to be taken in by His Majesty Richard Sunrise, close friend of the crown and godfather to the princess. They are to travel to the Crystal Kingdom in secret, and she will be placed in the Starkindlers' trust until Crystalynian is retaken. If we are unable to save our people, then the princess will remain permanently with the Starkindlers. In either case, only myself—the royal scribe of Queen Kestral—along with Her Majesty the Queen, King Richard Sunrise, and the Starkindler king and queen will have any recount of this action. I write these words here in hopes that I can burn this journal in a fortnight, when my Queen retakes our beloved kingdom from the maunstorz...*

Lord Darshel lifted his emerald eyes from the page. "This is quite the recounting. Yet, even if you can retell stories of Zerra Starkindler, how am I to believe she is you? You did live at the Crystal Castle for a time when you served under Commander Matar and the Crystine. How do you not know your memories are false ones created by stories you heard during your stay there?"

Zyanthena clearly had been prepared for Lord Darshel's rebuttal. She reached across the table to another opened compendium and lifted a small oil painting set atop it. This, she handed to the lord-governor. The painter had been skilled at making the portrait lifelike. The woman's regal stature, dark skin and hair, sharp and direct eyes, and gorgeous features looked only too familiar. "The Shi'alam always insisted I must be related to his distant cousin Kestral—even if Vauldin did not respond to me back then. I look just like my mother."

"Kestral was Tashek?"

"She had an ancestor that was Sheev'anee. King Trev'shel was full Tashek, from clan Tamar'in, a subclan of the Tem'arids. They met at the Citadel of Light when the Xraxrains were visiting. Kestral was sixteen when they married. The king took the Xraxrain name instead of Kestral taking his name—to keep the royal line alive."

"You seem to know an awful lot for having only been in this library half a day."

Zyanthena took Queen Kestral's picture back and gently set it in its place inside the compendium. She evaded Lord Darshel's prying questions—not yet ready to share all she had learned through Vauldin and the library. "Like I said, I had many questions when I woke up. The answers seem to find me the more I read and remember."

Darshel was quiet for a long moment as he thought over her words. Finally, he said, "And you honestly believe you are Arrez Xraxrain?"

"And Zerra Starkindler—or more precisely, Arrez raised as Zerra."

"Well then…" He let the words drift away. Setting down the scribe's heavy journal, Darshel moved away from the table.

"You do not believe it to be so."

"I don't know what to believe!" He spun back to face her. His discomfort had his temper rising to the surface. "To me, you are Zyanthena Sheev'arid, the Tashek woman my men captured crossing my lands. The same Zyanthena I have come to know as very loyal and honest and brave. The very one who fights for me even when she does not have to. And now you say you're… you're the heir of Crystalynian, or maybe the Crystal Kingdom itself, or—"

"But I *am* Zyanthena!" She rose to grasp his hands and stop his mind's spinning. The action worked, and Lord Darshel stilled at her sudden contact. "You think this is any less confusing for me? I am reeling, lost, in the enormity of it all. How could I possible be *that* girl? Yet Vauldin awakening for me proves that I am of the Xraxrain line."

It was strange to see Zyanthena so rattled. Usually, she was the most centered woman the Kavahadian had ever met. Was it her previous memories of Princess Zerra, now accessed, that brought out this new side to her, or was it just the extraordinary situation that had forced it up? Lord Darshel glanced down at her hands—white knuckled—on his and realized Zyanthena was afraid of the revelations. "You have every right to be astonished, Zy'ena. This kind of news isn't easy to take. Even if you had had a forewarning, I doubt this could be processed in a day, or—Stars!—even a season." He squeezed her hands and then released them. "Luckily, we will have a long winter stuck here to delve into this matter. So, let's go to the kitchens, and I will rustle up some dinner."

"A lord knows how to rustle?"

Lord Darshel laughed, relieved to hear her come back to herself enough to make her typical sarcastic remarks. "I've done a little in my day." He heard the disbelieving harrumph at his retort as he headed back down the staircase. It made Darshel smile.

At the bottom, he stopped to glance back at Zyanthena and watch her find her way down the wooden steps. Her movements were very cautious, and lost was the usual grace and lightness of foot. An unaccounted-for step had Zyanthena grabbing for the railing to keep from falling. "Zy'ena!" Darshel rushed back up to her side as she straightened herself and recovered her dignity.

"I'm still weaker than I'm used to."

"Yes, well…I think in this case, that's pretty normal." He slipped a hand around the warrioress's slender waist, taking her other arm across the back of his neck. "Though, I'm surprised you made it all the way here from your bedchamber without my help."

"I rested along the way. Yet, even knowing where I was going, it took me an hour."

"You knew where the library was?" Darshel asked. "Never mind. Maybe I don't want to know about that—yet. I've had enough surprises for one day."

§ §

After a dinner of potatoes and chicken soup, Lord Darshel helped Zyanthena down to see her beloved black stallion. The forty-horse stable was located at the western corner of the palace and boasted a stunning view of the mountains from its entrance. The Xraxrains had been considered the best horsemen in Syre, widely known for their studies in horse behavior and training techniques and touted as being the most advanced in horse husbandry of any of the kingdoms. Because of this, the stalls were unique in that they were twice as large as other stables, with runs that went to the outside. The divider between each stall was only five feet high to allow the horses a view of all their stable companions.

Unrevealed and Lord Darshel's courser, Tano, were comfortable in two of the roomy stalls, pastern-deep with straw. The tall black trumpeted out a greeting to his rider and pushed against his stall door in his excitement at seeing her again. Zyanthena's own beaming smile reassured the lord-governor that he had been right to bring her there, even in such a weakened state.

"Hello, my friend," the desert woman greeted her mount as she gave him some slices of apple she had snagged from the kitchen. "He looks well."

"Yes, if not contrite for throwing you before. I've let him and Tano run in the pens outside to let loose some energy. From the looks of things, his old wound is not bothering him at all anymore." Unrevealed had been injured the day Zyanthena had been captured by Lord Darshel's cavalry. An arrow had bitten deep into his hindquarters, preventing him from making a safe escape. Zyanthena had surrendered to Commander Raic instead of risking any permanent lameness for the horse.

"I am glad to hear you kept up with the horses while tending me."

"I know better than to neglect a Tashek's mount. Ill would have found me if I had."

Zyanthena chuckled. "Indeed, it would have." She stroked the stallion's broad cheek and smiled as the big black closed his eyes in delight.

"Here are some brushes I found. I don't think a romp outside is warranted, but this should not wear you out too much." She thanked him and entered her charger's stall. Darshel watched them awhile and then moved on to his own mount.

Time passed in a comfortable silence as they groomed their horses. When Lord Darshel finished up, he glanced across the stall divider to find Zyanthena sitting in the straw, looking wearied. "I know you could sleep here with Unrevealed any day of the week, but a bed would be better suited, don't you think?" asked Darshel.

Zyanthena looked up at the lord-governor's voice. She groaned sleepily. "Yes, My Lordship. That would be nice."

"Very well, then." Lord Darshel collected the brushes and set them in the aisle before coming back to Unrevealed's stall. "I can carry you, if you'd prefer?" The fact that Zyanthena didn't protest was testament to how tired she was. It still seemed atypical that she would let him dote on her so, but Lord Darshel reminded himself that the behavior was most likely temporary.

"All right, here we go. A nice, warm bed."

Zyanthena stirred herself awake and managed to keep herself sitting upright on the bed while Darshel stoked the fire. As he returned to her side, she asked, "Could you help me with this dress?"

"I, ah…certainly." Darshel reached around her to unbutton the back. "It's loosened."

"Help me lift it over my head." When he hesitated, Zyanthena matched his stare. "Since when have you been modest with a woman?"

"Only with you, Zy'ena."

"You carried me naked not so long ago."

"Half-naked. I did have the decency to cover you. And you weren't awake then."

"But I am now. And I am fatigued and in need of your assistance. Do I need to ask again?"

"No. No, you do not." Darshel averted his eyes as he helped her with the thick brocade of the dress. Underneath were cotton petticoats, comfortable to sleep in. "These are quite fine."

"Yes. The best for the queen of Crystalynian. I found them in the bureau in the closet."

"If I had known the dressers were stocked—"

"You were busy attending to other needs," Zyanthena interrupted. "And, for that, I understand. There are men's clothes there as well. I'm sure you would like to change into a clean set." She stifled a yawn.

"I'll let you sleep." Darshel motioned her to lie down and helped her under the covers. "You will promise not to disappear on me again if I leave you, right?"

A soft, weary smile answered him. "Perhaps," she said quietly and drifted off to sleep.

Lord Darshel watched Zyanthena for some time, finding himself lost in her beauty, her face softened in sleep. Finally, though, he tore himself away to search the closets for clothes. The rooms were indeed well stocked with almost any article of clothing a lord would need, and many were warm and thick for the cold winters and high-mountain elevations of the kingdom. Darshel was surprised to find that many of the garments fit him acceptably. "Well, I won't feel like a pauper on my winter stay here." He took a number of the outfits to his room across the way and changed into comfortable clothes.

Then, after checking in once more on Zyanthena, he headed away to the library, taking a candle along to light his way. He couldn't quite shake the feeling that something major had changed with the desert woman. Certainly, her beliefs about her past had not eased his heart. Worse, it seemed that more than Crystanian had been rebuilt by the obsidian stone, Vauldin.

Lord Darshel neared the table Zyanthena had occupied. He set the candle down and took to inspecting the compendiums she had collected there. Two codexes were about the history of Syre: one of the First Age, the other of the Second. An old, worn, leather-bound book was about the properties and histories of the Stones of Power, and a fourth was about the kings and queens of Syre. Zyanthena had also pulled down fifteen journals and two maps of old and new Syre. Lord Darshel doubted that all of the books had been on the same shelves. How, then, had she known where everything was without searching for days?

A noise startled the Shekmann, and he turned to see two beady eyes fixed on him in the night. Struggling to calm his racing heart, Darshel spoke to the alpha wolf: "Someone else who likes sneaking up on me with no warning. Can't you ever just be nice?"

The grey wolf sat on his haunches and tilted his head, watching attentively.

"Right. I'm talking to a wolf, silly me." He turned away to survey the contents of the table again. "And silly me to think I can understand any of this. Magic has changed this palace from ruins and pulled forth forgotten memories in a girl with no past. More peculiar things are bound to happen."

Lord Darshel glanced down to find his hands shaking. Yes, he had to admit, he was afraid. Afraid of Crystanian, afraid of the magic of Vauldin, and afraid of what changes had happened to Zyanthena Sheev'arid. "Stars, I am in way over my head!"

Chapter Two
§
Meeting Over Tea

It was a grey-clouded, rainy day along the coast. Despite the damp, the Sealand prince wandered the beach, his ocean-blue eyes fixed on the steady wash of waves against the golden-flecked sand. No one else was about, all of the populace having shut themselves inside the stone walls of Fortress Opal, which jutted out of the only cliffside to the south like a pointed crown. Prince Par Fantill preferred it that way. For too long, he had endured the subtleties of court and the flock of potential fiancées that came with them.

Since the prince's return to Sealand's capital, King William Fantill had made two ultimatums. The first had been for Par to learn how to use the stone, Serein, to protect Sealand from the maunstorz. The second had been to find a wife and future queen. Neither prospect was high on Par's to-do list. He was not comfortable using Serein's powers, especially the more he read and learned about the sapphire's abilities. Magic was a frightening thing and had not been witnessed in Syre for nearly three hundred years—or so the prince had thought. His father and Crystine Commander Matar said otherwise. The use of magic had destroyed the golden Second Age of Syre. For that one reason, Prince Par felt that the Stones of Power should be left well enough alone. However, King William, the previous wielder of Serein, insisted the stone's powers would be the only thing to save Syre from the enemy. It was something father and son disagreed upon.

As for the second command, Par tolerated a daily hour of tea with a lady of his mother's choosing. Yet despite some ladies being quite pleasing to the eye, the prince found their conversations exceedingly dull and their daily flirtations to win his affections annoying. Constantly, he was wont to remember the intelligent twinkle in the brandy eyes of his long-lost betrothed, Princess Zerra Starkindler of the Crystal Kingdom—the only lady Par had ever had any feelings for. Had the princess and her family not been taken in the maunstorz attack on their kingdom, Par knew, he and she would have long since been married—perhaps even had a child or two. But fate had not allowed such to be. Worse, the more Par pined for the should-have-beens, the more his father pushed new prospects on him.

And so, after having endured the fortress for one long month, Par had taken the opportunity the weather presented to elude his duties and enjoy a quiet stroll away from the prying eyes and etiquette his title demanded. Of course, the prince was not entirely alone. His golden-eyed shadow kept a watch on him from the grassy berms further up the beach. Lord Gordar Farrylin, his cousin and lord protector, would never leave Par completely unattended, but he knew when to give his charge some berth, which Par was grateful for. Just an hour alone was no small feat those days.

Yet it had not always been so. Not two months past, Prince Par had been heading the Sealand army in North Point, a command post in the northern reaches of the kingdom. He had fought alongside men wearied by a hard-won struggle against a force of enemy maunstorz numbering nearly ten thousand strong. Though the days had worn the prince thin, Par had found a comfort in leading his father's forces. Certainly, he had been given more respect and solitude, which his father and the court did not allow. Staring out at the grey waves of the ocean, the Sealander felt an ache in his heart for those days on the battlefield.

"My prince."

Par, startled out of his reverie, turned to his cousin. Lord Gordar had approached quietly and had caught him unawares, a faux pas during the uncertain times of war. "Cousin," he replied, slightly sheepish. Gordar would never judge his prince for being vulnerable when he was around, but Par felt the embarrassment nonetheless.

"Afternoon tea will be served shortly. The queen bids me to remind you to attend."

Par held in a sigh. "We will go soon." He started to look away but caught sight of his lord protector's disapproving face. "Yes? Did my mother say more?"

"To remind you to dress…decently, I believe her words were."

Par looked down at his garments, trying to find fault with them. "What's not decent with these?"

Lord Gordar tried to look serious but failed when a chuckle formed on his lips. "Lace, my prince, is in fashion—or so I believe—and those ruffles along the chest and sleeves."

"Oh, ghastly."

"Indeed, but I think the ladies would find you less ragtag if you wore their usual finery."

"Ragtag? This is the finest men's jacket of last year's set!"

"My point exactly," Gordar teased. "Your jacket's out of fashion."

"Bah! It's bad enough I'm humoring my father on selecting a bride, now he expects me to follow the ever-changing ways of courtly feathering too."

"Am I to believe it will be your military set today, then?"

"Yes, cuz. I do believe it will be."

§ §

The afternoon tea was taken in the queen's private sitting room, one of the largest and finest in the fortress. It was gilt in silver with inset sapphires, the colors of the royal house. Thick brocade in a rich blue covered the sitting chairs and couch and hung along the windows, enhancing the depth of the hues. Though the outside of Fortress Opal looked drab and military-like, this room, and all the others, spoke of the wealth of the Sealand capital.

Queen Kesnia was as fair as her only son. All of her fine, pale features had gone to Par—except for her hazel eyes. Par's eyes were the color of his father's. Kesnia looked as dignified as always, sitting so straight and proper despite her short stature. Prince Par loved his mother. She was the calming force behind the throne and as steadfast as the sun. Had it not been for the underlying reason for the afternoon tea, the prince would have enjoyed being with his mother that day.

A new lady and her mother were sitting on the couch, waiting politely for the prince's arrival. Joining them were two girls of the lady's choosing. The last person to arrive was the prince's only sibling, Lady Celeste, twelve years of age. As the prince entered the sitting room, this cute little copy of himself hurried from her seat to greet her big brother. The others rose respectfully as she rushed to him.

Par reached down to hug Celeste as she fell into him, clutching his waist tightly. He faked a protesting groan at her strength. "My, Celi, you've gotten quite strong!"

"It's good to see you, brother." She smiled up at him like an adoring angel. Par mirrored the look. He hadn't seen his sister for three *long* years, as she had been hosted at a countess's household in Darrol, one hundred miles east of Fortress Opal. The lady of the house was supposed to be teaching the young princess about proper etiquette—a task Par knew would be difficult, for Celeste was as rebellious as she was cute. Her running to him showed how little progress had been made. She said, "Mother says you've been back a whole month! You should be ashamed for not calling me home sooner!"

"Me, ashamed?" Par raised his eyebrows. "I think not, sister. I'd have had you back the moment I arrived."

"I wanted you to wait, Celeste," Queen Kesnia said, reminding the siblings where they were. "Now, please, bring your brother here. I would like him to meet Duchess Limonté and her daughter, Lady Yvonne."

Par straightened and let his sister pull him, reluctantly, to the couches. He hoped Lord Gordar was following closely, for the room held too much femininity. At least Celeste seemed oblivious to all the fuss. She grinned widely at the young Lady Yvonne, quite taken with her already. "This is my brother, Par. I'm sure he's excited to meet you."

The group chuckled nervously at the girl's boldness. Still, the small faux pas helped take the awkwardness out of the room. "Celi," Par berated quietly, though not too forcefully. He had too much affection for his sister for that. To be polite, he accepted the duchess's hand and then the lady's, laying a kiss lightly over each one's gloved knuckles. He also greeted the lady's two companions before introducing the room to his lord protector. Having a handsome cousin, especially one with stunning golden eyes, helped shift the attention away from himself.

The queen seemed pleased enough with the first exchange. "Now that we are introduced, may we have some tea?" She indicated the table set to the right of their seats. A maid was waiting to pour their drinks and hand out biscuits and cakes.

The distraction of food and drink gave Par just enough time to share a trapped look with his cousin before he accepted his teacup and found a seat in a chair between the two crowded couches. Lady Yvonne politely found her seat nearest his, her two ladies close to aid her in conversation lest she and Par not find it easy to converse. Par found it unfair that he was not accorded the same arsenal; Lord Gordar was made to sit with the queen and duchess as their "gentlemanly" entertainment.

The Sealand prince found himself at a loss for words. Trying to be polite, he asked the first thing to come to mind. "Are you from the capital, Lady Yvonne?"

Yvonne smiled shyly behind her cup. "Only for the past summer, Your Highness. I grew up in Permonde."

Par was surprised the lady spoke frankly, unlike the other ladies he had had to entertain. There was a hope their conversation would be less of a drudgery than usual. "Permonde. That's near Pearl Lake, if I am not mistaken."

"Yes, Your Highness." She seemed pleased the prince knew where her home was. "My father holds a large acreage of grapes there."

"That's right," Par remembered. "The Limonté vineyards are among the best winemakers in the kingdom. I know the place now. The Sia Hills must be full of snow about now."

"Well, yes. Though it's far too early. The sudden snows have harmed the last crop."

Prince Par could sympathize. More and more reports were coming into the capital of similar blights since the snowstorm caused by the wielder of Ravel, the crystal Stone of Power. Of course, the king and prince had not told the populace that their losses were from magic. Enough panic was going around without adding that. "I am sorry for your family's loss. Are your reasons for being south because of the snows, then?"

Instead of replying, the young lady did something that the prince had not expected. Her eyes got a little defiant, and she tossed her long, black hair behind one shoulder, suddenly looking anything but demure. Par blinked at the change and her bold answer. "My family is hoping I will be a suitable match for you, as rumors have it that you have yet to find a proper betrothal." She didn't state that her family thought she was indeed just the right bride for him. Still, her tone implied it—yet she knew better than to say such aloud, as it would have been too direct and rude. However, for Lady Yvonne to respond the way she had made the prince suspect the young woman did not agree with her family's wishes. Did she think him a pompous laughingstock from whatever rumors the ladies of the court had concocted about his previous betrothal pursuits?

The ladies accompanying Lady Yvonne gasped at her rudeness and whispered for her to behave more appropriately toward the royal heir. Par, however, was intrigued. Here was a woman with a smart tongue held under the sway of what society dictated. The idea was familiar to the princeling—it reminded him of a certain princess... Glancing at his mother, Par realized the hand she had dealt him. Queen Kesnia hid a pleased expression by responding to something the duchess said. *Clever as always, mother,* Par thought affectionately.

Enough time had elapsed to make the three ladies unsettled, certain Lady Yvonne had offended the prince. Par knew he must not let Lady Yvonne get away with such a smart remark—at least, with the other ladies present to witness the slight—but he couldn't help approving of the young woman's tactlessness; it was refreshing to be goaded. "Rumors can always be wrong, my lady," he said, deciding to play the game Lady Yvonne was dictating. "One would say there are rumors of you, too." If there were, Par had not heard, having been gone too long at war, but the prince knew how to approach this contest of words. Let the lady think he had evidence against her.

"But that wasn't true!" The second girl—Par would later come to know her name as Lady Collette—burst out in her friend's defense. Yvonne glared at the girl, willing her to be quiet. However, the bait had already been eaten.

"Oh? And what part was not true?"

Lady Yvonne answered, knowing it was her only recourse. "I did not have any *familiarities* with my father's man. David was a good friend, nothing more. The word was spread to debase my father, in hope that his competition would gain the royal approval for their wines."

There had to be more to the story, Par was sure, but he had heard enough of the rumor to know what the cost had been to the young lady's reputation. He decided he needn't expound on the issue. "I do not have enough evidence to say whether or not what you defend is true—and as I do not, I declare we are equal on account of the distress our rumors have caused."

"Are we?" Lady Yvonne replied shortly, then found her tact enough to add, "Your Highness."

"Pardon?"

"I am not sure of the rumors of you."

"Ah." Par cleared his throat. "And of what do you refer?" Being royal, he doubted there was only one rumor going around. He could only imagine what had been said.

"The princess. She would still be the one?"

Zerra, Par thought. Of course. "Princess Zerra Starkindler, you mean?"

Yvonne nodded.

"She would have been my betrothed, if she were still here."

Chocolate-colored eyes flashed, unhappy and validated. "And you think that makes us even, Your Highness? *None of us* will compare to the princess of the Crystal Kingdom. Any dreams of being the one, true love for you will never be allowed to grow within your heart. With you, we would always be second rank to a dead girl."

Now Par understood the lovely lady's temper. He could see how him still loving a lost princess might make the ladies resentful toward him. Par knew he might be dense when it came to some court politics, but on this matter he was not stupid. When young ladies' only hopes for a good life were bound to being married off to men approved by their family, it left most in a position of uncertainty. If Par had been in Yvonne's place, he would not be pleased with how all the facts aligned, either.

"Yvonne!" Duchess Limonté scolded between gushing apologies to the queen.

Par had been processing his thoughts. By the time he caught up to the panic in the room, the duchess was making to leave with the ladies in tow. "No!" the Sealander begged to stop them. His words shocked the room to silence. "Stay, please stay. Lady Yvonne has not offended. In fact, I find her words a relief to hear them said so plainly. Please, sit and relax. I ask of you."

The rest of the room hesitated, and then the women returned to their seats and slowly settled back into a routine. Queen Kesnia grinned, pleased with her son; she knew half the battle had been won if a lady could make Par extend the afternoon tea.

The two other ladies looked uncomfortable, knowing Yvonne had overstepped. Also, they were confused on the prince's pardon. Only Yvonne, still felling slighted by Par's admittance of his long-lost love, had any confidence to sit proud and somewhat proper. She had a look in her eye, as if she expected Par to continue their conversation—whether inappropriate or not—where it had stopped.

Yet Par was not sure he wanted to speak more on the matter of the princess of the Crystal Kingdom. No one, except Lord Gordar, understood his stubborn longing for Zerra Starkindler. Continuing the subject with a lady he had just met—and who would certainly not sympathize with his plight—was not something Par was willing to do. He cleared his throat and searched his mind for another recourse. "You said you were from Permonde. That's pretty country."

Yvonne's eyebrows rose at the turn of direction. "Yes, it is, Highness. Have you been?"

"Yes. I went on a hunting retreat near there a few seasons back. It was Levies and Storage Time, I think. The maples were orange. There had been a syrup-collecting party going on at the same time."

"You were there during the Harvest-Gathering Time," Lady Yvonne corrected. Her eyes softened some as she recalled good memories of her own from such a season. "That was a good time to visit."

"I thought so. Of course, the fox hunting didn't go so well, but the syrup I tasted was excellent."

His comment had the lady smirking. "Had I been with you, your hunting would have fared better."

"You fox hunt?"

"I do." Yvonne lifted her cup to sip some tea before continuing. "I'm trained in archery—at least as much as my tutors will let me learn. I go on hunts now and again to catch pelts. It's all the rage these days, having fox or minx fur on winter coats. They fetch a fair price here in the capital. I have a tanner I share my catch with in Permonde. It helps him feed his wee ones."

Par wondered if the lady had added the last tidbit to make him think of her as an altruist. If she was playing for political gain, it didn't make him like her more. "Do you help the townspeople often?"

"I do. I find it important in my role as the duke's daughter. Those of privilege should help those less fortunate than ourselves. Do you not agree?"

The prince's eyebrows knit. Yvonne Limonté was certainly going to be a woman who would challenge the status quo—for good or ill. If he decided to court her, as his parents wished, it would be a constant battle of wills between them and the court. If this was to be commonplace with her, was he really willing to keep playing this game, year after year? "I think all folk should have opportunities. It is their due. Whether that means I help them or not all depends on the situation, however. There are some who would do poorly to be helped by the more privileged."

"And you think yourself wise enough to be the judge of that?"

"I'm not perfect, my lady, but, yes, if I am to be their king someday, then I need to have that discernment. There will be times I cannot help someone and times I can. I will need to know how to give proper judgment on such matters."

His response was not haughty, as she clearly had expected of the royal heir. Prince Par could see her pause and reassess him. Whatever conclusion she came to seemed to calm her confrontational attitude. "I apologize, Your Highness, if I implied you could not lead judiciously. Indeed, a good king would know how to be discerning."

"As I said earlier, I appreciate candor, Lady Yvonne. It would do me poorly to become hardened to the counsel of others for my own ego. When I choose my queen, I fervently hope she is one who will help me to become best ruler I can be for the people of Sealand."

"Then you have no objection to my forwardness?"

"I—"

"Because, Your Highness, if you are looking for a queen who will speak frankly with you, I am the one fit for the task."

Her two ladies gasped at Yvonne's boldness, once again unrestrained despite protocol. In a way, though, her behavior amused the prince. Certainly, his mother had finally found a lady that could keep him on his toes. "You haven't been in the capital long, have you?"

"No. My family would not permit me."

With manners like that, I can see why, Prince Par mused. He chuckled. "With good reason, I am sure. But you have been out in society?"

Lady Yvonne's lovely brow furrowed. She seemed suspicious that the prince was looking to demean her for something. "Yes, for four seasons, since my eighteenth birthday. I have had suitors…" She frowned, knowing her admittance sounded bad. "But after the false rumor of my stolen virtue, there have been…few."

Par's eyes went to his lord protector, who—despite keeping a cordial conversation with the older women—had also listened in on Par's discussion with Lady Yvonne. His cousin knew the look well. Right after the afternoon tea, Lord Gordar would speed away to check on this false rumor and learn the truth. Knowing if Yvonne spoke true about her virtue would be important, as Par was beginning to suspect that the setup between Duchess Limonté and the queen had been because of the impact this rumor had caused the young lady. A girl thought to be deflowered had very little left to stand on once the dust settled, even if the rumor was proven wrong. "I do appreciate your frankness, Lady Yvonne. Perhaps within the next week, would you accompany me around the capital? I think you need to see it with your own eyes."

"Does this mean you accept a courtship, Your Highness?"

"I didn't say that." Par was quick to set the young woman straight. "As you also have some…objections to me, I think we should proceed slowly with our relations. I will see you around my city to introduce Opal to its new lady of the court and you to it. Shall that be enough?"

All the women seemed stunned that the Sealand heir had elected to do even that much. Queen Kesnia seemed pleasantly surprised at her son's change of heart, and little Celeste was beaming at her brother as if he were the greatest man in Syre. It took some moments more for Lady Yvonne to respond to the prince's invitation, but she finally found her voice enough to say, "Yes, Your Highness. I believe it shall."

Chapter Three
§
Bartering

The Red City was cold and dark under six feet of fresh snow. Its townspeople, now prisoners in their own city, huddled within their poorly insulated dwellings and found little relief from the biting cold. More than a few would lose their battle against the elements and starvation—not that their captors had a care about the ailing populace. To the maunstorz, the people of Rubia's capital were worth very little compared to what they controlled in the Red Palace.

Aptly named, the palace of red stone and bronze was the only well-lit building in the whole city. Its bright candlelight and fires sent out a mocking glow to the people, creating a subdued envy of the riches beyond reach. But that was how Mansocan, leader of the enemy army, liked it. Domination and suppression suited him just fine—and what better way to control all of Rubia than by killing the king and keeping the sole, sickly heir and his young son captive, locked away in the dungeons below the Red Palace, along with the other two princes of his Third's recent catch? If all kept going his way, Mansocan knew that he would be controlling both Rubia and Sunrise by the snows' thaw. He had the right leverage, after all.

Like all maunstorz, Mansocan was built to run and fight for days. His scar-laced skin was a testament to his prowess at war, as were the five tattooed lines on his right arm that noted his high status of *seka'vlr* within the maunstorz. Only one man, Zepthanial, was above him. Yet, far away from his sovereign, Mansocan was his own leader. He controlled the six contingents of maunstorz in Syre any way he chose. Two he had kept in Staria to harass the noble "Prince of War"; three helped him hold Rubia, and the last Mansocan had sitting pretty at King Raymond's command front in Sunrise. With the wielder of the Crystal stone keeping the snows high and cold in the North, Mansocan could see how ripe Syre was for the taking. He could be patient; all the years his ancestors had fought to take the eight kingdoms were nearing an end. Mansocan would take the country by the next turning of the sun, or one Syrean year's count of Seasons.

The *seka'vlr* snickered and turned away from the window overlooking the city. He grabbed up a flask of ale and a tray of sweet "counties" and flung himself into a plush chair in front of the roaring fire. "Chornauk!" he called out and waited for his Third to appear by his side.

His underling's waist-length, shocking-white hair made the man's eyes gleam red in the firelight as he bowed to his commander. Mansocan ordered him: "Bring me the heirling. I always like my chats with him."

"Yes, sir." Chornauk saluted and quickened away to the dungeons.

He returned with Prince Rowin Sunrise, one of several captives in the maunstorz' control. The Sunarian royal, his lord protector, and the prince's younger brother were prisoners of war, captured in a raid as their royal procession traveled south from the Citadel of Light, in Staria, after a War Meeting hosted there. Too good a bargaining chip to pass up, Chornauk had made sure to bring the royal hostages to his *seka'vlr* at Mansocan's claimed residence, the Red Palace, in the conquered kingdom of Rubia.

The twenty-six-year-old Sunarian had not lost the piercing glare in his midnight-blue eyes despite three weeks of torture and meager meals provided by his captors. If anything, the hardships had brought out a fortitude in the princeling that Mansocan would not have guessed the royal to possess. So much for Southern men being "soft and spineless," as Mansocan had surmised. The boy was very like his long-departed father, King Richard, a man Mansocan once had traded swords with.

"Sit by the fire. Have some ale and a blanket," Mansocan ordered, doing his best to sound polite. However, from the wary look in the Sunarian's eyes, it was clear the prince was wise enough to know that the hand that fed him was connected to a mouth that bit. He came to a cautious seat on the flagstones, outside of his enemy's reach. Prince Rowin accepted the blanket but forwent the ale—in case it was again laced with a truth serum. Once was all it had taken for the Sunarian heir to suspect any kindness as a trap. Yet it was for that reason Mansocan called upon him so often; Prince Rowin was a smart lad.

"How are the dungeons, oh princeling?"

Prince Rowin eyed Mansocan coldly. "The mice are plentiful and the straw good and wet."

Mansocan chuckled. "Sounds like a cheery time."

"The best."

"And does your protector still breathe?"

When Prince Rowin had been captured by Chornauk and his men, Rio Ravesbend, the prince's lord protector, had fought bravely to keep his prince from being taken. However, his efforts had been rewarded with a dislocated shoulder and a concussion. The injuries were minor in comparison to those of Sage Cooper, their third companion. Rowin's loyal servant had been skewered by the maunstorz and left in a heap at their feet. Mansocan delighted in reminding his princely captive of this loss—as it brought a flare of anger to Rowin's eyes—yet, the jab had been losing its potency; the prince was too intelligent and cautious to continue being baited. Mansocan had slowly shifted tactics to other means of entertainment as his foe learned to maneuver around his provocations.

"He's still alive." Rowin's tone stayed emotionless, though inwardly he had to be fuming.

Rio's dislocated shoulder had been slow to heal, and the concussion left him prone to piercing headaches. Beyond that, the lord protector and Prince Derek of Rubia suffered from raging fevers brought on by the damp and cold of the dungeons and the lack of decent food and drink. If either man suffered further, it was doubted they could survive past midwinter.

"A pity. I had thought the Sunarian would have died from his ailments by now. You Southern men are hardier than I gave you credit for."

Rowin didn't bother replying.

Mansocan smirked and took the opportunity to sip his ale—the best of Rubia's stores. He changed the subject to their "normal" affair. "Your king has sent another missive. It seems he and the Sunarian court are still open to bartering for your brother's return. It's now up to eight hundred dreites."

"At that rate, he's bound to empty all the royal coffers." No longer was Rowin infuriated that King Raymond Sunrise, his uncle, was only interested in his half-brother Connel's release. After a month of being the maunstorz commander's playthings, the royal heir now realized neither Connel nor himself would be bartered off. They were worth more as captives to hold over his uncle's head than any amount of gold bars.

"Is Sunrise so close to bankruptcy? I thought their pockets ran deeper."

"If you throw in the Estarian stars and the candlesticks," Rowin replied, not giving any real answer to Mansocan's probing. He had learned from the start to not reveal too much. The *seka'vlr* was a gifted fisherman of truths.

Monsocan allowed his foe to see his admiration at an evasion done tactfully, head-bowing to such carefully crafted words. "And what can I offer you to get a better account of said coffers?"

"The price for that would be quite high."

"Name it.'"

It was their other game, and Rowin was getting better at it. "Ten loaves of bread, fresh and clean. Four barrels of clean water. Blankets for each of us, all thick and whole. And the herbs feverfew and willow."

"My…you are getting more brash. Four barrels *and* herbs?" The red gaze slid downward to his captive at his feet.

"That price is low for what you ask."

"Hm." Mansocan set his ale cup between his knees and leaned over it so as to be eye to eye with Rowin. He studied the heir of Sunrise for any flinch in his resolve. Finding none, his look narrowed. "Six loaves, two barrels and blankets, and feverfew."

"Eight, three of each, and the herb."

"For a price on the coffers?"

"You first."

Mansocan sat back and returned to his ale. The room filled with the soft crackle of the fire. In the glow of the flames, the prince's face was cast in shadows, making him looked etched like a marble statue. Rowin stayed patient and resolute under his captor's red stare. Mansocan said, "Chornauk."

"Sir."

"Take the prince to collect his due and see that it is sent to the dungeons. Have him returned here for supper."

Chornauk frowned but did as he was ordered. The leader's Third was none too pleased to see their captive win a barter. In his eyes, the prisoner should not be given any leeway. The hulk of a maunstorz picked Rowin up roughly by his scruff, nearly choking their captive with his collar, and marched him away to the kitchens.

§ §

Once they were out of earshot of the *seka'vlr*, Chornauk made sure to club Rowin on the head for good measure. "Just remember your place, boy."

"My place is keeping my fellow captives alive. We're not worth much dead."

"You aren't worth anything, just eating good food stores. I'd have killed you long ago."

Rowin hid a smirk. He could see why Chornauk was only a third-ranked commander. He was too impetuous; Mansocan, on the other hand, was very cunning.

The pair reached the kitchens, and Chornauk ordered the cook staff there to ready the bartered items. They grumbled at seeing more food allotted to the prisoners but followed the order, laying out eight loaves of fresh bread and three barrels of water. A runner was called to gather the blankets and the herb. All this was closely inspected by the prince. Rowin watched as a taster ate of each of the loaves and drank of each barrel before Rowin sampled the same. Never one to be too careful, he would not let his fellows be poisoned so easily. Once everything was to his satisfaction, Prince Rowin followed alongside the porters back to the dungeons to see the order filled.

Rubia's dungeons were dark and dank, a testament to how the royal house treated its "guests." Rowin could safely say Sunrise kept theirs better; he had been inside his own before. He used a well-burnt torch to see the steep staircase that descended to the dungeon level where the maunstorz kept their prisoners. There were eight cells in total, each housing four men—those Mansocan had deemed important enough to keep alive. The only addition to that number was Prince Derek Chível's six-year-old son, Miguel, whom they had thrown in with the Rubian prince and the three Sunarians. The thirty-three captives had survived by eating the very watery gruel the maunstorz brought and by huddling together in the wet straw. Only Rowin's recent use of bartering state secrets had given them any added comforts.

Someone groaned at the torchlight, and Rowin shifted his hand to cast it into the cell he shared with the other princes and his lord protector. Rio Ravesbend and Prince Derek, lying there in fever, barely reacted to the sudden brightness. Young Miguel Chível squinted and went to hide behind his father, afraid to be picked on by a guard again. Only

Prince Connel bothered to glare at the offense. The younger Sunarian prince stood and neared the iron gate to better see their offender.

Prince Connel was six years younger than his half-brother. He wore the Sunrise arrogance well despite his medium build, and he sported more comely features. At that moment, his light-blue eyes blazed at seeing his brother standing there. Though the two brothers had become closer thanks to their recent trial, it was still a sore spot between them that Rowin was offering state secrets to procure better food and blankets. "Just what did that cocksucker want this time?"

Rowin was vague with his answer. "A measly account of our royal dreites." He knew Connel would not be pleased with the maunstorz's latest request. Rowin began handing out his winnings between the cells. He ended back at their own cell and handed the bread and herbs through. Rowin had made sure to sort the items more important to each group of cells. His own already had two blankets for their sick, but not enough water or food. It could anger some of the other prisoners, but he had kept a full water barrel for themselves; Rio and Derek needed it more than anyone else to combat their fevers.

"This is quite a bit," Connel commented as he took a piece of the bread.

Rowin would have said, *I'm getting better at pushing Mansocan*, but he didn't dare with Chornauk there. "I bartered for what I could. Please soak the feverfew in some water for Rio and Derek."

"Certainly it would be better saved for us."

Rowin glared back at his brother. "I will not have either of them die over a stupid fever! Were it you, I would do the same."

The Connel of before would have sniggered and kept the water for himself. However, having been a captive and gone through his own beatings made him appreciate his brother's compassion and common sense. "I will have it ready."

Rowin gave a nod of thanks to Connel before he was pulled away by Chornauk. He would much rather have stayed and attended to his lord protector, but his toll had to be paid in order to keep up his bargaining.

§ §

Mansocan had taken residence in the king's chambers. No one had bothered to wash away the bloodstains in the apartment's foyer where the *seka'vlr* had cut down King Corbin Chível. To Rowin, the red stain was his biweekly reminder to watch his step when around the maunstorz leader. He was led over the dirtied rug and into the main living area, where bronze ornaments highlighted the red colors of Rubia in the plush couches and rugs. A full oak table had been set up to the right of the room, next to the stained-glass windows depicting Estarian doctrine stories. The finest china had been set out for two. Mansocan was already at the south end of the table.

"Sit," he ordered, keeping his eyes on Rowin until the prince did as he was bade. As soon as Rowin had found his seat, a young boy came over and filled their bowls with a potato-leek stew. A warm slice of bread was placed along the side of each bowl. The boy returned and filled their cups with tea. "Eat, prince of Sunrise." Yet Rowin waited until Mansocan took the first bites of everything before he lifted his own spoon. Mansocan chuckled at his wariness. "After eight sittings of this, have you not accepted my good will?"

"Good will? That would not be the word to use on a prisoner."

"Then what would that be, young princeling?"

"Allowance, perhaps, or bribery."

Red eyes narrowed, but not for long. Mansocan let out a laugh. "I see. That is how you see all this. And here I was thinking myself generous."

"I am not complaining. I do not mind our arrangement."

Mansocan studied Rowin over his cup of tea. "I would have expected you to be outraged at betraying state secrets as you do, but you're rather calm about it."

"There is no love lost between myself and the Sunarian court. My brother spoke true of himself being more favored. For that, I'd rather keep myself alive than think them able to do anything."

A chuckle. "True, the Sunarian court does petition on Connel's behalf. However, I think it is loathing of your king that has you acting thusly."

Rowin's midnight blue eyes sparked. "And why do you say that?"

"Oh, come now! I have spies. King Raymond is not the rightful king, nor is he your father."

The look Rowin returned was as cool as glass as all emotion washed from his face. Mansocan knew he had hit a nerve. "I don't know what you know of anything, Mansocan, even of that."

"Well played." Mansocan grinned. "You are never one to give out much. A pity your king doesn't find you as valuable as your brother."

Rowin had finished most of his meal, so he let drop his "payment," as it were. "Yes, that king is a fool, and his pockets run thrice and thrice again as deep as the latest letter he sent. You were wise to turn it down."

"Seventy-two hundred more?"

Rowin nodded to the count.

"Hm…you are indeed one of the richer kingdoms. It's not so easy to topple with coffers like that."

"It's more than money that wins."

"Ah, but it seems to help."

Rowin's eyebrows rose. "You seem to find news like this intriguing."

"Yes, well." Mansocan pushed back and rose from the table. "My people aren't ones to value coin like yours. Might and military prowess are what make us leaders." He looked down on Rowin. "I'm sure that little tidbit will keep you entertained as you sit in your cage."

It was the cue for Rowin to leave and return to his cell. He knew it well. "Perhaps it will." He found his feet and took his exit, with Chornauk his constant shadow.

Chapter Four
§
A Sardonian Welcome

"If I get there first, you buy me hot soup and an ale."

"Hey, what kind of bet is that?"

"One to keep your cold ass going," Jacen Novano bantered back to Patrick Kins.

The two commanders' sons had broken off from their travel companions to alert the town of Sardon, in the northern part of the Golden Kingdom, of the arrival of forty-eight archers belonging to Prince Kent Argetlem's small force. Prince Kent himself had asked the two friends to go ahead of the company, as they were the least injured of the soldiers. Not ones to disobey a direct order—especially from a prince—Patrick and Jacen had urged their horses onward to alert the lord-commander of Sardon of the prince's arrival.

Travel in the Golden Kingdom had become easier once the whole party had passed over the Pika Mounts, the hills separating Staria from Golden. The heavy snows to the north did not trouble the area, though the biting cold still left a nip in the air. To Patrick and Jacen, both northern-born men, the day was a welcome balm from the ferocious snows they had left in Staria. Still, the frosted mud on the road to Sardon had been quite a mess.

"What I want, if I beat you, is a hot bath and a lovely girl to bed for the night," Patrick said as he reined his palomino charger to a clipped trot. "That would warm these ol' bones of mine better than yer ale."

"Oh-ho! Now you're talking. Maybe all four to the one who gets the missive to Lord-Commander Ivance first."

"You couldn't handle that."

Jacen tried to sock Patrick in the shoulder good-naturedly—or as well as he could from horseback. However, Patrick was quick to angle his mount away, almost sending Jacen to the mud. Jacen had to grab hold of Sapphire's mane to keep from tumbling. His dark-grey charger shook her neck at the offense as he righted himself. "Hey!"

Patrick chuckled at his friend's near-predicament. "Serves you right for your teasing. But I'm all for what we can find after reporting in."

They reached the town about half an hour before the others. Unlike most military posts, Sardon had no any defensive walls. It was open and inviting. Thatched-roof houses, of one to three stories and made of pine, lined the streets. Their natural yellow gave off a mellow cheer to the visitors. Surprised, Patrick and Jacen reined their horses to a sedate walk and melded in with the townspeople milling around the large main street. They paused to speak with a "peacekeeper" official and ask for the whereabouts of the man they sought. "Lord-Commander Ivance's post is two blocks up," the man said. "You can't miss it. It's the only building with an eight-foot fence around it."

The two friends shared a confused shrug and continued onward. When they came across the building, they realized the peacekeeper had been right: it was hard to miss a two-story livery stable that stretched three whole blocks. A few Golden officers were talking on the full-length porch out front; the soldiers saluted the visitors as they dismounted and asked for their leader.

"I am Lord-Commander Ivance." A tall man with greying hair stood from a rocking chair and came forward. The only one in full military regalia—he wouldn't be caught dead without all of it properly in place—Lord-Commander Ivance had the aura of someone in complete control.

Patrick said, "I am Patrick Kins, son of Commander Ethan Kins of Rubia, and this is Jacen Novano, son of Berret Novano, former general of Blue Haven."

"Good sirs." Lord-Commander Ivance saluted them politely.

Patrick continued, "We have been travelling from the Citadel of Light with Prince Kent Argetlem's remaining archers." He pulled out the missive Prince Kent had written. "He and his men are nearing Sardon. He asked us to go on ahead so that preparations are in order for their return."

Lord-Commander Ivance took the rolled-up missive and broke the wheat-and-scale seal, the heir apparent's personal mark. Everyone was quiet as he read the letter. Looking composed, Ivance turned to Patrick. "I see they carry with them the ashes of Lieutenant-Commander Eric Sloane and the other men who fell at the battle at the Citadel."

"Yes, sir." Patrick bowed his head in respect to the deceased.

Ivance's eyes looked pinched. "This is grievous news to me. Lieutenant-Commander Sloane was the greatest of our men."

"He passed away of his wounds he received defending Prince Kent from harm," Jacen said.

"I see." Ivance waved to his men. "Jerry, Marks, see to these men's horses. Kins and Novano," he addressed the two friends, "thank you for bringing the missive. Have you need of our barracks?"

"With all respect, sir," Patrick replied, "we've a need for some baths and a good beer. We've been on the road for nearly a month. With the snows, our travels were slow going."

The honesty seemed to break the ice; a smile teased Ivance's lips. "Indeed. Well, you will have quarters here whenever you return. For now, I believe you will be wanting the Salty Dog. The pub is on Erring Street, three blocks down and four to the right. Ask for Mrs. Farley."

"Thank you, sir." Jacen and Patrick gave a proper salute and headed away on foot.

The Salty Dog looked like any other two-story tavern. Its main floor was open and full of tables for patrons. A long bar was settled against the back wall, filled with all sorts of liquors. There was a stage to the right for dancing girls and live music. That day, a ragtag band of folk singers were performing to a half-filled room; it all seemed lively enough judging by the hollering and clapping. Upstairs was a loft, open-ended to the bar below, with twelve rooms for rent to travelers.

Patrick elbowed Jacen in the ribs. "I like this place already."

Jason rolled his eyes and led the way to the bar to ask for Mrs. Farley. The bartender bobbed her pretty, curly-haired head and went to a back room to collect the owner. A moment later, a squat, middle-aged woman, barely taller than the height of the bar, came out with her employee. Jacen thought Mrs. Farley looked like the kind of lady you didn't want to piss off. "Mrs. Farley?"

"Yes." She raised a pudgy hand to shake his hand. "You boys look like cavalry, if mine old eyes don't deceive me. Dragged in by the nasty weather we've been having?"

"Yes, ma'am."

"Ma'am. Now I ain't been called that in years, darlin'. Round here everyone calls me Fancy. Mrs. Fancy Farley."

"Mrs. Farley." Jacen wasn't sure if "Fancy" was the owner's real name. He wasn't going to say anything uncouth to find out. "We were sent over by Lord-Commander Ivance."

"Ah, Nicól, the sweet man. I guess that means you're in need of Sardon's full hospitality, then. Kitten, please ask that two tubs be readied with hot water and some dinner specials be ordered." The bartender bobbed her head and went away on the task. "And some good ol' Golder beer for you boys?"

"Ah, yes, Mrs. Farley." They started to fish out coin to pay for their ale.

"Oh, none of that now," Fancy berated. "Nicól always takes the tab for Syrean soldiers. You both just be enjoying yerselves. Kitten will come get you when yer baths are ready."

"Wow... Thank you."

The two had barely gotten a taste of their ale when Kitten returned to show them to their baths. They were shocked. "That was fast!"

Kitten bobbed her head to Jacen's comment. "We keep the water hot in the back. Many request a bath after being out in the cold."

"Makes sense."

They were led to a door underneath the stairs. It exited into a small room with four tubs, two of which were filled with steaming water. "It may be cold in here, but the water's hot," Kitten assured them. "We also clean your clothes, gentlemen. If you'll leave them here by the door, new shirts and trousers are provided. Your own vestments will be returned to the livery."

It was a lot to take in, Jacen and Patrick just nodded in shock and then waited for Kitten to take her leave. Once they were alone, they undressed and left their clothes where she had directed, then sank shoulder deep into the tubs.

"Stars, this is heavenly!" Jacen moaned as he sat back and closed his eyes.

"There's even razors here and"—Patrick sniffed a brand-new bar of soap the size of a coin—"and goat's milk soap!"

"As if you needed to smell it."

"Hey, you never know," Patrick replied.

"I don't know if I'm going to shave." Jacen looked in the small mirror that was provided. It had been two months since he had taken a blade to his face. Not one to grow a full beard anyway, he had a light fluffing of chocolate-brown hair along his jawline and nothing along his lips but a fine line of down on the cleft of his chin. With his hair long enough to tickle his neck, Jacen looked younger than his twenty-six-years. "I think I look kind of dashing like this."

"What a charmer." Patrick had already lathered up his face and was starting on his right cheek. "Clean or stubble all the way." It fit with the Rubian preferences for short-cropped military cuts and "macho" soldierly attitudes. Jacen had teased his friend over his daily exercise regimen of push-ups, sit-ups, and squats on numerous occasions; however, it was all in good fun. Being friends for twenty years gave Jacen the liberty. "Damn, I need a haircut, too," Patrick fussed once his face was done. He plucked at his strawberry-blond hair, annoyed at its length.

"I'm sure they have a barber in the town. Just relax and enjoy the water. It's getting cold."

Relenting, Patrick dropped his hands and sat back.

They managed another ten minutes before the water cooled too much to enjoy. After exiting and drying off, they found the fresh clothes Kitten had mentioned. The white cotton tunics and black trousers fit near perfectly, and there were fresh socks to go with their spiffed-up boots. It was much more than they had expected.

"Lord-Commander Ivance really pays for all this?" Jacen thought aloud.

Patrick shrugged. "Hey, I ain't one to complain."

Jacen still wasn't feeling quite right about it, but he let the matter drop. "I'm ready for dinner. I wonder what they serve?"

They soon found out the dinner special was a meat pie filled with cheese, potatoes, and root vegetables. A loaf of soda bread was also provided, and more ale. The two of them were ushered to a side table and left to their meals.

By that time, the Salty Dog was jammed full of patrons. The men were lively, enjoying being off work and away from their fussy housewives. It also seemed many had come for the "limited-time" entertainment. Intrigued, Jacen and Patrick looked to the stage to see what the fuss was about.

The stage had been completely cleared, except for a lone hand drum; lanterns made the area seem highlighted for the occasion. Two women came on stage, both dressed in flowing clothing made of the lightest and shiniest material. They looked exotic as only desert Tashek could. The first maiden bowed and then took up her starting position in a crouch on the floor in her billowing dark-blue skirt. The red sash about her slender waist and a single strip of silver, like a drop of moonlight amid the midnight blue silk, fully captivated the crowd's eyes. The maiden paused, her features cool and beautiful, and awaited the second maiden's cue to begin. The other came to sit upon her knees behind the painted hand drum. This one shuffled the long, red silk of her own dress out of her way and sat with the drum before her, her hands resting lightly on its skin cover. Then, a single word came from her lips and the drum beat began to build into a carefully timed tempo made to catch the audience's breath.

With the sound of the drum, the first Tashek shifted and a *kora* blade flashed silver in the air. She turned, and a second sword appeared from behind the first as she began a series of spins about the stage. Precise and mesmerizing, the woman and blades turned faster and faster to the building beat of the drum. The dancer skipped and kicked out and swung the blades right to left and around again until she came to a heart-stopping pause as the drum beats hit their final tempo.

The crowd inhaled as the sudden flurry stopped.

The maiden shifted slowly then, pulling air back into everyone's lungs as she moved the swords about her. The *kora* blades framed her lovely face above and below, intensifying the pull of the maiden's brown eyes, hollowed in shadow by the lanterns' light. Her eyes seemed to dare anyone to look away—no one could. The woman shifted again, and the dance began anew, always drawn forward by the drum. A final jump, spin, and crouch, and the pair finished their performance in silence.

Time stilled—then applause erupted. The two maidens stood and gave curtsies to acknowledge the whistles and clapping.

It was then the second Tashek maiden's turn. She set her drum aside and came to the front and center, where she gave the audience a true glimpse of her outfit. What had seemed a dress was a warrioress's suit in flowing red silk. Her torso, arms, and thighs were encased in a lightweight armor, delicate and intricate. Around her head was a band of silver, looking like a crown. It pulled the audience's attention to her big doe eyes and full, pouty lips. With her long hair allowed to run wild and features that looked like a doll's, this second woman seemed sweet and innocent.

She raised her arms to the sides in grand display, and the other woman stepped behind her to unbuckle the armor. Once it was removed, the crowd was shocked to find the maiden's torso laid bare to them. The Tashek smiled and took a *kora* blade from the other. Then, she paused with her left arm raised to hold the tip of the blade in front of her face; the other hand was close to her waist. The blue-clad maiden began using her feet and hand cymbals to create a tempo. The younger maiden took up the tempo, oscillating her torso to backward and forward like the slithering of a snake. Her left hand soon followed, moving outward and then up and down, like the head of a snake testing the air. Her hips slowly shifted into a right-and-left figure eight pattern and then went back to oscillating again. The maiden stepped out into a squat and waved the *kora* around, showing it off. A few swings later and she set the blade, blunt side down, atop her head. Still moving, the maiden balanced the *kora* as her body undulated and her arms snaked about her.

The woman came to one foot and danced it about back and forth with the rhythm. Mesmerizing the crowd, she even came to the floor, still moving and still balancing the blade. She walked about on her knees a full turn of the stage before ending in a backbend. Grabbing up the *kora*, she came back to her feet and began to spin about in a dance used to train *she-koum-o*. The red-clad maiden leapt about, sword flashing in a series of spins and kicks that ended in a split on the floor, the *kora* blade extended forward, following the line of her front leg until they were both extended outward to the crowd. The Tashek folded forward and paused in the astounding position.

Amid the roar of the crowd, the young maiden found her feet and presented the *kora* in traditional fashion, flat and laid across her two palms, as she gave a bow. The other Tashek came forward to join the other, and they bowed and waved to the enthused room. Whistles and hollering continued even as they left the stage.

"Whoa!" Patrick and Jacen shared equally astounded looks. They hadn't seen this side of the Tashek of Staria yet. No wonder the desert nomads were so highly spoken of! There was much they could do that stunned the rest of Syre.

"I see you gentlemen enjoyed our performance," a sugary-sweet voice said.

Jacen and Patrick looked up into the faces of the most beautiful women they had ever seen. It was the maiden in red who had spoken. "Yes, that was stunning," Jacen praised.

The woman smirked. "Yes." She waved to the empty chairs at their table. "May we?"

"Oh, yes, of course," Jacen blundered. Patrick did better by standing and pulling out the chairs for the women.

Once settled, the women in the red outfit, obviously the leader of the pair, introduced themselves. "I am Siv'arid Shaul'auna, sister to Siv'arid Kor'mauk." The two men's eyebrows rose in surprise at the news, they knew her brother from their trip into Staria. "And this is my cousin,

Siv'ala Kei'shkï. You may call us Auna and Kei. We do not expect you to be able to pronounce our names—at least not at the moment."

"And what brings you to Sardon?" Patrick asked. He had been confounded to find two Tashek—especially women—in the Golden Kingdom.

Shaul'auna giggled. "Why, you two, of course."

"Huh?"

Kei'shkï made a disapproving sound in her throat and clarified. "Siv'arid Kor'mauk requested us to be the two Tashek to accompany the eight men on the surveying expedition to the north of the Gap of the Forgotten."

During the men's trip to the Citadel of Light, capital of Staria, Patrick Kins and Jacen Novano had been enlisted by the Starian king to head up a small scouting expedition to seek out where the maunstorz (all of Syre's enemies) called their homeland. It had been a suggestion put forth by Tashek scout Terrik Sheev'arid, son of the Sheev'anee's Shi'alam. Terrik had proposed that knowing where the maunstorz were originating from could lead to Syre's war units being able to counter the invaders by taking them out at their source—if such a thing were possible. The scouting expedition was, perhaps, just a fool's hope, but it could lead to the conclusion of an age's old war between Syre and these invaders from the north.

"You?" Patrick asked.

Kei'shkï's eyes narrowed at his disbelieving tone. "Shaul'auna and I have extensive experience scouting the northern lands of Staria and the mountains of the region. Siv'arid thought, too, that two women would be…less alarming to the men of the party."

Patrick held back his prejudiced thoughts of women's capabilities by coughing into his hand and taking a sip of ale. "I see."

"So, you know about the reasons we're going?" Jacen asked.

"But of course," Shaul'auna said cheerfully. She tore off a piece of bread and dipped it into some of the leftover gravy from their dinners. "Master Peore Callé and his apprentice received the missive sent by the war council at Staria and accepted." The man in question and his apprentice where two notable surveyors from the Golden Kingdom, coming highly recommended by their prince, Kent Argetlem, who had suggested their enlistment. "They will arrive here within the month.

Kei'shkï and I have already begun interviewing potential candidates for the other positions. We will let you meet three of them in the morning."

"It sounds like you're both on it, but are you sure you want to be the ones to go beyond the Gap? There is no guarantee of us returning."

Shaul'auna giggled again. "One would ask the same question of you both. It's not like this is anyone's dream journey."

"Exactly," Patrick said.

Shaul'auna grinned at him, but her next words were cutting. "I hear the son of Commander Ethan Kins isn't known for his abilities outside of swordsmanship. How best can he help out an expedition beyond that?"

"Now you look here—," Patrick began.

"No, you look." No longer was she smiling. "This expedition may very well claim our lives if this unit isn't at its best. Survival smarts and fighting skills are imperative. Kei and I are ranked as ninth-level *she-koum-o* practitioners, and we have thirty-five years between us of experience scouting the Gap. Kei is also the best medic of clan Siv'arid. You both are here only because the Shi'alam and the council recognized you, but as for you having proved yourselves useful to us, you have little beyond your recognition. Why should we trust in you?"

Patrick was left gaping, fully scolded. However, Shaul'auna wasn't done. "We would appreciate you withholding your ideas of women being less capable. In this case, neither of you have the skills we do."

"As I'm sure you will show us tomorrow," Jacen cut in to stop her tirade.

"Indeed." Her brown eyes flitted from one man's face to the other.

There was silence as the four fighters studied each other, and then Kei'shkï cut in with words in Keshic to her cousin. Shaul'auna replied to her before speaking with Patrick and Jacen in the common tongue. "We will meet you at the livery in the morning. We are staying in a room upstairs—for free, I might add, due to how many customers we draw for the owner." That smirk was back on her lips. "Good evening, gentlemen, and welcome to Sardon."

Chapter Five
§
Set to Task

For forty days, he had been pushed beyond human limits. Young Decond, new *Khapta* to Terrik Sheev'arid, had learned the meaning of Tashek discipline and the many ways they ingrained such amazing skills into their people. He had sat beneath a waterfall for countless days on end, stood on a post barely wide enough for five toes (his other leg crossed over his knee for extra "difficulty") for many hours—which, at first, made him lose feeling in his legs—and done a four-point push-up over a stream bed until he was sure to drop from fatigue and fall face-first into the water. At other times, his teacher, En'ril Savam'eed, would get him lost in the maze of the Ar'heim and force the lad to run his way home while avoiding traps and hidden Tashek fighters. All in all, Decond's experience of the Tashek's sacred lands was a jumbled mess of being pushed for hours—or was it days?—beyond his limits, only to be allowed to fall exhausted to sleep on the nearest sand pile. It was the hardest and most grueling training, physically and mentally, he had ever beheld.

However, the regimen seemed to have worked. At forty-three days from his arrival in the Oracle's lair, Decond had learned to hold his own in fights against the twenty guards, as well as to find a place of calm clarity in a mind that used to contain endless chatter. He was even able to speak basic Keshic without too much difficulty; however, it was still up to the Oracle to approve of his transformation.

"*Khapta!*" Terrik called to Decond.

The farrier-turned-Tashek-warrior had been meditating under the spray of the waterfall. At his guardian's call, he pulled his head from the deluge and looked to the shore. Terrik Sheev'arid stood just off the bank, holding out a stack of new clothes for his student. "Coming!" Decond stepped across the river to join the desert man. Though Terrik was somewhat changed—being off the addictive spice had brought out a gentle side in the warrior—he was still prone to impatience. However, Decond found that, thanks to all his new training, he was no longer affected by Terrik's moods. The teacher and *Khapta* seemed to have come to an understanding of each other's strengths and weaknesses. Decond dared say they worked like a unit—almost.

"I've brought you your first official *saer'rek*." Terrik held out the desert garb and waited for Decond to dry off and take the pile of clothing. "En'ril has gone to speak with the Oracle. We may be called today."

"Do you think I am ready?"

Terrik eyed his apprentice. A man not one to give much credit in the first place—and completely doubtful forty days was enough time to transform Decond to what the Oracle desired—he had yet to praise Decond on anything. Yet, there was a look to the Tashek's features that gave Decond hope that his teacher might finally be seeing something worthwhile in him. Thinking back on his own journey, Decond was finally beginning to feel confident that he was growing into his own potential the Oracle professed he had. His muscles were toning up with the extreme regimen the Tashek demanded in their training, and there was a confidence to his posture and movements he hoped his teacher could finally acknowledge. To that point, he made sure to stand up tall and proud under Terrik's assessing gaze.

"You know best the answer to that question," Terrik replied, in typical elusive fashion of the Tashek.

Decond chuckled at the non-answer and pulled his long, auburn-blond hair back into a warrior's knot. Once dressed in the flowing clothes, he felt different and knew he looked different as well. No longer was he the "mountain goat" the guards teased him of being. Fastening a weapon harness across his torso, Decond settled his two battle-axes across his back and nodded to Terrik that he was ready to go.

The two of them jogged through the desert sand and into the maze of craggy sandstone arroyos of the Ar'heim, which protected the Sheev'anee's blind prophetess from the world. They came to the entrance of a deep cavern and paused to wait for permission to enter the old crone's domain. In usual fashion, they were made to wait half a day; however, on this occasion, Decond was able to stay awake and at the ready alongside his guardian; the last time he had come, Decond had been so exhausted from travelling from the Citadel of Light to the Ar'heim that he had slept the whole wait. Now, the young *Khapta* knew how disrespectful he had been before.

It was En'ril Savam'eed and his own *Khapta*, J'iya Tav'eem, who came to collect them. En'ril was Terrik's closest cousin; however, unlike the slender Terrik, En'ril was burly and wore his hair shaved off. Black Keshic tattoos decorated the man's skull with accounts of his bravery in battle. Only recently had Decond been able to read of the man's exploits. J'iya, unlike his teacher, looked like a more typical Tashek, willowy and graceful like a crane and just as clever. Thanks to him, Decond had learned to play the desert people's complicated board game *ko-dōr-eya*, which was supposed to hone fighters' strategic skills. Not once had Decond come close to beating J'iya at the game.

"The Oracle has approved an audience," En'ril told them. He gave Decond a fond fist-bump on one shoulder. "She seems to be in a good mood."

"Is she ever?" Terrik muttered. He was not one to hide his dislike of the old, shriveled seer.

En'ril quirked a smile but refrained from comment. "Come."

They were led deeper into the cave. It was nearly pitch-black, except for the sparse candles that lit the way. Only the visitors and guards had need of the light; the Oracle and her female seers were used to living underground. The way ended at the Oracle's main chamber, a cavern that spanned so deep that the lights failed to reveal it. Soft orange-red flames from oil lamps lit the cavern enough for the four men to see the Oracle and her eight seers near the crone's dais. En'ril walked them through the small ranks of guards and stopped below her seat. "Oracle," he said.

"Ah, Savam'eed, J'iya, *ahnamen*. You may sit." The fragile lump that was the Oracle motioned a gnarled hand to a clear spot below her dais. "Stay near. I will have need of you." Once the guardian and his *Khapta* had found their seats, the old crone turned her burned-out eye sockets to Terrik and Decond. "Sheev'arid's-son," she rasped. Terrik visibly braced in anticipation of what insults would come his way. However, the Oracle just sighed deeply and raised a hand for him to take. Clearly irked, Terrik reached for the bird-thin hand. The Oracle latched on to it with a surprising death grip. "No time! The lands shiver in the colds of Ravel. The North weakens. Your sister has awakened, Shi'alam's son. The earth has shaken in its wake. Vauldin has the power enough to break the world asunder—but Syre is in need of the other Stones of Power. Without them, all could be lost by the turning of this season."

Having been long away from the rest of Syre, Terrik had not known of the horrible snows from Ravel or the tumultuous awakening of the stone Vauldin. "Zyanthena was the heir of Crystalynian after all?"

"Yes, Sheev'arid's-son. It seems the stone was tipped by some recourse. Some debt or blood was paid."

Terrik was too shocked to respond.

The Oracle released him and turned her sights on Decond. "Orphan. Reborn," she called to him. As before, her eyes seemed to have a pull of majik. Decond stepped closer and raised his hand. The Oracle took his hand in both of hers and cradled it softly before she let out a sigh. "Yes—yesss. You have found your center. You are the calm within the storm. It is…adequate to work with Sevén."

The pearl, inlaid into an old, weathered ring, plopped into his hand. Decond opened his palm to study the ring's intricate artwork of rolling wheat grains and moons. The pearl itself was a mellow pink, almost light enough to be white. It had been polished smooth and well kept. A warm, safe feeling emanated from the Stone of Power. Decond was entranced.

The Oracle smiled. "Sevén will work for one with good and clear intensions. With her, you can 'feel out' the other stones."

"I—"

"Do not doubt, Orphan. I will teach you," she interrupted before Decond could voice his fears. A gnarled finger poked at his heart. "One must only think and hold intention of what one seeks. Savam'eed will provide a drawing of each stone and their names. On a map or by meditation, you will know where to go to find the stones and bring them together with their wielders. Only together can they defeat Ravel and the maunstorz." She turned her empty eye sockets to En'ril. "Bring Decond back to me after he has purified himself."

En'ril bowed. "Yes, Oracle."

Her face turned back to Terrik at the last. "The winds foretell that all of the stone-bearers must meet together in their Place of Power before the turning to Planting Time. This is imperative, Sheev'arid's-son! You, Savam'eed, and J'iya must help Decond in this task over all else. Syre depends upon it!"

Chapter Six
§
At First Sight

The Citadel of Light was lightly dusted with snow, so unusual for the area. Its fierce walls kept out most of the howling winds and storm; however, for the residents used to the dry heat of the desert, the cold of winter was biting. Nestled deep into the heart of the City of Light, the remaining forces of Staria and the Sheev'anee huddled together by fires started from dried horse dung—the only burnable material readily available.

"This blasted cold!" Captain Sean Woodman cursed as he huddled within his jacket and outer robes. With Staria's forces locked inside the city by the storms that raged through the North, the cavalryman had little to do. The Citadel had enough food to feed the trapped army, especially with the whole town evacuated south to Kavahad, yet with the persistent snowstorms that kept them inside, the men were becoming cranky, restless, and *very* bored.

"Ah, quit your griping, cap'ain," one of his horsemen said. "At least we're warm and well fed. Better than Terrance's men on watch right now."

"Yeah, but it's our turn next," another said.

"I still don't see why we watch day in and day out. Them maunstorz ain't been seen in a month," said a third.

"It doesn't pay to be caught with our pants down if they do ever come around," the first cavalryman replied.

"We know, Swanson," Sean cut in. "That still doesn't make the watch any easier. What I'd do for the sweltering heat of summer right now."

"Oh, yeah!"

The door to the long hall grated open, ending the huddled men's complaints. Prince Al'den Maushelik, heir of Staria, entered, accompanied by First Guardsman Meeg Thorsen and the prince's ever-present Sheev'anee shadow, Cum'ar All'ani. The three men had been out on a scouting run around the walls of the Citadel. Even though they were unaccustomed to the weather, the leaders weren't going to stay inside, warm and lax. They patrolled daily for an hour before coming back in to warm themselves and the horses; Prince Al'den wasn't one to put his men through such discomforts if he himself would not.

The cavalrymen were quick to their feet in salute. "Highness, sir!"

Al'den began to rid himself of his layers. He threw them on a rack by the fire to dry out from the melting snow that soaked them. "Men. It seems the weather is clearing. We may have stars tonight."

"That'd be a first in weeks!"

"Yes." Al'den warmed his hands over the fire. "Cum'ar says a Sheev'anee party is coming from Paragon with some spirits and novelties. We might be able to have a little party tonight to distract ourselves and celebrate the turning of the calendar."

"It's already past First Snows," a man replied.

Al'den chuckled. "But I thought a change of routine would be nice for everyone."

"What kind of novelties are we talking about?" another soldier asked.

Cum'ar answered. "My people bring aged brandy and southern ale. Plus, some dancers and fire throwers have joined to give some entertainment."

"Any women?" someone asked, despite the rudeness of the question.

The Tashek raised his eyebrows. "Yes...but not the kind you are referring to. Our women are not for hire, and they choose for themselves if they will bed another." He shrugged, helpless to explain Sheev'anee culture properly. "I'm assured you will find their entertainment to your liking." From the responses, it was hard to tell if the men were disappointed or not. "Anyway, they should arrive within the hour."

"So, men, help out when they arrive," said Al'den. "Sean, you're in charge."

"Always, Highness." It was their private joke. Most everyone called on Captain Woodman to get things done, despite him being lower ranked than other leaders. Al'den said it was his "stellar" personality.

They bumped hands in agreement before Al'den turned away. With the long winter and lack of the court and townspeople, the army protocols were more relaxed, which the prince preferred. More a man of the sword, he had long ago tired of courtly etiquette. "See you all in an hour. I'll be with the king." The prince then headed up the western staircase to his family's apartments.

§ §

He hurried through the freezing halls to King Merretham Maushelik's rooms. Stepping inside, Al'den found the apartment warm, but not warm enough—as if the fires hadn't been properly stoked. "Father?" the prince called out as he crouched by the living area's main fireplace and poked the embers. He placed two logs on the red coals and stood up to search out the king. "Father?"

"Here, Al'den." King Merretham finally called from his study. The seventy-two-year-old ruler creaked his way from his chair and waved his only child back to the warmer room. "Sit. Tell me the reports," Merretham said as he prepared a kettle over the growing fire. A cough escaped his lips.

"Are you all right, Father? Where's Kellen?" Al'den asked, referring to the servant man.

"This old man can get his own tea. I sent Kellen to the library for some books."

Looking around, Al'den noticed there were already stacks of compendiums in every flat corner of the living area. "I see you've been doing some light reading."

Merretham waved away his son's concerns. "Just trying to refresh my memory on a few things. Nothing but the need of revivifying this worn-out mind."

"You're not one to forget much."

The king coughed again as he poured two cups of tea and set one on the stand beside Al'den. "No, but there is a lot one forgets. I'm just freshening up the cobwebs."

"And that cough?"

"Ah, it's been with me only a few days. Ignore it. It's the cold against these old bones." King Merretham smiled and rubbed his old, injured knee. "The weather makes everything act up."

"I see." Al'den let the matter drop. "I've little to report. Besides more snow, all is quiet. The Sheev'anee are coming north with some supplies and entertainments. I thought it would help the men's morale."

"That's good. I've always enjoyed Sheev'anee hospitality."

"Then you'll join us?"

"No, no. I wouldn't want to spoil the mood. The men relax better without me there. I'll stay up here and enjoy the peace and quiet."

"It's been quiet for over a month."

"Trust me, Al'den, when you get my age, quiet is always welcome—no matter how long."

"I'll take your word for it." The prince smiled and enjoyed a sip of his tea. Sitting back, he picked up the newest compendium. "*Myths and Legends of Syre*?"

"Less myth and more legend, I'm afraid." Merretham leaned in cheerfully, as if sharing a private joke. "Most of those stories seem unbelievable—except to a wielder of the Stones of Power. Read and believe most of what is written there. I myself have seen some extraordinary things in my time as a bearer."

Intrigued, Al'den opened the book and began to scan the page. He looked up and said, "A person saw a white stag with glowing horns?"

King Merretham smiled at a memory. "Each stone contains the shape of a spirit animal that can be used to send messages to other wielders."

"And the stag?"

"From Sevén, the pearl of the Golden Kingdom. It was a beautiful creature to behold…as large as a horse and fast, like the wind."

Al'den still did not know much of the stones beyond what his father had shared. Since he had sent Amun, the citrine stone, away, he had felt little need to learn about its powers; in hindsight, he thought himself foolish for not at least humoring his sire and learning of his birthright. "And what of Amun?"

"A falcon, of course."

"Of course." The royal house of Staria did have a fondness for birds.

Merretham poked at the book in his son's hands. "You should read this. With Ravel and Vauldin awakened, you will soon witness events beyond anything you've seen before or can imagine."

"You think the stone-bearers will be skilled enough to do these things?"

The elder Maushelik had a knowing look in his eye. "Al'den, my boy, it takes only one properly trained wielder to do these things. There are eight stones…someone, at some point, will be able to."

§ §

The lesser hall had been transformed. Rich tapestries warmed the stone walls and created an indoor bazaar. Torches were set up inside red and gold lanterns the size of a man, to chase away the darkness, and thick rugs were thrown down to pad the floor and keep the creeping cold at bay. The illusion of the heat of summer was in full effect as all of Al'den's forces came and went to the festivities. By the time the prince himself arrived, the men were well into the party.

"My Prince of the Yellow Star," Cum'ar greeted, his arms out and palms up in full Sheev'anee honor.

Prince Al'den returned the greeting before adding a protest. "All these weeks you call me as a friend, and now—all of a sudden—I am your promised one again."

Cum'ar's mouth tweaked. "You are always our promised one, and tonight you are our most honored guest. I give you no other title."

"Fine, Cum'ar. Just lead me to some ale."

"Right away, sir." The Tashek seemed amused.

Cum'ar led the prince through the maze of tapestries until they came to a central room. Those men not on duty were there already well into their ales or brandies and fully enjoying the entertainments. Al'den was led to the center seat before a great fire pit. He was bid to sit, the All'ani leader coming to his right to pour the royal some ale. "Your timing is perfect. My people were just about to perform some fire dances."

"Fire dances?"

"One of our many talents," Cum'ar replied.

A minute passed. Then, tambourines and drums began to tap out, calling all the Starian guests to look ahead at the stage set before them. Dancers in flowing, bright silks padded out and spread about the floor. Two women in particular twirled to the front and bowed; their bright-blue silks glittered with gold coins. They were more scantily clad than the soldiers were used to—and more than one of Al'den's men pointed this out with a devilish grin.

"Gentlemen," the prince warned, even though he, too, was caught admiring the beguiling women.

The two women at the front giggled at the soldiers and sashayed their hips in exotic movements bordering on the provocative. They seemed not the least bit disgruntled by the stares. Stepping closer together, they mirrored each other in belly dancing. By the end, the soldiers were hooting and hollering at their amazing body control. Judging by their wide-eyed gaping and good-natured elbow prodding, it seemed the Starian men had never witnessed such dancing before

The blue-clad women blew the soldiers some teasing kisses before stepping back to let another performer come forward. Carrying two staffs forward, the man lit the ends on fire in the pits separating the audience from the performers. Once the staffs were ablaze, the fire dancer began to twirl them across his shoulders then down his back and chest, his body bending as needed to keep the props ever moving. The performer ended with one staff balanced on his foot, the other still being twirled about his upper body. In one fluid motion, he kicked up the staff and caught it, never once losing his cadence. The man finished by throwing both staffs in the air and catching them before folding into a bow to the shocked crowd.

His performance was quickly overtaken by another dancer, who twirled two chains with burning balls of cloth soaked in oil at their ends. This dancer moved about in perfect *she-koum-o* steps as he twirled the two chains about his body. At times, he would cross the chains only to twist himself back; at others, the man would wrap a chain about a forearm or leg only to reverse the direction and dance the other way. The Starian soldiers were entranced with the choreography; the movements were smooth and practiced and seemed more like a dance than a deadly art form. The male Tashek made a final turn amid his twirling chains and then snuffed them out in a bucket at the left of the stage.

The darkening of the stage area left the watching soldiers breathless and on edge in anticipation of the climax.

In the shadows, a lone woman knelt at the center stage, with a tray holding six candles balanced atop her head. Then, two women came up from behind the Tashek dancer. Each had a single, lit candle in one hand; these, they used to light the eight candles. As they were lit, the figure came into focus: a stunning Tashek maiden, her long, black hair kept in two braids. She slowly rose from her kneeling pose and began a sensuous dance whilst keeping her tray of candles level. She undulated about in a slow figure eight pattern with her hips, hands, and feet. The dance wove about the floor, and yet she not once lost her cadence or the balance of the tray. The maiden made a few passes about the stage, pulling the Starian men into a trance. She ended at the fire pit near the front row. Coming to a crouch once again, the Tashek's amber-brown eyes connected with Prince Al'den's, and she held the heir in her stare. The audience held their breath as she stilled. Then, the two women from before came and put the candles out.

The spell was broken.

Al'den blinked as torchlight was added back to the room. The lovely maiden who had held him entranced was gone. "Cum'ar, who was that just now?"

The Tashek man's eyes seemed to dance in amusement. "Come, my Prince of the Yellow Star. I will introduce you."

Al'den felt himself frown at his friend's lack of clarification, but he followed the All'ani leader, who led him around back to the room where the performers were. The All'ani clansmen greeted their leader as Cum'ar passed through. In return, their clan head bowed his head. Finally, he stopped at the gorgeous woman who had performed last. "Prince Al'den, may I introduce you to the eldest of my sisters, Lăn'esha."

Up close, Lăn'esha did look a lot like her brother. Both were tall and willowy and carried themselves with a presence that demanded respect. The way the maiden had moved during her performance reminded Prince Al'den of a cat stalking its prey; now, he could see her warrioress's prowess in the lines of her toned muscles under her thin silks. Having already met one other Tashek fighter, Zyanthena Sheev'arid, Al'den had no doubt that Cum'ar's sister was a highly-skilled *she-koum-o* practitioner as well.

"All'ani, Lăn'esha," he rolled the name off his tongue. Belatedly, Al'den remembered to bow to her in full, honorable fashion.

Lăn'esha's eyes seemed to dance—like her brother's. It seemed both were easily amused by the Starian heir. "My prince." She bowed, graceful as a bird of prey.

"Your performance…it was breathtaking."

The grin she flashed was full of pride. "I thank you. I am pleased that it moved you so."

"Lăna is our tribe's greatest fire dancer," Cum'ar explained, his words bringing Al'den back to earth. The All'ani warrior seemed to know what his prince's preoccupied stare was about. Leaning in conspiratorially, he said behind a hand, as if his sister could not hear, "And she is yet to be amalgamated." The prince recalled it was the Tashek's word for married.

Prince Al'den cleared his throat in shock at his friend's' forwardness. "I—"

Lăn'esha grinned, seeming pleased to see the royal so flustered. "Brother dearest, it is rude of you to tease our host so." She punched Cum'ar teasingly in the gut. "I am sure Prince Al'den has his eyes upon plenty of women. You needn't provoke him so." Turning politely away to help her clansmen with packing of their props, she left her brother and prince in peace.

However, Al'den felt himself already ensnared. Cum'ar had, perhaps, intended this infatuation all along, but Al'den knew that any chance for his redemption was lost. He was completely and utterly entranced by the All'ani woman, his heart stirred by her direct and daring stare.

"My prince?" Cum'ar leaned forward to catch Al'den's focus. "Prince Al'den."

"Hm, yes, Cum'ar?"

"Shall we rejoin your men? My sister will be along shortly."

Al'den nodded, still finding himself distracted. "Yes. We should get back to them. Can't leave those rascals around so many beautiful women unattended. Stars forbid what kind of trouble they are in already!"

Al'den was right. The All'ani women—and some men—had joined the soldiers. The Sheev'anee were a people comfortable in both their skin and their sexuality—unlike most in Syre. It was easy to see how the Starian soldiers could get lost in those direct stares and touches. Even though Prince Al'den had made sure to have his commanders instruct their men on etiquette, he could see some had been wooed by the Tashek.

Not that Al'den had fared any better. Here were women he could finally relate to, as many Sheev'anee maidens were apt warriors in their own right and accustomed to the ways of war. There was no need for courtly politeness and run-around conversations.

"More ale?" Cum'ar lifted a tankard in front of his prince's nose.

He accepted the beer. "I must apologize for my men."

"For what?" Cum'ar chuckled. "For their loose behavior? I assure you, my prince, they will not find any of these women easily taken advantage of. On the contrary, it is I who should apologize for anything my people may do."

Al'den snorted at the nonsense and gave an appropriate eye roll. "Sounds like we're all a sorry, lawless lot."

"Indeed," the Tashek man agreed with a grin. "Whatever will your people think when their mighty heroes come home so corrupted?"

Al'den made a face. "Don't remind me."

"Then I won't." Cum'ar wore an amused expression. It seemed the All'ani leader was having more fun than the whole Starian army. He glanced about the room and then looked back at Prince Al'den with his eyebrows raised in a tease. "And here comes the greatest trouble of the night."

It was Lăn'esha. She came into the room and all eyes were upon her. Worse, her eyes were only for two men: her brother and Prince Al'den. She sauntered up to them as if she were the one to own the Citadel of Light. "My prince, brother. Care if I join you?"

Lăn'esha's idea of "joining them" was challenging the two men to a game of *Cesellenés*, a royal board game of strategy. With her partner, a woman going by a nickname "Shauni," which Cum'ar said meant "thistle," the two men were soon schooled on how to play. Even with Lăn'esha taking mercy on them, it was easy to see who controlled the board. At twelve-to-three, even the most loyal of Prince Al'den's men were betting on the ladies to win.

It was almost a relief when a runner came to get Al'den sometime around midnight. Almost, that was, until the prince heard the news.

"Highness!" The man came to a knee, looking panicked. "Your father, King Merretham, has been found collapsed in his apartments!"

Chapter Seven
§
Maneuvering

With the early snows across the north, the Starian court had been moved from Kavahad to the demesne of the LaPoint family. Markus LaPoint, acting as lord-governor in Lord Shekmann's absence, had been the one to offer his estate to ease the burdens on Staria's temporarily established command post at Kavahad; however, it had been Commander Ethan Kins—appointed as the city's leading authority—who had been more than happy to have the whiny courtiers leave for other grounds. Not only was the large estate more luxurious than the military post—and more acceptable to the outcast people of privilege—it was also not as scarce for food and shelter. The second point had been Commander Kins's principal reason for moving the nobility from Kavahad to the LaPoint estate.

The headache, even without those extra souls, was still too great, however.

"These blasted numbers just won't add up!" Ethan Kins grumbled. He was a military man through and through, not some accountant, for Stars' sake! Yet with the northern armies stretched thin in every direction and Lord Darshel Shekmann's force presumed vanquished or lost to the storms, it had fallen on Kins to help out with Kavahad's daily needs. The centrally located military post had to remain functional for all the reports coming from every direction of Syre. Now, Commander Kins was more a desk man than an on-the-field commander—and his body, at least, was not happy with the change.

"Commander?" Lieutenant-Commander Curtis Marx poked his head into the room that had been Lord Darshel's main office.

"Enter." Ethan waved his man in as he set aside the numbers he had been calculating.

Marx, looking sharp and competent as always, came in and gave a brisk salute. In his pressed uniform and neatly cropped beard, the man of twenty-three years looked more the age of thirty. His motive for the fashion was to "keep the men in line." He said, "Sir, I've received three more missives," and handed the papers over.

"For Stars' sake, what now?"

Marx didn't bother responding. He waited for his commander to accept the missives and open their seals to read each one. Once those were done, Marx handed one more set of papers across the desk. Commander Kins raised an eyebrow questioningly. Marx said, "This one was personal, sir. I figured you'd like it separate. As for the others…is there anything you need me to inform the men about?"

It was what Ethan liked about his subordinate. Even though the mertinean lieutenant-commander was quick to temper on keeping the armies in order, Curtis Marx was efficient and never wasted energy on pointless activities. "No need," Kins replied. "These state that all fronts are still the same: no sign of the maunstorz in Staria or near North Point. Commander Grant's forces are hunkered down south of Raven's Den and still harass the enemy whenever the snows give them a chance. Grant does say he would appreciate some reinforcement soon. I'll need to write Commander Tyk to see if his force can lend a hand there—though the distance they must travel poses a problem." Tyk's men had been waylaid near the Noway Mountains, as the sudden snows had barred their passage east.

"Very well, sir."

"How are our men and Kavahad?"

Curtis shifted, his only tell that things weren't quite all right. "We are still sorting ourselves out. Kavahadians aren't altogether pleased with Rubian men stationed here in power with the LaPoints." Even if it had been King Merretham and Lord-Governor Shekmann's orders, Kavahad had been run by the Shekmann family and their people for centuries. Had Lord Darshel been around, the city would have been running smoothly. As it was, even with Commander Gordon, Lord Darshel's third-in-command, and Advisor Abrus available to help run the accounts, the situation was harrying.

"I want a report on any and all disputes. Any men that need to see me will be handled after lunch."

Curtis gave a sharp nod and shifted back on his heels. "Yes, sir."

"And the viscount? Has he left for his estate yet?" Markus LaPoint made frequent trips back and forth from his estate to Kavahad to keep his lord-governor's books in order, as well as assure the people that they weren't being overrun by Rubians. Most times, he stayed three to five days at Kavahad and then returned home for the same duration. The accounts had been far easier to manage and keep tallied with the man around.

"Yes, sir. He left as soon as the sun rose. He should be nearly home by now."

"Good." Ethan leaned back in his chair and surveyed the desk for any loose ends he could use his lieutenant-commander for; however, what was in front of him, only he could manage. "Very well. Back to rounds with you." He gave his second a salute. "Have that report to me by lunch."

"Sir!" Marx retuned the salute and left as quickly as he had entered.

Alone once again, Commander Kins picked up the personal letter Marx had handed him. The handwriting on the front of the envelope had him feeling relieved; it was from his son. Settling back, Ethan broke his family's seal and unfolded the paper.

Father, we have just reached Sardon. Our first trip to the Golden Kingdom has been one of ease and amusement. It is warmer here, no snows past the Pika Mounts, and the Sardonians are a jolly folk. For a military post, it is relaxed and welcoming. We have already met with the two Siv'arid scouts sent by the Sheev'anee—two women, if you can believe that! I may have more to say on them and the others of our party once we are more acquainted. Mainly, I wished to write you of our successful arrival at Sardon to ease your mind. Jacen says hello and that he has my back. May you stay warm enough in Kavahad. —Your son, Patrick.

Tears came unbidden, and he was happy there was no one in the vicinity to witness his lapse. He had been worried about his son's journey—even if he was accompanied by the soldiers under Prince Kent's command. Sardon was under control of Lord-Commander Ivance, a man Ethan Kins trusted over most other military leaders in Syre. His son and Jacen Novano were in good hands.

Yet, a father could worry. Wiping his tears away, Ethan set the letter aside and tried to pull himself together for work. There was so much to do and not enough hours in the day to get it all done.

§ §

Markus LaPoint's company arrived at his estate just in time for the evening meal. The dashing rogue left his courser in the capable hands of his stable master and made for the stairs on the eastern wing of his estate. He was met at the entrance by his young cousin, Jeremy Freedman.

The two embraced like brothers, then Markus let his cousin help him from his outer riding habit.

"You're just in time. Cook was setting out soup and pheasant in the main hall. I saw you coming up the lane and had them set out an extra place setting."

"Great, I am starved! A full day's ride from Kavahad every handful of days does leave one wishing for the comforts of home." They headed for the viscount's apartments so he could change into attire more appropriate for a host to Staria's courtly women. "What have I missed, cousin?"

Markus had taken in his eighteen-year-old cousin to teach him the ropes of running a demesne. With the Kavahad lord-governor missing—and Markus's duties being called to Kavahad so often—it had been a blessing to have someone the viscount trusted to keep an eye on his own estate. "There has been little to report. The ladies of the court have started creating popcorn-and-cranberry wreaths and knitted placemats for the First Snows' festivities—or so I've been told. I must admit, I am lost on such womanly plannings."

Markus clasped Jeremy's shoulders in sympathy. "Yes, the fairer sex does have a certain touch when it comes to parties. I'm sure the manor will be inundated with such frivolities that it hasn't seen since my grandmama's passing."

"Will there be a ball, then? I heard the ladies gossiping about it."

The viscount hadn't planned on one, but then again, he hadn't expected to host the elites of the Starian court, either. "If a ball is what the ladies demand, I will not be the one to discourage them. I'm sure the staff would also find it pleasing." Markus exchanged his riding clothes for an elegant jacket of green velvet and brown tweed pants. He slipped off his riding boots and replaced them with leather flats. It only took a quick glance in the looking glass for the rogue to know he appeared the part of a ladies' man. "And of our other guest? How does the lady of Blue Haven fare?" The eldest princess of the Havenese crown had been lumped in with the Starian court when the snows had forced her party to hunker down. Though weather would have been milder to the south, the Havenese had opted for comfort and warmth over dreary hours on the roads.

"Princess Éleen has been a restless sort. Polite but restless," Jeremy replied without tact. "I've taken her about the demesne on Bella," he said, referring to a grey mare of good breeding that Markus owned. "It seemed to settle her some."

"A princess so far from home and distanced from a betrothal agreement would be in some distress. I applaud you on taking such measures to comfort her, cousin."

Jeremy blushed at the praise. "It was the one idea I could think of that I was willing to do."

The young lad made the viscount proud. Markus slung an arm around Jeremy's neck and hugged him close to tousle his hair. "You did just fine. I'm going to make a gentleman of you yet." Whether Markus himself was a gentleman was up for debate—he was a known womanizer—but Jeremy was young enough and easily swayed by the other sex to find the idea exhilarating. His inexperience and enthusiasm gave Markus his own delight; the lad was fresh clay in his hands, ready to mold. "Come, to dinner with us! We mustn't keep such lovely womenfolk waiting."

The dining hall was the fullest it had been in years. Princess Éleen and her lord protector, Carrod Nexlé, had been given seats near the head of the long table, just to the left of Markus's own. Beside them and across sat many of the ladies of the Starian court: Diane Levine, Selena Durrow, Kaitlin Lepree, Catalina LaCroix, Rosa Quartlett. There was a Lord Zale Herth, and Lord William Greyson, with his sister Rosetta. Plus more lesser nobles besides. Further down were two young girls, Coltrine and Ainsley, given to the princess of Blue Haven for help and companionship—though the viscount thought they were too immature and "clucky" to bother with. Last were a few of the LaPoint's men, all he could count on to run the demesne smoothly. The meal looked to have just begun; it was on the first course of soup. The two men's timing was fairly acceptable.

"Viscount Markus," Lady Kaitlin Lepree cooed at seeing Markus and his cousin. Her words brought the gentlemen at the table to standing, in respect to their host's arrival.

Markus waved everyone to their seats as he and Jeremy found their own at the head of the table. "Lady Kaitlin," he acknowledged. "Princess Éleen. Lords and ladies." He included the rest before changing tack by surveying the food about the table. "Hm, this meal looks scrumptious! I am glad to see you have all started."

"Were the roads acceptable?" Lord Carrod Nexlé asked politely, taking up the conversation so the ladies were not required.

“Ah, fairly so. The winds have driven the snows into piles here and there. At least the sun has seen fit to peek through.”

“And words from Kavahad, my lord?” It was Markus’s commander-at-arms who asked, though the viscount could see others were also curious.

“Kavahad is handling the weather, and there has been no report of the enemy anywhere near here. The mertinean has done well to keep the maunstorz to the opposite banks of the Senna. There was report, too, that the Golden Kingdom will be able to send barley and potatoes north for distribution.” That last report had been a relief. It had come bearing Prince Kent’s personal seal. With much of the north buried in snow, many towns were starving for good food.

Princess Éleen dabbed her delicate mouth with a napkin before asking her own questions. “And news from abroad? Has there been word from the Citadel of Light or elsewhere?”

“I am sorry, Highness.” Markus made sure his voice remained endearing. “But it seems very few messages have reached Kavahad. Not too surprising, however. The temperatures, I suspect, north of here are too trying to chance birds, and our king will not risk a single runner to the weather. However”—he slid a hand inside an inner coat pocket for a letter he had received from Sealand—“there is a report from Sealand.” He held the letter out to the princess.

She took it with some speed, belying her anxiety for news beyond their little pocket of Syre. He continued with the details as Éleen’s china-blue eyes scanned the contents. “North Point claims that the snows are easing some along the coast. If such continues, they may be able to send boats north from Fortress Opal or West Port. They may even get as far as Port Al-Harrad. Their supplies and reinforcement of soldiers may take the strain off Staria.”

“This letter says the princes of Sunrise have failed to reach their kingdom!”

“Hm, yes.” Indeed, though the news was somewhat old, Markus had found it ill. “It seems the Sunarians were to reach their border three weeks past. However, their party was lost somewhere in the Aras. With this unexpected weather and the enemy running about Syre, I am not surprised this information comes late. I do fear what this means for Staria.”

“King Raymond Sunrise is not known to be forgiving,” Lord Carrod said.

"Indeed, he is not." Markus held himself back from making a face. His demesne abutted the northern corner of the Sunrise Kingdom. He knew well the insufferable moods of the other kingdom; the whole lot of Sunarians seemed like stuck-up pricks. Trade with Sunrise was rarely profitable as it was with the Golden Kingdom to the south or Rubia to the west.

"But for Staria to have lost—"

"The weather makes such matters hard to know, Highness," Markus cut Éleen off smoothly. "Even news such as this may not be true. That letter is many days old. Unfortunately, we are as deaf and blind to the events without this property as they are to us. Yet, I will continue to amass whatever details I may during my goings to Kavahad. Rest assured, Princess, I will try for word on Syre—and on Blue Haven—as often as I can."

His dismissal of Princess Éleen's fears may have been done eloquently, but Markus doubted it was had put to rest the matters the royal woman was determined to fret over. However, there was little more he could do than assure her of his attempts. Until Syre was not so encumbered with the early, heavy snows, they would remain in the dark. It was up to him, then, as the host to keep their minds from such matters. "Jeremy here tells me you have all begun plans for a ball here for the First Snows' festival." He clasped his cousin's shoulder affectionately.

As planned, the turn of conversation set the table in a better mood. The Starian ladies began to cluck out about what preparations they had begun and ideas they had for the event. Gone was the tension the Sealand letter had created. Only the princess of Blue Haven seemed reluctant to join in the glee of the festivities. At least the others were willing to play along with the viscount, and Markus was relieved. "I will have my staff prepare a suckling pig for the feast, then," he said as his own way of encouraging the nobles. "As for the details of the ball, I will leave that to you ladies' capable hands. I will provide anything you so desire." By now, they had come to the end of their final course. After giving his gracious permission for the women to do as they pleased with his manor, Markus wiped his mouth clean and excused himself to take care of other matters. He almost escaped the dining hall without incident when Lord William intercepted him for a private converse.

"Viscount Markus, sir?"

Markus held in a sigh and turned to the handsome Starian with a smile plastered to his chiseled face. "My lord?"

Lord William waved the viscount to the hallway. "A private word with you, sir? If you can spare the time?"

As Lord William was a Starian nobleman whose rank was well above the viscount's own station, Markus LaPoint knew better than to dismiss the other's request. "No, indeed. Please, let us speak in my private billiard room."

"My thanks, sir."

Markus led the nobleman down the hall to the billiard room, which was set on the southeastern side of his manor. The gaming room was long and narrow and had windows looking out to the archery range just beyond, settled before a thick stand of poplar trees. Under six feet of snow, the open range was only noticeable because of the raised lumps of target stands. The scene seemed enchanted and inviting while the men were kept warm by the fireplace.

"Bourbon?" Markus asked as he strode to his well-stocked bar.

"Please. Two cubes," Lord William said to indicate how many pieces of ice. His host easily obliged the man and handed him the glass. The willowy Starian accepted the drink and wandered away to sit his tall frame into a chair by a gaming table. He tapped a long, delicate finger on the board. "Play a set?"

"I'm always up to the challenge," Markus replied. He placed two logs on the fire before coming to a seat across from the fair-featured Starian lord. Being host to the nobility for nearly seven weeks had given the viscount a great appreciation for their love of gaming. Lord William was no exception in his fondness for rithmomachy, draughts, and darts. They set about repositioning the playing pieces back to the start of the game.

"You first," Markus bid.

Lord William nodded and moved forward his first piece. He then settled back as the other man moved his own. "So," he began after a sip of liquor, "it is quite unlike you to let the womenfolk worry over such matters that are military concerns, Usually, you are careful to keep them from such trivialities."

Markus glanced up from his move, calculating. "Yes, I guess I do handle them rather delicately. Yet there was little to relay beyond military notes. Kavahad has become overrun as a focal post in this war."

Lord William seemed amused by the viscount's subtle sidestep of the truth. He placed another playing piece before replying. "And I was of the thought that it always was a military post. The Shekmanns were martial intellectuals through-and-through. The LaPoints, however, are better known for their political maneuvering and commerce. I hear you are the strategist behind Lord Darshel's rule."

Markus's eyebrow twitched. "Hm, for one so well thought of in the Starian court, you come off rather smooth-talking and cunning yourself."

Lord William smiled. "I am still a courtier."

"Indeed." Markus moved another pawn.

"And I am no fool." Lord William took a sip of his drink and puckered his lips to get the brandy from his neat mustache. "You were maneuvering the princess of Blue Haven, as I have seen you do over and over these past weeks. You are looking for something from her."

"Looking, found. I am cautious with those from Haven. Their interests run deep among Sunarian royalties. Even that princess has more ties to them than is decent."

"She is Prince Al'den's betrothed."

"For how long do you think? I say by Snow Thaw, she is long forgotten. Our prince is short on keeping interest in such delicate, pliable ladies for long—no matter how lovely."

"She does have political advantages."

"Like what? Soldiers? Their king nearly spat on ours for bringing only fifty men as aid. Trade? Blue Haven shares in that aplenty with Sunrise. No, King Jarod has no real interest in Staria. It is a full span of Syre away and of little importance to that pompous liege."

"Princess Éleen does make a nice piece to mold as queen."

Markus laughed. "The lady is rather easy to sway to one's cause. No wonder she is easily batted around like a ship at sea. She has yet to find her port—and I am sure King Jarod knows this. Compared to his other offspring, she is…expendable."

"One would say you hate that woman."

"Ah." The viscount raised his pinky finger to wiggle it next to his nose, signifying that he had been caught in his white lies. "I dislike such lambs that are so easily herded. But she would make a fine morsel in bed, now and again."

Lord William chuckled and rolled his eyes. "I have heard that about you. Most of your better 'dealings' are done between the sheets."

"It's a talent the Shekmann lords have been using for generations. It is also quite effective. I would use such tactics on the Havenese princess if I thought it would come to good use, but alas, I have my doubts on that."

Lord William moved another piece and captured one of Markus's pawns. All in all, he was winning the board. "I will have to warn you," he said as he collected the token, "if you try to debauch her before our prince has made his decision, I will take all actions to discredit you. Our prince cannot have his name spoiled thus."

They shared a look for a long moment. "You have no need for such threats," Markus finally said. "I would never put Staria in such a compromising position. Only if these was a benefit to us would I ever pursue such matters."

"Just see that you do." Lord William pasted a honey-sweet smile on his comely features and moved his next playing piece. "Check."

The viscount's eyes pinched at being maneuvered into a corner. He studied the board a long time and finally found a move that didn't finish him. "I see now why the Greyson name is so valued at court," he said as way of praise. "You and your sister inherited your lands at a young age but have made your holdings prosperous. Only a man with a good head on him and a decent upbringing could be so successful."

"My sister, Rosetta, is the real mastermind behind the business. Her sense of foresight has kept us from many would-be losses."

A look of appreciation sparkled in the viscount's eyes. "Yes? Your sister is rather delectable in all regards."

"And spoken for, I might add," Lord William cautioned again and moved another piece. "Checkmate."

Markus tsked. "A pity, but I will keep my hands from her—on my word, my lord." He found himself unable to get out of his predicament on the board, so he sat back into his chair and knocked back the last of his drink. "We are going on a hunt tomorrow afternoon. You are more than welcome to join us."

"I would be delighted."

They rose from the rithmomachy board and shook hands for a game well played. "For now, I won't keep you from your business. Tomorrow, then?"

"Yes, tomorrow."

Chapter Eight
§
Interviews

It felt good to get Golden air back into his lungs; at least, that was Prince Kent Argetlem's first thought upon waking in Sardon. The second thought, however, was not as cheerful. Trying to stretch after a restful sleep had set the Golden heir's healing shoulder afire. "Ow, ow, ow!" he hissed out and clasped the injury with his other hand. After eight weeks, the deep gash he had received during the battle at the Citadel of Light was finally mended closed, yet it would be many weeks still before the limb was back to a useable state—exacerbations by its owner notwithstanding.

"Bloody limb," Kent muttered as, with more caution, he rose from the bed and made his way to the nightstand across the small room. Bending down to assess himself in the square mirror there, he took in his disheveled appearance, which was quite unbecoming of the sole heir of the Golden Kingdom; he was in desperate need of a shave and a warm bath. "How fine you look today," he said to his image—with much sarcasm. The long, cold haul from the Citadel of Light had left him somewhat gaunt and fully wishing he had stayed in the high walls of the great city, enjoying his newly formed friendship with Prince Al'den. There was still a hollow ache in his heart from the loss of the camaraderie between the two princelings.

"Highness, sir!" A call from without startled Kent from his reverie. Jumping, he turned to the door just as his man creaked it open. It was Colonel Jared Deed, of the prince's archers, second-in-command under newly appointed Lieutenant-Commander Charles Hadley (taking over the post for the late Eric Sloane).

"Jared," he greeted kindly. He and his men had begun to adopt the more lax protocols after their visit to Staria. Jared returned the acknowledgment with a casual salute. "Come to see if I am awake?"

"Sir." Jared grinned and gave a nod. "They were going to draw lots to see who would come wake you, but I said not to bother. I don't mind helping you dress and the like."

"Well, I appreciate it, Colonel. Stars know I'm thrice as slow with this healing shoulder. Any assistance is graciously received."

"Then I'm glad I came," Jared Deed replied and waved the prince to a seat on the bed as he rustled up some clothes. As their troop was still on the road to the Golden capital and travelling cavalry light, there was only a military wardrobe available for the royal—not that Kent minded. The sensible clothing was more comfortable for horseback, anyway. With Jared's assistance, they got him into the uniform without too much hassle.

"Shall I help you shave, Highness?"

"Well." Prince Kent was surprised and a little cautious, "I—"

"I've done so before, sir. I helped my late father when he became incapable. His hands, you see, from his arthritis. I promise I won't nick you, sir."

"Well, then, by all means. I'll allow it." Kent had been wondering how he was to accomplish the task adequately with his main hand out of commission—hence his disheveled state. Trying to not look nervous, the prince positioned himself as his colonel suggested and waited to feel the blade across his skin through the soap lather. True to word, however, Jared was skillful. The shave took only about ten minutes at the most.

"Hm. Well, I do say, Colonel, well done! Well done indeed!" Kent praised as he fingered his clean-shaven face. "I don't think I could've done better on a good day."

"Thank you, sir." The colonel seemed to blush. "Ah, I believe breakfast is in order, Highness, if you so desire?"

"I do, thank you," Prince Kent replied. He almost let Deed quit the room when he called him back. "Oh, Colonel? Jared?"

"Sir?" Jared returned to the doorway.

"Maybe it's not the place or time, but…as I am now without Lieutenant-Commander Sloane, I am also without a personal protector. I have a need for one like yourself who is willing to go out of his way to assist me. Would you consider yourself for the position?"

"Well, sir, I…" Jared looked taken aback. "The honor is, well…"

"It's all right. I don't need an answer today." The prince gave a disarming smile. "It was just a thought. Answer me whenever you are ready." He hoped this helped to dispel the sudden awkwardness. "Tell the others I will be down shortly."

"Yes, sir. Highness." The salute was brisker this time, and crisp. Jared Deed took his leave.

Alone again, Kent took in the last details of his room, making sure it was tidy. Then, with nothing left to do, he readjusted his arm in its sling and headed out for the mess hall.

He and his men had taken up rooms in the livery, thanks in part to Lord-Commander Ivance's insistence. Prince Kent knew better than to ignore his father's best military leader, in any case. Ivance had served their family going on forty years and had an exemplary record. More to the fact, Sardon was without walls, so being close to the lord-commander and his men seemed wise. Their rooms were on the west side of the livery, on the second story, while the kitchens were on the east, ground level. The walk there was outside, on a wraparound porch with a comfortable overhang. Even in the early morning chill, it was a pleasant walk. Plus, it gave the prince time to view the action of the military post: a farrier was checking two mounts' feet in the open stalls across the way; a few other horses were tied nearby and being tacked up for morning rounds; the rest of the yard was open—save for a small archery range and sparring square, set out of the way from the stalls and rooms along the back fencing.

There was where some real action was.

Two brightly adorned Tashek women were taking up all the attention on the sparring square. Their two opponents were putting up a defense against the fiery desert nomads, though it was plain to see the men were outmatched. Prince Kent couldn't help his focus sticking there, on their duel, as he wandered along the porch toward the mess hall. As there were about twenty soldiers also gawking, it meant the royal wasn't the only one amused by the fight.

"Highness," Colonel Deed greeted his prince as Kent finally made it to the bunch of soldiers enjoying the morning entertainment.

"Colonel. What have we here?"

"Those Tashek are from the Siv'arid clan. They are the two promised Sheev'anee who will aid in the expedition north to the Gap."

Prince Kent chuckled and shook his head at the women's masterful displays with their *kora* blades and spears. "As usual, it seems the Tashek are going to make a statement of their abilities."

"Indeed," a Sardonian soldier agreed from beside Jared Deed. "It seems the ladies had a bet with their opponents on who were better fighters."

"I'd say those lads bit off more they can chew," another commented.

The two "lads" in question turned enough for the royal to get a good look at them. Upon recognizing the Rubian and Havener, he couldn't help his own chuckle. "It seems Jacen Novano and Patrick Kins did not learn enough about the Tashek in Staria. Certainly they knew of the capabilities of the Sheev'anee?"

"I think it has more to do with their pride as men, Highness," Jared informed him.

Kent shook his head. "More the fools, then. From what I've seen, Tashek women are fiercer than the men. They've drawn poor lots."

"Indeed, sir. I think Kins and Novano have been hustled for a good half hour now. I'm surprised they're still trying."

"They are stubborn, we'll give them that. Still, my bet's on their losing."

"As are all of ours," the first soldier said. "Minus the lord-commander."

The mention of Ivance drew Kent's attention to the man in question, posted in a rocking chair and smoking a pipe just beyond the audience of soldiers. Prince Kent wandered over and asked, "The men are saying you think Kins and Novano will win?"

The lord-commander rose and saluted his prince respectfully. Kent waved him back to his seat, took up a lazy perch against a column, and waited for the commander's comment on the fight. "I do…or at least I think they'll get by. I'm always a sucker for the underdog, and I'm not about to underestimate the endurance of the Kins men ever again."

Kent took his meaning—he had underestimated them before. He said, "I don't know. Pardon my disagreeance, but I've seen the Sheev'anee in action. They are a force to be reckoned with."

Ivance withdrew the pipe from his lips and blew out some smoke. "You would know better than I, Highness, having visited Staria personally." It was a polite and uncommitted answer. Prince Kent chuckled and returned his focus to the fight.

§ §

Despite having fought for thirty minutes straight, the two Tashek maidens seemed barely winded, whereas Kins and Novano each had a fine sheen of sweat across their skin. Certainly, the *she-koum-o* style the ladies employed was apt at making the more traditional fighting styles of the Syrian soldiers' work too hard.

Jacen looked ready to call his defeat against Kei'shkï, and his footwork was beginning to lag. The Siv'ala woman sensed her victory and continued to force the Havener about the sparring area; she did have an advantage on range what with her use of a long spear. A full circuit later, and Kei'shkï got Jacen to yield. She backed away from his bent-over form and found a casual seat against some hay bales to watch Shaul'auna and Patrick duke it out.

The tall and burly Patrick should have had a great advantage over the tiny Shaul'auna; however, it became clear that the Tashek was better skilled with a blade. She had nearly disarmed Kins on a thrust and took him off his game almost immediately at their start. From that point forward, the game had been on. Now, a quarter past the half hour, both fighters were finally looking winded. Patrick's swings were becoming more erratic, but his stubborn pride kept him from yielding to the Tashek woman. Shaul'auna had thoroughly meant to school him on the practice yard, yet the fact that the Rubian was better with a blade than she had assumed seemed to have caught her off guard. Because of that, Patrick forced himself to fight to his best and beyond. He would force his advantage.

A sudden parry and turn on Patrick's part ripped the *kora* blade from Shaul'auna's grasp. Not to be outdone, however, she was quick to scramble into close range and trip the soldier up. She took advantage of his sprawl to kick his sword hand, sending his own blade flying. Patrick barely had time to nurse the ache from his hand before Shaul'auna was upon him, her arms and legs wrapping about his neck and about his waist to ride him piggyback. Patrick struggled against her firm hold, but Shaul'auna's grip only tightened. Flailing, Patrick sent them backward into the fence to stun her.

Shaul'auna's hold weakened enough for Patrick to pull her over his shoulder and flip her to the ground. His much larger bulk was over the Tashek's in a moment. She struggled fiercely as her opponent lowered himself further and got an elbow to her exposed neck. Waiting then, Patrick kept his pressure firm while Shaul'auna pelted his torso with punches and kicks. "Call it," he murmured, looking sideways at the Tashek's lovely face. Shaul'auna's eyes flashed in defiance against the order.

"It's a draw!" Lord-Commander Ivance's voice rang out across the yard. It startled the two fighters, who had completely forgotten their audience.

"I don't see how, sir!" Patrick yelled over his shoulder. He wasn't going to remove himself from his opponent until his victory was claimed.

"Look again, soldier."

In Patrick's haste to end their fight, he had forgotten one, very important thing: he was fighting a Tashek and not another soldier. Ivance's order to reassess the situation emboldened Shaul'auna to reveal why they were at a draw. A smirk formed on the woman's full, pouty lips.

Patrick lifted himself enough to see the dagger that she had managed to slide alongside his groin and much too close to his manly bits. He couldn't help the swallow of fear at having such a place compromised. Shaul'auna seemed to enjoy that weakness. She tapped her blade against his groin until the Rubian man jumped off of her, exclaiming, "Holy shit!"

The crowd of soldiers were laughing hard.

"As I said, soldier, it's a draw. "Lord-Commander Ivance pushed himself away from the railing and covered his own amused expression by yelling out, "All right, boys, fun's over! Get inside before the food's cold!" The whole group jumped to, knowing better than to argue with the man.

Prince Kent turned to Ivance and commented, "I see what you mean about not underestimating the Kins family." He and Ivance shared a nod in understanding before they too headed in for breakfast.

§ §

Shaul'auna was up on her feet and collecting her sword before Patrick could even think to be gentlemanly. It was hard to tell if she was embarrassed by her "loss"; the Siv'arid woman kept her face carefully blank as she joined Kei'shkï and started a conversation in Keshic. It wasn't until Kins and Novano came near that either maiden glanced their way.

"A good fight," Patrick started.

"Hm." Shaul'auna's lips pursed together as if she had an objection that she would not voice. Whatever it was, she said instead, "Indeed, Kinsson. You have shown me you have been trained well in the sword. I will not underestimate you in that again."

"So, we have an understanding?"

Neither woman looked like they agreed, but Shaul'auna did give a reply—of sorts. "We will be meeting three candidates at the Salty Dog in an hour. You are welcome to join us." She gave a Tashek bow. "Enjoy your breakfasts, gentlemen." With that, the two Sheev'anee moved away to whatever business they had. Patrick and Jacen watched them go.

"It seems like Auna doesn't like you much," Jacen commented as he handed over a waterskin.

Patrick smirked. "I think she's sore that she didn't beat my ass."

"You did kind of play dirty there, at the end."

"Hey, she duped me first!"

Jacen rolled his eyes. "You know, we're supposed to be making friends with the ladies, not proving a point."

"Though there was a point to prove."

"Yes, well…" Jacen shrugged the rest of the sentence off. "Let's eat. I'm starved after that fight. Plus, I'd like to be done in time to meet those people Siv'arid was talking about."

Patrick nodded. "I hope she has a better eye for choosing expedition candidates than she does on gauging fighters…"

§ §

Midmorning at the Salty Dog was quiet. Shaul'auna and Kei'shkï had picked the largest table at the tavern and were there waiting, dressed in the traditional brown robes of their people. Kei'shkï called to the bartender to bring some ales as Jacen and Patrick came over to join them.

The arrival of Jacen and Patrick seemed to signal to the only other patron that the meeting was nigh. The man, a wild-looking sort, stood from the back corner he had been hiding out in. Standing a full six-foot-six, he was intimidating at first sight as he came to loom over their table.

"Mr. Durrow, sir." Shaul'auna looked up into his hooded face, unfazed. "Please take a seat and stop scaring our guests."

The man's features softened immediately into a kindly smile. "Yes'm, Ms. Auna," he replied as he pushed back his hood and sat beside her. The subtle shift in his demeanor completely destroyed his tough-guy image; he looked like a real softy as he beamed at the Siv'arid woman. So, someone else was easily ensnared by the Tashek's charisma…

Auna said, "Jacen Novano and Patrick Kins, this is Paublo Durrow of Duncitt. He is a travelling blacksmith."

"Please, call me 'Paps.'" Mr. Durrow extended a hand to the two men. His own engulfed theirs in an iron grasp. "I am glad to finally make your acquaintances."

"A traveling blacksmith?" Patrick asked, getting down to business.

"Aye, sir. I had a shop in Duncitt but have long taken to the road to forget some personal matters."

Patrick felt himself become instantly suspicious. "Of what sort?"

Durrow's eyes turned sad. "A loss of my wife and child from fever. I couldn't bear to stay with their memories."

The words had Patrick contrite. "My apologies, sir, for bringing up such grievances."

"Not at all, laddy. You're here to interview me. It should be all out on the table to keep us all on keel."

Patrick was starting to like the man, just from his words. The blacksmith may have come off as imposing, but his character seemed to be the opposite. "Just so, sir, I appreciate the honesty. Tell us what work you're used to."

"I can do any type of iron work, but my best pieces are hunting weapons." With slow motions, he indicated he would be removing some of his own weapons to show the two soldiers. At Patrick's nod, he took out a long hunting knife and an ax, which he slid across the table for the others to inspect. The craftsmanship was among the best Patrick had ever seen, and he voiced as much. Durrow replied, "Thank you, sir. I was in the competition for his majesty's own farrier but lost to the man in the current position. Ah, it would have been a sight to have been proclaimed by the crown!" Blue eyes looked regretful at the memory.

"That's a tall accomplishment on its own," Jacen said, impressed.

"You lads are too kind." Durrow smiled. "It will be a pleasure working for you."

"You do know what our mission entails?"

"Aye. As I've no ties to any one place, I've no mind for where we need to go. I'm all ready to go north as far as ye say." His eyes turned to Shaul'auna as he said the last. It was easy to see that the farrier was completely taken with the Sheev'anee maiden. That Shaul'auna smiled kindly in response but kept from any further encouragement made it seem that she was aware of this but not willing to take it anywhere.

Patrick wondered if it would cause any problems down the line to have such a hulk of a man be so enamored, but he decided to forego any conclusions. He shared a nod with Jacen before he said, "In that case, I think we are all in agreement of your coming along."

"Indeed, sir?" Durrow glanced about the four of them before beaming a happy grin. "My thanks, laddy."

"It's Patrick, sir." They shook hands once more as Durrow repeated the name. Then, the farrier took his leave in a jolly manner. His parting made the tavern seem too quiet.

"Well, that was quite the character," Jacen commented.

Shaul'auna agreed. "Yes, he is. Maybe I'm too presumptuous, but we've taken steps to check his background—and the others'. Just for clarity's sake. I am…relieved you approved of him. We were in need of a blacksmith."

"His work looked exceptional—at least those pieces that he brought. I still want to see if your inquiries call attention to any issues."

She gave Patrick a look. "You are a cautious one."

"With good reason. I will always be wary of strangers."

Her brown doe eyes assessed him long enough to make him shift uncomfortably. By the time her gaze had moved from his person, the next interviewees had arrived.

A man and his youthful travelling companion walked right up to the table and gave their names to their party, getting straight to business. Shaul'auna waved them to seats—yet only the youth complied; the man declared he would rather stand. "Very well, Mr. Calhorn." Shaul'auna waved to Jacen and Patrick. "Micah and his son, Jean, are hunters and trackers by trade. Mr. Calhorn has experience trapping in the Crystal Mountains and Hills of Buckwin in the Crystal Kingdom."

"Are you from there?" Patrick asked.

"No, sir. I was born here in Sardon and have been back for fifteen years."

"And why did you return to Sardon?"

"On account of my boy here. His mum informed me of his birth through a letter. I came back so she wouldn't raise Jean alone."

Green eyes shifted to the youth. Jean Calhorn still looked wet behind the ears, though he was trying to act more mature. He didn't even have the trace of a beard yet! "And how old are you, boy?"

Jean gulped, making his features looked even younger and fairer. "Sixteen, sir." The age Patrick had been when he had gone from being an apprentice under his father's lieutenant to leading his first command—with too much pride and not enough wisdom, he remembered.

"I understand Jean is young, Mr. Kins, but I assure you I have taken him on many hunting trips since he was four years old. He can track with the best of them."

"We have seen their skills in action." Kei'shkï added, speaking in favor of the father and son. "We tested them tracking me north from Sardon. Even with all my skills to mislead them, they caught me in half a day. They did even better tracking a deer near the Pika Mounts."

Patrick gave great weight to her words. He had only one objection: "You do not find the details of our trip disturbing to you, Mr. Calhorn? Certainly, your son will be missing a life here."

That got young Jean to his feet. He slapped his hands on the table, shocking all of them. "My father's a good and honest man. He's done well to teach me the ways of his trade. I would go with him anywhere in Syre and especially on a trip sanctioned by a king!"

"Jean!" Micah put a hand on the youth's shoulders to subdue him. "My apologies, men, ladies."

However, Jacen and Patrick were greatly amused by the outburst. It reminded them of themselves at that age. After they stifled their chuckles, Jacen replied for them both. "It's quite all right, Mr. Calhorn. In any case, we aren't one to go against the Tashek's good judgment, especially when they speak so highly of someone. We will still give you the winter to change your minds, but you are welcome in our party."

"We won't change our minds, but thank you, sir." He reached out to shake their hands and bid the two Tashek a good day. Mr. Calhorn and his son then pardoned themselves to other engagements. The man was certainly prompt and very businesslike.

"The kid is rather young," Jacen commented, once they were gone.

"And cocky," Patrick added.

"But skilled. You won't be disappointed with the Calhorns." Kei'shkï continued to hold her good opinion of the hunter-trappers.

"Of five people, the Calhorns were the ones we liked the most," Shaul'auna added. "Even Mr. Durrow is not as skilled as they."

"And where are the other three you interviewed?"

"We did not think them worth your time. One, a young farrier nicknamed 'Kipper,' is a close second to the blacksmith. The others are not worth mentioning at all."

"I would like to see this Kipper," Patrick replied. Shaul'auna gave him a look, so he clarified. "It'll be a long winter. I'd like to have a backup or two just in case any decide to back out."

Her brown eyes narrowed. "And though you liked Mr. Durrow, you have your doubts about the man?"

He shrugged. "As I said, I would just like some backups. It's a long time until Snow Thaw."

"Very well, then. We will collect the young farrier and continue searching for others."

"I would advise we continue to meet regularly and practice our fighting and survival skills daily. The new members should join us," Kei'shkï added.

Jacen and Patrick looked to each other and nodded to the common-sense proposal. "Agreed. So, we will see you at the livery tomorrow then?"

"Yes, Kins-son." The barest smirk was on Shaul'auna's full lips. "We would not miss another chance to duel with you, though may I suggest archery or horseback for tomorrow's activities?"

"We can do both."

"Good. Tomorrow then, after breakfast."

Chapter Nine
§
Penitence

To restore her body, Zyanthena took to meditating twice a day and moving slowly through *she-koum-o* forms. The first few days left her utterly exhausted, and more than once Lord Darshel had found her asleep in a seated pose. He had to tuck her into bed on those occasions. Because of her weakness, she rarely ventured from her bedroom to the other parts of the palace as she had the first night upon awaking from her coma. Yet, it seemed that her knowledge and use of Vauldin were improving by the day, as were her insights into Crystanian.

The beyond-belief acts of magic she began to practice were somewhat unnerving to the Shekmann. Indeed, what Lord Darshel walked into that late morning had his gut clenching in anxiety. "Zy—" he began to say as he brought some tea for her. The sight had the name stopping halfway from his mouth.

Zyanthena had perched her *kora* blade at the base of her bed. She sat cross-legged before it with her arms and hands held to either side of the sharp blade. Eyes closed, she looked lost in meditation—except for the furrow of her brow. As Lord Darshel watched, the sword seemed to glow in a blue-white light across its length, and a humming sound buzzed in the air around it. A spark jumped from the blade a second later. Concentrating further, Zyanthena willed the metal to warm and glow brighter. Afterward, she murmured a word in Ancient Syrean, and the blade began to disappear as if it was a painting being washed away in rain.

Lord Darshel was in utter shock as the *kora* blade vanished. Forgotten was the tray in his hands. It began to slip to the floor, and he fumbled to catch it.

Zyanthena's attention flew from her task to the interruption. She spoke another word in Ancient Syrean as her right hand lifted—as if she could reach out to grab the falling tray. Inches before it crashed to the stone floor, the tray just stopped in midair. The abruptness shook its contents, and one cup teetered to fall and shatter across the stones. Zyanthena panted at the effort it took to control the tray's fall, yet she managed to bring it to a shaky rest safely on the ground. Despite the fact that her skin was beaded in sweat and her hand trembled at the effort,

Zyanthena looked pleased at her rescue. "My Lordship, you may stop your gaping now."

Darshel cleared his throat and bent to retrieve the broken pieces of the cup. "It's hard not to when you do such things."

"That was not just an honest staring," Zyanthena replied with a pointed glower. She slipped off the bed to help him collect all the pieces. "Give them to me," she ordered, her palms held out to him. Lord Darshel hesitated for just a breath before complying. As he had suspected she would, Zyanthena closed her eyes and murmured more words in the old dialect. In the time it took to count to ten, magic remade what had been broken. The cup became intact in her palm, minus one small chip from a shard they seemed to have missed. "Well, it's not perfect."

"You really are going to give me a heart attack."

Zyanthena chuckled and took the tray from Darshel, lest he drop it again. "These are but simple majiks. Vauldin can control electricity…a substance much like lightning." Lightning, at least, was a word they both could understand; the other word… well, Zyanthena only knew the term from the books on majik but even that made it hard to comprehend. "It also has the power to remake the 'cycles of beginnings and endings, life and death.'" She set the tray on the rugs by the fire and motioned the still-stunned Kavahadian to join her.

"And those other tricks?"

"Tricks? Hm, you mean the invisibility and levitation? Those are the powers of Bellor, the jade stone of Blue Haven, and Kevel, the ruby of Sunrise. In very limited ways, the other stones can borrow powers from each other. But—as for what I did just now—I won't be able to do more than that. To harness another stone's abilities takes a great toll on the wielder." Zyanthena poured them each some tea as if their conversation wasn't out of the ordinary.

Zyanthena's nonchalance seemed to calm the Shekmann's nerves—but only a little. He did accept the cup she offered, however, and came to sit beside her. "And what tolls do you mean?" Darshel asked. His emerald eyes roamed over her features and body, taking in the beads of sweat and the slight shaking of her hands. Were those signs of her "toll," or still the effects of coming out of a coma?

"Everything in its own time," she replied cryptically.

Darshel's strong features hardened as his temper rose at her lack of answer. "I think I'm owed an explanation. Considering you were on the brink of death for days, a heads-up on anything that can happen to you from using the obsidian is non-negotiable."

Zyanthena blinked at Darshel's sudden tirade. Then, her lips softened into a smile. "Indeed, My Lordship, you do have that right." Zyanthena's gaze shifted to the fire and seemed to look right through it—and it was not her first time going into such a stare. The look was one that bespoke of the warrioress pulling information from elsewhere not in that world. Every time she came out of that trance, she knew more about Vauldin, the Stones of Power, and Crystanian. Just as times before, Zyanthena finally shifted out of it and her eyes cleared enough to address His Lordship's question. "Tolls," she repeated, reminding herself of their conversation. "Majik—as in all things—relies on checks and balances. Life does not exist without certain requirements to sustain it. You cannot live without taking in breath or food and water. Even denying oneself pleasures and other human contact can create illness."

"So, I assume magic also requires certain properties to work?"

She nodded. "Energy. Majik takes energy from a wielder or, in a case of a proficient caster, from other living things. There must always be a give and take, though some majiks require more than others."

"And that brings me back to my question: What have you had to give up to work with Vauldin?"

"My quick healing."

Darshel stared at her until she elaborated.

"It's true that I was dead, yet Vauldin's price for bringing me back was not so great."

The Shekmann scoffed and raised his hands to indicate the reconstructed palace.

She said, "Even Crystanian was remade. In my case and the palace's, I believe there was stored energy from the destruction and deaths of Crystalynian's fall. This energy was reabsorbed for the purpose of the remaking."

"That doesn't make much sense."

Zyanthena shrugged. "The only other explanation I can think of is that Vauldin absorbs the energies released when people and living things die. If that is the case, it can store a lot of power."

Lord Darshel was silent for a long minute. "All right, we'll go off of your first theory."

Zyanthena could not fault His Lordship for the fear behind his words. After all, the Stones of Powers' magics were new to her too, and, at times, just as unnerving. "So, taking my awakening out of the equation, any majiks I practice from here on out will require a price to perform." Zyanthena rose, her hands still shaking. "It takes energy to focus Vauldin's powers. It gets easier as I master more, but in the early stages of learning, especially after just waking from a coma, the cost does run me a bit ragged."

"Is that why you meditate and perform the healing forms so often?"

She nodded and sipped her tea.

"If you're expending energy, then don't you need more than rest and meditation to restore yourself?"

Zyanthena gave him a look. "Your meaning?"

"I mean that the forms and meditation focus and store your energy, but they don't create much of it, right?"

"They can help me pull energy from my surroundings into myself."

The explanation seemed to startle him. "Really?"

She nodded. "And with Vauldin, I can feel that action more than ever before. There really is energy in everything." The words seemed cryptic again. "But I got you off track. You had a point you were making?"

"Right." Darshel cleared his throat. "I was trying to say that you need to eat and drink more to counter your expenditure. I did notice you were losing weight."

The Tashek looked thoughtful. "I find your reasoning…sound. Working with majik is like fighting on a battlefield."

"Then you won't mind me making you more meals throughout the day?"

"Lord Darshel," she teased, "who here is master and who is servant?"

"Our roles have been switched. You are the only living heir of Crystalynian and high above my station."

His words sobered her. "Perhaps, if one were to go off of paper. But, in my eyes, you are still my superior."

"Zy'ena—"

"If not, then can we agree to be equals? I cannot be higher than you. Not with the circumstances we find ourselves in."

Lord Darshel nodded resignedly. "We can be equals."

"I would have it no other way." Zyanthena became distant again, like before when she had looked into the fire. Yet, it was less over gaining new knowledge and more from depression over their conversation on whose rank was higher.

Still, the look was a reminder of the other questions His Lordship had yet to ask. "Zy'ena, what are you doing when you go into those trances?"

"Trances?"

"Your eyes look distant, as if you are elsewhere."

"Ah…you mean when I'm talking with Kestral."

"Kestral?"

"Queen Kestral…my mother. Her soul was trapped in Vauldin as penitence for using the stone to try to bring King Trev'shel and Prince Verrin back to life."

The words brought Lord Darshel to a steely silence, so Zyanthena went on, unbidden, to try to elaborate. "Some things, even if in the realm of possible, should not be attempted. Vauldin is the Keeper of Life and Death, but who are we to judge what the toll is on a soul? My coming back to life is an anomaly, and I do not understand why I was given not one but two chances to live... Yet, my mother is punished for her use of the stone out of grief. It also split Crystalynian asunder." Zyanthena shook her head, at a loss for the right words to express the confusing subject. Finally, she came up with: "I think Vauldin is a very fickle stone. It has chosen to give me life—along with a warning. Trapping Queen Kestral inside itself is a good reminder for me to not try and aspire to the power of the Stars."

Lord Darshel was still rendered speechless; Zyanthena could see that in his pinched expression and persed lips. *Was he angry at this revelation or scared shitless?* Lord Darshel looked away to the fire and drank his tea, absorbing this new—and scary—revelation without further questions. This detail about Vauldin seemed to unnerve him more than all the others thus far.

Yet, Zyanthena understood. *A power that circumvented death itself?* The Stones of Power were sounding more and more dangerous by the day.

Zyanthena shifted and pushed herself to her feet and, on unsteady legs, walked over to the glass doors leading her quarters to the open-air balcony outside. She pushed open the right door and strode out into the snow-drifted space, leaving His Lordship to his ponderings. When she was not quick to return, Lord Darshel finally rose himself and followed her outsid, as she had hoped.

The king's chambers were on the third floor of the palace, on the western side, overlooking the long horse runs. Currently, Unrevealed and Tano were out parading in the snow. Zyanthena had come to the railing to watch their antics. She gave the Kavahadian lord-governor a nod in acknowledgement as he joined her.

"They are happy enough, those spoiled mounts," Darshel commented.

Zyanthena smiled in agreement, but it lasted only a moment. Turning to face him, she said, "I apologize for telling you truths that are nightmarish to hear. Even I find myself apprehensive at the responsibility of handling Vauldin."

"Neither of us are here by choice, Zy'ena. As the Sheev'anee would say: this was fate."

She scoffed. "I'm not much for believing such things."

"Neither was I…until I met you."

Zyanthena's eyes widened at the statement. "Lord Darshel—?"

Lord Darshel silenced her. "Zyanthena. Yes, I am afraid of that stone—of all the stones, frankly. That Queen Kestral was sucked into it gives me no small comfort, but…" He paused to shake his head of the craziness of it all so he could speak more clearly. "What we have read of the stones shows that they do hold some awesome powers. The crystal, Ravel, has created this snowstorm out of season. I'm more worried about its wielder and his allegiance with the maunstorz than I am about you and yours. I know you, at least, have the control and willpower to use Vauldin's abilities wisely."

"Thank you for the vote of confidence."

"It's not confidence. I know this to be true."

"Perhaps." Zyanthena turned back to the majestic sight of the Forbidding Forest and the Crystal Mountains and lifted a hand to capture some of the falling snow. "Ravel's wielder is powerful," she commented. "But there are two things I have over him. The first is that I am learning from the most talented wielder of the last stone-bearers, and secondly, I am more respectful of the cycles of this world than he."

"Watch it. You sound arrogant," Lord Darshel teased.

"But I'm not." She closed her hand on the snowflake. "You see, nature abhors being out of rhythm for long. Even a forced snowstorm like this must bow to its true properties. Starting yesterday, I am going to keep nudging it back to its proper event."

"Even doing that won't save the people who are freezing to death or starving."

"Maybe not directly, but I can make the rest of the snow months milder." When Zyanthena looked back at Darshel, he could see the resolve in her brandy eyes. "It's the least I can do to help Syre while we are trapped here. Beyond that, I will research all I can on the stones and train myself. I must surpass Ravel's wielder by Snow Thaw."

"That's ambitious."

"It's imperative. As you said, Ravel is in the hands of a maunstorz supporter. I fear what that means for Syre. The maunstorz now know of the awesome powers of the Stones. I would not be surprised if we—the wielders, I mean— are targets. Therefore, I must be their worst threat so that the others stay ignored. The only other stone that is active is Serein—at least that I am aware of. And I doubt that Par Fantill knows how to use her."

"How do you know another stone is active?"

"A memory." Zyanthena clasped Vauldin in her palm and thought back to the one night she had seen Serein. "When I was Zeera Starkindler, the night of my coming-of-age, the prince of Sealand showed her to me. At that time, Vauldin answered Serein's call…the two stones glowed and sang the songs of their powers." Unconsciously, Zyanthena drifted away from their conversation, lost in the memories Vauldin had connected her to.

It was clear that the Tashek warrioress was distracted. Her blank stare had Lord Darshel reaching out to clasp her shoulder in concern. "Zy'ena…"

Even distracted, Zyanthena's quick reflexes kicked in at the intrusive touch. In the breath of a second, she grabbed the offending hand and twisted it about in a painful lock. Of course, she released him just as soon as Zyanthena realized what she had done. "I apologize, My Lordship."

"No need." Darshel rubbed his offended wrist. "I am relieved to see you cannot be taken off your guard so easily. Your mind drifts away to past memories or you converse with Queen Kestral often. It makes me worry."

Zyanthena took the critique seriously. "If I am drifting away as much as you say, then it is a problem that must be corrected as soon as possible. We are safe here in Crystanian, but once we are back in Syre, I cannot be so distracted."

"I'm sure this is temporary, just like the other symptoms from your coma."

"Maybe so, but I find it unsettling."

Lord Darshel chuckled. "Or maybe you're getting comfortable having me around."

Brandy eyes narrowed. "You'd like that, wouldn't you?"

He shrugged. "I've worked nearly two full seasons to get you to like me. I'd say this is progress."

"And I'd say you're getting too cocky, Your Lordship."

Darshel let out a deep-bellied laugh in reply. It was good to enjoy their verbal jousting; it certainly beat their more serious subjects of late. "Perhaps. You have said it was one of my faults. But a man stuck with a woman alone in a lost castle has to dream."

The Tashek's look darkened. "On that, My Lordship, I would say you need to keep such thoughts to yourself." She began to move back inside, to the warmth of the fires.

Zyanthena's fiery denial made Lord Darshel laugh again. "I'm patient, Zy'ena," he teased to the desert woman's retreating back. "The snows will last at least three good months, you know—that's one long Season. At some point, I'm going to look quite appetizing."

Zyanthena stopped at the door and turned back to the Shekmann. She was absolutely beautiful in her mother's winter-style cloak and thick brocade dress. Yet, there was a gleam in her brown eyes that warned the Shekmann lord that he had gone too far. "Patient?" she said coolly. "In that case, an hour or two stuck out here will be to your liking, My Lordship." She bowed and stepped back into her room. Darshel rushed to the door, but the Tashek had already shut and locked it. She stood just inside as he pounded on the glass.

"Zy'ena!"

"I think you need to cool down, My Lordship."

"Let. Me. In!" She stared back, her eyes saying, *Like hell I will.* With a final wave, Zyanthena turned and made her way back to the rugs by the fire. Sitting comfortably, she ignored the lord's insults and pounding and drifted into a meditative trance beyond the sounds of distraction.

Though annoyed, Lord Darshel would not let himself be outdone. He lasted only about ten minutes before he began to pound the glass again. When that didn't work, he searched about for a piece of granite that had broken off from the stone railing and came back to the thick door to shatter the glass. Weaseling his arm through the jagged crack, he found the latch and lifted it. He stalked back into the room to hover over Zyanthena's still form. All the while, the Tashek didn't move—even as his blood began to drip onto the rugs. Lord Darshel crouched down in front of her and stared at her hard while ignoring the burning from the cut he'd given himself from breaking in.

Finally, Zyanthena gave in with a sigh. "And you just had to break the door."

"You were the one who locked me outside. I say we are even."

She opened her eyes. "Touché."

"And next time, you won't try that."

"Next time, you will remember to not flirt with me in such a compromising place."

"I make no promises."

His truthfulness made Zyanthena chuckle. "Fine. You win this round." She reached out to Darshel's injured forearm and said a word. In an instant, the wound was healed. Lord Darshel flexed it to test the mending; it was impressive. Zyanthena rose and ignored him as she went to inspect the glass door.

"I'm assuming you can fix it too. Otherwise, I wouldn't have broken it."

"Indeed." Zyanthena sighed again. She swept all the glass pieces to her and made a pile on the floor. "Though this is not as easy as the cup or your arm."

"Consider it penitence," Lord Darshel said as he headed for the hall. "I'll have lunch ready for you when you get done. Enjoy training!" He gave a backward wave as he left Zyanthena to clean up the mess.

Chapter Ten
§
Master Harkland

Prince Par had chosen a day when the city of Opal was not being beset by rainstorms to take a loop through the streets with Lady Yvonne Limonté. As before, Par had his cousin with him, and the young lady had her two friends. On Lord Gordar's insistence, six guards were among their party, surrounding the open carriage the prince shared with the ladies—a fact the prince detested, as he would have preferred being horseback. "Think of the ladies' safety, my prince," Lord Gordar had reminded him. Resigned to the logic, Prince Par was stuck riding in the carriage while his lord protector and guards got to see the city from their mounts.

Opal sprawled about the fortress like a falling veil on a wedding dress. Whereas the fortress sat atop the lone butte, the rest of the city had been built down the gentle slope to the sea. Long, wooden docks made up the last vestiges of the port before Sen Sia took over to the unending horizon.

Prince Par had chosen to see the docks on their sightseeing route. It was not for its delights—the ladies would probably not be impressed by the overwhelming smell of fish—but for the practical reason that he had business with the port master. The man was an old ship commander and had been commissioned to put together a number of boats to sail to North Point or even Port Al-Harrad—if the waters were passable. Par would not heed his cousin's advice to do the errand at a later date. Already, he was behind in speaking with the port master. Pretty ladies be damned, he was not going to be deterred again!

Prince Par had his carriage stop just short of the docks. He disembarked with passing words to the ladies to wait for him in the tea house across the way. He had almost escaped his escort duties when he heard a commotion behind him. Turing, he witnessed Yvonne managing to talk her way past his guards and head his way. "Lady Yvonne—"

"Not you too, Highness," Yvonne snapped back as she neared. She had gathered the skirts of her pretty yellow dress into her hands to keep the hems from the dirt and ichor of the fish market. "My ladies are content to have their tea and avoid the fish markets of Opal, but I am not."

"Then they have more sense than you," Prince Par couldn't help saying. His patience with courtly correctness was wearing extra thin since he had shown the ladies—for what had to be a good two hours by then—the more illustrious shops in the upper-hill markets of the city. "This section of Opal is not for such fair ladyfolk."

That got Yvonne's temper flaring. "And Your Highness is so much better?"

Par would have replied with just as cutting a quip had not Lord Gordar arrived at his side to shake his head in caution. Instead, he continued with, "I just have some business to attend here, and short at that, Lady Yvonne. I will not hold you to this place for long."

Black eyebrows rose and Lady Yvonne set her jaw. "Prince Par Fantill, you promised me a chance to see the royal city. This fish market and docks are a part of that city, are they not?" She continued before he could gather a reply. "Therefore, I will go with you. I will not get in your way." Yvonne hiked her skirts up a few more inches, showing her white stockings and delicate heels. Without waiting for his agreement, she began to stride in the direction Prince Par had been heading.

Par let out a defeated sigh as Yvonne's retreating back began to gain some distance. "Certainly, she is a stubborn one."

Lord Gordar was grinning, even into his gold eyes. "You like them that way, cousin. Besides, the walk may do Lady Yvonne some good."

"What? To calm her vexations?" Par relied. He waved back to his guards that all was well and for them to enjoy some tea with the two remaining ladies. Then, he and Gordar started after Yvonne.

Gordar said, "Yes. She did seem to be less taken with the shopping and sights than her two companions. I dare say the lady is bored."

"*She's* bored!" Par guffawed. He had agreed to the outing only to ease his mother and father's desires, not his own.

Lord Gordar's mouth quirked. "Birds of a feather…"

Par raised a finger in warning. "Not that saying, and don't imply that Lady Yvonne is like someone else, either. Princess Zerra was rebellious—but in a cute, innocent way."

"Because she was thirteen." It was Gordar's way of getting in the final word before they reached Yvonne's company. The two cousins fell in beside the less-than-ladylike lady.

"This way," Par said shortly, lengthening his stride so Yvonne was no longer leading. They wove their way around multiple fish vendors and crates of still-alive and freshly gutted fish and sea creatures. To Lady Yvonne's credit, the young woman did not seem disgusted by the assortment of water life the fisherman had caught. Curious, she began to reach out to examine the large shell of a fresh scallop before Par's hand on her wrist stopped her. "Not now, Lady. There would be little in the ways of getting the fish smell from your skin until we reach the fortress again. For your ladies' sakes, I bid you look but do not touch."

Yvonne made a face but complied. "As my prince wishes."

Par continued on without comment. Lord Gordar was kinder. "Ignore him, my lady. Prince Par's mind is set on business. Most days he is loath to being so stingy around the docks. Fresh seafood is one of his delights."

"You couldn't tell from here," Yvonne commented under her breath. She did follow her two escorts, however, as they finally made their way to the last building by the docks. Lord Gordar held the door open as Yvonne followed the prince into the din of the dock master's weigh station.

Inside, there were still some fisherman relaying their catches to the weigh staff; however, for the most part, the weighing and record-keeping was done for the day. Prince Par ignored the men standing about for their turn and headed toward the dock master's private office to the back of the building. There, he tapped on the weathered wood of the door and squeaked it open a crack. "Master Harkland, sir?"

The door was opened further, and the old ship commander greeted his visitors. "Your Highness?" He seemed surprised but pleased to have the heir to the crown visit him personally. "Do come in, Highness. Sit. Er…" The man seemed flustered to find a lady among them but had only one chair besides his own to offer.

Prince Par waved Yvonne to the seat to correct the problem, then he extended his hand to the man as if they were old friends. "Master Harkland, I apologize for not visiting sooner. Duties at the fortress have kept me from pursuing my last missives."

Master Harkland seemed shocked and little distressed at being so accosted by the royal heir. "I did send reply to your letters. Were mine not received, Highness?"

"Oh no, they were received. I just desired to visit in person. My father had assigned you a very important task. I am only following up on the progress of the order."

Mr. Harkland paled, as if he were afraid he had done something wrong. "I am getting boats prepared as fast as I am able, Highness. However, there is word of ice to the north, and passage to North Point is difficult."

"As I was told as well. That is another reason I wanted to speak with you. I have heard you were a great ship's captain in your day. Certainly, a military man of your accomplishments would have some ideas for means to how we can get our boats north?"

There was a pause as Master Harkland gaped at the praise, and then he said, "Ah, yes, Highness. Actually, I do have some ideas—they are rough, though, mind you." He raised his hands in emphasis to that point. "But they just might work." His aged face looked more excited now that he realized Prince Par was not there out of irritation.

"I am open to any ideas that get supplies north to our ailing forces."

The dock master pulled down some boat blueprints and spread them out across his desk. With Par's assistance, they pinned down the papers with candlesticks, a compass, and a magnifying glass. Prince Par leaned forward in anticipation as Master Harkland began his narrative on improvements to the Landarïan boats; improvements that could, just possibly, get them through the ice-ridden waters blocking off the northern end of the kingdom.

"These may not be feasible though, Highness," Master Harkland said at the last.

"What are your estimates?"

Even though Par wanted to say price was no object, he knew better. The royal coffers were already being used for other supplements to Sealand. The early snows had hit hardest in the northern lands of the kingdom. Yet, even farther south, cities and towns lacked proper food and fuel. More than the military at North Point were in need of supplies. Boats would be faster but garnered more risk. It was that risk the prince hoped could be decreased.

"Hm, well…I would estimate these modifications would cost around the price of three dreites, give or take."

Lord Gordar sucked in a breath behind his prince. "Three hundred thousand in gold bars!?"

Master Harkland knew the news was bad. "'That would be to outfit all twelve ships you asked commissioned."

"That is a high price to outfit the ships with this ice-breaker design," Par said, though he was reluctant to admit it. "Is there no way to have just one ship be the head of the fleet?"

"One ship would not cut it. If the weather turns of a sudden, as it does in the north often, the ice would refreeze and block the path."

The prince was not ready to give up. "How many ships, then, would be necessary for that task, if not all can be?"

The dock master seemed intrigued by the idea. "Well—these are all still estimates, mind you—but you could get by with eight ships if you reduced them to skeleton crews and eliminated some weight."

"Some walls could be removed to add room and certain foodstuffs excluded."

He nodded. "Doing that could get you down to seven, maybe even six, boats needed for the trip."

"And at least a dreite less in costs. That is a price the king would be better able to approve," Lord Gordar agreed.

Prince Par nodded. "Indeed." His ocean-blue eyes narrowed as he studied Master Harkland's designs once more. "I give you leave to test this design on one boat. Work out its kinks and study its efficiency in the ocean. I hear there is ice just north of West Port. It may be enough to know for certain."

"It just may, Your Highness." Master Harkland seemed impressed with his prince.

"Can you make it quickly?"

"Highness." The dock master made it sound like he had said, *boy.* "I can get the best builders I know to work on this day and night. I'll have it ready for you within a fortnight."

Prince Par was pleased. "I will count on it then, Master Harkland." He extended his hand to the man. Relief at having someone willing to work promptly made his smile full and genuine. "Thank you, sir."

"It is I, Highness, who should be thanking you for your faith in me. I will not let you down."

Their party of three left the dock master's shortly afterward and made their way back toward the carriage. Prince Par noticed the way Lady Yvonne sneaked looks at him as they strode back through the fish markets. Finally, he could not contain himself any longer. "Lady Yvonne, I see you are no longer so enticed by the markets."

Chocolate-brown eyes dared to stay on Par's handsome face for a few moments too long to be polite before they were averted to the sights. "They are not as intriguing as what I just witnessed."

"I'm not sure what was so entertaining about my business with the dock master."

She gave a quirk to those red-painted lips. "Highness, I was impressed to see you take interest in that man's off-the-wall ideas about his 'ice breakers.'"

"Master Harkland is one of the most forward-thinking boatmen of his generation," the prince said as way of praising the man. *Where is Yvonne going with this, anyway?*

"He did seem to be, but that's not why I am impressed."

"Out with it," Par insisted, irritated by the lady's indirectness. Lord Gordar laid a hand on his shoulder to remind him to stay calm. "I'll not have you beat around your words. You said you liked being direct."

Lady Yvonne stopped, making the two cousins pause as well. She faced the prince resolutely. "I just didn't expect you, Highness, to take any interest in the man's ideas. You commissioned him for boats, and instead he gave you blueprints. Certainly, that man is not doing as the crown bids. Your actions seem…unconventional."

The Sealand prince's face hardened. "The crown commissioned him for boats to go north. As it stands now, they cannot get past the midpoint of Sealand. We need ideas like Master Harkland's to get to the northern borders before Snow Thaw." Not usually one to get angry, the royal couldn't seem to keep the heat from his tone. "As for me, Lady Yvonne, you don't know anything about me—and the Stars only know what kind of rumors you've been told! I care about my people very much. I am not the pampered, supercilious princeling you make me sound to be."

Lady Yvonne's cheeks were flushed a bright pink as the prince finished his little rant. *Did she almost look about to cry?* Lord Gordar touched his cousin's arm again. "I am sure my lady did not mean to offend, my prince," he said gently. "If anything, Lady Yvonne was expressing her admiration."

"That is as it may be, but she did say some offensive things—not to me so much as to the crown in general." He looked Yvonne straight in the eye. "Even bluntness needs tact."

Lady Yvonne blinked away a tear she wouldn't let fall. "As my prince wishes," she replied stiffly with a curtsy. "I will return to my ladies.

By your leave, Highness, my lord. I will not bother you again with such rudeness."

Prince Par was startled at her abrupt turnaround. Had he really spoken too harshly? He stood, stunned, as Yvonne hurried back to the carriage a block away. "Gordar—"

"I will return in a moment. Let me get the ladies escorted home."

Par sighed but let his lord protector race ahead and arrange everything. By the time he arrived at the street, the carriage and guards were gone and two horses were left for him and Lord Gordar. His cousin handed him the reins of one mount. "I've lost the art of speaking to women," Par lamented as he mounted.

Lord Gordar settled on his horse beside him looking amused. "Hardly, though, you too lost your tact."

Par wrinkled his nose at the fact. "Indeed. More, I've lost my patience for playing political games. Stars, I do miss North Point!"

Lord Gordar chuckled. "Keep up your sour mood, and your father just might send you back there."

"Truly?"

"No." His cousin doused the flare of hope. "His Majesty needs you to get Serein's powers under yoke. Until you do, I don't see you going anywhere."

The prince groaned. "Two tasks I've no desire for." He was quiet for a time as their horses clopped up the cobbled street. The lord protector let Par have his silence. "I suppose I should send an apology to Lady Yvonne," he said at last.

"That is, if you still wish to court her."

"Court her?" Par protested.

Gordar shrugged. "What else would you call it?"

He frowned. "I concede the definition, but I hadn't thought of our courting as such."

His cousin made a noise in his throat. "And I assure you that she did."

Par sighed. "This is why I hate court politics. Too damn conniving."

"You just don't like the reasons for it," Gordar replied, knowing him too well. "I remember you being quite taken with them when you asked the Crystal princess to be your betrothed."

"I thought we agreed that Zerra Starkindler was to stay out of the conversation?"

The lord protector shrugged the excuse away.

"Fine. Yes, I didn't mind it then. Zerra…she never acted like these ladies. I had nothing that needing proving or garnishing up with her. We were friends, and I had nothing to hide she didn't already know about. That—*she*—was easy."

"And are you not making all of this more difficult as an excuse to not choose another?"

"You know, sometimes I hate that you know me so well."

Lord Gordar flashed a smile. "I as well, my prince."

"You will help me write an appropriate apology to the Limontés?"

A chuckle. "Now that's a first. You were always better with words than I."

"Yes, but I don't seem to have the best politesse when it comes to Lady Yvonne Limonté."

"Indeed, my prince, that is the truth."

"Ah, bugger off!"

Gordar shook his head, sending golden locks flying. "Not until we've written an appropriate letter, I will not."

"Stars' blight on you and the damned letter!"

"Now, now, such attitude will not do…"

§ §

King William Fantill watched as his son and nephew walked their horses back up to the fortress's stable yard. He sighed as he took in the sight below; Prince Par had left with the ladies in the late morning but returned ahorse with only his lord protector. That boded ill for his heir's success in finding a lady to court. "That son of mine…he'd put off finding a wife forever if I hadn't a say about it. I just don't understand him sometimes."

"William, come away from the window," Commander Matar of the Crystine cavalry bade him. The Crystal Kingdom's horse commander was staying in Sealand as a favor to the crown instead of staying with his forces currently stationed at North Point. Being *Khataum* in the Guardianship to the Stones of Power gave him much insight into the magical crystals—Serein included. He had offered his services to Prince

Par and the Sealand crown when it had become known Serein was active at North Point; Matar had gone south to keep an eye on the prince and his sapphire. “You’ll find no good answer peeping at your son as you are. Leave the boy be. He’ll find his partner with time.”

King William made a noise in his throat. “I’m already aging and grey. I don’t have the luxury of waiting for my son to give me grandchildren.”

Matar chuckled. “As if you are so old.”

“I feel like it quite often these days, *Khataum*.” Still, William turned away from the window to rejoin his old friend around the piles of books strew about his work table. “Especially with Par so restless to be fighting again. Stars, was I ever so reckless?”

The Crystine commander’s midnight-blue eyes looked especially intense as he glanced up from the page he had been scanning. “I remember you being quite hard-headed in your day. Like that time you started a bar fight in Dapper, all because the drunk lord was questioning the size of your manhood. Or how about that time you leapt into the fray of thirty maunstorz alone all because we had gotten stuck climbing a cliffside to escape an ambush? You scared me shitless thinking you were done for.”

His majesty tsked as he sat down opposite his old war comrade. “Point taken, my friend.” Hie guzzled down a tankard of beer by his elbow and wiped the foam from his mouth and beard. He tipped his head to Matar to query if the other man needed a refill. The commander shook his head. “You know, it’s been some time since I’ve thought of those days long ago,” William said as he stood to get himself another.

“Nearly twenty-five years now,” the Crystine man agreed.

“Hm, yes. It’s good to see we are still around after all that time. Back then, I truly wasn’t sure I would be…”

“Had it not been for the destruction of Crystalynian by Vauldin’s majik, I doubt we would be the Syre we are today.”

“Such devastation as what Kestral wrought doesn’t seem like such a gift.”

“Vauldin killed many maunstorz during Crystalynian’s fall,” Matar reminded him. “Had it not, the maunstorz really would have taken Syre.”

“That’s what you believe, *Khataum*.”

"It's what I've witnessed," Matar countered. "Even though the stones all went dormant afterward, so did the maunstorz. It let Syre move on from all that bloodshed."

"Until now," William griped under his breath. "We're right back to that time when those vermin nearly took us over—except now, they have a wielder of their own."

"Of Starkindler blood. There is still a chance we can get Ravel and the Starkindlers back. At least one of them has to be alive to wield the crystal."

"That's only a small comfort. So far, only two other stones are active—"

"That we know of."

William frowned at the interruption. "And neither wielder is proficient as the person who wields Ravel. We're now outclassed and outmaneuvered."

Matar sat back. He looked proud and formidable and as confident as King William remembered him to be. The Crystine commander was a skilled tactician but just as equally charismatic in a political setting. He seemed unfazed by the facts at hand. "I have confidence in Vauldin's wielder and in your son. The tides will turn back our way."

King William looked at the heaps of compendiums they had amassed on anything they thought useful on the Stones of Power, magic, or even royal bloodlines. "For all your certitude, even you do not know who wields Vauldin. For all we know—and should assume—it's someone we may find an enemy."

"Such a naysayer, William," Matar teased. "No. The obsidian was protected by the Guardians of the Prism. Not a one of them would let it go to the wrong hands. Plus, there was a link to the Xraxrain bloodlines in the Tashek, so I've no doubt Vauldin is in the hands of an ally—an exceptionally powerful one at that, for us to have felt the effects of Vauldin's rebirthing all the way here in Fortress Opal."

"Pray that I have such confidence as you. I have been long without the use of Serein and her powers. I've forgotten much of how to wield her." William huffed at his incompetence. "For all the good I can be to Par. I hope you are indeed correct that Vauldin's wielder is powerful and our ally. I'm ready for some good news for a change."

"As am I, William. As am I."

Chapter Eleven
§
The Prince's Resolve

The room was hushed; the only sound was the steady crackle of the fire. In the early light of morning, Prince Al'den found himself passing the hours by reading *Myths and Legends of Syre*—as if the compendium could give him answers to the bleak case before him. His father, the king of Staria for nearly forty-six years, was still in bed and had yet to awaken. In the candlelight, by which Al'den read, his aged father looked hollowed out and wearied. The fine beads of sweat on King Merretham's face and the grievous, faint wheezing were the greatest testaments to the illness that consumed him. His faithful attendant, Kellen Lockslory, dabbed the king's face from time to time; however, it did little against the fever.

All'ani Cum'ar had send his clan's best physician to attend the king. Yet even that woman had given their Prince of the Yellow Star little hope on King Merretham's recovery. She had examined him and prescribed some herbal remedies but had warned Al'den that little could be done unless the liege awoke. Rest, keeping the king warm, and time were her best remedies against the sickness that plagued the Starian king's lungs and body.

It had been a full day and night since then, and Al'den was losing hope. "Kellen." He startled the attendant by breaking the long silence. "You may go. Rest and eat."

"Your Highness!"

Prince Al'den interrupted the protest. "I will stay with my father. You have yet to take to bed since his collapse. You will not serve him well if you do as well."

Kellen looked ashamed. He acquiesced to his prince's wishes. "I will send for the All'ani man," he said and then bowed and took his leave.

Alone, Al'den stood from his chair by the window and came to his father's bedside, where he sank to a chair. Gently, he scooped up the limp hand to hold between his own. "Father," he said quietly, knowing there would be no response. "You should see the sunrise today. For the first time all month, it dawned clear and bright. The snows are awash in its reds and oranges. I don't think I've ever seen anything quite like it here at the Citadel. Indeed, when have we gotten such snows before?" Prince

Al'den patted the back of his father's withered hand as he spoke. The motion was a small comfort to himself, as if, by the action, he could will his father's eyes to open. A haggard wheeze followed instead. The sound constricted Al'den's throat. It was getting worse and wetter…

He blinked back the tears that threatened to fall. "Father," he choked, "when have I ever seen you so weak? Never. Never can I remember you being so worn. You were always so strong. To see you like this…" *It breaks my heart.* The prince could not finish the words aloud. Instead, he took the wet cloth, dipped it in the water basin by the bedstand, and sponged off his father's skin just as he had seen Kellen do. It was all that could be done.

"My prince," All'ani Cum'ar announced himself before he came into the room. The Tashek leader entered humbly to show a deep respect for the sickly king.

"Cum'ar." Al'den replaced the cloth and then tucked his father's hand in under the bedding before he stood to address his closest ally.

The All'ani leader gave a polite head-bow once his prince was standing before him. "I came to assure you of the continued vigilance to your walls by your men and to say that we can see for miles this morning. There is no sign of the enemy anywhere." Usually, Cum'ar was more tactful regarding the delicateness of the situation, so it came as a surprise to have him address his prince as if nothing were wrong; however, the prince found the Sheev'anee man's words a relief. Being a leader of the armies of Staria had always been the heir's place, not sitting by his father's deathbed—if that was what is was. To have his mind occupied elsewhere had to have been Cum'ar's intention. It worked to give Al'den some pause.

"*Ahnamen*, Cum'ar. I am relieved to have you keeping watch over my people in my place."

"The men are all worried, sir, but have asked me to say their prayers are with you and the king. They bid me to repeat that you take what time you need to be with His Majesty. They will keep the Citadel running smoothly."

A wan smile came to the prince's lips. "Of course, they would say that." Al'den waved his friend to the table and its stacks of books. Seated, he filled two cups with tea and passed one to the desert man. "I have no doubts of my men's abilities to keep this city safe. With you and your people here as well, the Citadel is probably the safest place in the northern lands of Syre."

"Indeed, my prince." Cum'ar sipped his tea. His amber-brown eyes wandered to the sleeping king. "Even if the enemy knew of the king's condition, they would be unwise to attack us here. Other places in Syre are not so lucky."

Al'den felt his hopes lift on that front. "Have you had word, then?"

"No. But I sent birds at dawn. With the Stars' luck, we will hear from one of our allies soon." Cum'ar fingered the rim of his cup as if it was extremely interesting. "I fear the damage the maunstorz and the snows have wrought while we remain stuck here."

It had been a fear of Al'den's as well, though he had yet to voice such. "As you said before, we must wait out the snow and await word. But that was my father's decree…" Al'den looked across the room to the bed. "If—"

"There will be no *ifs*, my prince," Cum'ar interrupted, knowing what the heir's next words would be. "We will know in a few days, when the king wakes."

"Or that his time has come."

"Yes." Cum'ar had explained the Sheev'anee's version of "passing" to his leader. The Tashek believed death was a change of the person's soul to an ethereal form—as all Starians did; however, they were even more entrenched in ideas of fate and destinies being preordained than other people of the sands. They called it *Kavannen*. "The Stars write how each person's destiny will arrive and pass. They dictate how and when a person goes back to them, as well. Your father, king of Staria, has had an exemplary life, but also one of difficulties. His ending will be just as trying."

"I do not want to think such things." Al'den's features were hard, and he frowned into his drink. "But I am a military leader first and foremost. I know well how fragile the human body is. Even your healer looked skeptically on my father's case. The more the hours pass, the smaller my hope grows."

There was sympathy in the All'ani leader's eyes. "I, too, have watched a great man wither away and pass. Sometimes, the worst part is the waiting."

Prince Al'den nodded and refilled his teacup. The silence stirred between them until Cum'ar nudged about some of the books on the table. "There are all on the Stones of Power!" he commented, sounding shocked.

"Yes. Father had been making Kellen collect them from the library and bring them here."

"I had thought such works had been burned." The desert man reverently touched a few covers, clearly intrigued at the diversity of the titles.

"Not here." Al'den took up the *Myths and Legends of Syre* he had been reading. "My father loved books. He hid these away in a back alcove of the library so they could be preserved. I guess he had the foresight to know they would be needed someday."

"But without Amun, what can you learn?" Weeks before, Al'den had entrusted the citrine stone to the Havenese princess's care, hoping Éleen's travels southward would keep the stone safe. All'ani Cum'ar was the only other one to know of Amun's whereabouts—and he did not approve of distancing the stone from its wielder.

"A great deal, at least in the history of the stones and certain meditations that can strengthen a stone-bearer's mind." Al'den looked across to his father. "A fool I was, though, to let Amun go. With it, I could have healed my father." His frown was angry.

"And now you understand the reasoning to keep Amun close." The Tashek's words were harsh. "But you cannot fault yourself for not knowing better. We will have to find the Havenese princess once the snows melt enough to pass a great distance."

"If they let up that much, I would rather bring the whole of the Starian forces against our enemies and help the suffering of the people. Amun will not avail me until I learn to use it, and I am not so powerless as to rely on it solely. I will crush the maunstorz by force."

Cum'ar's thin mouth quirked at his prince's resolve. "And that, my Prince of the Yellow Star, is why I follow you. For you will make Syre tremble before you."

§ §

Another two days passed in waiting and watching. Two more days when the skies dawned clear and no more snow fell. It was both odd and a relief to know the unnatural blizzards covering Staria seemed at an end. With the calmer weather, two birds made it back to the Citadel of Light. Cum'ar was handed the messages by his sister—their clan's bird master. They shared a relieved smile before the All'ani leader hurried away to find the prince.

"Prince Al'den!" Cum'ar rushed to King Merretham's chambers and found the Starian heir asleep, curled over the compendium he had been reading. He almost sneaked away to let the exhausted prince sleep—but he knew the missives were greatly anticipated by the Prince of the Yellow Star. Cum'ar crossed the room and shook Al'den awake. "My prince, we finally have word!

Prince Al'den groaned and sat up groggily. His first reaction was to panic and stand to check on his father. Realizing the king still slept eased the prince's fears enough for him to listen to the desert man. "Cum'ar. I apologize for my state."

Cum'ar shook his head and started again, now that Al'den was awake enough to comprehend him. "We have received word from two of our allies." Al'den's eyes widened and he reached for the missives. "One is from Raven's Den, written by Re'shaird Aerrisson. The other comes from mertinean Commander Kins."

"Let us read these in the other room," Al'den suggested, and they shuffled out of the bedchamber. Then, the prince unfurled the two letters to find both men had written as much as they could on the small paper.

Aerrisson had originally left with Lord Darshel Shekmann and his Kavahadian cavalry to follow the maunstorz eastward. He had separated from the group when they had realized no word on their progress had reached the Citadel. Aerrisson had headed south, to Raven's Den, to try to meet up with Commander Grant and the mertinean stationed there to warn them of maunstorz pillaging and burning. Yet, even word on the Tashek scout's whereabouts and the mertinean at Raven's Den had not reached the Starian forces—until just then. According to Aerrisson, Raven's Den had been attacked by a maunstorz force before he had arrived. Commander Grant and most of his men had escaped to hide out in the Red Hills just outside the post. Once Aerrisson had joined with them, they had begun a strategy of guerrilla attacks to wear the enemy down.

"The enemy leader is a man by the name of Silvarron, Second of the generals in Mansocan's armies."

Al'den's eyes strayed to Cum'ar's face. "Your people know more of this enemy than we do. You even know their names."

"No." Cum'ar shook his head. "We only know four names: Zepthanial is their leader, a man we have only heard about but never seen. Mansocan is his First, leader of the maunstorz armies. The Third general is Chornauk. The Crystine and Sheev'arid's have had numerous battles against him. He is a hulk of a man, tall and iron-muscled. He can take on five high-leveled Sheev'anee by himself. There is rumor of a Fourth general but alas, he is not a man I am familiar with."

Al'den waved Aerrisson's missive. "Re'shaird asks what orders we have for them or any news. They sound as isolated as we are."

"I agree. Commander Grant is one to follow orders, but his direct commander, Ethan Kins, is stationed at Kavahad. More, I fear that if Grant has not gotten orders from Kins or the Red Palace, then the snows must be worse in Rubia than here. Getting word to them is easy enough if the birds can fly, but reaching them—or having Grant and Aerrisson retreat—may be out of the question if the snows are too deep."

"Let's not jump to conclusions," Al'den cautioned as he turned his attention to the other missive. Commander Kins seemed to have more details. He, at least, seemed to be able to communicate between most of the forces in the west—as the war council (held at the Citadel) had hoped. "Kavahad is, indeed, a more centralized location for our command base. Commander Kins has kept word between North Point, Sardon, Fortress Opal, and the Golden Place. He writes that he has been unable to hear from Rubia or Sunrise, however. Still, that the western side of Syre has stayed in contact shows that our plans to move our main communications south were correct. Now we are back in communication with everyone—through Kavahad."

"But what Commander Kins has to say on some things alarms me," said Cum'ar.

"Me as well. The groups leaving the Citadel all reached Kavahad—except the one with the princes of Sunrise. Prince Kent arrived at Paragon Oasis and then separated with his men to head for Sardon. Princess Éleen's party and the court of Staria arrived in Kavahad and were then moved to Viscount LaPoint's lands to give relief to their host-city. Prince Par and the Crystine reached North Point safely and are now south at Fortress Opal trying to find ways to get supplies north to the ailing villages…"

"Commander Kins writes that all communications from Rubia have stopped."

Al'den said, "That would have mainly have been Raven's Den and Wynward's Crossing."

"And one other—the forces of Kavahad."

Al'den frowned. "Lord Darshel and his party were having trouble getting birds to use before the snows. That does not mean that they have been lost to us. They could be hunkered down somewhere in Rubia."

"Perhaps you are right." But Cum'ar did not look pleased.

"What is it?" Prince Al'den asked. He knew the Tashek well enough to know when the man was holding something back.

"I still wish you had Amun."

"And what does that have to do with any of this?"

The desert man almost didn't say what was on his mind. Almost. "With Amun ,you could try to communicate with other stone-bearers. Not as well as the wielder of Sevén, but you could have a conversation with some success. I have my suspicions that the obsidian stone Vauldin has awoken and joined with its wielder, but we cannot know for sure unless that bearer comes here in person or you use Amun to try to reach them."

"That is interesting, but I still don't see how that is relevant to these missives and your worries over Lord Darshel's forces," said Al'den.

The All'ani leader's eyes looked distant, as if he had lost himself in thought. He raised a finger to ask his prince to wait, and then he reentered the king's chambers only to return with an old journal that had been set among the books collected there. "As leader of the All'ani, I am privy to details only given to the highest members in the Prism of the Stars." He was referring to title given to the Tashek that kept the histories of the Stones of Power. It was a tight-knit group that—as Al'den had recently learned from Cum'ar—rarely gave out secrets of the eight stones. The prince had been awarded the right to this knowledge because of his link to Amun. Only the royal blood of the Mausheliks could awaken and use the citrine, and Al'den was the only living heir, so there was no doubt to his inheritance of the stone.

Opening the journal, Cum'ar skimmed its table of contents and then flipped to a page he had discovered before. "Our Shi'alam was once cousin to Queen Kestral of Crystalynian."

Now *that* was news; Al'den's eyebrows rose.

Cum'ar went on: "The Shi'alam always insisted that Queen Kestral had two children, either of which would have the blood to awaken

Vauldin. This journal here states that Prince Verrin was mortally wounded along with King Trev'shel before Crystalynian's fall. The girl, Arrez, however, was given into the care of the wielder of Kevel. She—and that man—disappeared from record once the kingdom was destroyed."

Prince Al'den scanned the page but found little enlightening. He fixed his friend with a bemused expression. "You Tashek love speaking in wayward circles. You have yet to give me any answer to why I need Amun and why it is relevant to these missives."

Cum'ar looked frustrated. "I thought you knew, prince, that the Sheev'anee, most particularly the Sheev'arids, found and kept Vauldin—without its owner, sadly."

"Actually, I did not."

"Well, maybe I failed to mention that during our talks…"

"So, Vauldin, the obsidian stone?" Al'den kept Cum'ar from getting sidetracked. "Who guards it?"

"You know her. Sheev'arid Zyanthena."

"Zy'ena…" Al'den remembered a fact the Shi'alam and his adopted daughter had shared: Zyanthena had been one of the Nallaus—Tashek not associated with the Sheev'anee. The detail had been leaked when the Nallaus had attacked the Citadel to cause panic among the armies amassed around, giving the maunstorz a chance to pass by. The diversion would have worked had Zyanthena not realized the Tashek fighters were from that clan. "So… you are trying to say to me that Zyanthena was not Nallaus at all but the lost heir of Crystalynian?"

Both men shared a look that was both stunned and baffled. "It's the only conclusion I can come up with…unless she somehow ran into the heir and Kevel's wielder in the middle of nowhere." Cum'ar shrugged at his own befuddlement. Even he was not certain his reasoning was correct. "You know that shaking we felt a month ago, before the snows came? The only stone I know that has ever awoken or fallen into slumber so radically is Vauldin, and to have done that, it had to have awoken to its wielder."

"You still can't conclude the wielder is Sheev'arid Zyanthena."

"Hence why we need Amun. If Vauldin has awoken, then we have a link with the wielder, perhaps can even learn the goings-on in Rubia and the east. With such communication, we won't be so blind. And—if it is Zyanthena—then she can tell us why Lord Darshel's forces have lost touch and what they found following the maunstorz."

Prince Al'den looked back at the missive in his hands. "I see your reasoning for us to collect Amun and speak with this wielder of Vauldin, but until then, we must try to help our allies as much as possible. Certainly, Commander Grant needs to get his forces away from Raven's Den before they fall to the cold or this Silvarron."

"It sounds as if Kavahad could not support them in this, though."

"I get that feeling as well…we could handle their numbers, but the distance is too great, unless we ride at cavalry speed…"

"If Grant's men can, I would say send them south along the Senna River. They can be better supported in one of the towns in the Golden Kingdom or even Sunrise."

"I would prefer Golden." There was no friendship to call upon with the Sunarians, and Al'den doubted the king of Sunrise would protect or harbor men not his own.

Cum'ar agreed. "Prince Kent will find a way to get them supplies. We can try to get word to Sardon about their plight."

"I will write it." A letter to Prince Kent, newly acquired friend to Al'den, sounded like a way to lift his spirits. "Cum'ar, tell my men and yours of these missives. Knowing our allies are well will give them relief."

"Yes, my prince."

"And one more thing…"

The All'ani man raised his eyebrows, waiting.

"I will write a letter to Princess Éleen to be sent with the missive to Commander Kins. I am heeding your advice that we need Amun."

All'ani Cum'ar grinned. "Forget a bird, then. Lăn'esha and I will go retrieve Amun ourselves, with your leave."

"Without me?" Al'den protested.

"Or with. Only your father can answer that. I would have you not leave him."

Al'den nodded. The logic was sound.

Cum'ar added, "But you will see how useful Amun is once you have it back."

Chapter Twelve
§
Learning the Sight

It took four days to be "purified," a process that involved fasting, drinking only water and cactus juice, and meditation. By the final day, Decond was feeling delirious—a condition he suspected the Oracle wanted. En'ril Savam'eed collected him and helped Decond back to the Oracle's main chamber. That day, they were the only ones to grace her hall.

"Savam'eed, *ahnamen.* Leave Decond here with me." The old crone moved from her huddled mass of horse hides to reach out and pet En'ril's cheek. The Guardian held the hand to his face for a tender moment and then left on silent feet. "Young Decond," the Oracle continued and held out her hand in invitation. As before, the farrier-turned-Guardian reached out to take the delicate limb; he felt his own tremble from the lack of food. "You have purified."

"Yes," he replied, though she had stated more than asked.

"Then drink from the bowl at my feet."

Between them, on the dais, was a horse-hoof bowl filled with a liquid. Decond brought it to his lips and caught a whiff of the earthy pungency of the drink. "What is it?"

"Just drink, Orphan. It is a plant that will help you gain the Sight."

He didn't know much about plants, but Decond suspected the Oracle meant the liquid would give him visions—as he had heard some would. Still, it did not do to ignore the order of the Oracle. He took a sip and choked on the bitter taste.

"All of it."

Grimacing, Decond managed to drink the rest before he gagged and dry-heaved. Winded, he set the bowl back on the dais with a click.

"Now, you will carry me." The weathered crone came to a bent-over stand before him. Even on her feet and on the dais, she was still shorter than Decond. He hesitated but finally reached for the fragile woman; the Oracle was as light as a sack of dried root vegetables his arms and as delicate as a stick sculpture. He felt apprehensive that she would break in two if he squeezed too tightly.

"Go deeper into the cave," the Oracle commanded, her haggard voice having no such reservations. "Follow the oil lamps."

Indeed, there were just enough oil lamps laid across the floor to light Decond's way. He followed them into the long cavern, going deeper and deeper until they brought him into a final room about three hundred yards into the ground. There, an underground waterfall flowed down the back wall into a mineral pool at its base; the light from the small candles around it made the water glisten just enough for Decond to make out the fall of water. The candles also helped him see where a wide swath of horse hides had been set out across the bare sand of the cavern floor.

"Set me down beside the pool." Decond obliged and then stepped back as the Oracle settled herself. "Now, you will remove your clothes."

That time he balked, "Oracle—"

"It is not as if these eyes of mine can see you, boy," she interrupted. "You will disrobe and set your clothes aside and take a seat in the center of the room." Suddenly self-conscious, Decond did as he was told and removed the new *saer'rek* he had received. The cool, damp air hit his skin like a shock as he freed his foot from the last of his clothes. Completely naked, the young farrier piled his clothes at the entrance to the cave before taking a shivering seat where he had been instructed. The Oracle did not move or speak until she heard Decond still. "Now, young Orphan, you will soon feel the effects of the Seer's sage and datura."

So, she *had* drugged him!

"But you are in a safe place. These plants will help loosen your mind. At first, you will see images of your past, those that must be confronted before you can connect with Sevén." Then, she said, "Sevén, the ring I gave you—where is it?"

"Oh." Decond rose and collected it from the pocket where he had stashed it. "It is here."

"You will set it on the stone beside me." There was a flat stone to the right of the crone's knee. Decond placed the ring there and found his seat again. "Now, as I was saying…you should begin to feel the effects of the drink."

"You mean the hum under my skin and the flashes of lights?"

"Everyone has their own reactions." She didn't say yay or nay—so typical of a Tashek. "I will play my rattles, and my girls will drum for you, so that you may journey into these images of your past."

Startled, Decond realized that the Oracle's seers were indeed present. They came forth from the shadows and came to sit just off of the hides. He felt his face flush in embarrassment at having all the girls surround him, yet none of the seers seemed to notice his nakedness. They found their seats and began to tap out a rhythm on their drums, all business. Two took up the pace the Oracle set with rattles of their own, made from the hulls of nuts. The room was awash in the sounds of the instruments. The girls then added a chant, and Decond became entranced in the sounds. Soon after, the herbs took hold and the young farrier's body was rocked in a cascade of fire and ice. Knocked backward, Decond fell into the explosion of colors that took over his sight. He was pulled ruthlessly into a vision of his childhood:

Decond had been born in the town of Tarry, on the western edge of the Crystal Kingdom, the youngest of six children. He had tried to forget much of that time; however, the sage and datura would not let him. They pulled the memory forth, making it seem as if Decond was back there once again…

He was seven. It was Growing Time, and the town seemed contented in the lull of the summer heat. He was running about the walls of the outdoor furnaces of his uncle's ironworks shop. Beside one of the furnaces, his father—Decond barely recognized the man—was learning the ropes from his brother. A farmer until the acreage had been lost to creditors, Decond's father had begged his brother to take them in and for him to work the shop to pay off the remainder of his debts.

What was supposed to be a second chance at life had turned into a nightmare for Decond and his siblings. The uncle had a mean streak a mountain high. Frequently, he would get drunk and corner his brother's children to beat them—or worse. Decond's parents turned a blind eye to the abuse, as without the man's support there was nowhere to go and no way to make ends meet.

Under the plants' influence, Decond rewitnessed the final time he had seen his siblings' abuse.

It was the day Decond was running about the furnaces. He remembered feeling confused that his elder brother hadn't come back out of the storage shed from counting to ten in a game of fox-and-geese. Wondering why, Decond had returned to the shed to look for him. Entering it, he found his uncle standing over his brother's form, with his brother's pants down around his ankles. The boy was crying at what was being done to him. Of course, Decond had been too young to comprehend the truth, but he had understood his sibling had been hurt. Reacting, he had taken up a hook hanging by the door and swung it at his uncle in his brother's defense. The weapon impaled the man in the left kidney area and knocked him to the ground. Freed, his brother had run out, pulling Decond with him. They had run away from the shop and hadn't looked back until their fear had faded, which had been hours later. As fate would have it, that was the last time Decond saw the rest of his family.

His brother, Decond lost a year later…

The two brothers had wandered about as street orphans, eking out a meager life on scraps and trash. By winter, they had fallen in with a crowd of runaways; however, these boys were little ruffians, stealing from the wealthy and causing trouble just to do it. Unused to being among cutthroats ended up being the siblings' undoing. They got caught during one night's raid. Cornered, Decond's brother had tried to fight off the man who found them, but their target was a former war veteran turned black-market crime boss. The man gutted Decond's brother right there in the alley but allowed Decond to live; he "drew the line at putting down a boy under ten"—or so he reasoned. The blood and viciousness of that night terrorized Decond's dreams for years and created a mental and physical dislike of weapons—not that his Guardian, Terrik, had cared to honor Decond's feelings about such things.

The sage and datura let Decond lull in the darkness for a sixty-breaths' count, the full of a minute, before more visions plagued him. These next ones, at least, were not as full of terror or bile-causing. In the first, Decond finally left the streets of Tarry. He had been found by a drunk farrier and taken in to be the man's apprentice. It was this same man who had taught Decond all his skills with ironwork. The pair had eventually left Tarry for a more "lucrative" post, working at the capital in a shop just west of the Crystal Castle.

The image changed from their first meeting to one in the new shop. It showed Decond a time not two summers past. In the crisp, morning air of Harvest-Gathering Time came a horse and rider in need of servicing. The rider had turned out to be a woman with stunning brandy eyes and a poise that had made Decond fumble over his words. Thinking the lad would be incapable of pronouncing her alien name, the Tashek had allowed him to call her "Zee." Zyanthena, Decond recalled, on their very first meeting. Never before or since had he seen such an exotic, enigmatic woman; his heart had fallen for her completely in just one glance.

Zyanthena's beautiful face slowly dissolved, like water washing away clay, and he was left with one final vision. Before Decond was the irked face of Terrik Sheev'arid, having just been charged with teaching Decond to be one of the Guardians of the Prism. They were back at Terrik's tent during their stop at Paragon Oasis—the day Decond's life became no longer his own but one ruled by the Sheev'anee's "circle of fates." Terrik had cut his palm and made Decond do the same, and then they had grasped hands and become connected by blood to be brothers in the Prism.

In response to the image, Decond's hand stung, just as it had then. He fingered the scar in the memory of its making. The physical touch seemed to break Decond from the hold of the plants. Coming to in the barely lit cavern, the young farrier found himself cradled in the arms of a seer, his head placed gently on her knees. Slowly becoming aware, Decond realized he had thrown up and defecated on himself from the intensity of the drugs. It was utterly embarrassing.

Decond's moan alerted the Oracle to his return to consciousness. "Girls, help him clean up and pull the hides."

"Helping Decond" turned out to mean the seers did everything. Decond's purified and drug-ridden body left him incapable of holding himself up and at a loss as to shifting his limbs properly. In the end, the girls washed him clean without his aid and then dressed him in the *saer'rek* again. Decond was not sure he had ever felt so ashamed and self-conscious in his life. Yet there was little he could do. Fully robed, he was set back onto a fresh hide, his soiled one having been carried away. The seer who had held him stayed to prop his spineless form upright.

"Your visions show what is in your heart, what has molded you." The Oracle's voice sounded like a shout to the drugged Decond, though he doubted she spoke any louder than before. "It seems," the old crone continued, "that you had a traumatic childhood, mountain-born."

"I had a cruel uncle and a deadbeat father."

"And a brother murdered before your eyes."

Decond swallowed, tasting bile at the words. "Y-yes," he finally admitted.

"The plants hide nothing of your woes. I saw all with you."

"All?" How could that be?"

"All," she repeated, "even your desire for a young Sheev'arid woman, and your apprehensions of her brother and his duty to guide you."

"Of Guardian Terrik, yes, but that of which you speak of Zee—"

"Your body, boy, betrayed your affections." For the first time, the seers reacted with covered giggles of their own. Apparently, his enlivened manhood had been quite the sight.

Decond felt his face heat up. "Th-that's not really true," he stammered.

"Ah, you are human, young Orphan, and Sheev'arid Zyanthena has an allure not easily overlooked." Was the old woman jealous of Zyanthena's beauty? "Your feelings for her will make this next part a little easier."

"And what would that be?"

"Patience. Patience, Orphan."

Considering he hadn't eaten a decent meal in ninety-six hours and had just vomited and soiled himself from a drug-induced vision quest, Decond was beginning to understand why Guardian Terrik disliked the Oracle. The old lady could be condescending. Still, he kept the feeling to himself and murmured to the old crone to continue.

"First, you must understand what these visions teach you. What strengths and weakness are in your heart that limit you?"

"The vision of my childhood…all it reveals is a painful past."

"Ah, but such trials mold you into who you are."

The words let Decond be introspective. "Well…I can see that. My age kept me from understanding just how cruel my uncle was and how precarious the situation my parents faced was."

"So, your naivety protected you."

"Yes. It also gave me fortitude, the ability to withstand poor circumstances."

"Fortitude is useful, if used wisely."

He nodded, forgetting the old crone could not see.

"What else?" she asked.

"My brother's death…it horrified me. I used to be unable to handle weapons. Just the sight of a hand blade would make my knees weak, my heart race…"

"And now?"

Decond realized that his training with the Tashek had erased that gut-clenching reaction. Even holding a sword and dagger did not leave him shaking as it once had, though—in all honesty—he still preferred axes to swords for that very reason. "I see weapons as tools now. In the right hands, they can be used to protect someone, too."

"Still, they are for one purpose."

"Killing is not mandatory."

"That is a lofty goal, Orphan."

"It is a choice to keep such convictions."

She chuckled, a raspy sound. "Indeed." The crone shifted in her robe and pulled it around her bony frame tightly. "This farrier you worked for…"

"Tim Flander."

"Yes. Why see him?"

"He was the one to take me off the streets."

"A kindly man?"

"A drunkard and a lazy one. Yet he did provide a roof over my head and a decent meal—and my skills with iron."

The crone hummed at the information but didn't probe beyond that. "And Sheev'arid Zyanthena?"

"It was the first time I had met her—that vision."

"A profound encounter, it seems."

Decond felt his face flush. "Was it?"

"Your body seems to say so."

Decond heard the soft chuckle from the seer who held him; others had to be smiling, as well. "A young man's body wouldn't help reacting to such a woman on first sight," he managed to say in his defense.

"Hm. Perhaps…" The oracle didn't sound convinced. "Zyanthena…what is she to you? Obviously, she thought enough of you and your skills to hire you for the Crystine."

"And that's all it was. Zee has always had an eye for talent."

"Talent. You say that so benignly."

"Because it is—our relationship is just that between two friends."

There was a knowing look to the Oracle's features. "Your heart's secret is safe with us, Orphan. That you have such thoughts of Sheev'arid Zyanthena will help you connect to her with Sevén."

"Connect with her?"

"That is right." The Oracle waved her hand, and the closest seer rose to collect the pearl ring and take it to Decond. "This next part is all you."

"Ah. But are you really done analyzing my visions?"

"The last is between you and your Guardian, so, yes, we are done with your visions. But whilst you have the plants in your system, your reach will be enhanced."

"I…do not understand."

"Sevén has the power to connect with the other stones. It can link them together. The true wielder will be able to communicate with all the bearers. For you, it will give you short visions of each stone's surroundings. With the stone Vauldin, you may be able to do more."

"Do more?"

The first sign of frustration Decond had ever seen from the Oracle furrowed her brow. "It's not an exact science, boy. Imagine Zyanthena, everything you can about her. Think of her features, the sound of her voice, her mannerisms, her smell—"

"That's awfully intimate."

"It's what I'm counting on, Orphan. You know her better than any of the other known wielders and certainly more than any of the Stones of Power. Hold Sevén, concentrate on Zyanthena's essence, and you may just be able to reach out to her."

It sounded a little far-fetched, as if even the Oracle didn't know what to do and was shooting in the dark. Decond had his doubts.

"Erase all your reservations, Orphan. Sevén will be your guide—if you just trust its majik."

Therein lay the crux of the problem. Magic sounded worrisome and a sure bet to be against the Estarian religion—at least as far as Decond knew. He almost didn't take Sevén from the seer as she crouched before him, but he had been embarrassed enough by all the seers' attentions that it made him want to put an end to everything as quickly as possible—and that meant doing as the Oracle wanted. Reaching for the ring, Decond curled his fingers around the pearl and its gold band and prayed for forgiveness for his transgressions.

In the silence that followed, nothing happened.

Then, his palm grew warm as Sevén's powers flowed out. A calming feeling radiated from the pearl into his hand and up his arm to his heart. Sevén's powers of healing erased his fears, just like that, replacing them with feelings of protection, warmth, and peace. He looked down in awe at the golden-white glow that escaped through his fingers.

The Oracle breathed a sigh of relief. "Sevén accepts you, Orphan. Now, try to seek out Zyanthena. Certainly, by now, you miss her."

He did, more than any other person in his life. But how, in all the Stars of the sky, was he to "reach out" to the Tashek hundreds of miles away?

Sevén glowed again, erasing his doubts as soon as the question was raised. *Trust, believe*—those were the feelings Decond got from the stone, emotions more than words. "Here goes," he murmured and closed his eyes to try touching Zyanthena.

Slowly, pieces of his memories came together to create the Zyanthena Sheev'arid Decond knew. It was not the image of a toughened warrioress, capable of fighting off forty maunstorz. To Decond, Zee had been a servant of a lord near the Crystal Castle. He hadn't known she was a fighter—nor that her "master" had been Commander Matar, leader of the Crystine—until she had "hired" him as a farrier for the cavalry. Every time they had met before, Zyanthena had worn a lovely, brocade cape that concealed her desert clothing. In the summers, she had donned women's homespun shirts to blend in with the population of the town. Looking back now, Decond realized it had been Zyanthena's way of softening her fighter's spirit; in those clothes, most people barely gave her a second glance, which they certainly would have if she wore her desert garb.

Another memory helped Decond recall that Zyanthena had been one of the best listeners he had ever met. She was patient and astute to subtle changes in himself or others—a trait that allowed her to get people to open up about almost anything. She had been the only person Decond had ever told about his brother's death. There had been compassion in those brandy eyes as he had spoken of the event, and the soft touch of her hand on his arm had been so comforting. It was an action of sympathy he had never seen Zyanthena give to anyone else.

Yes, Decond admitted in retrospect, that one action had been the final clincher for his falling in love with Zee. He had felt like he was someone special to Zyanthena from the actions she showed to only him.

"Zee," Decond murmured, overcome with longing to feel that touch on his shoulder again. The phantom feeling of her hand's weight on his arm finally opened him to Sevén's powers. All of a sudden, Decond was thrown into a motion akin to tumbling—or flying headlong at an invisible wall. A breath later, a room came into focus and his world righted itself.

The walls were made up of blocks of granite stone, thick and strong. A fireplace roared, warming the room. To the left was a door made all of glass; its transparency showed snow falling outside. To Decond's right was a door to a hallway and, beside it, a walk-in closet full of clothes. The closet door was ajar just enough for the him to make out the items inside. Something large bumped into the back of Decond's knees, sending him sprawling to the black bear rug at his feet. Spinning about to land on his rear, Decond froze as he came nose-to-nose with the largest grey wolf he had ever seen.

"Ember?" Zyanthena rose from the bed where she had been meditating. She came to crouch next to Moon Ember, the alpha's mate, and placed a hand into the thick fur of her neck. Ember made some vocal chortles but kept her sights on Decond. "Someone's here?" Zyanthena asked the wolf. She looked at the space in front of the grey wolf but saw nothing. Ember chortled again. "A young man? Astral projection, you say?"

Decond was astounded that the Tashek woman understood the wolf; however, he was still too terrified to move. It seemed odd—or intriguing—that the wolf could see him, but Zyanthena could not. Now what was he to do?

"Reach out?" Zyanthena murmured, still speaking with Moon Ember. She seemed to trust the wolf's knowledge, for she raised a hand up beside the wolf's snout and paused. "If you really are here, Ember says you need to touch me to link your projection to this plane."

It seemed sound advice. Decond raised his hand and pressed it against Zyanthena's outheld palm. Their hands met solidly. Zyanthena's breath seemed to catch as his form became more apparent to her. "Decond?" she whispered.

"Zee!" Decond heard the awe in his own voice. He really had connected with Zyanthena!

"How—?" Zyanthena started, but she stopped herself with a head shake. "I sense Sevén, the pearl of the Golden Kingdom. You are using it?"

"I guess so." Decond shrugged helplessly. "It's my first time. The Oracle says I am 'pure' enough to use Sevén to track the other stones—whatever that means."

A fond smile formed on the beautiful Tashek's face. "Of course, you would be. I know of no other who is as kind-hearted and selfless as you."

A blush flushed up his face at the praise.

"You are with the Oracle?"

"Terrik and I were sent here by the Shi'alam. The Oracle ordered me trained to prepare to use Sevén. She believed from first setting eyes on me that I was destined for this—or, I mean, by first touch."

Zyanthena tsked under her breath. "That Oracle…always playing with people's lives. Even if she is right ninety percent of the time, she is rather infuriating about it."

Decond chuckled. "You sound like your brother."

Zyanthena wrinkled her nose. "Perhaps. I have my own reasons for disliking the Oracle—none of which I will bother to voice here." She continued before Decond could ask, "Is my brother treating you well?"

He shrugged. "Well enough. I've been in training with En'ril Savam'eed and the other Guardians more than Terrik. For a while, I thought they were trying to kill me."

"Hm. *She-koum-o* practices can get a bit extreme," Zyanthena agreed. Keen eyes looked Decond over head-to-toe. "But you seem to have passed more or less unscathed."

"I feel more capable," Decond replied, sitting up proudly. Indeed, the training had seemed to suit him—after he had gotten over the initial shock of it. "I've gone through forty days of non-stop training under Savam'eed's tutelage."

Zyanthena's eyes flashed in surprise. "That is indeed a small feat. I offer you my congratulations on surviving the Guardianship's strict training. I know well what that all entails."

"*Ahnamen.*"

The Tashek *thank you* seemed to make her even prouder. Zyanthena made a hum in her throat and then bowed to Decond as well as she could without breaking their contact. "You have grown into a man of great esteem these past weeks. I am happy to see this."

Decond rubbed the back of his neck self-consciously at such high praise. They had never been so formal before; it seemed odd and a bit uncomfortable.

Zyanthena must have recognized his behavior as embarrassment, for she changed the subject. "Is there something you were sent to ask me?"

"Oh, ah…no. The Oracle didn't say anything in particular, just that I needed to connect with you. She thought our familiarity with each other would make the linking stronger."

"Familiarity." Zyanthena tested the word, rolling it in her mouth. The word conjured up a different connotation that the old crone liked to use, one too potent for just their shared friendship. "It seems the Oracle was right. Your connection is coming through clearly—despite us being over seven hundred miles away."

"So far!" Decond was stunned.

"Yes. Lord Darshel and I are at the old palace of Crystanian in Crystalynian. We are trapped here by the blizzards but are well. We have been without word from the rest of Syre for nearly two months."

"I'm sorry. I can't offer you much in news. I've been here in the Ar'heim and without word too."

"I am glad to hear that you are safe and well cared for. To me, that is enough." The image of Zyanthena seemed to waver. His own must have as well, for Zyanthena frowned and said, "I think your link is weakening. You may lose me soon. Decond, if you are using Sevén's powers, then know this: using majik always comes with a price. Use the pearl sparingly, or you will find yourself exhausted. Rest when you can. Eat—"

Whatever else Zyanthena was going to say was cut off as the connection ended. Yanked back into the cave in the Ar'heim, Decond became surrounded by darkness again. He felt as if he was floating into nothingness, bewildered and unanchored to the world. The sudden shift had been too quick for his brain to comprehend. Alone, Decond lost count of how long he floated. When he came to, he found that the young seer who had held him was standing above him, looking panicked, as if she had been trying to rouse him for some time.

His groan settled her fears. "He's come around!" The seer's wispy voice called out to the others.

"Stars' praise," he heard the Oracle mutter. "Orphan, can you hear me now?"

"Y-yes," He found his voice, though it took some effort. With the seer's help, he found a cross-legged seat. He groaned at the massive headache that overtook him. Decond held his head until it eased. "What happened to me?"

"You collapsed," the seer said. "As if your body couldn't hold itself anymore."

That seemed about right. Even now, Decond felt wearied to the bone. "Zee was just warning me about something like that. A 'price to be paid' for using magic—or something of the like."

"You spoke with Zyanthena?" The Oracle sounded excited.

"We had a full conversation. It was like I was there in the room with her."

"Incredible! Your connection to her was that strong?"

"She called it an…astral projection." Decond stumbled over the weird terminology. "It felt real enough."

"Such a strong link does explain your fainting. I have never heard of a non-wielder having such abilities with the stones. You will need to handle Sevén carefully from now on. However, your use of the stone was a success. You are ready to search for the other stones with Guardians Terrik and En'ril. Rest the remainder of the day and night and eat your fill. Tomorrow, you will begin your search for the other Stones of Power."

Chapter Thirteen
§
First Snows' Ball

There was a freedom to the Northern lands that the South lacked, at least as far as Princess Éleen Eldon-Tomino had come to know. At first, with the loosened reins had come an embarrassment to let protocols become so lax. Afterward, the princess had experienced a profound joy as she explored all that was new and different. The feeling of being unencumbered was slowly awakening in the second child of the king of Blue Haven—for better or worse.

It was made more apparent by her choice of companions: Lady Rosetta Greyson was an enigma to the sheltered Éleen. Orphaned at seventeen and backed by her older brother, Rosetta had not only been able to keep the Greyson demesne from bankruptcy, she had reestablished it ten-fold. She was also responsible for numerous orphanages throughout Staria—and some in Golden—and was the royal crown's most reliable diplomat. Lady Rosa Quartlett was her esteemed partner in some of the Greyson holdings; a schoolteacher at heart, she loved tutoring at the orphanage at the Citadel of Light and helped organize fundraisers for the children. Of all the nobility sent to Viscount Markus LaPoint's grounds, these two women intrigued Princess Éleen the most.

"Look! Over there!" Lady Rosa pointed to a mother doe and a newborn fawn springing away into the underbrush. For all the ladies, the unusual wildlife at LaPoint's property had been a wonder.

"How darling!" Lady Rosetta grinned and eased her prancing horse back to a walk. She patted its winter-haired neck in praise for its behavior.

All four of the horses had all been enlivened at the sight of the deer; however, the dappled-grey mare, Bella, which the LaPoints had loaned Éleen, was the quietest of the bunch—much to the princess's relief. The mare settled quickly to the princess's hands on the reins. "I still can't get over seeing them!" Éleen commented as the doe and fawn disappeared. "In Blue Haven, the animals are too quick to hide. It's hard to catch proper glimpses of them."

"Indeed," Lord Carrod, Éleen's constant protector, agreed. "The sport we could have in Staria! I'd come back with double the trophies than from home."

"A drabble on you, sir!" Lady Rosetta told Lord Carrod. "You men are always so set on killing things instead of enjoying their beauty."

Lord Carrod blushed a fine crimson and blustered through an apology for ruining the ride. He then excused himself, pulling his mount back to trail the three ladies he was accompanying; however, Lady Rosetta wasn't about to let their only male companion get away so easily. Spinning about in her saddle, she fixed the young lord in her sights. "Lord Carrod, is it really a sport in your kingdom to hurt such fine animals?"

"It is, ma'am."

Lady Rosetta harrumphed. "I guess it's the same everywhere," she told her two companions. "Men are always out for the glory or prize of some pelt or other."

"I bet Selena would be thrilled with Havanese pelts," Lady Rosa said, regarding one of the other ladies of the Starian court. Lady Selena Durrow was well known for her "fashions," usually of some animal fur or expensive plume of the season.

Princess Éleen held her tongue. She wasn't one to gossip over anyone she barely knew, and all the Starians were bare acquaintances to the newly arrived royal. Lady Rosetta was not dissuaded, however. "Oh, Stars, that woman! You just had to bring her up on such a lovely break from her ramblings. The ball tonight is all she has been spouting about for days, and of her hack of good drabberies and enouncements."

Now that did make Éleen giggle. Lady Selena had been rather vocal of late, lamenting her missing wardrobe—most of it still at the abandoned capital. She and a number of the other ladies had been beside themselves for being out of fashion for the planned ball. Still, Éleen had her own reservations; it would be her first official ball since leaving Blue Haven. So many customs were different in Staria that she feared making an embarrassment of herself.

Lady Rosetta continued, appealing to their one accompanying gentleman to help them. "You will save us from Lady Selena's duress, right, Lord Carrod?"

Lord Carrod coughed into his hand. "I will do my best, ma'am."

"Ma'am. Now isn't that sweet," Lady Rosetta teased. She looked to Éleen. "You will have your man dance with us tonight, Princess Éleen. I've been told he is quite proficient."

"Um." The princess's china-blue eyes turned to plead with her lord protector, silently asking for his acceptance. She and her guardian had become rather close in their travels across Syre; Éleen dared say she trusted the young lordling with her life. "I am sure Lord Carrod would grace you with a dance or two."

"He had better if he knows what is respectable." Lady Rosetta returned her attentions to the man in question. "You had better, Lord Carrod. Besides my brother, you are the only decent man of the lot—Jeremy Freedman notwithstanding because of his youth."

"Viscount LaPoint seemed respectable enough," Éleen disagreed.

Lady Rosa warned, "You don't want to trust that man with a ten-foot-pike." Her brown eyes turned to include Lord Carrod in the advice. "Viscount LaPoint is as smooth as brandy and goes down just as fiery, but he's one man you'd rather do without—if you catch my meaning."

Éleen didn't, but she could see how the overly polite viscount could seem slippery. "I will dance with his host only if he requests such, as per your advice, Lady Rosa." With her protector behind her, Princess Éleen missed Carrod's nod of understanding to not let the princess out of his sight; he knew well enough what dangers the lady warned him of.

The ladies' route took them out of the thickets of the demesne and onto the fields. Usually, this time of year would be the final harvest of squashes, root vegetables, and wheat; however, the early snows had killed off the last of the plants. A fine dusting of snow had covered the cleared swath of ground in a blanket of white. It looked untouched as far as the eye could see. Far beyond, the distant rise of Pika Mounts showed how close the demesne was to the Golden Kingdom.

"We should turn around now," Lord Carrod said as he took in all that open ground.

"Yes. It's high noon. We've been out for a good hour," Lady Rosetta turned her horse to a second trail leading back to the estate. "Would you like to race?" Her robin's egg–blue eyes gleamed at the two ladies.

"Princess Éleen, you mustn't!" Carrod was dismayed, but his princess was the first to charge out like a young schoolgirl released for recess. Her lord protector groaned at the recklessness and cued his bay to catch up with the three women. With Lady Rosetta and Lady Rosa, Princess Éleen was proving to be a handful like her other Eldon-Tomino siblings—a trait she used to hold in reserve.

The horses made good time through the snows despite the thick powder being up to their knees. They seemed to be enjoying themselves as much as their riders on this crisp day. Still, the ladies wisely pulled up their frisky mounts to let their coats dry before they reached the stables.

Giving her mare some rein, Princess Éleen relaxed, turning to beam a smile at her lord protector. It was the happiest expression Lord Carrod had seen on her face in a long while; usually, the princess was the quiet, reasonable voice behind the arrogant chatter of her siblings and mother. The thought of the princess's newfound joy had the Havener lord feeling discontented. Her family had only seen their twenty-four-year-old daughter as a bargaining chip—and a poor one at that. Éleen was the yet-to-be-married nuisance; they used the word "old maid" on most occasions. If only they could see what a wonderful woman their daughter was…

The princess's situation hadn't helped by King Merretham of Staria, who had refused the betrothal between his son, Al'den, and the Havenese princess. Even the tentative engagement he had allowed did little to bolster the princess's reputation to her family. Prince Al'den was still open to choosing another, while the princess was stuck between a rock and a hard place. Worse, the maunstorz and Nallaus attacks at the Citadel of Light had forced the Starians' hand to send everyone southward—a blessing, it seemed, now that the snows had come. Separation from the Starian prince made Lord Carrod doubt whether the betrothal would happen at all.

Now, the princess was among the Starian court at the LaPoint demesne and not travelling further south as originally planned. Before, she had been asked to accompany Prince Kent Argetlem back to the Golden Kingdom; however, the serious snowstorms had started before their group had reached Kavahad. Lord Carrod Nexlé had pulled the Golden heir aside and begged him to let the princess find shelter with Kavahad. Lord Carrod hadn't said it, but Éleen had a delicate nature and suffered from limbs that turned a purplish-blue in the cold and hurt her terribly. Her lord protector did not want to see his charge suffer like that again. Luckily, Prince Kent had agreed to his request, and the prince and his men had left for Sardon shortly after, leaving Princess Éleen's safety in

Commander Kins's capable hands—which was how she had ended up with the Starian court at LaPoint's demesne.

Even with the precarious situation, Lord Carrod was relieved to see the princess open up more and more now that she wasn't smothered by her family. Without them, she was turning into quite the sweetheart—naïve but good-natured. Yet he hoped her little rebellion wouldn't get too out of hand; he wasn't sure what he would do if Éleen got hurt.

Getting on with his duties, Lord Carrod made sure he was the first to the stable yard and dismounted so he could hold Éleen's mare and help her down. Other attendants were there waiting as their party came in. "Your Highness." Carrod gave a polite bow as he took Bella's bridle to steady her and got a hand ready in case Éleen lost her footing dismounting.

"Thank you, Lord Carrod." Éleen smiled up at him once she was safely to the ground. "And thank you for letting us tease you so on our ride. I hope we did not offend."

Carrod felt his neck flush. "No need, my lady. I understand no ill was intended." Éleen smiled broadly again and stepped away to her two choice companions, leaving her protector to hand their mounts off to a stable hand.

"See you in a few hours for the ball?" Lady Rosetta asked.

"Yes," Éleen replied with a smile.

"Oh, I am so looking forward to it!" Lady Rosa barely contained a squeal. "Dressing up aside, I've heard the viscount has hired a string quartet to accompany us tonight!"

"Yes, the best group from the northeastern corner of the Golden Kingdom—or so I've been told." It was no surprise that Lady Rosetta knew the details; she was well versed in procuring any information she wanted. "Princess Éleen, we are going to have a 'political debate' in the ladies' parlor this afternoon, if you wish to join us."

"To pass the time, of course," Lady Rosa filled in. "You will join us?" She reached pleadingly for the princess's hands.

Éleen balked for just a breath. In Blue Haven, women weren't allowed a voice in the courts—minus the queen with her husband, in private. This was one of the practices that differed in Staria. In the desert kingdom, women could be political, run campaigns, even become diplomats or fighters if they so chose. Her family would be aghast!

Lady Rosetta sensed the princess's reserve. "You don't have to participate, Highness. You are welcome to observe."

"We will have some cookies and tea," Lady Rosa added as enticement.

That had the Havenese princess giggling and relenting. "Very well. I will come—but only to watch!" she added with a finger raised in emphasis.

§ §

Lord Carrod met Princess Éleen at the doorway to her quarters. He wore a disapproving frown, though he was too polite to say that her afternoon activities had been improper for a Havenese royal. Éleen ignored the look. She had found the event quite fascinating. It seemed the power to debate openly on issues gave everyone the chance to form their own opinions—or re-form, in some cases. There had been perspectives offered that she had never thought to ponder. It had been enlightening.

"All is ready, Highness." Lord Carrod bowed his head as he held the door for her.

"Thank you." Éleen curtsied before passing into her room. "You may go freshen up yourself, if you wish."

Lord Carrod shook his head. "I am ready for tonight." Princess Éleen took in his usual military attire. It was clean and pressed but not the kind of jacket one would expect to wear to a formal ball. Her look must have said it all because her lord protector said, "This is my best suit, Highness, and I have no other."

"I am sure another lord—or even the viscount—would be able to accommodate you."

"I'd rather not bother them, if I may say so, Highness."

Éleen almost tsked but caught herself. It wasn't uncommon for a soldier to wear his military uniform. She finally conceded. "Very well. I will be a short while getting ready."

"I will be right here," Lord Carrod promised.

A "short while" meant nearly an hour, but Lord Carrod was not unfamiliar with his charge's preparations, and the time was not wasted. When the princess reappeared, Carrod had to stop himself from gaping. The Havenese royal had chosen the family's traditional jade-green color for her velvet dress. It was accented by rich, gold threads and a fine dusting of lace at the neckline and sleeves. A beautiful, raw citrine stone was the only centerpiece around her neck; Lord Carrod recognized it as the gift the prince of Staria had given her. Though he disliked the man for not honoring their engagements, the stone did look magnificent around Princess Éleen's neck. With her hair coiffed into a high bun and her face powdered to resemble a china doll's, there would be no others as stunning as the princess of Blue Haven at the ball.

"Does it look nice?" Éleen asked, spinning slowly for her lord protector to inspect.

"It looks…" *Stunning*, he wanted to say. Instead, he chose, "Superb, Your Highness."

"Superb. My you are a man of few words," she teased and came near so Lord Carrod could take her hand to his elbow. The princess let out a breath. "I must admit, I am nervous."

"Ah, don't be, Highness. You know everyone here, and it is a small event." Carrod squeezed her fingers in encouragement. "Besides, I will be near you as long as you need."

"Thank you." She gave a more resolute nod for them to head out.

The estate had been transformed for the evening's festivities. Cedar boughs and mistletoe had been laid about on the windowsills and archways. A white candle was in each window. Fresh fruits had been placed about the main hall, on the small tables set about the room. Other foodstuffs and beverages were displayed on a long table taking over the west wall. A corner had been set aside for the quartet and pianoforte; the performers were already well into a song when the Havenese arrived.

"Oh, you made it just in time!" Lady Rosa came bounding over with a fruit punch in hand. The two Greysons trailed the young lady at a more refined pace. The enthused woman interlaced her arms around Éleen's free one. "The pianist has just arrived and was going to play next. I've heard she is fantastic!"

"Then, I very much look forward to it," Éleen replied as she was pulled from Lord Carrod's arm. Looking back, the princess mouthed an apology as the lady led her through the crowded hall toward the instruments.

"I apologize for the lady's enthusiasm," Lord William Greyson said. He and his sister had waited on the Havenese lord as his charge was whisked away. "Lady Rosa gets carried away at social functions sometimes."

Lord Carrod tried to keep his expression neutral, though he was sure he failed. "Ladies can be that way at times," he agreed.

"Some ladies," Rosetta corrected. She let go of her brother's arm and dismissed herself to go after her two acquaintances. "We will see you by the pianoforte."

Lord Carrod nodded and then accepted the drink a servant offered; with Éleen having been pulled from him so quickly, he felt adrift. Lord William made a motion toward the performers' corner. "Let's follow our womenfolk, shall we?"

"Indeed."

The hall was as filled as it could get, but the two lords managed to reach their destination without being pulled into other conversations. The three ladies had found places front and center to the piano and were boxed in by eight other women. The small crowd kept the two men from drawing nearer, so they reassured themselves that the women were within eyeshot.

The pianist appeared and bowed to her audience. Then, she sat amid a billowing of skirts and paused with her fingers on the keys. A breath passed ,and she began to play an accompaniment filled with lilting high notes and sorrowful lows. The piece lasted a good eight minutes in its entirety. By the time the lady finished, the great hall was quiet, lulled by the music. A silence lingered long past the last, fading notes.

Markus LaPoint took that silent gap to make his entrance. He strode to the pianist and helped her to her feet as the crowd finally applauded the performance. The viscount helped the lady curtsy and then gave her a peck on the cheek and whisper of thanks in her ear before turning to the assembled. "Ladies and gentlemen, I give you Mrs. Lafroy of Darholm." The woman curtsied again as the applause was repeated. "Mrs. Lafroy will grace us with more of her inspiring music in a moment. First, I wish to bid you all welcome to my family estate." The words were for other guests he had invited from around the demesne, workers and families not living within the manor's walls. For one night, he was allowing the common folk and courtiers to mix as one class. "I bid you all to enjoy the turning of the date to First Snows' Eve. My home is open to all. I have provided a roast pig in the dining room and a feast besides. Other foods and drinks are in this hall, as well. My parlors are opened to all of you. Partake of games in the billiard room or tea and crumpets in the sitting rooms. I hear Lady Diane Levine has prepared the necessary components for the creation of garlands. You may make your own in the sitting room to the east. Good sirs, I hear Lord Darber has called for a round of cards."

"You're on, you old coot!" a man shouted from the crowd.

Markus grinned at the liveliness of his guests. "Yes, indeed!" He paused to motion to the center of the main hall. "I remind you that dancing will be here in the hall—men, do make sure to give the ladies some of your time for that." There were some good-natured groans and elbow-poking in answer to his words. "I know, I know. Just passing on the message," Markus replied with his hands raised in the air. "Now, I won't keep you any longer. Without more ado, I bid you to continue enjoying the music provided by Mrs. Lafroy and the Darholm Quartet." Another round of applause was given to the musicians. "Eat, drink, and be merry this fine eve!"

A final clap was given to the host before the party resumed. Princess Éleen and her two friends found their two lords in the crowd. They were still gushing among themselves about Mrs. Lafroy's performance. "Oh, that was wonderful!" Éleen expressed to Lord Carrod. She accepted the wineglass he offered her.

"I found it moving," he agreed, though he wasn't sure how closely the princess was listening to him. Her attention had been pulled back to her lady companions' conversation.

"I say we make our own game of cards," Lady Rosetta had been saying in reply to Lady Rosa's question of what to do next.

"Ladies in Staria play cards?" Éleen asked, astounded. Here was another change from the South.

"Of course." Lady Rosetta's eyes flashed as she replied. "It's one of the best ways to learn how men tick."

Her brother made a cough into his fist. "Forgive her, Princess Éleen. My sister loves to gamble. In truth, she is quite good at it. Don't think you will best her in a game easily," he said to Lord Carrod in warning.

"That's right!" Lady Rosa exclaimed, smacking a fist into her other hand. "Southern ladies don't get to partake in such fun. Oh, we have got to teach you a game or two."

Lady Rosetta was more cautious on the offer. "That is, only if you wish, Princess Éleen. We can certainly find entertainment here, like the dances. We—"

"No, please, I wish to learn." Éleen felt excited by the prospect. Still, she looked to her lord protector for support on the matter.

Lord Carrod sighed at the inevitable. "Stars, your family will hang me for allowing such escapades…"

"Oh, thank you, Lord Carrod!" Éleen contained herself from jumping up and down at being allowed the freedom.

Lord Carrod found himself unable to say "no" to the princess. In allowing the forbidden, Lord Carrod cautioned they should play a game among themselves only. Stars forbid the princess actually learned to gamble at a real table! He was certain calamity would ensue as others took advantage of the first-timer.

"We can arrange that," Lord William assured him. He helped escort the ladies to the billiard room and wrestled a side table for their use. Amid boisterous games of craps, darts, and a game of twenty-one, their group of five began to teach Princess Éleen the basics of playing cards. Once she seemed to have a handle on it, they added "money" to up the stakes—using popcorn. An hour in, it was clear that the Havenese princess was having more fun than she'd ever experienced; gone were her aspirations for dancing. Princess Éleen had found a new thrill: gambling.

Chapter Fourteen
§
An Idea

The cool, wet nose startled her awake. Zyanthena came back to the present as if emerging from drowning. Panicked, she flew up from where she had blacked out on the bearskin rug and came to a huddled seat. Moon Ember cocked her head at the Tashek. The look reminded her to breathe. "Ember." Zyanthena reached out to touch the thick fur at her neck. The wolf rumbled a response. "Thank you for waking me."

Still in some shock, she glanced to the bed—where she had been before Decond's presence had appeared. Hunter, the pack alpha, lifted his large head from the thick quilt. He didn't look concerned with her condition in the least. "Was I out cold long?" His eyebrow ridges twitched—Hunter's bored reply of "no." She huffed at that and slowly found her feet to return to bed. She had already been tired from working with Vauldin well into the night, and Sevén's influence had made it worse. Now, she felt fully spent and bone weary. Heavily, Zyanthena fell to the bed beside the large grey wolf.

Yet, despite her fatigue, sleep evaded the Tashek's mind. It was abuzz with the new knowledge from Sevén's touch. Decond had been able to use the pearl to reach her, but how? "Is it possible for non-royal blood to use the Stones of Power?" she murmured to herself.

Hunter rumbled in his throat an answer that, no, he had never heard of such an occurrence.

"You say that as if you know so well." Hunter huffed and shifted his muzzle from one paw to the other, turning away from the disbelieving human. "All right. You guardians of Crystalynian have served the kings and queens for generations. I get that you passed your knowledge down from wolf to pup for all time."

Hunter chortled to her to go back to sleep—as if she were a young pup in need of the order.

Zyanthena socked him gently in the shoulder and then rolled onto her back. With her hands behind her head, she looked to the ceiling and pondered. *Each stone has certain powers. It is written that Vauldin has powers of influencing "life and death" cycles, controlling electricity, "vision of the night," animal speak, "caller of souls," and the ability to remake what was. Sevén is a healing stone…yet it can call to other stones from great distances?* She had tried to piece together details of the other stones, though her main focus had been on her own obsidian. Zyanthena was beginning to see how studying all of the stones' powers had its advantages. She said aloud, "Then…it stands to reason that I could do that to a miniscule extent as well. Right?"

Hunter harrumphed at her for bothering him; Moon Ember was more helpful. The she-wolf jumped onto the bed and snuggled in by Zyanthena's side. Her reply was that the Tashek could try the majik, but it would only work with someone she had a very deep connection with. Maybe. Chances were slim at best.

"Ah, I see. Well, that creates an obstacle."

A deep connection with someone…

"So, Decond has a deep relationship with me if he connected so well." The epiphany had Zyanthena sitting up quickly again as she put two and two together. Hunter griped at her disturbance and shuffled off the bed to a quieter corner. Zyanthena ignored him and continued her musing. "Decond said that the Oracle believed he and I shared a 'familiarity' with each other that helped us link. The only time I've ever heard the old crone use that term was when two people were paramours. She's not really suggesting—?"

She looked at Moon Ember. The wolf rumbled if that was such a problem. Mating was normal, after all.

"We're not like that." The grey wolf seemed unconvinced. "Whatever." She dismissed the matter. "Decond wasn't able to give me news on Syre. It'd be good to have some. Yet who do I know of the stone-bearers that I can link with?"

Moon Ember asked if any other of the stones were active—besides Ravel, whom the entire pack had agreed, along with Zyanthena and Kestral, was the cause of the snowstorms.

"That is true. When last the Guardians had spoken, Amun was not in the care of Prince Al'den. Sevén was—is—obviously at the Oracle's and not in the Golden Kingdom. Kevel was being held by a Guardian; Bellor and Sheveth are who knows where; and Serein was with Prince Par Fantill of Sealand…" Her voice trailed off as memories of her time as Princess Zerra Starkindler came flooding back. "Serein was active back then! That's right. I saw her glow and make a song."

Moon Ember found the information useful. The wolf asked if Zyanthena had known the Sealand heir well. "I knew Prince Par ages ago, when I was just a girl. Thirteen. Now, I only know him by introduction."

And how close had the prince been with Zerra? The she-wolf wanted to know.

"How close? He asked for my hand in marriage that year."

Hunter chortled that her words made them sound close indeed.

Zyanthena tsked at him. "That was a lifetime ago. I barely remember being Princess Zerra Starkindler. Only from what memories Vauldin has returned to me do I remember having been the princess."

Still, did that mean they had been close? Moon Ember wanted to know.

Zyanthena's frown was deep and disturbed. "If I decide to go down that road, it opens up so many doors that perhaps should remain closed." A whole pot of worms and all that. "My last run-in with Prince Par showed that he still remembers Zerra and longs for her. Even after eight years, he has refused to select another to become his future queen—just because of that engagement."

Moon Ember rumbled that she liked the sound of the young royal already and that he seemed deeply in love with her. It was a very loyal union.

"In love with Zerra Starkindler, you mean," Zyanthena reminded the grey wolf. Perturbed, she rose and began to pace the room, which only made Hunter flatten his ears to his head in irritation. She mirrored the feeling back to the alpha but returned to the bed to sit with his mate. Curling her fingers into the she-wolf's thick coat, she massaged the ruff as thoughts whirled around in her head. "But I can see where you would think that gives us a connection strong enough to try reaching out to him."

Moon Ember chortled that she should try.

"Maybe." Zyanthena was still frowning at the idea. "But I'd like to get better with Vauldin first. There is also the possibility that Prince Par doesn't know how to use Serein. If that's the case, would a link even work?"

Moon Ember pointed out that Decond had managed on his first try even though he hadn't been linked with Sevén for long. It more came down to if Serein was willing.

"That sounds awfully complicated," Zyanthena commented. "And it sounds as if Serein is as fickle as Vauldin can be." Moon Ember seemed to find that amusing. Zyanthena chuckled as well. "Well, it is a good idea to try, but I think I'm going to research more first and keep working with Vauldin." She stood. "I'm going to go to the library."

Hunter grumbled that it was good of her to leave, considering it was still dark outside and the sun had yet to come up. He was looking forward to some quiet to be able to sleep.

"You're just a grumpy old geezer," the desert woman teased the alpha as she went about collecting a robe and lighting a candle.

Hunter flashed his teeth at that and retorted that he was only seven. That hardly made him old.

"Yeah, but it's good fun teasing you," Zyanthena replied. Still, she made sure to stay well away in case the grey wolf decided to snap at her. "Please, send Darshel to me when he wakes."

Hunter gave her a sarcastic stare as she took her leave. Zyanthena heard the last of his griping to his mate that the Tashek treated him like her courier service. She left before she could hear Moon Ember's remark, but she was sure it was some kind of grandmotherly retort. Those two grey wolves reminded her of a cute old couple she knew in the Sheev'anee. Just like those Tashek, the wolves were amusing to be around. Zyanthena couldn't help grinning. It was certainly interesting being a wielder of a Stone of Power. Who else could hear the banter of wolves, besides her? It opened up a whole new world.

§ §

The snows had fallen deeper in Rubia than most of Syre. For the men of Raven's Den, now chased away from the shelter of the post by the enemy, the weather should have spelled their doom; however, their Tashek scout's ingenuity saved the mertinean from the worst of it. Re'shaird Aerrisson had been loath to let their circumstances get the best of the mertinean force. Upon his meeting with Commander Grant's force, the Tashek man had been adamant about finding ways for the two hundred-some infantry to survive the sudden winter.

The first order of business had been creating clusters of camps close enough to one another to keep the large force in communication but small enough to hide from the enemy. Each camp was sheltered within gullies within the Red Hills. The natural features gave the men adequate shelter from the winds and cold. Most had more than one escape route for such times when maunstorz forces were seen in pursuit.

The second idea Aerrisson had orchestrated was to have small force guerrilla attacks against the maunstorz holed up at Raven's Den. Though seemingly insignificant at the first attempts, a succession of attacks had whittled away valuable foodstuffs for both men and horses from the caches in the post. Besides somewhat successful hunts for wild game, those pilfered items gave the Rubian men a fighting chance to get through the snowy times. Better yet, it had the potential of starving out the maunstorz at the overrun Raven's Den. It could even force them to leave the mertinean post—at least, it was an outcome Re'shaird hoped to achieve. His and the mertinean's survival depended upon it.

Currently, Re'shaird Aerrisson sat atop a small hillock overlooking the grasslands around Raven's Den. Concealed by a thicket of coniferous trees, the Tashek scout analyzed the Rubian outpost as the dawn lit the snow-covered plain in orange fire. His keen, walnut-brown eyes searched for the one maunstorz he considered his greatest adversary: second-in-command of the enemy forces, a man he had heard called Silvarron.

The charismatic enemy leader was a usual fixture to the Raven's Den parapets in the morning. He was hard to miss. With a regal bearing and calculating features, it was easy to see why Silvarron had been picked to control the maunstorz force. More, the long-limbed man always had a large crow perched upon his shoulder as he went about his rounds. The black bird, nestled among the man's long, white hair and pale skin, was like a specter of doom.

Or, at least, it seemed that way to Aerrisson. That day was no exception.

"There he is," he murmured to himself as Silvarron came to the main gates of the outpost. As usual, the maunstorz scanned the open land around Raven's Den, looking for his adversary and watching for herds of deer to hunt. It seemed almost destined that Silvarron and Aerrisson happened to be within sight of each other. That they both looked for the other was becoming a habit of sorts. "Not today," Aerrisson continued his self-talk. "You expect me, so I won't come today…tonight, maybe."

Absently, Aerrisson fingered the red resin necklace at his neck. The blood-red pendant held within it a small rose from a desert bush. It was once a gift to his paramour, Sheev'arid Zyanthena, but the fiery woman had returned it upon their last encounter. Despite its sorrowful significance, Aerrisson cherished the memories the pendant brought him; Zyanthena certainly would have taken all precautions against this especially cunning foe. Her warning was what had given Aerrisson pause from attacking Raven's Den for the eighteenth time. *Silvarron is catching on.*

Just then, a horn sounded, drawing Aerrisson's focus back to the fort. He watched as a clump of maunstorz runners—eight in count—made it to Raven's Den. This cohort bore the flag of Mansocan, leader of the armies. So, they had run all the way from whatever point eastward the maunstorz leader was stationed. This was the first Aerrisson had seen of communications between Raven's Den and other enemy camps. It paid for him to pay attention; if the maunstorz were able to run across snow-ridden Rubia, then it was a safe bet larger forces could soon follow.

Aerrisson waited some minutes more, but he was not close enough to get any real, useful information from the maunstorz. Besides the fact that the eight runners reported to Silvarron, there wasn't more to see. The desert man finally concluded his watch and sneaked back off the hillock to where his dark-grey stallion, Lunier, was tied in a cluster of evergreens. Aerrisson gave his faithful companion an apple for waiting so quietly, and then he jumped atop his horse's back and aimed them back toward the Red Hills.

Their trek took twice as long. Aerrisson was not one for letting the enemy find their way to the mertinean, so he backtracked multiple times to leave a discombobulated trail. At least Lunier had the stamina for such measures; Tashek mounts were the best for long-distance travels, after all. Confident in his horse, Aerrisson took all the extra precautions as he could while he made for Commander Grant's hidden-away campsite.

Grant's main camp was cloistered in by a high canyon, though a single track to the back led to an escape route. The high walls were guarded day and night by archers. With Aerrisson's help, the men were extra vigilant to anything amiss. The lot of twenty archers were quick to call, "Who goes there?" as Aerrisson made his final approach.

"Manse, Davies," Aerrisson called out. "It's Re'shaird. Stand down your men!"

"Aye, sir." Manse saluted and waved his men to return to watch. "Tis good to see you, sir!" he called down to the Tashek. "Another hour and the commander was a getting worried."

"I took a turn by the fort before my return," Aerrisson replied. "The other camps are doing well. Major Tucker says he hopes you send some cheese along next time."

"Ah, those Carmey boys and their cheese! You tell him next time I'll make it a turnip for their complaints." Aerrisson chuckled and waved up to the archers before continuing into the camp. Their jokes about food were always in good fun. Some bread, potatoes, and root vegetables, along with whatever wild game they could catch, was normal fare. Dreams of cheeses, fattened pork, or—Stars!—even a decent poached egg were the men's ways of passing the time and trying to forget the cold. Aerrisson certainly didn't blame the mertinean their visions of fancies; he was hard-pressed himself to have some hot, desert sun while savoring *rassen*—spiced snake meat—with a side of Sheev'anee *kiwano* iced horse milk-cream. Now that was a meal!

Commander Grant came out from his tent just as Aerrisson stopped Lunier at the entrance and dismounted. The war veteran's lined face softened in relief at seeing their scout returned safe and sound. "Re'shaird, good." They shook hands, both men having become fast friends through their trials. "How does it fare out there?"

"The camps are doing well. Food and grain are leveling down, as we've tracked. The men are keeping warm enough and the enemy has stayed away. All is as good as we can hope for."

"Good, good. And Camp Three's men who had been under the weather?"

"Mostly recovered. There is one who needed a finger amputated from frostbite turning to gangrene, but he's the only one. Your doctor's with him, and the man seems to have stabilized. The three with fevers are over the worst. It seems their illness has not spread to the others. Your doctor reports that the situation he feared has passed."

Commander Grant had been just as concerned over Camp Three's situation. Sick men in the throes of winter usually meant a dead army; however, the way Aerrisson had broken their numbers apart had kept the fever from spreading. Whereas, at first, the separation had seemed impractical to the point of being suicidal, now it seemed a gift from the Stars. It had been one of many Sheev'anee practices that were becoming helpful.

"I also took a pass by Raven's Den," Aerrisson continued.

"Oh?" Commander Grant used to worry over Aerrisson's tours near their old post, but such excursions were becoming old news. Many had led to successful raids, in any case. "And what were those maunstorz up to today?"

The desert man shrugged and accepted a hot cup of tea as he and Grant settled around the firepit just beyond the commander's tent. He blew softly on the steaming drink, sending vapor into the cold air before chancing a sip. "That commander of theirs, Silvarron, is becoming more vigilant to these hills. I'd say we need to become more cautious ourselves. There is a chance of their leaving their lair to search for us."

"I don't like the sound of that."

"Neither do I." Aerrisson swallowed the tea and coughed on the heat. He cleared his throat. "More, a group of runners reached them. They came from somewhere farther east."

"East? Runners from another maunstorz camp?"

"Mansocan's sigil marked them."

"I haven't seen any runners communicate for months between their factions! And now from their leader, no less."

Aerrisson agreed. "And they came from deeper into Rubia. The snows must be easing for eight runners to make it to Raven's Den on foot. That bids us to take more caution. Tell me"—the Tashek posed a question of his own—"have we received another bird from the Citadel?" In truth, Aerrisson had been the most shocked by the arrival of the All'ani falcon. To have a second make it to them seemed improbable—as he hadn't expected a single one to make it past maunstorz lookouts.

"Not yet." Commander Grant shook his head. "As much as I wish it so. It was such a relief to finally hear from the Citadel of Light."

"We should not trust a second bird to get through to us, then."

Commander Grant made a face at the Tashek's words, even though Aerrisson spoke the truth.

Aerrisson continued: "Which means we need to make plans as if we're in this alone."

"I take it you have some more ideas, then?"

"I do. As I see it, we have two, maybe three, options open to us." Aerrisson pulled out a leather map of the area he kept in a breast pocket. He unrolled the worn leather and spread it out in the snow at their feet. "Kavahad lies one hundred thirty miles south-southwest of here. Maybe a difficult trek for all of our men to make, both with supplies and the issue of cover to hid from the enemy. Farther still is Paragon Oasis, westward at two hundred ten miles, and the Citadel of Light north-northwest at about the same distance."

"Kavahad makes the better choice."

"Yes, it does, but…it also leads Silvarron's forces straight to them. As much as I dislike Lord Shekmann, I don't feel like bringing a full enemy contingent to his doorstep. I doubt Kavahad could withstand it."

"Then, how about the Red Palace? That's the next city with the most military force."

Aerrisson shook his head. "I don't trust that way. If King Corbin had sent you a runner or even reinforcements, then yes. However, your king has stayed silent to all your requests. It makes me wonder what stands between us and the capital for word to not get through."

Commander Grant tsked. "You Tashek are always so skeptical."

"It's kept us alive," Aerrisson replied tonelessly to the criticism.

The mertinean commander shrugged, accepting the logic. "True."

The desert man got back to task. "That takes me to our other option."

"I'm not sure I like that look you've got. My gut tells me you're about to say something crazy."

Aerrisson grinned. "Now you're getting me!"

Commander Grant groaned and poked at the map. "So, what is it?"

"We stay put and do one of two things: either make a false trail like we packed it south and hide low or—"

"Don't say it!"

"Or we attack Raven's Den full on, more than we've done. However, we would need to win if we do that. For, if we lose, Mansocan's army will come right back to our doorstep and try to wipe us out."

"A leave-none-alive scenario. I really do hate those."

"Better than all the enemy breathing down our necks."

The aging Rubian sighed and shook his head. "I'm for the situation where we all stay very *not* dead. You think you can conjure me up one of those scenarios?"

Chapter Fifteen
§
What Southern Men Are Made Of

With his biweekly bartering for food and small "comforts," Prince Rowin was finally seeing an improvement in the health of his lord protector and the prince of Rubia. Rio Ravesbend was even able to sit upright and talk, though he was still prone to splitting headaches. Prince Derek, however, was slower to heal. Every other day or so—it was hard to tell time without sunlight—the Rubian prince would spike a fever again. At least the captives had saved enough feverfew to give to the prince, and the herbs seemed to be helping.

Today, Prince Derek wasn't doing as well. The pale-skinned Rubian was in another fevered state. His frail body shivered against the cold bars of the cell adjoining theirs. His moans and sweat stink alerted his cellmates to his illness. Prince Connel made a disgusted noise in his throat and shuffled about in the straw in his corner. "Not again. He should just die already."

Rowin glowered at his brother to withhold his comments, then, shuffling over, he wrapped his only blanket about Prince Derek—even though he already had one—and tucked Prince Derek in as gently as he could. "He's improving, Connel. It's just slow in these conditions."

Connel scoffed. "Sure, sure. As you say, nursemaid." The younger prince huddled deeper into his own blanket, not at all happy with the cold, wet draft of the prisons. "I just wish it was bartering day. Those maunstorz have been ignoring our needs again."

Rowin's eyebrows rose in shock to hear Prince Connel admit—out loud—that he appreciated his brother's efforts. Still, Rowin knew better than to acknowledge it. "We're managing. At least we still have water." Rowin took a small cupful to bring to Prince Derek, pouring slowly so the ill royal could keep the water in his mouth. "There, there. That's good," he murmured at Derek's success—as if he were a young foal Rowin was nursing back to life.

"Thank you, Prince of Sunrise."

The words had come from Prince Derek's lord protector, Yory Selèv, who had been placed in the adjoining cell. Being separated from his ailing prince disturbed the man, but he stayed as close to Derek as the prison allowed—which usually meant he was only able to grasp the prince's hand through the bars. Yory's gratitude for Prince Rowin's help was a daily utterance. "You're welcome." Rowin gave a warm smile and touched the lord protector on the hand. "His fever is low today. I think it will be short-lived." Yory managed a thin smile of his own, though his worry never left his blue eyes. He bowed against the cold metal bars and hugged his prince's hand as close to his chest as he could.

Rowin left the two Rubians alone to check on Rio. His lord protector was, thankfully, awake and alert. "And how's your head today?" he asked while helping his friend to a seated position. He passed him some water as Rio settled.

"Well enough I'd say," Rio replied before taking a drink. He coughed as water got stuck in his throat. In vain, he struggled to not upset the cup; water was precious these days. Rowin rescued the drink and then helped Rio brush some droplets from his soiled uniform. "Well, besides my clumsiness, I guess."

His prince chuckled. "I'd say you're in good enough spirits if you can make a joke. Care to take a spin about the cell?" Rio made a face but agreed. It was their way of getting some exercise for stiffened legs—if it could really be called such in a ten-by-fifteen cell. They stood, and Rowin supported his man by his uninjured arm.

"This is still embarrassing," Rio complained as they bumbled along around Connel, Derek, and little, sleeping Miguel, "That you are taking care of me when it's my job."

"Oh, come now! You've been by my side for ten good years. I'm just returning the favor."

A disapproving frown was his lord protector's answer. "This is still a blight on lord protectors everywhere. I'm sure to be the laughingstock of Syre."

"But an alive one," Rowin reminded him, "And a damn good-looking one, too."

Rio groaned, "Now you jest! I'm sure I look like a deadbeat ruffian and smell just as good."

"Well," Rowin teased with a sniff, "you could do with a little dash of perfume."

His lord protector punched his prince lightly with his free arm and then winced as his shoulder protested the abuse. "Stars, you'll be the death of me!"

"Oh, I hope not," Rowin answered and helped Rio massage the joint. "I plan on pestering you to a ripe old age of ninety-two."

"Ninety-two?"

Rowin shrugged. "First number to pop into my head."

"Ah, I see."

"You should both get a room," Connel told his brother and lord protector.

They turned to include the younger prince in their fun. "My, Rio, I think my brother's jealous of you and me!"

Connel's frown was sour. "Of you two?" He huffed. "It's not even decent."

Rowin laughed and crouched down in front of his brother. "And how would you know if you've never tried it?"

"Ah!" Connel made a disgusted face. "Seriously disgusting, Rowin!" His elder brother just grinned at getting such a reaction.

Rio cleared his throat and leaned down to the two Sunarian princes. "Ahem, actually…" He made a nudge to their cellmate's and his lord protector's direction. "They are together, so you might want to tone down those kinds of jokes—just a bit." He made a motion with his fingers.

Both Sunrises looked astounded; it was the first time the two brothers had ever looked related. Connel's light-blue eyes were wide in shock and he was speechless; while Rowin, on the other hand, mouthed, *"They are?!"*

Rio nodded. "I knew that ages ago. Why? You couldn't tell?"

The two brothers looked back at Prince Derek and Yory Selèv still huddled nearby. The desperate but gentle hand-holding took on a whole new light. "Huh. Well, that is…" Rowin started.

"All good and well," Rio finished for his prince. "Any man—or woman—should have their happiness. But you will both be a little more tactful from now on?"

"Oh, no problem there," Rowin assured him. Connel made a noise in his throat that could have been either yay or nay, but he did nod afterward.

"Good." Rio changed the subject. "Is there anything decent to eat around here?"

"What, besides bread, bread, oh and look," Rowin held up another piece of a saved loaf. "Another piece of crusty bread? We are a four-star establishment."

Rio chuckled "I'll take the extra-crunchy one. I've always had a thing for dried and sawdusty bread."

"Stars!" Connel commented again and selected the best of their fare. "I think you lads need to blow off some steam soon. Your jokes are getting raunchier by the day."

Rowin winked at Rio as he replied to his brother. "I'll be working on that, trust me. Give me a week and I'll have Mansocan lining up entertainments by the handful."

"Oh, I'm certain you will." Connel threw a moldy piece of crust at his brother. "I see how you wish us Sunarians to be taken as."

"Yes, the easily-bored-and-in-need-of-distraction types." Rowin popped a piece of bread into his mouth like it was candy.

Connel rolled his eyes. "You're incorrigible. You don't even deny you have deplorable pastimes."

"It's what makes me extra charming."

The younger prince ate the last of his bread and stared at his empty hands forlornly. The meager meal had barely counted as a snack.

"Here," Rowin said, passing the last of his loaf to his brother.

Connel glared at it. "I don't want your favors."

"I'm full." Rowin shrugged and kept the hand out.

"Liar," Connel replied but finally took the bread. "This still doesn't count as anything."

"Not a thing," Rowin promised and ignored his own stomach's growl as the last of their bread disappeared into his brother's mouth.

"What softhearted Southerners your lot is."

The three Sunarians jumped and scrambled to their feet as Chornauk appeared in front of their cell. The red-eyed hulk of a maunstorz had slunk near, staying in the shadows just to see how unobservant the prisoners were. So far, he was quite unimpressed with Syreans.

"Chornauk." Rowin said the name harshly—which suited the warrior maunstorz just fine.

"Heirling."

"What does Mansocan want now?"

A toothy grin spread on Chornauk's face. It was a frightening look on him. "Mansocan has made a bet with me. To fulfill it, we need you three and three others." A hand motion brought more maunstorz, who began to retrieve the prisoners. The three Sunarians, Prince Derek, Yory

Selèv, and a commander of the mertinean named Dane Price were pulled from the cells amid many loud protests. The three Rubians were the men with the greatest influence in the remaining Rubian court; if something happened to them, Rubia was in dire trouble.

"Shut up, fleas!" Chornauk ordered to the jabbering men. "Your precious prince and his men may be returned to you…if they last the day." The barb sent the prisoners into a frenzy, but that only made Chornauk chortle at their desperation. Cuing his men onward, the maunstorz leader forced his six prisoners out of the dungeons.

Connel stumbled against his brother as they were pushed up the stairs. To Rowin he murmured, "Now what?"

"We don't know enough," Rowin replied.

"Bullshit!" Connel hissed before his guard forced them apart.

Rowin wanted to agree, but he knew better than to appear in front of Mansocan with an expression of fear. Stealing one quick glance with his lord protector, Rowin sealed a mask of resolve onto his face and marched along, following the guards' lead. To his surprise, they were taken outside of the Red Palace to an outdoor sparring range reserved for the palace mertinean. Mansocan was there, his back to the arrivals. Below him—for he was on a second-story walkway—were twelve of his fighters, practicing hand-to-hand sparring and strength training. There was blood on the white snow from some of the fights. Apparently, maunstorz sparring was a no-holds-barred kind, and injuries were common, if not welcomed. Rowin gulped as the observation made him more apprehensive.

"Leader," Chornauk greeted with a fist salute to his chest.

Mansocan turned away from his men to look over the prisoners. "You bring me these?" he said, his face stoic but his words implying, *Why them?*

"They are the leaders among our prisoners."

Mansocan looked down his nose at the six men. Princes Rowin and Connel still had an arrogant air to their posture, while Yory Selèv and Dane Price were both soldiers; however, the last two… "These two are half-dead." He focused his hardest look on Chornauk as if he were schooling a young boy. "And the others may not be worthy of a good fight. It is not their people's way to have their most skilled fighters command."

"Why lead when one cannot fight well?" Chornauk argued. "No, they will prove why they are chosen to lead their people."

Mansocan was silent for some breaths as he considered. Finally, though, he relented to his Second's wishes. "Very well. Set them up on the eastern side of the field."

Rowin knew that what was coming next would not be pretty. Hoping he had enough rapport with the enemy leader, he spoke up before they were moved down to the yard. "You call this fair, Mansocan? Two of us are injured, and the prince of Rubia is ill with fever. You don't even give us a decent chance."

"Rowin!" Connel hissed for him to be quiet; the younger prince didn't want the maunstorz leader to be provoked and kill them all on a word.

But it was too late. Mansocan had already heard. He stalked to Rowin to stare him down. To the Sunarian's credit, Rowin didn't even blink. Mansocan assessed him head-to-toe to find a chink in his resolve. Finding none, he said, "Indeed, you are right, Heirling of Sunrise."

"Leader—" Chornauk protested. It was cut short by Mansocan's warning glare.

Turning back to Rowin, Mansocan continued. "How about this, Prince of Sunrise? I will let you fight in pairs. Certainly, together you can make a decent enough lot?"

Prince Rowin knew he wouldn't get a better offer. Plus, he could see that the bartering was pissing Chornauk off. He agreed quickly.

"Good." Mansocan's smile was thin and cold, and it didn't reach his eyes. He waved the prisoners away while Chornauk came near to protest.

"Sir—"

Mansocan lifted a hand to silence his Second. "Are you trying to say our men are incapable of a one-to-two match?"

Chornauk ducked his head; it was an affront to admit such a weakness. "No, *Seka'vlr.*"

"Then pick your best and get this over with."

"Yes, sir." The maunstorz Second bowed and hurried off to comply.

Mansocan came down at a more sedate pace. His men all took a knee as he passed by on the way to his observation chair. The seat was near the spot where the prisoners were being unbound and armed with hand weapons: knives, clubs, or fighting sticks. As expected, Prince

Rowin's midnight-blue eyes were blazing with deviance at the maunstorz leader.

"Why are you doing this?" Prince Rowin dared ask.

"Why?" Mansocan settled in his seat and took hold of a wine goblet. "There is a bet going on about you."

"What bet?"

Mansocan's smile lacked any warmth. "About what Southern men are made of." He took a sip of his drink and wiped off the excess wine with a swipe of his thumb. The wine stain looked like blood on his pale skin. "Chornauk believes you are all insufferable weaklings, incapable of any skills of battle. I, well…let's just say, I contended that."

"So, we have been forced here to entertain your whims?"

"Precisely."

Mansocan waved a maunstorz to collect the first two prisoners for their duel: Prince Derek and Yory Selèv. "You may need to go easier on these two," he instructed his fighter in a mocking way. "They aren't looking so well." The maunstorz in question gave a toothy grin and stepped to his side of the sparring yard with an arrogant swagger to his step.

Yory Selèv had kept a glower to his features since their departure from the prisons. It deepened further at Mansocan's words. Holding his prince to his side, he murmured something to Derek. The pale prince stayed huddled against his dark-featured protector and mouthed something in return. Whatever Derek said, it settled matters for Yory, for the lord protector took them to their corner, where they armed themselves with three provided daggers. Once armed, Yory stepped in front of his prince, fully intending to be his shield. He nodded their readiness to the opponent.

By the first two clashes, it was clear why Yory Selèv had been chosen as a lord protector. The Rubian was lean and moved like a dancer across the yard; however, for all his wiriness, his limbs had strength and speed to them. Staying in constant motion, Yory kept the maunstorz man effectively out of range of his fevered prince. It became a game for the maunstorz fighter to try to reach Prince Derek Chível.

Behind Yory, Prince Derek still looked dazed from his fever; however, he was certainly fighting to keep himself present in their deadly confrontation. He positioned himself whenever needed so his lord protector didn't have to concentrate on two tasks. Working as a shadow,

Prince Derek slowly crept up behind his man. He was so careful about it that no one—not even their audience—noticed until it was too late. On an upward block of Yory's, Prince Derek made a long lunge and struck at their opponent. The move was beautiful—and deadly accurate to its target. Just like that, the maunstorz man was impaled with a thrust to his heart.

The enemy fighter gaped and lost his rhythm as his hands went to the dagger protruding from his chest. Yory Selèv didn't give him any more chances to realize he was done for. The lord protector cut at the maunstorz's carotid in a single strike and watched as their opponent fell to the red-puddled snow. He turned away then, a stoic expression on his face, to steady his prince once again. They returned to their fellow Syreans as if very little had happened.

The maunstorz were stunned.

Mansocan cleared his throat in the silence and asked for more wine. Realizing that his leader was pleased with the turn of events, Chornauk ordered Mansocan's chalice filled and for two of his men to clear the yard of the corpse. Another fighter was called forward. Chornauk waved for Prince Rowin and Rio to come out.

"No," Mansocan said, and met Rowin's heated eyes as he decreed, "The other two. This princeling will fight last. I want to see the younger Sunarian and that commander next." Mansocan chuckled as if knowing his choice angered Rowin. They both seemed to know that, of the two brothers, Rowin was the fighter. Mansocan was curious to see just how competent—or not—the other Sunarian prince was. And if the outcome didn't favor the royal, well then, all the better.

"Connel—" Rowin started.

Prince Connel gave his brother a dirty look. "There is not a choice, Rowin."

"But—"

"Would you even care if I made it through this? With me out of the way, you are sole heir."

"Seriously? Of course, I don't want that." Rowin was affronted that his brother had such a thought.

His younger brother paused before flashing a cocky smile. "In that case, relax, Rowin. I wouldn't let you have your coveted throne so easily." His eyes hardened, though the grin remained, and he walked away to join Dane Price in the yard.

Mansocan chuckled to himself at the two siblings' banter. The two brothers—who were rumored to dislike one another—certainly argued like kin! Their situation made it all the more amusing. He raised a hand to wave the start of the second fight. "Fighters at ready. Commence!"

In the takeover of the Red Palace, Dane Price had suffered a sliced eye and a deep gash to his thigh. The mertinean commander never complained of his injuries, but the bandages, rarely changed from their imprisonment, couldn't be the cleanest after two months. Just how festered the wounds were remained to be seen, but it could spell the man's doom before the fight finished.

At least, Prince Connel seemed to think that was true.

Connel stayed to the commander's good side and let the mertinean man lead their charge against the enemy. Dane seemed to be a robust fighter; armed with his anger, his fighting was exuberant. Prince Connel was content to let the other have at their maunstorz opponent while he hung back and fingered his six collected knives nervously. It was true that Connel wasn't a fighter. His was a hunter, though, and had practiced with knives, bows, and an occasional spear on a regular basis. But with only knives available to him, his options were limited to staying out of the enemy's range. Which was not to Connel's liking at all.

Dane roared and charged the maunstorz opponent. They converged and started a fistfight, weapons forgotten. It was hard to see who had the upper hand, as both mertinean and maunstorz seemed to trade blow-for-blow. Then, the opponent got a right hook to Dane's blind side and connected with the commander's jaw. Dane's head was whipped around. Another blow sent him to the ground.

Using the distraction, Connel threw a blade at their enemy. It stuck firmly into the maunstorz's shoulder. The prince's second throw was off target as the maunstorz twisted to see his other opponent. The maunstorz launched at the royal before Connel could get off a third throw.

"No, your fight is with me!" Dane Price bellowed and leapt after the maunstorz. He floored the fighter and climbed up the body to straddle him, where he pounded the opponent's face in again and again. However, his advantage didn't last very long; the maunstorz tossed him off and rounded on him. Two serious blows later, the mertinean commander lay unconscious on the snow.

The maunstorz fighter rose like an ominous specter and turned to Prince Connel. He pulled the knife from his shoulder and tossed the blade aside. Flexing his muscles, the warrior began to stalk toward his second prey. Prince Connel turned deathly pale in panic as the maunstorz neared. He backtracked away from the fighter, only to trip over a straw bale left in the yard. Flailing, the prince tipped over, and his last blades slipped from his hands. Prince Connel reached out desperately for a knife to defend himself as he felt the enemy coming closer. His hand just brushed a metal handle as the maunstorz rose above him with a club held high, ready to bring it down at the royal's head.

A knife suddenly thunked into the maunstorz's temple, killing him.

The group of maunstorz screamed in fury at having the battle finished in such a way. Outraged, attention turned to Prince Rowin, who had used the distraction of the deadly fight to sneak a weapon from his guards. Once he saw Connel was on the losing end, he had surged forward and flung the blade to save his brother's life. Of course, once the deed was done, he was swarmed by Mansocan's men. Chornauk was the first, body-slamming the prince to the ground. Others followed soon after.

"He must die!" Chornauk declared.

"No!" Mansocan signaled for his men to clear. "Guard the others," he ordered five maunstorz. The other four Syreans were herded together as Prince Rowin was hauled roughly to his knees in front of the enemy *seka'vlr.* Mansocan reached out with a hand—his dominant one, adorned with steel nails that extended like claws from his fingertips. He curled his index finger under the rebellious prince's chin. Rowin felt blood drip from the wound. "These men will not be put to death. It defeats the purpose of having them."

"But, *Seka'vlr*!" Chornauk growled.

"He will be punished." Mansocan looked sideways at his Second. "A loss of one finger won't do any harm but may remind him to be more careful."

Rowin swallowed but wouldn't let himself be cowed in front of his enemies. "Go ahead. For my brother—or any of my people—I would defend them any time to keep them alive."

Mansocan chuckled at the prince's audacity. "Indeed, I believe you would, in a heartbeat, Prince of Sunrise." His red eyes bore into royal's blue glare as if the leader could reach the prince's soul. "And because of that, I won't punish *you.*" He turned and pointed. "Bring him."

When Rowin realized who Mansocan referred to, he took to fighting. He managed to elbow one maunstorz in the face and another in the throat before Chornauk and two guards pinned him to the snow. All the while, Mansocan looked on in amusement. Once the Sunarian was thoroughly subdued, the *seka'vlr* turned to his task. With his eyes on Prince Rowin, Mansocan took hold of the struggling lord protector's left ring finger and took out his knife. "Learn well, *Prince*. I am not a man to cross." He readied his blade above the man's Oath of Fealty ring.

Prince Rowin could only plead, "Rio! Rio, look at me! Look here! Rio!" as the blade made its first cut.

Part II

§

(First Snow 110 SC)

Chapter Sixteen
§
Request

The Sia Hills of northeastern Sealand were unique to Syre in that they had escaped the worst of the snows in the north. Because of this, passage for the lone priest and his horse was idyllic, almost a stroll in springtime. Priest Anibus, cousin to the Sealand crown, was on his way south to West Port. His only companion for those six weeks was a grey mare named Rain—a gift from the Crystine cavalry months back when his journey had taken him to the Crystal Kingdom.

Journeying would have been quicker had Anibus chosen to stay with his cousins Prince Par Fantill and Lord Gordar Farrylin; however, the one thing Anibus disliked most in all of Syre was boats. Unwilling to make the passage aboard Par's horse-transporting vessel, Anibus had broken from the rest to make the way on horseback. After a short stop at North Point—the fort of the northern Landarïan army—he and Rain had meandered along the Sia Hills to a small monastery just outside of the city of Ivor.

That was when the snows had come down. Waylaid while waiting for better weather, the priest had taken up residence with the monks. Yet, as the snows deepened and food became scarce, Anibus knew he should not overstay his welcome. (In truth, he was more worried the hungry populace would look at Rain as an available steak, and there was no way in the Heavens he was going to let the Crystal mare get eaten!) Taking what he and the mare could carry, Anibus had made a polite excuse to leave and taken the first clear day to continue on his way.

His choice to head out had proven to be a Stars' send. The weather continued to grow milder and snows turned to frost and cold rains as he trekked southward. Finding little knolls and nooks to hide in had kept horse and rider dry enough to prevent a fever chill. More, Anibus discovered a lovely trait in the little mare that fully melted his heart: on cold evenings, it was common for Rain to lie down behind her rider. Many a night, Anibus was kept warm and comfortable curled up alongside the horse's belly. There was no denying the chaste Estarian priest had finally found the love of his life in the Crystal mare; Rain's devotion to her handler was undeniable.

"Look down there," Anibus said to Rain as they paused on the last hillock of the Sia Hills. "That town there is Dolland—once homestead to the Dol family. I have an acquaintance family there. We should be able to rest with them and have a proper roof over our heads and soft straw to sleep on."

Rain pawed the ground as he spoke, as if she understood the priest's words. She certainly looked intelligent enough with those big, brown eyes of hers. Anibus laughed at her energy and gave the mare her head so she could pick a way down the slope toward the town.

They made Dolland as dusk was falling. The small town—Anibus would more accurately call it a village—was home to mostly farmers. The northern fields were less fallow than most he had seen in Sealand. Golden grains of wheat and barley swayed in the soft, orange light of the setting sun. A little girl of about seven popped her head up as the horse and rider approached. She stared, wide-eyed, for several seconds before taking off, sprinting toward her family's home, seen across the fields. There was no doubt that the whole town would be out to see the visitor by the time Anibus reached his destination.

Indeed, a small crowd had gathered in the main street by the time Anibus stopped at the mercantile. The priest ignored the curious stares as he tied Rain to the hitching post and stepped onto the boardwalk in front of the store. He was unable to enter, however, as an exuberant, teenage girl rushed out first and flung her arms around his waist. "Priest Ani!"

Anibus held in his groan as all the air was squeezed from his lungs, but he did manage to hug the girl in return. "Rosemary? You're so grown up!"

"Tis been four summers! I kept-a askin' Mum when you was comin' back t' visit."

"It has been a long time," Anibus confessed and gently untangled himself from the fourteen-year-old's hold. "I'm on my way through and thought a visit would be nice. Are your folks in?"

Rosemary nodded. "Mum is mindin' the store, and Pa's in the back wi' our pigs. Oo," she cooed. "Is that your horse?" She ran around Anibus before he could reply.

He turned to find the girl already petting Rain's head. "Yes. That's Rain."

"She's pretty."

"Yes, she is."

"Can I take her 'round back?" Rosemary asked, her green eyes pleading. "I'm old enough."

"I..." Anibus faltered, though he knew Rain would behave perfectly. "Yes, all right. I will be back to help you once I say hello to your mother."

A big grin formed on the girl's freckled face. Rosemary untied Rain and began to lead the mare away.

Anibus sighed, fatigued from his trip and the girl's enthusiasm. He turned away to find Martha Myler, the girl's mother, behind the store's counter. Yet, she seemed already privy to his arrival; as soon as Anibus's boot crossed the threshold, she was smiling and making her way over to greet him.

"Anibus! Stars' blessing, it is you, lad!"

"Mrs. Myler."

Martha greeted him with a motherly hug. "It's so good to see you." She squeezed his forearms as she backed away to study his prematurely worn face. "You must have been travelling hard. You look plumb tired."

He chuckled and nodded. "Across Syre to the Crystal Kingdom and then back around from Staria. I've seen it all except Blue Haven."

"My, the Eminary asks much of his acolytes these days!"

"Not at all. My journey was more for my king than His Eminence. Being cousin to the crown comes with certain...responsibilities."

"Well then..." Mrs. Myler's voice faded out. Even if she disagreed with the extent of the "jobs" Anibus did from the Sealand crown, she knew the priest cared too much for his family to heed any of her words. "Well then," she repeated. "Do come in and make yourself comfortable. Rest!" She ushered him though the store to their little apartment in the back. "Your timing's perfect, always. I was just having Rosemary finish up with the supper."

"I could smell your home cooking from miles away. It had my mouth watering all the way here."

Mrs. Myler blushed at the compliment. "Oh, you're too kind to this ol' woman."

"Not at all. As you know, I've travelled much of Syre. No one can match your cooking." She clucked, but Anibus could see his flattery was winning Martha over.

Mr. Myler was just coming in the back door as they came in from the storefront. He dipped his hands in a washpot by the door and wiped them clean before turning to offer the priest his hand. "Priest Anibus."

"Carl." Anibus shook his hand firmly and felt the man's work-weathered calluses scratch his skin. Carl Myler had always seemed a titan of a man. Having grown up a farmer, he was muscled from the hard work, and managing the store had not changed him. Rarely had Anibus seen the man stop to relax.

"Bad weather to be travelling through," Carl commented.

"Actually, I've missed most of it. The snows caught me when I was in Ivor. Since then, I've found the trek south pleasant enough."

"Hm." Carl grunted and found a stool to sit on to remove his barn-soiled boots—so Martha didn't scold him for tracking it around the house. "Well, lucky that, then. Others have complained of poor roads."

"I wouldn't know," Anibus replied. "I kept to the hills. My horse is very surefooted. She managed the back country beautifully."

"That grey mare?"

"Yes, she's mine."

Carly looked impressed. "She's no standard mount. Royal blooded, I'd say."

"A Crystal horse, of the Starkindler herd."

Both Martha's and Carl's eyebrows rose. "Worth more than a handful of docets," Carl said with a whistle under his breath.

"A gift," Anibus replied, skirting the mention of money. "And I should go help tend to her. My bags are still on her saddle, besides."

"Bring Rosemary back with you," Martha said before Anibus could take his leave. "Supper is almost ready."

"Will do, ma'am."

Anibus exited from the back and made his way across the tiny yard to the stable. The Mylers had an assortment of livestock: four pigs, a rooster and hens, a single milk cow, and an old plow horse. Rain had been put up in a corner corral away from all other animals, save the plow horse. The big Shire seemed quite taken to have the delicate little mare next to him. Rain, however, had a sour expression on her face thanks to the gelding's constant sniffing. Had Rosemary not been there, Anibus didn't doubt Rain would have put the old lug in his place.

The girl already had Rain untacked and bridle exchanged for a rope halter. Anibus's saddle and gear had been set on the rail of the pen.

Rosemary was busy brushing the grey down with a straw currycomb. She grinned as Anibus neared. "Rain's so sweet. Pa was worried she'd be too much for me t'handle, but she's stood like a lamb. We showed him!"

Anibus returned her grin and lifted his hands to stroke Rain's face. "Yes, she is as fair as they come. Spirited when it counts, but not a mean bone in her body."

"Pa said she must'a cost a fortune."

"No." He frowned at the thought of Mr. Myler putting so much thought into her worth. "Rain was a gift from Commander Matar of the Crystine cavalry in the Crystal Kingdom. I didn't pay for her—minus my promise to treat her well."

"I wish I was given a horse."

He chuckled. "I'm sure your folks wouldn't like another mouth to feed. Besides, isn't old Crow a good mount?"

Rosemary wrinkled her nose and gave a shrug. "He's old. And big. And slow. I'd love t'have a mare like Rain. Then, I could ride fast as the wind and beat ol' Timmy Goodings. He's mean t'me and picks on everyone. Course, his father is the mayor, so he gets away wi' it all the time."

"Sounds like a charmer."

"He's ugly and mean."

Anibus chuckled and finished petting Rain. He came into the stall to check Rosemary's work and to clean out the mare's feet—it wouldn't do to leave a stone in overnight. Lastly, he checked her hay and water. "Everything looks good here. Thank you, Rosemary. Care to head in for some supper?"

She beamed up at him and nodded enthusiastically.

Anibus gave Rain one last pat and then let himself and the Myler girl out of the small corral. He slid the rail back into place and walked with Rosemary back to the apartment. Following her lead, he kicked off his boots at the door and washed his hands before settling into a chair pulled out for him at the dinner table. Rosemary settled into the one to his right, leaving the last places for her folks. The elder Mylers came to the table too, and the woman of the house began to dish out food. Anibus thanked her as Mrs. Myler plopped down a loaded spoonful of mashed potatoes mixed with vegetables and gravy. "My, it looks good, Martha!"

"There's always more where that came from," she said in reply and then lifted another bowl. "Chicken?"

"Thank you." He forked out a piece.

Martha nodded and finally sat down. She slid her chair to the table and fixed her cloth napkin in her lap. A warning look to Rosemary told the girl to do the same and to mind her manners. Nodding to the two men, she said, "Anibus, would you grace us with a prayer?"

"Of course, ma'am." Anibus interlaced his fingers with those of the two ladies and bowed his head. "To the Stars that guide us, we thank you for this meal that gives us sustenance and strength. We may have only a little, but it is surely enough, and we are grateful for that. Stars, I ask you grace this Myler family for their hospitality and friendship. I ask that you join them here tonight and watch over them once I've gone. Thank you for your constant guidance and grace. Forever and always, blessings."

The Mylers whispered the ending to themselves, and then all straightened and dug into the meal Mrs. Myler and Rosemary had prepared.

The food really was delicious and as good as Anibus remembered. Nothing ever beat a meal prepared by Martha Myler. He finished two helpings of potatoes and three pieces of chicken before his stomach protested the abuse. Wiping his hands and mouth clean, the Estarian priest leaned back into his chair and proclaimed himself thoroughly stuffed. The Mylers looked full too, and Mrs. Myler seemed pleased that her meal had been so satisfying.

"We'll have some pie in a bit," Martha informed him.

"But first, I need to make sure all is closed down for the day," Carl said.

"I can help you," Anibus offered politely.

"No need, lad." Carl waved him down. "Your job is to rest. I will be back shortly."

"Make yourself cozy by the fire," Martha instructed Anibus. "I'm sure your traveler's bones need the heat. Rosemary, help clean the table."

Bereft of anything to do, Anibus made his way to the other room and the fire Mrs. Myler had mentioned. Alone, save for an old fuzzball of a barn cat, he sat down in the rocking chair closest to the flames and settled into the quiet.

Anibus wasn't sure if he had drifted to sleep or if he had just been lulled to complacency by the fire, but when next he realized it, the Mylers were about the fire too. Mr. Myler was smoking from a long pipe; Mrs. Myler was knitting; and Rosemary was on the floor, teasing the cat with a chicken feather. A piece of apple cobbler was on a stand to his left, next to a cup of steaming tea. "Oh," Anibus groaned, and straightened in his chair.

Martha smiled, "You looked like you needed that."

"Hm, yes." He blinked and rubbed his eyes. "I apologize for nodding off."

She chuckled. "It's fine. Though you should have at that tea and cobbler before they get cold."

"Of course. Thank you, ma'am." It took no more persuasion for him to gobble up the dessert. The cobbler was to die for, and the chamomile tea was soothing. Both were finished off in short order. Then, Anibus rose to take his dishes to the kitchen, not wanting to bother his hosts with the chore. When he turned back around from washing the plates, he was startled to find Mr. Myler behind him. "Oh, Carl, I apologize."

Mr. Myler waved it away. "Can I have a moment of your time, priest?"

"Ah... yes. All right." Anibus had the feeling the request wasn't for some small religious favor, yet he followed the man out of the kitchen and to a closet-sized study set off of the mud room.

Carl produced a key to his one drawer in the study and turned the antique lock with a clunk. After opening the drawer, he retrieved a wooden box far in the back. It was worn and dusty, cobwebbed even. "Priest Anibus. I—" He paused with a look of consternation on his face. "Priest," he began again, "are you headed for West Port?"

"That is the plan. I have need of meeting with the Eminary again after being absent so long."

Mr. Myler seemed to like the sound of that. "Then, may I ask a favor of you?"

Anibus balked, instinctively sensing that what Carl wanted would be more than a normal favor. "That would all depend, sir."

Carl smiled and huffed at his guest's cautious behavior. "I know I am not a man to ask many favors, and I can see you know this one may be big."

"Sir," Anibus replied as neither yay nor nay.

"This isn't easy for me to ask...." He shuffled the box in his hands. "Priest Anibus, I need you to take my Rosemary to a convent in West Port. I will pay for her passage and your time. I've got it all saved right here."

"Wait a minute, sir!" Anibus raised his hands, taken by surprise. "Carl, I need to ask why you want this."

Mr. Myler nodded and sat down in his chair, suddenly looking as if the life had left him. It seemed he had known it was a gamble, in any case, to ask such a huge task of an acquaintance. "Really, Priest, it comes down to that I'm scared. Scared of what may happen." He rubbed his fingers over the old wooden case absently. "The stories I'm hearing from travelers out of Golden and Staria…they cause me grave concern."

What kind of stories?" Anibus shifted to sit on the desktop.

"War stories." Carl looked up. "I've lived through a war before—and all the atrocities that come with them. Soldiers taking all the food stores from the towns, women raped, whole families cut down for not sympathizing, businesses running dry as people are scared off…"

Anibus frowned. "But there is no war in Sealand. It's all far north and east of here."

"In Rubia, I hear." Carl shook his head and pursed his lips. "Tradesmen say Rubia is impassable, completely cut off from the rest of Syre. And it's not the snows but them maunstorz. They've managed to cut right past the military might of Staria and straight to the heart of Syre. You can't tell me that's no small cause for concern."

Anibus felt his chest constrict. *How did that happen*? The maunstorz had been stopped at the Citadel of Light. He had seen the aftermath with his own eyes! *It must be those maunstorz who vanished from North Point—but how did they get past all that desert without being spotted*? "Carl, sir, I don't think it is best for Rosemary to be separated from you and Martha, nor do I think West Port is the safest place to take her if she did leave you. If the maunstorz are in Rubia, then you have a whole host of armies between them and here: the Starian army, Sheev'anee, Kavahad, plus the soldiers of Golden. Those armies are far more likely to be attacked than this little town."

"That may well be, but we are a farming town. If our armies are starving, they will come here for our harvest. Those are the men I fear."

Anibus looked dismayed to hear a fellow kinsman speak of their soldiers with such little faith. Still, he could not deny that war did bring out the worst—and best—in people. "Your Rosemary is still so young. To be taken to a convent—"

"It would keep her safe and innocent!" Carl argued. "Younger girls than her have been taken in. Please, Priest, surely you see the logic?"

Anibus could see himself slowly losing the argument on that point. "And how is she to travel?"

"I will sell my old Crow to a neighbor in exchange for a little mare he has."

"I won't let you sell your horse. You need him for plowing." Anibus held up one hand against further objections. "Can your savings cover the cost of the mare?"

"Well, yes, but barely. There will be nothing left over for you—"

"Then, that's what you will do, though I still don't think that this is the best idea," Anibus cut in. "But I will not take Rosemary without your wife and daughter's agreement."

Carl could see it was the best he was going to get. He nodded. "We will discuss it in the morning over breakfast—that way, Martha has time to think it over tonight."

Anibus made an unhappy line with his mouth and held in a sigh. "Very well. Tomorrow then." Silently, he prayed the answer would be no; however, by late morning, the decision was made. Anibus had underestimated the Mylers' fears of the possibilities of war coming to Sealand. Martha was adamant to see her daughter to safety, and Rosemary was ecstatic for a trip to such an esteemed city. Hands tied, Anibus found his next day filled with preparations to take the Myler girl with him to West Port.

Chapter Seventeen
§
Soul Majik

For the first time in two-and-a-half weeks, the snows were thawed enough to be passable. Taking advantage of the weather, Lord Shekmann and Zyanthena tacked up their mounts and rose the two stallions outside of the castle proper.

They were soon joined by the whole pack of grey wolves. Amid the excited yips of the twelve predators, the two horses trotted along with an air of tense alertness; however, the still-deep snows quickly took down their adrenaline, and Tano and Unrevealed were forced to settle. The wolves became the leaders of their little group in short order; none seemed to flounder in the deep snow. Relying on their knowledge of the area, Zyanthena signaled to Lord Darshel her desire to follow their insights. She called out to Swift Hunter to show them the lands around the castle, which neither she nor Darshel had yet explored.

The true grandeur of Crystanian became apparent as they rode around the western wall, heading northward. The outer walls of the palace were made of obsidian and white quartz, while the foundation was of granite. In the morning sun, the walls gleamed like black ice and snow against a grey background. There were seven separate spires to the heights of the palace, making it one of the largest royal houses in Syre—only the Sunlight Palace in the Sunrise Kingdom was larger. There was just enough gold gilded into the framework of the windows, archways, and turrets of the outer walls to make the entire structure seem unusually opulent for such a military-like fortress. It was a thing to behold.

Lord Darshel shook his head as they paused to admire Crystanian. "And you are heir to all this." He meant more than just the palace. All around them were the deep forests and Crystal Mountains of Crystalynian. It was a backdrop that took his breath away.

Zyanthena was less inclined to be wooed. "I am heiress to a dead kingdom," she replied, and looked away from the sight to give him a look filled with irony. "Maybe in its time, Crystanian was the seat-head of Syre, but now it has a population of two—and a pack of wolves," she amended when Swift Hunter harrumphed at her.

"You're rather droll," Darshel commented at her negativity. "A kingdom can be rebuilt as long as its ruler still lives. Certainly, you cannot be the only Crystani alive. Once they hear of your return, the people will return home."

Zyanthena frowned. "I'm not sure that's the best for those who have etched out a life elsewhere for a quarter of a century…"

The Kavahadian lord-governor shook his head at her and tsked. "I see you are still fighting with yourself over your birthright."

Sharp brandy eyes narrowed. "I am Sheev'arid, Zyanthena first and foremost. Whatever Vauldin makes me besides that is still up for debate." She turned Unrevealed away from Crystanian and cued him into a walk to put an end to the discussion, which they had gotten into a number of times by that point. Behind her, Lord Darshel sighed and rejoined the Tashek as they headed into the first line of trees of the Forbidding Forest.

The forest itself was not daunting as stories foretold. Instead, it was a healthy place, completely free of human touch, its tall pine and aspen trees making the whole area ethereal. It was the wolves' familiar haunt, and Hunter—with his mate—knew all of its secrets by heart. The alpha shared his insights with Zyanthena as they travelled northward, telling her of animal paths a human eye would miss and ancient tales of past battles and natural disasters still written into the landscape.

There was one particular location Swift Hunter wished the Heir of Vauldin to see. Leading the way, he took them all to a clearing about a half mile northwest of the palace. The enormous, empty vista opened up onto a hillock overlooking the rest of the Crystal Mountains. The view of the high, snow-capped peaks was the most spectacular view thus far; however, that was not why the pack had gone in that direction. The twelve grey wolves mingled about on the open field, making noises Zyanthena had never heard from them before. Uncertain, she asked Swift Hunter and Moon Ember about the vocalizations. *Is something happening?*

Yet before the leaders could reply, the area became suddenly charged as Vauldin was activated by the lingering magic that had been used on the spot twenty-four years before. What had seemed a warm, sunny day turned instantly cold, making their breath cloud in the air. A lonesome howl whipped about them, screaming on the winds that picked up out of nowhere. It was an unearthly sound, that wind, and promised a kind of doom. Sunlight was hidden beyond a swirling cloud that formed from above and sank over the hillock until all was dark. The howl turned to the shrieks of human screams, while lightning cracked in the magically changed air. Panicking, Tano reared at the storm, nearly unseating Lord Darshel. Beside the man and horse, the other horse and rider seemed completely still: statues amid the chaos. Then Zyanthena and Unrevealed disappeared into the cacophony of darkness and lightning.

The screams grew louder until Zyanthena, following an impulse, lifted her hands to the whirlwind. At her command, the chaos found order, and all of the spirits in the storm swirled around her. The screams stilled to become apparitions of warriors and mounts of a battle long ago. They stayed frozen before the wielder of Vauldin, their master. Thousands upon thousands of departed souls were held in the sway of the Stone of Life and Death.

Awe filled Zyanthena's eyes as she realized what was happening. "*É shăud'en ē*," she whispered to the ghosts of battles past, saying in Ancient Syrean, "I release you." The words came to her as if by an ancient decree. There was a rightness to them that she could not deny.

The hordes of warriors bowed to her command. It was as if they were able to finally find peace at the ancient battleground where majik had held them to the earthly plain. Just as suddenly as the ferocious torrent began, there was a *crack* as the death-majik disappeared. Just as suddenly as it began, the cold turned to warmth and the darkness to light.

The aftermath was poignant.

"What the…!?" Lord Darshel felt himself and his brave mount shaking as the event dissipated. He glanced to his right to witness his companion's expression. There was a gleam of power in Zyanthena's brandy eyes that constricted his chest. The power of death—and controlling the souls of the deceased—had given the desert woman's gaze an eerie glow. There was a potential of addiction to that kind of euphoria that chilled his heart. "Zy…Zyanthena?"

She shifted, as if becoming aware of her stillness. Zyanthena lowered her hands and turned those glowing eyes on the lord-governor of Kavahad. "Lord Darshel," she said, so simply.

At that moment, Lord Darshel Shekmann knew true fear…

Chapter Eighteen
§
Praise

"They've arrived!"

Patrick startled at the abrupt arrival of Jacen at his mount's stall. He had been lulled by the soothing, repetitious motion of brushing the palomino's coat. Candor, too, had jumped at the interruption, so Patrick knew he hadn't been the only one dozing. "Stars, a little warning next time!"

Jacen chuckled and ignored the chastisement. "Come outside! Master Callé's wagon just arrived." He bumped his hands against the stall door in his excitement and turned to go, not waiting for his friend's reply.

Patrick forced a sigh to bring down his heart rate. He patted Candor and said, "Be back later, boy," before letting himself out of the stall. Patrick, unlike his Havener friend, was not very excited to meet the great surveyor and his apprentice. Jacen loved to study maps for hours, so he was anxious to meet the best mapmaker in Syre. For Patrick, the arrivals meant more strangers to be introduced to and interact with cordially. Some days—and today was one of those—the task seemed a bit too tedious for his liking.

The growing numbers of their party were all there too, curious to meet the esteemed surveyor, a man employed by the royal crown of Golden itself. Mr. Durrow was the farthest away, leaning against the stable wall, as Patrick exited. He bobbed his head the Rubian's way, and Patrick returned the hello casually before continuing on. Beyond the blacksmith were two new faces: twins by the names of Sammy and Reed Ritter. Interviewed just two days prior, they were there for a trial run for the weekend, when all the group was together. Past them were the Calhorns, sitting to the side on some straw bales. Young Jean's eyes were wide in excitement at the goings-on of the livery; his father was more reserved, taking the activities in stride. The two newer additions to the group were near the Calhorns. Young farrier Kipper leaned against the fence with a foot raised and propped against the boards and an ax—his weapon of choice and always in his hands—gently tossed about. Beside the farrier was a slightly older man named Maximillian Rosailles. The tall and skinny-as-a-bean man went by the nickname "Pickle." He had been picked for his cooking skills, which he'd gained from his time under Lord-Commander Ivance's own personal squadron. Maximillian had been quite ready to retire from regular military duty and was eager for a prospective trip to lands beyond the regular borders of Syre. Last were the Tashek maidens. They stood ready but patient as Master Callé's loaded-down cart was being unpacked—overly supervised by the cantankerous surveyor, who was worrying over his equipment getting jostled. Somehow, Jacen, the man's apprentice, and two of Ivance's men were humoring the old man and obeying his every little nit-pick.

Patrick shook his head at the absurdity.

A box slipped out of the man's pile as Patrick neared. Rushing to save it, the Rubian stopped its inevitable plummet—only to find Shaul'auna had also rushed in to stop the box. The Tashek woman seemed shocked to have a second rescuer of its contents. Flushing, she murmured, "You've got this?" and let the box go as Patrick righted it and set it safely on the ground. Patrick chuckled to himself as the desert woman retreated to a safe distance from him.

"Thank you, young man!"

Patrick turned to shake hands with Master Callé. "You are welcome, sir. I am Patrick Kins of Rubia."

"Peore Callé, of the Golden capital. You must be our other leader along with lovely Siv'arid there."

Patrick rose his eyebrows in Auna's direction. The Tashek shrugged at his silent question. "I… yes, sir, I am. We're in charge of this crazy expedition."

Master Callé nodded. "Good, good. Well, I'm looking forward to speaking further on our orders and discussing our routes of travel. This old body of mine has this one last expedition in it, and I intend to do my part."

"I'm sure you will, sir." From all the rumors, Patrick knew Master Callé was a stickler for getting details right; however, even with a perfectionist personality, the master could outpace younger men on a journey. He was quick and efficient, the epitome of a professional.

It took nearly half an hour to unpack and transfer the contents of the cart to the master's rooms. Thankfully, Callé had been given quarters closest to the street entrance—a foresight of the lord-commander's. By the time the surveyor and apprentice were settled, the rest of the party had moved on to daily weapons and survival skills practice. Elder Callé settled into the rocking chair outside his quarters to watch and bid his apprentice, Peter Schelling, to join the others.

Patrick wandered over to the surveyor as Jacen took the lad in hand and spoke to him of his strengths and what he needed to learn. "Your apprentice seems young."

Callé chuckled. "Peter is a wet-behind-the-ears sixteen, but I've had the boy with me since he was four. He's a better surveyor than men thrice his age."

"I'll take your word for it, sir."

"You're very socially polite, young man." Callé eyed him from the side as he continued to rock in his chair. The words seemed to imply Master Callé didn't trust him at face value.

Patrick answered as truthfully as he could. "Sir, I'm mertinean through-and-through. Most of our company—save Rosailles there and my friend Jacen Novano—are civilian personnel. I've learned to temper myself for their benefit."

"Kins, you said the name was?"

"Yes, sir."

Callé's eyes narrowed, and he really looked Patrick over this time. "There was a great mertinean lieutenant by that name once."

"Commander now, sir, of the mertinean's eighth battalion. Commander Ethan Kins."

"Commander…hm. Men of ambition you Kins-men are."

"Sir?"

"Your father rises in rank, while his son leads an expedition to Northern Syre. You were picked by the Starian king himself."

"Technically my appointment was by the Shi'alam of the Sheev'anee and approved by the entire war council at the Citadel of Light."

"That's what I mean, boy." Callé stared at him. "You're from the up-and-ups."

Patrick pursed his lips, unsure how to reply to that.

"And those women…" Callé continued. There was skepticism in the master's features. The look compelled Patrick to speak out on their behalf.

"You mean the Tashek? Auna and Kei are skilled fighters and know the northern territory of Staria like the back of a hand. I am of the

North, Master Callé. Tashek women have made ferocious fighters, more so than you men of the South have ever seen."

That had Callé laughing. He waved a finger at Patrick. "*That*, young Kins-son, is the attitude I'd expect of you! And well played. As leader of our little party, I would want you to speak up in favor of your people."

So, the man has been testing me? "I don't know everyone well enough for that yet, sir, but I do want to have faith in our party. As the Tashek have said, our survival depends on it."

The chair squeaked as Master Callé rose from it and offered Patrick his hand. "That we can agree on, Patrick Kins. I had my doubts when I saw the young age of the people leading this company, but no more. You have a level head on you."

Patrick didn't reply with more than a "sir," but he did take the surveyor's handshake. Master Callé would be a hard master to please, he sensed. *All the more reason to have a united unit,* he thought, which brought him to another detail he needed to hash out. Patrick waited for Master Callé to retire to his rooms for a post-travel "nap" before he turned to find Shaul'auna.

The Siv'arid woman was over at the throwing weapons corner of the livery. She was explaining a point to young Jean as Kipper and Maximillian threw their own weapons. Jean's eyes shone with glee at seeing Kipper's skills with the ax, though Auna had him practicing with knives. She was berating the young Calhorn about his distraction when Patrick neared.

"Auna."

Shaul'auna almost looked relieved to have the excuse to leave Jean to the two men's attentions. "Kins-son."

"May we speak?" *Privately,* he had meant to add, but Patrick didn't want to with the others there. The two Sheev'anee women were already pined over by most of the men in the company—not that any said so beyond whispers over a beer now and again. Heedful of that, Patrick never addressed either maiden out of eyeshot of the others.

Shaul'auna waved them to the hay bales near the stables. They sat and leaned back against the stable wall and surveyed the practicing group members without speaking. Finally, she shifted to eye the Rubian, her doe eyes catching details in his features even Patrick doubted he was aware of. "What was it you needed to speak to me about?"

Cool and direct as always. Without Kei'shkï or Jacen there, Patrick wondered if they would get along; there was a certain tension between him and the Tashek maiden that would need to be addressed at some point. "We need to discuss who here are the leaders of the group."

"Are you and I not?"

His eyebrows knit into a frown. "We never really discussed it, but it seems you said so to Master Callé."

Shaul'auna licked her lips, looking much too innocent for his liking. "And tell me where in my reasoning am I wrong? You and Jacen were assigned by the king. Kei'shkï and I by clan Siv'arid. We make up the initial four of the party. Kei and Jacen are not ones to readily lead, however, as you and I are… So, are we not the leaders of this group?"

Patrick really hated arguing with the Tashek. They always twisted their words to their advantage. "Some discussion on the matter would have been nice," he grumbled.

A giggle escaped her throat. "You do like your 'discussions,' Kins-son."

"It keeps things clear," Patrick said in his defense.

"Indeed, it does." It was hard to tell just how much Shaul'auna was mocking him. "But if you agree with my logic, then I say that is concluded." She started to rise.

"And why not Jacen? He has led his own troop before. Most get along with him better."

"And whose fault is that, Mr. Taciturn?" Shaul'auna stood before him, her hands clasped at the small of her back. She didn't look like a dangerous fighter in this meek pose, and it made Patrick wonder if she took the stance to keep him from losing his temper.

His frown deepened. "My question stands, Shaul'auna." He said her full name without butchering it. The effort was not lost on the Tashek.

"Jacen Novano may have the experience to lead but not the charisma. It is one thing to lead a troop of trained soldiers and quite another to lead a group of rag-tag volunteers on an expedition to the wilds. As I will be so bold to say, Kins-son, you meet those qualifications. This group needs you to lead it." A less self-assured woman would have blushed when giving such praise; however, Shaul'auna's features stayed steady, composed and resolute.

Patrick had not expected the warrioress to see him as so highly qualified, and he felt himself gaping rudely. Realizing it, he knocked his jaws together. Shaul'auna seemed to sense she had surprised him to speechlessness. She bowed respectfully and said, "As we both agree, I will get back to train the others. Perhaps you should mingle as well, and get to know your group members better."

§ §

There was one errand Prince Kent would not let anyone else do, and that was visiting the late Eric Sloane's family. The lieutenant-commander had owned property ten miles southwest of Sardon, a distance Lord-Commander Ivance insisted he accompany the Golden heir personally. Together, the two men who had known Sloane the longest traveled with the sun and a six-soldier escort to bring the grievous news to the family.

Prince Kent had not seen his lord protector's land before. Having met the man through his father's commission, he had never found the time to visit the out-of-the-way town his lord protector had called home. Now, with hindsight, it made the prince feel as if he hadn't appreciated his most loyal soldier enough.

At least Eric Sloane's position had offered his family a comfortable living. The Sloane property was a good thirty acres of fine farmland just outside of a small town called Greendale. They made enough to support a second home, reserved for their workers and a maid. It was a pretty acreage nestled near the Pika Mounts, where the rolling green hills were peaceful and lush.

"The main house is just over that rise," Lord-Commander Ivance informed his prince. He pointed out the direction. "It's built by a little spring and fishing pond. Quite the spot for a retreat. Eric and I enjoyed it a time or two in years past..." The leader's voice sounded distant as he reminisced. In truth, only one or twice would either man have had a reprieve from their duties; they were married to their military careers.

Ivance ordered a man ahead to inform the family of their arrival. Though he had sent a letter a week before, the Lord-Commander thought it best if the Sloanes were given notice before receiving their prince. It was out of courtesy to Mary, Sloane's widow, who could be an anxious woman if taken by surprise. A young lad took off as the rest of the party continued at a casual walk.

A handful of people were standing in front of the quaint cottage when their party arrived. Mrs. Carter, Eric Sloane's eldest daughter, was the lady-in-charge. She stood front and center with her son, Isaak, cuddled in her arms. Eliza Carter's fifteen-year-old son, Trevor, stood just behind and to their left, with two of their farmhands. Farthest back was the maid and the two young daughters, Kelly and Trina.

Prince Kent had forgotten that his lord protector's son-in-law was enlisted in their army and stationed at the capital. That meant all the responsibilities of the household fell to Mary and her daughter. Seeing Mrs. Carter in her father's place was a strong dose of reality and a hollow reminder of the loyal retainer he had lost. Kent dismounted and handed his reins to Lord-Commander Ivance. "Mrs. Carter." He removed his cap in respect.

Eliza stepped around her son to give a proper curtsy to the prince. Despite being five years his senior, she seemed flustered at meeting the royal. "Prince Argetlem."

"Prince Kent will do, Mrs. Carter," he corrected gently and flashed a disarming smile. The look softened the young lady's features. He extended his greeting to the others, not missing any. The heir's casual and personal greeting seemed to take everyone back, shocked at how down-to-earth their highness was. "I came to pay my respects to your mother, Mrs. Carter. Is Mrs. Sloane here?"

"Ah, yes, High—Prince Kent." Eliza seemed reluctant. "Please, Highness, Lord Commander, if you will follow me."

"Mother—" her son Isaak started.

"Go with Trevor," Eliza murmured to him. To Trevor, she added, "Help the girls set the table and manage the fire. We will be to the kitchen after seeing your grandmama." The four children were off before Prince Kent could insist that a meal wasn't necessary; he shut his mouth in a reminder to be polite.

Ivance and Kent were shown to the master bedroom of the cottage, the only room in the upstairs. The space was dark, lit only by a candle, and it took a moment for their eyes to adjust. Once they did, the men found Mary Sloane sitting in a nook in the far corner. She was absently knitting, though how the woman could see in the dim light was anyone's guess. Eliza didn't motion them forward to greet her. She leaned toward the men instead and whispered, "Highness, Lord Commander, as you can see, my mother isn't well. She took to bed after news of my father.

Since then, I've only managed to get her to her chair. She is lost without Father."

Guilt filled Prince Kent at the words. He had grieved his lord protector's passing in Staria, having been with Eric Sloane to his last breath. The family, however, had heard the news from a missive after not seeing or speaking with him for some time. He could only imagine the extent of their grief. "Does she hear?" he asked softly.

"In a way," Eliza replied. "But Mother doesn't say much anymore, just my father's name, over and over."

"May I?" Kent indicated that he wished time with Mary.

Mrs. Carter hesitated, but Lord-Commander Ivance took her by the arm and motioned them out. "We will be below, Highness."

Prince Kent nodded his thanks and continued into the room unaccompanied. He made his way to Mary's side and kneeled before her as she rocked in her chair. It had been some years since Kent had spoken with Mary Sloane. The wife of his lord protector was loath to leave her little estate, especially for duties at the capital. In just that time, Mrs. Sloane had become so frail. Saddened, he reached for her boney hands and paused them from their busywork. Mary seemed to stiffen at the touch, but she barely turned her eyes.

"Mrs. Sloane. Mary, it's Prince Kent Argetlem." Kent had been hoping for some response, but Mary gave none beyond a slight change in her breathing. "I…I came on request of your husband to bring you his last words." The prince pulled the letter he had carried all those weeks in his breast pocket. The hard-stock envelope he pressed into Mary's hands. To his surprise, her fingers closed upon the letter with some force. "He also wanted me to return his ring to you, and this brooch." The two items had been with the letter. Prince Kent assumed they were the most important items to his lord protector—Sloane hadn't had much else besides that he cherished so.

A tear slid down Mary's cheek as the two items were pressed into her palm. Gently, Prince Kent dabbed the wetness away with his sleeve. "Eric told me to tell you that he loved you. You and your family were always in his thoughts. I'm sure his letter had more to say, but those words were the most important." Still, Mary had nothing to say, but her tears told Kent that she had heard.

It seemed rude for him to stay longer, so he made a quiet, "Excuse me," and made his way from the room. Mary needed the space to grieve, he sensed, and Kent wasn't sure if his presence was a comfort to her in her moment of need. Returning to the kitchen below, Prince Kent joined the rest of the household for tea.

Lord-Commander Ivance and his men had headed outside to bring the ashes and belongings of the deceased. It left Eliza and her girls, plus the maid, to tend to household needs unencumbered. Mrs. Carter was at the fireplace, fumbling with the heavy iron kettle hanging over the flames. Prince Kent moved across the room quickly to help her, lest she get burned. "Let me," he said as his hands curled to either side of Eliza's on the coil handle.

"Oh!" Eliza was startled. "But, Highness—!" she began to protest.

"Kent, please, Mrs. Carter, and where shall I set this?"

"Oh, ah, on the board, center of the table." Eliza flushed at being helped by the royal, but she was stuck between the dilemma of heeding the Golden heir's words and being a polite host.

Prince Kent wasn't going to give her much of a choice. He could see that Eliza Carter was overwhelmed with everything as it was. "Shall I fill these cups?" He indicated the fanciest cups the household owned and proceeded to pour, silently thanking the Stars for having met Prince Al'den of Staria. Al'den insisted men were—and should be—capable of helping womenfolk out with such tasks whenever the possibility presented itself.

Bereft of the task at hand, Eliza turned away to gather up a tray with cookies, jam, and sugar that she set beside the teacups. Done, Eliza began to untie her apron as she instructed her girls to go wash up; the maid left with the girls to keep an eye on them. Alone with the prince, Eliza seemed more flustered. "I apologize, Prince Kent, that we do not have much to offer."

"On the contrary, your family provided more than enough." Kent went about preparing his tea as he liked and collected a second drink, which he handed to Eliza. "May you and I partake of this tea on that bench I saw by your pond?" Mrs. Carter flushed but agreed. Together, they took their cups and biscuits to the seat beside the water.

Eliza Carter settled herself beside the royal and seemed uncertain how to behave—if she should wait to drink and eat or make small talk. Considering how nonchalant her father had been, Prince Kent found his daughter's behavior amusing—not that he would say such out loud. "Your family really does have a pleasant place here."

Eliza glanced up from her teacup at the comment. "Thank you, Highness… Kent. It was father's employment to yourself that made all this possible. He felt proud to make such a home."

"I am sorry I kept Eric away so much. He spoke of you and this property often."

"Father did?" Eliza seemed shocked.

"All the time. You and your mother were in his thoughts every day."

She smiled politely. "To us, you were first from his lips. Father seemed honored to be picked to serve as your lord protector."

"I could not have asked for a better man."

Eliza studied him hard at the words, as if she was skeptical of a royal who spoke such praise of a man in his employ. Whatever conclusion she came to had Mrs. Carter blushing and turning her eyes away to the pond. "Thank you, Highness, for being so good to my father."

"It's the least I can do for all Eric did for me. My only regret is taking up all of his time from you and yours."

A wan smile formed at that. "Father would say he regretted it none. He would have continued to serve you all his life if…" Her voice faded out as Eliza realized her father *had* served his prince his whole life. A tear formed in her eye.

Prince Kent pulled a handkerchief from his pocket and passed it to her. "I've no doubts on that, Mrs. Carter." He waited for her to accept the cloth and dab her eyes with it. "Would it be too much if we shared our memories of your father? I'd love to hear about Eric and how he was when he was home."

"I'd like that, "Eliza agreed.

For the next hour, they spoke of the greatest man Prince Kent had ever known.

Chapter Nineteen
§
The Wager

"Let us see what you've been practicing."

Prince Par huffed at the words. In front of Commander Matar and his father, he felt like a schoolboy again—and the words were a bad omen of a test he was going to fail. He gave the Crystal leader a sour frown and took Serein from his cousin. "Here goes," he muttered.

What he had been told to "practice" was how to control water with Serein's powers. The *Khataum* had said it was the first of the sapphire's powers and the easiest to control. *Yes, easier said than done. To think that moving water in a glass was even possible!*

Serein felt warm in his hand as Par looked at her. The stone's lovely blue facets began to glow and hum with a soft ocean song. It was the most Par ever seemed to get from the Stone of Power.

"Relax your mind, Prince," Matar instructed. "All is possible with calm."

Par tried. He did find all the Tashek exercises Matar showed him to be helpful, but the concept the commander wanted just seemed…wrong. "I—I can't!" he said after attempting to get the water to spin. It didn't matter how he thought about it; moving water didn't seem like something he could achieve.

The Crystine commander gave him a sharp look. That direct, midnight-blue stare made the prince blush. Matar sighed and sat back. "The trouble is with you, Prince Par, and not that stone. Your unwillingness makes Serein unwilling."

"I'm not trying to be obstinate! It's just…this seems crazy!"

Matar raised a hand as if to say, "Case in point."

"Maybe we should try a different approach?" King William Fantill said, coming beside Matar.

"I'm all ears, William," Matar agreed. He was doing well at hiding his frustration at the heirling's lack of progress, but after nearly three months of training the royal, it was getting difficult.

"You could try something else of Serein's powers," the king told his son. "Serein could do other things besides water magic. Try scrying, calling out memories, or separating matter."

"I don't even know what that means!" Par replied to the last. He was grateful his father hadn't said shapeshifting. Now there was power that seemed plain insane!

His cousin reached out to clasp his shoulder in a reminder for Par to calm down. Despite his own reservation about the Stones of Power, Lord Gordar had been a constant anchor for Par when practices seemed too off-kilter. "Maybe calling memories would work, my prince. You and your father, or you and I, could try to find a past event to explore?"

Par looked up at his lord protector in surprise. Gordar was even less enamored with holding Serein than he, but he was volunteering? Gordar shrugged at the prince's look.

"That is a good idea," King William agreed. "Let's try with each other." He came to sit across from his son, taking Matar's place. "Serein may not respond to me anymore, but we are familiar with each other. It may help."

Par was doubtful, but he placed Serein between them and then held out his hands and laid them over his father's palms. The two royals locked gazes, and Par willed his breath to slow to match his father's. He didn't know what else to do beyond that—and his father was little help to him—so they ended up sitting there in silence. After some time, Par shifted and said, "I don't think this is working."

"You don't want it to work!" Matar berated. He had stayed quiet and out of the way until the prince spoke.

"Matar, please," King William bid his friend to keep his peace as he slid his hands from his son's.

"I will not," the commander said in return. "Prince Par, you need to confront yourself and your fears. Serein will not help you until you trust in her. You are the only one holding this back!"

William gestured to silence the *Khataum*. Matar huffed his frustration, made his excuses, and stalked away for a reprieve out on the balcony. "Ignore his words, Par," William told his son.

"No, it's all right, Father. I understand Matar's frustration with me. He is right, after all. I am the one holding back."

"Still, working with a Stone of Power is not easy. We've asked a lot of you."

"And with good reason. Having Ravel and Vauldin awake has made all of us concerned. I'm just not sure throwing me and Serein into the mix is going to help."

"Only you can answer that, son."

Par nodded and let his father go speak with the vexed Crystine man. Really, the prince was surprised Commandeer Matar had made it so long without blowing up. He looked to his cousin as Gordar passed him a cup of tea. "I really am a failure with all this—and Syre is counting on me to control Serein."

Lord Gordar slid into the seat beside his prince. "I think you are putting undue pressure on yourself, cousin, and I'm not so sure using Serein is going to help with everything, in any case."

"But her powers could help!"

"And they could make things worse," Gordar countered. "I know that is what worries you the most. But in *that,* Commander Matar is right: you are the one who needs to decide whether or not to use Serein. It is your choice."

"Not according to them."

Gordar chuckled at Par's sulking. "Uncle and Matar can cajole you all they want, but you hold all the cards. That's where their frustrations lie." He bumped his cousin's shoulder with a fist. "Don't take them so seriously. You do what you have to do."

"Thank you." Par smiled at last and finally took a sip of his tea. It was a relief to have one person completely on his side. He fingered the sapphire stone still in his hand. "Everything about Serein seems so surreal," he admitted. "Most of this feels like shooting arrows in the dark. My father, bless him, doesn't remember much of how to use Serein, and Matar… How can a Guardian understand all the apprehensions of having such power? They are much more comfortable with all this than I am."

"I think—adding my two docs—that you will make a fine wielder," Gordar replied. "That you are willing to look at the negatives of using these stones, and not just their assets, means you will use it wisely. That is, if you do decide to use Serein. I do not worry that you will do anything to harm Syre."

It was the first time Gordar had said anything in favor of Serein's powers. Par was shocked; however, it made the hesitant royal a little relieved to hear the words from his lord protector. As usual, his cousin had hit the issue on the head: Par *was* afraid he would do something to hurt the people of Syre. "Thank you, Gordar."

"Any time." His lord protector flashed a smile and accepted the sapphire back into his keeping.

§ §

When the prince's session was over, Par and Gordar took their leave to the archery range. Though Par was first and foremost a rapier wielder, he enjoyed the other weapon for its meditative qualities. After all, one could clash with a sword as madly as they wanted, but a heated arrow shot usually went wide. There was no "faking it" on a target.

Somewhat to their surprise, Lady Yvonne Limonté was there with a friend and her family's escort. The Prince of Sealand and the lady had yet to speak since their argument at the fish markets. Chocolate-brown eyes flashed at the royal as he and his cousin neared, and then Yvonne turned away to nail a perfect shot—just for spite, Par assumed. "Ladies," Par greeted shortly and made his way past her to some targets farther down the line.

"Oh, Highness!" The retainer seemed flustered at his arrival. "We will be out of your hair quickly, Highness. Please, just a moment."

Par felt his eyebrows rise at the man's behavior. "There is no need, good sir. My cousin and I will take the targets down the way. Lady Yvonne need not leave on my account."

"That is indeed right," Yvonne muttered as she lined up another shot. "We have no need to leave, Mortensen, just because His Highness comes for practice."

The retainer gasped in astonishment.

Prince Par knew the lady meant to offend, but he decided to ignore her. He motioned Gordar to continue with him. "Good day, ladies, sir." He tipped his head and started to head off again.

"Is that all?"

The question made the two cousins stop and turn back to Yvonne. *Her audacity really knows no bounds!* By all means, Yvonne Limonté looked ready for a fight. "I received your letter, Prince Fantill. It made bare passages of contriteness for our last encounter."

"Ah, yes… that." Par turned to give her his full attention. "I felt the words were clear enough, my lady."

"Oh, they were clear." Yvonne's attitude had her friend and retainer looking wide-eyed. The other young woman put her hands to the lady's forearm and whispered for her to be politer to the royal.

Of course, Par didn't expect it. "And what in my letter did you find lacking? Perhaps I can correct it?"

"Hmph." She made a noise in her throat. "Do you wish to correct it?"

That time, everyone but Par moved to protest; even Lord Gordar stepped forward to offer a resolution. However, the prince was the first to reply. "Then I shan't, my lady. As you've read my words and made your decision, I will leave it be as I wrote."

"You are a very smooth talker, Highness."

"And you are as tactless as ever." Prince Par and Lady Yvonne ended up staring at each other amid the others' expressions of worry. Finally, though, a smile formed on Par's face. Then, Yvonne broke out in a smile and laugh herself. Prince Par motioned to her bow. "Are you finishing your practice, or shall we have a round?"

"I am up for another, Prince Par." Lady Yvonne readjusted her grip, shifting her arm sling. "If you think you can keep up."

Those were the words Par was used to. Soldiers were often competing and cajoling each other. To have a lady use the same tactic made him suddenly feel better about his interaction with Yvonne. *Who would have thought an archery contest would help*?

"Are you sure about this?" Gordar leaned in to whisper as he helped ready a bow and quiver of arrows for his cousin's match.

"Surer than anything else to do with Lady Yvonne Limonté."

Lord Gordar studied his cousin's face for a long moment. "All right, then." He handed the bow over and then stepped aside.

Prince Par took his stance to Yvonne's right, enough distance to be polite but close enough to be able to hit the same target. "Shall we?"

"If I am allowed to go first?"

"By all means."

"And we will make a wager with each other."

It didn't surprise the prince that Lady Yvonne wanted to make a wager. "Name your price."

"Five shots each," she said. "If I win, you must promise to court me properly for the exact number of seasons as arrows I best you."

He chuckled at her confidence. "And if I win, Lady?"

Lady Yvonne shrugged. "That shall be up to you, Highness."

"I sense you doubt my abilities."

A smile quirked her lips, but Yvonne kept her words civil. "On that, I would not know, Highness, but I am well aware of mine." She stepped up to the line and proved why she had felt so bold. Ignoring her audience, Yvonne readied her stance and notched an arrow, keeping another in hand. The first, she released, and she immediately had the second in place. Turning, Yvonne aimed and let loose her second arrow to the next target in line. A third, fourth, and fifth were shot in quick succession to the next targets, the last being a good one hundred meters and an angle away.

All hit near the bull's-eye.

Par cleared his throat in astonishment at the woman's prowess; she had plenty to brag about if that was her skill level. It also reminded him why he shouldn't make wagers with women: they usually won. He made a silly face, like he was both embarrassed and impressed, and turned to share a look with his cousin. He winked at Gordar with his eye hidden from their audience. "I see you are quite the marksman."

Yvonne puffed up, happy to have shown off. "I've had a great deal of practice."

"Indeed." The prince shared one last look with Gordar before setting himself up where the young woman had stood. Going still, Par took a breath and pulled back on the string. Another breath-count later, he released the arrow. It flew to hit the exact center of the target. Not stopping, the heirling nocked another arrow, turned, and let loose again. Though Par's timing was slower than Yvonne's, in the end, all his shots hit accurately—and a little more centered than his opponent's. He turned to see Yvonne's annoyed look.

"Again!" She challenged and stepped beside Par. The prince chuckled as she forced him aside.

As Par had expected, this time Yvonne upped the ante. Instead of staying still, the lady chose to walk down the line, aiming while moving. Each shot was as good as before. Despite her dress, the young Limonté had been striding out, nearly jogging, so Par made sure to do the same. Again, his aim was just as true.

By then, the three onlookers sensed that the two opponents were getting heated in their bid to beat the other. Yvonne's lady and retainer seemed disquieted by the unladylike display of their charge. Should they step in to save face? Lord Gordar, by contrast, was amused by the whole event. He, at least, knew of Par's competitive streak. His prince would not stop until he had won—or lost miserably.

"One last time," Lady Yvonne said, her teeth gritted. She reset at their start, aimed, and looked away. The act was repeated on every target, and all but the farthest were centered.

Par sensed he had met his match but stepped up to the task. Following the lady's lead, he prepared and looked away. One target, two, three, four… a gasp made him look back to his marks. The final arrow had flown wide! He heard himself curse under his breath.

Yvonne Limonté was jumping up and down in her excitement and victory. She spun to her companions in a happy dance, clutching the poor lady's hands in glee. Prince Par was too stunned at his miss to notice her poor behavior. He was still blinking as Lord Gordar came near to clasp his shoulder. "We'll keep to ourselves that you didn't lose just to be gentlemanly," his lord protector teased.

"Stars preserve me! What did I just agree to again?"

Gordar laughed. "Courting Lady Yvonne Limonté for one season."

Par felt his face flush.

"I do say, my prince, that you've just made your father's day and made all the eligible ladies in Sealand cry."

Chapter Twenty
§
At a Crossroads

"We could take this route here." Cum'ar leaned across the map of Staria to point out where he meant. "If Aerrisson and the men could head just slightly north, we could meet them coming down the Senna."

"You're assuming we could get another bird through."

"Not exactly." The Tashek lifted a finger to halt the Prince of the Yellow Star's pessimism. "A bird we could send, but I had more of a mind for riders. The snows have slackened enough to make passage."

Al'den frowned. "I'm not up for sacrificing more of your men for this. The All'ani have done more than their share already."

"Then let another of the Sheev'anee take the brunt."

The two leaders glanced up to find the Shi'alam entering the war room. The Sheev'anee leader was an impressive man, as tall and broad as the Prince of Staria; he looked as robust as men twice his junior. With his grey-peppered beard trimmed to a warrior-acceptable length and his robes of office equipped with two *kora* blades on its belt, there was no question that the Tashek man was a ruler in his own right.

Al'den was shocked to see the man. The Shi'alam had moved his men to Paragon Oasis, a more central location for patrols around Staria. His departure had signaled to the tribes that he was allowing All'ani Cu'mar's title of being the prince's guardian. "Sir, had I known you had arrived at the Citadel, I—"

"There was no need, Prince Al'den," the Shi'alam interrupted. "Had I wished a formal greeting, I would have sent men ahead." He came near the table to see what the two men had contrived. "I had heard of your plants to travel south to rescue the soldiers of Raven's Den and to continue further to procure Amun." If the Shi'alam was angry that the citrine stone was not in the prince's possession, he showed no sign of it. "I came to offer my tribe's support."

"*Ahnamen.*" Cum'ar bowed his head to the Sheev'anee leader. "We were just reviewing routes to travel."

"There is the need for continued surveillance of Staria, as well," the Shi'alam reminded. "Your focus has been east. I intend to check areas north and west of here."

"That sounds wise," Al'den commended.

The Shi'alam nodded. "I know you have been preoccupied with other matters, Prince Al'den. My well-wishes for your father. I have served alongside him for many years. His illness had me saddened."

"Thank you, Shi'alam."

They shared a sad look until Cum'ar called their attention to the map. "Do you concur, Shi'alam, that this could be our safest route to intercept Commander Grant's men?" He traced their spoken path eastward to the Senna River and south until the two forces met.

"I would suggest a more direct angle toward their force." The leader pointed out the way. "The snows are more thawed this way. Plus, it will be quicker, in case the maunstorz have become aware of Grant's hideouts. This advancement is less reliant on surprise and more on reinforcement. There are some risks with distance between supply stations, but it could save more lives in the end. At cavalry pace, you would be successful."

"That leaves me with the problem of the foot soldiers and archers."

"Your Lieutenant-Commander Terrance and Captain Woodman seem capable men to defend this post with their armies. Though I am sure they would all appreciate heading south to warmer weather as opposed to staying put to protect the capital. It's a matter of whether you wish to keep your stand here or let your forces go south as the court had. I would offer two of my *kala*, Skík Savam'eed and Cum'eri, to ride south with your forces for extra protection."

"You suggest leaving the Citadel entirely," Al'den said rather than asked.

The Shi'alam nodded. "At this point, I would. The North is entering Deep Snows, with less in the way of supplies available to us than is normal. Fewer demands would be put on our allies if we were to retreat back to Kavahad. Most of the mertinean and Starian forces are concentrated there as it is."

"This would be a temporary abandonment of the Citadel of Light," Cum'ar continued, "And I do also concur that this would lessen the strain for goods to our forces."

Al'den had thought over that very idea too, but he was reluctant to leave the most defendable fortress in all of Syre. The snows certainly didn't help the decision; Starians were unused to such phenomena as snowstorms. The prince sighed, feeling weighted down by the full immensity of all his burdens.

"This need not be decided tonight," the Shi'alam said reasonably. "My men are fresh, as am I. Take tonight to rest, Highness. The winds could bring you an answer on the morrow."

Prince Al'den was inclined to agree with the Sheev'anee leader. The day had been long with his task of sitting with his father, patrols, and meetings. *Have I even eaten three meals today?* His body was heavy with fatigue, more than ready for sleep. "Perhaps you are right." He straightened as well as he could manage and gave a respectful head-bow to the All'ani and Sheev'arid Tashek. The two desert men promised to keep a careful watch through the night and bid their prince a good and restful sleep. Al'den then took his leave to find a bed.

To the prince's surprise, his chamber was warm and cozily lit by a roaring fire. On most occasions, he went to his bed with low embers and icy sheets. The welcome relief of the heat had Al'den moving toward the fireplace before he registered the other changes to his quarters. "Ah," he sighed as his hands thawed from the cold.

"It is good to see you finally relax, my prince."

Al'den startled at the voice and turned to find Lăn'esha sitting comfortably in the high-backed chair to the fire's left. The stunning desert warrioress looked amused to have caught her lordship off guard, though she hid the look behind a hand. Standing, Lăn'esha grabbed up the tumbler of wine she had set on the table to her right. Al'den couldn't look away as the exotic woman sashayed closer and handed him the drink.

The shine in the Tashek's eyes deepened as he received the glass, his gaze captured in hers. "All'ani—"

"Just Lăna, Highness. We are alone." Al'den felt himself swallow at the implications of those words; it had been some time since he had been so sequestered with a woman. Lăn'esha continued with a smirk: "I made sure to have bread and cheese for you…and the wine, of course. As you and my brother have been at the maps for hours, I assumed you missed out on dinner. Again."

Shaking his head at being mothered, the Starian prince grinned before knocking back a large gulp of wine. He set the near-empty cup on the mantle and wiped his goatee dry before replying. "*Ahnamen*, Lăna, for the food and wine. However, this hospitality comes as a shock."

"Does it?" For just a moment, the desert woman seemed to be flirting. Or was she?

Al'den cleared his throat. "I—yes. Since we met, you've kept a respectful distance, honoring the title and station your people have granted me, your Prince of the Yellow Star."

"Yes, I have, but—" Suddenly, the alluring woman was a hair's-breadth from the prince. "I've no more wish to stay away. These past few weeks, I've seen your interest in me. I've a desire to show you my own interest in you."

Lăn'esha was close enough for Al'den to smell her lovely, rosewood perfume mixing with her sweet womanly scent. It wafted up to him as he breathed in her proximity. The royal felt his body thrill in anticipation of what Lăn'esha had just proposed; no longer did he feel fatigued. Al'den could barely get his boggled senses to say the correct things. "Lăn'esha." He tried to find his wits by taking a step away; however, her scent lingered in his nose. "I must warn you that I cannot give a woman such as yourself a happy marriage. As a prince of Staria, I will need to wed a woman of the courts."

The words would have had most ladies fuming; however, Lăn'esha found the excuse amusing. She laughed and closed the gap again. "First, my prince, I never said anything about marriage. It's much too soon for such talk. And secondly, you are much too far away from your courts to be thinking of such duties." Her eyes gave a daring flash. "All I am offering you is as much as you desire."

Prince Al'den was enraptured as the Tashek woman began a slow, backward step toward his large bed. He felt blood rush to his face as Lăn'esha made deliberate work of ridding herself of her clothing. By the time the desert maiden was at the foot of the bed, Lăn'esha was presented to her prince in all her pure, naked prowess. The warrioress saw Al'den's nostrils flare in excitement at seeing his bounty and knew she had him hooked. Taking the final step to sit on his mattress, Lăn'esha baited him one final time, "Tonight is all for you, My P—"

The word was left unfinished as Al'den captured her enticing mouth with his own. He drank Lăn'esha down as if she were the last drop of water in Syre.

§ §

"Prince Al'den!" Attendant Kellen burst through the prince's door sometime in the dead of the night. Al'den bolted awake at the intrusion. Beside him, Lăn'esha was at ready with a blade in hand. If the scene was a shock to King Merretham's attendant, Kellen made no indication if it. "Highness, you must come quick! Your father, sir!"

"How is he?" Al'den was on his feet and throwing a blanket about his shoulders as he searched for his pants. The attendant's white face had him fearing the worst. "Kellen," he repeated, "how is he?"

"Your father, sir, he's—" Kellen's voice caught, and Al'den knew the answer without the words spoken. He hastened past his father's man and sprinted barefoot down the hall to the king's chambers.

The door had been left open. He slammed it the rest of the way and rushed through the main sitting room to the bedchamber beyond. Candles lit the scene in haunting shadows. There were dark hollows, newly laid, on the elder Maushelik's features that showed an unnatural emptiness to the great king's body. Al'den's heart went cold.

"Father," he breathed and took the lifeless hand of his sire from its place on the mattress. There was the barest lingering trace of warmth. "No…no, Father. This cannot be! You've left me far too soon!" Tears came unbidden to his eyes, and Al'den felt his throat clench as he choked on the truth: King Merretham Maushelik of Staria was dead.

A comforting hand touched his shoulder, and Al'den turned to find Lăn'esha dropping to his side. Her face was somber. She stayed quiet as the prince felt the depths of his grief.

"I came for you as quickly as I could, Highness," Kellen choked out. "He was here and then gone so fast…"

The prince shook his head. "No, Kellen, it's all right. We already knew this could happen… Father and I made peace with it days ago." Still, his passing left Al'den feeling shattered.

Lăn'esha touched him again. "I will go tell the others. Stay here as long as you need." She stooped to whisper words to the dead king in Keshic and then took her leave.

Left alone, the prince let himself feel the reeling of his heart and the complete breathlessness from his grief. His father's passing changed everything. There was no going back. Al'den was uncertain of how much time passed, but when he uncurled himself from his father's bed, the sun had risen. Spent of tears and numbed, he finally addressed Kellen. "Call all the men to the courtyard. I will set the pyre myself."

"Sir." Kellen bowed stiffly and took his leave.

Prince Al'den turned his gaze from his father's lifeless body to the sun. "I know now what I must do, Father."

§ §

Prince Al'den took his time washing his father's body before he carried him the long distance to the courtyard. There, he found his men had already prepared a pyre. Reverently, the heir placed King Merretham upon the bed of sticks and stepped back.

First Guardsman Meeg Thorson, brought a torch to his prince. Al'den accepted the flame and turned to address his armies. "This morning marks the passing of King Merretham Dashēn Maushelik, king of Staria. Long had he reigned! His soul rests now in the arms of our Mother."

The warriors began to chant the king's name as Al'den lifted his torch in the air. Keshic titles for the great ruler were sung as he turned away and touched the flames to the pyre bundles. In Starian fashion, the great leader of the kingdom of sand was sent to the Stars by fire.

The great armies of Staria and the Sheev'anee watched the flames rise and burn until the last of the pyre was ashes. They stayed silent until the last of the coals burned warm. Then, as one, the leaders of each unit came forward and knelt down before their new king, the only heir of Staria. Solemn to the last man, the entire force vowed their undying allegiance to the Prince of the Yellow Star.

When the oath-gathering was complete, Al'den stood before his great force, crowned for all to see. With a final look shared between Cum'ar, Lăn'esha, and himself, King Al'den Maushelik gave his men his first decree. "Prepare yourselves, my armies of Staria. In three sunrises, we march from the Citadel of Light to meet our enemies. There will be a reckoning to pay!"

Chapter Twenty-One
§
Say My Name

Since that day on the field, majik seemed to flow easily. Zyanthena Sheev'arid found once-hard tasks were now as natural as breathing. The true heart of Vauldin's great powers had knocked open a door inside her mind and illuminated the Tashek to unlimited possibilities. Gone were her fatigue and shaking limbs; the warrioress's fluidity returned, and Zyanthena took up practicing her *kora* blade again.

That was how Lord Darshel Shekmann found her that late afternoon, in the throes of a lively practice. The fiery woman thrust in an interchange of sword maneuvers and spins. Zyanthena seemed an apparition in the open snow she had chosen to occupy. Lord Darshel found himself entranced by her display; no other fighter could still his breath as much as her.

A final jump and spin brought the Tashek around to see her audience. Zyanthena paused in her downward thrust to eye the lord-governor of Kavahad. "My Lordship," she acknowledged.

"Zy'ena," he returned.

Though Lord Darshel hid it well, he had been avoiding a closer interaction with the wielder of Vauldin since its most recent activation—not that Zyanthena blamed him. Vauldin's powers seemed to be the most awesome and fearful of the Stones of Power. Its abilities to influence not only the plain of the living but also the veil of the dead made it fearsome indeed. However, there was a feeling of lonesomeness in their interchanges that left the warrioress's chest feeling hollow. Did His Lordship feel the same?

"You need not stop on my account." Lord Darshel continued. Indeed, he hoped she wouldn't. Zyanthena was alluring on most days, but now her control and precision in the forms was nearly surreal. There was a discipline to her movements that was flawless.

"Why don't you come practice with me?" Zyanthena bade him. "I am finally able to hold myself upright. It would do these limbs of mine some good to move them properly."

Lord Darshel looked skeptical. "I am not sure I would be an adequate sparring partner for you."

"That I doubt, Your Lordship. You are a Shekmann. Certainly, you lack not in swordsmanship." Still, she removed her obsidian pendant and allowed Moon Ember to take it The two pack leaders were her constant companions and observers—and perfect guardians for the powerful stone.

The motion was not lost on Darshel. He took the removal of Vauldin to be the Tashek's gift of courtesy toward his wariness. More emboldened, the Starian cast about for his own weapon, finding a second *kora* blade among Zyanthena's discarded outer robes. He pulled the Tashek blade free of its scabbard and tested its balance.

"You will find its weight less than your Kavahadian broadswords," Zyanthena said of the weapon. "They are lighter to accommodate our speed."

"I've seen your *she-koum-o* in action and can see where it has its advantages."

Zyanthena nodded at his observation and then took up a defensive crouch as she signaled to the lord-governor to begin. Sinking into a battle-ready mind-set, Zyanthena Sheev'arid waited for the Shekmann to make the first move.

Lord Darshel swung the *kora* blade a few more times, feeling its weight and warming up his wrists as he circled his opponent. Then, striding into Zyanthena's range, he tested the woman's reactions. True to form, she met him thrust for thrust. There was no hint of hesitation or fatigue in her movements. Grinning, the Shekmann took a two-handed grip on the sword and increased his speed: downward thrust, across, parry. Uppercut, parry, diagonal slash, thrust, and parry. Darshel slowly increased his pace until they became lost in a series of attacks.

Across from him, the desert woman let loose a devilish grin as she blocked and then spun around another thrust. Zyanthena came about in a slash to his back, which Darshel blocked overhanded-and-down, following his spine. She spun back around to thrust at his exposed ribcage. That time, Lord Darshel barely managed to spin away as the second attack came quick as lightning. He came out of the spin into a parry, anticipating the downward thrust of his opponent's sword. Their blades clashed loudly in the calm morning air, and the two fighters stood staring eye-to-eye.

Zyanthena grinned at the thrill of holding a weapon again. The glint in her eyes was the only warning to her sudden, devious sweep at the lordship's ankle as she attempted to side-kick him to the snow. Lord

Darshel floundered and barely got his sword up as she thrust downward at his falling form. He rolled out of the move and readjusted to another parry at his chest. Blocking, the Shekmann found his center again and managed to block another one-two-three attack from the desert woman. They stepped around the last parry and ended up with their blades at each other's' necks. Pausing, Darshel sucked in his breath as he acknowledged her skills. "I see you haven't lost your touch."

"Neither have you, My Lordship." She bowed her head before straightening and sheathing her sword. "It feels good to have a decent sparring partner."

"Decent," Darshel repeated, with a snort. "I'm more than decent, as you well know."

"Indeed," Zyanthena agreed, not calling him out on his prior reluctance. "I look forward to further engagements. I would hate for my skills to dull over the snow seasons."

Darshel chortled. "As if that is possible, Zy'ena."

He was rewarded with a grin. "No, I guess not."

"Shall I prepare us lunch now?"

Zyanthena eyed the Shekmann, considering something, though what it could be, he could not fathom. She said, "Not yet, My Lordship. There is something I think you would like to see…"

When she didn't expound, Darshel had to ask, "And what would that be?"

The tiny, knowing smile was infuriating. "That's for me to know and you to discover."

Lord Darshel gave her an annoyed frown. Though—he had to admit—the knowledge Zyanthena knew from Queen Kestral's memories were useful. Whatever she had in mind had to stem from that knowledge. Still, that superior smile was condescending. "Again, Zyanthena, what is it?"

"Oh," she teased, "I've angered you."

"You cryptic nature has worsened since your coma."

The words amused her. "Indeed, My Lordship." She extended a hand to the *kora* blade. "I will take that and return it to my room. As for you, go through the East Wing. There you will find a staircase at the end of the hall that leads to the most unique place in the palace. I think you will find it quite to your liking."

Darshel tsked at her. “Fine, I’ll go there, but because I am curious only and not because you’re suggesting it.”

Brandy eyes danced at his tone. “Of course, My Lordship.” She gave a half-bow at the Shekmann as he started to take his leave. “I will join you shortly.”

The Kavahadian reached the location the Tashek had directed him to in about ten minutes’ walking time. It wasn’t hard to find, as the stairwell was the only feature on the wall. The rest of the eastern wall was natural bedrock. The Shekmann couldn’t help reaching out in awe to trace the perfect chiseling of the stone tunnel as it cut deeply into the obsidian and granite. Only majik could have shaped the passage so precisely. “Now, I really have to see what this is about,” Darshel murmured as he passed into the staircase. He shook his head ruefully. “She knew I would, of course. That feisty woman.”

The staircase wound down, going deeper and deeper into the bedrock; however, landings and observation windows had been carved into the left side of the tunnel, allowing in light to show the way and give a view of the outside world that was breathtaking. The eastern side of Crystanian was built right up to a thousand-foot cliff that made up the side of a deep gorge going off into the wilds of Crystalynian. All in that one glance, the snow blanketed the Forbidding Forest, which stretched endlessly onward into the Crystal Mountains.

At one particular landing, the roar of a waterfall drew Darshel closer. It was the falls from the main river that wound around the eastern flank of the palace. Coming to the large window carved behind it, the Shekmann was awed to find the powerful cascade at arm’s reach. Its powerful spray had prevented it from freezing. Being so close, he couldn’t help reaching out a palm to feel the winter-cold water. “Incredible.”

That sight would not be the most spectacular, the Starian would soon discover. Not long past the waterfall, the stairs finally ended, bringing him into an enormous, natural cavern, open on the far side—one hundred and sixty feet across—to more of the gorge. It was not the expanse that had the Kavahadian stopping in astonishment, however. It was the curtain of steam he walked into. Breathing deeply of the warm, moist, air, he came the rest of the way into the palace’s hot spring baths. “Now this is luxury!” he said, and laughed out in wonder.

Despite the fact that the palace was kept decently warm against the freezing temperatures outside, Lord Darshel was desert-born and had yet to shake the cold from his bones. However, one touch of the spring's water and the lord knew he would finally feel back to normal. It took him only the time to strip naked before he was shoulder-deep in the hot pool. "Ah," he groaned and sank back against the stone side of the pool. "This is glorious!" Darshel basked in the heat as it unworked muscles he hadn't realized were sore.

Minutes slipped by in comfortable silence. Then: "I see it took you no time to partake of Crystanian's best feature."

Darshel shifted and searched around for Zyanthena in the mist. "By the Stars, woman, you could have told me these existed ages ago!"

As sweet laugh answered him. "Yes, but everything has its own time. I, for one, was not ready to make the distance here until now." The lord-governor followed the sound of her voice until he made out the Tashek's shape coming toward him out of the mist, across the length of the pool.

The desert beauty let the shawl wrapped around her shoulders slowly slide down to the floor, revealing that all else had been removed. Zyanthena made her way to the edge of the pool with all the grace of a wild predator and paused at the edge to meet Lord Darshel's emerald stare. In return, the Shekmann found he could not take his eyes from her as the warrioress's lithe body was revealed to him. Somehow, he felt it would be rude to look away from that daring gaze.

"Zy—"

Zyanthena shook her head, breaking the spell, and stepped into the pool. Boldly, she came closer. "There is a tension between us that has yet to be addressed." The desert woman stopped just out of the Kavahadian's reach.

Darshel blinked. Was he reading the situation correctly? There had to be a trap in this sudden offering. After four months of his pursuit, there was no way her behavior meant what his thoughts had jumped to. "Zy'ena, I'm not sure—?"

"I'm referring to how you look at me now, since my reawakening. I see it in your eyes: your fear of me and what I've become. No longer am I the Tashek you captured. I am the heir of Crystalynian and wielder of Vauldin." His Lordship swallow nervously at the reminder. "I much preferred us as we were becoming. There was a respect and camaraderie from the trials we've endured."

"I didn't mean to make you feel that way." Darshel felt himself trying to shrink back against the stones of the side and cursed his weakness. Only this woman could disarm him so!

Brandy eyes narrowed. "And yet you do." A look came to his eyes that mirrored that of a trapped animal's panic. His chiseled features pinched and he licked his lips absently in his discomfort.

"What is it you wish me to correct, Zyanthena?" His voice was just as haggard as he looked.

"I would have you see me as a woman again, that woman you wished to conquer, My Lordship."

"Trust me, *shika*," he said, using the polite Keshic word for woman. "It is not possible that I cannot see you as a woman. But we don't need to—"

"Lord Darshel Shekmann of Kavahad never backs down from a lady's invitation."

"You are more than a lady." Even to his ears, the rebuttal sounded weak, so Darshel tried again. "Zyanthena, what you are asking...this is more than a lady's invitation." The lord-governor knew it from the daring in her domineering eyes. "*Paramour* is the term of your people. I think you mean me to be that. Certainly, you can't demand this today and then expect it to only be this once." There were still two seasons of snows to keep them trapped together at the palace, after all, and afterward, all the travel time after the snows melted.

"On that you are correct. This would have to be seen as a contract of paramours. Anything less would be debasing of such a pact." Those perceptive eyes held him breathless. Lord Darshel could have sworn she was reaching down to touch his very soul. "What I must know is, why you are so unnerved? Is it my power—or the possibility of congress you've waited for so long becoming real?" She seemed to loom closer until those brown eyes took up all his attention. "Which is it?"

"Neither, Zyanthena." The formal use of her name set the desert woman back. Just like that, the spell of her hold seemed to break and she pulled away.

Without her stare's influence, Lord Darshel could think. The lord-governor motioned for the Tashek to sink into the water and let it cover her nakedness. That she complied showed her willingness to talk it out. "Trust me when I say this: I am very interested in you. I have been since you were first 'chained' to me." He echoed the words she had used at their beginning. "If anything, my attraction has grown since I've come to know you—but so has my respect. To be paramour… I don't think we are there yet," he admitted with a stolid shake of his head. Zyanthena looked ready to argue his words, so Lord Shekmann reached out to cup her cheek.

The Tashek's eyes widened in shock at the sudden, gentle contact. "My—my Lordship?"

There, there it was. The reason for his hesitation. Lord Darshel could see, then, that Zyanthena's bravery was still stronger than her desire, and that was not how the Shekmann wanted the exotic woman of his dreams. "If I do this—if *we* do this—you will call me by my name."

Her eyebrows rose at his order, but it was clear the request was considered. "Very well… Darshel." His name slid off Zyanthena's tongue like honey. The way she said it made the Shekmann feel warm and his body thrilled with anticipation. Only her way of pronunciation could elicit such a feeling.

It strengthened Lord Darshel's resolve that his intuition was right: they weren't quite ready to become more intimate. "Thank you, Zy'ena. For your respect, I give mine in return. We will not do this. I will not be your paramour." Zyanthena opened her mouth to protest. "Shh." He silenced her with his thumb across her lips. "Zy'ena, your request must go both ways. I understand its need. I do admit I have been avoiding you more than I should. It's my fault, my apprehension's fault. However, I cannot grant you this as long as you do not also see me as a man, I mean. I have my own wants and needs, and, in this, I want to be selfish."

Lord Darshel removed his hand and scooted back, leaving her blinking in ambivalence. "Seeing as I have ruined the moment, I am going to retire to my quarters. Take your time here. I will make lunch when you have had your fill."

"My L—" Zyanthena cut herself off. "Darshel, you need not leave."

The tall Starian had been exiting the pool, but her words had him pausing. Keeping himself partially turned away, he replied to the desert woman, with a chuckle to lighten the mood, "Yes, Zyen, I do. The sight of you coming to me as you have has excited me more than you need to know. If I stay, my resolve will crumble. I go to prevent that."

He was rewarded with a smug, knowing smile that carried all the way to her lovely eyes. "Very well… I think I understand."

Darshel nodded and continued away to collect his clothes and depart from the temptation she presented. He left the woman of his desires alone in the heat and steam of Crystanian's baths.

Chapter Twenty-Two
§
Playing Decoy

"Commander! Commander Grant!"

The leader in question was startled from his morning tea. It was barely light outside, and already the camp's peace was disturbed. "Stars and tarnation! Ensign, what is all this racket?"

Ensign Tyler Cabet apologized with a salute—a little behind protocol. "Commander, sir, apologies. We have another bird from the Citadel, sir. Scout Re'shaird said you'd want to read it immediately."

The mertinean was on his feet in an instant. "Well, don't just stand there. Lead on, boy!"

"Sir, yes, sir."

Bemoaning his yet-to-be-eaten breakfast, Commander Grant settled for grabbing a buttered toast and his coffee and followed his overexuberant ensign across the camp to the small trail leading up the canyon. Hoofing it up the snow-packed walk, they finally reached the top where the Tashek man was settling the falcons. Commander Grant huffed out a cloud of air at his exertion but made it to the desert man's side.

Aerrisson was still calming their newest messenger bird; its mate was beside the falcons on a gnarled old tree, blindfolded by a leather cloth and tethered. The Tashek continued to coo to the large bird of prey on his forearm as he fed it pieces of fish. He did acknowledge the mertinean leader with, "Good morning, Commander."

"What was so urgent to send this boy running and hollering all through camp?" Even to his own ears, Grant sounded grumpy.

"Trust me, Commander, you wouldn't want this to wait one second," Aerrisson replied as he stroked the falcon's chest. "Ensign, leave us."

Young Cabet gave the Tashek man a sharp salute and headed off. Aerrisson waited until they were alone before setting his falcon on the tree and tethering it. He turned back to the commander and waved him to a seat overlooking the canyon. "This missive is from the Citadel again." He handed over the parchment.

From the scout's actions, Commander Grant sensed the words were different from the last missive. He gave Aerrisson a look before settling in to reading it. By the time he was done, his greying eyebrows had risen nearly to his hairline. "His Majesty King Merretham has died!"

Aerrisson nodded. "The Prince of the Yellow Star now commands all the armies of Staria and those of the North still in his borders. He no longer wishes to sit idly by in the Citadel while we are stuck in this snow-laden state. He understands our precarious position being chased out of Raven's Den. If we can make it just over one hundred klicks north–northwest of here, they can rendezvous with us at the Senna River."

Commander Grant reread the letter. "This says he is sending ahead one of the Sheev'anee groups to meet with us ahead of him and reinforce our men and mounts."

"Yes." Aerrisson pointed out the name. "Skík Savam'eed and his nephew, Kăt'ta."

Commander Grant was already thinking. "How fast can the Sheev'anee travel?"

"Without snow, they would be here in five suns. With deep snows… about a fortnight to twenty suns."

"Staria's deserts shouldn't be as snow-packed as we are on the east side of the Red Hills."

"They have better mounts, too."

"Good point." Grant didn't take offense to the fact. It was true, after all. "Let me see your map." Aerrisson handed it over, and they hunkered down over the leather map checking angles and distances—as they knew the Citadel would be doing the same. "If we assume your horsemen will travel faster than us—"

"Then we had best head straight west of here, and we should hit the Senna forty klicks north of the East Bridge. From there, we would follow the river north."

"That seems possible."

"However, we have a few issues they do not."

"Being skeptical again, I see," Grant teased.

"Practical," Aerrisson argued. "We are down a handful of horses, and a number of the men are wounded. This route is shortest to the Senna, but we still have to consider the possibility of the maunstorz tracking us, especially once our raids stop." At least to Aerrisson, Silvarron seemed the kind of leader to scout out a silenced enemy.

"What do you have in mind?" Commander Grant knew the Tashek was still thinking of their previous conversation a week before.

"This may slow your forces down too much, but if I take a large enough number of horses with me and trek south, I can make it look as if we have abandoned our camps in hopes of reaching the Red Palace. If we leave some equipment strewn about—as if we left in haste—it might work."

"It would work better if we left some corpses behind. A number of the fallen have gone from gangrene and illness. It would look like we were running from a plague."

Aerrisson actually blanched at the detail—something the mertinean man had not expected of the Tashek. "You would really court such a thought?"

"I can be practical too, Re'shaird, and I've lived through more of this war than you. My experience tells me we need the maunstorz to buy our ruse. I will not do this on half measures."

The words gave the desert man pause. "Yes. I can see that."

Commander Grant stood. "We will prepare immediately. I want you in charge of the horses. Pick out those you can use as we pack essentials. I leave it to your discretion on if sending a bird can be risked."

"On that, I will wait three days before sending a bird, and I will take the less able horses. They will be loaded down to mimic human weight. I will trek south two suns and then turn westward and circle back around. The horses will be loosed where I can guarantee their survival."

"So be it." Grant handed back the missive. "We will leave by first light tomorrow morning. Until then, I will have runners communicate with the camps. Once you have your horses, I would like you to keep a watch on Raven's Den."

"That I will do."

"See you at lunch," Grant said in parting and left the Tashek to his orders.

§ §

Aerrisson rose well before the sun and packed up the last of his tent and essentials, which he put on a pack horse hitched beside Lunier. Then, he took special care to check over his dark-grey mount's body and tack; with Lunier, he would take no chances on ruining the horse's endurance. The others were looked over as well, but only his steed and pack horse were critical for his forthcoming trek. Satisfied that all was as it should be, Aerrisson wandered away from his herd of horses to check on the mertinean.

In the torchlight, the main mertinean camp looked to be in scattered disarray, though most of that was intentional. The last details were coming together as the groups of mertinean met back up with their commander. The remaining one hundred and ninety men from Raven's Den were surrounding their great war veteran when Aerrisson arrived.

"There you are," Commander Grant said as way of greeting as the desert man slipped his way fluidly to his side. "All is organized here. How is it on your end?"

"Ready to go. I'll just wait for you to all take your leave." Aerrisson had wanted to make sure the soldiers' passage was as erased as they could make it. It wouldn't do for their force to be easily followed. To that end, the horses the mertinean were to use had been tethered a quarter of a mile deeper into the Red Hills. The men would hike there following in each other's footsteps, and the last of the men would be responsible for covering the tracks as well as possible. Once the men were safely away, Aerrisson would let loose the remaining horses and push them south.

All of it depended on the mertinean leaving soon, however, before maunstorz patrols were out and about.

"We're going then," Commander Grant assured. "You just make sure you stay safe, lad." He extended a hand to Aerrisson. "I expect to see you in five days' time."

"At the latest," Aerrisson promised. Despite the fact that the Tashek did not usually shake hands, he accepted Grant's handshake. He respected the mertinean commander enough to dismiss tradition.

Commander Grant called out to his force to proceed. They left Aerrisson standing there in the mess of their camp until the last man made the top of the canyon. Grant paused one last time at that point to wave the Tashek off, and then the last of the mertinean disappeared over the ridge.

The sudden silence had Aerrisson feeling unusually fidgety. Turning away, the Tashek warrior busied himself cleaning away the last of the tracks on his side of the canyon. He used branches of coniferous trees to brush the signs away. Luckily, the canyon was a natural wind trap. The continual gusts helped stir the snow to settle over the imprints.

It was just before the rising of the sun, when the skyline was beginning to lighten, when Aerrisson finished his work and returned to the horses. He freed them all, except for Lunier and the pack horse, and then mounted.

The herd began their trudge south before the sky was full of dawn's colors.

§ §

Hours into the morning, the first of the maunstorz scouts came across the evidence of the horses. They signaled back to their main force and began to follow the deep tracks back to the source. It was just after lunch when Silvarron and his force came to the deep canyon the mertinean had made their home base.

The long-limbed second-in-command removed his snowshoes and surveyed the disarrayed campsite with discerning eyes. His crow came back to its usual perch from its once-over pass about the canyon; it carried a dropped buckle in its beak. Silvarron held out a hand to accept the silver piece of metal. "Search the camp," he ordered of three of his men. Two more he sent to further investigate the surrounding area. Another group was out looking for other campsites—their leader suspected others to be about.

Fingering the buckle absentmindedly, the charismatic maunstorz strode slowly up the camp's main trail, taking in the neglected equipment and abandoned corpses of humans and horses. He toed the closest one. "Vsenk!" he called out, and all his fighters paused to listen. "Esh elothēem! Jē calr vulth!" *My people, do not touch anything! These people are sick!*

His well-disciplined force was quick to respond. They carefully handled the rest of their investigations, using the ends of their weapons. With danger averted, Silvarron bent over a corpse and studied it with the same care. Once he had satisfied his curiosity, he continued deeper into the camp, all the way to the ridge of the canyon. Standing at the top, he found evidence of falcons and boot prints of at least four people. The spot had an excellent view of the canyon and Red Hills—all the way to the distant Raven's Den, a dark spot far beyond.

"They had a perfect vantage point," he murmured. His crow, Kautch, seemed to agree. Silvarron petted him to settle his cawing and then let the bird occupy itself with a falcon feather. He, meanwhile, continued to ponder the enemy's camp and the tracks leading away.

His second returned to him and gave a breast salute and bent a knee.

"Report," Silvarron ordered. The maunstorz began to speak in their tongue. "In Syrean-basic, man! Our Mansocan demands us to learn their words."

The second dropped his head, chastised, and began again in choppy Syrean: "All găne. Trăck sauth all hărse."

"Horse," he corrected.

"Hoarse. Thirty-two vulth."

"Sick," Silvarron supplied.

"S-seek. S-săven caumps faunt." The second pointed where the other camps had been found. Their distances, he indicated by hand signals.

"Other tracks?"

The second shook his head. Silvarron waved him away, silently taking pity on the man's poor language skills. He had learned enough to make a general assessment, anyway. "Kautch, it seems our prey goes toward our leader. Certainly, they must think their capital is safe? But…" He eyed the surrounding area. "One of them was clever." He stopped the absentminded jingling of the silver buckle and lifted it for his crow to capture again. "Vsenk!" he called out to his forces milling around below. "Runners return to Mansocan. An enemy force may be heading south." He pointed to his second. "You, go with them, with thirty men. Track the horses. The rest will stay with me. We explore these hills!"

§ §

Aerrisson finally stopped the horses in a small valley. The herd settled quickly, foraging for grass beneath the snowy ground while their herd-master turned his two mounts to settle under a tree.

The Tashek took his time checking out Lunier and the pack horse, making sure their legs were not showing signs of injury and that the tack was not rubbing. The two falcons, also, seemed to be faring well in their cage atop the pack horse. The birds of prey returned to napping after a meal of fish and snake meat while Aerrisson removed the cage from the pack horse's back. Afterward, he allowed the two horses to forage while he settled himself with a meal of jerky, dates, and pieces of hardened bread. As he ate, Aerrisson reviewed his route south, using the sun and landmarks to calculate how far he had travelled: seven klicks through the snow was a good amount of distance on horseback. "I wonder if the maunstorz took the bait?" he murmured.

Not sure if he would see anything through the trees, the desert man still attempted to scope out the situation. He shinnied up a tall pine tree until he reached the highest branch to hold his weight and then carefully took out a spy glass. All around were the vast forests and rounds of Red Hills. Steadying himself and slowly adjusting his scope, Aerrisson looked back the way he had come.

The horses' tracks were a blaring testimony to his whereabouts. That the maunstorz wouldn't follow at some point seemed preposterous; however, for the time being, there was no sign of pursuit. Even with a packed-down trail, the afoot maunstorz had to be having some difficulty caching up. Still, it wouldn't be good to give them too much time to make up the distance…

Aerrisson stayed on guard long enough to give the horses time to eat and rest. By midafternoon, the desert man climbed back down the tree and called Lunier and the pack horse to him. "Time to go, my wings," he murmured to the grey. "We go until sundown." It was quick work retacking the two horses.

Re'shaird, Aerrisson looked back one last time, feeling uneasy at being unable to see across the Red Hills; the landscape certainly wasn't the wide expanses of the Aras Desert. He settled himself atop the desert war charger, clearing his mind for the task at hand, and took up the pack horse's lead in his off hand. It was time to continue pushing the horses south. With luck, time would soon show that the maunstorz had taken the bait—Grant's forces counted on it. For now, the warrior had to bid himself patience and continue with their plans. "Farther south, Lunier. Let's go!"

Chapter Twenty-Three
§
Finding

The sight that greeted the four Guardians of the Prism was startling. Transformed were the arid desert and deep arroyos of the Ar'heim. What waited beyond was not golden sand but crisp, white snow dusting the entire Aras as far as the eye could see. "W-what?" J'iya said for them all.

"We had heard of the snows brought on by Ravel," En'ril said as he reached out to scoop up some of the cold substance in his palms. "But this is more than I had expected. Rare is snow in the Aras…"

Terrik gazed out at the never-ending, inch-deep blanket of white with narrowed eyes. "This bodes ill for the health of Syre's people and crops."

"At least with Vauldin awoken, we have a strong ally to combat Ravel's majik."

"There is no guarantee Zy'ena can control it to the extent needed to counter these snows," Terrik replied to his cousin.

"You doubt Sheev'arid Zyanthena?" En'ril sounded shocked. Terrik didn't give a reply, just a sour frown.

"Zee will be able to," Decond said with certainty. Only he, mountain-born and acclimated to the cold, found the snows of little concern. He had led his horse out a little farther into the white Aras to study the snow's depth. Despite it being a shock to find after the sheltered Ar'heim, he didn't see it as being a problem, at least in Staria. The desert's heat looked to be winning its own accord—without any magical influences; at least, Decond could sense that through Sevén's connection. Nature was taking back its natural course against the abnormal snows set down by one of the Stones of Power.

"I like your *Khapta*'s optimism," En'ril teased Terrik. "It's a nice counter to your sullenness."

Terrik tsked and then strode over to his apprentice. "Decond, we need to search out the other stones."

He had no idea how to go about that, but still, he pulled out the pearl from its place on a chain around his neck. He unclasped it and took hold of the ring, feeling its warmth in his palm. "What do you want me to do?"

En'ril and J'iya came over too. "The Oracle said to try a scrying method using a map of Syre." En'ril produced a leather map and unrolled it at Decond's feet. "She thought that if you reached for Zyanthena again, you could become familiar with how the pendulum-scrying works. From there, you could try for Serein—as we know where she should be."

Decond took a cross-legged seat in the snow and held the chain and ring over the map. "Like this?"

"Yes." En'ril adjusted his hand so that the pearl was centered over the map. "From here, keep your hand still and close your eyes. Seek out Zyanthena and Vauldin as you did before."

It sounded simple enough—in theory. Decond already knew what the signatures of his friend and the obsidian stone felt like. Centering himself as he had been taught, he reached deep into a calming trance and searched outward for that link again. That space felt empty at first, but then, the familiar connection with Zyanthena started to grow. *Show me your location*, Decond commanded in his mind.

J'iya gasped at Decond's right shoulder. "He did it!"

Decond opened his ice-blue eyes to find Sevén had shifted of its own accord to point toward Crystalynian. Readjusting his arm slowly allowed the pearl to gravitate until it was straight over the capital, Crystanian.

Terrik frowned at his *Khapta*. "You're not just doing that because you know where she is, right?"

"Terrik." En'ril elbowed his cousin's side. "Decond's not one to cheat or show off." To Decond, he said, "That was a good start. Did you make sense of it?"

"I felt how to use Sevén." Decond wrapped a hand behind his neck, rubbing it self-consciously in embarrassment. "But finding Zee is easy. I'm not as confident about the other stones."

"You won't know until you try," En'ril encouraged. "You may find Serein similarly easy. After all, you have met the Prince of Sealand before."

"Yes." Decond remembered Par Fantill's openness and honesty. The Sealand heir had been anything but pompous; he had treated even the lowly orphan with kindness. Such a person did leave an impression in the mind. "I can try," the farrier-turned-Guardian said as he centered himself again. "Sorry if this takes me a few minutes."

A few minutes it might have been, but Sevén seemed pleased with Decond's control, for the pearl was excited to reach out to Serein. Much in the way that the moon could control the tides of the ocean, Sevén called out, and Serein moved to answer. Almost, Decond could feel the Prince of the Evening Star beyond his stone's powers. "Here," he said confidently and pointed at Fortress Opal. Once he had, though, he frowned. "Prince Par went home?"

"Yes." Terrik straightened from his crouch, satisfied with his *Khapta*'s work. "It was thought best for him to be away from the North—away from Ravel. The *Khataum* guards him."

"The *Khataum*?"

"Commander Matar."

"Ah." Decond gave Terrik's usual response back at his Guardian. The Tashek man didn't seem to notice. "Well, it felt like Prince Par has been working with Serein. I couldn't touch him, like I did Zee, but I could sense him…"

"That's impressive," En'ril praised sincerely.

"Can you sense any other stones?" J'iya asked excitedly. "They should be coming awake one by one."

"Well…" Decond didn't know any of the other wielders; he didn't think reaching out be easy.

"Sevén knows the imprints of every stone," Terrik reminded him. "If you trust in that, you should be able to find each one, even those without wielders. That's why the Oracle was tasked with guarding Sevén in the first place—so it could call the Stones of Power together."

"We'll give you time." En'ril touched Decond on the shoulder before standing. "You just do whatever you need to do to find them all. No rush."

The three Tashek backed off, then, taking Decond's horse with then, and allowed the *Khapta* all the room he needed. Left to his own devices, the young mountain-born stared down at the leather map and recentered himself. He closed his eyes and concentrated on slowing his breathing so that he could communicate with Sevén. Stilling, Decond allowed himself to fall into the pearl's calming warmth…

§ §

"That's all of them," Decond called out as he opened his eyes. To his shock, he came back to the world to find it nighttime. A quarter moon softly bathed the snow in a blue-white glow. "Stars, it's evening!"

J'iya was the first to shift from the campfire the three Tashek had made. He hurried over to Decond's side with a cup of hot tea. "You were dead to the world. We almost thought you were asleep, except you'd move your other hand now and then to place markers." The markers in question had been objects Decond had on his person: a small crystal he'd brought from the Crystal Kingdom, a shell from Port Al-Harrad, a pense coin, a leather cord, a small ointment tin, a farrier nail, a goose feather the length of his thumb, and a pocket watch: eight objects for the eight stones.

Terrik and En'ril had joined them. "You've finished?" Terrik asked.

"I think so." Still, it was hard to tell if he was right. Some of the objects fit over a large area.

"Tell us what you felt," En'ril encouraged.

Decond nodded and adjusted the blanket they had placed around him at some point. "So, I think this is how it is. The feather is Amun—at least in my mind, I see Staria's citrine associated with birds. I sense it here, just east of Kavahad." The two Guardians frowned at each other but didn't interrupt. "The ointment is Sevén, here where we are, and Vauldin is the pocket watch at Crystanian. It was a gift from Zee on my latest birthday. From there, I feel Serein—the shell—at Fortress Opal along with… I think it's Kevel? The pense represents Sunrise in my mind. The crystal is just east of us, between the Citadel and Ar'heim. The nail feels like Bellor in my mind. It's here at the Crystal Castle…that's weird, right?" Decond commented. The others agreed. "Well… lastly, I think this is Sheveth—the leather cord piece—located here between the two splits of the Senna River in Rubia."

Terrik eyed the map skeptically. "Are you sure about all this?"

"Um, it's not like I've had any experience," he defended himself. "But I did just spend the day letting Sevén guide me."

"I don't think your *Khapta* is wrong," En'ril said, siding with Decond. "His placement of Serein, Sevén, and Vauldin are all accurate."

"Yeah, but Sheveth is in the middle of nowhere, and Amun and Kevel aren't where they should be. Stars, look at where he's put Bellor! The jade stone's at the Crystal Castle for Stars' sake!"

"I'm more worried about how close Ravel is to us. We should move away from here as soon as possible."

Terrik didn't look convinced, but he did agree their enemy was too close for comfort. "Mark those locations, Decond. You'll check them again once we've gotten to Paragon. For now, let's ride southward, away from Ravel." The Sheev'arid turned away to begin packing.

"You did well," En'ril praised before he too turned away.

"Thanks," Decond mumbled as he began marking where Sevén had shown the stones' locations to be.

"Cheer up!" J'iya encouraged. "You've felt all the Stones of Power. I'll wager you're right and they're all in those spots. Sheev'arid and Savam'eed are just worried because they're not where they expected them to be. But that's not your fault."

"Thanks, J'iya." Decond gave his fellow *Khapta* a smile and watched the lithe youth skip away to his horse. Then, he shifted from where he sat, finding his body protesting at having been frozen in one shape for hours. "Ai, this really bites!" he whined as stiff legs uncurled. "I hope this doesn't happen all the time. I'll feel like a cripple if this keeps up!"

§ §

Evening in Crystalynian was quiet in the near-abandoned palace. Lord Darshel found himself feeling alone; somehow, even the pestering wolves and their alluring master were leaving him be. Perturbed, he searched out Zyanthena only to find her not in her rooms. Ever since Vauldin had awoken to its full powers, the Tashek woman had been studying with a fury in her quarters of the library, seeming to find new books to consume right and left. Where could the heir of Crystanian have gone to this time? Back to the mountains of tomes, or soaking in the hot springs? There was, of course, a third possibility that Zy'ena had gone to visit Unrevealed. Of the choices, the library was closest, so Lord Darshel tried there first.

As luck would have it, Sheev'arid Zyanthena was in the enormous library. The entire pack of wolves were lazing about the floor level while the desert woman read an old tome by candlelight. It was quite the sight, that lone warrioress amid the furry shapes of the predators and the flickering shadows from the candles against the towers of bookshelves. "Zy'ena."

Keen eyes rose from the text to become shadowed orbs in the light. "Darshel." Her voice thrummed against the lord-governor's eardrums in a seductive caress.

He neared the table. "It's late."

Her eyebrows rose. "Is it? I've lost track of time." She leaned back in her chair and stretched. The casual pose took away the illusion of otherworldliness around her.

"I suspect it is nearing the middle of the night. Aren't you tired?"

"Aren't you?" Zyanthena redirected in typical fashion.

"Woman," Lord Darshel growled in protest as he came around the heavy pine table, "Stop evading my questions."

Zyanthena smirked. "Temper, my Lord Shekmann." She looked amused.

The Kavahadian decided to ignore her teasing. "What had you so preoccupied this time?"

"I've found a book inside a hidden compartment in the walls," Zyanthena replied. Darshel's eyes narrowed at the news. "From what I can place, it's as old as the start of the Second Age. There are things written here of a Syre you would not believe." She turned the book so the Shekmann could see the page she was on. "The Second Age was a golden age for majik. The Stones of Power were held by the first rulers of Syre and used to assist the people with day-to-day troubles."

He said, "This says they used Sheveth to create a well in a town that couldn't find water...and here, Serein was used to shift the tides when some ships got beached after a storm..."

"And here, Ravel was used to create rain when a year was too dry."

Lord Darshel shook his head. "A part of me thinks this all so preposterous—but then again, I've seen some of the things you can do with Vauldin."

"In that age, the stones were seen as bringers of prosperity and relief. It wasn't until the end of the Second Age that they were used for more nefarious means: battle, espionage, mind control..."

The last words had the lord-governor making a face. "Leave it to the human condition to create such vile ideas."

Zyanthena murmured an agreement. "Had we kept away from such actions, the populace would never have condemned their majiks. Fear drove Syreans to protest their use and demand they be destroyed."

"Can the stones be destroyed?"

"On that, I cannot say. I haven't come across any texts that speak of such, but they can, obviously, become dormant." She shifted to face the Shekmann. "Why do you ask? Do you wish to destroy them?"

His emerald eyes assessed her critically; she had clasped Vauldin unconsciously when he had made the suggestion. It seemed the wielder was already very attached to the stone and its powers. "I don't, but even you can agree it may be smart to know if that is a possibility. People do very stupid and evil things with power. You never know if such knowledge would become necessary."

Zyanthena nodded in agreement. "Yes, but that the Stones of Power have existed for over two hundred or so known years may be evidence enough that they cannot be destroyed. That doesn't mean that I don't understand your caution. Syre has been without their majiks for some time now. I can't say that's been a bad thing. The more I read, the more I worry of what could happen if one of the wielders does use them inappropriately." The warning of what had happened to her mother, Queen Kestral, was clearly in the forefront of the Tashek's mind.

Darshel recognized that look in her eye. He touched Zyanthena gently on the shoulder so that she looked at him, and then he crouched down to take hold of her hands. "I cannot lie to you, Zy'ena. These stones do not seem worth the risks of using them, and mostly certainly, some of what I read scares me. Yet I know you well enough to trust you will be discerning in your use of Vauldin. Perhaps we have to trust in the goodness of the wielders and believe the stones will not go to a person undeserving of such power."

A wan smile came to the Tashek's lips at his words. The sad look made the Shekmann squeeze her hands more firmly. He said, "Come. I think you are ready for bed. Sleep should soften your mood."

"It is amusing to see you be a caretaker."

"Yes, I know all about your pastime of making fun of me," Darshel replied.

"No," Zyanthena shook her head. "I mean it. The great lord-governor of Kavahad waiting on a Sheev'anee is quite the sight."

Lord Darshel huffed and pulled her to her feet. "And I'm sure my father is rolling in his grave about all I've done for you. At least we are far away from Kavahad. My people would be having a laugh over all this."

Zyanthena chuckled. "Still… *ahnamen*, Darshel. I do appreciate the assistance."

"Yes, well…" For just a moment the Shekmann was embarrassed at her gratitude. "For now, it's a little one-sided, but I guess that's to be expected."

"I did offer you—"

He cut her off. "I know, Zyen. I just don't think we are ready for that."

For once, Zyanthena didn't make a wisecrack at the rogue of a Shekmann for losing his nerve. Instead, her keen brandy eyes studied the man before her, as if reaching into his soul. "My Lordship." She ducked her head into a bow and then turned to collect the old tome. "To bed it is, then. More discoveries can wait until the light of day."

§ §

"Here, breakfast is ready." Lord Darshel plopped a plate before the distracted Tashek. Blinking herself back to the present, Zyanthena pushed aside the old Syrean text—so it didn't become soiled—then looked over the meal of eggs over-easy, potatoes, and polenta. "Our meals get more sophisticated by the week."

Darshel chuckled. "I'm getting better at cooking, and the palace's stores are never-ending." He set his own plate across from hers and settled onto the bench. "What distracted you this time?" he asked, tapping the book.

Since he had found her that morning, Zyanthena had been nose-deep in the ancient secrets of Syre's Second Age. It seemed the knowledge within its pages was new to even Queen Kestral's memories. "There is so much from the Second Age that was lost to us. Their uses for water storage, irrigation, removal of refuse, and advances in medicine were intriguing. Half these seem improbable in today's world."

"I'm not sure what the benefit is on looking back at the past as you are, especially if it has no place in our time."

Zyanthena made a face. "A lot of it would be helpful—once I figure out how it worked."

"But you're using majik. The citizens would not be."

"Actually, a lot if this doesn't need majik. At least, once it's constructed."

"Well, that's news…" Darshel wondered when he would stop being surprised by it all. There was too much to take in.

"There's something else, too," Zyanthena continued. "The book says there was a way all the stone bearers could travel across Syre in the blink of an eye—beyond the use of Ravel's powers. Something to do with the stone obelisks throughout the kingdoms, set at 'strategic interception points.' It makes me wonder…"

"I'm not sure I like that glint in your eyes." Darshel pointed his fork at Zyanthena.

She gave an innocent look. "What? It's just a thought. I've seen these obelisks, like the one here, in the queen's garden." The area in question had been revealed a week before as the snows had receded.

"That can wait until you've eaten. Seriously, woman, your food is growing cold!" Zyanthena laughed at the lord-governor's frustration, but she did take the not-so-subtle hint to start eating. Lord Darshel gave a satisfied nod as she stuffed a forkful of food into her mouth. "All of it, or you're not leaving the table to your experiments."

"Yes, Mother." An irked eyebrow rose, making her grin widen. She cleared her throat after swallowing and faked being more contrite. "I'll eat it all. Promise."

Lord Darshel harrumphed and continued with his breakfast.

True to her word, Zyanthena finished all her food—because she had been starving—before standing and hand-washing all the dishes. After completing the task, Zyanthena turned to find Darshel collecting the old tome from the table. "I know what you're off to do," he commented as he held the book aloft and twisted it about in his wrist. "So, I will join you. Stars know what kind of trouble you'll dig up on your own."

"Me? I'm only going to look at the obelisk."

"Yes, with the stone Vauldin along, I'm sure nothing could possibly happen." His voice dripped with sarcasm.

Brown eyes rolled as Zyanthena reached for the tome. "I'm just looking. There's no harm in that." She started out of the kitchen, her constant wolf shadows at her heels. Darshel sighed and shook his head before following the Sheev'anee outside to the garden.

It wasn't hard to imagine what wonders had grown in the queen's garden; there were bare dried plants and trees throughout the large courtyard, now revealed after the snow had melted. Untouched by human hands for a quarter of a century, the plants had somehow thrived on their own accord and spread outside the normal borders of their planters.

In the center of the enormous courtyard was the object of Zyanthena's latest obsession: the towering, obsidian obelisk, remnant of a time long gone. "Van'allíer," Zyanthena murmured the name her mother had called the structure. Ignoring everything else, the Tashek neared it as if entering a place of reverence. Behind her, the wolves settled around the courtyard to sleep or nose about. Completely forgotten, Lord Darshel found a wooden bench to sit back upon and set his emerald eyes on the woman's back as she walked toward the old stone formation.

Zyanthena finally reached the obelisk and touched it respectfully. Up close, Van'allíer's surface was not smooth, as it had looked from afar, but runed in ancient Syrean symbols. The heir of Crystalynian traced the marks with her fingertips as she slowly circled the stone structure. Somehow, old words began to come to her, and Zyanthena whispered them under her breath as she walked. An image of Rast'enn, the crystal obelisk that stood at the first cobbles leading to the Crystal Castle—accessed by her memories as Princess Zerra—flashed across her vision.

Suddenly, the runes felt warm under her touch. The feeling was followed by a glow as the ruins went alight in response to her intonation and Vauldin's magical influence. In the blink of an eye, Zyanthena felt Van'allíer's powers activate. Just as quickly, she felt her body being sucked into its glow. Another blink and she was just—gone.

"Zy'ena!" Lord Darshel was on his feet and running at the obelisk as Zyanthena was lit in a glowing light and then pulled into the stone, all within a single breath. His hands slapped the obsidian surface as the last traces of power left the runes. "Damn it!" he swore loudly. He had known it was a bad idea to let her near the ancient pillar. And now, she had vanished within it, to whatever end he could not guess at! Choking back his anger and despair, Darshel pounded his fists against the obelisk until he had exhausted himself of emotion.

Powerless, he turned about to lean against the hard stone and slid until he was sitting at its base. To his surprise, Moon Ember and her mate came near to lick his face and hands, as if offering him solace. Lord Darshel allowed it for a short time and then pushed their muzzles away. Still, the wolves remained and came to lie beside him. Alone in their care, the lord-governor said to them, as he stroked Ember's hair, "Now she's gone and done it!" He felt tears well up, unbidden. He tried to wipe them away before they fell. "Stars, what does this mean now? Damn it, Zy'ena, at least take me with you when you leave!"

As if the wolves agreed, they all mingled around Van'allíer and howled to the sky, echoing Lord Darshel's fears.

Chapter Twenty-Four
§
Letters

The prince's entourage made it back to Sardon at dusk. After their overnight trip to Greendale, Lord-Commander Ivance insisted the heir of Golden return to Sardon and await reports of safe travel to the capital—not that there needed to be such concerns that far south of the Pika Mounts, but it was the prince's life on the line. Prince Kent suspected it was more because Ivance felt obligated to provide a better escort than for any other reason. Still, the Goldener was relieved to return; his men had been poorly equipped for nights in winter conditions, and they lacked extra rations if their travels were delayed in any way.

A third reason awaited Prince Kent upon his return to Sardon: a letter from Prince Al'den Maushelik.

"This arrived this morning." An officer saluted and held out the parchment. "It came by a Tashek bird."

Prince Kent recognized royal house of Staria's family seal: a sword wrapped in a falcon's claws and beak. He took the letter in exchange for his tired horse's reins and headed to the wrap-around porch to sit in a rocking chair. Excited for news from his Starian friend, he broke the golden wax with a knife and unrolled the letter.

As he had expected, Prince Al'den's letter was informal and to the point as only a man used to military procedure could be. It spoke of the snows in the north, the first birds finally getting through to Kavahad, North Point, and the men from Raven's Den. The biggest event of it all: King Merretham's passing and the prince's ascension to the throne. Kent was stunned.

The look on his face must have been something, for Lord-Commander Ivance, who usually stayed out of royal affairs, had to comment. "What word is there from the Citadel, Highness?" His face was neutral except for the tightness to the leader's jaw as he thought of the worst news a letter could bring.

"Prince Al'den says the Starian king has passed."

The few men in hearing distance all stopped to gape in shock. Even Lord-Commander Ivance lost his composure. "This is ill news indeed." He fumbled to his own seat, distracted by the jarring news. "King

Merretham was a courageous and just leader, and a wise man besides. He raised an able son to take his place."

"Did he fall in battle?" an officer nearby asked. From the number of eyes upon Prince Kent, it seemed many wished to know.

Kent shook his head. "Not according to the letter. It seems old age and the cold were the best of him."

The men removed their hats and held a moment of silence for the fallen king before Ivance reminded them there was work to be done. As his men scattered, the lord-commander continued their conversation. "Does Prince—I mean, King—Al'den have any other news for us?"

"There is some. The North seems quiet because of the snows, but birds were able to get through to different command posts within this past sennight. Kavahad continues to keep tabs on forces as best it can. North Point and Staria are in a lull from maunstorz harriers. Only Commander Grant's men from Raven's Den have seen any action. They have relinquished Raven's Den to the enemy and are hiding out in the Red Hills. Grant writes that all assistance from Rubia has gone unanswered. Their force is cut off from the rest of the mertinean."

"I don't like the sound of that," Ivance commented. "Does the Citadel respond?"

"Yes. Prince—ah, King Al'den is sending all his cavalry and Tashek forces across Staria. He will help Raven's Den's forces get to safety and has already sent riders ahead for reinforcement. He and his own force will meet up with them on their way to Kavahad."

"King Al'den will ride personally?" The lord-commander sounded worried.

Prince Kent shrugged. "Al'den never struck me as the stay-behind-safe-walls type. He is a man of action, used to being in the fray of battle."

"Yes indeed." Ivance shook his head ruefully. "Much like his father of old, before injury forced Merretham to stay aground. A Maushelik ahorse and leading an army is a terrifying sight to behold. Stars know, we've needed such bravery on the battlefield."

"You speak as if you have seen it."

"I have." Ivance sat back in his chair and looked across the yard with distant eyes. "I fought alongside Merretham Maushelik when he was the heir-apparent of Staria. No man fights like a Maushelik. No man."

"Hm." Kent felt his lips curve into a smile as he was warmed by the lord-commander's words. It seemed he was not the only person who had been won over by Maushelik charm. Ivance's praise was a relief too. Their alliance with Staria had been the correct path to have taken all those months ago.

"I will keep my men at full readiness," Ivance continued as he pushed himself up from his seat. "If Staria needs our assistance, we will be ready for it—by your leave, Highness."

"You think it will come to that?"

"Not right away, but I'm willing to bet that Golden's forces will be called upon at some point after Snow Thaw. That's where you come in, Highness. It's time you returned to the Golden Palace to report on the North. That council you sat at the Citadel of Light had to have provided us with some news. If nothing else, our lead economic advisor can help the crisis of food storage in the North. I know our allies need it badly."

Though Kent would have liked to disagree about returning home, the lord-commander was correct: he had better influence at court than writing missives from Sardon. So far, all the letters he had sent had been answered with inaction and skepticism, the respondents saying that matters weren't as bad as he proclaimed. Yes, being at the capital was imperative to making Golden's reluctant advisors move into action. "Very well, Lord-Commander." He rose and offered his hand to Ivance. "I will head home at dawn."

"And I will order your men to get packing. Get a good supper and sleep. I will see you off in the morning."

"Sir." Prince Kent nodded his head and watched the tall military leader head away to bark orders. Left alone, Prince Kent reread the letter one last time before tucking it away. Then he headed inside to see what the cook had made for dinner.

§ §

Morning came with its usual struggle: how to dress, shave, and pack one-handed—even if his arm was improving. Yet Prince Kent was saved, once again, by his diligent colonel. "Let me, Highness." Jared Deed stepped in just as Kent was about to go at his facial hair with a blade. "We can't have the king thinking you got into a fight with a cat."

The Golden heir chuckled and handed over the sharp blade. "My constant savior. I'm beginning to feel like a damsel in distress."

Jared seemed to blush. "Not at all, sir. A little extra help after a war injury is just par for the course."

The two men paused their banter so the colonel could get through the shave without nicking the prince. When finished, he stepped back to allow Kent to pat himself dry while Jared took care of cleaning up the basin and putting away the shaving kit in the prince's satchel.

"Ah," Kent sighed as he viewed his man's work in the mirror. "It looks wonderful, as always, Colonel. Too bad I still can't convince you to be my lord protector. Then I wouldn't have to bother training anyone to accommodate me and this bum shoulder."

There it was again, Jared's usual reluctance to be given such an advancement in station. "You won't be so encumbered a few weeks from now, my prince."

"Even still, I'd have to find a protector as able as Eric Sloane."

"That will be very hard to come by, sir," Jared replied. "Lieutenant-Commander Sloane was in a class of his own."

"Indeed." Prince Kent was also thinking fondly of the man. "Yet I need my dilemma solved, and soon. I could just fight you for it—offhanded, of course. Best of three swordsmanship rounds to conclude the winner?"

Jared chuckled. "Highness, even if we both battled offhanded, I would still let you win. You are our prince, after all. It would be déclassé of me to beat you."

Kent tsked at that. "Letting your prince win just to save face benefits me not at all."

The colonel tried to hide his amused smile but failed miserably. "How about we wait until you are well so we can compete in archery? You'd fare better in that than with the sword, in any case."

"If archery it is, then let's have a round right now," Prince Kent said. Much to his archery colonel's surprise, he headed out the door, bag in tow, to do just that.

Gaping, Jared Deed hastened to follow with a protest on his lips. "Highness, we need not—"

Kent turned back to give his man a look—which, on his scholarly face, wasn't all that commanding. "I say that I can and we will, Colonel. If I win today, you become my lord protector. And if you win—no cheating—I'll let the subject drop once and for all. Deal?" He turned away and continued to the ground level without waiting for a reply.

§ §

Jared sighed and chuckled at his prince's resolve. "I've got to hand it to Prince Kent, it's hard to tell him no. Stars bless m that I don't screw this up." Especially in front of the entire militia of Sardon. The gossip would be flying across Golden if he put himself to shame this morning. Resigned, the colonel followed his prince's route to the archery range.

As expected, Prince Kent was at the armory speaking with the master. Rumors of their contest seemed to have already spread among the soldiers—which the colonel didn't put past the prince spreading himself—and a good number had stepped out from breakfast to watch. More than a few hoots and hollers were sent Jared Deed's way for coming to their prince's challenge.

The colonel stepped up to the archery range and picked out a practice bow to string up. He was joined shortly after by the Golden heir, who carried with him a child's bow about half the size of the adult recurves. It had a pull under twenty pounds. Jared raised his eyebrows at the weapon. "You think that will reach the distance to the target, sir?"

Prince Kent shrugged good-naturedly. "I guess we'll find out, Colonel."

The soldier wore a skeptical, embarrassed face, but he waved his prince forward to their starting line. It still wasn't too late for him to back out from the crazy contest…

In typical Golden fashion, the soldiers were already calling out bets before either man had notched an arrow. Despite the prince's bum arm, the Sardonians still thought Kent was going to beat the colonel. Their yapping had the archery colonel blushing beet-red and their prince laughing in good humor.

"Ah, just get on with it!" Jared muttered to his prince.

If I had known his morning was going to turn out that way, would I still have gone up to assist Prince Kent? The thought passed the colonel's mind as his prince stepped up and lifted his bow. The shaking and weakness in Prince Kent's form answered the question: *Yes, I still would have.*

Prince Kent stuck his tongue out the side of his mouth as he fought to hold his injured arm steady. Concentrating hard, he pulled the child's recurve back and let his arrow fly. It flew at the target… and dropped short by ten yards. The anticlimactic finish had the soldiers fall silent.

Jared tried to keep a straight face, but it finally cracked as he met the prince's blue eyes. A single giggle escaped before he could clamp his lips shut. To the colonel's credit, Prince Kent was also laughing. "Ahem." Jared managed to hold back another giggle. "I think you should try that again, sir."

"Indeed I will!" Kent replied, undeterred. He pulled free another arrow and notched it. Readjusting his aim, he let the second arrow fly. This one struck true, a perfect bull's-eye. Redeemed, Kent turned back to his archery colonel and lifted his chin. "And there we go."

Jared held back another laugh as he stepped up to challenge. "We'll say the other was a practice shot."

"Indeed."

The colonel readied his own arrow and took aim. Just a second before he released, Jared felt his bow twist from pressure at its base; however, he had already committed to the shot. The arrow flew wide as his repositioned recurve directed it. Colonel Deed spun about amid a chorus of laughter to find Prince Kent casually turning away, whistling none-too-innocently at having messed with the shot. "I thought you declared no cheating, my prince."

"Me?" Kent faked being affronted. "Never, Colonel. Though, I think you missed your practice shot."

Jared Deed shook his head at his prince's mischief but accepted the words; it did make them even, after all. He turned back for the second shot but kept an eye out for another interference. His distracted focus proved to be his undoing. With all the soldiers at Sardon bearing witness, Jared missed the bull's-eye by a ring.

Prince Kent Argetlem had won his wager for the colonel to become his lord protector—all over that one, lousy shot.

§ §

The ladies of the Starian court were passing their day with a game of "debates," forming two teams of four women. Three others, senior ladies, were elected to judge them on diverse subjects like diplomacy, ethics, philosophy, and social issues. Their game was lively, as Lady Rosetta Greyson and Lady Diana Levine, as team leaders, were well-versed in battles of words. One was a diplomat herself, the other an educator, and they helped their ladies pick away at the arguments until each had exhausted the round's question.

Princess Éleen was participating for the first time that day, having been cajoled by her new friends to come from the sidelines and put all she had learned to work. Even with Lady Rosetta as her sponsor, the princess was nervous on speaking out for herself. Still, Éleen promised herself to give one round her all—even if she failed miserably.

"Our next round will be on social issues," Lady Rosetta said as she pulled from a stack of cards with topics written on them. "Princess Éleen, you will play against Lady Catalina LaCroix."

The princess gulped, intimidated to be put up against a lady who was so well travelled in the world, but she stood up bravely and took her place at the head of the room beside the alluring, blond-haired Starian.

Lady Rosetta continued, "Please flip the coin, Princess Éleen. Lady Catalina, make your call." The teams flipped for the right to pick their side on the issue: *for* or *against*. Éleen was handed the coin she was to toss and waited for Lady Catalina's decision.

"Heads."

Word said, the Havenese princess flipped the coin and the room watched it fall and spin about on the floor. "Heads," she declared in favor of Lady Catalina being "for" the issue.

Lady Catalina crowed her victory along with her teammates. Then, she and the princess of Blue Haven settled in to hear which debate card Lady Rosetta had drawn.

"Ladies," Lady Rosetta began and flipped the card over, "you will be battling on this topic: You are city council members approached by a citizen to gain permission to build a pond on his land. Adversely, his neighbor downstream states that this man doesn't need the extra water and that the citizen petitioning is doing so out of an old resentment and is assumed as payback. You, as the two main council members, must argue for the approval or denial of the petitioning citizen's request."

Princess Éleen shifted nervously as she heard the scenario. She had hoped for something easier to start with; even her team seemed to agree. Yet she squared her shoulders and gave Lady Catalina a brave nod. "I will accept the question."

"Very well," Lady Catalina agreed and stepped forward. She addressed Lady Rosetta first. "May I ask if there are any other details given to this case before we begin?"

"Yes, you may. I do have facts on both parties. Do you have a particular inquiry?"

"I do." Lady Catalina bobbed her head. "Citizen with the proposal: I need to know where you live and the usage of your land, so that I may make an appropriate reply to my council."

"Yes. Council, I reside on an estate just west of the Red Hills, bordering on the Aras Desert. I have a dairy cow and some chickens. The land is a small acreage for my own personal use. I am a law-abiding taxpayer and pay my share as required."

Lady Catalina nodded. "And you have need of this pond, citizen?"

"Yes, , I do."

Princess Éleen felt herself frowning and realized she had a question for the citizen herself. "Citizen, if I may?"

Lady Rosetta nodded.

"Please, expound for our council on your use for this pond."

"Oh, ah..." Lady Rosetta scanned her card for the detail. She shook her head. "The citizen does not expound."

The princess's frown deepened. "Very well, then. Does it say what the citizen does for work? He did mention being a taxpayer."

"Correct. The citizen is retired. He was a former cobbler. His land is paid off, and any recent taxes comes from a stipend of saved earnings."

Lady Catalina nodded, agreeable to the citizen, as she was supposed to be. "Very well, citizen. Thank you for answering my other council member's questions. I make a motion to approve your proposal for a pond on your property."

"And I object!" Éleen called out, startling herself and the others. Her startlement had her blushing pink in embarrassment, especially when the others couldn't help laughing.

"Very well." Lady Catalina squared her shoulders and put a hand on her hip. "May I hear your reasons for his objection?"

"Ah." The Havener felt herself begin to shrink in on herself—until Lady Rosetta made a hand gesture for her to stand tall and be confident. Emboldened, Éleen pushed herself to continue. "Yes. We have only heard from the one citizen, yet there is another before us today who is asking us to deny the proposition. I wish to hear more from this man on his reasons against the pond." Éleen looked to Lady Rosetta for assurance. Lady Rosetta smiled back and nodded as she passed the information card to Lady Diana to play the second citizen. "Other citizen, please explain why you come here today."

"Certainly. I am a farmer who lives downstream from my neighbor. This is not the first time this man has tried to get more water through council approval. However, he doesn't need this water for a recreational fishing pond! His pond will take water that I need for my crops."

Princess Éleen's eyebrows rose. The second man had provided the information the first had omitted. She shared a glance with Lady Catalina. "It seems that the situation is not so straightforward as it seems… Does this second citizen have anything else to add to help shed light on this situation?" Lady Diana shook her head. "Very well. Thank you, citizen. Lady Catalina, I think this council should reconsider our approval to the first citizen. However," she added before anyone protested, "I think the council should investigate this proposal further. The farmer will need adequate amounts of water to produce his crop for the town and himself, yet the other citizen still needs to feel as if we have addressed his needs."

"And what do you propose to be fair, Princess?" Lady Catalina challenged.

She hesitated. "First, I would send an official to investigate out the situation and get the facts straight. There seems to be a long-term dispute at play that is not just from this instant. Neither party has been fully forthcoming on all the details."

"But what if a decision needs to be made now?"

"Then…I would approve of a pond *only if* it were built on both neighbor's properties," she replied, startling herself. Éleen flushed, embarrassed and lifted a hand to her lips to cover the look. "I was supposed to be against the motion, not creating an alternative."

The ladies giggled at her faux pas, but Lady Rosetta gave a supportive smile and encouraged the princess to proceed. "Yes, that was the exercise, but I think we are all intrigued by your compromise. Please, tell us more details."

Éleen collected her thoughts and then said, "I would think both parties would benefit from a pond: the retiree would get his fishing pond and some water for his animals, and the farmer would have water in reserve for his crops, as well as access to some fish—which I doubt he gets much of from working his fields every day. I think the council should approve the action—but only under certain conditions: the two neighbors should be the ones to create the pond and stock it. If one of the other does not do their part, the council has the right to fill in the pond and void the approval."

The room was quiet. Princess Éleen looked around and wondered what was wrong. She turned worried eyes to Lady Rosetta. "Lady Rosetta, please tell me my err?"

Lady Rosetta rose and collected the card back from Lady Diana, and then came over to put her hands on Éleen's shoulders. "Nothing is wrong, my dear friend. Your decree was not the kind a city council member would give—but, as a royal, you would have that kind of authority to direct a city council to act thus. Though it was not the exercise, your solution sounds fair and well thought out. Not only did you address both citizens' concerns, you also put contingencies on the neighbors learning to work together. If they do not, the situation goes back to how it began. The proposal would be denied a second time, and the first citizen would lose his credibility to ask further help from the council, as he proved he could not compromise with his neighbor or think of the farmer's water issues. Your broader approach could help the personal development of both parties to get along."

Even if Éleen had proposed a good compromise, the princess was not satisfied with her result: she hadn't completed the exercise by the rules dictated in the game. Perturbed, the Havener took her seat again as the next two ladies rose to compete. Éleen resolved to pay close attention to their debate. *There is still so much to learn!*

§ §

An hour later, the ladies finished up their debates and went their separate ways for lunch. Princess Éleen slipped from the room, after thanking Lady Rosetta for her help, and leaned against the closed door. The Havener was exhausted from all the discussions and daunted from all she still had to learn. Sighing, Éleen felt herself sag against the thick wood of the oak door.

"You don't need to put yourself through this, Highness."

Princess Éleen looked up to find her lord protector waiting for her from across the hall. "Lord Carrod, how long have you been standing there?!"

"Since you went in," he replied, as if it waiting two hours was nothing. Lord Carrod pushed away from the wall to come near. "I'm not sure why you are spending so much time on these Starian ladies' pursuits. Certainly, you have other activities better suited of your time?"

The princess frowned. It wasn't like her protector to say such a thing; it was too close to her family's disapproving rhetoric not to irritate her. "What is it to you how I spend my time? We are stuck at this demesne until the snows ease."

The Havenese soldier's face was almost stoic except for the permanent frown he wore on his brow. "Your only task in Staria is to win the heir's favor."

Éleen was already tired, and this sudden conversation had her on a short fuse. "So, that's all I'm expected to be?" she raged and pushed past her guardian to head for their section of the mansion. "I'm only around to procure a political tie to another kingdom and bear their offspring?"

Lord Carrod kept up easily as she fumed down the hall. "That is your purpose to the crown of Blue Haven."

Her china-blue eyes flickered sideways to glare, but the princess kept marching forward. "Spoken like a true Southern man and soldier loyal to his crown."

Lord Carrod's eyebrows rose. "Highness!" he protested and stepped in front of her to stop her forward stride. "Since when do you speak like that? Being around these women has made you lose your sense of propriety! Your family would be aghast to see you like this."

"Being around these women has opened my eyes! I've been pampered all these years, told what to do, how to act, and what to think. Worse, I accepted it all without question! Only now do I see how little I know of the world and how sheltered I was from it."

Lord Carrod could not reply; his mouth hung open in shock. Éleen forged on, emboldened by his silence. "Like orphanages, for instance. I've never visited one. Nor have I helped teach the underprivileged how to read and write. Both Lady Rosetta and Lady Diana have. I've never thought about the commoners' issues with taxes and laws. Did you know that in some places, if a person can't pay their taxes, their children are taken away to work it off?"

From her lord protector's suddenly saddened expression, Lord Carrod had known.

"Do you see? I was sheltered from all that. It's something you know, but I—the daughter of a king!—was sheltered from it? Do you think that is right? As someone of privilege, shouldn't I be aware of these things and try to fix them?"

Eyes still averted, Lord Carrod had to say, "But as a princess of Blue Haven, that has not been the calling set for you. Being the eldest of three daughters, you must be the one to wed and create political advantage for your family."

"And just who decided that?" Éleen put her hands on her hips.

Her lord protector lifted his gaze to her fiery eyes. "Queen Élise."

Princess Éleen frowned. "Yes, Mother. Herself a product of an arranged marriage. She, most of all, should understand the fears of being wed off to a stranger, but Mother does not care for me. She happily sent me away to Staria."

"But you wanted to come, Princess."

"Yes, I did. Now, more than ever, I am grateful for leaving Blue Haven. I've learned more in three seasons than all my years at the palace."

"But still…you *are* a princess of Blue Haven. Such actions are not permissible for those of your sex. Acting this way is—"

"What? Disreputable? Shameful? Contemptible? Is it shameful to want to teach people to write so they cannot be taken advantage of in the workplace. Is it contemptible to want to manage water storage correctly so the populace doesn't get sick? Is it disreputable to want women to be treated with more respect for taking care of the home and children or, Stars, those who want to run their own businesses to support their families? Is it—"

The princess's words were cut off when Lord Carrod suddenly, and quite unexpectedly, threw his arms around her and pulled Éleen close. Hugged against him, the princess could barely make out the words he muttered into her hair. "Highness, it is not shameful to want those things. But…the more you run headlong into learning such truths, the more I must shelter you from them. Before, I knew you felt trapped by the rules of your station. Yet to see you try to break free… it makes me worry for you, Highness. There are a great many things I cannot protect you from. Going down this path will only lead you to heartbreak and contempt."

Princess Éleen had been shocked to be pulled in so intimately to her guardian's body; however, his words were the sweetest he had ever said to her. *He worries over me…* Slowly, she reached up to grab fistfuls of his jacket. "Lord Carrod… thank you."

§ §

Viscount LaPoint poured himself a glass of brandy and then settled into a chair by the fire. As ice tinkled in his glass, he mulled over the letter he held. It bore the golden wax seal of a sword in a falcon's talons and beak. *Seal of the Mausheliks.* It wasn't addressed to him but to a certain obnoxious princess of Blue Haven.

"To open, or not to open?" he murmured. Redoing the seal would not be all that hard; Markus LaPoint had a lot of practice in hiding evidence of tampering. It was one of his ways of procuring information. Yet, this was the royal house of Staria. That was the main crux of the matter. However, the viscount was too curious about what the crown wanted from the princess. Curiosity won out.

Markus set his drink aside and took out a knife to carefully loosen the seal holding the parchment. Gingerly, he unfolded the letter and leaned closer to the fire to read Prince Al'den's fine script:

Princess Éleen Éldon-Tomino,

I hope this letter finds you and that you are well. The Citadel has finally been freed of snowstorms. Myself and the Sheev'anee are riding southward as you read this. I have word that you were waylaid at Viscount LaPoint's property. Please stay there, Highness. I am coming for that piece I gave to your protection. Please, keep it safe until I arrive.

—Al'den Maushelik

Markus had to laugh. So much for it being a love letter between betrotheds! It was as straightforward and boring as any military report. "The poor, poor princess—to be thought of as lowly as a package courier."

Still, Prince Al'den had entrusted something to the princess of Blue Haven? That seemed important. Markus wondered what that item was. "Such a clipped letter for it to be addressed to the princess," he mused. "And…the prince is coming here so quickly?" Markus hadn't heard that news. Perhaps even Commander Kins had yet to know? "This is all quite peculiar…but I will make do with keeping this knowledge to myself." He stretched forward and reheated the wax carefully over a candle flame and reset the tampered seal. "I have something new to think about..."

Chapter Twenty-Five
§
Only the Stars Really Know

A fortnight into their travels brought the priest and his charge halfway across Sealand's grasslands; in another fortnight, they would reach West Port. Despite the Myler girl having never travelled before, she was handling the trip without the whining and foot-dragging Anibus had expected—especially with riding a cantankerous mare and taking back roads and sleeping out in the elements. What the Estarian priest had anticipated as a horrible chore was far less an inconvenience he had imagined. Young Rosemary, he finally decided, was a very brave and strong-willed young woman.

Still, such travels would take their toll on anyone, and Anibus had already been at it for over a season…so when wet rains came pounding down on them about ten miles south of a little farming town called Tabbit, the priest made sure to find them a decent shelter to hunker down in, with a promise to stay overnight. As they came to the little lean-to shelter—possibly intended for a travelling merchant or a hunter's camp—Anibus became aware of his charge's "issue," which she had withheld from him out of sheer stubbornness and embarrassment.

It had come about when she had slid from her mare's back and then groaned and clutched at her belly. Anibus noticed her reaction, but the girl had been quick to hide her discomfort when she saw him watching. Two more occasions of that as they unpacked and settled into the shelter had the priest concerned.

"Rosemary," Anibus said once he had fluffed their blankets into a dry corner, "why don't you lie down for a while?"

"But I need to get this fire going and start cooking."

Anibus couldn't keep back his fond smile. She was such a diligent worker. "I can manage that. We've been on the road for a number of hard days. You deserve a break for putting up with me."

She rewarded him with a shy smile. "All right." That Rosemary agreed without further remark confirmed that something was wrong.

Anibus took in the girl's flushed and pinched facial features once more and then helped her to bed. "You should remove your outer dress," he ordered her gently. "It's wet and needs to dry by the fire. You will warm up better with it off." Unlike the first time he had suggested it, Rosemary no longer was embarrassed to remove her drenched outer clothing. She turned away to unbutton the thick, wool dress and then handed it back to the priest's waiting hand before scooting under the blankets of her makeshift bed. All but her pretty red curls were hidden from view.

Anibus shook his head at the girl's stubbornness at not telling him of her condition. Yet he left her alone to finish grooming Rain and Buttercup and to start boiling water over the fire. He also heated some rocks; these, he carefully pulled from the flames and wrapped in leather, so as not to be too hot. Then, he returned with them to Rosemary's bedside. "Rosemary," he murmured. She groaned but finally rolled around to see him. "Here are some warm stones."

Rosemary gave him a look. "What for?"

Anibus cleared his throat and forged on. "Maybe I am being too presumptuous…but you're on your moon-cycle, right?"

The girl blushed a bright crimson in response. So, he had guessed correctly.

"I have been around other women who suffer on their time. It seemed heat always helped, so I thought you would like these. And there's hot tea with rock sugar. I've heard it can help with the pain."

"I…" Rosemary looked embarrassed as she sat up to take the hot cup of tea and stones. Her hair fell over her face, hiding it from the priest.

Anibus smiled disarmingly. "It's something that's a part of nature and nothing to be uncomfortable about. Just know that next time, you can tell me if you're not feeling well. You've done well this whole trip, not complaining at all and helping me out. A lot. But you don't have to suffer in silence."

Rosemary ducked her head, still sheepish, but she did give a small nod. "Thank you…"

Anibus nodded and took back her cup once she drained it. "Now, you lie there and rest. I'll have dinner ready in a bit. Are you staying dry enough?"

"Yes."

"Good. Now, sleep." He helped her pull the blankets up to her chin. Relieved that a moon-cycle was the girl's only problem, Anibus resumed the regular evening task of making supper and drying the clothes out. He settled into his seat against a rough log, listening to the crack of the flames and sizzle of roasting hunks of dried, salted pork and potatoes. Evening fell about them in a slow slackening of the rainstorm making its way into shrouds of mist…

A rustling startled Anibus awake. Turning, he found Rosemary pulling some clothes from her packs. She paused at his look and then slowly closed her bag and tiptoed near the fire. She settled next to the priest and huddled in her petticoats. "You dozed off."

"I guess I did." Anibus looked away from the girl to the fire. To his relief, Rosemary had saved their dinner, pulling the skewers aside to cool. He reached for the food and passed the girl her portion. "Feeling better?"

Rosemary flushed but gave a nod.

"That's good to hear. I'm glad the heat and tea helped."

Rosemary looked the priest up and down with critical hazel eyes. "It doesn't bother you?" The way she said it sound as if it should.

"No."

She harrumphed. "The boys at school said it was gross."

Anibus chuckled. "Those boys are being immature."

"Mum says it marks my womanhood."

Had he been taking a drink right then, Anibus knew, he would have been choking on it. Luckily, his mouth had been free of food or drink. Rosemary could go from being embarrassed to bold in a hot minute. "That's only one mark of becoming a woman. Other things still take time."

"Like growing breasts and wide hips? Pa seems to love Mum's hips."

The priest had to send up a little prayer for strength from the Stars before he could reply. "Those are all marks of your body maturing, but to be an adult takes more than that."

"Like what? Layin' down with someone? Makin' babes?"

Stars, why lead the conversation there of all places? "No, that's only the physical aspects of maturity," Anibus replied. "To be an adult is to learn responsibility, patience, wisdom, experience—"

"You ever sleep with someone?"

Anibus had to cough into his hand. "I'm a priest of Estaria who made a vow of chastity until I reach the age of thirty." At which time he could take a wife and start his own worship house, if he wished.

"So, you're like a…a virgin?"

He gave her a look. "How do you even know that word?"

"I hear things. People talk." Rosemary shrugged and looked away to her food. She seemed sheepish again.

"People may talk, but that doesn't mean you need to understand. You're still young, Rosemary. Stay a child for a little longer. Trust me, you're not missing out on anything."

"But..." Rosemary choked out, and Anibus realized she was trying not to cry. "But I have t' grow up, don't I? I mean, Mum and Pa have sent me away... so I have t' grow up."

The words pulled at Anibus's heartstrings. He had wondered why the girl had not pouted about leaving. Now he knew why: Rosemary was trying to put on a brave face that this little "adventure" was just for fun. Yet her words showed she had realized that she might never see her family again. It made the priest wish he had said no to the Mylers about taking their beloved girl south. Rosemary could well have lived out her days in Dolland and not seen any of the war...but only the Stars knew what would be the little town's fate.

Sympathetically, he put an arm around her shoulders and pulled her into his side. "Only a little growing up," he said gently. "You'll be at a convent. Think of it like a boarding school. They'll teach you any skills you want. You never know, this war could end in a year and you'll be home to quiet little Dolland again."

Rosemary wiped at her tears as she spoke. "But this war has been goin' on since long before I was born."

Anibus frowned. "That's true."

"Still." Rosemary gave a courageous smile, though it was still shaky. "I guess a convent don't sound so bad. You think I can learn t' bake pies an' cakes an' things? I always wanted t' do that."

"Well, I know an abbess named Cādene at Westharborne who loves making desserts. I'll be sure to introduce you."

"Thank you. That sounds wonderful!"

Anibus gave a wan smile and pointed at her food. "You should eat before it gets cold. Besides, we've got a whole two weeks to talk about West Port and a whole lot more of Sealand countryside to see besides." Rosemary agreed and took to her dinner with a renewed voracity.

Their hearty meal was soon gobbled up, and the day's long ride caught up with the girl. After reheating the rocks, she took them with her to bed, where she promptly fell asleep once more. Anibus was left alone, watching the girl dream by the light of the fire. His thoughts were still perturbed.

Standing, Anibus went to Rosemary to make sure she was well tucked in, and then he stepped around their lean-to to be by Rain's side. In the coldness of the night, he stroked the grey's silken coat and looked into her deep brown eyes, haloed in a rim of flames from the glow of the fire. "Do you think I did the right thing?" he asked quietly. Rain turned her head to nuzzle his cheek with her velvety nose. The touch made the priest smile. "I hope so. Only the Stars really know, after all. Thank you, girl."

§ §

He pushed the horses southward until the Red Hills began to clear of snow and relent to fall grasslands. Finding a lush valley with many plants to sustain the herd, Re'shaird Aerrisson finally stopped the mertinean mounts and unloaded the packs from their backs.

Three days had passed since his departure from Commander Grant's forces. Three long days of uncertainty as to whether their plans had succeeded on diverting the enemy forces. The Tashek could barely take the worry; he had checked his passage for anyone tailing with no sign of any pursuit. Not that maunstorz on foot could keep pace with horses at marching pace, but the lack of any commotion behind him had the warrior-scout fearing the worst. Still, Aerrisson kept to the plan, just to play a good cover.

The horses seemed content to stay in the valley he had chosen, and after the forced pace, even Aerrisson had to admit it looked like paradise. Yet such a rest would not be for himself and Lunier. The pair had to backtrack and see what catch they had snared…

"Take a break, my friend," Aerrisson said fondly to his loyal mount as he pulled the tack from the grey's sweaty hide. He watched as the stallion trotted away with the pack horse. Aerrisson turned to his second task: the release of the falcons.

The two birds were restless from being kept in a jostling cage for four days. They were cantankerous—especially the larger male—as he removed them from their prison and noosed them to a tree. Freed, the two birds of prey fanned their wings and chirped in relief. "Soon. Soon, you will feel the skies," Aerrisson cooed as he carefully stroked the smaller male's breast. The larger one he pacified with scraps of meat, knowing full well it was prone to biting in irritation. The two birds settled.

The Tashek built a small fire to cook hunks of meat and to make tea while composing quick updates to be placed on the falcons. Once he'd eaten, Aerrisson returned to the two birds and attached his missives to their legs. With final words to them to reach their mates safely, Aerrisson released the two males to the skies and watched them disappear into the air.

"Only the Stars know if you make it home," he muttered to himself as the falcons faded from view. Their departure made him feel suddenly more alone and cut off from the Sheev'anee than ever before. Perturbed, he whistled his steel-grey back to him. Lunier came to him at a trot, his near-black mane tossing wildly about as the refreshed mount came to his master's call. "You ready, boy?" he asked. Lunier pawed the melting snow and shook his mane, looking energized and ready for more miles under the saddle. "Good. That's good." Aerrisson patted his neck and fed him and the pack horse some grain-pressed treats for energy before starting to retack his steed. There were hours still left in the day and forty miles to make up to rendezvous with the mertinean upstream, on the Senna. There was no time to waste.

§ §

A night and half the morning later brought Aerrisson across the path of those he desired. Through a scope's glass, he finally saw the maunstorz force he had hoped would pursue—except it was not all he had hoped for. "Silvarron sent eighty men. That's hardly half of his force." The maunstorz man was too smart. Had he seen through the mertinean ruse? The thought chilled Aerrisson more than the winter temperatures covering Syre.

If Silvarron anticipated their sudden departure to be a cover-up for the men heading west on foot, then Grant's forces could well be in danger.

The desert man sent a fist into the tree he had hidden behind before he sneaked back to Lunier's side. His stallion was used to the scout's coming and going and barely made a start as he exited the trees, though the pack horse started at the sudden appearance. His main steed was all fire once his rider was mounted, with the other's lead in hand. Heading northward at the hard pace their master set, Lunier and the pack horse charged through the ever-deepening snows as well as they could manage. Despite Aerrisson's reservations, he pushed his horses to speeds meant to cover their previous distance in half the time. It might very well break the mounts, but the mertinean's safety was paramount in Aerrisson's mind—and that was a thought as sacrilegious as any of the Sheev'anee's codes ever were. Horses were their lifeblood. To push his partners to such ends was unthinkable. *Stars' strength that all comes out well in the end…*

Chapter Twenty-Six
§
Truth Uncovered

"I'm courting someone. How—by the Stars!—am I courting someone! This is insanity!" Prince Par argued with himself as he paced his rooms at night. He strode back and forth on his rugs, alone save for the flickering fireplace, candle flames, and his befuddled thoughts.

Had Lord Gordar Farrylin been there, he would have heard his cousin saying: "It was all your fault, my prince." But his lord protector was not there to chastise him on being so competitive. As it was, his dashing, golden-eyed cousin was away on duties, and Prince Par was alone in his misery. Though usually not one to throw tantrums and break things, the heir of Sealand felt like trashing his quarters.

In the turmoil of his emotions, Serein flared to life, startling its wielder with a dazzling blue glow.

Dumbfounded, Par clutched the sapphire and pulled it away from his chest to stare at its brilliance. "Oh, now you decide to do something!" he growled at the stone. In his hand, the sapphire warmed as its magic sought him out. In the past, when this happened, the royal usually took the cowardly route and refused the feeling; however, this night, Par was in a more receptive mood to accept offered power. He absorbed the warmth as if he were drinking in a hot beverage.

The result was exhilarating. Serein enveloped its wielder in a power so strong it matched the ocean's pull, and yet the prince found himself far from drowning. The overwhelming powers flowed from the Prince of the Evening Star as quickly as a wave's crashing and left its bearer in a puddle on the floor. In the next breath, Par came back to himself and reoriented to his quarters, which felt suddenly very cold and lonely without Serein's nature around and within him.

"Par! My prince, are you all right?" Gordar came running from the doorway as he found his cousin in a heap on the rugs. "Par!"

A groan was his answer. "Softer, Gordar, please."

His lord protector put a hand on the prince's back to steady him. "I can, but tell me what happened!"

"You didn't see?"

"See? See what, Par?"

"Serein." Par rubbed his aching temples. "Serein just flared to life."

"She did?" It was hard to tell if Gordar was shocked or worried—perhaps both, judging by the way his golden eyes cast about the room for anything amiss.

"It's the most incredible thing I have ever felt, cuz. The power…I understood why my father calls it is the 'commander of the seas.'"

"Did she hurt you?"

"Hurt me?" After sharing Serein's essence, the thought of her using her powers to do him harm suddenly seemed sacrilegious. "No, Gordar. I am fine. Amazed beyond words, but fine." And to his surprise, Par realized he really was *fine*. His previous anxieties were gone.

Lord Gordar seemed less than appeased. "You're down on the floor as if you've passed out."

"Just aftershock, I think."

His lord protector frowned. "I like this not at all. No one was here to keep an eye on you in case something did happen." He helped his prince stand on unsteady feet.

"I think that's why I accepted Serein this time. I actually *welcomed* her into me."

"That sounds even worse."

Prince Par laughed at his cousin's very serious expression. "Perhaps, cuz, perhaps. I promise I won't be so reckless next time and will have my father or Commander Matar around to watch over me."

"I'm holding you to that." Lord Gordar had that stubborn fix to his jaw that said he would make sure the prince would not forget the promise—for he certainly would not.

"Did you find our contact's information useful?" Par asked, switching subjects to avoid a longer explanation of his recent experience. He meant the man he'd sent to Permonde to tie up loose ends about the Limontés' background.

"He's been more than thorough," Gordar replied somewhat cryptically. "He brought you a little gift."

"Gift?"

"I think you should see for yourself—if you are up to it."

Par fixed his cousin with a stare. "Is this going to take some time?" He only cared to know because he was scheduled to meet Lady Yvonne

Limonté for a hunt early the next morning, and it was already well past dusk.

"This…may take a little time, Highness, but that all depends on you."

"Oh?" The prince's eyebrows rose. Now he was intrigued. "Well, let's get to it."

Lord Gordar turned away and headed for the door. He stopped only long enough to collect the prince's woven capote and hand it to him before continuing into the hall. In the dim light of the hallway candlesticks, the two Sealanders made their way through the fortress. They avoided the staff and other residents by taking back passages. It was rare for Lord Gordar to take such paths, and he only did so when he needed to hide his prince's secrets. The "gift" was becoming more and more intriguing to Par by the minute.

They exited out of the scullery door and headed around the back of Fortress Opal's stone exterior until they came to the rear of the stable yard. The lord protector helped his prince through a hidden door they had installed along a back wall. By that time, Prince Par was giving him looks, but Lord Gordar remained silent on any details until they reached a tiny alleyway the stable hands used to remove horse manure from the fortress. Beyond the piles of dung, they came to a secluded cubby set aside for staff rest breaks. Sitting on two boulders were the informant and the "gift."

Prince Par looked the lad up and down, assessing him from tousled brown curls to field worker's boots. There was a bulk to the young man's shoulders and thighs that spoke of someone used to hard labor. Beyond that, the prince could only guess at the worker's career or age.

"Your Highness!" The informant was quick to his feet and into a bow as he realized who the approaching shadows were.

"You may be at ease," Prince Par bade him. The man complied by sitting back down, though there was a tension in his posture that showed he could not entirely relax in front of the heir of Sealand. "What news have you brought me?"

"More than news. I bring you David Carter himself, Highness."

Prince Par was impressed that his informant had found the man behind all the rumors about Lady Yvonne Limonté's improprieties. "Is this the truth?" he asked the young man.

Youthful-seeming David swallowed hard enough to make his Adam's apple bob. He said nervously, "M-my P-prince. I…I am David Carter."

The words were not an answer at all. "Yes and…? Who are you to be brought to me all the way from Permonde, good sir?" Par refused to give him any details. He would only pursue the matter further if this David Carter was the man he was looking for.

The man's next words came as a shock. "I am Lady Yvonne Limonté's beau. I love her, Prince Fantill! She is the only one dear to my heart. Please, please, Highness, release her from this forced betrothal and let her come back to me." The lad's sudden bravado must have taken a lot of courage—or it had been bottled up for weeks—for him to have confessed so strongly to the man stealing his lover away. And a prince no less!

Prince Par was stunned to silence.

"You dolt!" the informer yelled, and pulled David roughly from his seat to force him to kneeling. "This is your prince you are speaking to. You have no authority to speak to him in such a manner!"

"Stop!" Par ordered. His lord protector was there in seconds to remove the informant's hands from the lad. Lord Gordar sent the man back a few feet and then returned to David Carter with an apology as he set him back on the boulder. Prince Par came near once the field worker was settled. He came to sit across from him and took in the lad as David shuffled his shirt back into place and eyed his prince with wary eyes. "And how long have you been seeing Lady Limonté?"

David seemed shocked to have his prince acknowledge the relationship. "I've courted her for twelve seasons." A year-and-a-half. "I—I was going to build up my savings and buy my own homestead before offering her my hand. I was nearly there when she was called away to the capital, Highness."

Prince Par took it all in with a neutral expression. "And the lady's father, good sir. What was his opinion of you and this match?"

By the sudden change of expression, the prince knew the news was poor even before David confirmed it. "I am seen as only a worker, Highness. Lord Limonté does not see all that I can provide Lady Yvonne—especially when I procure the acreage. I am capable, Highness!"

It sounded like overconfidence of youth and headiness from love. "But certainly, if you love Lady Limonté, you must understand her family's reasons for not approving of you?"

David's reacted as only someone who had been put down on a regular basis could, his brown eyes flashing. His resentment made his next words short and angry. "No man can be as good a catch as *the Prince of Sealand*, so of course, one's honest love is never considered. After you, I am no more than horse fodder."

Prince Par had hoped to speak to David Carter as equals, but the other's words regarding the gap in their stations meant that such was not possible. Mr. David Carter had been reminded of his lot in life hundreds—if not thousands—of times over. There would be no common ground to find. "And what of Lady Limonté?" he prompted. "Certainly, she had the right to seek her best opportunities?"

David only frowned and stubbornly refused to answer.

Par held in a sigh. "Beyond that, Lady Limonté needs to seek a proper husband for her station."

"My love is greater than anyone's, and I would prove it to her every day."

On that matter, Par had no standing; he certainly did not love Lady Yvonne yet, and maybe never would. "That is not the argument here," he said instead.

"But how are love and admiration not better than all the gold in the world?!"

The point hit home for the Sealander heir. He himself was still stuck on a love eight years in the past, so he knew full well the power of love.

A shifting of his lord protector's weight to the prince's left helped break the stalemate. "We digress, Highness," Lord Gordar reminded his cousin. "You came here for a different reason." *Remember* was the word the lord protector left out, but Par was grateful for the reminder.

"Yes, Lord Farrylin, you are correct. Thank you." Par returned to his conversation with David Carter. "There really is only one reason I had need of speaking with you, Mr. Carter." He hoped the change in his voice and intonation were not lost on the young man. "Lady Yvonne Limonté is currently in the limelight of the Sealand court. Therefore, she cannot afford to have such rumors about her floating around."

"Rumors?"

"Yes. Of her improprieties."

David Carter made a sour frown. "Spoken in such poor taste. You of the privileged use such terms for an act normal to all creatures?"

"Normal it may be, except that it slanders a woman of age who is coming out to the court. To be labelled as such is ill to her indeed. I have need to know if such is true of Lady Limonté."

"In this, I will not grant you. Such an act should only be done with the utmost respect and secrecy—if it is done at all before matrimony."

It was as if David Carter had meant to say that he had slept with Yvonne Limonté, but without the direct yes or no, Prince Par could not use the confession as proof. Yet, before he could push the lad on the matter, the answer was given to him by a far more honest source—though entirely by accident.

Serein flared to life beneath the prince's shirt, responding to his unsteady emotions once again. Just as quickly as she had the time before, the sapphire flared into her wielder, giving him the answers he sought through her powers to access memories. In a flash of warmth, Prince Par was bequeathed the memories of David Carter and Lady Yvonne's union: thoughts, feeling, and physical sensations in their entirety. The insight was too intimate and detailed for the Prince of the Evening Star to deny. It rocked him forward to his knees and left him disoriented and out of breath.

"Highness!"

The prince came back to the present to find his lord protector at his side, again needing to steady him as the aftershock of Serein's powers left him unbalanced. The lad and informant looked stunned to see their heir in such a state. "I am all right," Par murmured to Gordar as he righted himself and slid back up onto the rock he had been using as a seat. The prince forced his head to clear and body and ground himself back into the present moment. *If these spells are going to become a normal thing, I hope I get used to them. It won't do to have the whole fortress thinking their prince is ill.*

Finding himself, Prince Par readdressed David Carter. "Where were we? Oh, yes," he continued without pause, "We were speaking on improprieties and their acts being kept in secret." David was giving him a look, as if his prince's change of tone suggested he had the knowledge the lad was refusing to supply. Indeed, after what just happened with Serein,

Prince Par knew too much. "You are correct to keep any such acts from becoming public. However, as there are already rumors, I would suggest—for Lady Limonté's sake—that you keep a low profile away from her family." He lifted a hand to stave off David's rebuttal. "In this, you have caused enough trouble for the lady. From here, you must let her decide her own future."

"But with you—"

"I am saying that I will give Lady Limonté her own freedom to choose," Par interrupted. "And that is the only assurance I can afford you, good sir. If your love is indeed greater than the desire for wealth and comforts, then it is her choice whether to accept it."

"But—"

"Are you really so indifferent to her problems that you would argue this with me?"

That question finally shut the young man up. Contrite, David Carter hung his head and murmured an apology to the prince.

"Very good," Prince Par concluded, seeing he had finally won the argument. "I suggest you return to Permonde and continue your work. If you are indeed close to securing your property, it would be best to continue. You would be wise to keep yourself out of the way for this season—just my opinion, Mr. Carter."

Prince Par rose and motioned to his cousin. Lord Gordar came near and bent close to hear his prince's command: "Please, take care of arrangements for these two gentlemen at an inn on the outskirts of the city. See that our man understands they are to leave before sunrise in the morning and make for Permonde."

"Highness," Lord Gordar agreed. "As for you—?"

"I will return to my quarters. If you still have a wish to check on me, come after all is through."

"Very well, Highness," his lord protector conceded. He gave a bow. "By your leave, I will take care of things here."

"I give it," Par granted. To David and his informant, he said, "A good night to you, gentlemen."

"And to you, Highness." Both men had the sense to bow to the Sealand heir as he took his leave. Upon parting, Par prayed that the two of them would continue to keep their heads and stay quiet about the meeting, peculiar as it was. Mr. David Carter seemed like a troubling complication attached to his betrothed…

§ §

"Highness."

Not at all surprised, Prince Par turned away from his mirror to say a good morning to his lord protector. Though Lord Gordar had surely checked on him in the night, Par had been fast asleep and had missed his presence. All the magic-work had been more draining than Par would have thought. "I was just preparing to sit for breakfast, cousin. Care to join me?"

"Of course, I would." The golden-featured Sealander came the rest of the way into his prince's bedroom and came to help Par adjust a piece of his riding habit. "You were dead to the world last night," he commented.

"Yes. I think Serein's powers tired me."

"Did she do it again, when you swooned while talking to that lad?"

"Swooned?" Par teased on the wording, but he was quickly sober. "Serein showed me the memories of their union."

Gordar's eyebrows rose in incredulity. "The whole thing?"

Par felt himself blush. He cleared his throat. "Yes. In just a few breaths."

His cousin guffawed. "That would be a sight…"

Par reached for one last cufflink and then motioned them to his little breakfast table in his second room. "It was something I'd rather unsee." Even hours later, Par could still feel the physical sensations in places he would rather forget. *Are all of the sapphire's memory-calling powers so detailed?* Stars, he hoped not!

Lord Gordar must have been talking and noticed he was being ignored, for the lord protector was giving him a look. "Ah, sorry, I was a little distracted."

Lord Gordar tsked as he poured them both some tea and passed a cup to his cousin. "I said, you need to speak to your father and Commander Matar about this. Certainly, they will know how to help you."

"I know that I need to update them on this new development, but…I think this is Serein's way of rebelling against my reluctance. She seems frustrated on my lack of commitment."

"You make the stone sound like a remonstrating wife."

Par laughed. "Indeed, sometimes she feels like it. Why get married when I've got all I need from a magical stone?" Lord Gordar shook his head despairingly at his prince. "Still," Par continued, "if this is going to be happen regularly until I'm willing to use Serein, I may have to limit my public appearances."

"We can't have the people thinking their heir is ill," Gordar agreed. They lapsed into silence long enough to dig into their breakfast of porridge with milk and honey. After a few bites, Gordar continued with their other issue. "About Mr. Carter, Highness. I've made sure he and our informant are on their way. However, he does pose a problem." Ocean-blue eyes glanced up, a question in their look. "He thinks himself your betrothed's lover. His existence will continue to cause you grief."

"Cousin, certainly you are not suggesting some misfortune befall him?!" Par was shocked. His lord protector was not that sort of man.

"No, of course not. I am just pointing out that your failure—your ethics—to make further constraints against his case will come back to bite you."

The word *bite* had the prince thinking of a particular moment in the two lovers' memories. The sudden flashback had him losing his appetite. Par made a face and dropped his spoon. "That may be, but I've no wish to pursue it further—*for the time being*," he made sure to add, seeing that Gordar was going to argue the decision. "I have my answer on that matter, and it is more accurate than any rumors."

"And does it not bother you, Par, knowing your betrothed is not untouched?"

"No, Gordar, it does not." His reply seemed to surprise his lord protector. "Why should we men think that only we can spread our oats before matrimony but women cannot? Are we really so superior?" Par shook his head in dismay. "This matter of improprieties indeed! Perhaps that young field worker has the best sense of the lot of us."

Gordar huffed at his prince's logic but then agreed with it. "Indeed, Par, we men are a little too pompous about such matter. Though, I am relieved to hear your stance on the subject. So…I take this to mean you will continue to court the Lady Yvonne?"

"For the agreed-upon one season, yes, I will."

"But not after?"

"On that," Par replied, "I will have to decide when the time comes."

§ §

Done with breakfast, the heir of Sealand and his lord protector headed for the large ward at the front of Fortress Opal. The open space was packed with soldiers, retainers, vassals, and horses—all the protection detail and men needed to keep the royal hunting party safe and fended for. If Prince Par had his way, he would have dismissed most of the staff and left the fortress unencumbered, but such behavior would reflect poorly on the House of Sealand and slight the Limontés.

"Just for today," Lord Gordar reminded the prince quietly as they exited the fortress through the main entryway.

"I know," Par replied and pasted a pleasant smile on his face as everyone turned to acknowledge the heir's arrival. All bowed until their prince bid them to continue with their duties, and then he continued down the steps to where the Limontés waited for him.

"Highness." Middle-aged Duke Limonté greeted him with a proper bow.

Prince Par offered the man a hand instead, forcing the duke to straighten. "Good morning, sir. It seems a fine day to go hunting."

"Indeed, Highness. The skies are cloudless and the breeze slight. I hear our scouts have already found some bucks for us."

"It is good news to know we will have an opportunity for a real chase," Par replied but he made sure to step past the duke in case he continued with droll pleasantries. He continued to Yvonne's side. The fiery young lady was already astride a dark bay courser, sitting sidesaddle in a fancy riding frock. Par wondered how she would keep up with the hunting party. "My lady."

"Highness." Yvonne nodded and settled her frisky mount with a light touch on the reins. "Are you ready for today?"

Direct, forthright, and refreshing. "I am, Lady Yvonne. Give me time to get ahorse and we can be on our way."

"Delightful. I am relieved to see you do not desire to tarry long. I'm told that our herd is a half hour's ride from here."

"Then I will hurry." *Why hadn't anyone informed* me *of that fact?* Par frowned. Because he was the prince, that was why. Unlike Prince Par's military commanders, the court would cater to his every whim. "If you'll excuse me to get ready." Yvonne nodded and kept her eyes on his person as Par strode over to his horse. Luckily, only a few men stopped him for more morning pleasantries, so Par made acceptable time to his cousin and their two horses.

"I'm about ready to charge out of here myself," Gordar mumbled as he passed Par his charger's head. "This fanfare seems exorbitant today."

"It's all because it's the lady's invitation," Par replied as he checked his horse's girth. Not that a groom hadn't, but his mount, Constable, was notorious for holding his breath. He then mounted the lanky chestnut. "It seems Lady Yvonne loves to hunt in a large party."

"I will do my best to be accommodating, then."

Par chuckled. "I'm just hoping they will tire of chitchat by the time we reach the scouts, so we can get on to real business."

"Stars can only hope, my prince."

Idle chitchat it ended up being, but the Sealand heir was still relieved to be away from the fortress. The weather was warm and clear, not a rain cloud to be found, and the road they travelled through the open grasslands gave a panoramic view of the southern lands of the kingdom. They passed through a few small farming villages outside Fortress Opal. The populace, excited by the potential glance at royalty, came out to wave at the prince's procession. Their glee was infectious.

Prince Par made sure to ride near his people and greet them. In return, the villagers seemed to appreciate his affections, as more than one person whispered to another their shock and delight at being greeted by their heir.

His behavior seemed to surprise Lady Yvonne as well, for she commented on it once they passed the villages. "You have a way with the people," she said offhandedly.

"I like to know my people are happy and well. There's no better way than speaking with them directly. Besides, most people that I've met are pleasant and tell me interesting tales."

Lady Yvonne gave him a critical look. "Commendable of you." Her words seemed perfunctory.

He chuckled at the remark. "I'm not doing this to win your favor, Lady. I truly do enjoy meeting the people. My lord protector can vouch for me, if you still disbelieve."

Lady Yvonne shifted in her saddle to eye Lord Gordar. The lord protector had held his horse back to speak with Duke Limonté, in Par's stead, as the prince played his part of courting the daughter. "No need,

Highness, I believe you." She let the matter drop and instead pulled out a scope to train on the horizon. "I see we are nearly there."

"Are we?" Par was relieved. He accepted the instrument from Yvonne and looked ahead as well. In the distance, he could see the flags set up by their scouts. "Very good. We made good time reaching them. I'm ready for a good hunt."

"Three 'goods' in a row, Highness," Lady Yvonne teased. "You *must* be ready for some action after all our polite banter."

"I am ready for a hunt, my lady, but it is not from our talk."

Lady Yvonne giggled. "Indeed, Highness?" she said in tones of disbelief. "But I know it is from our pleasantries. Being so civil wears on me, too."

Lady Yvonne rose a gloved hand to signal a vassal to her side as their party finally reached the scout flags. Her man came up the line of horses and passed over her prized hunting falcon onto her leather-protected arm. She tossed a devious grin the prince's way as she settled the bird and began to release its wings. "I'd love to make another wager with you, Prince Par."

He groaned, though he had to admit, the challenge in her eyes stirred him. "I worry what you have in mind, Lady Yvonne. I fared poorly against you in our last contest."

"It's nothing of that sort, Highness. I promise."

"Then, by all means, what is it?"

"The winner of our hunt gets to choose our next couple's activity."

Couple? Par let the word go; they were technically courting. "Very well, Lady Yvonne, I accept your challenge."

"Perfect." With that, Yvonne Limonté called her people to her and released her falcon into the air.

Chapter Twenty-Seven

§

A Matter of Guilt

"It's a beautiful thing, is it not, Prince?" Mansocan's keen eyes were on the prince as the maunstorz flashed the new ring he sported.

"That's not worth a retort."

Mansocan chuckled. "Oh, come now, princeling! Certainly, you have an opinion on the matter." By the young man's twitching jaw muscle, Mansocan could see his teasing was having the desired effect.

"As the enemy, you should be showing off your winnings. That does not mean I need to respond to your gloating."

"Ah, so you do know what I'm doing." Mansocan took a sip of red wine and then fingered the fealty ring once more. "And how does your lord protector fare today?"

Rowin Sunrise's eyes were so cold that they looked nearly black. "He's alive, which may be a disappointment to you."

"Indeed not, good prince. I actually like keeping my prisoners alive—those that are suitable. Your lord protector falls within that category." Three others in the cells had been less "suitable" and had finally succumbed to the cold, damp conditions and their own bodies' weakened states. The corpses had been pulled from the cages after the maunstorz were certain the impact of the men's deaths had sunk in; one of the dead had been Dane Price.

Rowin set his expression in a careful, neutral mask; his stoic manner was a testament to his fortitude. He was quick to change the subject. "And what do you want me for today? I doubt I have anything worth bartering about." It was true; he was running out of state secrets to levy with.

The words amused the maunstorz leader. A flash of a smile graced his lips as the enigmatic warrior rose from his chair. "You are a man of many means, so I doubt we have touched on all the information inside that cunning head of yours." He came before the Sunarian royal and looked down at the half-eaten loaf of bread and untouched cup of tea he had provided. Reaching down, Mansocan scooped up the cup and took a sip; all the while, the royal's sharp eyes kept a wary study of his actions. "Mm. Rubian berrybrush tea. My people have no such wonderful plants to make these delicate flavors with. I've come to appreciate the finer aspects of your Syrean delicacies." He replaced the cup. As expected, the young Sunarian lifted it to finish off the tea. *So, the prince still thinks we are drugging him.* "With our open and honest communications, princeling, I have no need for the truth plant. Bartering with you for your people's needs is much more to my style."

"You still haven't said why you wanted me here."

"A man directly to the point. I like that about you. Among my people, you would rank high for your warrior's prowess, cunning, and resolve."

"In my kingdom, that's just par for the course for surviving the court."

A noise of agreement thrummed from Mansocan's throat. "Yes. Your Sunarian court…I have my greatest commander keeping an eye on your king—that usurper, King Raymond Sunrise." He made a face.

It was the first Prince Rowin had heard of the maunstorz having made it to the capital of Sunrise. Before, all he had been taunted with was the fact that the command front had been overrun. It boded ill for Sunrise's people...

A look must have passed over his features because Mansocan tapped the tabletop to regain his attention. "I give that information freely, prince of Sunrise, to warn you of just how completely I have your kingdom in my hold. And, with the snows as they are, your greatest military powers will not know of this until the time of Snow Melt. By then, I will have split your great lands of Syre in two."

There was no mockery in those words: just cold, hard truth. And, unfortunately, Prince Rowin was likely to agree. Syre hadn't exactly been unified before these recent maunstorz attacks. The North had been more so, thanks in great part to commanders such as Matar of the Crystine and Ethan Kins of the mertinean, as well as the great warrior-king Merretham of Staria. Those were three men with enough influence to move the northern armies on a single call; however, the other kingdoms had fewer men of action. Sunrise and Blue Haven were the worst, always ignoring the fighting in the North; the Golden Kingdom had been a great force nearly twenty-five years ago, but it currently held itself in reserve. Only Sealand, having suffered attacks to its northernmost border, had shown any resolve against the maunstorz. With only three of the seven kingdoms—he didn't count Rubia, as it was occupied by the enemy—having any mettle to fight the maunstorz, Syre did look lost.

"I see we understand each other." Mansocan's voice pulled Rowin back to the present. He made a motion for Rowin to stand and follow him. "Bring your bread, princeling," he ordered. "I will make sure your people are fed as long as you grace me with your time."

§ §

Rowin had learned enough over nearly two seasons as a captive under the maunstorz leader to follow his instructions on food—limited as it was. He pocketed the bread and followed Mansocan out to the hall.

As usual, it seemed all but Chornauk believed Prince Rowin Sunrise was not a threat to their great leader—a testament to the man's skills, if Rowin was to believe that. Having only the hulk of an enemy around to guard Mansocan's back, the trio started down the halls with Mansocan leading the way with a casual air. "Have you seen the Red Palace?" Mansocan asked.

"Only a little," Rowin replied. "And only on three occasions. I had to keep some relations with kingdoms on Sunrise's borders."

Mansocan took note of the information with a nod. "I see." His red eyes trailed across the elaborate trappings on the walls of the hall. "Just as in your Sunrise, I see that your"—he fished for the word—"royals like their finery. All of this." He gestured to the delicate red jasper stonework, ruby-encrusted sconces, gold latticework, and painted ceilings. "It would easily feed all your kingdom's people a country-thoroughfare over. Your love of material possessions confounds me. That you place such importance on objects over your people's health and fruition…" Mansocan shook his white-haired head. "It is baffling."

"The more we speak, the more I am surprised by your people's lack of wealth."

"Wealth, young princeling? Your definition of wealth is a peculiar one. How naïve you Syreans are."

"Well, what would you have?"

The faint smile Mansocan returned reminded Rowin of a grandparent looking down on a child. There was a wisdom behind those eyes, though the prince could have sworn the maunstorz leader was barely forty—if that. *Why? Why that look?* "Prince of Sunrise, there ae plenty of ways to be wealthy in life—and gold is not one of them. According to you, it is useful in securing position, prestige, reputation. But all of those things can be attained other ways. No…true wealth is in simpler things. Things your people have forgotten."

They had come to the east entryway. Mansocan pushed through the heavy, ornate doors to the courtyard and royal stables outside. The cold air was a shock compared to the warmed inner halls. Rowin pulled in his breath and tried to hide his sudden shiver. The astute maunstorz leader was not fooled, however. "Chornauk. Your ulster." The second-in-command made a face but handed over his fur overcoat to the princeling. Mansocan said something else in their language—to which Chornauk argued. Mansocan turned on his man with a deadly glare. "You will go fetch him now. This princeling of Sunrise is no fool. To do me any harm will mean all the prisoners' deaths." The words were for Rowin's benefit and most definitely a warning. Chornauk eyed him up and down in obvious threat before saluting his leader and turning heel back into the palace.

Mansocan turned away and resumed their walk. "Now, where were we? Ah yes, our perspective on wealth…"

Rowin hugged the ulster to his body and followed Mansocan out into the yard; however, the state of the place, not the enemy leader's words, held his attention. All about the stable yard were carcasses of livestock—or what was left of the butchered beasts. The maunstorz, it seemed, left little of the animals to rot. There were still bloodstains on the snow and some bones and organ matter, but most of the carcasses were as bare as Rowin had ever seen.

Mansocan must have sensed the Sunarian's preoccupation, for he stopped to eye the royal. "What is it, heirling?"

"The livestock."

"Yes?" Mansocan scanned the yard, as if looking for the reason behind the words. "My forces eat the animals as needed. They are sustenance during this weather."

"But you ate all of them?!"

A scoff. "We freeze the meat and use it sparingly. It saves on resources."

The prince's face was crestfallen. Many of the carcasses were horses; he could tell by the skulls. "Many had better uses than as food."

"Ah." Mansocan finally seemed to understand, "You mean the creatures your armies ride to war and cover much distance with."

"Horses. They are horses, and there are many ways they are useful—many beyond being eaten."

"Horses." Mansocan tested the word before shaking his head. "I still do not understand the appeal."

Rowin's love for the creatures made his next words heated. "Horses are the greatest of creatures. With their size and strength, they can perform feats that men alone are incapable of. They can pull heavy loads, plow fields by acres, carry a man thrice the distance he alone can walk—"

"My people are capable of running near as far as your horses."

"But with the exertion all on yourselves. With horses, the distance is taken up by them, with much less cost to the body."

Mansocan was quiet for a time before he relented. "Yes. On that, I have noticed the advantages. Still, these creatures, *horses*, are a mystery to me." He waved the prince on and they entered the stable.

To Rowin's relief, there were still around twenty good horses the maunstorz had not slaughtered. Mansocan said, "I am not one to detest something just because I do not understand it. Therefore, I did not let my forces kill all of the horses for meat." He strode up to the nearest stall and put a hesitant hand to the mare's neck. "I wish to become familiar with these creatures, so that I can understand your people's fascination with them. You will teach me about these four-legged beasts, Princeling."

Rowin was shocked. *Mansocan wants me to teach him about horses?* He felt his eyebrows rise nearly to his hairline. "Um…well, that is unexpected," he managed to say.

A dry chuckle. "Indeed. My forces think this a folly of mine to want to know so much about you Syreans: your language, ways, creatures. However, I find the knowledge useful."

Prince Rowin felt himself balk. His enemy's acquisition of knowledge only served to improve the maunstorz campaign—and this request would give them a huge leg up. Horses had been Syre's one big advantage against the maunstorz, who always stayed afoot. Should this be where he finally drew the line and refuse?

But that was where leverage came in, and Chornauk was on time with the bait.

"*Seka'vlr*," Chornauk announced himself at the door and pushed the prisoner in ahead of himself.

"Good timing," Mansocan replied with praise, but his eyes were fixed on the Sunarian prince and not his commander.

Rowin kept his face a careful mask, schooled as anyone of royal blood had to be; however, he felt his cheek muscles begin to clench.

"Bring the prisoner," Mansocan ordered Chornauk.

"What do you need him for?" Rowin stepped boldly in front of his enemy.

Mansocan smirked as if knowing he had hit the prince's weakest spot. "Your lord protector? I don't need him for anything. As long as you are willing to teach me about these beasts, I will let your man sit in the dry straw and warm himself with a blanket and tea. I've even had clean linens and ointment set aside for his injuries."

Comprehension dawned in Rowin's mind. Mansocan was bartering with him again, only this time Rio Ravesbend was the leverage. "Fine," Rowin agreed. "I will teach you about horses, whatever you want to know. But I will see Rio's hand cleaned and treated first."

Mansocan's returned smile lacked any warmth. "As you wish, prince of Sunrise." He waved Rowin to the stall where the supplies were arranged. There was obvious glee in the leader's red eyes as he watched the prince doctor the lord protector's hand, injured by Mansocan's own. Rowin felt guilt flavor his movements as he cleaned and dressed the empty space where Rio's finger had been. His movements had to let on to the maunstorz leader that Mansocan had won.

Prince Rowin Sunrise wondered if he just might have broken, and all over his lord protector's finger…

The hunting party met back up at the royal hunting lodge four miles south of where the deer had been scouted. It was late, and the sun was nearly setting when the large group gathered to show off their tallies.

Prince Par had brought in the largest buck of the day; however, it was his only saving grace. Besides the deer, he and Lord Gordar had only managed a few conies and one pheasant. Duke Limonté had procured eight conies, three squirrels, two does, and a turkey. Two others of the Limonté party had come back with two more turkeys and three ducks. It was Lady Yvonne, though, who won the hunt by numbers. She singlehandedly brought down a boar and eight ducks. Her falcon brought back three conies and five squirrels, plus it scared up a fox that its master shot for its fur. With a final count of three additional turkeys and two pheasants, the lady had made an impact. The crowd clapped at her bounty.

"Congratulations." Par joined the applause as he strode over to the proud Permonde woman.

"My thanks, Highness. Though, your buck wins for its beauty and size."

"Perhaps," the prince said to avoid either agreement or denial. He helped Lady Yvonne collect up some of her bounty and carry it to her vassals to begin cleaning them. His own buck was being handled by his best flesher—less likely for the meat and hide to be ruined that way. By the way the young lady was acting, Prince Par wondered if she would join in the processing of the carcasses, and he said as much.

"Usually I do, Highness," Yvonne replied, "but these pelts are to go to a tradesman in return for helping me with moving some of our family wares."

Par had to remind himself that the Limontés were wine makers. "Yes, I did notice that your father brought some barrels for our hunt." Cumbersome as they were.

Yvonne looked across the yard to where her father was already a few glasses into the family vintage. "I see that Father is up to spinning his tales again."

"I was noticing their ostentatious nature."

Lady Yvonne rolled her eyes. "My father loves telling tall tales. They make him think he is more dashing and valiant than he is." She shrugged. "They keep my mother entertained."

The Sealander prince noticed Duchess Limonté's absence but had not commented on it. He took the opportunity to keep their conversation going. "I noticed Duchess Limonté was not along. Is this not her event?"

"No. Mother hates these functions. Killing and skinning helpless animals and all. She is, most likely, off to the markets looking for new textiles or jewelry."

"I see now who you take after."

Brown eyes studied the fair Sealander a moment, weighing his question for any hidden criticism. "Yes, I am like Father," she finally agreed. "He bore only three daughters and no sons. One of us had to fill in for the loss."

"You say that as if it was a duty only," Par teased. He judged the situation differently.

"It's not—" Yvonne began to protest until she saw his grin. "Why, you—!" She slapped the prince's arm with her glove.

Par laughed heartily, not taking any offense at her ladyship's lack of protocol. "I can see you like the freedoms of these activities. Certainly, normal women's affairs must seem tedious."

Lady Yvonne agreed. "I would take a lively hunt any day."

"Good. That takes the pressure off of our next activity's selection."

"You say that as if you won today."

Prince Par grinned at her challenge. "You did say my buck won in terms of mass."

Lady Yvonne conceded the point. "Indeed, Highness. Besides, I am curious on what you would find to do as a couple's activity."

"Hm, well…I had a thought before our hunt, but your words have swayed me otherwise. I will need a few days to rethink my course."

"Very well, Highness. I will give you such time and await your invitation with anticipation."

Lady Yvonne's words sounded like a conversation ender, so Prince Par bid her a quick excuse to "relieve himself" and strode away to the trees. He noted that the young lady turned away to the fleshing of the animals and to speak with the party's head cook, overseeing the butchering. The young woman looked perfectly at home among the men.

"I caught you staring, my prince."

Par startled as his cousin materialized from the shadows of the trees. "Great Stars above, Gordar!" he exclaimed as he tried to slow his racing heart.

The lord protector chuckled. "It does not do you well to be so unobservant. I must stick closer to take up your slack."

"I'm too accustomed to having you at my side. Though you have been rather generous with your berth today, cuz." Par found himself a secluded tree to do his business as his cousin turned away to politely eye the surrounding trees and guests.

"Giving you space seems to have helped in regard to your confidence in speaking with Lady Yvonne."

"Ah, so that's your intention." Par finished and returned to his cousin's side. "Always the sly one, you are."

"I know you too well." Gordar grinned back. "And I could see you were subtly flirting with the lady. Long has it been since I've witnessed that!"

"Don't sound too pleased." Par gave him a warning look. "I'm trying to behave in accordance to expectations. Though, I dare say, it can get a bit compulsory at times."

"Oh, that was not force, my prince," Gordar continued to tease. "You were enjoying yourself."

Par didn't have a good rebuttal for that. If truth be told, the hunt had made it easier to speak candidly with Lady Yvonne. "Yes, well…we will see if it is lasts. I have yet to bring up the business with David Carter."

Lord Gordar shook his head, sobered. "And here I thought you had planned to keep it to yourself?"

"I had, but I do need to understand where Lady Yvonne stands on that topic. My decision rides on it."

His lord protector was disapproving, Par could sense. "Just so long as you approach it delicately, my prince."

"On that, most definitely." Par straightened his riding habit and turned to Lord Gordar for approval. Once it was given, he waved them on. "Back to the battlefield."

"To look at this party like that bodes ill, cuz."

"Oh, bugger off! Go find yourself a good port and a card game, or something of the like."

Gordar just chortled and stuck to his prince's side. "No, Highness. You are stuck with me until death do us part."

Inwardly, Par was pleased. Having Gordar as his constant shadow was the best relief he could ask for—and the buffer he needed as he waded into the fray again to rub elbows with the invited nobles.

Duke Limonté was one of them. Well into eight cups of wine, he was becoming the center of the party. Everyone there was well aware of his delight at having his "finest, tomboy daughter" catch the eye of the heir of Sealand. The man's etiquette was rough at best and debasing at the worst. Lady Yvonne and the retainers tried their best to settle the man's outbursts—and dilute his wine—but it seemed they were on the losing end. At least the other noblemen who had accompanied the hunting party were also heavy drinkers; it would do well if tomorrow's hangovers kept the gossip about of Duke Limonté's faux pas from spreading back to Fortress Opal.

"Highness, should I—?" Gordar asked at a particularly loud outburst.

"No need, cousin. I will turn a blind eye to tonight's ruckus."

"But—"

Par gave his cousin a sideways look.

"Very well, I will ignore this mess for another time." Which could mean that the cleanup would be more work.

Par nodded. "Let the men have their fun." It meant he had to say less and did not need to watch his tongue. Indeed, the lively atmosphere was a welcome relief from the stuffy weeks at court.

"The deer! The deer has arrived!" a retainer called to the party as large hunks of venison were carried into the clearing and set on the middle of the table.

"Prince Par gets the first choice!" a noble cried out. More voices followed into a chant until Prince Par humored them and stepped forward to choose his steak. He pierced a good-sized hunk and held it aloft before tearing into the meat. An applause followed as he nodded his satisfaction to the cook. The Sealand heir didn't need to bother with a speech; the men were already eating by the time he swallowed. Relieved, Par took his bounty back to his seat and shared with Gordar.

"It's like a victory feast," he commented into his cousin's ear.

"Yes, they are all quite exuberant tonight."

They shared a laugh and a shrug before clinking a toast together and feasting on the deer; if the noblemen wanted to stay informal, so would they.

The night grew deep as the hunting part ate and drank in the light of the raging fire. It felt as if the party were the only people in the world, cut off from the rest of Sealand by the dark and the wandering poplar forest. The moon rose before Lord Gordar poked his cousin in the ribs. "She's coming back around."

Prince Par craned his head about to see Lady Yvonne bringing in a hot plate of smoked boar. She passed an allotment to the table and then came around to offer the prince and his cousin some of her catch. The meat was still sizzling and dripping fat. Par whistled as he forked up a piece.

“Highness.” Lady Yvonne curtsied. “It was smoked over a fire pit these past five hours.”

The prince was impressed. “And seasoned well, I see.”

A slight blush came to the lady’s cheeks. “Yes, a Limonté family secret recipe.”

“You did this yourself?”

“The sauce? Yes, Highness.” Yvonne looked pleased but embarrassed at the admittance of a woman’s activity—cooking.

“Stars!” Par shared with his cousin his amazement before he bit off more.

“It is delightful, Lady,” Gordar replied more politely.

“Thank you, Lord Farrylin.”

“Come, sit with us!” Par patted the seat beside them. The two cousins were just far enough away from the nobles to be polite but not too close to be the center of attention, so having her join them would not be seen as inappropriate. Yvonne hesitated but finally acquiesced and set her plate of boar on the table before them.

“I apologize for my father,” she said after an uncomfortable pause.

“No need, Lady,” Par bade her. “I, too, am enjoying the freedom of our camp and being away from Fortress Opal.”

“Still.” She fingered a thread on her riding frock. “His manners are quite poor when he takes too many cups. I apologize for his lack of propriety.”

The wording had the royal remembering his own use of the phrase. “As I have said, Lady, I will dismiss it for the time being. However, there is a different subject I do wish us to discuss.” Par could feel his lord protector’s eyes pleading him to let the matter be; he ignored him and decided to blame his obstinance on the wine.

“And what would that be, Highness?”

“A worker of your father’s…a Mr. David Carter.”

In the firelight, Prince Par saw the lady’s expression freeze.

Chapter Twenty-Eight
§
A Little Clarity

"A...Mr. Carter, Highness?" Lady Yvonne's brown eyes looked pinched.

"That's right." Prince Par remained casual, focusing on the boar more than the Permonde lady beside him. "He's stated an interest in you, Lady Yvonne."

"Me?" The word came out breathy and soft.

Par nodded and took a sip of wine, allowing the pause to continue so Yvonne Limonté could sort through her thoughts. Setting down his mug, he wiped his mouth and hands on a cloth before continuing. She certainly wasn't supplying any words to further or end his inquiry. "Would you care to expound on the man's offer? Shall I see it as legitimate or a false claim?"

The Limonté woman was silent for a long while. She swallowed nervously and finally said, "It all depends on your reasons for asking, Highness. Is such a man in danger of losing his life or his livelihood?"

Prince Par was shocked. *Lady Limonté really thinks the worst of me.* "It's nothing of the sort, my lady, I promise. I am not the kind of man to find a rival a threat. I do, however, wish clarity on the matter."

"Clarity." Lady Yvonne looked away to the drunken men. None seemed to notice their conversation on the quiet side of the table.

The lady's pause had Par prompting her to speak further. "Yes. This Mr. Carter seemed fervent on his declaration. There was no doubt in my mind that he meant every word."

Tears brimmed in her eyes. "That fool," Lady Yvonne croaked out, and she fisted some of her frock into her hands.

"Highness," Lord Gordar said in a bid for his cousin to back off.

Again, Par ignored him. Instead, he reached for one of the lady's hands. The contact, he found, was striking in that Lady Yvonne didn't have a woman's hands; they were calloused from bow and spear. "Lady Yvonne, please do not misunderstand me. I bear you and Mr. Carter no ill will. I only desire to hear the truth from you. When we first met, you were angered over my attachment to the princess of the Crystal Kingdom. Can we say your situation is one and the same?"

Lady Yvonne let out a single sob and then patted at her eyes furiously with her free hand to dry them. "The same, Highness? I dare not say that such is so, but affection...there was that, yes." There was a heartbroken echo in her voice.

That emotion, Prince Par could understand. "Yes...I gathered as much from Mr. Carter."

"You spoke at length?" She sounded shocked.

"Yes, for some minutes, in person."

"He—he is at the capital?!"

"Was, and he has gone back to Permonde. You must understand the complications that would have ensued had he stayed longer." She nodded. Still, the fact that David had journeyed all the way to see the prince seemed to calm her. "We spoke of the man's options and plans for his future—and yours."

Yvonne glanced warily at Par's face.

Par continued: "The Limontés having three daughters and their eldest, at twenty-two, unmarried...I'm sure that has the duke and duchess worried. I can see how their bid to have their eldest win the hand of the crown would make them dismiss all other suitors."

"You are the *catch of our generation*, Highness." The lady's statement sounded like words directly from the duke's mouth. At least Yvonne's lips quirked at the statement.

"Yes, well..." Par coughed and released her hand to drink more wine. "I'm sure my lord protector here can name a few traits to make me less worthy of such praise."

"He does have some flaws, my lady," Gordar supplied as prompted.

It elicited the giggle Par had hoped for. "Oh, most certainly not, Highness! The ladies of the court have a list of over two hundred and fifty attributes of your eligibility. They recite it weekly."

The prince groaned. "Stars forbid, those ladies will be the undoing of me!" Yet, the turn in their conversation had eased the tension. It was a relief to feel it dissipate.

"Thank you for your care and concern, Highness," she said.

Ocean-blue eyes turned to regard her, and closed as Par nodded at her words. "Yes. I do speak to you with care."

"Then, I need to give Your Highness my reply."

"No," he said, and saw her shock at his answer. "No, you do not. Look, Lady Li—"

"Yvonne, please, Highness."

"Lady Yvonne," Par started again. "I just wanted to make you aware of my knowledge of your relationship with Mr. Carter."

"Previous relationship, Highness."

Par sighed. "Are you going to keep interrupting me?"

Lady Yvonne giggled and then clamped a hand over her mouth. She shook her head.

"Sure, you won't," he teased back. "But I will tolerate it." A warm smile softened his features. "As you and I are both bound by great loves before now, I propose this to you: I will continue to court you as our wager has decreed. However…if after that time, we find no affection has grown between us, I will release you to follow your heart where it leads." She opened her mouth to argue, but Par raised a finger to silence her and forged on. "That is a respect I can give to another whose stars are crossed. It's the best I can do for you, Lady Yvonne."

"Highness. I…I'm at a loss of how to reply."

"Just say that you understand where I am coming from and thank me for being so courteous."

She giggled again. "Certainly, Highness. My words exactly."

Prince Par flashed a dazzling grin and lifted his wine mug to salute the lady and his lord protector. "Then, let's set this conversation aside for a later time and enjoy the Limonté boar and wine."

"On that, I can agree, Highness. Cheers!"

"Cheers," he replied and included Lord Gordar in his toast. Then, a thought came to the prince. "Ah, I've got it now!"

"Got what, Highness?"

"What we will do on our next outing."

"Oh? And what would that be?" Even Lord Gordar seemed interested in what the heir of Sealand had in mind.

"To see my bladesmith's workroom. Master Ferris Galandrés is the best sword maker in Sealand."

"Are you sure of that?" Gordar whispered into his cousin's ear.

Yet, the prince had judged Lady Yvonne correctly. Her smile was broad and enthusiastic. "I would love to see his work! Do you think Master Galandrés would let me visit?"

"I know it. He enjoys showing off to such sweet company."

"Oh, stellar! I accept your assignation, Highness."

Par hesitated at the word assignation but, then again, such an activity with the lady was exactly that. "Then, so it is. I will contact you as soon as I secure a day."

"I look forward to your correspondence, Highness." Lady Yvonne squirmed with glee before standing to help her father's staff. She left skipping.

"That's the oddest courting outing I've ever heard of," Lord Gordar commented as he watched the lady flit away.

"Odd it may be," Par replied, bobbing his eyebrows in victory. "But the lady likes the idea—and, I admit, so do I. Now *that* is a worthy activity to occupy my day."

Lord Gordar tsked at his prince. "You're hopeless, Par. Charming but hopeless."

Prince Par just smiled and knocked back another mug of wine.

§ §

Their small party was out on a tracking-and-scouting run to test their skills and to see how the unit operated. A week in the Pika Mounts, forty klicks north of Sardon, seemed like an adequate amount of time to find any kinks in their group. Patrick relied on Maximillian Rosailles's knowledge of the region to find decent places to camp. The former Sardonian soldier had practiced in the hills for years under Lord Commander Ivance's watch. His grasp of the lay of the land was brilliant.

"A small valley is to our west," Pickle was pointing out to Patrick and Jacen. "It's got adequate water and shelter for this time of year."

"We will head there, then," Patrick agreed and turned Candor away from the vista to address the rest of the crew. The ten others of their expedition were lazing about the latest campfire—their third one since leaving Sardon. The Kins-man gave them all a skeptical look; most seemed to view this outing as a way to relax and enjoy a week's reprieve from the training and drills they had practiced daily. For Patrick, battle trained in the field, the nonchalance sounded warning bells in his head. "Shaul'auna!" he called to the Siv'arid maiden.

Quick as a cat, the alluring Tashek was on her feet and to him. "Kins-son."

"A word."

Shaul'auna raised her eyebrows at the directness of the order but followed the Rubian away from the others' ears. "What is it?"

Patrick sighed and looked back at their group. "None seem to take this trip seriously."

"As seriously as they can. It seems only the Calhorns are excited by the prospect of spending more nights in the cold and rain."

It was true; the weather had been a bit unpredictable. He asked, "Even you and Kei?"

Auna scowled. "I may be desert-born, Kins-man, but I have travelled extensively."

"Well then. Fine."

She studied him intensely. "What is it, Patrick? Did Maximillian say we should turn around and rethink this outing?"

"No." He was shocked at the line of questioning. "Actually…" Patrick looked back to their party and waved at them. "There is no sense of urgency or caution with them. If this was real, we would not survive long in enemy territory."

Shaul'auna took in their camp with that perspective in her gaze. "Indeed, I see the problem."

"I'm at a loss on correcting it. With soldiers, I could yell at them and threaten them with running, night watch, or—Stars!—even a loss of rations. I don't think that will work here."

"No, not with these men," Auna agreed.

"I will have to think on this, then."

"As will I."

Patrick gave the Tashek woman a look.

"You are not the only leader here," she explained. "You can rely on me, Kei'shkï, and Jacen to back you up. There is no need to lead alone."

"Hm." He accepted her reminder. "Thank you, Auna."

She nodded her pretty head. "Shall we go, then?"

"Yes." Turing to the group, Patrick said loudly, "Everyone up! Get your gear onto the horses and that fire out. Pickle knows a sheltered valley where we will station ourselves. We head out in five."

"So prompt, Kins-man," Shaul'auna teased as he finished. Her pouty lips turned up in a cocky grin.

"Five means you, too," Patrick replied stoically. He still wasn't fond of the Tashek woman's teasing.

Auna chuckled. "Already on it, Kins-man. *Beat you* in five."

§ §

They trekked for three hours and finally made the valley by midafternoon. It was a pleasant spot, sheltered from the worst of the winds and containing ample tree cover and grass for the horses. A small, stream-fed pond was a short distance from the forest. It was an idyllic place for a long-term camp. For their small party, it would make for an easier stay than the first part of their week.

Patrick motioned the expedition members to gather around him before they all had a chance to break and lounge again. "Now, I want to remind you all we are out here to prepare ourselves for next Snow Thaw's expedition. That being said, I want to spend these next four nights in practice taking turns on watch, as well as packing up in the mornings and reassembling the camp. Trained soldiers can be ready to go in under ten minutes. I want to see if all our work until now can beat that time."

There were a number of unhappy faces at hearing about the drills, but Patrick chose to ignore them. Until he needed to put more pressure on those individuals, he would leave well enough alone. "As we are commissioned for a scouting expedition, we will also practice surveying, scouting, and tracking during the daytime. Master Callé will rely on the intel from our scouts, Kei'shkï and Shaul'auna. I want everyone to act as if we are in enemy territory. For once we are up North, there will be maunstorz." He was silent then, to let the warning sink in.

"I trust in clan Siv'arid"—he pointed to the Tashek women—"to know how to detect and avoid our enemy. The Calhorns will be on lookout for tracks of people and game, but neither of you are to do any scouting. Your job will be to stay in the vicinity of our party." Micah Calhorn nodded his understanding. "The protection of our detail will fall to those of us who can fight: Jacen, Pickle, Kipper, Mr. Durrow, the Ritters, and myself. Our objective is to protect Master Callé and Peter."

Patrick turned his gaze on the Tashek maidens. "Auna and Kei, I encourage you to only act as backups in a fight." The two women were glowering at the order, so he went on to explain, "In this group, gentlemen and *ladies*, the Tashek are our backbone. If you want to get home alive, we need them to stay alive." He pointed at the desert women. "Kei'shkï is our medic. Without her, we stand a poor chance. Shaul'auna is our most experienced scout. She has fought against our enemy and knows the lands in the North best." He set serious eyes on each member to emphasize the point. "Understand that if you want to come back from the Valley of Death, then these two—of clan Siv'arid—are your best bet. Your life depends on their survival."

The sobering words seemed to knock some sense into the group. Awakened eyes took in the Tashek and then each member as they all sized everyone up. Patrick hoped the situation had sunk in. If it didn't, their chances of success would do down by a great margin.

"Shaul'auna and I have picked each of you for the skills you possess. I'm counting on all of you to help me lead this expedition to fruition. For our families affected by the maunstorz, for the people killed, homes lost, and our peace and happiness destroyed…what we have agreed to do for Syre is go forth to find the lair of our enemy. If we are successful, we could become the reason for our side's victory. Let these days, then, prepare you for that task."

His poignant, emerald eyes tried to communicate to each person their significance to this mission. "Take these few days, when we are not at the front lines, to find your fortitude and resolve yourselves for what lies ahead." Patrick finished his speech and let the silence grow between them. He had pieced together all the words he had thought from that morning's spoken concerns to Shaul'auna on through their trip to the valley. He hoped what he'd just said was enough to stir some urgency into the party.

Jacen seemed to sense the gravity of Patrick's rousing speech. He stepped forward to usher commands, as everyone else seemed dazed. The clap of his hands broke the reverie. "So, we must assemble a camp as quickly as possible, eat some lunch, and start our surveying of the area. Let's beat the time of a trained troop of soldiers! Hustle, hustle!" The group broke up, and there did seem to be a change in their energy. All started in on different duties as if time were not on their side.

"That was quite the speech," Jacen murmured to his friend as they watched the others start on their tasks.

"I just hope it was enough."

"Relax, Commander," Jacen joked. "Your words even had me ready to tackle the wastes."

Patrick lifted an eyebrow at the Havener. "Then, why are you still standing here joking with your commanding officer?"

A hearty laugh was the reply. "Because you had me rooted speechless." Jacen winked and turned away to his own duties of unloading the supply horses.

Patrick chuckled, finding his friend's words had, indeed, relaxed some of his tension. He turned away to his own job of untacking Candor and Sapphire and setting up the tent he and Jacen shared. By the time he finished, the others were nearly done with their own tasks:

Pickle was nearby making a makeshift fire ring out of rocks he had found near the stream; Kipper, always near the Golden soldier, had an armload of sticks and dead evergreen branches to start the fire. The two men bantered gaily at some joke or other as the young farrier took to the wood with his ax. Farther away, the Calhorns had finished their own unpacking and tent-building. They had turned to assist Master Callé and Peter get the surveyor's equipment under his own tent, lest it rain.

Across the clearing, the two Ritter brothers were at a game of knife-fighting—or had been until an annoyed Shaul'auna came over with a harsh reprimand. She sent them away to water the horses and fetch buckets and waterskins to fill with water. Then, the Tashek rejoined her cousin on guard duty, looking over the camp and valley with keen, watchful eyes from atop a small hill.

Only Mr. Durrow was not directly seen about. His absence had Patrick moving across the campsite to the two desert women.

"They are moving well enough," Shaul'auna remarked as he neared.

"Yes," Patrick turned back to give the crew a once-over. "It seems I found the right words for that effect."

"You did accomplish your goal with poetic panache."

"Poetic?"

Shaul'auna shrugged. "I thought it bordered on the dramatic."

"It did its job," Kei'shkï said and flashed her cousin a warning look. As the more serious of the two, the Siv'ala woman did not seem to like the uncomfortable prodding of their banter.

Patrick ignored Auna's remark and focused on his real intention of coming over. "I was wondering where Mr. Durrow has gotten to."

"He mentioned the need to...relieve himself." Kei'shkï made a face, unhappy to be privy to the event. "He went into that stand of trees a short while ago."

"Ah, I see." Patrick cleared his throat. "I guess I will speak with him when he returns from that."

"Speak of what?" Shaul'auna looked suspicious.

"To sharpen a hunting knife of mine. It's dulled thanks to my use of it on some timbers." Their first night out, they had come to discover that not all the tent stakes had been packed. Patrick had helped fashion some wooden stakes to fill in the last of the bracings. Sadly, it had been his one good hunting knife he had used. The blade hadn't seemed right since.

"I have a whetstone," Kei'shkï offered.

"No, keep it." He gave a short smile. "I'd like Durrow's expert hands on the blade." Patrick shrugged. "Use the man's skills while he's around."

"That's a good idea, actually." Shaul'auna said. "We should inspect everyone's weapons and let our blacksmith and farrier have a turn at them."

"Then we'll ask for that as everyone gathers for supper."

"You do know we should assign watches now."

"Of course." Patrick wasn't sure why the desert maiden brought it up; it was procedure.

"Then not everyone should eat at the same time. I will go assign pairs now that the packing is done."

He was taken aback by her abruptness. "I suppose."

"Good." She gave a sharp nod to her maiden-sister and headed back down their small overlook to the camp below.

Shaul'auna's departure had the Rubian looking to Kei. "What did I do?" Obviously, he had missed something.

Kei'shkï's features stayed neutral to the point that it seemed she wouldn't reply, but then, she said, "Siv'arid Shaul'auna is irritated that you didn't consult her on your 'little speech.'"

He tsked at that. "I spent all day going over what to say! I even asked her opinion earlier."

Kei'shkï shrugged. "What can I say? She's a fickle *kyesh*," she said, using the Keshic word for woman.

"I'll say."

Kei'shkï said nothing more on the subject. Instead, she got back to business. "I will stay on guard for now, Kins-man. You should get back to organizing the camp. It will be dark soon."

"All right." His emerald eyes slid sideways, critiquing the Tashek for a moment. "I'll get back to it, then. I'll have Jacen or Auna bring food, once it's ready."

"Very well, sir."

Patrick nodded and turned away, relieved one Tashek warrioress was willing to be professional. As for Shaul'auna's stiff upper lip… well, that was just another item on his growing list of things yet to solve.

Chapter Twenty-Nine
§
The Wielder of Ravel

Ill news reached Fortress Opal that late afternoon, while King William Fantill and Commander Matar were having a late lunch in the king's study. A servant brought the missive from the aviary master. The detailed note was written in tiny script, small enough for need of a magnifying glass. It was from the king of Staria.

The *new* king of Staria.

"Long have we awaited news from their front…but of this type?" King William was saddened.

"King Merretham was not a young man," Matar agreed. "But he seemed healthy, robust even, last I saw him."

"It's those damn snowstorms! That weather is rare in Staria. The king must not have borne them well. Darn it all!" Frustrated and grieving, William Fantill slammed the missive on the table between them.

The Crystine commander gave the Sealander a look and then picked up the letter calmly. "Certainly, our new King Al'den has more to say than that…"

"They're riding out," William responded before Matar found the contents in the letter. "Pri—King Al'den is loath to sit around in the cold and without proper word from the other forces."

"Yes." Matar smiled at that. "That sounds like Al'den. With the All'ani and Shi'alam's forces at the Citadel, I can see why he would decide to pursue action over waiting out the snows. He is also, likely, anxious to see his people again with his own eyes. I know I would be if I were in his position."

"You *are* in his position," William reminded him. "You could return to North Point, if you're concerned."

"No. I trust your Commander Averron and my second, Wix, to keep my forces in Sealand healthy and safe. It's the Crystal Kingdom I worry over."

"We haven't gotten any word from farther eastward than the Golden Palace and Kavahad," King William agreed. "It's bad enough to not hear from Raven's Den, but now Sunrise as well." He shook his head mournfully at the omen.

"And the weather in Rubia is severe by reports from Commander Kins. All of Syre east of the Senna River is cut off."

"King M—Al'den," he said, still uncomfortable with former prince's the new station, "says he knows of the condition of Commander Grant's forces and rides to meet them. Besides Commander Kins, Grant is the only mertinean we have the whereabouts on."

"If this was a game of rithmomachy, we would be losing."

"And I thought you hated that game."

"I do." Matar sighed and rubbed his face with a hand. "What I hate worse is being cut off from our comrades. The snows from Ravel are more effective than any route the maunstorz could have created. Being holed up and isolated makes me itch for some action."

"You always were a man of action," King William commented. "Being at Fortress Opal must rankle you."

"I chose this as *Khataum* of the Guardianship. Seeing Serein active and with your son blindly naïve and unaware made the need great for me to stay at his side."

"But his ineffectiveness is putting a damper on things."

Matar nodded. "Had you not already tried Serein on yourself and Celi, I would have asked if you had another son around. Par's reluctance surprises me for a man of such convictions."

"Sadly, I think it's those convictions that make him reluctant." It was a fact both men could agree on. "Too bad Amun is not active. Prince—King Al'den would be a force the wielder of Ravel wouldn't want to reckon with."

Commander Matar shook his head and scanned the missive again. "Alas, we don't even know if Merretham told his son of Amun or kept it near. Merretham wasn't forthcoming to me about it, except a very long time ago."

"And all of this still leaves us country-deep in snows and holding only one stone active against our enemies. You're right…I don't like these odds. Let us pray the Starian cavalry can reach Kavahad and reunite with our forces. The North is unnervingly empty right now."

Matar nodded and stood. He set the missive down and collected up his coat. The commander looked to be a man on a mission.

"And just where are you going now?" asked the king.

"To pray and, then, to knock some of your men around at practice."

In other words, the Crystine commander was too disturbed by the news from Staria—and too proud to show it—to sit still a moment longer reading Syrean messages. "Please, go easy on them, my friend. My soldiers are not as tough as your Crystine brethren."

"All the more reason to practice with them. You Southerners need a taste of the North now and then to remind you of the real world." Matar winked as he closed the door behind him.

"And that's what I'm afraid of," William Fantill murmured to himself as he looked out the window to the calm, western coastline. Fortress Opal seemed so peaceful and so very far away from the ravaged frontlines of northern Syre. Yet, the king knew well how quickly serenity could be shattered. "Stars preserve us that such does not come too soon…"

§ §

The entire Starian cavalry and all of the Sheev'anee but Shík Cum'eri's forces were grouped around the outer walls of the Citadel of Light, awaiting the king's orders. Still inside, King Al'den, Cum'ar, and First Guardsman Meeg Thorson helped the remaining foot soldiers and archers board up the entrances. Beamed up tightly and locked with an intricate stone locking system—a part of the Citadel's defenses since its creation—the king made sure his remaining men would be under minimal threat of invasion from their enemy. The Citadel's high walls had never been successfully climbed in history, so it left the gates as the entries to most invaders. Even still, the commanders guaranteed their king that they would keep constant watches and that "the walls will hold, Majesty, until you return." King Al'den had the utmost faith in his forces.

Then, travelling alone with only All'ani Cum'ar and Meeg Thorson, Al'den headed through the maze of city to a small tunnel hidden in the walls. "The passage is only known to the kings of the Citadel and his closest men," he informed his two companions. "This is the only exit out of the city, besides the main gates." The fact that these two men were being gifted the secret was not lost on the Tashek and guardsman.

"We honor this knowledge with our lives," Cum'ar replied. He and Meeg took a knee and bowed.

"Thank you. I trust both of you and extend this knowledge in sign of that trust." Al'den waved them onward, and the passage narrowed as it went into the city's outer walls. They followed it through corridors that were passable only when squeezed through sideways—a very tight fit for men in armor. Finally, they reached its exit to the outside.

The king paused there and studied the rock indentations until he found the four points needed to activate the door's opening. He had to use some force to push the invisible levers inward, but they finally moved. The barren and snow-covered outside was visible through the small door. The three men crawled through, and King Al'den resealed the exit. The wall looked impenetrable once again.

Their exit took them half the distance between the southern and western gates. The forces waiting for them to the south were barely visible from that point. "Now, we walk," Al'den said, and started toward the cavalry and Sheev'anee horsemen.

"Certainly, by now you know you have no need of that," Cum'ar stopped the king and pulled out a whistle, which he blew without invitation. A minute later, the men witnessed two horses pull from their handlers and come galloping their way. It was Cu'mar's chestnut mount, Casheem, and Al'den's new Tem'arid mount, Kesh. Snorting and fiery, the pair reached their masters and reared in excitement. Cum'ar stepped forward and calmed them with words in Keshic then handed Al'den Kesh's reins.

Al'den took the white horse in hand and went about checking that his tack was in order. He and Cum'ar mounted, and the king helped Meeg swing up behind him; though, the Tashek horses were not capable of carrying an extra rider for long, the short distance back to the forces would not hurt Kesh's back.

The Shi'alam was shaking his head at them as they returned to the horsemen. "A little communication would have been nice, Majesty."

"In this, I could not say," Al'den replied and held out an arm to assist his guardsman in dismounting, "but our forces are now tucked securely into the Citadel. At this rate, they'll fare better than us over Deep Snows."

"Stars, I hope so." The Shi'alam glanced over the great, stone wall of the Citadel of Light, looking fretful. The Sheev'anee leader was reluctant to leave men at the capital, cut off from the rest of the forces.

"I trust in them and this city to hold for a season." Al'den made sure his own countenance looked strong and resolved; he had to be for the choice he was making. Getting Amun back was first in his mind; second was securing Commander Grant's forces from the enemy's clutches. Speed was required for both, and foot soldiers could not cross the Aras Desert in the time required.

"And I trust you." The Shi'alam bowed his forfeit of power and signaled his own forces to prepare to leave. Clan Sheev'arid was heading westward to search for enemies along the way to Port Al-Harrad, the Tem'arids would head directly east, and the All'ani would head south with their king. "Stars' speed, Majesty."

"And to you, until we meet again." Al'den extended a hand to the great Sheev'anee leader. The Shi'alam accepted it with a grip of iron.

Releasing the handshake, the Tashek leader set hard eyes on Cum'ar, "And you, All'ani, keep our king safe."

"On my word and my life, Shi'alam." Cum'ar ducked his head and extended his arms outward in typical Tashek abasement. "At Stars' speed, sir."

The Shi'alam returned the greeting and then signaled his forces away. They broke from the rest of the cavalry and galloped away.

"Shall we?" Cum'ar asked his King of the Yellow Star.

"Yes. Signal the riders." Al'den gave Cum'ar the lead and took one last look upon his great city. He saluted his men sitting high atop the walls, watching their departure. "Keep safe, my people of Staria," he murmured before turning Kesh away and rejoining the front of his cavalry. "Cavalry of Staria, clan All'ani, we head for Paragon!"

The great force of horsemen took up an excited cry and followed their great war-king southward, to guaranteed action.

§ §

The Shi'alam's forces reined in their mounts about one mile from the Citadel of Light and paused to take a final look at the majestic city. The dark shape of the king's cavalry could be seen moving away from it on their way south. It seemed surreal to see the sight after weeks of staying locked in behind the walls by the snows.

"Shi'alam, sir." Shy'tin, attendant to clan Sheev'arid and newly returned from keeping an eye on the Shi'alam's son, Terrik, cued his horse alongside his leader's.

"Shy'tin…I feel as if I'm making a mistake leaving so."

"You were all in agreement this morning."

"Yes, we were." He gave his retainer a hollow smile. "We had been unable to travel away from the Citadel for some time. It was beginning to feel a bit like home…"

"Nostalgia doesn't suit you, sir." The words brought a welcoming chuckle to the Shi'alam. "Besides, sir, we are nomads of the desert. Being cooped up too long will make you soft."

"Well said." The Sheev'anee leader squared his shoulders and turned his mount back the way they had come. He had elected to go westward so he could make a stop at the Ar'heim, to speak with the Oracle and his son. It had been over three moon-turns since he had had any word from that direction, and he felt lost without the guidance. "Head out!"

The riders were on the move again. They parted only long enough for the Shi'alam to retake the lead and then came together again like a wave on the ocean. The horses took up a ground-eating trot and continued across the snow, traveling as easily as if it were sand.

The Shi'alam pointed them toward a landscape that looked familiar; however, there was a prickling to the back of the leader's neck that had him pausing his forces about another three miles westward. *Something feels off…* The Sheev'arid clan leader gazed about the open land, not seeing a thing, but caution rang through his head and gut. He opened his mouth to make an order but never got the chance…

Out of thin air, arrows came raining down around them. The horses panicked, rearing and whirling about, many colliding with each other. The next moment, a whole host of maunstorz were right there, close enough to pull riders from their mounts and skewer them with their jagged swords.

"Leave that one alive!" a voice called out to the maunstorz men who had pulled the Shi'alam to the ground. The four warriors seemed annoyed at the order, but they obeyed. Seeing as the maunstorz had taken out an entire Sheev'anee force in less than a hand count, they could afford to keep one Tashek alive long enough to torture him for information.

"Collect the horses," the voice said again.

The owner of the voice spoke Syrean well, better than the common maunstorz. The Shi'alam wanted to see who this enemy was, but his face was pushed to the snow. It was probably best, elsewise he would see the carnage of his forces around him. Over sixty skilled horseman dead in short order. Unthinkable!

The leader's boots came into view of the Shi'alam. "Bind him and bring him back to the tents. Make sure none else live."

The maunstorz grunted their obedience. Strong arms pulled the Shi'alam to his feet and roughly bound his arms behind his back. Other ropes were tied to his ankles; if the Sheev'arid tried to run, they would inhibit his escape.

Upright, the Shi'alam saw the work done on his forces. Blood carpeted the snow in a red blanket of sorrow. Words of grief and prayers for their souls' safe return to the Stars came to the Shi'alam's lips. Yet, the maunstorz were quick to silence him. The maunstorz then pushed the Shi'alam along in the direction of their camp. Up the dune they all went. The maunstorz camp was revealed with a step over an invisible line. Just like that, the majik concealing the enemy was behind them.

The Shi'alam recognized it for what it was: he was in the enemy camp and among the wielder of Ravel.

"Over here." The man's voice again, dictating where the prisoner was to be brought. The Shi'alam looked there, to the largest tent, and to the young man and Tashek before it. Nallaus and...only one of the Starkindler sons had dark hair. Zeek Starkindler.

The young Crystal-born waved them all to his command tent. Inside, it was warm from a fire and thick horsehide blankets along the walls. The tent followed Tashek fashion; practical and efficient. About two dozen Nallaus accompanied the wielder of Ravel. The lad himself took up a seat at the center. He looked to be in control.

"A traitor to your people," the Shi'alam began.

"The Shi'alam of the Sheev'anee...not the prize we had thought to come by, but still a good one." The words were monotone, mentioning facts only. "But for a ruler of the so-called Guardians of the Truth, you seem to not remember enough."

The Shi'alam replied with a Keshic curse. It only amused the prince, who said, "Denial is dismal for a leader of your caliber."

"What do you know of truths? One serving your people's enemies knows only lies."

"As much as I would love to agree with you, I cannot." Zeek rose from his chair and came near. He dropped to a knee to center his gaze on the Tashek captive. His eyes blazed red. The Shi'alam gulped. "Your histories have left out a thing of two. Syreans are not as innocent as we would like to think we are." Zeek stood and returned to his chair.

"And you think this knowledge justifies you?"

"I know it does."

"You and Ravel are killing more Syreans than all of the maunstorz combined!"

"That is what happens when magics of this power are brought into the world. These 'enemies' of yours have suffered far greater from the Stones of Power than any of the people of Syre. Having Ravel on their side finally evens the odds."

"The Stones of Power were created to protect the people of Syre, not kill them!"

"The Stones are only a conduit for people's rage and hatred. Using them at all only brings destruction." Zeek's face distorted into anger. "They created this cycle of enemies and fighting. And now, the worst of the stones has been activated. Vauldin's powers flow once again. The Stone of Life and Death is the harbinger of chaos."

The Shi'alam couldn't argue that point; he knew well the destruction Vauldin could exact. But the obsidian stone could also bring much good into the world. "It is the intentions of the wielder that bring good or evil. The stones themselves only give access to the powers of the Stars."

"Exactly. As long as people have these powers, evils will always exist. I cannot trust in the goodness of any of the wielders' intentions. Even good intentions can bring about bad results."

"You cannot even trust in the goodness of your sister, Prince Zeek?"

The Crystal-born was silent, a cold frown on his face. "Just what do you mean?"

"Zerra Starkindler, your beloved sister, was the lost daughter of Arrez Xraxrain, heir of Crystalynian and wielder of Vauldin."

The frown deepened. "You lie. Zeera died in the wastes of the Aras nine years ago. I saw her die."

"And Vauldin helped her live." The Shi'alam believed that now wholeheartedly.

A Nallaus woman came closer to whisper in Zeek's ear. The prince listened and then nodded to her. "Perhaps my sister did live thanks to the magic of Vauldin, but I won't know until I face the wielder myself. Yet, you, Shi'alam of the Sheev'anee, won't be around to witness it." Zeek waved to the maunstorz at the Tashek's back. "Zephthaniel, do as you wish with him. The Sheev'anee will not be a problem for a while."

The Shi'alam gaped at the sudden dismissal. He fumbled for words to keep their talk going, but the prince's red eyes staring back, emotionless, haunted his vision as the Shi'alam was pulled from the tent and away to slaughter. It was his last sight beyond the silver of maunstorz steel.

§ §

In the darkened cave, the air currents shifted, and the lone oil lamp's light was buffeted about until it could no longer last. Once it was snuffed out, only the scent of burned oil and the moistness of the caves remained.

The Oracle shifted in her robes, wakened from a light sleep by the passage of the winds. Within her mind's eye, an image took shape, and the old crone *knew*. "The Shi'alam is dead." But the where and why were lost to her. The deep ache of his passing left a gnawing void in her belly. The great Sheev'arid clan leader was gone—and there was no rightful heir to take his place. *The Sheev'anee cannot suffer a fool*, she thought of young Terrik. Yet it was unthinkable to have another clan head take over; the Sheev'arids had led for centuries. There was hope of the girl, Zyanthena, taking over…but even that thought made the webs of fate constrict the Oracle's heart until it skipped a beat. "The balance is broken. Our Shi'alam has passed before his time…the prism is breaking."

The crone's mutterings woke the young seers, and one came near. "Oracle?" The girl's voice was wispy and sweet.

"Rouse the Guardians. I have news that needs to be carried to the clans on swift feet. Go, girl! Quickly!"

Part III

§

(New Year 111 SC, end of First Snow)

Chapter Thirty
§
The Havenese Coup

"Hey! She's coming to!"

The group huddled around and peered down at her with expressions of hope and relief. They were rewarded with a groan. "Back off!" Zyanthena growled as she clutched her head. Her vision cleared to the image of a small, candle-lit room, the basic cot she had been laid upon, and the shadowy shapes of eight men. All, at least, ones she knew. "Lieutenant Madden, report," she said

"That's our commander's 'Night Fox' all right." The men chuckled and stepped back to give her room.

Another Crystine soldier, Ensign Garret, came near and offered her a cup of water as Madden updated Zyanthena. "We are very happy to see you, Zy'ena. Happy and shocked. It's been nearly three seasons since we've seen you and the rest of the Crystine, and one-and-a-half seasons since we lost contact with the mertinean and command front."

"Worse, you just appeared out of nowhere near that old pillar. It glowed and then 'bam!' You were there," said the young page boy, Chris Foller, a bare-wet age of sixteen. The others hissed for the boy to be quiet and made signs of protection.

"Yes, well…" Zyanthena pushed herself to a more proper seat, ignoring their protests to take it easy. She took in the room and the men again. "Where are we? This is not the castle."

Glances went around as the men seemed to debate over how much to tell her. "We'll tell you more once you get your strength back," Madden said. His jaw clenched in anticipation of a fight with their Crystine scout. "You've been out cold since this morning."

Over twelve hours unconscious?! Zyanthena felt herself panic for a moment. It did seem to be dark outside. She could only imagine Lord Darshel's anger and worry at her folly; he had been against the whole idea of scoping out Van'allíer. Also, it was not a good sign that she had blacked out from the teleportation. *Stars, I could have died. Losing consciousness should be the least of my worries!*

Lieutenant Madden seemed to take the Tashek's silence as a form of agreement, for he stood and motioned the others out. "I'll have a stew readied for you when you feel up to it." The Crystine man paused at the door. "There is a lot you probably have to tell us. There are more than just the Crystine who are anxious for word." He saluted his exit, leaving Zyanthena alone to wonder what his words meant. Everything seemed off.

The warmth and glow of Vauldin had her reaching for the stone, and the contact made Zyanthena aware of Kestral's own worry. Apparently, her mother had been calling out for some time. Connected, finally, the queen set about on a tirade of concerns and questions. Zyanthena let her vent until Kestral seemed to have exhausted all avenues of her inquiries. In the silence that followed, Zyanthena asked her mother if blacking out was normal after a jump through the pillars.

I attempted to activate the obelisks back in the day, but my ancient Syrean was poor. As you have discovered, you must be able to pronounce every pillar's name correctly to jump to their locations. What I hadn't learned was the rest of the "call" — all the script you used when you touched Van'allíer. Arrez...

Zyanthena hesitated at the name.

Zy'ena, you've done something beyond my comprehension, so I cannot give you any definitive answers. That ancient codex would have been more informative of such inquiries. You'll find out more once you return to Crystanian.

Zyanthena felt herself balk at the mention of another jump. Even if she did need to return to Crystanian, the bruises all over her body, the headache, the dry mouth and nausea were pretty good reasons to postpone it for the time being. At least, it seemed her limbs could move.

"It's time to see what's up," Zyanthena said aloud and swung her legs over the edge of the cot. Sheer stubbornness had her coming to her feet and grabbing the wall for support; however, the thought of a good stew in her empty belly had her reaching for the door and heading outside before she could think to abort the mission.

In the faint lights of the campfires, Zyanthena made out the place the Crystine were using as a base. It was an old grain-and-hay barn in the far western pasture of the Crystal demesne—far enough from the castle that fires would not be spotted. It was not one of the locations she expected the Crystine to set up a camp.

The suspicion of something being horribly off had her turning to the nearest campfire and finding Lieutenant Madden's familiar shape in the light. The soldier looked resigned to answering her questions as he took in Zyanthena's countenance, set for a "no-nonsense" conversation. Wordlessly, he stood to fill a tin bowl with stew and motioned Zyanthena to a seat around their fire.

Seven others were there as well, and four men the Tashek did not expect. "Lieutenant Dawson!" There was also a man named Cal and two more Kavahadian cavalrymen she had not been introduced to but whose faces she remembered.

"Ms. Zy'ena." The lieutenant saluted her out of respect.

"How many made it?" was her first question to the men from Kavahad. Temporarily, the desert woman forgot about the Crystine's problem as she was confronted with soldiers whose survival she had been unsure of.

"Thirty-five," Cal replied before Dawson could. Zyanthena's brandy eyes shifted to the elder soldier's face. "That's how many men reached Wynward's Crossing and the Crystine. Of those elected to go southwest toward home…"

"We don't know," Lieutenant Dawson picked up as the veteran's voice faded. "The enemy left us alone, it seems, but that first snowstorm came out of nowhere."

"Yes. Yes, it did." Zyanthena heard sadness in her tone. It was her (and Vauldin's) fault for riling up Ravel's wielder, and she hadn't been awake to take any measures against the other's majik. "Still, to find you alive—Lord Shekmann will be relieved."

"Our Lordship is alive?" "Where is he?" "How is he?" "Why isn't he with you?" The questions came out in a garbled mass from the concerned Kavahadian cavalrymen.

"He is safe and well," Zyanthena reassured them. "His Lordship and I are staying at Crystanian."

"Crystanian?" It was Lieutenant Madden again. He had kept quiet, knowing the men of Kavahad had needed their greetings first, but this news was odd. "There is nothing up there but ruins. How are you surviving these snows?"

Zyanthena pursed her lips and set her stew closer to the fire to keep it warm. This was going to take a long explanation. With a request for their open-mindedness and to refrain from questions, the desert warrioress began her narrative of the happenings in Crystalynian. By the time she finished—all the way to the use of Van'allíer—the men's expressions were filled with disbelief; some were even a tad bit unnerved. "All of this would seem impossible had I not lived through it all." She pulled Vauldin free and clutched the obsidian Stone of Power before holding it out for all to see. "The old majiks of Syre are awakening to those whose blood they call. This will become a time beyond the fight of soldiers."

The men looked stunned. Finally, Madden cleared his throat. "Improbable it may be, Zy'ena, but I've heard you Tashek speak of the power of the Stars before and their fates before. Commander Matar believed in it too. I never imagined this power to be so…real, but I'm not about to dismiss something just because it sounds off-the-wall crazy."

"It's no crazier than seeing me pop out of nowhere in a flash of light." Zyanthena kept her tone light to dispel the soldiers' anxieties. Her words brought chuckles to most of them.

"Well, compared to your adventures, I'd say we've had it pretty quiet."

Her sharp eyes narrowed to pin the Crystine man down in a direct stare. "Now, *that* I do not believe. You're not at the Crystal Castle, as you should be, which makes me wonder why you aren't there holding it for the late Starkindler family?" Even if the family had been gone from the castle for nearly nine years, the Crystine—under Commander Matar's direct order—had laid claim to it in hopes of their return. Even the people in the town kept that belief, despite it becoming less of a possibility by the year.

However, one was alive. There was no other explanation for Ravel to be active. Not that Zyanthena was willing to tell the soldiers that. Yet.

Madden rubbed the back of his neck self-consciously, as if guilty of letting his commanding officers down. Still, it was his responsibility to report to Zyanthena on their situation. "Well, you're not going to like this much…"

"Humor me," Zyanthena prompted dryly.

"The pompous prince, Jace Éldon, showed up with a full company of foot soldiers. He had a decree that said the Crystal Castle must come under Blue Haven's control while the main force of the Crystine was away to Sealand—as if we were inadequate for keeping it safe! It was signed by King Jarod himself and accompanied by a raven-and-sword emblem. I'm the highest rank here—which isn't saying much. I didn't have much footing to countermand him. He is a prince, after all!"

She replied, "Yes, a prince of a foreign kingdom." Her voice smoldered with held-in anger. "Pompous indeed! These Havenese bastards are taking full advantage of the chaos to the west." In the past forty years, the Blue Haven crown had claimed territory to their northern border—a mountainous part of Crystalynian—as their own to flaunt their superiority as those with the most land of all the kingdoms. So, it came as no surprise that they were willing to try for the Crystal Kingdom while it sat without a proper king or regent.

"Their timing is sickening. While we are off protecting their asses from the maunstorz, they go and do something underhanded like this!"

Zyanthena made out the soldier who had said that from across the flames. He was a longtime veteran of the Crystine, having lived through the maunstorz sacking of the kingdom, as well as all the fighting since. He wasn't the kind to lie down and roll over to a foreign power. In fact, none of these men were. "And that's why it cannot stand," she said.

Shocked expressions stared back from around the fire. "But… how?"

A baneful look came to the Tashek's features, a promise of retribution for the grave insult to a place and people she respected. "Oh, I have a few ideas. I think I'll need to visit this pompous ass before the morning." The men's worried faces made Zyanthena say, "Relax! I'm not going to do anything untoward to an heir of Blue Haven. I'm just going to make it clear that a Havenese takeover will not be tolerated."

§ §

Before the light of dawn, the Crystine took Zyanthena to the forest cover just outside of the Crystal Castle proper. They blended into the shadows of the pine trees just past the cobblestones and huddled together in small groups to assess the grounds. Already, the Blue Haven soldiers were up and about, stationed in squadrons to patrol the perimeter by torchlight. They seemed neat and organized.

Madden said, "Though the prince said we were allowed on the grounds, it has been uncomfortable working under their commander, Dorian Hartford. His ways are too Southern for my tastes, and he doesn't play well with others. We elected for patrols farther from the castle and at Wynward's Crossing to avoid him. It's kept us cordial enough, though I hear the townspeople are not as gracious toward their men."

"Good," Zyanthena replied. Indeed, she was pleased by the Crystal people's obstinance. "Now, tell me: Where does Prince Jace grace the castle, and what of this Hartford?"

Madden pointed out their positions. "It seems the prince prefers to stay in the king's quarters and study on the third floor, west wing." The warmest place in the castle. "He has an escort of four guardsmen with him at all times. Commander Hartford tends to vacillate between the main grounds, war room, and lesser hall, sometimes even the billiard room. He's taken a liking to the Crystal ales."

"What charmers." Zyanthena's eyes wandered over the castle walls, remembering all the ins and outs of the keep. She was the best one there to sneak in; the main problem was that the Crystine refused to let her go alone—even if she could be most effective by herself. In an argument (that she had won) about keeping the Crystine out of trouble with the Havenese, Zyanthena agreed to the aid of the Kavahadian men. The Starians did not look like the people of the Crystal Kingdom, so using them in a ruse of bandits taking advantage of a royal so far from home would be more probable to pull off. It had been a logical enough plan to subdue the Crystine's occupier.

Zyanthena motioned to the seven Kavahadians she had selected to come with her. "We will go through the dross entrance. The soldiers should be the least concerned with it. Only the castle staff ever use it."

"Yes, because it smells like shit and garbage," replied Madden

"All the better reason." The Tashek grinned at Madden and then returned to a more serious demeanor. "It seems that there is a ten-count pause between patrols. More than enough time to get there. Prepare yourselves. We leave after the next patrol."

They waited in silence as the next Havenese guards marched around the castle and into view. As they passed, Zyanthena shifted her eyes to the men beside her and gave a nod as the Blue Haven soldiers' backs were facing them. With a silent finger-count to her comrades, Zyanthena began her own breath-count to manage their time. With a final nod to Madden, in trust of their support should it be needed, she waved their infiltrating party into action. As silently as possible, eight shadows ghosted across the open cobblestones to the cold granite stone of the castle. Zyanthena led them swiftly and unerringly to the dross door.

She found it locked. Motioning for eyes on lookout, she slid two lockpicks from a pouch at her waist and got to work on the weathered lock. A minute later, it clicked open, and she pushed the door inward. Finding the coast was clear, she waved her comrades inside and barely latched the door behind them.

In a huddled mass by the entrance, Zyanthena issued more orders. "From here, we are in the servant quarters. I've no idea how many remain, but we must silence any we find. In all ways we must act like bandits. Leave it to me to knock these people out. I don't want to kill anyone."

"We're with you all the way, Zy'ena," Lieutenant Dawson said for them all. Loyal to the Tashek for keeping her promises, they would follow her through any hells; it was why she had chosen these young men to come.

"Thank you," she said. "Now look sharp!" They all nodded and kept weapons at the ready.

As luck would have it, Zyanthena only came across a young maid leaving her room and an elderly butler who had just risen for household work. The two servants were quickly dispatched with a Tashek sleeping powder and left in their beds as kindly as could be managed. Beyond their quarters, the west hallway opened to the main halls. The warrioress had her men wait in those shadows as she peeked into the next room. Satisfied that all was quiet, she and the group crept along until they came to a large tapestry on the wall. Behind it was hidden an old entrance to secret passageways in the walls: the perfect mode to move about the castle unhindered. It catered to the Tashek's preference for stealth.

"Hurry." Zyanthena waved the men through and then pushed the old, wooden door closed. "Up the stairway. It gets wider on the next level." As it was, Zyanthena could not squeeze past to lead again; two of the Kavahadians barely fit up the passage as it was.

"These are useful," Officer Jim Danvers murmured before he was shushed.

"Don't think on it too much," Lieutenant Dawson cautioned. "It's doubtful you'll get to raid a castle like this again."

"Quiet!" Cal told the younger men. "To task, men! Jerry, get up those stairs."

Zyanthena huffed her amusement at their banter. It would be hard for their voices to carry through the walls—hence why she wasn't reprimanding the men—but their easy exchange reminded her of another time among the cavalrymen. They all got along quite well and made a good team. All their communications were light.

"I'll lead again," she commanded as they cleared the next landing.

Zyanthena hurried forward to turn them right and up another staircase. She ignored the other passageways in favor of the most direct one to the king's quarters. They made the next landing and continued into a western passage that led to their destination.

At a particular wall, she motioned for silence and then located the peephole she needed to see into the king's bedchambers. The room was empty, though oil lamps from the room beyond indicated the study was occupied. The bedroom would be a good extraction point. "We're here," Zyanthena whispered back. "I'll go first and take out any of the prince's guards. Lieutenant, follow me after I clear that first hallway."

"Understood, ma'am."

Zyanthena ignored the title and prepared herself to sneak into the bedroom. She waited a half-count to recheck that all was clear before pulling the wall inward; this entrance was made of heavy stone, but it slipped free quietly enough. Tiptoeing forward, Zyanthena came to the door and peered around it. There was two of the guardsmen Madden had spoken of at the study's doorway. She paused long enough to motion about the number to the others and waited for an opening to pounce. Now, it was up to her speed and efficiency to take out the guards before an alarm was called.

The Tashek bided her time until the guards were not focused her way. Then, she crouched and rushed the distance between them. Zyanthena came out of the first guard's blind spot to catch him near the point of the jaw, delivering a direct strike to the upper jugular to knock him out. She caught his weight on a spin and slid him lightly to the floor while moving toward the second man. The timing gave the other guard little time to comprehend the attack, and he was out cold before his lips could part in shock. This body was lowered just as quietly, and Zyanthena was already on alert for the other guards by the time Lieutenant Dawson came around the corner.

Eyes, Zyanthena signaled to the Kavahadian men as she motioned that she would check out the study. Trusting the soldiers, the Tashek moved ahead and sneaked a look inside, seeing only the lone form of the prince. Though Zyanthena didn't know Prince Jace firsthand, she was sure it had to be him: short-cropped and coifed black hair, strong jaw and brow line, clean shaven (except the sliver of a goatee), and wearing an opulent overcoat in Havenese hunter green with white lace trim. Only a spoiled royal-born would think to wear such clothes in the cold of winter in the Crystal Kingdom.

Signaling the men to keep watch, Zyanthena motioned that she would go in with Lieutenant Dawson and deal with the prince. One Blue Haven princeling would be no trouble at all. Striding forward, the Tashek made it to within striking distance before Prince Jace noticed anything was off.

The prince had been reading by an oil lamp on the old, cedar desk. At the movement to his back, he said, distracted by his book, "Has the cook gotten breakfast already, Jauken?"

"On that, I would not know, Prince Jace," Zyanthena replied as she neared. The royal had barely enough time to register his surprise when she was upon him. Effectively, she incapacitated the prince in an arm lock that folded him over the desk and set a blade to his throat before a shout could get out. "If you want to live, prince of Blue Haven, then you will stay quiet and cooperate while my men gag and bind you."

"You will pay for this!" Jace hissed.

"That, I very much doubt," Zyanthena replied. "By the time your kidnapping is discovered, you will be far from here and unable to be found."

§ §

"You made quick work of that!" Lieutenant Madden praised as their force hastened away from the castle.

"It's all thank to Zy'ena," Cal said. "Leave it to a Tashek to make us all look outclassed!"

Zyanthena shrugged at the comments and kept one eye on their bounty and the other on the landscape. "All in a day's work, gentlemen. Now, let us hope my ransom letter from the 'High Fork Bandits' keeps the Havenese occupied. Your men's safety requires it."

"We'll be fine, Night Fox. You just get this princeling far away from us."

She flashed a smile. “That’s the idea.” Zyanthena planned to go back to Crystanian through Rast’enn. Taking Prince Jace with her would solve a lot of problems.

Pushing their mounts to a gallop, the Crystine and Kavahadians circled around the demesne to where the old crystal obelisk marked the arrival at Starkindler property. They made Rast’enn just as dawn colors broke the grey of morning.

“Off you get, Prince,” Cal told the royal. The gagged Havener glared and made muffled, angry retorts. Seeing that he was going to be obstinate, Cal and Jerry pulled him off and half-dragged him to the desert woman waiting at the pillar’s base. “He’s all yours, Tashek.” Cal pushed him forward. “Good luck with that.”

“He’s nothing I can’t handle,” Zyanthena assured them, ignoring the emerald glare of her unwilling companion. “You all take care.”

“We will. Though I think you should take our brave lieutenant with you, Zy’ena.”

The desert woman wanted to protest, but Dawson was already at her side with a remark that changed her mind. “Our Lordship will believe we made it when he sees and speaks with one of us. It should be a great relief for him.”

“And this doesn’t scare you?” Zyanthena eyed the young man. She had explained to them all of the obelisks’ and Vauldin’s powers, even if most of what she said was circumstantial at best.

“You made it through,” the lieutenant countered. “I trust you.”

“I don’t trust myself,” Zyanthena muttered inaudibly, but she wasn’t going to argue further. They didn’t have the luxury of time. “Very well. Hang on to me and don’t let go.” Dawson nodded and set himself up. His bravery was worth an applause.

Zyanthena said to Madden, “Tell the Crystine to be strong and patient. I will get word to our commander, and he will reach you latest by Snow Thaw.”

Lieutenant Madden saluted her. “We can hold until then, Night Fox. Your appearance was all the fortification we needed.”

“Very good, Lieutenant. Thank you.” She bowed her head once and then focused on the task at hand. “Leave quickly once we’re gone. At Stars’ speed.”

“At Stars’ speed, Tashek.”

Closing her brandy eyes, Zyanthena sank into Vauldin's powers and felt the stone call to Van'allíer, now recognizable. Amid gasps of surprise and awe, Zyanthena, Lieutenant Dawson, and Prince Jace were surrounded by a flash of white light. In the next blink, they were gone.

Chapter Thirty-One
§
A Royal Kidnapping?

Van'allíer's activation set the queen's garden aglow and scattered the wolves sleeping around its base. As its light reached its zenith, it spit out the three portal users and went dark. The wolves were already milling about the trio by the time the light faded.

Zyanthena, already prepared from her first experience, found herself still conscious, though her body and mind were addled from the abrupt change of location. Her stomach rolled and emptied itself of the light breakfast she had consumed earlier. The acidity of bile in her throat had the desert woman making a face. Luckily, Moon Ember and Swift Hunter were there for comfort; a couple of wolf tongues against her hot cheeks were enough to bring her back to the present. "Ember, Hunter. Sorry for worrying you. Everything went well."

Hunter laid his ears and grumped back his irritation at her recklessness.

"Yes, I agree. I was careless," she soothed.

The alpha seemed to find her admission satisfactory, for he turned away to the other two humans. Both Lieutenant Dawson and Prince Jace Éldon were being thoroughly sniffed over by three packmates: Howler, Too Soon, and Quiet Stalker. The three young males backed off as their leader came over.

"Don't scare them too much," Zyanthena said as she found her unsteady feet and came over. "They could be unconscious. I was the first time." Yet, neither was.

Young Dawson was awake but too weak to move. Plus, having wolf snouts poking about him was a bit unnerving, especially when he hadn't been expecting it. Hunter smelled the young man's fear and nipped his packmates to back off. The appearance of the Tashek's boots emboldened the lieutenant to groan and attempt to sit up. "Easy," Zyanthena cautioned. "It takes a few minutes for the mind to catch up to the body." She helped the lieutenant sit and leaned him back against Van'allíer.

"I feel the need to blow chunks," he said.

The warrioress chuckled. "Yes, well… that is understandable. Do so if you have to. It does get better in a minute." Still, she was impressed. So far, she was the only one who had suffered a blackout from a portal jump. Being aware of it seemed to help counter the effect…

A sound of heavy, bumbling boot thuds and someone crashing through dried plants had her turning to see Prince Jace upon his feet and trying—flailing really—to run away from them. Taking the opportunity of Zyanthena's turned back (and seeing an exit), the Havener had struggled to stand and jog toward the garden's archway. His attempt got him nowhere—the pack of twelve wolves coming to block the exit was a pretty intimidating deterrent.

Zyanthena shook her head at his foolishness and stood to face the prince of Blue Haven. "It's pointless, you know. You're miles from nowhere."

"I'm the first prince of Blue Haven, I'll have you know." Jace turned away from the wolves to give his kidnapper a scowl. It was a brave face considering Hunter and the others could smell the fear coming off the royal in waves.

"I know exactly who you are." Zyanthena removed her fisted hand from a hip and came forward. "The thing is, I don't take kindly to Blue Haven setting an upstart princeling at the Crystal Castle while its protective detail is off saving Syre." She was close enough to poke the Havener in the chest. "Your rudeness knows no bounds."

"You're one of those Crystine. My people will see you pay for this."

Zyanthena matched the prince's snarl. "Your people will be too busy trying to find your ass to know the truth. All of the evidence will point to a group of bandits taking advantage of a royal prince so far from home."

"My men will see through your ruse."

The Tashek's smile didn't carry to her eyes. "Even if they try to pin this on the Crystine, you will not be found in their care, Prince Jace." She spread her arms wide. "You're up north at Crystanian and far from any aid."

He snickered. "You love lying to keep your condescension, don't you?"

"Lying, Prince?"

"There is *no way* we are in Crystanian. That city is in ruins and nearly four hundred miles from the Crystal Castle. In no *sane* world could we have travelled so far in just a few minutes."

The desert woman's features went neutral, though her eyes stayed deep and penetrating. Zyanthena assessed the arrogant royal before her as if he was nothing more interesting than a cockroach walking across the floor. Finally, she shrugged. "Suit yourself. I'm sure a few hours trekking the wilds of the Forbidding Forest will change your attitude. You're welcome to run. I've gotten you far from the Crystine and any more damage that you can do to them." She turned away to the lieutenant. "Can you stand?"

"Yes." Dawson began to push himself to his feet. Zyanthena stepped near to help him and then waved him toward the palace's entrance. They headed for the snow-covered staircase while ignoring the Havenese prince; their movements signaled the wolves to follows. From there, it would be up to Prince Jace to decide if he would run or not, though Zyanthena hoped the royal would have enough sense not to be so stupid.

The door to Crystanian banged open just as the Tashek and cavalryman made the top of the stairs. Lord Darshel rushed out, Zyanthena's name on his lips. He stopped in his tracks at the sight before him. "Lieutenant Dawson?"

"My Lordship." Dawson straightened, pulling himself from the Tashek's stabilizing arm, to give his lord-governor a proper salute. "It's very good to see you, sir."

Lord Darshel was dumbstruck. He looked between Zyanthena and Dawson with disbelief in his eyes. "But—but how?"

Zyanthena stepped closer to the Kavahadian lord. "I traveled to Rast'enn, the pillar by the Crystal Castle. The Crystine found me...and your men." Lord Darshel still looked stunned.

Lieutenant Dawson said, "There are fifty of us with the Crystine, My Lordship. We're as safe as we can be."

"Oh, thank the Stars!" the Shekmann whispered. He had worried all his men had been lost between the snowstorms and the maunstorz.

"I'm sure the lieutenant will have plenty to tell you," Zyanthena prompted, "but may I suggest we find some tea and time to sit? Portal jumping isn't the easiest thing to do."

Lord Shekmann's eyes took in their haggard forms and let his questions stay unasked. "Come, I'll get something ready."

"*Ahnamen.*" Zyanthena began to say more but was interrupted.

"Did I hear them call you a lord?" It was Prince Jace, shadowing them and not staging a rebellion by running away from his captors. He came up the stairs without waiting for a reply and began again. "If you are a lord, I demand you tell these underlings of their folly. I am Prince Jace Éldon of Blue Haven. I must be returned to my men at once, and this—this *wench* must be properly punished for abducting me!"

It was hard to imagine Lord Shekmann looking more shocked than he had already been, but the addition of the Havener had his eyebrows rising nearly to his hairline. His emerald eyes shifted to Zyanthena. She shrugged and murmured out of the corner of her mouth, "A certain complication at the Crystal Castle that needed to be dealt with."

Lord Darshel murmured an "uh-huh" in his throat, knowing more would be said as they settled inside by the fire. Still, this was an unusual turn of events. "I am Lord-Governor Darshel Shekmann of Kavahad, in Staria," he addressed the royal. "But as for me having rein to send you back to the Crystal Castle, I am not the authority here. This palace belongs to the Xraxrain family."

"Then I demand you take me to the ruler of this place," Prince Jace continued, not missing a beat.

Lord Darshel tried to keep the amusement from his face, but it was hard. He turned his focus to Zyanthena, who her head, too fatigued to continue arguing the matter with the pompous prince. "I will see what I can do," he said instead and stood back to wave the trio through the doors. "In the meantime, why don't you come in out of the cold and warm your bones? I am sure recent events have you wearied." The prince huffed, lifted his chin in defiance, and stepped through the threshold. He continued deeper into Crystanian, finally slowing to take in the marvel of the ancient architecture as he ventured farther down the main hall. Prince Jace left the others at the door. Lord Darshel gave Zyanthena a look. "Really? You abducted a prince?"

"That will be explained as well," Zyanthena evaded as she stepped passed the Starian into the warmth. Her pack of wolves were quick to follow. They padded after her as she started for the kitchen, peeling layers of winter clothing as she went.

Lord Shekmann had to shake his head at the nonsense of it all. "And here Zy'ena acts as if she just went out for a stroll..."

"I assure you, My Lordship, she did not." The lieutenant's voice had the lord-governor remembering his presence. "She may underplay it, sir, but Zy'ena was unconscious for a full day after we found her. She looks to be faring better now, though."

The Kavahadian lord frowned at the news—not that it shocked him that Zyanthena would deny the severity of her condition to him. They definitely had a lot to talk about once they got time alone... "Come, Lieutenant. Let me show you to the kitchens."

"Aye, sir. Thank you, My Lordship."

§ §

It took some time to sort out the events of the past twenty-four hours and then settle the two new additions to Crystanian into rooms. Lord Darshel expertly evaded answering the Havenese prince on the whereabouts of the ruler of Crystalynian; some things could wait a few hours.

Finally, the Shekmann found himself alone with the desert woman, in the hallway just outside their quarters. No longer able to contain it, the lord-governor let himself succumb to the emotions he had held back since the Tashek had returned. "Zy'ena!" he started, putting a hand out to stop her from entering her rooms.

"Dar—" Zyanthena's reply was cut short as the Shekmann pulled her to him and hugged her close. They stayed that way for some time before Darshel let his arms loosen. He slumped, his forehead coming to rest on her shoulder and against her long, black hair. Zyanthena made a noise—a hum in her throat—to show her shock, but she followed it by lifting her arms to cradle the lordship's head and shoulders gently. "I am sorry that I worried you. In hindsight, you were right that having Vauldin around the obelisk was a bad idea. I activated Van'allíer's powers unknowingly. It was reckless of me."

"You left me!" Darshel's strangled voice murmured into her hair. The sound was muffled. "You left me here alone with the wolves! I imagined the worst."

"Yes, worse could have happened."

"That's not very encouraging."

She chuckled, just once, before returning to a more somber tone. "I apologize again. I will try to be more cautious in the future."

Lord Darshel pulled himself upright. "That's like telling the sun not to shine."

The words had both their countenances softening into smiles. "Indeed," Zyanthena agreed.

"Yet I'm holding you to that. There'll be reckoning to pay if you try something so rash again."

Zyanthena lifted her chin in mock defiance. "Now *that* I'd love to see you try."

"Woman!" Lord Darshel growled. The protest only served to bring a smirk to her lips. "You're really something. I'd like to wipe that smile off your face."

"Well, I do know a few ways that can be accomplished." Her eyes flashed with mischief.

"So do I," the Starian challenged back. "And I doubt we've got the same ideas."

An eyebrow rose. "Of course not, Lord Shekmann. My thoughts were on swordplay. Yours well…were on a different kind of sword." She looked down knowingly.

"Oh-ho, now you've done it! We are taking this outside."

The Tashek's grin widened. "Now, that's what I'm talking about."

§ §

Within the hour, the Havenese soldiers were in an uproar over their prince's disappearance. First Guardsman Jauken Lautvine was the first to come across the two guards knocked out cold in the hallway. Alarmed, he rushed into the study to find it empty, not an object out of place. It had seemed odd to him for Prince Jace to not have put up a struggle, so he had dismissed a kidnapping out of hand. It wasn't until neither hide nor hair of the heir was found that they suspected worse. Returning to the study, Jauken and Commander Hartford turned the place over looking for clues. They found a ransom note knifed into the wall above the desk—which they had missed before in their panic.

The culprits were surprising.

"The High Fork Bandits of Buckwin!" Commander Hartford growled. It was a notorious group that his people had been trying to subdue for two years. Rarely did they venture beyond the Hills of Buckwin, north of Blue Haven's royal estate and southern Crystal; however, he would not put it past them to go after the Blue Haven heir so far from home and lacking his normal protection.

"This is outrageous! Such audacity!" Jauken tore the paper from the wall to scan the wording more closely. "I knew we should have dealt with those miscreants more thoroughly. Argh!" He crumpled the paper in his hands. "We must chase after them and get word to our troops stationed at South Keep."

"Everything must be done quietly," Hartford cautioned. "The people of Crystal have not been welcoming. They will find us a laughingstock if they hear we have let our prince get captured out from under our noses."

"Don't be so hasty, men."

The soldiers turned to find Prince Jace's personal advisor, Camu Doln, at the door. The slippery-as-a-snake inferior bent down to retrieve the balled-up note Jauken had thrown on the floor. "This is an urgent matter, Advisor Doln," the commander protested.

"Oh, yes, that it is," Camu replied, "But don't let the words fool you into error." Spindly finders stretched the note to its proper size on the desk, and the advisor pulled the oil lamp closer—though the dawn light through the northern windows was nearly adequate enough to read by. "Some letters can be deceiving."

"I don't see how that is," Commander Hartford grumped. "The Buckwin bandits are a known enemy to us. They had motive for this abduction."

"Indeed," Camu replied. "But there are others who would stand to gain from this." Slate eyes snaked about the room. "This abduction was well planned. How did they even get in this room?" It had been an unanswered question during their search. "Only those with intimate knowledge of the Crystal Castle could have evaded our detection."

"Then we ask the staff."

"Yes…and one other group associated with the castle."

"The Crystine."

Camus smile seemed better suited to a reptile. "Exactly."

It didn't take long to assemble two mounted parties to head for the Crystine's known camps at the demesne's edge and at Wynward's Crossing. Commander Hartford headed up the first, heading for

Lieutenant Madden's troop, while Captain John Corbus went the longer route to the bridge; First Guardsman Lautvine stayed to help interview the staff. The men dashed off, their horses kicking up snow as they hurried on their way.

Lieutenant Madden's forces were around the fires having coffee and breakfast when the Havenese arrived. Commander Hartford made a face; disciplined soldiers should not be lazing around so. No wonder his prince had been taken, with such casual lookouts! Or perhaps they were lazing because they were responsible. "Crystine," he acknowledged gruffly.

"Ah, Commander Hartford! You're just in time for breakfast." It was the leader's second, Cole Hayden, who greeted them. He held out a teapot blackened by the flames to show the coffee was hot.

"I ate before sunrise," the Havener replied as he dismounted. He ignored the lad and turned to the Crystine's leader. "Lieutenant, we need a word."

"Oh?" Madden's bushy eyebrows rose, but he stood from his seat to comply. The brawny Crystine man waved them away from the others so they could speak in private. As usual, he seemed to view the Havenese commander with reserve. "What brings you out our way so early, Commander?"

Commander Hartford regarded the other man with eyes the color of darkened rum. He seemed to be studying the Crystine for deception. "We've encountered an…issue this morning."

"An issue, sir?"

"Yes. A group of bandits broke into the castle and took Prince Jace captive."

Madden's eyes widened in shock, as they should after hearing such news. "That bodes ill, Commander!"

"Yes, it does…and if it is the Crystal's fault—"

"Don't jump to conclusions and threats, Commander Hartford! I am as alarmed over this as you are. It has been a while since we've had rebels take advantage of the castle's lack of security, but we are undermanned right now. We will help you look right away, sir. Do your men have any idea on the direction the prince's captors headed?"

"A vague idea. Southward, toward the border, though anywhere along the way can make an adequate hiding spot."

"And you went around the demesne looking for tracks?"

"Yes, though your forces will be better equipped for the looking."

"Then we will get on it immediately, Commander."

Hartford looked doubtful, though much of his countenance remained stoic. "You're quick to help."

Madden frowned. "And you seem quick to suspicion. My people cannot afford to lose face to another kingdom. Your prince's retrieval has become our top priority." To prove that, the lieutenant turned away to issue commands to tack up.

Still suspicious, Commander Hartford returned to his mount and climbed aboard. "Ensign Danver," he called out to one of his own, "stay with the Crystine and help them search. Keep your eyes on them."

"Yes, sir, Commander, sir." The ensign saluted and reined his mount to stay as the rest of the Havenese galloped off.

For the Crystine, it would end up being a very long day.

Chapter Thirty-Two
§
Fight in Desperation

Just ten clicks south of the East Bridge, his mighty mount's legs gave way. Lunier went down and rolled in the snow, and Re'shaird, Aerrisson was tossed away. He came up from his face-plant into an ice-cold snowbank in a hurried panic. "Lunier! Lunier!" Rushing to the steel-grey's side, he held the struggling horse down until he calmed. Keeping up a steady, soothing string of Keshic, Aerrisson began to inspect his horse's legs, praying that one had not been broken. It was by the blessing of the Stars that none were. Beyond relieved, he let Lunier come to his feet.

"I hear you." Aerrisson petted the grey's sweat-soaked coat. "We've run as far as you can. *Ahnamen.* You did well." Taking care of Lunier would have to come first before continuing the distance to the East Bridge. Putting his anxieties on hold, the desert warrior focused on helping his horse.

Off came the packs and then the saddle; only the blanket remained. Aerrisson removed his bedroll and covered Lunier with it, ears to tail. The horse sent steam into the air from the heat caused by his exertion. It would be execrable if the desert mount suffered pneumonia or colic from cooling down too quickly in the frigid air. Next, Aerrisson collected dead grasses, digging them up from under the snow, to make curry brushes. He spent the next hour currying the horse's coat dry and slowly massaging and stretching the mount's legs and back. By the end, Lunier was looking better.

"You rest now, boy. Eat and recharge." Aerrisson rubbed under Lunier's cheekbones, in the deep hollow between them. The stallion closed his eyes in pleasure. "I'll get about fashioning some snowshoes while you do. We'll walk until you catch your strength."

The task of fashioning snowshoes out of pine boughs and a rope woven of horsehair distracted him from the time passing by. If his thoughts strayed to it, Aerrisson knew he would panic that the wasted minutes meant Commander Grant's men were found and massacred—and that thought was despairing. Finally, the equipment was made. Returning to Lunier, Aerrisson retacked him and fed them both a compressed trail bar made of dates, oats, honey, and seeds. It would be the last of his stores unless an animal came across his path. At least water was plentiful with the snows...

"All right, let's go."

Trudging through snow deep enough to come past Aerrisson's knees made the next part of their travel long, slow, and laborious. By the time the sun was setting, the Tashek doubted he and Lunier had made more than two clicks. Resigned, he found a sheltered hollow to bed down in for the night and got a small fire going. Then, leaving Lunier, he searched the darkness for other signs of fires or torchlight; however, all was dark. Sighing, he said to himself, "I hope I'm not mistaken and I really am close to the bridge. But where are Grant's men? Stars, please say they've made it that far!" If they hadn't, it could mean Silvarron's forces had caught up. That thought made his gut clench.

Returning to the camp, Aerrisson tried to force his worry down by taking care of Lunier and checking his equipment. A small meal of roasted rabbit was enough to settle his stomach. Afterward, the Tashek tried to find some sleep—but it was slow to come. Barely refreshed, the desert man and horse set off again, just as the dawn light made the darkened skies grey. Riding once more, albeit with less reckless haste, Aerrisson and the stallion continued to the East Bridge.

The Senna River was iced over as the horse and rider came upon it. Snow stretched into Staria as far as the eye could see. As with the rest of the North, it seemed even the desert had been turned into a plain of snow and ice. The great bridge, signaling the border between Rubia and Staria, was untouched by any foot traffic. There were no old, filled-in tracks across its expanse, meaning no Sheev'anee or mertinean had come by.

Aerrisson cursed and looked about the land with his spyglass. In the far distance north and west was a dark shape on the horizon, but it was still too far away to know what it was. To the east, the forest looked empty of life. "Damn it!"

Grabbing a horse hide and creating a stick of charcoal by burning a branch, Aerrisson wrote in Keshic and attached it in plain sight on the Starian side of the bridge. Turning away, he remounted Lunier and headed straight east at an easy gallop. With luck and a prayer, Commander Grant's men wouldn't be too far away.

Nearly three clicks into the forest, Aerrisson heard sounds all too familiar: the clash of metal and people yelling, screams too. In dread, he cued Lunier to faster speeds until they were near the area where the noise came from. Pulling the steel-grey up, he dismounted before the horse had truly slowed. Sneaking forward from there, the Tashek hunkered into the shadow of the tree until he had gotten close enough to see what was going on.

It was just as the warrior feared. Commander Grant's forces had been caught by the maunstorz. The one hundred and ninety men were forced to make a stand in a bowl between two hills. It seemed, at least, that they'd had some time to prepare. Stacks of felled trees had been placed about the camp in a ring of protection against the enemy. The supply horses were at the center, and the mertinean were hidden throughout the circle with small fires at each station. Rounds of arrows—readied to be lit on fire—were plentiful among the soldiers. Too, it seemed some traps had been placed about the perimeter; a number of skewered maunstorz hung from some already sprung. Commander Grant and his men were not going down without a fight.

"You remain here, boy," Aerrisson murmured to Lunier and signaled him to stay as he crouched away. The desert man knew he made a poor backup to a full cavalry of horsemen, but he would do all he could to help Grant's forces. The first step was thinning the enemy's numbers where he could—a task the Tashek were masters of.

Keeping to the shadows of the trees, Aerrisson sneaked around to the left edge, where he could hear the maunstorz were concentrated. There were a fair handful of corpses already lining the snow from a failed attempt at surrounding the mertinean. Even so, some braver—or just more reckless—maunstorz remained about the perimeter in wait for an opening to rush in; these men were now Aerrisson's targets.

The Tashek warrior knocked two maunstorz unconscious and slipped them to the snow. Only when they were stilled did he finish them with a slash to their throats. Then, he crept forward to find more. Another three were taken down in similar fashion; however, a fourth managed a warning cry before he was felled. The closest handful of enemies were alerted to their man's death, leaving Aerrisson suddenly very occupied with defending himself.

The five reinforcements came to surround the desert man with guttural words exchanged between them. They flashed their jagged weapons in challenge as they readied themselves about their prey. In reply, Aerrisson took up his two *kora* blades and came to a calm, ready stance at the center of their circle. He paused in a half crouch and let his eyes flit between the five maunstorz surrounding him. His pause seemed to signal to the enemy to pounce.

Yelling, the five maunstorz broke into action. The first came from Aerrisson's back. The Tashek stepped about in an arc to bring a sword up to block. He whirled around the other's sword to slash out at the maunstorz's thigh, cutting it deeply, and continued away to the next attacker. He slashed the next in a one-two-three clash of metal to deflect another's blade before he could finish the attacker off. Aerrisson kicked the third maunstorz away and renewed his thrusts at the second one. He finally dispatched this enemy on a turn and thrust. The second maunstorz crumpled to the snow as the Tashek whirled away to take on the other three.

The next two came in a pincer attack. The first took Aerrisson head on, distracting him enough for the other one to come around behind. The sting of a blade across his shoulders alerted Aerrisson to the danger. Ducking to a knee, he struck out in both directions to take the maunstorz out at the knees. Blood sprayed as the two enemies crumpled to the snow. Following through, the *kora* blades flashed a deadly silver as they came about to finish off the downed maunstorz.

That left only one.

The last maunstorz seemed infuriated by the loss of his companions. He came at the Tashek in a rush, abandoning his sense of caution in favor of revenge. Aerrisson was able to block his thrusts easily, matching the single blade move for move. On an eighth stroke, he slipped under the blade to the opening of the enemy's exposed side. From there, the maunstorz was quickly put down. Re'shaird, Aerrisson came to a pause, winded but otherwise unharmed.

Still, there were sounds of battle all around the clearing. It seemed some of Grant's men had taken to the trees, just as he had, to fight the enemy one-on-one. The rest of the mertinean stayed hunkered down behind the piles of logs and sent out volleys of flaming arrows into oncoming maunstorz. There were a number of men down on both sides and still a whole host of the enemy forces pouring out from the trees beyond.

Aerrisson assessed all of this quickly and made sure to move back into the cover of the forests. The maunstorz, it seemed, were doing the same, so he would have to pick down their forces in small groups, one by one. Somehow, the Tashek knew, he had to make his effort count.

§ §

"*Seka.*"

Silvarron turned from his vantage point on a boulder above the bowl the enemy had made as their stand—a poor footing, in his opinion. *Only fools go to lower ground like that.* Still, the fools were making a good effort to keep the maunstorz at bay. The traps and flaming arrows were a deterrent, but even that only delayed their inevitable defeat. "Speak."

The underling saluted and continued in rough Syrean basic. "There are two hands of enemy in forest." He pointed out where in the circle. "One to far right real good. He take many."

"Oh?" Silvarron stroked Kautch's chest as he considered. "So…it may be *that* man. Show me."

"*Ka.*" The maunstorz saluted again and led the way with five others as escort. They continued around the side of the hill cautiously, staying well back form the opposition's arrows and men. It was only as they reached the area where a number of their elite had been posted that the man leading them move their party closer to the fighting.

Silvarron's best fighters had been felled some time recently. Bending down, Mansocan's Second-in-Command felt their blood to find some puddles still warm, as were the bodies. The blade cuts were not like those from the enemy's mertinean; they were thinner and deeper. "Desert sword," Silvarron murmured, finally recognizing the wounds. He had seen enough of the injuries from fighting the desert dwellers of Staria to know that now. Yet he had not expected one of the desert men to be among the Rubian forces. That explained a lot of the raids against Raven's Den.

"*Seka?*"

"You will return to your task of watching our forces," Silvarron said to his maunstorz henchman. "These two will stay with me." He pointed at two fighters he trusted to cover his back.

The man refused to say, *"Are you sure?"* Though the question was in his red eyes.

Silvarron rose from his crouch to his intimidating height. "I said go. I have prey I need to hunt...the little snake is taking naughty bites out of our forces."

§ §

Aerrisson was past the count of fifteen enemies slain when he got a tingling up the back of his neck. Feeling watched, he crouched down in the snow by his recent kills and looked warily to the stands of trees about him. The main fighting had moved deeper into the bowl and closer to Grant's men, but there were some maunstorz still trying to pick at the perimeters. Yet none had given him the sense of a predator watching. Was it really the gaze of an animal or maunstorz? His gaze centered on a shape on the hill above him. Aerrisson narrowed his eyes and focused there.

Suddenly, a large crow flew at him from the shadows, its claws aiming for his eyes. Aerrisson let go a yelp—unable to hold it in—and reacted to the dark shape. Rolling and slashing, he managed to get the bird away from him; however, he now knew the enemy coming for him.

Yet, it was not Silvarron that appeared, only two of his underlings.

They came charging from the right and left, using their leader's bird as a distraction to get into position. They closed in as Aerrisson found his feet but were already a stroke behind the Tashek warrior. He slashed right and left in a deadly cadence with his continuous footwork, weaving a circle between them that kept their blades from ending his life. The two enemies fell under his barrage.

A hollow clap filled the air. Aerrisson turned to meet its owner.

"You desert men live up to the stories. I'm quite impressed. Those were two of my best, and you cut them down as if they were poor fighters." Silvarron's cultured voice was smooth as silk and as sweet as mountain honey. He seemed more like an aristocrat than a soldier. He was not as Aerrisson had expected. "What? So sullen. Do you not wish to thank someone for their admiration?"

"Admiration?" It wasn't a word he had expected a maunstorz to use—nor had Aerrisson expected such well-spoken Syrean. It was nothing like the guttural language of the enemy.

"Yes, admiration." The crow came back to Silvarron's shoulder, and the maunstorz leader petted it absentmindedly. The bird continued to peck at his fingers until he turned to study the object in its beak. "Ah, one of your people's emblems," he said as he took the silver piece the bird had taken from Aerrisson's hair. "An interesting way of marking your people's rank and status… do you know the Nallaus do the same? Though they say they are nothing like you." He huffed. "Traditions die hard, it seems, even for those forsaken."

"The Nallaus were once Sheev'anee."

"Yes." Red eyes rolled up from the emblem to the Tashek's face once more. "Which is why I know what skills your people possess. Of all those we oppose, you are the main thorns in our side—much the same as the Crystalynian leaders of old. Of Tashek blood, were they not?" Silvarron's hard line of a mouth turned into a charming smile, but only for a moment. It became a tight line again as the long-limbed man tossed the emblem through the air back to its owner. "The desert warriors will fall as the original kingdom did. Your race into fighting will be your undoing."

"You say that only because you fear our strength." Aerrisson caught his emblem without taking his eyes from his opponent. If Silvarron had wished it to be a distraction, it was not. Quickly stashing it away, the Tashek began a slow, calculated step around his foe.

Silvarron seemed amused. "The only thing I need fear is death itself—but that will not be for me today." He lifted his long cane and twirled it expertly in the air before him.

"That is no weapon for a warrior."

A corner lifted of Silvarron's mouth. "Know this, young Tā-shek: no descendant of Xercon ever walks without a weapon. Ever." The Second-in-Command of the maunstorz armies closed in the blink of an eye and met Aerrisson's sword with the edge of his cane. They clashed with the sound of metal on metal.

Aerrisson knew, then, that the cane was built for fighting. It would be no surprise if it contained a blade concealed inside as well. He parried and stepped around the enemy man in a beautiful but deadly dance of skill. For once, however, Re'shaird Aerrisson was not the tallest or the longest-limbed in a duel—his usual advantages. Silvarron had to stand at a tall six-foot-three!

"What's the matter?" the enemy taunted. "I know your skills are better than this. I had hoped for a more entertaining fight."

Slashing quicker and spinning around his opponent, Aerrisson growled his frustration at being unable to find an opening for an attack.

He tried to force an advantage, but the maunstorz commander was showing why he had won such a position in the army. For the first time, Aerrisson realized he could be outmatched.

That seemed to amuse the maunstorz. Silvarron grinned as he shouldered the desert man, coming through his defenses to make impact. It jarred the Tashek and sent him stumbling. "On your guard!" Silvarron warned as he lunged into range again. The end of his cane was missing its cover, revealing a knife point headed straight for Aerrisson's heart. Reacting by instinct was the only thing that saved him from being skewered. Aerrisson tumbled away and tried to find his footing, but the enemy was still at him. He rolled just as the weapon almost caught his inner thigh. The weapon spliced through his pants instead, drawing blood.

The warning was not lost on Aerrisson; Silvarron had nearly gotten him in the femoral artery—a mortal wound. If he couldn't keep up with the other's attacks, he was a dead man. Chilled at the thought, Aerrisson kicked himself away to roll down the hill. He whistled loudly as the roll jostled him through the snow and landscape hidden underneath. His descent ended in the bowl between the two hills and nearly to his ally's defenses.

Yet not close enough.

Behind him, Aerrisson thought he sensed Silvarron coming near, running and sliding down the hill toward his prey. Time was running out. He rolled to face up to find Silvarron nearly upon him. The maunstorz had his cane raised for a killing blow. Time seemed to slow as Aerrisson watched the specter of his death close the gap between them…

The next second, a grey form came between them, and Lunier reared and lashed out at the man trying to kill his owner. The stallion touched down with feet still slashing and teeth gnashing at the enemy. Silvarron was effectively blocked from Aerrisson by the fiery steed. Shocked, the maunstorz man retreated, nearly falling in the snow in his panic. Lunier kept after the leader until he was chased farther away, up the hill. The stallion only turned away when Aerrisson whistled him off. The steel-grey came galloping back, and Aerrisson swung aboard and kneed his mount toward Commander Grant's barricaded defense. Jumping into it over a pile of logs, Aerrisson made his return to the mertinean.

Chapter Thirty-Three
§
The Snows Are Thy Prison

"You crazy Tashek!" Commander Grant greeted, turning away from the watch to find the desert man. He still couldn't believe the entrance he had just witnessed: first, Aerrisson had fallen down the hill to escape an attack by the enemy, only to be saved by his horse at the last. The six-foot jump over the defensive log pile had been the last insane part of the whole deal. Thank the Stars that Lunier was such an extraordinary mount. Most of the mertinean horses would not have made the jump.

"I had to make a grand entrance, just for you," Aerrisson bantered back. It beat admitting just how screwed he had been just a few moments ago. "Besides, I figured you could use a little reinforcement."

"A cavalry would have been better," Commander Grant griped and waved them back to the protection of their log walls.

"Well, I wish I had that for you, too."

"Was that Silvarron you were fighting?"

"Yes." Aerrisson felt his jaws clench. It had nearly been the death of him, matching weapons with that maunstorz. "And his skills are greater than I anticipated." Grant's eyes narrowed to hear the admission. "He will be one enemy to watch out for."

"An enemy with skills to overpower a Tashek? That is ill news indeed."

They hunkered down against the defensive log pile and sneaked glances at the enemy. The volley of arrows and traps had kept the maunstorz away all that morning, but it was becoming evening and they were still trapped. Against an enemy known to fight even into the night, it seemed the mertinean were on the losing end.

"Tell me what I can do," Aerrisson asked.

"Help keep the men awake and on guard. Let us hope we don't run out of arrows too soon. I fear we will not fare well to take on close-quarters combat."

"I will make a run to collect arrows as openings allow."

"I would not risk you on such a task."

The two men shared glances. "And I would," Aerrisson argued back. "We need them to keep the maunstorz at bay."

A shout brought their attention back to the forest as another round of maunstorz neared. The firing of the arrows began again. This new enemy group was thwarted just as those before it had been, but there were more maunstorz to take their place.

"We will have to engage them at some point," Aerrisson continued his argument. "I will go with a few men under cover of night and take down another round about the perimeter. I took down nearly two dozen before Silvarron appeared."

Commander Grant was surprised. "So many?"

"And I will take more."

"Later, then, but only when the enemy tires and gives us space."

Aerrisson doubted such a time would come, but he wasn't up for wasting breath when there were more important things to do. "Very well. For now, I will go support the other side of this wall. I won't leave the defense without telling you."

§ §

By supper, the Blue Haven princeling was beginning to suspect that the deflection of his inquiries to the Crystalynian rulers was a ploy to distort the truth. The Kavahadian lord-governor was respectful and polite but very obtuse on the whereabouts of the king and queen. As for the rest of the staff…the great palace seemed far too empty. It was fully furnished and stocked with top-shelf comforts any royal could want, yet the whole place seemed only a figment of a dream without the bustle of residents. Something was terribly wrong, and Prince Jace was determined to know what that was.

Resolved, he finally got the courage to wander from the fine apartments he had been situated in and strode down the hallway to the grand staircase leading to the main level of Crystanian. Turing the direction he remembered, Jace made his way to the dining hall. It ended up being easy to find with the delicious smells coming from the kitchen; however, the entrance had him pausing in trepidation.

The young lieutenant was there, scratching behind the ears of a motley brown-furred wolf. Dawson turned at the sound of the prince's footsteps. "Oh, there you are. I was just going to come find you for dinner."

Prince Jace stared down his nose at the Kavahadian's lack of decorum. "I am not a *you.* I am Prince Jace Éldon, heir of Blue Haven."

Lieutenant Dawson wasn't cowed. "Yes, as you've said several times, Prince."

"It's *Highness*, Lieutenant. If I need to remind you again, I will ask your superior to reprimand you."

"Yes, Highness," the soldier replied and turned away before the royal could see him roll his eyes. Pompous princeling indeed! "Come, on. His Lordship and Zy'ena are waiting."

"Um." Prince Jace cleared his throat and waited for the young man to look back at him. "These…beasts. Can they not be moved?"

"They're not going to do anything—not unless Zy'ena tells them to." Dawson continued into the dining hall, leaving the royal to come through the pack or be a coward and head back to his rooms.

Prince Jace made a face as his request was ignored; however, his stomach ached from hunger. So, he had to puff himself back up and creep through the bundles of fur blocking his entrance to the hall and its feast. Once through the gauntlet, he breathed a sigh of relief at not becoming a wolf's lunch and came the rest of the way into the dining hall.

It was empty, save for the three people he had been introduced to already—his kidnappers and that lord-governor.

"There is soup and bread, Your Highness." Lord Darshel rose and bade the Havener to a seat. "And good Crystani wine."

"I'm relieved to hear it," Prince Jace replied as he came to the table to take an empty seat across from the Kavahadians—as the woman was at the head of the table, he had to make do with the empty left side. "I had begun to wonder if I was to be subjugated to poor, docate faire."

Zyanthena made a huff in her throat. "His Highness should be grateful for food at all, as I doubt he could accomplish the task if left to himself."

"Zy'ena," Lord Darshel warned.

Still, Prince Jace glowered at the remark. "I may be your prisoner here, *woman,* but I am a royal of Blue Haven. You must treat me well if you expect the ransom to be paid."

That had the Tashek chuckling sarcastically. "And he's still going on about this ransom business," she murmured to no one in particular. Then, Zyanthena looked back at the Havenese heir with eyes of liquid, brandy fire. "And I am not *woman,* Prince Éldon. My name is Sheev'arid, Zyanthena. Though you may use its shortened version, Zy'ena. For all intents and purposes, I am ruler here, *Prince.*"

"You are not the queen of this castle."

"It's a palace, Prince, and I am its heir—just so we can get that out of the way once and for all."

The prince gaped at her tirade.

But she wasn't finished. "You may stop requesting Lord Shekmann for an audience with the king and queen of Crystalynian. I am right here, so you may speak to me at your leisure."

It was almost a shame to see the Havener's aristocratic, dark features turn blotchy with forming veins and red hues as his blood pressure rose with his stifled anger. Certainly, he and Zyanthena seemed to bring out the worst in each other at every encounter. It boded ill for future fights to come. The peace of Crystanian was ruined. "Y—you! It is not possible that you are the ruler of Crystalynian! Y—you." He sputtered and glanced to the Shekmann lord. "She…?!"

Lord Darshel wiped his mouth clean on a napkin before motioning Prince Jace, who had risen in disbelief, back to his seat. "Zyanthena speaks the truth, Highness. Her bloodlines have been confirmed to be those of the Xraxrain's daughter, Princess Arrez."

Prince Jace sputtered again. "I—I can't believe this!" He gulped and tried to patch together some semblance of authority. "So…your kidnapping of my person has created a political entanglement worth full repercussions! My family has footing to disparage you to all the other kingdoms of Syre."

Zyanthena looked bored. "Threatening me will get you nowhere, Highness, and, as you were the one to make a political gaffe first—by taking over the Crystal Castle—I don't see you winning any favors to help save you from this situation."

"I was there to hold down the kingdom in the Starkindlers' stead."

She scoffed. "I'm sure Commander Matar will not see it that way. Until the true family can take the Crystal throne once again, the castle has been in the care of the Crystine. Everyone in Crystal knows this. Your takeover reeks of a Havenese coup to take over the Crystal Kingdom."

At least the prince has a sense to look offended. "I—we—were doing no such thing! Blue Haven and Crystal are allies, and the maunstorz our enemy."

"I'm glad you've got that straight," Zyanthena replied, deadpan. She raised a glass of wine to take a sip, using it to create a pause, though her sharp eyes never left his face. The warrioress continued after swallowing the wine and replacing the glass. "Your seizure of the Crystal Castle will be thwarted thanks to your disappearance. Your men will have a whole season to think over their actions against another ally, while their search for you will continue to have no good leads. They will have to pronounce you lost at some point." It wasn't hard to imagine how King Jarod would take that news. "As for you, Prince Jace, you are not a prisoner here, except for the snows that bar your passage south. I suggest you learn to enjoy your stay. It's going to be a long few weeks with us all together."

§ §

Prince Jace finished his meal in a heated silence. His first grievance was the woman. There was no way in all the stars above that she was ruler of Crystalynian! Besides, wasn't the kingdom long dead and in ruins? Though he had to admit that Crystanian seemed pretty solid in all respects. His second grievance was the food. They had provided him only one course of soup and bread. There hadn't even been a main meal! It boded ill for any better service in the days to come. Worse still, the Kavahadian lord-governor had no quarrel with a royal being treated in such a way. Now that his hands were washed of the duty of granting an audience to the ruler of the keep, Lord Shekmann seemed content to follow the woman's lead. It was all so dastardly!

Zyanthena was the first to leave the table; her pack of wolves following her was the only good news to her parting. The Shekmann was next, leaving the dishes in the care of his young lieutenant. Dawson seemed hesitant to leave the royal at the table alone; however, the prince made no effort at polite conversation and left as soon as the last of his wine was drunk. Ignoring the other man, Prince Jace began to wander down the halls.

He still didn't believe that he was free. Despite their assurances that the prince was no prisoner, Jace could not help thinking of his state as otherwise. Yet, the long and empty halls of Crystanian seemed an unusual prison. It was more like house arrest in a grand Southern mansion.

And there were wonders to be found in the palace. A full, heated sitting room with windows overlooking the deep gorge and wilds outside showed the great expanse of mountainous terrain outside Crystanian's walls. Another room with shelves upon shelves of books and old tomes was the most extensive library the royal had ever seen—if he had time for books. There were other apartments, all as large and well furnished as his own, on both the second and third levels of the palace. On the fourth story, he found evidence of an aviary and a full open-to-the-air training room equipped with weapons of all shapes and sizes.

Prince Jace became lost, then, in a maze of rooms and hallways. He found a winding staircase on the eastern side that ended back on the main floor. Was it a passage for servants? With no one about, it was hard to tell. His wandering ended back at the kitchen, which was, astoundingly, stocked full to the rafters. The sight had him thinking up an idea—one he was quick to enact. Finding an empty sack, Jace filled it with foodstuffs that would not easily spoil. Finished, the prince sneaked back to his assigned quarters and shut the door.

"I will give it until nightfall," he muttered and stuffed the food sack into a corner. From there, he began to prepare a bundle of clothes to layer. "They make it far too easy." *Idiots.* The Havenese heir finished by propping his door open—so his captors could peek in on him—and put himself to bed. Feigning sleep, he kept an eye on the failing light outside his window and bided his time.

When it seemed enough time has passed, Prince Jace rose and tiptoed to his door. The hallway was empty and dark save for two candles. The coast was clear. He turned away to collect the clothes and food and then left his rooms. As he sneaked down the hall, the prince could not believe his luck at not being discovered. Still, he crept through the palace all the way to the front entrance. He pulled the heavy door open only enough to pass through and came out into the frigid mountain air. By the time he reached the stables—he had seen them from the aviary—Prince Jace was shivering and breathing on his hands to warm them.

At least the stables were warm, like most of the palace, and well lit. Prince Jace took advantage of the warmer air to set down his provisions and put on layers of the Crystani wools he had pulled from his closet. He then turned to the task of tacking up a mount to carry him southward.

There were two horses in the stables; a broad-boned grey with dark mane and tail, and a black courser. The first looked strong and able but—Stars!—the black was beyond stunning and well suitable as a prince's steed. It was the second horse that Jace chose to approach and tack up. Though it took some coaxing, Prince Jace managed to saddle and bridle the black stallion. He then tied down his food and clothing bundles behind the saddle and led the courser from the stall. The black snorted at the stranger handling him but tolerated the prince leading him to the stable entrance and mounting. Getting outside was another matter, however.

Unrevealed was having none of it. Without his master, he wouldn't leave the warmth of the stable to go out into the cold and night. His refusal quickly escalated into a battle with the Havenese prince—which the man lost. With a final say on the matter, Unrevealed bucked the rider off and trotted back to the comfort of his stall. Prince Jace came to his feet, furious, and marched back to the courser. That time, however, the black stallion would not let him near. Ears pinned back, the horse rushed the royal with teeth bared and front feet slashing. Finally fed up, Jace threw up his hands, cursing profusely, and marched away. He would have to find another way home.

Defeated, Prince Jace returned to his rooms and proceeded to throw clothes and bedding about in a frustrated rage. Nothing was going his way, damn it all! Yet, somehow, some way, he was going to escape and return home. Somehow.

§ §

Zyanthena waited in the shadows until the angered prince was gone before going to her mount's side. "Unrevealed," she murmured softly and held a hand out in signal for the stallion to come near. "You're so good," she continued to praise as she proceeded to hug her horse's strong neck. It was still true: Unrevealed wouldn't let anyone but herself aboard his back—a fact the Tashek had counted on when the Havener had tried to take him. "Let's get all of this off of you," she said of the tack and gear. "The prince was rude to leave it on you after all that."

"You were right that Prince Jace was going to try and run."

Zyanthena turned her head to see Lord Darshel from the corner of her eye. Still, she continued to unload the Crystine horse as she replied. "He was too predictable and gave up far too easily, in my opinion."

"For a man used to being waited on hand and foot, I'm impressed he made it this far."

"Right," she scoffed. "We should be relieved he has an eye for excellence. If he had chosen Tano, I would have had to chase him down."

"Oh, don't underestimate my old man," Lord Darshel said fondly of his war charger. "Tano would come back to me at a whistle. I trained him for that. The prince would not have gotten far."

"Perhaps."

Lord Shekmann chuckled at Zyanthena's reluctance to agree. "At least we now know that the prince gives up easily. There's little else he can do to get out of here."

"That doesn't mean I won't be vigilant. Prince Pompous will be watched day and night."

With the wolves around, Lord Darshel didn't doubt that. "I still would like to know why you brought him here. Surely you knew he would be a problem?"

"Not this much of one," Zyanthena admitted. She became silent for a time, staring at a spot on her black's coat as her mind wandered. "Really," she continued, "I hadn't thought past helping the Crystine and my anger at Blue Haven for their actions."

"That's unusual for you."

The warrioress turned to face the Kavahadian lord. "Indeed, but I do not regret getting him away from the Crystine. Those men fight hard enough as it is. To be subjugated to that…" She shook her unruly raven hair. "I could not allow it when I had a chance to correct such a wrongdoing."

"It will not end Blue Haven's control of the Crystal Kingdom."

"But it will give them something else to do until I can get word to Commander Matar and the rest of the Crystine."

"That'll be over a season away."

"No, it doesn't have to be. I plan on reaching out to another stone bearer, one I know whose stone is active."

"Oh? And who would that be?"

"Prince Par Fantill of Sealand. If I can find a way to reach him using Vauldin, we could get word to our allies in the west."

"That is quite the gamble."

"Yes, it is."

"And you think it will work? Contacting him, I mean." There was an underlying current of worry to the question.

"On that… I do not know, Darshel." Yet Zyanthena looked as determined as the Shekmann had ever seen her. "But I will try to get through. I am loath to staying penned in all these seasons without word to our forces. Now that I know I can travel about Syre, it seems remiss of me to just sit here and wait."

"Will there be risks to contacting Prince Par?"

"Yes, with everything there is always a risk, but I am the wielder of Vauldin. I won't let a little snow from Ravel hold me back for long. Syre is still under siege. The maunstorz and Ravel's wielder will learn to fear me."

Given the dangerous look in the Tashek's eyes, the lord-governor of Kavahad did not doubt her words. Lord Darshel wondered (as he had times before) if all of Syre could come to fear Sheev'arid, Zyanthena and her obsidian stone, if she truly unleashed its awesome powers on the world. The thought was too worrisome to contemplate.

Chapter Thirty-Four
§
Extrication

"Okay, bring her around again. Like that, right! Lower your hands and give her her head," Rowin called out as he watched the maunstorz leader trot a mare about the stable yard and circle back around. What had started out an odd and awkward request to teach the enemy man about horses had begun to be a welcomed time of the prince's day—at least he was around his favorite animals again. Plus, the Sunarian was finding that Mansocan was a talented man and a quick learner; he seemed to master any task the prince assigned him in a matter of hours.

This latest task of teaching horseback riding and horse husbandry was also a breath of relief from their previous leverages of Sunarian state secrets. There wasn't any need to tiptoe around details or feel guilty for selling out just so he and the other prisoners could eat and stay warm. All in all, it was a much better arrangement—not that Rowin wasn't careful to watch himself.

"Stop," Mansocan said to his mount as he reined back the dun mare and came to a halt by the Sunarian prince. The maunstorz leader dismounted like a veteran and turned to his prisoner. "I am beginning to appreciate these creatures' strength and speed. You people are clever to use them to cover great distances."

Prince Rowin nodded politely and took hold of the mare's bridle so he could pet her broad cheekbone. "Yes. They go farther than a man can travel by thrice the distance."

Mansocan eyed his prisoner with a penetrating gaze. "You seem reserved today, Princeling. Has something happened to dull your enthusiasm for this task?"

"No, there has not…" he continued after a pause. "I just envy you the freedom of being atop this mare. Long have I been without a decent ride."

The maunstorz stared back stoically for some moments before he shifted and handed the prince the horse's reins. "Then you will be given that small freedom."

"But?" Rowin was shocked.

"I need to see the proper way of doing things. You will ride this horse and show me all you are able to do with her."

"I... well." Rowin dared not get too hopeful. "I will, then, but this mare is only for a lady to ride, quiet and behaved. She will not be able to do all that horses are capable of."

The news seemed to intrigue the enemy man. "And what else do you mean?"

"Horses are very versatile. They can be taught to pull a cart or plow a field, jump over obstacles, made to dance, or even to fight on a battlefield."

"Ah, yes. That I have witnessed." Mansocan nodded. "Those...what did I hear them called? War chargers?"

Rowin nodded.

"They were as spirited as their riders. Very intimidating. Is there a horse here who can do all that?"

Rowin shook his head. "Not that I saw."

Mansocan bobbed his head at the mare. "Can you do some of those advanced things with this mare?"

"Yes, some."

"Then show me. Make me see this animal's worth."

There it was, that small reminder that the maunstorz were always gauging a human's or animal's value to see if they were worthy of life. It almost made Rowin balk; however, he wasn't going to let this small opportunity to ride a horse again go by. Even if his body protested afterward, his soul would be overjoyed. Slipping the mare's reins back over her head and coming along her side, he lifted a foot to the stirrup and mounted. It felt like heaven to find his seat at the last.

Mansocan nodded, his red eyes always tracking his charge and picking up notes on how to sit and use the body to perform cues. It was like the maunstorz was memorizing Rowin's every action to put it to memory. "Use the yard as you see fit," he bid, as if the royal needed permission to move the mare forward.

"Sir." Rowin bobbed his head and asked the mare forward with his seat and legs. The mare was quick to respond—more than he had expected. Feeling the lightness of her response made the prince test her paces on gaits and lateral work. That each maneuver was quickly executed changed his opinion of the mare's capabilities; she was almost as well trained as a courser. With a delighted grin, Rowin asked the mare to a canter and began to make more advanced maneuvers about the tiny yard.

Horse and rider seemed to fly across the snow, skipping to different leads effortlessly as the prince guided her into figures. He found a few different piles of objects—two water barrels here, hay bundles there, a broken gate by an open pen across the way—to jump the horse over. She flew over each with ease.

The prince pulled the mare up, then, until she was nearly cantering in place. He studied the yard until he spotted a bone left over from a carcass, sticking up out of the snow. Signaling the mare to a gallop, he steered her toward it. Coming near, Rowin slipped to the side of his saddle and bent low enough to scoop the bone up from the ground. It snapped off easily. Righting himself, the prince saw a bucket set out on the other side of the yard. They charged toward it, and Rowin deposited the bone within it without pause or upsetting the bucket. He pulled the mare up short again, feeling her prance excitedly after their exhibition. Rowin grinned. He was as happy as the mare to be performing.

"One more thing," he muttered and pointed them to the barn, where a pitchfork had been left carelessly against the outside wall. The pair galloped past, and Rowin grabbed up the utensil to hold aloft in a ready position for a throw. Coming back around the yard, he aimed for a hay bundle and let the pitchfork fly to spear the target in a perfect throw. "Good! Good girl," Rowin praised and brought the horse back to a walk. He patted her warm neck and exhilarated in a ride well done.

It was only as the afterglow faded that the Sunarian realized he may have overdone it. There was a small group of maunstorz gathered at the palace steps as he walked the mare about the yard to cool down. Most looked wide-eyed at the unusual display; however, it was Chornauk's sullen glare that tightened the prince's chest. The maunstorz Third was not pleased to see their prisoner so free and contented.

A clap to Rowin's left brought his attention back to the maunstorz leader. Mansocan had not moved from his spot at the center of the yard. "Truly outstanding, Prince of Sunrise! You outdid yourself with that little event."

The royal came near to dismount. He knew better than to gloat. "I am surprised myself." He turned to pat the dun's neck. "This mare was trained better than I had surmised."

"You seem to have a talent for riding."

"Yes. I've ridden since before I could walk."

"So young?" Mansocan sounded impressed.

Rowin shrugged. "It's just in my blood, I guess."

The maunstorz leader made a noncommittal noise in his throat. "In any case, Prince, I will have you teach me more of those maneuvers. They seemed impressive."

"Only after you learn the basics," he argued back—even if it wasn't wise. "Riding is a process like learning to wield a sword."

At first, it seemed as if Mansocan would deny his point, but the comparison to swordsmanship seemed to sway him. "Then I would know the skills to advance to those."

The Sunarian bowed his head. "Very well."

The two of them shared a long look before Mansocan broke the silence with a satisfied nod of his head. "This is enough for today. Do what you need to put this horse away. You will join me for lunch."

Rowin nodded—as if there was a choice in the matter—and turned away to cool the mare down with a few laps about the yard. He returned to the barn to untack the mare and brush the dried sweat from her coat.

A sharp dagger thunked into the dirt by their feet, startling horse and man alike from their task. Rowin turned to find its owner at the barn entrance. Of course, it was Chornauk. "Prince," the Third hissed as he stocked closer. The royal ignored the dagger and enemy man, getting back to his brushing as if there wasn't a threatening presence to his back. "You cocky little upstart," Chornauk started in. "If I see you pick up another tool you could use against my leader, I will kill you."

Yes, that was stupid, Rowin admitted to himself. "Mansocan asked for a demonstration, so I demonstrated."

The hulk of a maunstorz leaned over to retrieve his dagger—probably more irritated that the Sunarian hadn't tried to pick it up and give the Third a reason to slit his throat—and came to loom over Rowin's shoulder. "Even still, watch yourself, Princeling. Once you lose favor, I will be delighted to gut you for Mansocan."

"That, I do not doubt."

Chornauk sniffed, clearly annoyed he had not gotten more of a reaction. Still, he finally backed off to wait for the prince to finish so he could escort him to his leader's room. Prince Rowin knew better than to make him wait. Quickly, he finished his grooming and led the mare back into her stall, with fresh water and hay. Rowin returned to Chornauk so the other would know he was done. The Third glowered but waved the prince to follow him back into the palace. From there, they returned to the king's chambers and Mansocan.

The leader was not alone.

"Take a seat," Mansocan indicated the open chair between Rio Ravesbend and himself. The table had been set for three, but only dished for two. Rowin worked his jaw but came to sit; he was already concerned about Mansocan's motives if Rio was in attendance. "Chornauk." Mansocan waved his Third to leave the room and waited until they were alone before waving his servant-boy to bring them lunch.

The boy came and deposited two bowls of soup—potato and leek, Rowin was beginning to suspect, was the maunstorz's favorite—and three pieces of bread. Only Rio wasn't served the soup. Rowin's midnight-blue eyes narrowed. He eyed the enemy leader and then purposely slid his meal to Rio after having a spoonful for himself. His reaction amused Mansocan. "You Syreans are something else. No man of Xercon would serve his underling better fare than himself."

"Where I come from, it's called being *polite*," he retorted and ignored his lord protector's worried eyes. "Besides, my lord protector serves me well. He deserves good treatment."

Mansocan looked between them, as if storing more academic information in his mind for future purposes. "So, you use rewards for work well done?"

The prince frowned, finding the question unusual. "Yes…people become more motivated by sugar than vinegar."

"I do not understand this phrase."

"It means pleasure versus pain."

"Ah." Mansocan fixed his red eyes on Rio. The lord protector had yet to touch his soup and seemed shocked at their conversation. "Is it not to your liking?"

"Ah… what?" Rio blinked, blindsided at not being ignored. "Oh, no…it's ah…"

"Just eat it," Rowin coaxed his friend. "You could use a little more sustenance."

Rio still seemed more wide-eyed than usual, but he did pick up his spoon and began eating the hot soup. The movement seemed to satisfy Mansocan, for he continued his talk with the Sunarian prince as if they had been discussing the weather. “This use of…sugar seems strange. Certainly, you lose credence for being so lenient?”

Rowin was beginning to suspect a cultural difference was in the way—again. “I’ve not seen that to be a problem.”

“Really?” Mansocan sounded skeptical. He shook his head. “You Syreans are so soft.”

“You say that as if our graciousness is a weakness.”

“It is ineffective.”

“Then what is?” Rowin asked, turning the conversation so he didn’t have to hear more insults against his people.

“Cutting off fingers…or other body parts.”

The prince blanched, which made Mansocan grin.

“There are other punishments too, but I think you understand.”

“I do.” Rowin’s eyes travelled to Rio. His lord protector had paled at the mention of finger-chopping—not that his prince could blame him. Rowin still couldn’t help his throat closing up at seeing the empty space where Rio’s ring finger had been.

“But that is not why I have you both here today,” Mansocan continued, calling the royal’s eyes back to him.

“Then why?”

Instead of answering, Mansocan slid a letter Rowin’s way. Rowin hesitated at the trillium-and-crown seal: the royal seal of Sunrise. “They sent another plea.” Finally, Rowin picked it up and took his time reading the flourished sentences. He was frowning by the end of it. Mansocan said, “As you see, Prince of Sunrise, your court wishes to pay such a price to see Connel returned to them. Fools, are they not?”

Prince Rowin tossed the letter to the table. “They offer you an exorbitant reward.”

“Yes, they do, and for it, I would return their insolence by sending them the young prince’s head.”

“Oh, please don’t!”

“And why not?”

“For the first reason, Connel *is* my brother. We may not get along most of the time, but I would never wish his death. Secondly, such an action would be counterproductive. You would anger the Sunarian court and bring their revenge. Don’t you already have enough battles against the Northern kingdoms without adding the Southern ones as well?”

Mansocan spread his arms. “I’ve effectively cut off the North.”

"Only for the winter seasons. By Thaw, the Northern armies will realize what has happened. They will come here to take Rubia's capital back—even if only for principle. I've seen the effectiveness of the Northern armies. They won't stop until you've been pushed back from Rubia."

The enemy leader seemed amused by Rowin's faith in the Syrean forces. "I've had plenty of battles against your North. In fact, a number of generations of descendants of Xercon have fought your armies. We get better with each turning of the seasons. My father's generation took down your great Crystalynian Kingdom, said to be at the height of its power. Then, my own forces went straight to the heart of its neighbor, the Crystal Kingdom, and plucked the ruler and his heirs from the castle—*just on a whim*, to see if it could be done." He grinned at the growing shock on Rowin's features. "I had my forces leave with the royals before a proper counter could be made. Without the head of the Crystal Kingdom, it has become near ineffectual, just a remnant of a territory. That was when I knew...to take your kingdoms out, I only needed to control those at the highest positions of power. You Syreans and your levels of power and prestige," he chuckled, "are so easily influenced. Unlike us. When one falls, the next steps into place. There are none of these petty fights after a leader is gone. We all know who is in succession to whom. Far more effective."

Prince Rowin was dumbstruck to be given so much information on the maunstorz; Mansocan wasn't usually so generous. The Sunarian's silence prompted the great leader to continue speaking. However, it was in a direction not to Rowin's liking. "So then, Prince of Sunrise...you warn me against sending your brother's head home in a sack, but how will you extricate him and save the younger princeling from his fate?"

Certainly, Rowin could sense the hint of warning in the words. Mansocan had made sure to placate him with their conversation until he could go in for a distressful stab between the ribs. Rowin's midnight-blue eyes tightened in his worry—the only other outwardly sign that the maunstorz man had taken him off guard. Still, Rowin was a cautious man and well versed in their usual parley. "What price would you seek to be adequate for such a boon?"

Mansocan made a happy murmur in his throat, pleased Rowin had thrown that back at him. "A few things could be arranged." The prince's face darkened as he thought about all the possibilities that would make the maunstorz leader smile so, some of which had to include someone else's sacrifice… "But there is one I like best: you prove to me your conviction by being your brother's champion."

"Champion?"

"Yes." The grin was predatory. "I like the idea better than sending the courts someone's head, don't you?"

"And just what is a champion?" At least by a maunstorz's definition.

"One who fights for another's right to live."

That had been Rowin's suspicion.

"My prince!" Rio whispered in horror.

The lord protector had almost been forgotten until his protest. "Are you volunteering in his stead, good protector?" Mansocan challenged, knowing Rowin would not approve of his man being used as a shield once more. "The other lord protector already met his end for his prince upon your capture. Are you saying you'd take his place?"

Rio gulped and turned white as a sheet, but he still looked chivalrous enough to volunteer, even with the mention of Elis Thorpson's death.

"No one is taking another's place," Rowin countered, "least of all Rio."

"So, no killing of the Rubian royals or courtiers, then?"

Rowin made a face. "Definitely not. This is a Sunarian matter, after all."

"So good to see you take your share," Mansocan goaded.

"Of course." He wasn't going to do anything less—except die, that was off the table. Rowin squared his shoulders. "And just what will I need to do to win mercy for Connel?"

Now the grin looked delighted. "You will need to fight your way up my ranks; a man a day from my weakest to my strongest." He indicated the last as himself. "Every *vsenk* you defeat will lighten his cost."

"And for each one who defeats me?"

Mansocan had that look of *now you understand.* "Another body part gets sent home."

"Oh, Stars above!" Rio cursed.

Rowin wasn't fazed. He had suspected as much. "Fighting a man every day seems excessive for someone imprisoned for two seasons."

"Not at all, young princeling. I have to get you back in shape for fighting my best. If you can't defeat those lowlifes, then you're not worth much to me except as a stable boy."

Which, to the maunstorz, meant he was worth next to nothing.

Prince Rowin sensed how high the stakes were. Still, he raised them by making concessions. "For this position, then, I ask you continue providing adequate food and water in the amounts we've been given, twice weekly—and any medical supplies I need for myself to be decent to fight. I know your people are thusly cared for, so I demand the same attentions as they."

For just a moment, it seemed that Mansocan would say he had pushed too far and would call off the whole scheme in lieu of finishing off Connel. The look in his red eyes said had been dangerous enough to say all that. Yet, Mansocan replied, "Then you will also concede to continuing teaching me the ways of your horses. In return, I will keep the prisoners fed."

Prince Rowin straightened in his chair to become more regal. "Very well, Mansocan. I can accept that."

§ §

Back in their cell, Rowin was hearing an earful not just from Rio but Connel as well. The other two Sunarians were aghast at this most recent "request" of Mansocan's.

"You certainly have a death wish, brother, bartering with that *thing*!" Connel growled.

"Would you rather it be your head sent to Sunrise?" Rowin argued back.

"Of course not! But I'd not have you fight day in and day out on my behalf."

"On your behalf keeps you alive."

"Maybe, until you *lose*." Rowin and Rio hadn't kept that fact from Connel. "Each time you do, I get chopped to pieces."

"Then I won't lose."

Connel shook his head furiously. "Would that I had such faith in you, brother."

"I don't ask you to, only that I have it in myself."

Prince Connel huffed and turned away to sulk in the corner.

"And what of us, good prince?" Yory Selèv asked of the Rubians. He and Prince Derek had been conversing with each other when Rowin and Rio had been returned. Until that pause, they had kept silent while the three Sunarians had their heated discussion. The break had given the lord protector time to speak.

"You will be left alone and provided for."

"We owe you a great debt, Prince Rowin," Prince Derek said.

"No, you don't." Rowin came closer to put a hand on the sickly man's boney shoulders. "Rubia has suffered greatly as it is. You owe me nothing to stand in their way and be a shield. I am capable of that, so trust me to do so."

"You are very brave. I will find a way to repay your valor…when we find our freedom again."

It was good to hear another have faith in the possibility. "And that is what I fight for," Prince Rowin promised and gave both men a nod of respect. He let his voice carry to all the prisoners. "We are not done yet! They keep us alive because we have more value than if we are dead. I won't let the maunstorz forget that. If it takes me fighting and bleeding every day to be that reminder, then so be it! We will make it through this and find our freedom. On my word!"

§ §

In the king's chambers, Mansocan was hearing his Third's normal rants against his decisions to give the Sunarian prince so many freedoms. Chornauk was finding these latest additions too much to bear; he thought it unseemly that a prisoner was given such free rein and handouts. "This undermines all your power, *Seka'vlr*! It was bad enough to have the boy bartering for supplies, but this?"

Chornauk had already been at it for some minutes while Mansocan was turned away, looking out at the pathetic Red City through the stained glass windows. However, he was at his limits on hearing his Third squawk at him over his decisions. Spinning, Mansocan came at his underling with a dagger at ready. He made it past Chornauk's defensive block and held the blade at the other's throat. "I will not warn you again," he said tightly. "Last I checked, I am still *seka'vlr*. My rules and decisions stand."

Though the maunstorz Third was taller and bulkier, he knew there was no way to beat Mansocan in a fight. Just the fact that the leader had gotten in for a neck cut was proof enough. Chornauk glowered but kept still—in case Mansocan went through with the move. "*Seka'vlr.*"

Mansocan's dangerous gaze stayed locked on his Third's face for some breaths more. He waited for the other's acknowledgment that he could take Chornauk's life whenever he chose. The other finally gave it by closing his eyes and pressing into the blade to draw blood. "If you cannot follow my orders, you can go replace Chaenyeu," he said, referring to the armies' Fifth-in-Command. A demotion.

"There is no need, *Seka'vlr.*" Chornauk stepped away and ignored his bleeding neck. He bowed. "I will continue to do as you command."

"See that you do…or it will be your head I send to Sunrise."

Chapter Thirty-Five
§
A Day of Courting

Master Galandrés's workshop was off the main street, tucked away through a back alley; most passersby would not have known it existed—unless they knew what to look for. The master swordsmith preferred it that way.

The inside of the shop was anything but small and drab, however. The entrance came through three archways that slowly expanded the building space until they emptied patrons out into a spacious, open floor plan. The old stonework gave the place a feel of permanence and solidity, while the shine of silver, steel, and bronze pulled the eyes to hundreds of swords and rapiers about the walls, all in various states of completion.

Ferris Galandrés was a wonder himself. He was a humble man upon acquaintance but with a wit and good humor to entertain. The sword maker was especially delighted to host his apprentice, the royal heir, and the prince's guests. As he always did when Prince Par Fantill came to call, Ferris dismissed his staff—so none could send gossip through the town of the prince's activities. Par appreciated the anonymity. Rare it was for anyone to receive private instruction from a master bladesmith known throughout Syre for making the most detailed weaponry.

"Come in, Prince Par!" Ferris called to their entrance from the far side of his shop. "I'm just finishing up the final touches on the fuller of a rapier. I think you will find this design much to your liking."

Prince Par led the way through the archways and helped Lady Yvonne down the few steps to the main studio. He then continued on to the master, leaving the Limonté woman to take her time admiring the room, accompanied by Lord Gordar. "I don't know a work of yours that I have not appreciated, Master Ferris."

Master Galandrés laughed and turned from his task to shake the prince's hand. "Indeed, but this piece is truly magnificent." He lifted the finished rapier so Par could study it closely. Tiny sapphires had been inlaid into small, white-gold rosettes across the intricate spires of the fuller and handle. The metalwork itself was more elaborate than any piece Par had seen the man make thus far—and yet, the balance of the blade was perfect when held on two fingertips at the base of the blade.

Prince Par shook his head at the perfect weight, not unbalanced by the addition of the gems and spires. "This is truly a masterpiece."

"I designed her with you in mind, Highness," Galandrés commented with a smile as he took back the rapier. "I figured your other blade will be in need of a proper tuning, what with your person being stationed at North Point for a season. A prince needs a proper rapier at his hip. This one could do finely in that respect."

"Ah, but such a beautiful craftsmanship should not be sullied by blood."

Ferris tsked at his refusal. "A blade even as lovely as this is only useful for one purpose." He swatted Par's backside with the weapon, as if the royal was nothing more than a young boy in need of a lesson. "Besides, your blade is not as strong or as balanced. It does not become our prince to fight with such a thing."

Prince Par looked to the blade he had brought with him. It was the sword he had fashioned himself after hours upon hours of training under the master swordsmith. It was not as lovely or as perfectly crafted as Galandrés's, to be sure, but it brought back fond memories of the long hours under the man's tutelage. The blade was steady and dependable in a fight too. "That may be, Ferris, but I've become attached to this one."

They shared a laugh as the bladesmith carefully set aside his latest work, and they turned their attentions to the lord protector and the lady. "I see you have brought along your own beauty," Master Galandrés praised as he came over to Lady Yvonne to introduce himself properly.

"You are much too kind, sir," Lady Yvonne replied, smiling sweetly at the man's charm.

"Oh, not at all, fine lady!" He took her gloved hand and kissed the knuckles politely. "I have an eye for things of beauty and would never lie when I see such." Lady Yvonne blushed at the praise but covered it with a curtsey. Master Galandrés gave her time to recover by greeting Par's cousin. "And Lord Gordar. You are well?"

"Yes, Master Galandrés." Lord Gordar accepted the man's handshake.

"Good to hear. I am relieved, as always, to have you so close to our prince."

"As I am his shadow, I fear Prince Par is stuck with me." They laughed at the private joke. "But I am happy to be invited along today."

"And I am pleased you all decided to call on me." The words were extended to the prince and his lady. "Now come, come! Please, enjoy looking about my shop." Master Galandrés reached out to take Yvonne's hand. "I would be delighted for you to see whatever fits your fancy, m'lady."

"Well," Lady Yvonne started a little shyly, "would it be too much to ask to see how you work, master?"

"Why, not at all, Lady Limonté."

"Yvonne, if you please."

"But of course." The sword maker waved her along to see his forge room with its molds, hunks of precious metals, and large bellows that were two-and-six paces long.

What started out as a discussion on the process of sword making slowly transformed into a small practicum of sorts. Lady Yvonne's enthusiasm and intelligent questions led Ferris into continuing the work on a sword he had started that morning. The master showed her how to run the bellows and even allowed her to help pound some of the reheated blade into shape. It was many, long minutes before the two of them realized the prince and lord protector had left the forge room for their own explorations.

"My prince," the lady chastised as they found the royal and his cousin in the small practice yard to the back of the workshop. "You would leave a lady so unattended to come practice sword play?"

Prince Par bowed his apology with a sweep of the sapphire-studded rapier. "My apologies, lady, but I know Master Galandrés is ever the gentleman. You were in no way of harm."

"Still—" she began but then relented when the sword maker touched her arm to calm her. "It was really nice to see you at work. Thank you." Yvonne gave the bladesmith a smile.

"Of course. It was my pleasure, m'lady." Galandrés brought her hand to kiss her knuckles as he had before. "I am always ready to show my work to those so willing." He indicated Lady Yvonne take a seat on the small bench by the practice yard and turned away to get them both some wine. Ferris returned and passed her a goblet, then joined her on the bench. He indicated the two cousins should continue their fencing. As the two Sealanders began again, he said to Yvonne, "I am surprised, with your interest in weapons, that you do not fence yourself, Lady Yvonne."

"She's an archer," Par spoke first as he and Gordar traded some strokes.

The words prompted Yvonne to roll her eyes. "I may excel in archery, good prince, but I have been given rudimentary lessons in fencing. It just happens to be something I've not become good at."

"That's the same thing as saying you're lousy at something," Par bantered back.

"My prince." Gordar warned his cousin to hold his tongue.

"Indeed, Highness," Yvonne replied and took a sip of wine to try to conceal her offense; however, she did say saucily to her bench partner, "But that's his way of trying to make himself seem superior after losing to me in an archery contest." As expected, it prompted the sword maker to join her in a giggle at Par's expense.

"Yes, yes," Par replied back. "I know you'll never let me live that down."

"Indeed, Highness, I don't intend to."

The prince returned her eye-roll and then focused on his next attacks against Gordar. Par seemed to be struggling with finding openings; his cousin's defenses were solid. After five minutes—and only two touches for himself—Par called a break from their fight. They came closer to their observers and accepted the goblets of wine to wet their throats.

"You seem to be lacking at attacking, Highness," Galandrés pointed out. Being the prince's instructor at the rapier, he had the right to critique his student.

"Yes," Par agreed between catching his breath and having some wine. "Actual battle demands a different kind of swordplay, however. I've had to adjust to using the standard military swords. Also, fencing fares ill against maunstorz attacks."

As Ferris had never fought the enemy, he took his prince's word on that account. "I would be intrigued to see your other practice, then,"

"Another time." Par exchanged his master's rapier for a towel to dab off his sweat. "We have taken up enough of your time. Besides"—he flashed a grin—"I can't have Lady Yvonne see me beaten twice by my cousin in a day." He reached over to give Lord Gordar a companionable one-armed hug.

"Indeed not, Highness," Ferris agreed, laughing. "Well, then, let me see you all out. Lady Yvonne, it's been a pleasure.

"For me as well, Master Galandrés." Yvonne stood with the sword maker and let him take her hand through his offered arm.

Par and Gordar shared a look as the master bladesmith and lady headed back to the front of the shop. "They're getting on nicely," Gordar said.

"That they are," the prince agreed. "I had hoped this outing would keep the lady well occupied, but now, I fear, I've created a new way for her to torment me."

"The lady does absorb information rather astutely." They came to the workshop, and Gordar returned the prince's rapier and his own to the main table. "This sword is impressive," he turned the conversation. "You really should accept it from Galandrés."

"Maybe." Par didn't look convinced, but he did run his hand over the gilded hilt and sapphires. "Unfortunately, I've no time for competition duels right now. This rapier would sit untouched for seasons."

"We can always hope the maunstorz are defeated within the next turning of the seasons."

"We can only hope..."

"Highness!" Lady Yvonne called from the archways. "Shall we get on our way?"

Her words called the two Sealanders' attention back to their real business. "Yes, my lady," Par replied and motioned Gordar to follow him back to the front door. "Master Ferris," Prince Par continued, shaking the man's hand, "I thank you for letting us grace your workshop."

"Of course, Highness. I always enjoy your company. You may call at any time." Galandrés bowed to his prince and then gave Lord Gordar his own farewell. He waved the three visitors off as they paused on the stoop-side of his doorway. "Don't be strangers. I expect to see all of your again soon."

"We will try. Thank you, Master Ferris." Par waved once more and then led the way to the main street. The usual hubbub from the main market seemed muted as the crowd began to thin for dusk. "My, it's late!" the prince realized as he looked about. "We should be getting you back."

Lady Yvonne frowned at the prospect. "But you have not graced me with dinner, Highness." Par opened his mouth to argue the point, but the lady forged on. "It would only be polite, Highness. And besides, Lord Gordar is accompanying us, so there are no improprieties to staying together a little longer."

Prince Par blinked as his main argument was refuted. That Gordar didn't disagree showed that Lady Yvonne was correct on her points. "However, it's not wise for the royal heir of Sealand to walk into an establishment out of the blue. The fuss would be horrendous." Not to mention the place would boast for weeks afterward.

"Then I suggest you choose wisely."

Lord Gordar sensed an argument pending and stepped in to head it off. "A meal does sound appealing, my prince. I do have a suggestion, which I think all will agree on..."

"And what would that be?" Par looked a little irritated.

"That seafood street vendor you like on the wharf."

Par was incredulous. "It's hardly a place to bring a lady!"

"I'm all in," Yvonne countered immediately. "I would love to enjoy some fresh seafood." She stepped through the two men and caught Par by the arm. "Lead on, Highness."

Par wanted to be flabbergasted and protest, but it was a losing battle with the Permonde woman. He resigned himself and motioned his lord protector to lead the way onward, trusting Lord Gordar to keep them from too many eyes but also out of danger of shadier side streets. Luckily, Master Galandrés's shop was only one street up the hill from the section of the city that spilled into the wharf, and it wasn't a long walk to enter the bay area. Another plus was the coming night, which made it harder for the common folk to recognize their prince. The three of them managed to make the docks without creating a fuss.

"Your family will frown upon this," Par murmured as he scanned the small market of food vendors on the main walk to the docks.

"What they don't know won't hurt them."

"Stars," Par replied, "that's even worse!"

Lady Yvonne chuckled and released the prince's arm to skip ahead to his cousin's side. She peered curiously at the vendor's wares. The place Lord Gordar had led them to was one of the oldest street markets in Sealand. All the stalls were lively and competitive as they tried to sell the best fish and seafood to the moderate crowd.

"Do you have a preference, Lady?" Lord Gordar asked. He seemed pleased to have a willing dinner to share in the assortment of fresh catches.

"Ah, what's best, Lord Gordar?"

"Those scallops are always a delightful starter, and that vendor over there makes a mean flounder over seasonal vegetables and porridge.

There's also some sea urchin at that place—with good liquor, too—or lobster bisque in a bread bowl there…" The two of them wandered about the small block of vendors, leaving the prince sulking at the first stall. They finally returned to a small bench table the prince had snagged, loaded down with an assortment of dishes.

Prince Par eyed it all in dismay and shook his head. "Far too much food."

"It looks good to me," Lady Yvonne said cheerfully as she sat down on the bench across from him. Alone, without her family or attendants, the lady was overly casual, yet her behavior could (almost) be looked at as endearing and innocent. Lady Yvonne Limonté seemed to not notice her two companions' shared glances as she dug into a seafood soup, tearing off break chunks like most commoners would. "Mm," she hummed and sopped up more liquid with abandon.

Lord Gordar had to stop his cousin's staring with an elbow bump. "Eat up, cuz."

"Uh…yes." Par went back to eating his fish on a stick while keeping his eyes on the lady across from him. He couldn't believe how unpolished Lady Yvonne could be—yet it was a breath of fresh air compared to a stuffy dinner in a top establishment. The thought had the prince finally easing his attitude and joining in on a conversation about Master Galandrés's shop.

It was well past dusk—and several dishes through—that they finished up with their meal and escorted the fair lady home. In the lone light of a lamp, the prince and lord protector saw Lady Yvonne returned to her family, hopefully without any rumor of a scandal to follow by the next morning. The heir and protector returned to Fortress Opal by a back passage, and Lord Gordar stayed with his charge through a glass of fine brandy and a game of rithmomachy.

"Your second official courting seemed to go well," Gordar broached the subject carefully and only when Par seemed relaxed by the alcohol.

The prince made a noise in his throat accompanied by a frown. "Perhaps…though taking dinner at the docks was rather gauche for a proper assignation."

"Ah, come now!" his cousin scolded as he moved a piece on the board. "You liked the casual atmosphere, and Lady Yvonne seemed intrigued by the street vendors."

"Still, it's not the place to take a lady of the court."

"As if you're one for all those pleasantries and rules," Gordar teased.

"No. But I do need to act accordingly. Bypassing the rules could lead to scandals galore."

"Check," the lord protector said as he got a winning move on his cousin. Gordar sat back to enjoy his drink while Par studied the board with a deep frown of concentration. He continued with their conversation, "And here, just a few seasons ago, you were bemoaning court policy."

"I have forced my hand into this position." Par meant his courting of Yvonne Limonté, but the statement also included his losing the game against his cousin. "Thus, I have to act accordingly. Whether I like it or not, I can't keep flouting the rules. Next time, I must invite at least one of her lady companions along to keep some semblance of propriety."

"That is a wise idea."

Par shook his head in defeat at the game and sat back into his chair. "If only wisdom had a part in that."

"No, I guess not. More, the voice of the king and queen."

"Yes." Par gave Gordar an exasperated look and picked up a cigar to cut and light. He settled back to enjoy a few puffs before passing it to his lord protector. "I guess, though, that courting Yvonne Limonté has not been all bad."

"See, you do like her."

"Only as much as a man in my position should."

"You're just being stubborn."

Par nodded solemnly. Then, his cousin's expression had the prince chuckling, unable to hold the stoic pose. "You can stop looking at me like that. Yes, I had fun with the lady today, and, yes, she is beginning to grow on me."

Lord Gordar passed the cigar back before rising from his chair. "Just so I've got that admittance from you, my prince." He gave a mocking bow to his heir and charge. "With that happy news, I am going to take my leave. I will have Brantley and Kennet posted at your door."

"Good night, Gordar. Sleep well!" Par raised his voice for his retreating lord protector to hear.

"And a good night to you. May your dreams be filled with a certain lady tonight."

"Ha! And may yours!" Par bantered back in friendly defiance. He knew Gordar, at least, would have an actual lady in his bed that night—if the rumors of the lord protector's secret affair with a certain lady of the court was true. It was hard to know when the loyal protector wouldn't confirm it to his prince.

Settling into his quarters alone, Par finished off his drink and cigar until his body dictated he needed sleep. However, rest and happy dreams were not to be. An unusual and vivid dream came to the prince of Sealand—as if his recent run of happiness was not meant to last while his heart carried the lost love of another…

"Prince Fantill of Sealand? Prince."

The voice was commanding but lovely and seemed to drift into the Sealander's dreams like a soft caress. Though oddly, it was as if the presence was speaking through a wall of glass.

"Who is it that calls me?" Par asked and heard his voice echo, as if in a grand Estarian cathedral.

"I am the Queen of the Black Star, wielder of Vauldin, and heir of Crystalynian, good prince—however, you know my by two other names…"

"I do?" In truth, there was a nagging familiarity to the woman's voice that he could not place.

"Yes, Prince of Sealand." The voice paused, and there was a sound akin to knocking against the wall separating the prince from his mind's intruder. *"I see you have yet to accept Serein, Prince Par Fantill. Without such, we cannot speak together more than this. Serein's defenses will not let me."*

Wielder of Vauldin…Heir of Crystalynian… Par was still musing through the woman's claimed titles and didn't catch the hint to let Serein's barrier dissolve. *"My father and Commander Matar said Vauldin was controlled by one of the Tashek."*

"Yes." She sounded irritated to not have the prince's help in breaking the wall between them.

"Who?"

"You know me, Prince of Sealand. We met at the Citadel of Light."

"Being obtuse, I see."

"No, I…" The words were offered reluctantly. She started again: *"Back then, you mistook me as the princess of the Crystal Kingdom."*

"Zerra," Par murmured.

"Yes."

"Zyanthena Sheev'arid. So, you control Vauldin?"

"The obsidian stone awoke for me when I was placed on the spot where it went dormant at Crystanian twenty-one years ago. It needed to return to its resting place..."

"Are you alone, so far north?" Par interrupted. Though Zyanthena's story of how her Stone of Power activated could be entertaining, he was far more interested in matters that affected the state of Syre. Here was the chance to learn about the situation in eastern Syre; Zyanthena had been in the party tracking the maunstorz eastward from the Starian capital, after all. She could know more of Rubia and the Crystal Kingdoms than his people in southern Sealand.

"I have Lord Shekmann with me, but we are far from any other forces. The snows have cut us off from Syre."

"Then you know as much as we do of the Northern kingdoms and allies," he concluded.

The Tashek paused and turned the conversation, unsatisfied with where it had led thus far. *"You mentioned Commander Matar. Is he in Sealand?"*

"Yes. He came southward with me to Fortress Opal when he realized Serein was active."

Zyanthena huffed and murmured, *"That sounds like the Khataum."* Louder, she said, *"And you have been made aware that the wielder of Ravel is among our enemies?"*

"Yes. I know, too, that he controls the storms raging over Syre."

"He? You know who the wielder is, then?"

"No. Sorry, it just slipped out that way."

The vague shape of Zyanthena Sheev'arid beyond the protective barrier shook her head. *"I understand, Prince of Sealand. Your logic is sound that the wielder is male."*

Prince Par reached out to the shape of the woman and pictured her as well as he could remember. Zyanthena had been so beautiful and exotic—and reminded him so much of the Crystal princess. *"How are you speaking to me like this? I thought only the pearl, Sevén, could speak between stones? Are you just a figment of my imagination right now? Am I dreaming this?"*

"You are in a dream-state, Prince, so, yes, you can say you are dreaming me. However, you had to be semiconscious for me to access your mind." She sounded amused by the fact. *"As for your other questions: on the concept of Sevén, you are mostly correct. To very limited amounts, each stone can pull a quality of another—but to do so takes great effort for only a small ability. For me to speak to you like this right now is quite difficult."*

"Then how—?"

"Because we know each other, Prince of Sealand," Zyanthena interrupted. *"And I mean more than just from our one meeting."*

Par frowned in confusion. *"But I don't see how that can be."*

"I will tell you—but, first, can you give me news of Syre?"

"I already said—"

"But you know more than I. I can sense that, Prince. You left the Citadel of Light after Kavahad was long gone. Certainly, you must have heard some things in three seasons?"

"Well...actually, that's probably true." He shouldn't assume Zyanthena had any knowledge of the goings-on in Syre since her travels eastward. *"We've had a letter from Kavahad, written by Commander Kins stationed there."* That she should remember. *"Staria's forces will mobilize as the snows lessen—if they lessen,"* he corrected. *"Oh, and King Maushelik has passed."*

"And that is not news?!" Zyanthena replied sarcastically.

"I'm still shocked over it myself," Par said sheepishly in his defense. *"Beyond that, the court of Staria and dignitaries of Blue Haven made Kavahad before the snowstorms. They have been moved to Viscount LaPoint's demesne, just east of Kavahad."*

"*Is that all?"* She sounded a bit annoyed by the mention of LaPoint.

"Ah, no...there was word that the Sunarian party didn't reach Kavahad. Plus, the mertinean forces have been cut off from Rubia."

"Rubia has been hit hard with the storms, then," Zyanthena surmised to herself. She seemed to find all the news disturbing. *"Prince Par?"*

"Yes?"

"I have a message for you to pass along to Commander Matar."

The sudden change of topic confounded him. It was as if the desert woman was trying to exchange as much information as she could in a limited amount of time…or maybe it was the dream-state altering his perception and making their conversation hazy. He wasn't sure which.

"Tell Matar I found a way to travel across Syre. I will try to reach Osh'ēēn as I can."

"Ocean?"

"Osh'ēēn," Zyanthena corrected and spelled it out. *"Matar will know what I speak of. Tell him, too, that the Crystal Kingdom needs him to return as soon as possible. Blue Haven has betrayed us and occupied the castle in disguise as political succor."*

"What?!" That news was beyond incredible.

"You will tell him I have dealt with the situation as much as I was able."

Prince Par was becoming more confused, but he promised to pass along her message. The sense of time running out made him feel that arguing would be pointless. *"I can do that, Zyanthena."*

"Very good. Thank you, Prince of Sealand." The Tashek's voice sounded strained, as if it came through clenched teeth or as if the Sheev'arid woman was suffering from hypothermia. *"Prince Par,"* she continued haltingly, *"I will tell you now how I am able to speak with you without Sevén."*

For some reason, the words made the Sealand heir's chest constrict, as if his heart knew the answer before he had heard. *"Tell me, Sheev'arid."* Prince Par used her last name out of instinct, sensing it was more respectful.

The Tashek's silhouette moved, and she settled a hand over the prince's own through the glass barrier. There was a warm tingle through Serein that hit Par's palm; it was as if Zyanthena's will to touch the Sealander passed his protective shell. *"P—prince Par… there was a night, nearly nine summers ago, when you promised a young girl on her Berneisse to accept your hand as Sealand's future queen."* Par's shocked intake of breath had Zyanthena pausing for a moment. *"I am here to tell you: she does remember that now. Even if time and destiny have star-crossed your love, the Princess Zerra Starkindler does recall that night and your vow…"*

"Zerra is alive?"

Zyanthena paused and replied in typical Tashek crypticness, *"Of a course, Prince of Sealand. She asks that you stop holding your grief in your heart and breathe again."*

"But she's alive! Zerra is alive!"

Prince Par wasn't listening anymore, so he wasn't sure if Zyanthena Sheev'arid said anything more on the matter. His head was spinning, consumed by shock, disbelief, and pure joy at the words he had longed eight full years to hear: *Zerra is alive!* He was so overwhelmed that it took the prince some time to realize he could no longer feel Zyanthena's presence in his mind. His loss of concentration seemed to have broken their link. Still consumed with emotion, Prince Par Fantill opened his eyes and looked around his bedroom.

Nothing and everything was the same. Zerra Starkindler was still alive in Syre!

Chapter Thirty-Six
§
Frozen and Crying

The lord-governor had been against it, but "no" was a word the desert woman was resolute in ignoring. So, despite Lord Darshel's protests, Zyanthena had set herself up in a meditative seat, snuggled into the thick rugs before the roaring fire in her quarters. Irritated with her, the Shekmann had resigned himself to sitting on the bed and aiming a hard frown at the Tashek's back.

The wielder of Vauldin had gone into a sleeplike trance and disappeared deep into her mind. She sunk into an "astral projection" of herself as Princess Zerra Starkindler, when the girl had just turned thirteen. Her hope was that the connection between the Crystal princess and the Sealand heir would give her access to the royal's mind—if he was sleeping and dreaming, which was the only way Zyanthena had found in the tomes to connect to another wielder without Sevén.

As the minutes passed by in silence, Lord Darshel could not tell if the connection was a success; however, there was a sudden change that had the Kavahadian rushing to his feet. Without warning, Vauldin flashed a brilliant, white glow that made the whole room turn cold and frost-bitten. A moment afterward, Zyanthena gave a voiceless cry, her head thrown back in apparent agony, and she slumped over to the floor. Swift Hunter and Moon Ember, her constant guardians, went to the Tashek immediately, whining in worry at her unconscious state. The lord-governor was quick to follow, yelling out, "Zyen! Zy'ena!"

The desert woman was cold to the touch and there was a blue hue to her skin as the Shekmann reached for her. Her condition had Lord Darshel muttering a prayer for help. "Zyen! Damn, it, you did it again!" Another risk to herself by using magic beyond its normal boundaries. What had happened this time? Had Zyanthena finally pushed too far?

But no, her breath still came out, light as a feather against his cheek as he leaned close to check. She was alive but so very cold. "Heat," Darshel assessed and picked the Tashek up to set her under the thick covers of her bed. Hunter and Ember jumped up to lie on either side of their master, helping to warm her with their body heat. Meanwhile, Darshel turned away to restoke the fire that had been chilled by the stone's magic. The lord-governor returned to Zyanthena's bedside as the fire blazed high once more.

"Foolish woman," Lord Darshel murmured as he pulled a hand free from the sheets and tried to rub some warmth back into her limb and fingers. "Of course something had to go wrong! Playing with forces beyond human control had to backfire at some point."

Ember whined a protest and shifted away so he could pull back more of the covers to massage other parts of her freezing body.

"Oh, don't start arguing with me!" Darshel spoke back—even if he wasn't sure what the wolf's vocalization meant. "I'm the one who's always warning Zyen to slow down. Stars, I can't tell if this is helping!" He continued his ministrations anyway, massaging the Tashek's limbs one at a time to coax blood to flow through them.

Still, it was hard to tell if Zyanthena was thawing; a majik-cold was different from real hypothermia. There was one more thing he could do…but that would be an awkward conversation for later. "I'm not doing any funny business," Darshel said to the two wolves as he undressed to his under layers. "So, you tell her that if this works." The alpha and his mate chortled some reply as the Shekmann slid himself under the sheets, next to the desert woman. He floundered with removing her own outer clothing and then pulled Zyanthena flush against his body. The shock of her cold back against his chest and abdomen almost made Lord Darshel think twice about the plan, but their contact did seem to warm her. With Hunter and Ember at the Tashek's other side and feet, it seemed Zyanthena Sheev'arid was slowly beginning to thaw…

§ §

There was a piercing cry that shocked his mind and sent Decond toppling from his horse to the snow. The hard landing was just as addling to his senses as the scream. It took the young *Khapta* a few moments to realize his three companions had dismounted and were huddled around his person.

"Decond? Decond are you all right? Can you hear me?" The pain in his head made the young farrier-turned-Tashek-apprentice groan and clutch at his temples. "He seems to have come to." Savam'eed touched his *Khapta*'s shoulder and motioned J'iya to give Decond some space.

"And what in the heavens above happened anyway?" Terrik griped from behind his cousin. "The fool can't even keep ahorse."

"Keep your tongue," En'ril warned him and then returned his attention to Decond. "Are you here with us now, Decond?"

The lad squeezed his eyes closed to help reorient himself. When next he opened them, their clear ice-blue color looked more focused. "I think so… What happened?"

"That's what we'd like to know," Terrik replied. "One second, you were riding alongside us fine. The next, you stiffened and fell over."

"Then you didn't hear that cry?"

"What cry?" En'ril prompted.

By their bewildered expressions, Decond knew that the sound had been only in his head. The voice had been all too familiar… "Zee. I heard Zy'ena cry out as if she was hurt." He shook his head in shock. "I—she…"

"Zyanthena? You mean my sister?" Terrik finally came to crouch down by his *Khapta.* His features looked pinched at the news.

"Yes." Decond shook his head to clear it of the aftermath of the desert woman's cry. "Zee must have been doing something with Vauldin…that is what I sensed. Something must have gone wrong."

"Was it a confrontation with Ravel's wielder?" En'ril asked.

"No… I don't think so, anyway," Decond replied. "At least, that's not what I felt. It's all vague, though. I can't tell you more than that."

"Well, that's just great," Terrik growled and stood to stalk about their small perimeter in the snow.

"Then we should get moving again," En'ril prompted. "If you are able?" Decond nodded and accepted En'ril and J'iya's help in finding his feet. "There's little we can do from here but keep heading southward." Savam'eed didn't add any words of hope—just in case something had gone wrong. They wouldn't know, in any case, nor could they do anything from so far away.

Decond clutched at Sevén and made a little prayer for his friend to be safe before climbing back aboard his horse. He managed to concentrate enough to turn south and continue on their way. Still, his thoughts turned to Zy'ena…

§ §

The prince was startled awake by a loud cry resounding through his dreams. Opening his red eyes to stare at the woven ceiling of his tent, Zeek Starkindler oriented himself to his surroundings as he thought over what had just happened. *A woman cried out to the night?* However, he soon realized the voice had not come from the maunstorz or Nallaus camp around him. *The wielder of Vauldin.* She had sounded like she had been in pain. Perturbed to have been so linked to someone he called *enemy*, Zeek rose from his cot and grabbed up a light tunic to cover his bare chest. He slipped silently to the entrance of his tent and leaned against the pole there to look out at the night sky.

The blanket of stars was clear and bright, as no clouds or moon were around to obscure them. Zeek's eyes sought out the eight stars from whose power the stones had been born. They all blazed in brilliant color, brightest among the twinkling of lights that jeweled the dark in beauty. "No matter what happens down here, the Stars never lose their constancy," Zeek murmured.

"And let their reminder give your soul resolve," a voice spoke from behind the prince.

Zeek turned to acknowledge the maunstorz *xercon'vlr*, or great leader. "I am as resolute as first I was when Ravel chose me."

"I'm sure you are," Zephthaniel came closer to his stone bearer and took up a casual pose on the opposite tent pole. As always, the first descendant of Xercon seemed too calm and carefree to be leader of the warrior-born maunstorz. However, Zeek knew better than to underestimate the *xercon'vlr*; there was a reason he ruled over all the commanders of the people of Xercon. "Yet—something seems to have disturbed you. You are not one to easily lose your sleep."

The prince heard the unspoken question. Zephthaniel was as observant as ever. "A cry woke me." The maunstorz leader raised his eyebrows and waited for the Crystal-born to tell him more. "The wielder of Vauldin…something happened to her."

"To her?" Sharp eyes narrowed.

"Yes, a woman controls Vauldin, just as its owner before. The princess of Crystalynian must have been hidden, to keep her safe during the fall of the kingdom."

"Young she would be, only a babe when the kingdom was conquered."

"Perhaps the Shi'alam was right and Zerra Starkindler was the lost princess, Arrez."

Zephthaniel's eyes shifted sideways to study the prince for weakness. "And does such knowledge make you waver?"

"No." Zeek fisted his hands. "It is only another lie to cover up the truth. To think my sister was not of the same blood…"

"A hard truth to live by—but still, it does not lessen your affections for the girl."

"I don't know about that."

The *xercon'vlr* flashed a broad smile and laughed. "It is good to feel divided over such an issue, young Starkindler. Such truths make us all delve deep into our souls until we are able to find our proper footing." Zephthaniel reached out to lay a hand on the prince's shoulder. "Your time will come to confront the truth. Only then will you know your answer." He turned away and left Zeek Starkindler alone to his thoughts and the stars.

§ §

Zyanthena came to, feeling hot and stifled. Instinct had her start to panic at being unable to move, as if bound. Only the Tashek's training kept her from giving in to the trapped feeling. Forcing calm on herself, she took in her surroundings to find some semblance of sanity.

In front of her was a wall of fur; however, that moved to reveal Moon Ember's familiar gold-and-blue eyes. The female vocalized her relief at having her master awaken. She rolled up to her paws and came to loom over the Tashek to sniff about her person. Through the alpha female, Zyanthena learned of her condition—and why she felt so encumbered: Lord Darshel's and Hunter's weight still had her pinned in place. She groaned. "You think you could get these two to roll away from me, Ember?"

Zyanthena's voice startled the two males awake without needing Moon Ember to prod them. "Zy'ena!" Lord Darshel exclaimed and pushed himself to his elbows to see around her back.

"I am awake, Darshel."

The lord-governor let out a sigh and collapsed back to the pillows. "Blessed Stars, that's a relief!"

Zyanthena extricated herself from the sheets enough to sit against the headboard. Yet, even that amount of exertion had her world spinning. Forcing the feeling back by sheer will was the only reason her protesting stomach didn't empty onto the sheets. She groaned instead. "Serein's power really backlashed on me," Zy'ena muttered through her hands, which she held against her mouth to keep from vomiting.

"Serein?" Lord Darshel sat up and looked to her. "Did the sapphire's powers cause you to become so cold?"

Zyanthena nodded. "The prince of Sealand is not comfortable using the stone. His reluctance makes Serein extra protective. Had Prince Par been more cooperative, I doubt anything would have happened to me."

"This is why you shouldn't take such risks," the Shekmann berated. "You're already capable with Vauldin, but you can't expect the others to be as able to perform at your level. Please promise me that you will not try that again—at least until you can meet all the other wielders in person and know their abilities?"

The wan smile she returned was anything but reassuring. "As it stands, I won't be trying that particular majik again. Still"—her brandy eyes looked distant—"I was able to learn a few things."

"Like?"

"Like King Maushelik is dead, and Prince Al'den holds the crown." Lord Darshel's expression was stunned; it seemed he couldn't find words to reply. "Also, Rubia and Sunrise are not responding to missives from Sealand or Staria. Our assumption of a coup by the maunstorz could be correct, after all. The snows prevent our allies from a proper investigation into their silence. There seems to be a good motive, though…the Sunarian princes never reached Kavahad."

"Stars, it sounds like Syre is falling apart! The maunstorz might actually win at this rate, especially with Syrean allies."

"That is possible." The admission was tiring. Zyanthena's lovely features looked worn and hollow. "Unless we think of a way to get ahead of these developments, any movements by ourselves or our allies at Snow Thaw will be too late."

The war-trained Shekmann looked suspicious at her words. Just as calculating as she was, Lord Darshel also knew their options were not as limited—with the use of Vauldin and the obelisks—as other forces. He hated to bring that up, though. This most recent brush with magic made him reluctant. "Do you need me to make some soup?"

Zyanthena looked up as he hurried to action, rising from the bed as if they hadn't just been speaking of Syre's defeat. "Rather quick to dismiss this discussion, aren't you?"

"Just trying to be practical." The handsome Kavahadian turned back enough to wink at her. "With you out of commission, one of us has to be."

Zyanthena huffed and shook her head ruefully. "Taking my lines from me is not fashionable."

"It just means I've heard them too often." Darshel grinned. "But you do feel warmer, right?" He started to come back to check her skin's temperature.

"From what Ember told me, I was beyond hypothermic. Compared to that, I feel well." Zyanthena wiggled her fingers and toes, feeling the lingering stiffness in her joints from the chill. "I believe I am over the worst of this affliction."

"You should still take it easy. I'll be back with some food and water."

She didn't bother arguing. Her exhausted and pained body was enough indication of just how badly she had miscalculated the astral projection link with the prince of Sealand. Severe injury or even death were possibilities when working with high majiks; her latest use of Vauldin had been stupid. Zyanthena was lucky to have sustained so little injury for her risky action. For her, it was unprecedented.

Chapter Thirty-Seven
§
Baited

It was a relief to see Sardon again. A week of cold weather and daily, rigorous drills had all the unit pining for a hot meal, plenty of ale, and real beds. The thirteen-person scouting unit got through their final unpacking—on Patrick's insistence—and groaned themselves to bed for post-travel naps before dinner time.

In the quiet of the stables, Patrick and Jacen stayed with their Crystal-gifted mounts to groom them well and check for injuries. Candor and Sapphire had been with the two friends since their journey to the Crystal Kingdom, nearly four seasons before, and still the war coursers seemed to be in excellent shape. There was something to be said for Crystal-bred horses; in comparison, one of the unit's packhorses had not fared so well.

"Do you think we should trade in for a different packhorse?" Jacen asked as he combed out the dark grey's thick tail. He could see Patrick in the adjoining stall massaging down Candor's back muscles.

"I'm not sure." Patrick frowned at the task. "That mare was one of the sturdier horses Ivance allowanced us. We may have to seek a boon with him, if we do that."

"I think we should trade her for that mule."

Patrick glanced across his stallion's topline to give the Havener a pointed stare. "The mule was a bit too stubborn for my tastes."

"He wasn't a problem for me."

"You're just fond of those big, floppy ears."

Jacen chuckled. "Possibly. I thought they were endearing."

"Right." They were quiet for a time, then Patrick added, "The braying would be a disadvantage. Not the best feature to have along on a convert mission."

"That's true." There was a reluctance to the admittance. "I guess that's a good point for rejecting the idea."

"Hey." Patrick caught his friend's attention. "It wasn't a bad idea. On any normal trip, a mule like that would be beneficial. I'm just overly concerned about details that could call us out to the maunstorz."

"I know."

"I'll let you and Auna handle the issue of the mare," Patrick continued, to Jacen's surprise. "You're better at picking out horseflesh, anyway."

"Thanks."

Patrick nodded and continued his inspection of his palomino. Bending over, he was sure to check each leg and clean every hoof; it wouldn't do for a stone bruise to abscess and lay up his partner for a good month. Afterward, he rubbed down the legs and saddle area with a liniment the two Tashek maidens had introduced them to. It smelled of lemons and pine and warmed the soldier's hands as he applied it. Candor seemed to approve of the stuff.

"Commander, Lieutenant."

The two friends looked up to find Maximillian Rosailles at the stable door. "Pickle," Patrick acknowledged and waved the Goldener closer.

"Sir." Pickle saluted, though casually, as Patrick insisted. "The group is all headed to the Salty Dog for drinks. I just thought I'd check to see if you were in the mood to join us."

Jacen and Patrick shared a grin. "Of course! We wouldn't pass up a good Golden ale! Let us tidy up here and we'll be right behind you."

"Sounds good." Maximillian saluted again and turned away to head to the tavern.

With the thought of the beer and tavern food, it didn't take long for the two soldiers to put away their grooming supplies and do a quick wash-up to be fit to enter Mrs. Fancy Farley's bar. In less than a quarter-turn of the dial, they were at the Salty Dog's front steps and filing in with other patrons who had come for the evening's entertainments. To their shock, Lord-Commander Ivance and four of his soldiers were on the stage, a fiddle, beat-box, spoons, and two four-stringed gallo guitar in their hands. Apparently, the group had performed at the tavern before, which was why it was so full.

Jacen and Patrick shared impressed glances before filing deeper into the Salty Dog to find the rest of their unit. The Ritter brothers had secured a table near the end of the bar that allowed their twelve members—Master Callé declared it folly for a man of his age to be out at that time of night—to either stand at the bar or sit. Kei'shkï and Shaul'auna were sitting, per usual, with the Calhorns, Kipper, Pickle, and Peter, while Sammy, Reed, and Mr. Durrow stood with their backs to the bar and discussed the entertainment. Pickle had snagged two chairs for their last companions; he had reserved them by sprawling his long legs across the chairs and glaring at patrons who tried to snag the empty seats.

"Thank you," Patrick said to Maximillian as they neared and plopped into the chairs.

Pickle nodded and slid tankards of ale their way. "It was getting a bit hard to keep them, but I managed. At least most of the folks here tonight didn't want to deal with the uniform." By "uniform," Pickle meant his cavalry clothes, which still bore the lord-commander's insignia and metals of office. Most of the population of Sardon knew their safety came from Ivance's men and treated them with the appropriate respects.

"That's good to hear." Jacen lifted his beer to clank it against his fellows' tankards, cheering them all for a week well done. After a swig, he motioned to the stage. "What's up with that?"

"Surprising, isn't it?" Pickle grinned. "The lord-commander and his 'Rag-Tags' are well-known in Sardon. As you see, the town turns out when they'll be playing. It can get rather rowdy in here, but Mrs. Farley loves it."

"I'll bet. It's nearly as packed in here as when Auna and Kei perform."

"Yes, well." Kei'shkï joined in when she heard Jacen mention the Tashek maidens. "Our certain…charms can bring out a crowd. Men never can get enough of leering at two exotic maidens from Staria." She sounded anything but amused.

Shaul'auna giggled at her cousin's words—or it could have been the alcohol making her jovial. "Forgive Kei'shkï, she does love her anonymity. Me, I like the attention."

"Oh, I'll bet," Patrick muttered, finding it hard to believe the Tashek could be anything but noticeable.

Unfortunately, his voice carried enough for the desert woman to hear. Shaul'auna's eyes hardened and sparked at his words. However, instead of retorting as she normally would, Shaul'auna stood, with tankard in hand, and made her way around the table to the Ritter brothers. "Buy another tankard for you boys?"

"Aw, Auna, that's our job." Sammy grinned and flagged down the bartender to order more drinks.

Reed continued their charm by saying, "And it's our job to ask you, m'lady, for a dance. If it pleases you?"

Shaul'auna beamed back a smile and accepted the offered hand. "I would be pleased."

"I'll watch your drinks," Sammy promised. "As long as I get the next dance." The Tashek maiden was already being pulled away to a spot on the cleared area before the stage, leaving her unable to agree to Sammy's terms, but the younger Ritter seemed satisfied nonetheless. He grinned like a schoolboy skipping class as Reed and Auna started in on a country jig. Sammy leaned back against the bar and casually sipped his beer, grinning at their victory of getting a dance from the desert woman.

Patrick studied their little exchange, noting that not only the Ritters seemed to be in good spirits that evening. The alcohol and lively music had their whole party carefree and open—all good things—but the combination of everything centered around his concerns of having two, alluring Tashek maidens in their unit. More than the Ritters could get "cozy" with the ladies that evening…

"Hey." Jacen bumped his friend's knee with his own. "You're being too serious."

Patrick turned away from his misgivings. "I'm just watching the room."

"Right." Brown eyes rolled. "Join us in a game?" Jacen meant the card game being set out about the table. Micah Calhorn had brought them along in case others liked to play.

"Yeah, I'll take a hand."

"Bet's a docet—or whatever you have comparable to it."

Patrick shook his head but provided his allotment to the center. "I can see you're trying to rob me of my payday again."

"Of course." Jacen grinned. "I like having the full purse in hand for the weekend after."

Patrick huffed and picked up the cards laid before him. Mr. Calhorn's deck was made from pressed-wood grains so fine they gave a leathery texture to the little squares. The wood had been pressed into a papery form from the pressure of heavy boulders. Afterward, pigment had been painted on the smoother sides in numbers and Syrean rankings: academic, war advisor, court advisor, and ruler. The Rubian recognized them as a type of card game from his home kingdom, but he himself had never spent the coin to buy a deck. Still, any good Rubian knew how to play a game of pontoon.

"All right, let 'er rip, gents!" Kipper called out, enthused to be competing for a pot of money. The young farrier was notorious for his sly underhandedness. Yet, Pickle—to his right—was usually quick to pick up on his sleight of hand and call him out. It had become a game unto itself for Kipper to trick the Sardonian.

In earnest, the first round of cards commenced.

§ §

An hour later, Patrick was pulling out of the fifth game. Between Jacen and Micah Calhorn, he was losing too much money to their carefully crafted plays. He pushed away from the table to let Sammy and Reed, finally exhausted from dancing, take a turn. He sidled up to the vacated end of the bar, where young Jean had been found a stool by Mrs. Farley. The young Calhorn had left their game a round before and must have looked lost enough for the bar owner to take pity on him. "Can I get you another cider?"

Jean had been fiddling with the rim on his wooden cup, absently paying attention to no particular detail in the Salty Dog. He jumped at the question. "Ah, no…I'm still working on this one."

Patrick nodded and waved the bartender for a refill of ale. He turned his back to the bar as she filled his order. The Rubian followed Jean's gaze to Shaul'auna. The Tashek maiden had her own crowd of wooers—as usual. She seemed to fawn over all the attention, soaking it in like a good perfume. "She would agree to a dance, if you were so inclined to ask," said Patrick.

Jean seemed startled at the idea. His cheeks blushed, followed by an embarrassed duck of the head. "I don't know… there are so many men around."

The words had Patrick hiding his grin of amusement. *Ah, a young crush!* "Auna would always accept your offer of a dance over those strangers." That fact he was sure of; the desert maiden had always made sure to acknowledge the young Calhorn.

"Well." Jean looked uncertain still. "Maybe after I get back from the head."

The excuse put off the need to be bold a little longer. "Suit yourself," Patrick replied as Jean slid off his stool and began to wander to the back entrance of the bar and the crude facilities in the back alley. He watched the young lad for only a moment more, just until the arrival of his next beer—brought by the beautiful Katie—turned his attention to other conversation. In his distraction, Patrick missed Mr. Durrow leaving his quiet corner to follow young Jean out the back…

§ §

Shaul'auna had set herself at a strategic vantage point in the room—her Tashek instinct to always be aware of her surroundings. From her place, she could continue to partake in the entertainments while keeping an eye out for trouble. As a woman, she knew better than to let the partaking of alcohol dull her senses.

Because of that, Shaul'auna saw the problem: young Jean was slipping out the back to relieve himself. Though not a cause for concern, the shadow that ghosted Jean was. Shaul'auna had always made sure to keep her distance from the hulking blacksmith. His oozing sweetness, which he'd sent the desert woman's way on multiple occasions, had reeked of ulterior motives. Those motives were why Shaul'auna began to follow Jean and Mr. Durrow out the back—just in case.

§ §

Her misgivings ended up being well founded.

Coming out of the busy bar into the quiet of the back alley, Shaul'auna heard muffled protests and the sounds of a struggle. She rushed around the corner of the Salty Dog to make out Durrow's huge shape pressed up against the side of the tavern. Of Jean, there was no sign.

The lack of the young Calhorn's presence meant Jean could only be in one place: behind Peore Durrow. Shaul'auna hurried closer to the shadowy hulk. As she neared, the desert maiden could hear Durrow's voice: "Easy now…if you stop struggling, this will be over quickly and we can go about our business. If you play nice, I'll continue to keep this secret between just you and me." It was all Shaul'auna needed to hear. What was going on was bad. Very bad.

In a breath, a knife was in the Tashek's hands. In the next breath, she was launching herself for an attack at Durrow. "Let. Jean. Go!" The weapon plunged hilt deep in into the blacksmith's lower back; however, it was too short to fully penetrate his clothing and wide girth and reach the kidney. The attack did get Durrow off of Jean, though. He bellowed and spun away, exposing the young Calhorn. Shaul'auna registered the unbuttoned shirt—revealing a chest wrap—and the pants pulled down to Jean's boots. She was infuriated to see tears on the youth's face and blood on Jean's thighs.

"Monster!" Shaul'auna hissed and turned to shield Jean.

By then, the blacksmith had pulled the knife from his back and was flashing it at the Tashek. He was grinning. "Ah, now here's the real sport. Not the unseasoned girl but the sex-taught Tashek maiden. I've heard of your people's rites of passage into adulthood."

Shaul'auna's tongue ran over her pouty lips in an unconscious signal of apprehension. She gulped back her uncertainty of taking on the hulking man alone. Ignoring the blacksmith's barbs, she said, "Jean… are you well enough to get out of here?"

There was a sniffle, but the young Calhorn responded. "Y—yes." Jean's voice cracked.

"Then I need you to slip around behind me and get help."

"I—"

"Jean." Shaul'auna steadied her voice. "Go." Behind her there was a shuffling as Jean managed to get her clothes in order enough to run. A moment later, there was the sound of Jean's light footsteps.

Meanwhile, Mr. Durrow seemed to find the situation amusing. "By all means, *boy*, go fetch a few people. By the time you return, I'll have subdued Ms. Auna here and taken her someplace more…private."

Jean's footsteps paused,

"Jean, you must go. I will hold here until you get back. Trust me on this."

Finally, the youth's feet moved again. That Mr. Durrow didn't try to go after Jean showed he had his true prize. Shaul'auna realized this a moment too late; she had been baited—and either way, Durrow would have won.

Mr. Durrow grinned again and stepped closer. "Awfully confident you always are. I like that about you the most. It made setting this stage—and all those weeks of holding back—so delightful."

"When I'm done with you, you won't have that smirk or that prick to enjoy."

The returned chuckle was low and husky. "Oh, I wouldn't count on that, darling. I've got plans for you."

§ §

Jean's disheveled appearance and alarming accusation had the rest of their group hurrying from the bar, game forgotten. In the muted light of the back alley, they came across the aftermath of Shaul'auna's struggle. Blood and scuff marks showed the desert maiden had not gone down without a fight.

Patrick touched a puddle of blood, feeling his chest catch with concern. He rose from his crouch to face the Calhorns. "Only Durrow had a knife?"

Jean shook his head. "It was Auna's. She stabbed him in the back to get him o-off o-of m-me."

The choked words made the Rubian realize he had to speak more gently. *Jean had been the original target?* He took in the youth's clothes and realized a few buttons were out of place and there seemed to be stains on the inseams of his pants. "Kei'shkï," he called out.

The Tashek was there in a moment. She had been studying the ground and walls for signs of Shaul'auna's and Durrow's passage. "Kinsson."

"Please take Jean and help he—him." He almost slipped. "Get cleaned up."

That Kei and Micah shared a glance between themselves showed they had kept a secret about Jean. It solidified Patrick's certainty. "And inform the lord-commander, discreetly, of this matter with Durrow."

Kei'shkï raised her eyebrows at the word *discreetly*—weren't all Tashek discreet?—but she acquiesced to his order. "Of course, sir."

"Thank you. Micah, I'll need your skills to track Durrow." Mr. Calhorn nodded. "The rest of you spilt into teams and search the area. Use extreme caution. I'm not sure I trust Durrow to play nice."

"Got it!" They all nodded and leapt into action. Pickle headed up a team with Kipper and the Ritters, promising to stay close to each other so they could come to assist the other team once Peore was found. Liking the idea, Patrick asked Jacen and Peter to do the same.

At the end of the alley, Micah found traces of blood smeared on the fence. Farther down, there was more. "Smart woman, Auna is," Micha commented. "She left us a trail."

“Let us hope Durrow doesn’t notice,” Patrick replied. He felt his jaw clench in worry over what could be happening to the desert woman. “Let’s hurry.”

Chapter Thirty-Eight
§
Saved

Savam'eed's cavalry reached the East Bridge as the sky was lightening into dawn. His nephew, Kăt'ta, dismounted and inspected the wind-blown tracks over the bridge. He returned with a Tashek-made horsehide note and handed it to his father. "Re'shaird," he said, referring to the note's writer.

"He was here and gone again," Shík Savam'eed murmured. He quieted to read the note. The words were not heartening. "We continue east. Kăt'ta, Shet'aumen, ride to the fore and follow Re'shaird's tracks. Eyes to the land!"

Everyone shouted agreement as Kăt'ta mounted. Then, as one, the horsemen of clan Savam'eed continued across the East Bridge and into Rubia.

§ §

Dawn came cold and despairing. The light across the snow revealed the number of dead scattered around their little bowl. Those of the mertinean that had not died from the maunstorz attacks had finally succumbed to their injuries and exposure to the cold of the Rubian night. Of Grant's one hundred ninety men, only seventy-eight looked to have survived. The knowledge had the war-hardened commander sickened.

"Aerrisson, my friend?" Commander Grant patted the Tashek man awake as the light grew. The warrior had gotten about an hour's sleep after staying up all night fighting off enemy attacks and sneaking out to resupply their force with arrows.

True to form, the desert man was awake in a heartbeat at the tap on his shoulder. His alert eyes cast about for danger. "Commander?"

"Easy," Grant calmed him. "The maunstorz have continued to give us a reprieve. I figure they'll start back up sometime soon."

Aerrisson groaned and stretched himself fully awake. "I suspect you're right." His keen eyes glanced around, taking in their causalities. "Once they see how weak we've grown, their attacks will get stronger."

"Yes, I imagine so."

One of Grant's men scuttled near, a warm mug of diluted coffee in his hands. "The last of our stores, sir, and, sorry, there was only one cup."

"One cup? Stars, lad," Grant teased. "My world has come to an end!" The mertinean man chuckled and hurried away to bring more to others down the line. "Well, it's warm," the commander said to his Tashek scout and offered him a drink.

"Beats drinking horse piss," Aerrisson replied. Though it sounded like a joke, Grant couldn't be sure. One couldn't put it past a Tashek to do just that in an emergency. After a gulp, the warrior handed the cup back and said, "I'll go check on Lunier while there's time."

"All right. See if you can rustle up some road tack or something to fill our stomachs while you're there."

"Will do."

Lunier seemed to have fared the best in the force. The silver stallion stood calmly under the tarps erected to protect the thirty remaining horses and their dwindling supplies. His influence seemed to ease the others during the fighting; like a king giving orders of confidence to his men. Yet Lunier was happy at seeing his owner. His nickers greeted the Sheev'anee as he entered the tent.

"Hey, boy. It's good to see you, too." Aerrisson fed him a rock sugar as he reached out to his mount. Just seeing his stallion gave the desert man hope—and a reason to keep fighting. "You continue to keep safe in here, all right?" Lunier bumped his owner's hand, looking for more food. "I know. Later, all right? That means for all of you." The words were extended to the other horses. Silently, Aerrisson prayed that there was a later.

Shouts alerted Aerrisson to action brewing outside of the barricades. With a hurried pat of good-bye, he turned away from his pride and joy to rejoin the mertinean forces. Outside, the camp seemed to be in confusion. Men were scrambling to their posts or waking others, but there seemed to be no attack.

Aerrisson hurried back to Grant. "What is it?"

"The watchers are uncertain. There is movement in the trees." Commander Grant pointed in the direction of the alert.

"We should be prepared for another assault—maybe one underhanded."

"I agree. They've had all night to prepare a counter to our barricades and arrows." Both men thought Silvarron cunning enough to contrive an alternative attack.

"Western side!" a watcher called.

Grant and Aerrisson rolled into position and notched an arrow each. Still, the air seemed calm, too calm. Then, there was movement in the top rim of trees on that side of the bowl. The maunstorz were hurrying down the side of the hill—only they weren't focused on the mertinean trapped at the bottom. One after another was felled on their way down the hill. Their dying screams alerted the rest of the maunstorz to their plight. More of the enemy seemed to converge there until—

A wall of horseflesh plowed over the remaining enemy lines and galloped toward the camp. The enraged maunstorz continued to converge on the moving horsemen, their trail starting to cut diagonally down the bowl face.

"Arrows! Arrows there!" Aerrisson directed loudly, pointing Grant's men to fire at the maunstorz trying to intercept the horsemen. The mertinean near enough to hear were quick to focus their weapons on the second group of enemies. Maunstorz began to fall by the dozens.

"We've got them pincered!" Commander Grant bellowed for encouragement. Indeed, between the Tashek and the mertinean, the maunstorz force seemed to be thinning. By the time the Savam'eed's forces reached the open area in front of the barricades, the snow was rich with blood.

A horn from the other side of the rim sounded, alerting the maunstorz of something.

"A retreat," Aerrisson noted. A quick and effective one. "They pull back! The maunstorz fall back!" The area was clearing of enemies. Concerned that they would successfully escape, Aerrisson clamored over the barricade and ran for the nearest Tashek horse. "Silvarron. The enemy leader is that way!" He pointed to the direction of the horn call.

"Then we will pursue!" Savam'eed yelled back. "Shet'aumen's men, stay behind to protect the mertinean. Riders, forward!" The Shík's men folded apart fluidly, not one rider protesting the order. A third of the Sheev'anee remained behind as the rest followed the retreating backs of the enemy force. Left behind were the exhausted and relieved mertinean and their Tashek scout.

§ §

The blood smears led to a rundown shack on the outskirts of Sardon. With a number of the townspeople at the Salty Dog for the night's entertainment, the city seemed unusually quiet, especially here. Micah nodded his belief that Durrow had stopped at that building and waited as Patrick crouched closer to inspect the place.

Nodding back to Mr. Calhorn, Jacen, and Peter, he motioned to the other two entrances he had seen. Using military code, he indicated that he thought he heard Shaul'auna and Durrow in the room to the right, first of the rooms, his position near the back door. Jacen murmured details to their other team members. Quickly and quietly, they slipped into position and awaited Patrick's mark.

Now. Patrick signaled and began to move. Staying as covert as he could, the Rubian tugged the rope door handle and prayed it would open soundlessly. True to a place run by a blacksmith, the well-made hinges turned silently. Patrick shouldered inside and kept alert for Durrow, in case of an attack. As it happened, however, the hulking blacksmith from Duncitt was too preoccupied with Shaul'auna to notice.

Beaten and bloodied from knife cuts, the Tashek maiden was still not submitting to her fate. Durrow had gotten her topless and had tied her hands behind her back. Such a handicap had not left the warrioress defenseless, however. Blood colored her lips and trailed lines down her chin as Shaul'auna glared up at her captor and spit out the body part she had munched off.

When the piece rolled closer to Patrick's position, he realized it was the tip of a body part he couldn't fathom having bitten off. Choking back bile, he consoled himself that, at least, it was a small victory for the Tashek maiden to have defied her captor enough to have accomplished that.

Of course, such an action sent Mr. Durrow into a pain-induced fury.

The enraged hulk of a man began to punch and kick Shaul'auna, but that was as far as the four men would let him go. They rushed in as Durrow's back was turned. Patrick led, being the most suited to an initial attack against such a large opponent, and he struck out to hamstring the blacksmith. His blade cut cleanly through the large tendons above the man's knees and floored him. Patrick continued past Durrow to get in front of Shaul'auna and be her shield. His actions were just in the nick of time.

As the Rubian had expected, a maimed Mr. Durrow was not a finished one. His fall had gotten the man close enough to his abandoned hunting ax. Once his fingers came around the hilt, Durrow went up to his knees, swinging it in abandon. Patrick Kins barely managed to keep his feet against the blow of the ax against his sword. Luckily, Jacen was behind Durrow at the next opening. The Havenese soldier came down hard with a blow that split their opponent's head in two.

Mr. Durrow fell to the worn boards of the shack, quite dead.

"Auna!" Patrick spun about to inspect the desert woman. Overall, she seemed in better shape than he had feared, but he would save it for Kei'shkï to decide for certain. The Rubian took off his outer jacket, which came to his knees, to cover Shaul'auna and give the maiden proper coverage of her bared torso.

Shaul'auna curled the jacket around herself out of an innate need for comfort and safety. "*Ahnamen.*"

"Auna, are you—?" Jacen rushed over in worry.

"I am all right," she assured and looked at her rescuers with gratitude in her big doe eyes. "I had no doubts of your coming."

"I had doubts we'd make it in time," Patrick admitted.

"Your blood spatters were well planned," Micah Calhorn praised.

"A Tashek's defense."

"Still," Jacen prompted, "it helped. Now, let's get you out of here." He helped her stand and supported the maiden all the way back to the Salty Dog and her quarters. Kei'shkï and Jean were still there, the former an impatient, concerned mess. The lord-commander was there, as well. He seemed relieved that there was no live man left to hang.

"Had he been still breathing, I would have given him the Tashek justice of removing his manhood and balls," Shaul'auna said in her anger. Though the words left the men in the room squeamish, it seemed Lord-Commander Ivance completely agreed with her.

§ §

Savam'eed and his men returned about a full hour later. They had lost eight horses and twelve men to the maunstorz but came back in victory. The Shík reined his horse to a stop in front of Commander Grant and the huddle of mertinean men. "The maunstorz have been defeated! We left none alive.'"

Aerrisson approached and, without offering a proper courtesy, said, "Did you see a tall maunstorz man, seventeen hands high, with a raven-bird companion?"

Shík Savam'eed frowned at the scout's rudeness but motioned for any of his men to reply. None spoke of seeing such a man.

"Then Silvarron may not be dead. He is cunning and easily able to evade out attacks."

"I repeat what I said, Re'shaird scout. We left no bodies alive."

Aerrisson opened his mouth to protest, but Commander Grant stopped him with a touch. "We are grateful, Sheev'anee, for your rescue, and we do not contest your words. Now, we tire of our wearied march and battle. I think we will all be relieved to put a foot into Staria at this point."

"Indeed." Shík Savam'eed bowed his head in agreement. "We will help you with your wounded. Riders, dismount!"

Only the perturbed Tashek scout was left standing there, stewing, as the Sheev'anee went about helping the mertinean. Commander Grant finally came to Aerrisson with Lunier in hand. "He may well be dead, as the Shík said."

"And he may not be."

"But you would risk a ride out to find him?"

"No," Aerrisson relented. "We have fought enough."

"Then console yourself that his force is defeated. As for me, I'm ready for Starian ale." Aerrisson finally agreed to that offer and followed the commander in getting their reduced force ready to head to Staria.

The preparations took only a half hour to complete. By full sunup, the mertinean of Raven's Den and the Sheev'anee headed away from the corpse-laden bowl, heading back west to the East Bridge and safety. By noon, their march took them across the Senna River into Staria. More good news found them at that location: a runner for King Al'den was waiting. The Starian and All'ani forces were only an hour's ride away, he said. There was little to no chance of another maunstorz's attack with such a strong force coming to their defense. Able to let go a breath of relief, Commander Grant's exhausted men fell to the ground to weep and to give the Stars their gratitude for the rescue.

Chapter Thirty-Nine
§
A Pact Not Honored

By the eighth day, the prince had had a thorough course in the ways of a maunstorz champion. The first few fights had gone easily, though Rowin had paid with bruises and knife wounds. But the last three fights had not ended until each *vsenk* was dispatched—as those fighters would not submit any other way. This morning's fight seemed to be following that same course.

The fights were held on the open ground of the Red Guards' training yard. It was slicked down with frozen blood and packed snow, making the footing treacherous. As with the time weeks before, the prince had been offered his choice of weapons. For this eighth fight, he had chosen a typical sword to combat his opponent's long spear; however, Prince Rowin was finding the choice cumbersome.

Already, his skin was glistening with sweat that gave his new wounds a painful, salty bite. Small punctures lined his legs and arms: the price for ineffective blocks against the spear. The maunstorz man was harrying him across the slick field in an attempt to topple the royal and make a final stab. Rowin was almost ready to give it to him.

Still, the Sunarian was stubborn. Though his arms ached and his breath was heavy, he refused to yield. Doing so meant a cost to his brother.

As luck would have it, a too-long thrust from his too-confident opponent gave Prince Rowin an opportunity to kick downward onto the spear shaft and break the point from the wood. Taking advantage, he rushed the distance to his opponent and readied an ending swing. The maunstorz attempted to parry with a hand blade, but the weapon did little against the downward thrust of the sword. The *vsenk* fell to the snow, defeated.

Fatigued, Rowin went to his knees beside the maunstorz's cooling corpse and tried to ease his breath to stop cold, burning air from hastening into his chest. Sweat dripped off his face from the exertion of the fight, and already the air was freezing his soaked clothes to his skin.

An amused laugh came from his audience. "And yet again, you make a fool of my man." Mansocan came near to inspect the final blow. "I see I have underestimated your skills, Prince of Sunrise. By now, I had hoped for at least one price to be paid."

"They underestimated my conviction, is all," Rowin countered and pushed himself to unsteady feet. Already, the cold was stiffening his limbs into a painful spasm.

"Yes, well…" Red eyes seemed to assess him. "I would say their efforts have not been without some effect."

Rowin refused to admit his weakening state to his enemy. "Only to a slight degree."

Mansocan's lips tweaked into a knowing grin, as if he recognized the lad's arrogance as only for show. "I'll give you an hour to refresh and care for yourself. You will find your lord protector is awaiting your return."

It was another lesson Rowin had learned about champion fights: one must come and go from the arena on his own power. Failing to do so meant a forfeit or a loss of the allotted rest period. Trying not to hobble, the prince headed back the long distance from the fighting yard to the small "officers" room above the dungeons. The walk did his legs some good, but the effort made Rowin exhausted. He came to Rio sweaty and bloodied, and fell to the floor cot in a heap.

"Stars, Rowin!" Rio was aghast at his prince's condition. Each day he looked worse.

"Don't worry about it," Rowin pushed himself to lie on his back and put a hand to his forehead. He barely looked up at his loyal friend. "I haven't lost a match yet."

"Maybe, but you're getting closer."

Still, Rio began his ministrations to help nurse his prince back to health. He had found the herb and tar mixture the maunstorz provided to work wonders on overstressed muscles—especially if it was heated to an almost intolerable temperature. Warning Rowin of this, he started on the royal's legs and worked quickly to coat them, despite the patient's hisses of pain. The process was repeated until all of Rowin's limbs were covered in the stuff. They waited, then, for the decoction to cool before rolling the prince over and doing it all over again. By the end, Prince Rowin was too exhausted to complain, but his muscle soreness had eased.

Rowin groaned and pushed himself to all fours so he could remove his dirtied clothing. He accepted the clean tunic and pants Rio passed him—as they were following maunstorz's protocol, each *vsenk* was given new clothes after each fight. Afterward, the prince felt good enough to sit up and help Rio check and apply ointment to his wounds.

"This is lunacy," Rio muttered as he took in the new blotches of bruises and multitude of cuts. "I think they're trying to kill you slowly so they have one prince to send home."

"They won't get that pleasure," Rowin promised, though he knew he would be hard pressed to see the conviction through. Rio just glared back his answer. "How do the others fare?" Rowin asked, changing the subject. Since he had started the fights, he had been sleeping in this room above the prisons. It meant he was sheltered from the cold and wet but also bereft of news.

"Mansocan has continued to provide according to your terms. Everyone is much as you left them—if not jealous of your accommodations."

"Yes, well," he chuckled "The upscale resort comes with a steep fare."

Rio didn't think it was funny. "That is does. One I still think you shouldn't be paying."

"Rio—"

"I know, it's for Connel. Stars help us that he understands your sacrifice."

Rowin smiled fondly at his lord protector. "I think he does, Rio. Besides, the little twerp couldn't fight like this if his life depended on it."

"Which it does," Rio agreed. He finally gave a begrudging smile. "That little twerp has a very admirable older brother. I think I'm jealous."

They laughed. "Just don't let him know you said that."

"These lips are sealed, my prince."

"Good." Rowin groaned and stretched himself back across the cot. "In that case, I'm going to take a little nap. Wake me when they come."

"Yes, sir."

§ §

The hour came and went with no arrival of a knock—not that the two Sunarians knew. Time could not be counted easily in their nearly barren room. It was the arrival of the maunstorz *seka'vlr* that startled the two Sunarians from their peace. "I see you did not care to honor my horse lesson this afternoon, Prince of Sunrise," his voice full of well-contained rage.

"Wh—what?" Rowin started awake and rolled to his feet.

"It is a quarter past our hour, Prince Rowin," Mansocan said.

"But no man came to take him to you!" Rio protested.

Red eyes glared back. "That was not what I was told."

"I—but we—"

"No man came." Rowin motioned Rio to silence and came to his feet. "Rio awaited the summons. None came. Your accusation stands false."

"My accusation?" The maunstorz leader's features became dark and deadly. He stalked closer to the royal and seemed to be enjoying the prince's resolve to stand firm. "Careful of yourself, my good prince. You walk precariously."

Rowin didn't bat an eye. "You have come for your lesson, so we will go to it now."

"It does not work that way, Prince of Sunrise. A pact not honored is a pact that needs paying."

"I am ready—"

Enough!" Mansocan growled and lifted one of his decorated, taloned fingers to prick Rowin's chin. "You follow my rules of this exchange, Princeling. I give no quarter to their allowance."

The Sunarian's jaw clenched. Rowin could feel his argument losing its weight.

Mansocan sensed the small waver. "*Vsenk!*" The order called in enough maunstorz to handle the two Sunarians and Prince Connel. Before any of the fellow kinsmen could comprehend the exact nature of their fate, the groundwork had been laid: Rowin and Rio were bound and controlled by four guards, two more had Connel, and a seventh brought in an empty water barrel and trough of snow. The guards holding Connel took him to the barrel and lashed him firmly upon it. Mansocan came to hover over the young prince's form.

"I will make my point, Prince of Sunrise." He turned and slashed Connel's shirt open, exposing his back.

"No!" Rowin began to struggle and bellow. "This is not honor! I've done nothing but what you've asked of me! I won today, as every day, and I did not miss out on our lesson on purpose. You know I speak the truth. What you do now is not honoring our pact. You're going around it!"

The leader's eyebrows twitched as Rowin finally hit the mark. Mansocan's smile lacked any warmth. "Prince, you astound me with your perception. Too bad it will not change your brother's penalty."

"Mansocan, no!"

The enemy leader turned away and took a prepared knife from his underling's hands. In his other, he grabbed up a heap of snow and pressed it to the large tattoo Connel had hidden on his upper back—one Mansocan knew about from a previous torture session. It was a beautiful image of the Sunarian crest, with finely detailed trilliums around a woven circlet. Prince Connel's two prized hunting dogs had been sketched into the center as testament to their victories at competition. It seemed almost a shame to ruin such a piece—and so Mansocan kept it intact. "Know that this goes in payment of your life, Prince."

It was hard to know to which prince Mansocan referred.

§ §

It was a relief when all was done. Connel's screams had been an agony, yet there had been no way to ease his misery. The absence of their sound was proof that Mansocan's ministrations were finished. The three Sunarians were left unbound and alone in the small room afterward.

Rowin wiped his tears from his face and finally found the courage to come near his brother. Connel's features were slackened in blissful unconsciousness, the shock of his skinning having put him under. The young prince looked like the boy Rowin had once known, long before King Raymond had created a rift between the two half brothers. His face made more tears trail down Rowin's own.

"He's found release in sleep," Rio murmured, coming near. "It's the Stars' one saving grace to all this."

"The Stars have nothing to do with this." Rowin's anger returned. "Mansocan wanted a message to be sent, to us and the Sunarian court. He made it loud and clear."

"I had not known Connel to bear a tattoo."

"There's a lot Connel kept hidden that would surprise you." His fondness for his brother resurfaced.

Rio glanced to his prince, taking note of him, before he said, "We should move him to the cot and bandage that wound before he wakes."

"Yes."

It took excruciating work to move Connel from the barrel to the bed, but at least the younger prince did not return to a conscious state. Once he was finally settled and properly cared for, his two kinsmen collapsed against the wall near him and absorbed the aftermath of the horrific day. In the quiet, Rowin said, "Tomorrow, there will be blood to pay…"

§ §

Mansocan really did hate the tedium of a proper skinning. Even if the results were superb—and that tattoo had been removed flawlessly—the cries of a live creature were not pleasant. Yet they did make a good point.

That point had been for more than the prisoners' sake; the Sunarian court as well as Mansocan's underlings had needed a lesson. There had been too many mumblings and jostlings for his concessions, and the *seka'vlr* had tired of them. But now, those annoying buzzings in his ears should ease—for a time.

Mansocan looked to the tattoo, which had been set over a pile of snow for some minutes, before he called on the last, annoying pest on his docket. "Chornauk!" His Third appeared immediately and saluted. "We have our response to the king of Sunrise."

Chornauk's eyes wandered to the bowl. "Yes, I see. Shall I have it delivered immediately?"

"Soon." Mansocan turned to face his subordinate. "First, I need a preference of an ear."

His man frowned "An ear, sir?"

"Yes. Certainly, you have a preference?"

Mansocan came closer. To his Third's credit, Chornauk came to a knee and bowed over. Looming over him, the maunstorz leader slipped a knife down a sleeve and placed it above Chornauk's left ear. "After all, you don't really need an earlobe to hear my instructions, now do you?"

Chornauk was one of only a handful of maunstorz not fazed by his superior's ways of exerting power. He was a proud warrior, and his one-handed limb was testament that a little hacking of body parts was no hindrance. "If my ear would better serve you in a box sent to the Sunarian scum, you may have it, *Seka'vlr*."

In some ways, Chornauk's behavior was quite boring. Mansocan pressed harder against his skin to draw blood and then turned away. "No need. You'll find I've already exacted a price from you in your quarters." It was the *vsenk* who was responsible for procuring Prince Rowin that day. His failure had been in response to his superior's counter-command to get the royals in trouble. That insubordination would not happen again. If Chornauk were smart, he would heed the warning—if not, well, he was no longer useful as Mansocan's Third. "You can go now."

Chornauk saluted and stood to stride out the door. It was hard to tell if he had been rattled.

As for the Prince of Sunrise… Mansocan turned back to the tattoo and studied it some more. If the recent skinning didn't prompt the royal heir to fight harder, there were other options to achieve such an end.

However, that next day's fight showed the effort had not been in vain. Prince Rowin Sunrise defeated the next *vsenk* in a matter of minutes. The young man had potential…if Mansocan could cultivate it. *Carefully, though, very carefully.*

Chapter Forty
§
Rubia

Their argument was audible clear out to the hall as Zyanthena and Lord Darshel debated the validity of scouting out Rubia using the obelisks' majiks to jump between locations. Their lively words carried to Crystanian's two other human occupants as they came down the stairs for breakfast. Because they were facing the ovens, Zyanthena and Darshel didn't notice the arrival of Prince Jace and Lieutenant Dawson until they had heard an earful of the discussion.

"So, you're going to leave us here?"

The question made Zyanthena pause her recent arguing points to turn and answer the young lieutenant. "Not leave you. I would travel through Van'allíer as I did before and scout out Rubia to see why it has been so cut off from the other kingdoms. I would come back afterward."

Lieutenant Dawson gave her a withering look before he plopped into a chair by a prepping table. "On that, I agree with Lord Darshel. You shouldn't be going anywhere alone. From what I heard among the Crystine, Rubia is overrun with the maunstorz and snowed-in. The roads were barely passable by horse near Wynward's Crossing."

Lord Darshel seemed pleased with his soldier's reasoning. "See, even he thinks you're taking too many risks. *Besides* the point that you're still recovering from your last run-in with magic."

The warrioress gave both men a stare before her brandy eyes shifted to the prince leaning against the door frame to the kitchen. "Are you of the same opinion, Prince Jace?"

The prince shrugged. "Personally, I hated that trip from Crystal to here the last time around. However, if we're getting out of the middle-of-nowhere to be back among civilization, then I'm all for it."

"I doubt it'll be the trip you're imagining. My money's on falling into the center of a maunstorz's nest."

"At the Red Palace?" Jace came closer to find a seat. He crossed his arms over his chest, looking too casual for such a serious discussion. "Now, I doubt King Corbin would be so easily overrun."

"The South is clearly ill informed of the number of maunstorz still running around in the North. This last wave was not made up of small raiding parties but of infantry numbering in the thousands," she said.

Prince Jace glowered back. "I did hear of the estimated numbers, *woman*." He continued with the derogatory tone despite the Tashek's warning glares.

"Then you—"

"Zy'ena," Lord Darshel stepped in. "In this, I think we all agree but you. If you leave Crystanian, we go too."

Her frown deepened. "This won't be more than a few hours away to reconnaissance the Red Palace and other territories of Rubia. I *am* planning on coming back here."

"I'm not sure I trust you on that," Prince Jace replied before the lord-governor could say anything. "You did already kidnap me once, after all. I will not let you vanish to another kingdom without me there to keep an eye on you."

Despite Darshel's motion to not go at it with the royal, Zyanthena rounded on the prince. "And my thought is to keep you here where you can't cause more trouble. Al least here you'll stay warm and well fed until Snow Thaw."

"As your prisoner."

Lord Darshel stepped forward to plop a basket of freshly baked biscuits in the Tashek's arms to keep her from an exasperated retort. "*Breakfast*, I think, is needed in order to cool our tempers. As for you going alone, it's just not happening, Zy'ena. So stop trying to persuade us otherwise. Now, can we all sit down to a nice, *decent* meal and speak of this later?"

Grudgingly, Zyanthena took the biscuits to the table as Darshel and Dawson collected up butter, jam, and a jug of milk. They all sat down and ate in a strained silence. The decision to use Vauldin and Van'allíer was postponed until the food was all consumed and dishes were washed. Afterward, the foursome reconvened the meeting in the warm billiard room down the hall, keeping tempers cool over a game of billiards and tumblers of Crystani wine.

"I'm not hearing the argument of not trying it," Zyanthena began as she tapped a ball into a corner pocket. "At the rate the snows are falling, Snow Thaw will be a long way off. Our allies lose valuable information as long as riders and birds can't get through. As the one wielder with a working stone and the gift to use it, I can counter that problem in just one or two jumps."

Lord Shekmann raised his hand to halt her tirade. "I'm not against your using the pillars, Zy'ena. You've already made two successful trips through them. I'm just saying that you're not going alone, and neither are you going without a thorough plan."

"The Lord Shekmann and his plans."

"They're more efficient than your haphazard gallivanting."

Zyanthena raised her eyebrows in indignation. "As if my trip through Van'allíer had been planned."

"My point exactly!" The Shekmann's irritation made him miss a shot. He cursed and reached for his wine.

Lieutenant Dawson stepped into the opening they gave. "I don't think this is about that anyway, Ms. Zy'ena, my lord. We all are ready to go through with this, so the real question isn't *how* or *if,* but what we must do to prepare and when we leave. Right?"

A chuckle from Prince Jace, who seemed amused at the round-and-round banter, followed the young soldier's question. He took a puff of his cigar before saying, "The kid's got more sense than the both of you. No wonder he didn't get lost in the Forbidding Forests whilst you both did." By now, Prince Jace had been informed of the past months' events.

Zyanthena glowered. "Being lost and being chased are two very different things."

The prince grinned and leaned down for a shot, sinking it. "I'm sure it is, Tā-shek." He made sure to massacre the word.

The desert woman growled but held her tongue as Lord Darshel came near to look down at her meaningfully and shake his head for silence. As Zyanthena obeyed his lead, he said, "The choices of going deeper into Crystalynian have led us to this moment. The Tashek would say it was preordained." The statement made the royal scoff but did settle Zy'ena's ruffled feathers. "Seeing as Zy'ena does have access to such a power that can shift what the Sheev'anee call Tides of Fate, that's what we will do. We will prepare food, weapons, and medical supplies for a three-day trip through the pillars. As for when we go, I want to study the maps of Rubia thoroughly and know it as well as we can before heading out. This is good enough for you, right, Zy'ena?"

The Tashek's features played through several emotions before folding into a stoic mask. "Yes, My Lordship, it is." The change to the

Shekmann's formal title was not lost on the Kavahadian: Zyanthena was angry.

The lord-governor ignored the fact. "Very well."

"I still think you're all being overly cautious in all this." Prince Jace couldn't help the comment. "You'll see. King Corbin will assuage all your concerns once we have an audience. The lack of communication will be from the snows and the snows alone."

"And thank the Stars there'll be a prince around to get us admitted to such an audience," Zyanthena mumbled sarcastically. In truth, she still believed Rubia was in a bad way, but she couldn't resist the dig back. The prince really was such a sententious ass.

§ §

By the next dawn, the party was ready to attempt a jump from Van'allíer to Veth'aun, the obelisk closest to the Red Palace. What had started out as just the four humans had grown to include the twelve wolves and two war horses. The reasoning: Hunter and Ember would not be persuaded to leave their master's side. Under the threat of them eating the two scrumptious-looking mounts, Zyanthena had caved to their demands. Having Unrevealed and Tano along did make sense anyway, as both horses could carry quadruple the amount of a man. As for the wolves, there was no disputing that a pack of giant predators would be a great deterrent against enemy attacks.

Still, there was one issue…

"Are you sure you can travel with so many of us?" Lord Darshel asked. Carrying two extra people across seemed different from three people, two horses, and a pack of wolves.

Zyanthena shrugged. "The theory's the same. As long as everyone keeps hold of each other, we will be together at Veth'aun."

"And if you don't?" Jace asked jeeringly.

The Tashek's face darkened with sincerity. "On that, you don't want to know."

"Great." The prince sighed and clutched his bag tightly.

Zyanthena glanced back at him wryly. If she didn't know better, the prince was ready to mess up his high-docet pants. "So keep that warning in mind and hang on. I'm going to activate Vauldin and Van'allíer now."

The group settled around Zyanthena and linked with each other either by hands or body parts around the desert woman as she steadied herself and called for majik. Intonating in ancient Syrean, Zyanthena began to call on Vauldin's power to connect to the obsidian obelisk. In a flash of light, the deed was done.

They arrived at Veth'aun only a breath later. The sudden shift of realities left a number of the group addled: Unrevealed and Tano were skittish over the new surroundings until Zyanthena talked them down; four of the wolves had arrived unconscious—just as Zyanthena had the first time—and two more had to empty their stomachs. Lord Shekmann also needed to vomit, and even Dawson was looking a little green. Only Zyanthena and Prince Jace held on to their dignities—through tenacious pride to outdo one another.

Battle trained, Zyanthena was the first to scope out their location and check for enemies. Veth'aun was in an old cathedral on the northern outskirts of the Red City. It seemed abandoned, an old relic from another time. The courtyard it had been set in was crumbling and piled high with untouched snow. The desert warrioress crept through the near-empty cathedral to the front door, where she quietly slipped outside. The view from the small Estarian church's hilltop of the Red City beyond was both beautiful and despondent.

The capitol of Rubia was a large sprawl compared to the smaller capital cities of Crystal and Staria; however, what should have been a bustling center that clear morning seemed to be a ghost town. There were few signs of human—or animal—traffic on the streets, and most of the buildings looked shuttered. The lack of the usual city hubbub made Zyanthena frown. She turned back to the cathedral to check on the others.

Who she met first was a cursing prince of Blue Haven, pinned down in the snow by Swift Hunter. Zyanthena crouched down by his prone form. "You won't be running for sanctuary with the Chívels any time soon," she said.

Prince Jace turned his head to glare up at her. "And why is that?"

"Because something is very wrong with the Red City. Whether it be our enemy, or plague, or something else, I cannot tell from here, but it is not all right."

Her words seemed to reach the prince and knock some sense into him. He calmed. "So I won't be running off haphazardly."

"Very good." Zyanthena rose to check on the others. All but the unconscious wolves had recovered.

"Well?" Lord Darshel asked.

Zyanthena shook her head. "What I see of the city is not encouraging." She continued past the Kavahadian lord-governor to Unrevealed's saddle packs to pull out a scope. Her next words were for her three human companions. "Come and I'll show you."

Once they had all had a scope's look at the city, they were in agreement that something was off. "This is not the city I remember," Prince Jace began.

"No, it's not," Zyanthena echoed. She had been to Rubia's capital with the Sheev'anee two summers back, on their way to the Crystine. It had been a courtesy call to the royal family, and the city had never seemed so dead. "The snows have made a prison of the city. There's no telling, without going down there, just how famished the populace have become."

"But the lack of activity paints a poor story," Lord Darshel continued, his chiseled countenance looking pinched. "This will not be an easy task, scouting the city."

"Yes, it will," Zyanthena countered. "This is where my skills come in. I can get into the city without being noticed."

Prince Jace snorted. "Your exotic features are the most noticeable of all of us."

She glared back. "Hardly, *Prince*, Your arrogance reeks of royal standing. You'd be discovered in a hot second."

"Enough!" Darshel commanded and passed the scope to Dawson to keep track of. "In this I do agree, Zy'ena. A Tashek scout's abilities to pass through unnoticed will get you to the palace. I do suggest the cover of dusk, however."

"Agreed." She looked relieved that she and the Shekmann weren't arguing. Jace stared between them, lost for words and aghast.

"But you won't go alone, will you?" Lieutenant Dawson asked, concerned.

"I won't be alone." Zyanthena turned to eye her two wolf-shadows. "Hunter and Ember insist that I take five wolves with me. At night, they'll be more effective than any of us. Plus, twice as deadly." The others had the sense not to argue.

§ §

Their presence went unnoticed all that day. They took shifts at the cathedral entrance. The reports were the same: not much changed in the Red City from dawn to noon to late afternoon. By dusk, Zyanthena was well prepared to infiltrate the capital's muted confines. She covered herself in a plain brown travel robe and met the others at the entrance to the cathedral.

"Keep a lookout at all times," she warned.

"We're on it." Lieutenant Dawson grinned and saluted. Zyanthena smiled at his words and reached a hand out to squeeze his shoulder—in reassurance of her own safety.

"Do take all precautions," Lord Darshel said with more seriousness.

"And have you known me not to?"

He raised his dark eyebrows. "Your excursions with Vauldin have been lacking in a Tashek's common caution."

Lovely lips pursed at that. "Point taken, My Lordship. I will do better to be mindful of that handicap." At that, her brandy eyes shifted to the last person there. "I hope that this is just a city under snow-siege, Prince Jace. If it is so, I will have you granted the audience with King Corbin Chível you desire."

"You had better."

Zyanthena refrained from a reply beyond an eye-roll at the royal's haughtiness. "Darshel." She looked back to the Shekmann. "Keep Unrevealed safe."

The lord-governor understood the request. The black war horse was the desert woman's one, true heart. "I will, Zyen."

Relieved of the pleasantries, Zyanthena flipped her robe's cowl over her head and blended in with her five wolf escorts into the darkening shadows. They disappeared like a mirage.

"Whoa," Prince Jace commented as they vanished into the surroundings.

The Lord Shekmann and his lieutenant looked gratified at the prince's sudden sense of awe. Darshel said, "And that's why Zyanthena goes. No one beats a Tashek at infiltration. No one."

Chapter Forty-One
§
Hopes

A letter arrived by bird to Kavahad. With it came news the mertinean commander had hoped to hear: Commander Grant's forces had been rescued from a maunstorz harrying force! Commander Kins's eyes filled with relieved tears that he batted away to keep falling. "Stars bless the Sheev'anee," he murmured. The horsemen had made it through the cold and snows they were not accustomed to. Nevermore would the mertinean leader question their fortitude and resources. The Sheev'anee came through every time.

"Lieutenant-Commander!"

Curtis Marx arrived at the door in a prompt fashion. "Sir?"

"We must send birds to Fortress Opal and North Point. The Tashek of Staria have rescued our comrades at the border."

"Thank the Stars!" Curtis Marx looked as relieved as Ethan Kins felt. "I will get missives night away, sir."

"Thank you, Marx."

The lieutenant-commander saluted his commanding officer and hurried away. For the first time in three seasons, the two mertinean men could pass along word of good news to their allies. Hopefully, more was to come.

§ §

Pounding came to the king's door in the dead of the night, startling awake the ruler and his queen. King William Fantill groaned and rose to find a cloak to warm himself from the night's chill. Still in bed, Queen Kesnia asked if she should rise as well. The king bade his wife to sleep and kissed her on the cheek before turning away to answer the door. He hoped the knock wasn't for some horrible disaster.

"Father." Prince Par was standing in the hallway, heedless of the cold that should have seeped through his thin sleepwear. The king had never seen his son look so disheveled. "Father, something's just happened!"

King William motioned for Par to wait as he closed the door so the queen could sleep. Then, William ushered Par across the way, to his study. There, he lit a candle and began to awaken the fire from its slumber. The growing light showed him just how stricken his son was. King William turned away to get his finest brandy and two glasses. He passed the drink to Par, who took it and downed the offered drink in one head-toss. The sting of the alcohol seemed to wake the heir from his shock. His father passed him a throw before finding his own seat before the fire. "Now tell me, my son, what troubles you?"

"Father…do you remember much of being a wielder of Serein?"

King William sighed in relief. *Was that all this was? More of my son's insecurities with magic?* "It has been some time, and not since you were little—but the use of the stone's powers is not easily forgotten."

Par nodded mutely, staring into the flames. His ocean-colored eyes were distant. "Then you would know if a stone bearer could reach another without the use of Sevén, the pearl?"

The question startled the king. "Magic does have limits—to my knowledge. Did you not just have a bad dream, Par?"

"This was no dream! I had a full conversation with the Sheev'arid woman about Syre and events around us." He touched his palm; his father noted the gesture. "She said the powers of each of the stones can be siphoned to another in a very limited capacity. It was how she could find me and sneak into my mind during sleep…"

His son still didn't seem all there. King William frowned. "I have never heard of such a possibility. Are you sure this was not a dream, or perhaps a premonition?"

Par's gaze, hard and serious, focused on his father. "This was no premonition! I spoke to the wielder of Vauldin. She called herself by the titles: Queen of the Black Star, Heir of Crystalynian, and Tashek Sheev'arid Zyanthena. I know her. That desert woman isn't one to do anything by accident. Using our past, she found a way to connect to me."

"Connect to you? What past do you share with a Tashek of Staria?" The king couldn't completely put it past his son to have fraternized with a woman while visiting the desert kingdom—he had heard the desert nomads were especially wanton—but the conclusion didn't seem sound; Par barely made passes at women in his home city! King William couldn't see any other connection for his son to have to a Tashek woman of Staria, however.

Though, so far, this conversation seemed all-around strange, so that wasn't out of the realm of possibility either.

"Princess Zerra Starkindler."

The girl's name seemed to steal the breath from the room. It was the name William had hoped his son could let go of. "Z-zerra, you say?"

"Sheev'arid says Zerra is alive."

After eight-and-a-half years? The king sat stunned to silence. He finally lifted his glass to drain it dry and knock some sense back into his mind. "I think you need to start from the beginning and tell me everything, Par."

§ §

And so, Prince Par did. He found the conversation still so clear, as if Zyanthena had imprinted their words into his mind—or maybe Serein had. In either case, Par laid out what they had spoken of; there was much that seemed more vital when spoken aloud. By the end, King William was convinced it had been a real visitation by the desert woman and not a dream.

It was dawn when the prince got through his telling. Without any preamble, his father insisted Commander Matar and Lord Gordar must be woken to hear the retelling of the message. A page was sent to procure the two men, and the four men met back at the king's study to hear of the event again.

Commander Matar seemed more receptive to the news than King William. He was pleased to hear that Zyanthena was the wielder of Vauldin. "It's so like my Night Fox to find a way to contact someone while stuck in the middle of nowhere."

Par found himself grinning at the Crystine commander's fondness for the Tashek woman. "Funny, she said the same of you, *Khataum*." He almost pronounced the title correctly.

"It's not funny." King William frowned. "Everything she reported has me concerned! Only herself and Lord Shekmann survived out of one hundred and fifty good cavalrymen sent from the Citadel of Light. Blue Haven—those bloody fools!—have overrun the Crystal Kingdom. And now the Starkindler princess is found alive!"

Matar's midnight-blue eyes narrowed at the last. "Highness," he said to Par, "was that really what she said about the Crystal princess?"

"Ah." Par closed his eyes to remember it properly. "I had said: Zerra is alive? And she replied with, 'Of a course, Prince of Sealand.'" The royal heir frowned as he said the reply out loud. Spoken, it sounded different from what he remembered.

Commander Matar, however, seemed to find a relief in the words. "I see that Zy'ena is being vague on the matter." He chuckled to himself.

"What, sir?"

"Oh, nothing." Yet the smile remained. "But I do believe her when she says to be at Osh'ēēn and to await her there."

"Osh'ēēn? That old pillar by our Estarian church?" Lord Gordar asked.

"Yes. It is interesting that she refers to that pillar. Zy'ena must have found a way to activate them. The former queen of Crystalynian had an interest in those old relics. She insisted they could be used by the stones in some way…"

"But they never were," King William continued. "So why does your Tashek scout mention it now?"

"I have no idea." Matar shrugged. "But I assume Zyanthena had a point when she used the name. I'm not one to question her intent on such things."

"So, what will we do?" Prince Par asked. He liked the Crystine commander's words of action and acceptance of the unusual.

"I would say we set up a post at Osh'ēēn, as she suggested, and wait."

William snorted. "Nonsense. It would have to be Par stationed there, and my son has many duties to attend to."

Matar, not agreeing, shared a deadpan look with his old friend.

"Most of those duties can wait, Father," Par countered. He looked to Lord Gordar to confirm. His lord protector nodded. "All but one: Master Harkland says my eight ice-breaker ship are commissioned and the prototype already tested. I have a skeleton crew ready to embark today. I would see them off."

"Yes, and you should," Matar encouraged. His word over the command of Sealand's king had the ruler frowning at the poor etiquette. "What?"

King Fantill stared between his son and the commander, frustrated at their willful collaboration. "Fine," he relented. "I will pardon

Par from his duties for the course of one week. If Zyanthena does not communicate through Osh'ēēn by then, then Par will wait no more."

"Agreed."

"Of course, Father."

The aging ruler shook his head ruefully. "I really hate it when times are dictated by magic. Human lives should not to be molded like this, following its course. Pure insanity."

§ §

By six o'clock, the Sealand heir and his lord protector made the docks, arriving just in time for the official maiden voyage of the new ships. The vessels' commanding captain, Dorian Hightree, was standing at the helm of the lead ship. Recommended by Master Harkland, the former Royal Fleet commander turned tradesman had been eager to try out the new vessels despite their royal commission; Prince Par had been warned of the man's dislike for "people of high social standing." He hoped it would not lead to an issue with the captain that morning.

Captain Hightree and Master Harkland were finishing up their final checks on supplies and equipment when the prince and his cousin arrived. The old dockmaster was happy to see his prince, though the captain seemed irritated by the interruption. "Highness!"

"Master Harkland." Par grinned and shook the dockmaster's hand like they were old acquaintances. Indeed, with all the discussions back and forth, Par felt he knew the man well enough. "I see all looks ready."

"Yes, it is. The crew are all aboard and supplies are below deck. We can set sail by your leave, Highness."

"I'm glad to hear it."

Captain Hightree finally made his way over. Dressed in thick, wool homespun that was lined with silver fox-fur at the neck and waist, the man made an imposing figure. His frown was sour until Master Harkland introduced him. "And this is Captain Hightree, whom I wrote you about. He's the best sea captain on this side of Syre, Highness."

"I trust your commission, Master Harkland," Par replied as he reached a hand out to the stoic captain.

Captain Dorian Hightree was studying their exchange, as if the conversation was of great importance. He only stepped forward when his name was called. "Prince Par," he began, "you had Mr. Harkland here draw my commission?"

Par was surprised at the question. "Well, yes, Captain. As I have no experience aboard a vessel—other than as a passenger—my knowledge of who would be best to hire as captain and crew is limited. So, I gave leave for a man of more repute to make the call." The prince wondered if the man was irritated at that. It was hard to read the captain's expressions, except for that annoyed look.

Captain Hightree grunted an answer and released the prince's hand. His grey eyes swiveled to the dockmaster. "I see now why you let me choose my crew." He turned away without another word to Master Harkland or the prince.

Par wasn't sure what to think of that. Had he just been given the cold shoulder?

But Master Harkland was grinning. "It seems that you've changed the captain's mind about you." He shook his head. "I never thought I'd see the day Dorian Hightree praised a royal."

That was praise? Par was dumbfounded. "Well…that's good, then." He shrugged helplessly at his cousin. "Seeing as all is accounted for, Lord Gordar and I will take our leave so that the ships can be off."

"But there is the bottle to be broken on the *Fair Maiden*'s bow!"

"I think the honors are all yours, Master Harkland."

"Nonsense!" But the dockmaster did look pleased, and humbled, at the privilege.

"I insist," Par continued. "And I've brought some citrus wine and barrels of lemons for the crew to celebrate as they see fit. Please, pass the goods around for me."

"Highness." Master Harkland bowed at the gifts. "You are most generous!"

"It is thanks from all of Sealand for your commissioned boats' success on reaching North Point, Master Harkland. Your men deserve better once they return. Stars' speed to them." He took up the Tashek blessing, having found it useful and accurate.

"Our thanks, Highness!"

Par nodded and disembarked. He and Lord Gordar hung around, out of the way, as the christening ceremony was performed. Afterward, the eight ships left the port under much fanfare from the local wharf population. It seemed most there understood the important undertaking of the special vessels and their crew. The health and hopes of Sealand's northern soldiers relied on the success of the mission. Prince Par Fantill's hopes were the highest.

§ §

Princess Éleen groaned and stretched her aching neck. "My, I think I need a break!" The other ladies, all still occupied with their needlework, murmured that they had heard as the Havener set her project aside and stood. Used to each other's coming and goings to walk the halls for relief, the others barely looked up as she slipped out of the sitting room.

Alone in the coolness of the hall, Éleen shivered and rubbed her arms to warm them. The shock of going from the heated sitting room to the cold hallway helped clear her head from the tedious threadwork she had been at all afternoon; however, her fatigued neck and hands quickly stiffened in the cold. "Hot tea is in order, I think," Éleen muttered to herself, and started down the hall toward the kitchens.

Though the sitting room was supplied with a kettle and teacups, the provided tea of the day had been Lady Diana Levine's choice of a rosehip and lavender blend—much too relaxing for being shut inside and working on a repetitious task. Princess Éleen craved the hearty and warming "winter" blend the head cook had introduced her to. Not only was its robust taste warming, it eased the princess's "cold-limb" symptoms as nothing else had. Still, Éleen hadn't quite been able to coax the woman's recipe from her. It was a work in progress...

Midafternoon was a lull period for the kitchen staff: a few hours' reprieve before the evening meal needed to be started. Usually, the kitchen was empty as the staff took afternoon naps in their quarters. Yet the head cook had shown the Havener where the container of the winter blend was and welcomed the royal to a bag of it whenever she was in need. Princess Éleen made the kitchens in good time—encouraged by the chill of the halls—and made her way to the pantry where the tea tins were stashed.

She was in the midst of procuring some of the tea when voices in the kitchen made Éleen pause and peep out of the pantry. At one of the high stools before a preparing table, a young kitchen maid was being kissed passionately by the amorous viscount while the rogue pulled back her dress to get at a particular body part underneath. Though the woman's skirts hid most of Markus LaPoint from the princess's view, the maid's moans and viscount's exertions made the princess realize what was happening. Stifling a gasp, Princess Éleen whirled back inside the pantry. In awkward silence, she realized her dilemma: the two lovers were blocking her escape to the hall.

Of all the luck, and why now? Éleen flushed at the noises without. Keeping still, she waited in pained anticipation for the little kitchen romp to be over.

Even though it seemed to end in short order, by the time the maid had satisfied the viscount, the princess was feeling hot and queasy from embarrassment. It was a relief when she heard the maid speak to the viscount in polite tones and take her leave. The silence afterward was a Stars' send. "Oh, thank goodness!" Éleen breathed and pushed herself from the huddle she found herself in over the tea tin. She straightened herself and shook out her dress before rounding the corner out of the pantry. Her relief was short-lived.

"Enjoy your little voyeurism, Princess?" Viscount Markus LaPoint purred.

Éleen stopped dead in her tracks. The viscount was leaning back on the just-used stool, a roguish grin on his face. Though his clothes had been tidied from his little conquest, there was a stain on his trousers and a bulge in his pants, both in open display to the princess. The pose had Éleen blushing and trying extra hard to not look again. "Mr. LaPoint," Éleen said as neutrally as she could muster.

The grin widened. "Try as you might, Princess, I know that you were hiding in the pantry just now." Markus rose and sashayed closer to lean down by the Havener's ear. "Did you enjoy the sound and smell of our little afternoon delight?"

The viscount's breath on Éleen's skin had her shaking. She caught her breath. "I—I do not know of what you refer, Your Grace. I have only been here but a moment to procure some tea." She held up the tin as proof of her activities.

Markus chuckled and straightened. He took the tin from her hand, despite the princess's protests, and began to warm a kettle over the kitchen stove. Then, he found two cups and filled them with the winter tea, spooned into cloth bags. During it all, Éleen Éldon-Tomino dared not move. "Being the perfect guest, I see," Markus continued and saw the princess startle at his words. "Very polite you are. I know a few ladies just like you."

"I... Your Grace?"

"Sit." Viscount LaPoint waved to a chair beside him—not the stool, thankfully, but still a reminder of what the man had just done. The princess responded woodenly, caught between wanting to flee but complying to correct protocol as the viscount's guest.

By the time she sat, the kettle was hot. Markus removed it from the fire and carefully poured the water into their cups. "A lady, such as yourself, only knows the pleasures of a union by stories...or a sneaking glance at the act... so I will pardon you your naivete." His eyes observed the princess' nervous swallow. They seemed to say: *Oh, how fun the young and virtuous are!*

Princess Éleen straightened herself with as much dignity as she could muster. "Again, I think you are mistaken, Your Grace. To what do you think I am privy to?" In her nervousness, Éleen reached out to her cup only to bump it. Hot water spilled over the sides to scald her fingers. She hissed and pulled back only to find the viscount's strong hands about her waist.

Markus was already pulling her toward a cold-water barrel by the back door of the kitchens. He plunged her hand into the ice-cold water before she could think to protest. Éleen gasped at the shock. "Keep it in!" Markus ordered, his body keeping the princess pinned over the barrel. Despite his rakish nature, or maybe because of it, the viscount did seem to understand the seriousness of a severe burn.

"Your Grace!" Éleen protested.

"Keep it in!" he ordered firmly. "I've seen what burns can do. A young kitchen boy permanently injured his hand in this very kitchen. The gruesome sight is not easily forgotten."

The words stopped the princess's struggles; though, she felt thoroughly pinned by the viscount. His body across her entire back side was discomforting. The princess squirmed, trying to move away, but Markus refused to move until her hand was well iced. Even then, he only let Éleen remove her limb but kept her in place as he leaned over to inspect the injury.

"Your burn looks minor, Princess. How does it feel?"

"It's fine, Your Grace." The princess heard her voice reply steadily, though she felt anything but calm.

"Good." Slowly, Markus removed his weight. Yet, his hold on her wrist remained. "I have some lavender ointment for it." He began to lead the way back through the kitchens.

Princess Éleen balked and tried to pull back. "I am not letting you use this as an excuse to get me alone with you in your rooms."

The words only made her host laugh and turn back to address her. "Princess, in case you haven't noticed, we are already alone, nor am I unable to take advantage of you right here—if I so chose." Markus turned away and continued to drag the princess back to the table. From a drawer, he pulled out a jar of ointment with his free hand. "But what I was getting is right here. I provide it to my staff as they work."

"Oh."

Markus chuckled as he applied the lavender ointment to her fingers. To his credit, he was good with his hands. "There, that should do." Markus finally released the limb back to the princess. Éleen looked at it doubtfully. "With that, it will heal in no time."

"Ah…thank you," Éleen replied, reluctantly.

"Of course," Markus wiped up the water spill. "But it does not excuse you from your eavesdropping."

"I was doing no such thing!" Too late, the princess realized she had betrayed herself with her exclamation. She felt her cheeks begin to burn.

"My dear." The words turned velvety in the viscount's mouth. "Your persistence is commendable but far, far too telling." He grinned. "But no matter, we both know the truth. An honest admission is unnecessary."

"What is it that you want?"

"Oh, so direct," Markus teased. He threw a towel by the sink before leaning closer. "What I want, Princess, is what I always want: to let women enjoy our carnal pleasures. Such egregious pursuits should be the privilege of all women."

"It's deplorable."

"Only for one who's never had the pleasure, especially from an experienced lover."

Éleen huffed. She was finally getting enough courage mustered from hearing LaPoint spout off about his *talents.* "Whatever."

"Whatever?" The smirk was back. "Princess, you're destined to be the breeder of someone in high status. That does not mean you'll be enjoying it."

The reminder had the blood draining from her face. It hit the mark on one of the issues she wrestled with, being the first-born daughter to the crown. "Even you do not know that."

"Oh, but I do. Do you know the number of unsatisfied, married women that find my bed?"

"I have no concern to know."

Markus wagged a finger at her. "Whatever you're thinking, it's thrice that number."

Éleen made a face.

"So, Princess, your chances aren't very good."

"I'll take my chances."

The viscount shook his head. "Ah, Princess...well, once you meet with the prince of Staria, I'm sure you'll change your mind."

Éleen felt her pulse speed up. "Wait, what?"

Markus shrugged and slipped a note from his pocket. He handed it over to her. "Prince Al'den Maushelik is on his way to us. It seems you have something of his that needs returning."

Éleen's china-blue eyes were scanning the letter in a flurry.

"Of you, there is no mention. Peculiar is that not?"

Panicked at the words, Eleen's hand reach instinctively for the citrine-stone necklace she kept around her neck, secretly cradling the prince's secret she bore. *Did Markus know?* She gulped and decided to keep her tongue in a brave—or foolhardy—stance of defiance. "This letter proves nothing," Éleen managed.

"Perhaps," Viscount LaPoint countered. "Or maybe it is exactly the point. I'm sure you're soon to find out. If the news is poor, you know where my room is. It'll always be open for you, Princess of Blue Haven."

Chapter Forty-Two
§
Discovery

The shuttered city seemed more deserted than it had from afar. Padding deeper into the heart of the Red City, the wolves of Crystalynian and their master found much vacated, though a few weary souls still eked out a living on the outskirts of town. Still, there were few candles and fires. Most of Rubia's capital stood cold and empty.

Further inspection showed that a number of households contained corpses; whether they had perished from the cold or starvation, it was hard to say. "Just what happened here?" Zyanthena murmured as she hovered over a young woman holding an infant. Both were frozen statues turned blue and frosted.

Long Scar, the beta swift that Hunter had loaned to Zyanthena, took on the customary human head-shake—he was the best at imitating human behaviors—and chortled that the others had not found much better in the buildings beyond. Disconcerted, the beta and the Tashek left the latest house to join the other wolves: Howler, Too Soon, Far Tracker, and Silent. Like ominous harbingers of death, the pack of wolves and the warrioress continued deeper into the city in search of answers.

Their path took them all the way to the palace's gates. At least here, in the heart of the city, some homes still showed signs of living people. Yet that also led to the discovery of the occupation of the enemy. Far Tracker came upon the maunstorz first as the *vsenk* was exiting a sentry station. Before the man had time to alert the others of the wolf, the maunstorz was silenced and his body dragged to a dark corner.

Zyanthena whispered her thanks to the elegant grey wolf before studying their catch. "He's definitely one of their lower ranks," she said, frowning, "but this does mean the enemy has taken this city? It explains the poor condition of the citizens."

Too Soon vocalized a question, and the Tashek answered. "Yes, we'll need to get into the Red Palace. I have to know what was done to the king and his family."

The five wolves chortled among themselves and decided to send Silent for a look-about the palace gates. The near-black she-wolf disappeared into the night shadows before Zyanthena could have a say. Cramped into the corner, the others waited until she returned.

Silent came back with good news: there was a livery gate still left unattended by the stable yard on the east wing of the large estate. Guiding the pack there took less time than she had been gone. Just as the black she-wolf had said, the stables' manure gate had been left open. It was too easy to sneak into the grounds.

"Stay away from the livestock," Zyanthena ordered gently. "One whiff of wolf could set the animals off."

Long Scar huffed that the human stated the obvious. Then, in silent communication, the five wolves slunk away to find routes around the stables while Zyanthena continued her search through them. By the time they all rejoined near some carts on the other side of the yard, more details had been noted.

"The stables are frequented regularly, and the horses are cared for—which I do not expect from maunstorz. There are about two dozen horses left in the stables." Of the rest, the wolves had sniffed out carcasses numbering nearly fifty animals: horses, cows, pigs, and sheep. "The maunstorz are hard up for food, too. Though, I think it's more a process of planning than necessity." The five wolves concurred. "We need to find a servant door into the palace; not the main one to this wing. I—"

Silent vocalized that she had already found such an entrance. Heading west from the stable yard, they all stalked down the wall to a small doorway sunk into a cubbyhole that had been dug halfway below ground level. To the wolves, it smelled like a dump-door for kitchen leftovers.

"From here I should go alone." As expected, the wolves' response was an immediate no. "Look, the five of you don't exactly blend in as household pets."

Long Scar grumbled that this was the entire point.

Zyanthena gave the beta a look. "To that end, I will accept Too Soon's aid. Of you all, Soon is the least threatening-looking." Too Soon was the runt of the litter of Hunter and Ember's newest adult pups. His smaller size, however, did not hide his wolfish glower at being called *the least threatening*. Zyanthena socked him on the shoulder and continued: "For the rest of you, keep searching out here for signs of life or any clues about the maunstorz's movements. I'll have Soon call to you when and where we exit."

At least the wolves did not argue a plan that was straightforward but instead trusted in each other's abilities to get around safely and discreetly. Without preamble, they all headed off to scout different areas of the palace. Left alone, Zyanthena and Too Soon made eye contact before entering into the scullery door.

§ §

"It's been an hour. What's taking her so long?" Prince Jace whined as he stomped around the fire in an attempt to stay warm. Their "fire" was barely large enough to cook with and little brighter than a candle, so as not to attract unwanted attention. For warmth, it was rather lacking.

"One hour is barely enough time to get into the city, let alone search it," Lieutenant Dawson answered. "These things take time."

Prince Jace huffed. "Time, my ass. She could have spun up some fancy idea of a shelter for us with that magic of hers before she left us out in this blasted cold."

"Zy'ena doesn't need to be wasting such energy on useless things as that," Lord Darshel said in the Tashek's defense. With the borrowed clothes from King Trev'shel's room, the Shekmann was adequately warm against the night's chill. He politely ignored the scowl that the prince sent his way.

"There are more blankets in Tano's packs," his lieutenant supplied, being more helpful.

Prince Jace Éldon tsked but spun on his heels to go retrieve the blankets. He returned with a thin wool one and hunkered down with it by the fire. Now that he was better equipped, the spoiled Havener seemed less sour. "I just hope this business can be concluded soon."

Lord Darshel hummed at that. "As do we all, Highness. I'm missing those hot springs at Crystanian right now."

"Wait, Crystanian has hot springs?" Dawson sat up.

"Right in its walls, on the eastern side of the palace."

"I wish I had known that yesterday!"

"Maybe, when we return, they will be our first order of business."

"Right!"

Prince Jace made a face. "It's reprehensible that you are both talking about hot springs in a place like this."

Lord Shekmann countered, "You're the one who didn't want to stay behind."

The prince's face grew darker. "Touché, Lord-Governor, touché." With his sour frown deepening, the handsome prince readjusted his wool blanket and hunkered in closer to the fire.

Above them, the last vestiges of dusk faded to true, starlit night…

§ §

Having Too Soon along proved to be an advantage. The wolf's keen hearing allowed him to pick up conversations within the palace's many rooms from a distance that was safely away from enemy eyes. Some of what he heard was the run-of-the-mill banter of palace staff—from those who had learned to survive by following maunstorz orders and keeping their heads down and mouths shut. Other speech was from maunstorz underlings. Among the latter were a group of soldiers who were participating in the daily fights their leader required of them. It was this group that captured Zyanthena's attention.

"That bloody prince is making a mockery of us to our *seka'vlr*."

"That's right!" another agreed, banging an ale onto the table. "It's all because of that Sunarian that we sacrifice one of our own daily. He's influenced our *seka'vlr* somehow. As long as he has our *seka'vlr*'s favor, we'll have to continue humoring that Syrean scum!"

"Yes, damn that cock-start!"

Yet there was one maunstorz with a brain in his head. "You lazy fools! Our *seka'vlr* has been playing by our rules this whole time. We should be ashamed that this royal scum has bested us in every fight. We deserve just punishment if we cannot defeat him." The words seemed to hollow out the room.

"Fine. You have a point, Chauk'enn."

"Still, it doesn't mean I like it."

The wise maunstorz, Chauk'enn, sounded amused. "Of course not, but we do have to follow Mansocan's orders until Zephthaniel decides he is no longer worth leading the armies of Xercon. Every *vsenk* has a time of glory and a time of fall. Our *seka'vlr* is daring our traditions too much. It may make his undoing."

"I wish we were still serving under our *xercon'vlr*."

"In time, my fellows, in time. Our great Zephthaniel has plans laid out for the long term. Patience has always been his virtue. Until then, these princes of Syre make good bargaining chips to keep the kingdoms in disarray..."

Too Soon nudged Zyanthena's thigh and laid back his ears in concern. The desert woman nodded and motioned for them to move away from the guards' commons. They had heard more than enough. The Prince of Sunrise (or at least one of them) was here at the Red Palace. He could be kept in a room somewhere on the main floor, but Zyanthena doubted it. The maunstorz weren't ones to single out ranks and afford noblemen special privileges. Her bet was on the dungeons. She murmured as much to Too Soon.

The Tashek remembered being shown the guard quarters during her last visit to the palace. It only made sense that the holding cells were a level below that wing. The hardest part would be getting to the dungeons. There were about seven guards posted at the stairwell and another set was sleeping in the quarters provided—or so Too Soon could sense.

"Quick and quiet," Zyanthena told him in a barely audible voice. They would have one chance to silence the posted guards without waking the others. Blade in hand, the Tashek motioned for Too Soon to go first. She relied on his speed and power to overtake the guards. The desert warrioress followed behind to take out the remaining guards that were not body-slammed by the large grey wolf.

Luckily, the seven maunstorz never knew what hit them.

Zyanthena finished dragging the last corpse into a maintenance closet while Too Soon kept alert in the hall. Once the place was cleared, she motioned the wolf to join her at the door; more guards could be on the other side. Taking a final, steadying breath, Zyanthena nudged the door aside and they hurried through.

The room beyond was nearly empty—save for a cot against the far wall and a water barrel. A single form was sleeping on the cot. The man's eyes opened at the commotion at the door and widened in fear as the wolf came toward him.

"Not him, Soon," Zyanthena warned the wolf off. She recognized Prince Rowin of Sunrise despite his bruised and battered form. Quickly, she closed the door and turned to the shocked royal.

"Zy-zyanthena Sheev'arid?" Rowin pushed himself to a sitting position. His midnight-blue eyes, wide as saucers, showed his disbelief.

"Prince Rowin of Sunrise." She came near to kneel and give a customary Sheev'anee bow of respect, arms extended from her sides and palms skyward.

"By the Stars! But how?"

"That is a very long story, Highness. One we do not have the luxury of time for. Are you well?" The royal looked beat to hell and underfed.

"Let's just say it's been a shitty few months." Rowin groaned himself to standing. His eyes shifted to look past the Tashek. "Your friend here can give one quite the scare."

Zyanthena turned to smile affectionately at the grey wolf. "This is Too Soon. 'Soon' is fine. He is one of twelve wolves I have the privilege of having at my side." The prince looked warily at the large wolf of Crystanian. "But never mind him. I need to get you out of here. Are you able to move?"

"Me? Yes. I may not look it, but I'm in better shape than some. The others are being kept in the dungeons below."

"Then we will go to them." Zyanthena turned away and strode back to the door to pull out the large hoop of keys she had taken from the guards. She worked through them until one matched the keyhole to the guardroom door, and then she locked it.

"You're blocking our escape?" Rowin asked as he came near and helped the Tashek move the water barrel in front of the door.

"I have another idea for getting out of here. For now, I am more concerned with being cornered in the cells without warning."

If the prince planned on protesting, he knew better than to argue common sense with a Sheev'anee scout and knew Zyanthena had proven to be useful to her commanders in the past. "Then let me show you to the others."

"Yes, I am anxious to see who has survived."

He looked back at her momentarily, as if he found her words a warning to the situation beyond the palace walls. Looking away again, Rowin continued across the small room to the stairwell beyond. They descended into the darkened dungeons, stopping only long enough for torches.

By the light of the flames, Zyanthena Sheev'arid got to see the handful of Rubian nobles deemed useful enough to live. Of the original thirty-three lives packed into the cells, twenty-seven remained; though, twelve were sick with fevers from starvation and the poor conditions. Those twelve were in the first three cells, having been "quarantined" away from the others. The Tashek held back a gasp at the sight of their pasty skin and emaciated bodies. These men would not survive long in the state they were in.

"I've done as much as I could to get food and medicine provided," Prince Rowin murmured by her side. "Still…"

Zyanthena touched his forearm. "To survive under maunstorz imprisonment at all is a feat, Highness." She handed him the keys. "But now you have the honor of releasing these souls from this place." The prince took the keys and quickly found the ones to the match each of the cells. By the time they had moved to the fourth door, the prisoners were all awake and trying to make sense of the commotion.

"Rowin, what trouble are you getting into this time?"

The desert woman squinted and came closer to the next cell to make out the face of the man who asked. "Ah, Prince Connel," she said as he peered through the squares of his cell. It was priceless to see the shock on proud Prince Connel's face.

"T-tashek!"

"Zyanthena, Highness," she reminded.

Prince Connel was too shocked to correct the mistake. "Wh-what are you doing here?!"

"I thought it was obvious."

"Zy'ena!" Another man came forward from the shadows.

She said, "Lord Protector, it's good to see you."

"And it's great to see you!"

Rio and Connel came to the door as Rowin sprung them from the cage. As they stepped out, a tall prisoner squeezed passed them to get to the prince and the boy who were still in the cell. "That is Prince Derek Chível and his son, Miguel," Rowin informed Zyanthena as he came back to her side from releasing the others.

"And I'm Prince Derek's lord protector, Yory Selèv." The tall man said as he glanced up at the Tashek while checking on his prince.

"Yes. I remember you, Lord Protector." Zyanthena came in to see the prince of Rubia for herself. He seemed sickly, like the first men.

"Prince Derek has always had a poor constitution," Yory explained as she bent down and studied the pale royal. "But I've seen him pull out of worse."

Zyanthena nodded. "And the king?"

"My father was killed in his quarters by their leader at the beginning of the takeover," Prince Derek answered in a wispy voice. Still, there was steel in the tone.

"I see." Zyanthena clenched her jaw. "You and your son are very important to Rubia, indeed. We must get them far from here." She gave Yory a hard stare in promise.

"That's great, but how do you propose getting out of here?" Prince Connel said from the aisle. "I've seen the number of maunstorz between us and freedom."

"Yes, and how many reinforcements are with you?" a noble asked from the back of the huddled group of men.

Zyanthena's features became hard as she rose to address everyone. "There is only myself and three others here."

Scared, angry whispers began at that.

"But you got here, Zy'ena," Rowin said favorably.

"I came by a way you would never believe, Highness, and we will leave the same way—if we are able."

Just then, the shape of Too Soon returned from his sniffing about deeper into the dungeons. His unnerving presence sent a number of the men skittering backward in a frightened huddled. Ignoring the humans, the grey wolf came to Zyanthena's side to tell her of his findings.

His master stroked the thick hair at the wolf's withers as he spoke of his insights. "Thank you, Soon," she told him before looking to the others. "There is a passage that leads deeper into these dungeons."

"Yes," Yory Selèv agreed, "but it leads to a bricked-off cellar on the northern side of the palace."

"That is no problem," Zyanthena replied cryptically. "We head there now. There is no time to waste."

She and the wolf ghosted through the prisoners. They paused only long enough for Zyanthena to warn them all to follow or stay in the prisons and die. Finally, her harsh words seemed to knock some sense into everyone. The motley bunch of men began to follow.

"I can lead the way," Lord Protector Yory said as he caught up to the desert woman and her companion. "I know this route. It was an emergency passage."

'Then, by all means." Zyanthena waved him forward. She did not mention that the lord protector was too encumbered by his sick charge and the young boy; the Rubian protector seemed more than capable of the multiple tasks at hand.

In the Rubians' wake came the three Sunarians, Rowin helping Rio to walk while the proud Prince Connel was trying his hardest to not eye Too Soon as if the wolf would strike him down at any second. Behind them came the nobles, weighted down by the sick numbers of their group. Her frown must have been severe, for it prompted Prince Rowin to comment, "We can't leave them here, Zy'ena." The words were a bare whisper.

"I know, Prince. I would not ask it of them, but the Red City is a very pitiful sight. The cold and snows may be their undoing."

"I have been to the training yard and stables. I know the depth of the snows. It makes me wonder how you—"

"You will see soon enough, Prince Sunrise." Zyanthena cut him off. She had heard the doubt in his question. Looking resigned, the Sunarian continued the walk in silence.

"This is it," Yory finally announced after countless twists and turns. "Beyond this wall is the abandoned cellar."

Zyanthena nodded and moved toward the wall. "How thick is this?"

Yory shook his head.

"It should be two feet," Prince Derek supplied as he was helped to a seat against another wall.

"Very well." Zyanthena ran her eyes across the bricks for a few moments longer. "Then I need everyone to stay well back from here as I work."

"But what—?"

Zyanthena turned to glare at the skeptical Prince Derek. Her look shut him up. "I need room."

"We will give it," Prince Rowin promised and began to wave everyone back.

The Tashek ignored them all as she turned to the immense task before her. Closing her eyes and centering her breath, Zyanthena reached into Vauldin's powers and searched for something she could use. If it had been the stone Sheveth, she could have simply cut through the bricks. As it was, however, such a working would drain her body's reserves past a healthy level. Yet, there was a power Vauldin held that could work: to "remake what was broken." In all intents and purposes, the cellar entrance had, once upon a time, been open. Calling upon that image, Zyanthena reached deep into the obsidian stone's powers and began the process of remodeling the doorway.

Time and place drifted away from Zyanthena as she worked. Only when the task was finished did she open her brandy eyes to see what progress she had garnered. Before her, every brick had been removed and set in an organized stack, as they would be before use; the mortar was also separated into piles by material type. It was as neat as a construction site would be in preparation for the building of the wall.

More than few men were making signs of protection at the strange act, and all were dumbstruck.

"Zy'ena, you never said you were a stone-bearer!" Prince Rowin exclaimed as he came closer to the reworked wall to study it.

The Tashek was surprised to hear that the elder Sunarian prince knew anything about the Stones of Power. "This has been a fairly recent occurrence, Prince. I suggest we move quickly from here," Zyanthena said. "You'll find the city outside to be anything but a cheery sight."

Chapter Forty-Three
§
Escape

It was nearly dawn when the Shekmann made out shapes coming toward the cathedral from the city proper. Alarmed, he roused the others, and they all waited with weapons drawn as the dark shadows neared their position. It was the appearance of the five wolves at the fore that let the men know it was Zyanthena returning.

Lord Darshel hurried forward to assist some of the freed men the final way up the hill. His cavalry lieutenant was quick to follow suit. "Zy'ena!"

"I am here," the Tashek spoke from the back of the group. She and a nobleman with swordsmanship skills had trailed the group to be the first line of defense against an enemy, should they attack. Fortunately, such action had not been necessary.

The lord-governor of Kavahad looked stunned to see how many men the desert woman had come back with. "These—"

"We will speak inside the cathedral," Zyanthena suggested, and turned away to keep watch on the city. As the men disappeared into the building, she used a subtle working of majik to erase the signs of their passage in the snow. Only when she was satisfied of their cover did Zyanthena turn away, leaving the wolf pack to stand guard.

Inside, the rescued men were finding seats around the shabby interior. Still, the cathedral was a good wind block against the elements and probably as comfortable as the prisons they had been in for months. The two Kavahadians were busy getting the men blankets and hot water to sip; Prince Jace was already conversing with the three princes over the conditions of Rubia's capital.

Prince Rowin was the first to notice the Tashek's arrival. "Zy'ena." He rose from his crouch by his lord protector and brother.

"Prince of Sunrise." She bowed.

"Enough with the pleasantries, Tashek. It is we who should be gracing you with such honors."

Zyanthena nodded. "As you wish, Highness." She came closer and made a motion of permission to touch the royal. "Now that we are free of the palace, tell me of each of your ailments." Though the trip through

Van'allíer had been only a short-planned venture, she had had the foresight to bring medicines from Crystanian. Anything would be helpful to the men at that point.

"Never mind my condition," Rowin commanded. "I have been in better care than others here. Rio suffers from a dislocated shoulder, poorly set and healing, and headaches from an injury. His finger…" The prince choked on the words. "Well, there's nothing for that anyway. My brother had a tattoo skinned off his back five days ago…"

Zyanthena could hear the torment in his voice. She reached out to squeeze the man's arm in sympathy. "Who else?"

"Well, Prince Derek has been suffering from fevers, so have most of the men here." They turned to study the room. "Everyone has been tortured or used as punching bags in one form or another."

The Tashek nodded. She could see the picture of traumas on every man. "Let me see what I have with me. You should take your rest as well, Prince, while I prepare some herbs."

"Thank you, Zy'ena."

She bowed her head. "My only regret is not thinking of coming to Rubia sooner and easing your suffering. For now, I will do what I can for all of you."

Zyanthena turned away to gather supplies and update Lord Darshel of all she and the wolves had seen. There was plenty in her telling to concern the lord-governor.

"This many men, Zyen! We're not prepared for this."

"This is too few," she argued back. "If you saw the city, you would be relieved to see this number. The maunstorz cared not for the people of Rubia. There were too few to find and too many frozen corpses in their stead. Even half of these men may not make it." This last, Zyanthena whispered.

"And the enemy?"

"Has control of the Red Palace and its food stores. Mansocan leads them. He barely kept any of the nobles and Prince Derek alive—and, probably, only as a means to keep the populace who remain in check. The two princes of Sunrise would be used for similar purpose against their own kingdom."

"This explains everything we observed three seasons ago."

"Yes, it does." Zyanthena's lips formed a hard line. "At this rate, Syre is split completely in two by the maunstorz and the snows of Ravel."

"It's worse than we surmised."

"Yes."

"Then we need to get back to Staria and warn King Al'den!"

"First things first, Darshel." Zyanthena grabbed up her bag of herbal remedies.

"You're right, of course. But once this is done, we need to get ready to leave. There are too many maunstorz here."

"Agreed. Have Dawson begin packing while we work. Discreetly." At least Unrevealed and Tano were still in the courtyard, so packing would be out of the sight of the others. "From there, we'll discuss our options. The princes may want to be part of it."

They returned to the cathedral and began handing out ointments and making teas for the sick. Zyanthena came back to the princes to minister to them herself. "Here is an ointment for your wounds. Prince Connel, this one is specifically used to numb your skin." Though the royal had hid it well, now that Zyanthena was aware of his skinning, his cautious movements and inaudible hisses of pain made sense.

"I'll help my brother," Rowin offered and reached out for the jar.

"And I'd prefer the Tashek," Connel protested with a glare. Rowin raised his eyebrows at his brother's obstinacy.

"Let Rowin do it, Highness," Zyanthena soothed. She came before the Sunarian and knelt to take his hands. "Let me hold your hands instead and take your pain, Prince Connel."

Prince Connel seemed shocked at the desert woman's touch and phrasing, and he relented to the kindness with the barest nod and pulled his hands away only long enough to remove his shirt. Afterward, he braced himself against the coming contact to his abused skin. Zyanthena helped by steadying the prince with her eyes and hands. Inaudibly, she began to chant words of majik to help dull his pain. It must have worked, for Rowin finished the application of the ointment and dressing without making his younger brother hiss in pain.

Finished, Zyanthena squeezed the prince's hands once more and then released them. She walked on her knees over to Rio. "And now you, Lord Protector."

"I'm afraid there's little to do for me, Zy'ena. My injuries are seasons old."

The smile she returned to Rio Ravesbend was full of warmth and a glimmer of humor. "Let me try, at least."

Rio glanced uncertainly at his prince and only acquiesced when Rowin encouraged him with a nod. "As you say, Sheev'arid. I will trust you in this."

"Thank you, Ravesbend."

A hand reached out to the lord protector until Rio gripped it. Zyanthena's other one hovered first over his injured shoulder and then his head as she chanted soft words of ancient Syrean. As with the brick wall, the minutes ticked by as if there was no thought to them. It was only when the last bone, tendon, ligament, muscle, and skin cells slid into place that the Tashek lowered her hand. She felt the majik was done by the feeling of rightness in her gut. "That is all to do, Lord Protector."

Rio blinked out of the warm cocoon he had found his mind enfolded into. For some strange reason, his world seemed brighter, more serene, and—unexpectedly—pain free. "W-what?!"

"How are you?" Rowin knelt by his loyal friend and reached out to him with hopeful trepidation. The prince could only guess as to what Zyanthena had done for his lord protector, but if it was as he dared believe, then…

"I…I feel fine, my prince."

"Move your shoulder," Zyanthena prompted.

The Sunarian soldier did so, first with care and then more assuredly. The joint moved without a hitch, as if it had never been injured. "It's—"

Prince Rowin and Zyanthena shared a look. The latter bobbed her head at the prince's unspoken question. "With Vauldin, I have returned his body to its correct positioning. He had a break in his skull and tissues not in their proper place. I healed them as they should have been."

"Then I have more to repay you for, Zyanthena Sheev'arid," Rowin replied in gratitude.

"Your thanks is enough, Prince Rowin, Lord Protector." Zyanthena rose to see to the others; however, despite her being a stone bearer, only one other man could benefit from Vauldin's powers. Most of the injured and sick had to be treated with herbs, proper nutrition, and rest. By the time dawn rose over the Red City, the twenty-eight men rescued from the palace had been assessed and treated.

§ §

"What is the problem?" An irate Mansocan growled as he and Chornauk reached the commotion outside the dungeon door. His underlings had been scrambling to find a way into the locked door ever since the corpses of the absent guards had been discovered in the maintenance closet.

A brave *vsenk* came forward to kneel and bow. "*Seka'vlr*, this door has been locked and the guards killed. We are searching for the keys now."

Mansocan narrowed his eyes. Was this the work of Prince Rowin Sunrise? "Forget the keys. I want that door down. Now!"

"Yes, sir!" His fighters saluted and rushed for tools to undo the hinges. It took them fifteen minutes to accomplish the task. As they worked, Mansocan ordered Chornauk to check the palace and grounds for signs of an escape.

"It is down, *Seka'vlr*."

The great maunstorz leader nodded and ordered his fighters through. They pushed passed the water barrel into the empty guard room and continued to the stairwell to the dungeons. It took more time there to collect torches, as those that should have been in the holders were missing. After that, the maunstorz discovered the cells open and emptied of their prisoners.

Mansocan was furious. "Find them! Find them now!" He turned away from the scene with red eyes blazing like fire. Heads and body parts were going to go flying once he got his hands on the emboldened prisoners—but at least it was guaranteed. There was nowhere for the Syreans to run.

§ §

"We return to Crystanian," Lord Darshel said. "Everything these men need is there."

Prince Rowin looked skeptical. "Crystanian is far away and in ruins."

"Actually, Prince Rowin," Prince Jace corrected, "the palace is fully intact and stocked. Compared to here, it's like paradise."

Prince Rowin looked at the other man as if he had sprung three heads.

"In that, Prince Jace is correct," Zyanthena confirmed, to settle the matter. "Majik has reformed the structure. It has everything we need from medicine, to food and clothing, and proper comforts."

"But is far away from any allies!"

"That does make it safest," the Havenese prince countered again.

Prince Rowin looked exasperated. "There are men fighting the maunstorz as we speak! They need to know what we know. And Mansocan boasted of my men—men absolutely loyal to me!—being held prisoner at the Command Front. Certainly, they fare no better than we did up here. I cannot leave them to such a fate!"

Zyanthena and Lord Shekmann shared a glance. The lord-governor seemed to know the desert warrioress's thoughts, for he cautioned her, "That is even riskier than infiltrating the Red City. I would advise against it, Zy'ena." She frowned and turned away to pace. Darshel continued, "Besides, there are too many sick men with us. They will only be a hinderance if we go anywhere but Crystanian."

"And I say we do both." Zyanthena stopped her pacing long enough to give the Kavahadian a look of defiance. "We left Crystanian to search the lands closed off from our western allies. Now we know what's happening here, and we can do something about it! I want to see the command front as Prince Rowin asks."

The Shekmann's emerald eyes turned dark in anger. "And what of you, Zyanthena? Jumping that much, using so much of Vauldin's powers—don't tell me that doesn't cost you. I won't see you so close to death again!"

The words made her turn on Lord Darshel, eyes blazing in their own anger at his tactlessness. "It is my choice to use majik when it is best suited. And it is my choice and judgment to know how much I can do. *Do not tell me* that I am incapable in this!"

"As if you judged so well the last time."

A growl escaped Zyanthena's lips as she prepared for another volley of words.

"Ah..." Princes Rowin and Jace shared a glance as they found themselves caught in a personal argument they knew nothing about. The former cleared his throat. "Ms. Zy'ena, Your Lordship?"

The reminder of their small audience had the Tashek and Shekmann cooling down. "Our apologies, Highnesses," Lord Darshel said while Zyanthena turned away to continue her pacing.

"Well, I know very little of the eight stones of magic," Prince Rowin said. "So I am no judge of their limits. Yet, I do know a few things about them. One is that only the stone made of Crystal can move objects great distances. It makes me wonder, then, how you used your stone to get here."

"She made use of those pillars we see set at strategic points across Syre. You know the ones? There's that ruby-encrusted pillar outside of your Sunrise Palace. We have a jade one near Azure Palace."

Prince Rowin frowned at the Havenese royal. "Those ancient things? There's no magic in those."

Prince Jace shrugged helplessly. "I don't know what to say about that, except that I've seen that woman 'magic' me through two pillars in less than a week."

Prince Rowin looked intrigued.

"That's another, long explanation," Zyanthena interrupted. "And we need to get everyone away from here. I'm willing to jump to Crystanian and then the Command Front." She glowered at Lord Darshel to indicate no more arguments were allowed. "To see what has become of Sunrise. We need to get going. The maunstorz may already have discovered their prisoners are no longer theirs."

Coming back into the cathedral, however, the four of them found that the Rubians had made their own decisions regarding what actions they were going to take. The entire lot of loyal subjects had gone to a knee before their royal heir and his young son. All were saying that the prince should leave with their rescuers and get far away from the Red City. The nobles would stay and search out their families and the populace. Not a single man would leave despite the threat that their capture would result in death.

Zyanthena strode to the fore. "If you stay, the maunstorz will kill you for getting loose." She looked aghast at their choice.

"Beautiful, courageous lady." The designated leader of their little group shuffled, still on his knees, to her feet and reached out for a hand. "We care for our families as much as Prince Derek. We believe that you will keep him safe. Yet leaving with His Highness does not give us comfort, not while our families remain to suffer. We all know that staying may mean we all die, but I would rather leave this world with my arms around my wife and daughters than in a place far away from them." The man's eyes turned to include Prince Derek Chível, "Please, respect us for our choice and get the prince free from here."

There was a long silence after the words. Zyanthena shifted, slowly reclaiming her hand from the official. Yet she didn't give them an answer, nor was it hers to give.

"Officer Kiroy." Prince Derek rose to his feet, with his lord protector's help, and addressed his subjects. "Know that I wish you would come with us for your safety, but I do understand why you stay. I pray that you and yours stay alive until I can return with an army to wipe out the maunstorz that have overrun our lands. I will take back the Red City for them."

"We know, Highness. We will stay strong and await you."

The Rubian prince blinked back the tears that threatened to fall; they would do little to help these brave men. Instead, he gave them a proper salute—most were soldiers. "I will not forget you. Stay with the Stars' grace."

"And go with their will, Highness." The men bowed down and touched their foreheads to the cold ground. Afterward, they rose and began to collect up the meager supplies Zyanthena and Lord Darshel could provide. Officer Kiroy turned, at the last, to the Tashek warrioress once more. "We will leave after you. I want to see Prince Derek safely away before we track up the area leaving this hill."

It was plain to see that Zyanthena did not agree with their plans, but she kept the words to herself. "With Vauldin's powers, I will have your prince far from here in only a matter of moments. I hope that is enough to console you."

"It's all that we could hope for, my lady."

She nodded. "Then let's begin." Zyanthena turned away from the Rubian men and motioned to Lord Darshel and Prince Rowin to join her in private conference once more. "Now that they stay, I say we try for the Command Front first."

Lord Darshel frowned. "That's not getting the prince of Rubia—or Sunrise, for that matter—to safety."

"I second your plan," Rowin countered.

"Of course, Prince Sunrise would," the lord-governor griped under his breath.

"Darshel." Zyanthena berated him in a whisper and nudged his elbow. Aloud, she said, "My suggestion is, the pillar near the Command

Front is a quarter mile away from the fort. I can hide everyone there and go to the fort under the cover of darkness, just as I did here? Quick and quiet."

The Shekmann couldn't disagree with that; Zyanthena had been successful on her recent scouting. Reluctantly, he nodded his agreement.

"I agree—except that I will go with you." Rowin lifted his hand to stop an argument. "I know the Command Front in and out as you do not. Bringing me along gives you the advantage." He waited with bated breath as the Tashek and lord-governor shared a look. Their agreement came shortly after. "Now, show me what this magic with the pillars is all about. I am excited to experience it myself."

§ §

In a flash with the brightness of lightning, the rescued princes of Rubia and Sunrise were carried away from the enemy that held way over the Red City. By the light of dawn, they were a hundred miles eastward and into the border of the kingdom of Sunrise.

Part IV

§

(Year 111 SC, Deepest Snows)

Chapter Forty-Four

§

Westharborne

They came upon West Port from the north, following the mild cliff line against the coast until it ran into the city outskirts. The tall-spired buildings came to them out of the fog like a dream. Young Rosemary gasped at the wondrous sight of the seagulls fluttering between the peaks and valleys of the seaport city. Between the fresh spray of salt water and the sweet tang of the beach grasses, there was much new and glorious to see. Despite the long ride from Dolland, the girl was reenergized enough to slide from Buttercup's back and run ahead to the sand. Anibus, well accustomed to the sights of the Estarian-run port, took up Buttercup's reins and eased after his charge.

"Priest Ani, look at the ocean! My, isn't it fantastic!" Rosemary was beaming, a grin spreading ear to ear. "And there are ships!"

"Yes, West Port is one of the major trading ports in Sealand. You can find almost anything from Syre in its markets."

"Like Sunarian silk or Havenese teas?"

"Of course." Anubis found himself chuckling at the girl's awe at such simple *exotics.* "And much more besides, but we'll have to save seeing the markets for another day. Our business is with the head abbess at Westharborne."

Rosemary's face turned melancholic, "But it's my first time seein' the ocean."

"Let's see how our day plays out," Anibus compromised gently.

"All right," Rosemary agreed dejectedly. She came back to Buttercup more subdued and was quick to mount. Anibus released the mare's head back to her then pointed the way into the city proper.

There was a pair of gatemen checking travelers into the north entrance; the Estarian priest knew them both. They gave a good-natured start at seeing the long-lost acolyte. "Dare mine eyes deceive me, or has the great cousin-priest of the crown finally returned to grace our fair city?"

"It is I, Terry." Anibus grinned and bent down to shake the older man's hand. "And I see you're as poor with your poetry as always. Cal," he greeted the other man.

"Oh, ho! A smart lad you think you are, Priest Anibus! Two minutes in our fair city and you're already making crass remarks about my work. I'll have you know, I've gotten twenty-and-eight more of my poetry books sold at market since you've been gone. Some find my work worth a reading."

"Twenty-and-eight? My, Terry, in the near six seasons I've been gone? You've finally accomplished selling them for the price of your wife's hat."

The guardsman tsked and threw up his hands. "And there you go again, tellin' me the low worth of my art. I ain't missed that about you! Nope, not in the least! I'll have you know, my darlin' Corline loves that hat as much as my poetry, and she tells me of it every night."

"That she may, but this devout priest didn't hear of such from you. Tell Corline I say hello."

"Will do, Priest."

"And, Cal, I'll be looking for you in a day or so. I've got some yellowwood pieces from Staria I'm sure you'll enjoy."

"Aye, that I would." Cal tipped his hat. "Yellowwood is something special. I'll keep the door open for ya."

"Thanks, Cal."

Uncertain of the men, Rosemary had hung back while Anibus did the talking. She finally came to realize they must have been joking when the gatemen let them through with only a little more fuss. Hurrying up to the priest's side, she turned once more in her saddle to study the two men. "Are all men from the city so dilly?"

"Dilly?" Anibus repeated the word. "No. Terry and Cal are long acquaintances. I can't really help a tease at Terry's expense, though. He's always up to one play or other to get money. His idea of poetry is his newest. It's more like spouting nonsense than lovely rows to 'stroke the mind.' Still, I have to applaud his audacity."

"Yes, but…" She was still frowning their way.

"But?"

Rosemary spun back around in her saddle. "Never mind."

The girl's behavior had Anibus chuckling. "Keep with me," he instructed as they moved deeper into West Port. "The streets will get a bit crowded the closer we get to Westharborne. It won't do for Buttercup to get upset and kick out at the populace." Rosemary nodded and firmly urged her cantankerous mare to keep close to Rain. Steering them as best he could, Anibus made sure to keep the unruly horse to the center of the streets as much as possible. They managed to make the convent without any serious mishaps, despite the midday bustle. Relieved, they entered the quiet inner walls of the Estarian grounds and made their way to the east entrance. A young stable hand was there to take their horses' heads as they halted at the side gates.

"Nevill, it's good to see you."

"Priest Anibus, sir!" The boy's smile was broad and cheery. "It's good to see you return from your trip."

"Yes. I'm happy to be back." Anibus squeezed the boy's shoulder in friendly greeting. "It was a long road and not without much adventures," he said, knowing that Nevill did like a good tale. The stable hand was certain to find him again to hear all about it. "Nevill, this is Rosemary. She'll be joining Westharborne as a new acolyte. Rosemary, Nevill Connors."

The boy's brown eyes were quick to swivel to their new arrival as she dismounted. "That's great! Welcome to Westharborne, Miss."

With the Myler girl's poor history around boys, Rosemary seemed to regard the overly gracious Nevill with a wary air. Still, it was hard to stay aloof when his big eyes continued to stare back so innocently. Finally, she relented. "Thank you… sir."

The simple words were enough. Nevill's grin widened and he hurried to accommodate his new friend. "I'll take your horse, Miss, and get your bags to your rooms. Priest Anibus, may I do the same?"

"Sure." Anibus gave Rain one last pat on her cheek and an apple before handing over her reins. "Rain will need some extra rations for a few days. She's been on the road with me for three seasons."

"Don't worry about a thing," Nevill promised.

Anibus trusted the boy to do just that and did not say anything more on the matter. Instead, he turned to motion Rosemary to his side and headed from the gates into the convent. They passed through the high, iron entrance and came into a small alleyway that was devoid of anything but cobblestones and brick walls. Anibus continued to lead his young charge deeper into the recess to old, plain door. He didn't bother knocking, just headed right inside. The door led them into a side hallway off of the main entrance. Here, there were benches made of beechwood and sconces with tall candles for reading. Farther down, the hallway opened up into the chapel house, while other side passages led to the kitchens, dining hall, and public scriptorium. The kitchen was their first destination.

As Anibus had expected, the four main sisters responsible for the convent's food and drink were there, huddled around hot cups of tea and a loaf of rye bread. The women squawked at his entrance. "Anibus! Boy, you've finally come home!" Sister Nadine was the first from her chair to embrace their missed acolyte. The other ladies—Cādene, Sari, and Giselle—were quick to follow suit and smother their lad.

Anibus greeted each in turn and accepted the rib-crushing hugs of his convent mothers. Afterward, he introduced the shy Myler girl to the quartet of sisters. "I would like to introduce you all to Rosemary Myler of Dolland." He stepped behind the girl so that she couldn't hide behind his travel cloak. "Rosemary, these are Westharborne's sisters: Nadine, Cādene, Sari, and Giselle."

Rosemary ducked her head and murmured a soft greeting.

"My, Ani, Dolland is halfway up the kingdom!" Sister Nadine berated. To Rosemary, she said, "You're so far from home, girl."

"Y-yes," Rosemary agreed. She looked up enough to see the sympathy in the woman's eyes. It gave her courage to show a timid smile.

"But what beautiful eyes you have," Giselle praised. "And such lovely hair!"

"And cute freckles to boot!" Sari agreed.

"Ladies." Nadine frowned. "Don't overwhelm the girl! Come, Miss Rosemary, sit while I pour some tea. Ani, fetch me some wood for our fire, if you please."

Anibus grinned at being bossed around so soon at his arrival. *Yes, I am definitely home!* He helped Rosemary to a chair and then headed out to the wood pile behind the kitchen building. Not to his surprise, Sister Cādene was on his tail.

"Out with it," she demanded. "It's not like you to bring a young girl so far south—on a trip for His Majesty and Our Eminence no less!"

Anibus continued collecting an armful of firewood while he talked. "No, but the girl's parents are good friends of mine. They feared for her safety, what with the tales of war coming into Sealand's borders since Levies and Storage Time."

"But to bring her all the way here—"

"Rosemary was very brave. She didn't complain once on the road."

Sister Cādene glowered at facts thrown at her. "Still, it wasn't a trip to slog such a young thing through. I know you don't like to travel common roads."

"No, I didn't," he agreed. His soft words took some of the fire from the sister's eyes. "But there was belief enough of her town coming to some sad end during this war. For her innocence, her parents begged me to bring her to safety. They will pay for her boarding and learning from the mare she rode in on. You'll find Rosemary to be a hard worker and able to pull her weight to pay besides."

Sister Cādene shook her head sadly. "Is it really so bad out there, Anibus?"

Anibus straightened and looked the convent mother straight in the eye. "There is war, yes, but not in all parts of Syre—not yet. Most of it is still concentrated against military powers. However, the snowstorms will upend the delicate balance. People will starve, and that will lead to other problems."

Cādene made a sign of help to the Stars. "A prayer, then, for the people of Syre."

"And our own action besides," Anibus reminded. "The Estarian brother- and sisterhoods will be needed for aid. It is for that that I must go to the Eminary as soon as I know Rosemary is settled." The sister nodded her understanding. "Rosemary wishes to learn to bake cakes, cookies, and the like. I told her you would lend a hand in that."

"Two," she promised with a soft smile, "as often as I can spare them."

"Thank you."

They returned to the kitchens to find Rosemary already warming to the other sisters. They were busy talking of gardening and of tending herbs and vegetables in the plot outside. It was a subject Rosemary knew well. Still, her face lightened considerably upon the priest's return. "Priest Ani, the convent mothers say I can garden here too, and bake all I want."

"I'm sure you will come to love your time here, then." He smiled back before setting down his armload of wood. "And there's more to do than that—but I'll save the suspense to our mothers."

"Are you headin' off somewhere?" Rosemary, well accustomed to reading him after weeks of riding with him on the roads, sensed the change in him.

Anibus knew he had been caught. "Yes. I have other business to attend. But"—he came over to tap the redhead on her cute nose—"not before I see you to the rectory mother and your room."

She stood up. "Then, we can go now." The sudden change in her stature seemed to surprise the sisters, who had yet to see the girl's resolute side. Rosemary's show of courage had Anibus smiling in pride.

"Then, come. I'll show you the way to the dorter." He put out a hand and helped his young charge stand. They headed away, and Anibus gave Rosemary a quick tour of the convent as they went.

The dorter was on the other side of Westharborne, with small windows on its side that looked out to the sea. The rectory mother's humble dormitory was the first of the rooms on the walk there. Young Nevill must have already come with Rosemary's bags, for the rectory mother was waiting on her bench in the cloister as they arrived. Abbess Catlene came off as stern and aloof. Though Anibus knew better, it would be for Rosemary to find out that looks could be deceiving.

"Anibus, boy, do you plan to tarry with that girl all afternoon?"

"Mother Catlene," he greeted. "Rosemary Myler is from Dolland, up north. She deserves some time to be introduced to our enormous convent in small pieces."

Abbess Catlene harrumphed at the priest's smooth-talking way of warning his rectory mother to go easy on the newcomer. "I'll be handling her arrival as I do all the others, Anibus."

"Just so, we've had a long journey in wet and cold weather."

"So I've heard." Hazel eyes turned to study the Myler girl. Their direct stare had Rosemary huddling in on herself. "Then you'll be needing a hot bath and new clothes," she said. "Though you'll have to help with the bath water." It was one of the abbess's tests: lazy or industrious?

"That's no problem, ma'am," Rosemary murmured quietly. She was used to hard chores.

The answer seemed to soothe something in the rectory mother. "Very well. Come with me, Rosemary, and I will show you to your room and then our bathhouse." She turned to Anibus to wiggle her finger at him as he started to follow. "Here is where you depart, boy. Our Eminence has heard of your arrival. He awaits you in his study."

Anibus was hesitant to leave Rosemary, but he knew better than to ignore his teacher's summons. He finally nodded and bid his young charge, "I'll see you later, promise." Unbidden, Rosemary turned to hug his waist tightly one last time. She seemed to be as hesitant to part from him as Anibus was from her.

"And the girl's pay?" Abbess Catlene asked, at the last.

"I've already spoken to Mother Cādene."

The rectory mother nodded. "Then be on your way, Anibus." She turned and waved Rosemary to follow deeper into the dorter. There was no time for the redhead to look back in longing.

Bereft of any more responsibility, Anibus turned away to his other tasks. The first was to change out of his travel clothes; the second was to seek out the Eminary.

There was a small handful of men and young boys at the convent though, mostly, Westharborne was run by women. The men's dorter was back the other way, close to the stables and head chapel house. Only six priests and three boys resided at the Estarian convent. Priest Anibus had his own dormitory set to the west of His Eminence's—to be close for the leader's needs. The humble apartment boasted its own separate sleeping room from its study and lavatory, and it smelled and looked as if it had been neglected in its owner's absence. Anibus made a face at the mustiness of his room. "Home sweet home."

There was a note from Nevill on his desk, apologizing for not freshening up the room and that it would be gotten to shortly. In the meantime, new Estarian robes of office and undergarments had been set on a cleaned corner of the bed. Anibus took them with him to the washroom and tried to make himself presentable as much as possible without a full bath. In the end, the image in the looking glass didn't seem too bad: angled face, clean-shaven; long, brown hair combed and pulled into a mid-length ponytail; deep-blue eyes clear and fairly well rested and seeming bluer with the fresh indigo robes. All in all, Anibus almost looked back to his normal self after seasons on the roads of Syre.

It was—almost—a shame to be back in boring, quiet Westharborne. Anibus had to laugh at his melancholy. "Stars, I've been amongst my cousins and fellow Syreans too long if I'm pining for action already!" The Eminary was certain to notice his acolyte's restlessness and chastise him. Sighing, Anibus collected his impresa and slipped it about his neck; then, he headed away to this master's study.

The aging Estarian Eminary was reading from a predecessor's journal when Anibus arrived. A man of willowy build and poor eyesight, His Eminence seemed more like a bookish monk than the esteemed leader of the Estarian faith. Yet, his young acolyte knew better. Paulrē ("just call me Paul") Esquire had been an active participant in the fight against the maunstorz in years past. Just as he allowed Anibus now, the Eminary had travelled across Syre as a younger man, helping support the kingdoms and their populace with needs of faith and healing. Less known, Paulrē had powers of foresight in the form of visions and dreams. He was not a man to dismiss the powers of the supernatural but called them "gifts granted by the Stars themselves." In the last battle of Crystalynian, he had seen a vision of the great kingdom's destruction, as well as the victory against the maunstorz—even if it had not lasted. Paulrē insisted that Anibus Farryl was "destined" to be his successor and was grooming him for the part. Now, with the maunstorz threat again on the rise, Paulrē Esquire believed in the need for a strong successor to his seat.

"Eminence," Anibus greeted.

Paulrē looked up and proceeded to close the journal before motioning his acolyte closer. "Anibus, you finally returned to us."

"Yes. My road led me farther than I had expected."

"I've heard there was much afoot to keep you away." Paulrē stood and waved his student to follow him to the small portico in the back of the chapel house, overlooking the ocean. A small, round stone table and two log seats were in the quiet nook, and a teapot and cups set at ready. The Eminary and his student sat, and Anibus proceeded to fill their cups with winter tea. "Tell me all of what transpired on your journey."

Anibus nodded. "There is much to tell."

"We have the time."

Time there was, but still, it took four hours to speak of his trip from Westharborne to Fortress Opal then through the Golden Kingdom to the Deluge Marketplace in Sunrise. There, Anibus had met up with acquaintances of his, the soldier Rio Ravesbend, protector to Prince Rowin Sunrise, and the two friends, Jacen Novano and Patrick Kins. The three soldiers had been partaking of the summer competitions at Deluge, yet the challenge of protecting a priest of Estaria and getting him safely to the Crystine of the Crystal Castle had been too good to pass up. With the aid of a merchant—who was later revealed to be the heir of Sealand himself—they had crossed into the war-torn Crystal Kingdom.

From there, Anibus had delivered his message from the Eminary and King William Fantill to Commander Matar of the Crystine. His speech had set into action the Crystine's movements westward to aid Sealand against the maunstorz of His Eminence's vision. Events had quickly transpired to change Crystine's (and Anibus's group) focus to the Citadel of Light in Staria instead, where Anibus had assisted in burying the dead soldiers from the fighting's aftermath, as well as, sitting in attendance in the first War Council the North had seen since the fall of Crystalynian nearly twenty-five years before. The time afterward had included the priest's attendance at the Kavannen banquet before he and the others were ordered to disperse from the Citadel after enemies attacked the capital.

Afterward, Anibus had headed for home. He hadn't taken the route home with his cousins (Prince Par Fantill and Lord Gordar Farrylin, instead taking roads back. Because of that, he had learned of more of the devastation brought about by the maunstorz attacks and the out-of-season snowstorms. Of this, he could say that northern Sealand was hurting for supplies and protection.

Paulrē looked grim as Anibus spoke of the last. "Yes, I have received reports from the far reaches of Sealand and beyond. This abnormal weather bodes ill for the people of Syre—and it's not just the cold to worry over."

"Raids and pillaging haven't happened yet," Anibus agreed. "But that only takes time for desperate souls to find ways to carry on. Desperation makes people do stupid and cruel things."

"I know that only too well," the Eminary agreed, a wan smile barely forming on his weathered face. "Times like these will need our presence and faith all the more."

"I am ready to go wherever you need send me."

"I know." Paulrē's smile warmed in affection. "But not now. At least, not yet." He stood and motioned Anibus to follow. "For you, my closest and greatest acolyte, I have a different task. You are finally ready to be initiated into the final, innermost circle of the Estarian priesthood. With this ascension, you will know the principal reason out faith was born and our deepest secret that only sitting Eminaries know."

Anibus felt his face form into a frown. The Estarian religion had always been about believing and trusting in the powers of the Eight Stars of the Heavens that had created and presided over Syre. For the Eminary to say that such wasn't the faith's principal function seemed peculiar and incongruous with his understanding. "Eminence?"

Paulrē Esquire seemed to understand his confusion. "I have stood where you are now, my acolyte, and have had the same predilutions as you. Your apprehensions are sound but, I promise, unnecessary. I know the young man you are. You are exactly the predecessor I have waited for. All you need is to have faith."

His Eminence had never given Anibus any room for doubts, so—even in this—the priest chose to believe. "Very well. I will follow you into the very heart of our faith and prove I am qualified of your trust in me."

"Of course, you will." Paulrē gave his acolyte a slap on the back to ease the sudden tension his words had caused. Casually, he waved Anibus to follow and continued back into the chapel house. There, he lit one of the candlesticks at the main altar and lifted it. Then, he crouched at the old Estarian symbol on the floor. "Certainly, you have noticed these lines do not match up," Paulrē asked.

"I have." Anibus had thought it strange that the founders had mismatched the symbols of the Eight Stars to their corresponding positions and Syrean scripts.

His master grinned. "That is for you and I to line up." He motioned the priest to the other side of the circle of the Stars and showed his student how to shift the ancient seal about until the pieces locked and air popped out of the released triggers. A moment later, the floor shifted and shuddered to reveal a staircase leading into the ground. Anibus gaped. "Hurry inside. It closes itself within a breath-count to sixty."

Anibus hurried with the Eminary into the old stone stairwell and helped the aging leader down the steep, narrow steps. They wound down and down some more into a seemingly endless spiral until they were well into the cliff side. The way finally ended and gave way to a natural cavern. The darkness began to slowly fade into an eerie shade of purple.

"Eminence—?"

"Wait and observe," Paulrē said and continued ahead until their way opened into a cavern so large, the floor fell away to nothingness. A single stalagmite, the width of a small tree trunk and height of a young boy, was before the drop. Upon it was the reason for the purple glow: a single amethyst stone in the shape of a prism was pulsating an unnatural light, as if created from living flame—or the beating of a heart.

"What is this?" Anibus asked in a whisper, leaning closer but not touching the abnormality.

"This is the embodiment of the Stars' powers here on this world," the Eminary explained rather cryptically.

Anibus felt his eyebrows rise in disbelief. "This… stone is a manifestation of celestial powers?"

"I understand your skepticism, as I had mine so long ago. However, I know this to be true. My powers of foresight and the visions I receive are from this amethyst."

Anibus stared back at the purple stone and tried to see the might in the little rock that could fit in his palm.

"This stone is only known to me—and now you," his teacher continued. "More importantly, my acolyte, I believe this is the reason why the maunstorz have come to Syre."

Chapter Forty-Five
§
By the Cover of Night

The jump to Kest'orín was over in a second. The obelisk at Sunrise's border spit its travelers out about its base in a blaze of red and then went cold. In the first light of dawn, the group stayed groaning, some vomiting, on the snow around its great base.

"Zyen?" Lord Darshel recovered himself better than he had on his first jump. He rolled to his knees and crawled to the Tashek's side. The wielder of Vauldin was coughing up light spots of blood. "Zyen!"

"I'm all right, Darshel," she assured him as she wiped blood from her lips.

"Like shit you are!" He grasped the stubborn woman's shoulders and turned her to face him. Zyanthena looked thin and unnaturally pale. "The magic needed to make the jumps is taking too much out of you. The next one could kill you."

"Enough." Zyanthena glowered. "Check everyone else. We need to be alert and finding cover before the maunstorz search out the unnatural light from Kest'orín."

Lord Darshel glared back with eyes that promised the discussion was not over, but he did relent and turn away to check their party. Luckily, no one had passed out this time—even their new additions seemed relatively unfazed. As the party came to their senses, Zyanthena and the wolves spread out at their perimeter and kept alert eyes on the horizon.

"I know a place just to our south where we can hide ourselves," Prince Rowin said as they all convened to discuss options. "It's a natural furrow in the ground. With the snows, it should be well sheltered right now."

"I like the idea of that," Prince Jace Éldon murmured. His emerald eyes were roaming the open land fervently, not liking how exposed they were in lands controlled by maunstorz. Everyone else had the same concern.

"I think we're in agreement," Yory Selèv replied as he studied Prince Derek Chível. "Prince Derek needs rest after what we just did."

"Then we go now," Zyanthena agreed, joining their group. "Hunter says there is no one about. Neither the wolves nor the horses see any dangers over the mile they can see." A few quizzical looks were cast the Tashek's way, but she ignored them. It wasn't the time or place to explain her ability to speak with animals. "Prince Derek and Miguel may use Tano," she elected without asking Darshel's permission, "and Prince Connel may ride Unrevealed. The rest of us are well enough to walk."

They all agreed and headed from Kest'orín, following Prince Rowin and Rio Ravesbend as they led in the general direction of the landmark they sought. Zyanthena sent Far Tracker and Too Soon ahead, trusting in the wolves to find the location fastest, and indeed, they howled their discovery of it long before the group reached the site.

The natural furrow was large enough to shelter all ten humans plus the two horses, and left all but three wolves to the winds and snow—not that the grey wolves minded, with temperatures milder than those of their northern kingdom. The majority of the wolf pack stayed outside, however, to keep watch on the landscape. Only Moon Ember and Tiny remained to snuggle up against the sickly heir of Rubia and his son.

"This is better than I imagined," Lord Shekmann commented as he set his packs down and began to unload some supplies from Tano's packs.

Prince Rowin nodded. "I've used this before once, when I was caught in a rainstorm. I figured snow wasn't much different."

"It's still a bit cold, seeing as it's Deepest Snows," Prince Jace griped and huddled against the two chargers for warmth.

"While it's daytime, we can make do with a small fire."

"Actually." Zyanthena turned their attention her way. "I can use majik to illusion the signs of the fire away, but only if it stays small. Is should continue to shield this place even as night falls."

"Fancy toy, that."

The desert woman's eyes narrowed at the Havenese royal's remark. "It's not an easy trifle for me to do—Vauldin doesn't use the power of illusion. But to keep us from freezing to death, I will try. It'd be nice if you appreciated the effort." She gave the arrogant man a cold glance and then, she turned to a more receptive royal. "Prince Rowin, may I have you show me where we are in relation to the Command Front?"

"Of course," Rowin agreed and accompanied the Tashek back out onto the open plain of snow. Lord Shekmann followed them. "The Command Front lies to our east, about two clicks."

"A little over a mile," Zyanthena confirmed to herself.

"Yes."

"It looks to be easier going here in Sunrise," Lord Darshel added his own assessment. The snow was about six inches deep.

"It's better than I had hoped. The walk won't be too tiring." Yet Zyanthena already looked fatigued.

"You could ride to the camp?" he suggested.

Prince Rowin shook his head. "That would lack surprise. As you see, northern Sunrise is open and flat. The enemy would see us coming."

"I wouldn't ride it, either," Zyanthena agreed. "But we will have the pack with us. They'll be better eyes and ears than any of us."

"Then, I say you rest now until sunset." Lord Darshel took charge. "Both of you will have a long night. Let the rest of us keep watch."

The prince and the Tashek shared a look and nod. "That sounds wise," Prince Rowin agreed and turned to head back into their natural shelter.

"Zy'ena," the lord-governor stalled her. "A moment?"

A sigh of resignation escaped the desert woman's lips. "What is it?"

"You need to stop using magic so often. You know it's wearing you down."

"Of that, I know better than you." Her hackles were up. "Was that all, Darshel?"

The Shekmann stared at Zyanthena; his eyes were filled with unsaid words. Reluctantly, he said, "Yes, that is all."

Zyanthena bobbed her head. "Then, I will go find sleep and leave you and Lieutenant Dawson to the watch. Wake me when the sun has moved toward dusk."

"Of course." *Zyanthena.* Lord Darshel kept the name from his lips. With the growth of their party, their time to be candid with each other seemed over. For just a moment, the Shekmann lord wished for the solitude of Crystanian once more.

§ §

Prince Rowin and Zyanthena Sheev'arid were woken just as the sun made its descent to nightfall. Small packs of food and supplies had been bundled for them while they slept. The two rose, ready for the task that awaited. They ignored the concerned glances of their friends as they prepared to leave. Neither allowed any persuasion to abort the mission or to take any more men along in support. With only a final word of parting for their party to be ready to move at a moment's notice, the heir of Sunrise and the desert warrioress began their trek to the Command Front.

Prince Rowin waited until they were well away from the others to speak with Zyanthena. "Thank you for electing to do this, Sheev'arid."

The Tashek bobbed her head. "Of course, Highness. To safeguard Syre from the maunstorz, I would do anything to foil their plans."

"Still." Rowin gave a lopsided grin in fondness for her tenacity. "You've done much for me and my people. Rescuing us, healing Rio, bringing us here..." He shook his head. "I cannot imagine the price you pay to do such things."

Zyanthena's hand had gone unconsciously to the obsidian stone about her neck. "It is a price all stone bearers will wrestle with, Highness. However, I would pay it gladly any time I am able."

"To that end"—he motioned for them to stop and face each other—"Zyanthena, do say *no* if you are at your limits." He raised a hand to silence any objections. "You are unbelievably talented with your stone, but I know you to be just as capable as a fighter without it. Pardon my bluntness, Tashek, but I overheard you and Lord Shekmann talking. He fears you are overdoing it. If that is the case, then I concur that you need to not rely on the Stone of Power quite so much. If the word of a lord-governor is not enough, I hope you will believe the word of a prince."

Zyanthena seemed sullen to hear the order. For some time, she did not reply. The quiet of the night filled her silence—but only until Moon Ember slipped closer and bumped the Tashek's hand with her nose. The wolf's touch seemed to soften her attitude. "Very well, Prince of Sunrise. I will heed the words of warning from my comrades."

"That's all we ask." Rowin motioned them forward again and they continued toward the Sunarian fort. "As for your wolves," he asked out of curiosity, "can you really understand them?"

"Yes." Zyanthena looked to the giant she-wolf still by her side and set a hand on Moon Ember's ruff. "Vauldin gives me the power of animal speech. I can hear and understand them as easily as we can talk."

"That's incredible! To have such a gift…" Rowin shook his head ruefully.

"The ruby of Sunrise gives the power of telepathy not unlike the power of animal speak—though I guess you already know about that."

The words seemed to shock the royal. "How—?"

"A memory," Zyanthena replied. She pressed her fingers to her forehead, as if the prior memories caused a headache. "I…met you when I was young." The Sunarian prince looked doubtful. "You were visiting the Crystal Princess's Berneisse and touched her. You had a conversation about her needing to not fear your powers of mind-speak and that you wished her a happy coming-of-age. Not long after, we argued about breeding your lovely mare, Blue Galleon, to my black stallion."

Prince Rowin was staring, dumbfounded, at her. "You're the lost princess of Crystal?!"

The Tashek refused to stop moving, continuing toward their destination. Despite her earthshaking news, she waved for the royal to keep up with her. She stayed nonchalant. "Princess Zerra was the baby Arrez Xraxrain, raised in secret as another kingdom's daughter." She huffed at the irony. "My guardians kept me hidden in plain sight and under a similar title."

"But you're a Tashek of Staria!"

"I am both of those things and more, Highness. My road to who I am today has been long and not without many twists in my destiny."

The prince was still in shock, and it took several minutes of their crunching through the snow for him to work it all out. "So," he said at last, "doesn't that make you higher ranked than me? I mean… aren't you the heir—or *queen*—of Crystalynian?"

Zyanthena chuckled. "When you say it like that, it sounds so incredible."

"So, I'm right?"

Brandy eyes turned to regard the prince before returning to watch her footing. "A queen of a dead kingdom means very little. And besides that, I haven't decided if I will take up my birthright."

"But you use the stone Vauldin?"

"Yes. And with it comes quite the dilemma."

The choice of words seemed to convince the royal of her plight. "Yes, that it does. It is a choice all who are destined for greatness must make."

Zyanthena's mouth quirked. "Spoken as a true son of Sunrise's throne."

Prince Rowin tsked. "And now you make fun of me."

"Only to a point." Yet she was quick to sober as Moon Ember warned of their proximity to the Command Front. "We need to be quiet now, Highness. We are close."

Their conversation ended, and they concentrated on sneaking up to the walls of the fort. The wolves had already scoured the area and reported where the maunstorz sentries guarded the entrances. From the pack's description, much was being run as it had before. More to their surprise—or alarm—was that Sunarian infantry were watching the gates alongside the enemy.

"So, my uncle did sell out to those *monsters*," Rowin growled, barely audible. His face was set in a deep, angry frown. "Sunrise is completely compromised."

Zyanthena motioned for the royal to keep his head. "Perhaps not all are on board?"

"I know they aren't," he whispered back. "Commander Loris and his men would never agree to it." His midnight-blue eyes cast about the walls to the south. "Come. There's a back tunnel entrance only those of the crown know about."

Prince Rowin led them southward, keeping to the shadows of the fort walls. They crept past the watchers easily by relying on the wolves' keen senses to alert them of anyone near. Their destination ended up being beyond the keep's refuse pile—which was, thankfully, frozen and lacking its normal stink. In the ground just beyond, the prince paused and searched about on his knees until he found a hidden pulley line under the snows and dead grasses. It took some effort, but he and Zyanthena got the small tunnel entrance open. "This goes to the back alley of the main officer house."

Zyanthena seemed pleased with the ploy. "This is one thing I approve of Sunarians—you like to keep all your options open."

"I'll pretend I didn't hear your remark," Rowin replied, "because that's one thing I don't like about Starians. You look down on the men of the South."

They shared a tense glance. "On that, I concede, Highness, and apologize."

"Apologize better by getting my men out of here."

Zyanthena agreed and motioned for Moon Ember, Tiny, and Autumn to climb into the tunnel first; the other wolves would stay without to keep the area clear. Though the three wolves disliked the small space, they were not about to let their master go into the Command Front alone. Therefore, the smallest of the pack had elected to go. It was Moon Ember that insisted the wolves lead the crawl through the passage.

Climbing through an old, earthen tunnel in the dead of Deepest Snows was not the most enjoyable experience, but the trip went without event. Their party of five reached the officer house in good time and crept out onto the empty back alley. From there, they trusted the Sunarian prince to lead the way through the fort. Prince Rowin angled them toward the large jail house and soldiers' barracks. They kept to the shadows to avoid detection and came to the back of the clay-and-straw structure in good time. The royal motioned for Zyanthena and the wolves to wait as he chanced a glance into a barred window in the back.

Imprisoned in a sparse room were a good number of men, huddled in bundles to keep warm. One soldier shifted near the window, and the prince recognized the man's face. "Officer Colton! Officer Colton!" Rowin called out quietly. The man was known as a light sleeper, so it was no surprise that he came awake easily and glanced about. "Officer Colton, window."

The Sunarian soldier rolled to his feet and came near. His tired eyes blinked in disbelief at seeing his prince. "Prince Rowin?!"

"It's me. I've come to see what's gone on here. How does everyone fare?"

"Highness, it is dangerous for ye to be here. The enemy, sir. They're here."

"I know," Rowin assured. "I snuck in out of concern for you all." By then, more men had roused at the voices. They too looked elated to see their heir but also voiced concerns for his safety. "I've come to get you away from the maunstorz. How many are here, and who is still not with them?"

"Everyone you see here refuses to work with Thane Cornell and the enemy leader Chaenyeu. We've lost good men, those who've stood before their command."

The news constricted his chest. "And Commander Ravesbend?"

"He's being kept in the prisons below the command post, though it's been some time since we've seen him, Highness."

"He was taken well before the snows came," another clarified.

That was very poor news. Rowin feared for his lord protector's father. "Let's get you out of this disgrace of a fort and to safety."

"Not until you rescue the Commander, Highness. We will not leave him."

The words were valiant and everything Prince Rowin expected of Loris's men. "There'll be time for that. Right now—"

"Highness," Zyanthena had listened long enough. She could see an argument costing them precious time. "We will go to Loris Ravesbend. Keeping these men here will rouse less suspicion." She wasn't entirely happy to leave men who could, potentially, alert the fort to their presence, but Zyanthena had to trust them to stay loyal to the heir of Sunrise. To the men, she said, "Stay down and quiet. Wake everyone with as little movements as possible. We will be back with your commander."

The Sunarians were shocked to see a woman accompanying their prince, but the Tashek's words were so sure that they brokered no doubts. "We will do so. Please, just get the commander out."

Zyanthena pulled Rowin away with a promise to return. She asked Tiny and Ember to remain at the barracks and used Autumn as an alert as they headed away to where Commander Ravesbend was being held.

"The prisons are in the backmost rooms of the command post. There'll be a lot of enemies between the entrance and his cell."

"Are there any windows or vents?"

"Yes, but they're barred against escape."

"Lead me," Zyanthena commanded. She was already thinking of an alternative way in that didn't involve calling attention to themselves or taking crazy risks.

The vents to the cells were at ground level, looking like storm drains on the side of the building. The half-circle holes were barely large enough for a grown man to wiggle through. Zyanthena got on her belly and pulled herself into the bars as well as she could to look down into the cells. The third one, to her right, looked to have a single occupant, though it was hard to tell in the near darkness. She rose and walked on hands and knees to that cell's vent. Indeed, there was someone there. "Is that him?"

Prince Rowin got down beside her. "Yes. The drop down is over fifteen feet, though."

"No problem." Zyanthena rolled to her feet and went to Autumn. She instructed the wolf to find rope while she worked on removing the bars. "Keep watch, Highness. I won't be aware of the fort while I'm working."

"I thought you agreed to not use so much magic?"

The returned look was flat. "You want to break your way in through the front?"

"Not really."

"Then, watch my back." The warrioress turned away to her task, expecting the prince to cooperate. As before, she called on the powers to remake what was broken, knowing it would require less of a price than borrowing other powers again. Imagining the iron bars between her hands as they were before their making, Zyanthena willed them back to being heated liquid and then reshaped into iron disks once more. Though the process brough pain and injury—as the heat of a forge had to be a part of the process—the wielder of Vauldin managed to remake the twelve bars into disks. Finished, she set the iron aside and packed her palms with snow to calm the burning of her skin.

"You hurt yourself!" Rowin reached out to inspect the Tashek's hands. They looked raw and blistered.

"Relax, Highness. This is temporary." Zyanthena proved so by using majik again to heal her flesh, which remolded in a breath. Still, the effort had the warrioress swooning.

Rowin steadied her and helped Zyanthena to a seat against the wall. "You really do like overdoing it."

"It's all worth it in the end." She flashed a grin. "Besides, now it's your turn to break a sweat." Zyanthena tipped her head to indicate Autumn was back with rope. "Go, rescue your protector's sire."

Rowin collected the rope and found an anchor to tie it to. Leaving Zyanthena to rest and stand lookout, he squirmed his way into the vent and rappelled down into the dank cell below. The royal dropped to the wet straw and turned to the man most loyal to the Sunarian crown. "Commander Ravesbend, sir? Loris?"

Fevered eyes fluttered open and took some time to center on the prince. The great commander of Sunrise's armies looked beat to shit, starved, and left to rot. A man known to be meticulous and proper, he now resembled a vagrant in his unkempt uniform, ragged beard, and matted hair.

"Just what did they do to you?" Rowin murmured sorrowfully.

"M-my p-p-prince…"

Rowin lifted a hand to cup the commander's head tenderly. "Yes, it's me, Loris. I've come to get you out of here."

A wan smile answered him. "I never doubted you'd come."

Rowin's chest constricted at the man's faith in him. "I just wish I had come sooner."

"Not likely, Highness," Loris cracked a joke. "You princely types always have your own schedules to keep."

"I see keeping you locked up hasn't dulled your humor," Rowin tsked back. "Now, come on. Let's get you up and out of here."

It took some time to get them both back out of the cell, especially with Loris's poor condition, but in the end, the commander was breathing fresh air again after nearly four seasons of imprisonment. Things were looking up.

Supporting the wasted commander, Rowin trusted Zyanthena and Autumn's lead back to the barracks, where the soldiers were all awake. Upon seeing their commander rescued, favor toward the Tashek woman and her honest word seemed to create a trust in them that, indeed, they had a fighting chance of getting out.

Releasing the barrack locks was an easy enough task, or so Zyanthena proved with skills of lockpicking the irons in less than a minute. Yet, they needed a plan and escape route. A number of the men were wounded or swooning from lack of proper nutrition. The Tashek very much doubted they'd get far on foot. "The horse stables?"

"Western side. There's a gate there, but it will be guarded."

Zyanthena's grin was one of pure daring. "Closest to our return anyway. Leave the guards to me."

"But horses won't be quiet," Rowin argued.

"Prince of Sunrise, just who do you take me for?" Zyanthena dared to ask. "You get these men across this fort and to that gate without discovery. Leave the horses to me." In a breath, she slipped into the shadows with the wolves, leaving all the men to sneak out of the barracks and make the rendezvous she requested.

Prince Rowin turned to the men they had just released. "You heard the lady. Let's get out of here!"

§ §

Getting around the Command Front and setting up their escape was fairly east for the Tashek woman used to sneaking around. Using her skills, the wolves' senses, and majik, she easily subdued the guards in the way of the prince's group. The gate guards never had a chance. Leaving the wolves at that location, Zyanthena crept into the long horse stable and began the task of speaking with its occupants. By the time she finished, the soldiers under Loris Ravesbend's command had arrived to find the mounts already tacked up and waiting obediently.

"Everyone mount," Zyanthena ordered. "And do not touch your horse's reins." The men were shocked to be ordered thusly but complied. "Keep silent," she reminded them one last time and signaled the first horse to lead. One after another, the mounts exited their pens and fell into a line behind their neighbor. In an eerie silence, the horses filed out of the Command Front's west gate and continued away as Zyanthena had instructed.

At the last, Zyanthena closed and majik-locked the gates behind them and fell into the single-track line the horses had created. Her wolf pack formed around her, and they all jogged along until over half a mile was between them and the fort. Zyanthena turned at that point and concentrated Vauldin's majik on the line of tracks. In ancient Syrean, she erased the signs of their passage all the way back to the west gate.

Then, having to lean on Hunter for support, Zyanthena and the wolves continued to follow the horses' single-track line to where the others still waited. She was greeted by an angry Shekmann lord, his arms crossed over his chest. "Wearing yourself out again, I see."

"And rescuing thirty-four soldiers on top of it."

"Yes." Darshel's eyes slid to the horses. "I think you've fair spooked some of them, getting horses to act so perfect and quiet and head here unerringly."

"It worked out in the end. Besides, now we don't have to track on foot while our enemy are down their cavalry."

"It will be a help," Lord Darshel agreed reluctantly. "But we will soon need supplies."

"To that end, Prince Sunrise says there is a town west of here that he will ask for food, and the wolves can hunt down game. For now, we need to put distance between ourselves and the Command Front."

"Everyone will get ready to go, then. We'll make up as many miles as possible before dawn."

Zyanthena nodded. "Inform everyone we're to leave in ten."

The Shekmann gave the desert woman a look. "And what do you have planned?"

She made a face at being found out. "I am going to send a written message through Kest'orín to the pillar Osh'ēēn. As we can no longer use that method of travel, I thought that, at least, we could get a message to allies west of here."

Lord Darshel frowned. "Zy'ena—"

"It'll be the last use of majik, I promise."

He sighed. "I'll trust you on that. Besides, having someone know of our plight would be nice. But will it work?"

"Of that, I do not know, but I *believe* it will. If Commander Matar is with Prince Par, then I have no doubts he'll find a way to get military support sent our way."

The Kavahadian studied Zyanthena for some time. Finally, he said, "Then I will trust in your commander as well. Just don't use too much magic and make sure you eat afterward."

Zyanthena nodded. "Thank you, My Lordship... *ahnamen*, Darshel." His Lordship turned away to help get their ever-growing party under way, leaving Zyanthena to her last task. The Tashek turned away to gather leather and charcoal to write the *Khataum* a note. As the others started off, heading south and west toward Sunrise's border with Golden—and allies they still trusted—Zyanthena pointed Unrevealed northwest to Kest'orín.

She arrived in ten breath-counts and slid from her black's back before the obelisk. Steadying her breath, Zyanthena focused on awakening Kest'orín without accessing its powers to jump her away. Uncertain if the half measure would work, the Tashek relied on the ancient Syrean dialect to direct Vauldin and the obelisk to heed her wishes. Then, being careful not to touch Kest'orín, Zyanthena threw the leather piece at the ruby obelisk and watched it disappear as it hit its side.

"Well, that looked like it worked."

The warrioress turned to find Lord Darshel and Lieutenant Dawson standing behind her. They had followed out of worry. "Yes. I dare say it did. Still." She looked at Kest'orín one last time. "We should ride as hard as the horses can handle. It's a long way to Golden and we cannot trust Sunrise to be safe."

Lord Darshel strode forward and placed a hand on her shoulder. "It's not the first time we've had to move at cavalry pace with maunstorz on our tail. We also have two Sunarian princes on our side—plus you and Vauldin, of course. I think we're more prepared this time around."

"The Stars can only hope."

The Shekmann laughed. "Now that's the Tashek I know! Come on, the others are getting ahead."

Chapter Forty-Six
§
Message

It had been four and a half days since Prince Par Fantill had spoken to Zyanthena Sheev'arid through a dream. Though his father didn't approve, the prince and Commander Matar believed the desert woman when she mentioned trying to use Osh'ēēn, the mother of pearl–decorated silver obelisk in the abandoned courtyard in the southern gardens of the fortress grounds. Somehow, Prince Par sensed the words hadn't just been gibberish spoken by a figment of his imagination, and the Crystine man concurred.

Resolved to see what the woman had in mind, the heir of Sealand, his lord protector, and Commander Matar had camped out by the pillar and waited. However, after the hours and days passed with nothing happening, King William was becoming more adamant that they all return to pressing business of the capital and court. That day, he visited the three men in a state of annoyance. "It's pointless being here, Par."

"One week, Father. That's all I ask," the prince pleaded.

"And then, no more nonsense."

"Of course," Par promised and watched his sire walk away, busy with affairs of the state. "She will come, right?" he asked once his father was out of earshot.

"Relax, Highness," Commander Matar replied over a book he was reading. "I've never known Zy'ena to go back on her word. She said to 'be at Osh'ēēn,' and so I believe her."

"It's not like you mind," Lord Gordar picked up. "You hated all the work you've been doing. Loafing around here is quite to your liking."

"Not the loafing part. If I could just *feel* like I'm doing something, it wouldn't be so bad."

"You are doing something," Matar said again, his eyes on a page. "Sometimes, there's a lot simmering underneath when it appears as if nothing outwardly is happening."

"That was cryptic." Par rose to snag an apple from a basket of fruit they had brought along for snacking.

"I have lived among the Tashek a large portion of my life. You come to find their wisdom can be very profound—if you get through the puzzles they speak."

The prince bit into the apple and took to walking a lazy circuit about the yard. The garden Osh'ēēn was placed in was in full neglect, so it lacked any good plant viewing. Still, it was a lovely day, sunny and warm. The view of the ocean made it peaceful, and the coming sunset would be well worth the wait. "I still find the words Zyanthena spoke to me humming around in my head. Is that normal, Commander?"

Matar glanced up from his reading, took a good look at the royal, and then sighed and sat up. "I see you will not let an old man be," he reprimanded and set the book aside. "Come, sit." Par complied, feeling chastised for his disturbance. "Your… memories of that night are a unique feature of being Serein's wielder. She is the master-stone of memory, and so everything will be clear and concise as long as it is majik-al written."

"I've… found that to be the case."

Matar studied the prince, finding the words to carry a hidden message. His eyes narrowed as he pinned the young man in his midnight-blue gaze. "Tell me, prince, have you used Serein to access memories? Last you tried, it did not work."

"I…" Par picked at a seam, feeling like a schoolboy trapped in a lie. The Crystine man always had a way of nailing him in place.

"Tell me, my prince," Lord Gordar urged, coming to sit with his cousin.

"Tell me what?" Matar looked between them. The prince was still reluctant.

"Serein has been activating of her own accord this past season," Lord Gordar provided. He, at least, was concerned.

Forced to speak, Par added, "She's flooded me with power on two separate occasions. The first, I woke in my room. The second, Serein pulled memories from a vine worker I was interrogating."

"And neither time was of your volition," Matar concluded.

"No."

The commander sighed. "I'm not too surprised. The sapphire has been known to respond to wielders' emotional reactions. Still"—there was that disapproving look again—"you should have mentioned it to your father or myself sooner."

"I know. The power… being out of control… I can see it causing problems. Zyanthena said Serein is acting like a shield around me."

"And with your reluctance, she will protect you against any foe—no matter the provocation. Prince, Serein will kill for you if you do not direct her."

The words shocked Prince Par. "But I don't want that!"

"It's not about what you want. Serein will do what is necessary." Commander Matar looked dead serious. "I suggest, since we've the time, we take what's left of this afternoon and work on controlling your emotions and breathing. There are some exercises I know that can help with that."

"Not work with Serein?"

"No. In this, you must control yourself first. Beyond that, only you can decide to connect with Serein and control her against such actions. Sit up," Matar ordered. "We will start immediately. Repeat after me…"

The commander taught the two cousins for hours; however, the time in his solo tutelage was a pleasant one. Matar was a patient man and very knowledgeable. Too, without the pressure of King William by his side, the lessons seemed less formal. By dusk, the three men had gone through multiple Sheev'anee forms of breathwork, yet their bodies felt supple and energized.

"I feel like I could go for a run right now!" Par flexed his fingers in surprise at his energy.

"These forms were created for health and healing, not just for control." Matar seemed pleased with their progress. "Practiced daily, you can extend your life span and even heal minor ailments."

"Will this really help with Serein, though?" Lord Gordar asked.

"That is all up to your prince." The cavalry commander rose and stretched, putting an end to their session. "I'm in need of some dinner. Shall we reconvene our watch in an hour?"

"Yes. Thank you, sir," Prince Par bowed.

Matar waved away the courtesy. "Save your thanks for when you keep Serein from trouble. Until then, you will tell me if she activates again?"

"Yes, sir."

Satisfied, Commandeer Matar turned away to search out some food.

"We should find our own," Gordar said, pulling Par's focus from the Crystine man. "It wouldn't be fair for us to ask the kitchen staff to come all the way here."

"You go." Par was anxious to leave the obelisk unattended. "Bring me something easy to carry."

His protector shook his head at the nonsense. "It's not like the pillar is going anywhere."

"I just feel better staying."

"Fine. Suit yourself. I'll be back." Lord Gordar waved and headed away.

Alone in the growing dark, Par took to sitting on an old bench overlooking the sea. His hand came to Serein, and he felt its slight warmth seep into his palm. "So, you're emotional, huh?" he asked the stone. "I guess I don't blame you… if I was in your stead—and my wielder was pathetic—I'd act out too. Still, I can't have people getting hurt. You understand that, don't you?" Par shook his head as the calm of the night surrounded him. Of course, Serein couldn't respond back. She wasn't human! Volatile like one, maybe, but not of flesh and blood—or soul.

The royal glanced down at the sapphire in his palm. Her blue glow was soft and soothing—if only her power was the same. "Reluctant indeed… I'm scared shitless of the potential I hold in my hand. If only I come to terms with it." *Like Zyanthena Sheev'arid seemed to be*, he thought. The feel of the Tashek's confidence, so certain and commanding, still flowed through him as their conversation did. To have someone like that to confide in…

Par turned his attention to Osh'ēēn once more. "Come on, Sheev'arid! Use your magic. Come to us… to me. We're here, waiting…"

§ §

In the heart of the City of Rubies, the great king of Sunrise sat on his heavy throne and stared out into the room full of courtiers. His court was coming to the end of its day, and he was loath to be amongst their annoying chatter for much longer. The main topics of the day had been the coming Festival of Lights, held on the darkest night of the year, and of the cost of the banquet to be held at the palace.

It was all frivolous talk—and useless. His people were all fools.

Behind the scenes, King Raymond Sunrise was in contact with the maunstorz's representative. Negotiations with the enemy had led to prosperity and peace throughout the kingdom, but the price—the price!—was far greater a concern than a stupid festival. Had his subjects known that their princes were being held prisoner, would the court still talk of such things as festivals? Yet their safety entailed that no one knew of the heirs' capture.

It put Raymond in a mood. "All right, out with you! Out!" he thundered at his subjects. "Court is done today. Leave me! Now!!" The courtiers stopped and stared like mice caught in the grain bins before they scurried from their liege's presence. King Raymond was notorious for his temper, and not a one among them wished his wrath. Satisfied at their flurry, Raymond sat back in his chair and took up a wine goblet.

"They respond so well to your orders," a silky voice said through the screen panel behind the king's throne. It was the only voice that gave the mighty ruler any pause.

"Guards! I wish to be alone," King Raymond ordered. His royal guards all bowed from their places about the enormous room and turned away. The doors slammed shut to prove the ruler was alone. "I see you've returned."

A chuckle as the maunstorz came out from his hiding place. "I was gone but a day. Did you miss me so, Majesty?" The enemy was not a man at all but a boy barely over eighteen—or so Raymond guessed. He still looked soft in all the places yet to grow with maturity, and yet there was a power to the lad's musculature that spoke of hours of practicing with sword and fists. And scars—what scars he had on his bared arms! The tattoos—four lines about a bicep—denoted some ranking withing the enemy hierarchy. Rokell, the maunstorz's dignitary, was proving to be quite the headache.

"I didn't rather miss your breath upon my neck."

Rokell smiled, a grin predatory in nature. "On that, I will try to stand less close, Your Majesty."

"You have word on my latest correspondence?"

"I do."

Raymond expected a scroll to be handed over, but the boy did not move to extend one. "Well?" He spread his hands to say, *"Where is it?"*

The maunstorz blinked. "Such impatience you have—for a king." The words elicited a growl from the ruler. Rokell just smirked and stepped before the leader to extend a rolled-up piece of leather. "Mansocan sends his reply."

"Your sire is a bit archaic," King Raymond jeered as he took the rolled leather in hand. He hastened to pull the cord and unwrap the sheet. Unfurled, he stared at it a moment before yelping and tossing it away to the steps. "What is this?"

Rokell raised an eyebrow and strode casually to pick up the message. "I thought the reply was rather clear and quite artistic."

"But that's, that's—"

"Yes. The young prince's tattoo. *From. His. Back.*" The maunstorz lad spread the skin out and admired his father's handiwork. "It seems he is not satisfied with your latest offer. More pieces could be forthcoming if you don't negotiate better terms."

Raymond felt himself seething. He blamed it on the shock. "If you harm Connel again, our—"

"Our what?" There was a warning in those red eyes. King Raymond snapped his jaws closed. "That's right. Think wisely on what you say. Mansocan is not the most tolerant of leaders. He'll return your sons when he is ready. Until then, he asks you stop insulting him with such low bargains. I hope he has been clear, Majesty."

King Raymond set his face into a careful mask. "Perfectly."

Rokell grinned. "Good. Very good."

§ §

It was deep in the night, and the prince was too restless to sleep. Par flung his bedroll aside and stood from his cot. He tried to be quiet so as not to disturb his cousin as he slipped on an outer layer of clothing and shuffled to the tent flap in the dark. Stepping outside, the royal found another unable to sleep. Commander Matar sat at their small fire and was carving a figurine by the light. He looked up as the royal approached.

"Commander."

"Highness. Awake again, I see."

Par found a seat on a stool and hugged his arms about himself. "I've been restless since Zyanthena came to me."

"She does have that effect on people," Matar said of the desert woman. There was fondness for her in his eyes.

"You said to be patient, sir, but I find it hard when we don't know the *when* or *how*."

"Yes." The commander lowered his hands and took to staring at the fire instead of his work. "It isn't usual for her to neglect to give some indication of her timing, but…"

When the words drifted off, the prince asked, "But?"

Matar shook himself out of his thoughts. "But Zyanthena must be trying a majik-al practice I've only heard in theory but never seen mastered."

"And what is that?"

The next words were given with reluctance. "The former queen of Crystalynian had a theory on the pillars of Syre. She thought them to be some kind of… interconnected byway system—or something." Commander Matar shook his head. "It sounded crazy, the ideas she had. She believed the ancient Syrean scripts on the pillars' sides meant something, like an instruction book. But there are few who can read ancient Syrean, let alone speak it. I barely am able, and I've tried studying it for years."

Prince Par looked quizzical. "You're an interesting man, Commander."

"Oh?"

"You know my father and the queen of Crystalynian, yet you come from a humble background. I'm intrigued by how well versed you are in the citizens and history of Syre."

A cautious mask came to Commander Matar's face. "I am *Khataum*, a position of honor in the Sheev'anee, and a well-traveled soldier of Syre."

"I'm not sure anyone's ever explained what that Sheev'anee word means, exactly."

"No, I guess not." The admittance softened the commander enough to show pity on a stranger to Sheev'anee culture. "*Khataum* has no direct translation to our words. It's likened to such phrases as 'a man of much knowledge,' 'master of the world,' 'far-seer,' and 'friend of the people.' In some ways, it depends on which rank of the Sheev'anee is saying it of me to get the proper inflection."

"Those are high titles to be afforded."

"They are very lofty," Matar agreed. "For the longest time, I thought it was a way for the Tashek to make fun of an outsider—they do rather have an odd form of humor. Yet I've come to appreciate the respect they afford me."

"But that still doesn't explain how you know such esteemed rulers," Par pointed out.

Matar tsked at his stubbornness. "Of that, Highness—"

A commotion before them cut off Matar's words.

Osh'ēēn burst into white and blue light, fully engulfing the surrounding garden in its color. Something was expelled from its power to fall to the cobbles of the courtyard. Afterward, Osh'ēēn went back to dead stone again.

It took some moments for either man to move. Commander Matar recovered first. Shocked at the burst of magic, he found his feet and rushed to the pillar to touch its surface. There was a lingering heat in the stone. "Of all the...!" He couldn't believe it had worked.

"Commander!" Par called his attention to the object. Matar turned back and came to crouch beside the prince. "It's a piece of leather with writing."

Matar recognized it right away. "It's a Tashek's message—horse hide and charcoaled symbols."

"Zyanthena managed to send this through Osh'ēēn?!" Ocean-blue eyes were wide as Par looked to the ancient obelisk he had thought decorative. "So, the pillars *are* magical?"

"We saw it plain as day... but I still don't believe it."

They gaped a few moments longer. "What does the message say?" the Sealander recovered enough to ask.

The commander scooped up the leather piece and motioned them back to the fire. With still-shaking hands, he read the words. "Zyanthena was able to travel to pillars in Rubia and Sunrise. Allies have been rescued from the maunstorz at both places. Yet, there are too many men to use Vauldin anymore, or the pillars. They are riding from the Command Front toward Aura Lake, the larger of the two Halo Lakes, in Golden and request aid from any allies west. Maunstorz may be pursuing. They ride at cavalry pace."

"Cavalry pace from Sunrise's northern post...? How many men? Is everyone safe? Who did she rescue?"

"It's all Zy'ena could write safely." Matar looked perturbed. "As usual, it seems she's gone and outdone herself in enemy territory.

Highness, we must send a bird to the Golden Palace right away asking for their aid."

"Agreed. I'll get a man roused." Par stood, then paused and turned back. "Commander, what time frame should I give Golden?"

"If Zyanthena's right, she could get to the border in as little as ten days. However, with sick men or injured horse, a fortnight would be more accurate."

"Golden can move their men sooner—or so I hope."

Matar nodded. "And, Highness, please excuse me, but I wish to head there as well. I need use of three horses and supplies."

"Relax, Commander." Par grinned. "You're not the only one who want to go east. We'll take my horse-transporting vessel to Goldview and ride from there. It'll save us three days."

"I doubt your father will agree to letting you go."

"We'll leave before he wakes up."

"Stars preserve me, I'm going to piss William off again!" Matar muttered to himself as he took in the prince's resolved features. "Fine, but your lord protector will make sure to bring along a handful of men."

"I wouldn't let him go any other way."

They turned to find Lord Gordar standing there, having overheard everything. "Still," Prince Par said to his cousin, "no word to Father."

"Oh, the king will get word," Lord Gordar countered. "It'll just be a few hours too late. We'll have everything ready and be gone before sunrise. You have my word, Commander."

Matar looked between the two Sealander cousins and considered for another minute all the ways such an allowance would cost him. "Very well, Highness, Lord Gordar. In that case, let's get a move on. There's no time to waste!"

Chapter Forty-Seven
§
Reunited

"I see the flags of Kavahad!"

King Al'den looked ahead to the Sheev'anee scout cantering back to their force. They were the words he had hoped to hear. "We've finally made it." He shared a relieved smile with Cum'ar and Lăn'esha.

"Still, Majesty, you know we of the Sheev'anee should not travel farther," Cum'ar warned. His striking, amber-brown eyes looked pinched as they spotted the flags of Kavahad flying over the city gates in the distance. "Many forces are there, but so are the Kavahadians. With our history, it would not be wise to bring the All'ani closer."

It was an issue Al'den had been avoiding. "That blasted treaty is making things overly complicated! I wish there was a way to order it nulled." However, today was not that day.

"A time will come when you may, Majesty," Lăn'esha reminded him. "For today, let us leave be reasons for bloodshed."

"I know." Al'den reached out for the lovely Tashek woman's hand to squeeze it tightly. "Cum'ar, make camp here. Meeg and I will go ahead with Commander Grant's men and speak with those in Kavahad. Afterward, we will leave for the LaPoint property and Amun."

All'ani Cum'ar gave a Tashek bow of respect from his horse and turned away to issue the order to their force. His sister was quick to follow suit, leaving First Guardsman Meeg Thorson and the five other royal guards to watch their king's back. Time would be of the essence to keep Kavahad from panicking at an unidentified force coming their way. In short order, the six guards and the king of Staria were cantering toward the rugged, desert outpost, the rescued soldiers following on foot.

At Kavahad's gates, Meeg cued his horse ahead and yelled out to the guards there of the king's arrival. The men were quick to respond to the royal order, and a man was waiting to lead the king's party to the lord-governor's keep. Another waited to take Commander Grant and his men to the hospital and soldier barracks. Word must have been sent ahead to the keep, for Commander Kins, Commander Gordon, and Advisor Abrus were waiting on the main steps as the king arrived.

"Majesty!" The two Starians in charge of Kavahad were quick to a knee in greeting; the mertinean commander was just a step behind.

"At ease," Al'den bade them as he dismounted from Kesh and allowed a retainer to take the fiery horse's head. "I've travelled from the Citadel to see how you all fared with my own eyes."

"You've had a long journey, Majesty."

"We did. Long and cold, but not without some good news." Al'den greeted Commander Gordon and Advisor Abrus first, and then he centered his attention on the mertinean commander. "I have brought with me Commander Grant and his rescued men from Raven's Den. They are being seen to at the local hospital."

"Thank you, King Al'den," Commander Kins said, relief visible on his weathered face.

"It is I who should be thanking you, commander. Reports you sent north were enough to relieve me of my worries about Kavahad and my people. Yet I could not help making my way here. It's been too quiet in Staria. I needed to see my kingdom personally."

"It has been quiet," Commander Kins agreed. "But I'm not about to be ungrateful for the respite—against the maunstorz and the weather."

"Neither am I." King Al'den lifted his attention to the keep, which was less snow-ridden than the capital. "Do you all really fare well here?"

"My liege," Advisor Abrus came forward and bowed again. "The people complain of the military and foreign forces here, but no fights have erupted to that end. The people do appreciate the extra protection. Yet…" The man paused, as if knowing all his words sounded whiney. "Yet they wonder if any word of the Lord-Governor Shekmann has come to you?"

Al'den set a calming hand on the man's shoulder. "I am sorry to have put your people under such duress, Advisor, but I am grateful none have caused any trouble—on either side. I wish I could give you good tidings on Lord Shekmann's whereabouts, but I cannot. Still, I assure you, men are keeping a lookout for him. Kavahad needs to continue to be patient while the snows remain to block our searches."

"Thank you, Majesty." Abrus didn't look consoled, but he knew a royal order when he heard one. It was not the time to argue the joint control with the mertinean as long as the king said it was necessary.

"And are the populace in need of anything else, Advisor?"

"No, sir—ah, Majesty. Food has been sent from Golden as relief."

"Good. I am indebted to the South for giving us aid at such a time."

"Yes, Majesty. We all are." He nodded his head in agreement.

"Shall we go inside, sir?" Commander Kins interrupted in the gap that followed the advisor's words.

"Yes, we may. I wish to see how everything runs here and the reports you've received from our allies. I will stay long enough for that, then I have need of speaking with the Starian court."

"All the nobility have been sent to the LaPoint manor," Advisor Abrus said.

"So I have heard. I'll make my way there once I am done here."

§ §

It took nearly two hours to see Kavahad and review all the reports the Starian king desired to review. By the end, he and his royal guards were thawed of the cold, and the thought of returning to it was tiring, but it was not enough to dissuade Al'den from leaving for his other business. At a quarter past noon, he returned to the All'ani.

"How did it go?" Cum'ar asked as the ruler joined him by the fire and accepted some tea.

"Kavahad is not the happiest with the arrangements. Without Lord Shekmann there, the city's walking a fine line. However, as a military post, it is fulfilling its purpose above expectations."

"It sounds as if you need to ask the mertinean to leave—even though you just brought more."

"That may well be." Al'den gulped down the hot tea, enjoying its warmth settling into his core. "Yet we've no word from Rubia. I can't force their soldiers—who came to our aid!—to leave for their homelands without word of their safety. Plus, Grant's men will need to rest after their ordeal."

"I'd say the mertinean could join us, but we're not ones to wait for foot soldiers."

"No," Al'den agreed, "and I wouldn't ask that, anyway. I'll just keep trusting in Commander Kins's skills at diplomacy. He's the easiest leader for the general public to deal with. It seems that he's kept the peace working with Viscount LaPoint and Advisor Abrus."

Cum'ar made a face at the mention of LaPoint. "Now there's an unsavory sot."

"I'll pretend I didn't hear that," the Starian royal teased, hiding a smile behind his cup. "Otherwise, I can't take you with me to the estate to procure Amun."

The Tashek man made a hand signal that he would behave. "I'll be as tactful as a politician while I'm there."

"You'd better." Al'den tossed some snow at his Sheev'anee right-hand man. "Get up. We're going to LaPoint's now."

§ §

The LaPoint estate was a six-hour ride from Kavahad. It was set in beautiful countryside near the Senna River; the demesne was lush in trees and rolling grasslands and not surrounded by desert like its liege city. The snows were beginning to thaw there, making the horses' way easier and revealing how truly fortunate the viscount was for his location.

King Al'den and his small entourage rose straight up the main lane to the LaPoint manor and reined in their mounts at the wide staircase at the front. It didn't take long for a butler to exit the mansion and come to see about the visitors. The middle-aged man turned pale and procumbent at learning the new king of Staria was there. He hurried to accommodate the royal, his First Guardsman, and the two All'ani. They were ushered into the main foyer while the other subordinates were shown to the stables. "Wait here, Majesty, as I find Lord LaPoint."

"As you say." Al'den dismissed the man and took to unencumbering himself of his winter outerwear, which another staff member was quick to take from him.

"A rather opulent manor," Lăn'esha muttered as they surveyed the front room. It was gilded in gold leaf amid emerald silk wallpaper and marbled floors. Rich mahogany furniture gave a solidness to the foyer while elaborate chandeliers provided both light and intrigue.

"The LaPoints made their mark in trade of silk and marble. They have a quarry on the demesne with the highest quality of stone in Staria."

"And aren't afraid to show it off," Cum'ar also commented.

Al'den raised his eyebrows at the two siblings' words. "I do have your assurance of getting along with the viscount?"

"Of course," Cum'ar replied. "We're not here to start anything, only to collect your stone."

"Just so you remember."

"We do, My King of the Yellow Star." The proper title assured the Starian more than the other words. His two All'ani allies hadn't lost their perspectives despite prejudices against the LaPoints.

Viscount Markus LaPoint appeared soon after, looking distressed that the king of Staria has not been settled in a sitting room. "Majesty, your sudden arrival is a pleasure to my family and estate."

"Viscount LaPoint." Al'den accepted his handshake and followed where their host waved. It was a private sitting room off of the foyer. Hot tea and biscuits had been set out on the glass center table in the otherwise red-satin-and-mahogany-furnished room. Al'den took a place, standing, before the fire while his three subordinates found their seats. Markus LaPoint took to mirroring his king next to one of the chairs, a hand to its tall back. The viscount kept a careful mask over his features at seeing the Tashek in the king's party. "We have come from Kavahad. I was visiting to see how southern Staria fared."

"I believe we've managed more than your forces in the North, Majesty. The snows have been milder, and we've been able to receive aid from our neighbor kingdom to the south."

"Yes. I have heard of Golden's generosity—and of yours, Viscount."

"Thank you… Majesty."

Al'den gave the man a polite smile. "The thanks should be mine for your harboring the entirety of Staria's court here at your manor. I'm sure it's been a burden on your staff and stores to have so many guests at your home."

"Nothing we weren't able to manage."

"Still, you will not be without recompense. I've come with five dreites' worth of gold coins for your service to the crown."

Markus actually looked shocked at the amount awarded him. "That's a king's reward if I've ever heard of one, Majesty."

"Yes, well… I am a king to award a decent man for his service to the kingdom's people. You have shown your quality."

"Thank you, my liege." Markus LaPoint bowed deeply at the praise. "Your generosity will not be forgotten." There was a pause as a maid passed out tea. Once everyone was served, he began again. "And may I expect you to stay the night, Majesty?"

"Yes, and sorry for the intrusion. I appreciate any room you can provide."

"Consider it already done. I will situate you on the third-story apartments, and dinner will be served shortly. Shall I expect you to need my main hall to have the court's ears tonight, Majesty?"

Though Al'den wasn't looking forward to the oath-gathering, it was long overdue since his father's death. It was possible the opportunity would not come again for some time—what with the Deepest Snows and war upon them. "Yes, thank you, Viscount."

Markus nodded and straightened. "Then I will go make sure all is ready. My butler, Verrance, will see you to your quarters. Dinner will be served at six."

The king's small party was seen to their rooms and settled. Yet there was barely any time to change out of riding wear to apparel more appropriate for a dinner. Once they had changed and washed the road from their faces and hands, another staff member arrived to show Al'den and his men to the dining hall.

They were the last to arrive; however, the entire table had remained standing to wait for their king. Al'den felt himself balk at the courtesy—he was not one to demand such respects—but he chose to seat himself as quickly as was appropriate and bid the room to find their own chairs. The screech of wood against the marble floor and sounds of men and women settling to their places took away some of the tension underlying the room.

Markus LaPoint was the only one to remain standing. "Majesty," he began and kept the room from conversation, "may I say, we are happy to have you join us from the capital. It must certainly have been a long travel to reach Kavahad and this manor. But to see you safe and in person gives this kingdom relief. I offer a toast to that."

King Al'den nodded and took up his own wineglass. He stood and extended the drink toward the viscount. "Thank you, Lord LaPoint. I graciously accept your toast." They clinked glasses and then turned to indicate to the table to lift and drink their own. Al'den settled back into his chair and hoped it was the end of it.

"And I apologize for such a measly feast, Majesty. My staff had already prepared dinner before your arrival."

As the meal was a course of winter squash soup, followed by roasted duck with potatoes and sprouts, and a pudding dessert, the new king of Staria found the table more opulent fare than he had seen for three seasons. He said as much to Markus LaPoint. "This meal is to my liking, Viscount, and I would not have wanted your cooks to prepare a whole new menu just for me. Tell your head cook I appreciate the effort and look forward to trying their version of the roast duck."

"Very well, Majesty."

Markus LaPoint's agreement seemed to settle the tension at the table. If felt as if the entire Starian court had forgotten, with his absence and change of status, how down-to-earth their heir was. That their king was willing to eat "such meager fare" reminded them he was not a snob. Slowly, conversation resumed as the first course was brought out and wineglasses refilled. The room settled into a relaxed dinner.

King Al'den made sure to keep the conversation turned toward nonconsequential topics: hunting, how the markets fared with early snows, which horses had labored early foal. Those were all subjects he knew the viscount and his people were interested in. Any turn to questions of the war or plight of the North were quickly turned around. The ruler of Staria made it clear that dinner was not the place for such talk. It took only a few, failed attempts before the others followed his lead. Only when the last of the dishes were cleared did the king finally broach the subject.

King Al'den rose from his chair to address the room. "Now that we've enjoyed such wonderful cuisine, I ask for a little of your time." The room turned quiet. "My father, King Merretham Maushelik, passed away at the beginning of this season. Merretham was your king for forty-two years. He served Staria honorably, and I hope I can be true to his memory." He paused and ran his ice-blue eyes over the courtiers. "Now, I have heard from the lords and commanders in my service at the Citadel of Light and gathered their oaths of fealty. Tonight, I extend to you your oaths—if you will take me. I will be in the LaPoint's main hall for this, and I have a scribe commissioned for your seals and signatures. We will convene there in twenty minutes."

His dismissal started the room abuzz with questions. Al'den held in a sigh and raised his hand for silence. "Afterward, we will speak of your concerns for this kingdom and my plans for this season through the coming year. I will not speak to anyone privately at this time." He paused and motioned for his three closest subordinates to rise and follow him. "That is all."

Thankfully, the courtiers stayed their words, at least until their king took his leave. Al'den waited until he, the All'ani, and his First Guardsman were alone at the main hall before releasing his frustrated breath. Only to these three would he admit his irritation at the tedium. "Let the fanfare begin."

§ §

When Princess Éleen had heard King Al'den was at the mansion, she had made sure to put on her most elaborate gown and jewels so as to be the loveliest woman at the table; however, it was as if the Starian royal did not see her. The newly crowned Al'den Maushelik had been more concerned with trifling matters of the season than any political affairs. All of that had been saved for after the meal and was only extended to those men of title in the nobility: the viscount, counts, barons, and lords. Hardly any of the ladies of the Starian court attended—save Lady Rosetta Greyson and two others holding diplomatic license by the crown. As the talks were about Staria and not the rest of Syre, it was not Princess Éleen's place to attend.

That had made it hard for the Havener to sleep that night. Thoughts of failure and disgrace to her family plagued Éleen and kept her from any decent shut-eye. Therefore, it was a shock to her when Lord Carrod knocked on her door early the next morning to say that they had an audience with the Starian king. Lord Carrod Nexlé took a critical eye to her disheveled form and suggested she take a moment to put herself to rights but warned they only had ten minutes to appear. With no time for any decent wardrobe, the princess had to make do with a splash of water on her face, brush her hair, and put on a simple day gown; it was a poor showing of any resemblance to her station. Still, the two Haveners made the appointment in acceptable time.

King Al'den was standing before a window, his stature erect and commanding, making full effect of his six-foot-two frame. Despite the fact that he wore his light armor—a wardrobe that fit the man's character precisely—there was no doubt that this was the rightful king of Staria. Princess Éleen felt her heart beat strongly against her breastbone as she was ushered to the ruler's presence. It was worsened when she realized their talk was not altogether private: the First Guardsman and two Tashek shadows were there as well. The impromptu talk seemed less informal and more daunting than previous ones of their making. Without their friend, Prince Kent Argetlem, there to buffer the two royals, Princess Éleen wondered if Al'den Maushelik would be more imposing.

"Princess Éleen." The king turned from the window to address the last matter on his docket. "Thank you for coming."

"Highness… I mean, Majesty." Éleen curtsied deeply and felt the man's ice-blue eyes studying her.

"You look well. I had worried when I got word you were still in Staria that something had befallen you."

The words took the princess by surprise, but their warmth was encouraging. "Not at all, Majesty. We decided to pause our travels when the snows came."

"Yes. Many found themselves waylaid at different parts of their trip. I am relieved you were able to find acceptable accommodations."

"All in thanks to Viscount LaPoint, Majesty."

Al'den nodded before waving them to chairs and morning tea. "As we are in private, Princess Éleen, please call me by my name. I've heard enough 'majesties' this morning to last a week."

The request seemed foreign to the Southern-born—no man in lower Syre would be caught dead with such a request—but Princess Éleen gave a timid smile and acquiesced. "As you wish."

King Al'den was already pouring their tea, a habit the princess remembered of the Starian heir. She allowed herself to be doted on and accepted the cup gracefully. "Princess Éleen," Al'den began after they were settled, "I have come with two requests." A pinched look that came to the corner of the woman's eyes at the words, but he forged on. "The first is the return of my pendant, the heirloom I asked you look after."

"Yes. I have it right here." Éleen pulled the silver chain and citrine from her bodice and unclasped it from around her neck. "I showed it to no one, as you asked, and have kept it safe."

"Thank you." Al'den took the stone in his palm and held it tightly—as if it was the last piece of heritage he owned. If he had noticed any of the princess's own reluctance at letting Amun go, he did not show it. "Éleen, I was right to put this necklace in your care all these seasons. Thank you for giving me that faith."

"Of course, Maj—Al'den." The king seemed distracted now that he had his family's citrine back, so the princess asked, "And the second matter for me, King Al'den?"

The question pulled the Starian back to the room. "The second is for you to stay safe, Highness, and return to Blue Haven as soon as you are able."

"But I—"

"Staria is not safe and will not be for some time. My forces and I will be scouring the north for the maunstorz, and that means few men can be spared to protect you. War is no place for a princess, and I cannot guarantee your safety now."

Princess Éleen felt herself panic. It was as if they were back in King Merretham's apartments once more, the time she had been denied the betrothal. "Highness… Majesty, does this mean our betrothal…?"

"I am sorry, Éleen, but I cannot court a betrothal agreement at this time. My people need me to protect them, and I must rid the North of our enemies. If I must suffer King Éldon's disapproval, then I must for Staria's sake." He paused to take a sip of his tea. "As for you, Princess Éleen, I fear what could become of you staying here in the ravaged North. Our ways are very unkind and not something you need endure. Please, promise me you will get home."

It was her worst fear coming true. Éleen had worried that being called away from the prince would null their betrothal, and so it had. She found herself unable to get any air. "I, I…"

"The princess understands, Majesty." Lord Carrod stepped forward and gave a formal bow. "And I promise you, the princess will return home by the quickest route."

"My thanks, Lord Nexlé." Al'den rose and shook Carrod's hand, but his eyes strayed back to the unmoving princess. Concern was written in them. "Then I must take my leave. My forces wait in Kavahad, and I must return to them. Please, head south as soon as you are able. The Golden crown will honor our pact for your safety." He passed over a token signifying permission to move about Golden, given to Al'den by the heir himself. "Prince Kent has assured me this pass will get you anywhere."

"Majesty, thank you." Lord Carrod bowed as the royal stepped around him.

The four Starians began to take their leave, then, as matters of the state were pressing the king to leave for Kavahad. Lord Carrod waited at the door for his charge to come to her senses, but Éleen was slow to do so. Finally, her lord protector asked his dismissal by saying he should go and see the king of Staria off. Even then, Princess Éleen did not stir.

Only when she was alone did Éleen find herself again. Realizing her idiocy, she slapped herself awake and followed where the others had exited. *Perhaps there was one more chance to change His Majesty's mind...* With the last moments to alter the course of her fate, Princess Éleen rushed toward the front of the mansion; however, she arrived at the front windows to see the king's small entourage trotting away down the lane. The princess held in an upset gasp and forced her tears to stay in her eyes; she had only herself to blame for handling the situation so poorly. Too late, she had come to her senses too late!

"Ah, now, aren't you a sight," a voice whispered into her ear, causing the princess to jump. Of course, it was Markus LaPoint, come to gloat at her misfortune. "By such a look, I know that you've lost your favor of the Starian crown. His Majesty didn't want you, after all."

"He came to ask me to stay safe when I ride south, nothing more," Éleen found herself saying.

"And most certainly a lot less." Markus smiled. "No betrothal for you, I suspect."

It didn't seem wise to agree with him. "Such a matter was not discussed. His Majesty came for something else."

Markus chuckled. "A king won't bring up such a proposal if he has no intention of ever calling for it. Our Starian liege has forsaken you—and you know that." He paused to bend close enough for Éleen to feel his breath on her skin and whisper into her ear, "Whenever you've recovered yourself, remember that my door is always open to you. I'll make a real woman out of you —one who won't be refused by any man again." Markus's lips skimmed the nape of her neck. "Come calling when you're ready to learn, *Princess*." The viscount let his touch linger on Éleen's collarbone before slipping away to other duties.

Princess Éleen waited for the viscount to disappear down the hall before saying, "Pig." Markus LaPoint was a man to make her skin crawl.

"Highness!" Lord Carrod appeared, coming in from the front steps where the king's departure party had met. His voice and expression were tight and worried, as if he knew something was terribly wrong.

"Lord Carrod." Éleen schooled her stricken face to neutral and let her lovely, china-blue eyes looked out beyond the window, "I think we've overstayed our welcome in Staria. Let us pack and leave at once for Golden." *We have another friend there who may be more welcoming…*

After the reception they had just received—or lack thereof—from Staria's king, Lord Carrod knew better than to counter the princess's order. He bowed. "Right away, Highness."

Chapter Forty-Eight
§
To Make Haste

The ride from Sardon to the capital had seemed so easy after the desert of Staria. With level roads and many wayfarer stops along the way, Prince Kent Argetlem's small party made the city limits of Golden's capital in six days. Despite it being Deepest Snows, the weather had been pleasant and warm, making their journey seem like a stroll. It was almost a shame to see the large sprawl of the Golden city after such a lovely week on the roads.

"Well, we made it," Prince Kent commented as the first outbuildings came into view and then the darker mass of the capital.

Colonel Deed grinned back. "And not an incident to be had. I'll take our Golden Kingdom over Staria any day."

"It is more pleasant."

"And yet you say that with such a gloomy expression, Highness."

"No." Kent tried to lighten his features. "I'm just thinking of the mounds of reports that are sure to be collecting on my desk. My advisors do love saying certain matters are mine and mine alone. I can only imagine what they've decided to deem as 'only the prince's concern.'"

"It sounds as if I should have a word with your men."

"Perhaps. I just might let you loose on them." The scholarly prince grinned. The thought of the court advisors getting a "talk" with his colonel sounded more entertaining by the second.

"Are we to enter through the main gates?" Another of Kent's men asked, shimmying around in his saddle to call back to the royal.

"No, let's take the west gate." The soldiers' gate, some called it. The entrance would have less foot traffic, and Prince Kent did not want to draw much attention to himself upon his return. That all the men in his party agreed showed that they too preferred the idea.

The party turned their horses away from the main road to a smaller one that wrapped around the outskirts, making the west gates just before noon. The prince's arrival elicited a little fanfare, but Prince Kent calmed them and asked to pass into the city without an official running to the palace. "There's plenty for you and your men to do without running about on my account," he ordered gently.

The two gate guards were flabbergasted, caught between protocol and a prince's order. Colonel Deed settled them with an order of, "Hop to, men," that seemed to knock some sense into them. Colonel Deed waited until they'd passed into the streets beyond before muttering about their incompetence. "Flabbering buffoons, making a fuss of nothing."

"Still, you handled them well, Colonel. I didn't know you had such audacity in you."

Colonel Deed flushed at the praise and shuffled himself straighter in his saddle. "I am your lord protector now. I have big shoes to fill and won't let you—or the lieutenant-commander's memory—down thanks to any incompetence on my part, Highness."

"At ease, Jared," Kent bade him. "You've proven to me time and again, since you agreed to this appointment, that you are capable. Still"—he let himself frown back at the gate guards—"I must be too accustomed to Staria and Sardon's militaries. Our people here seem a bit too lax and out of practice. Or maybe I am projecting a problem that does not exist."

"No, Highness. I concur. Those two soldiers were unusually flustered. With your leave, I will investigate the rest of the men stationed here and see if they are the only ones or if all the men act the same. I am sure Lord-Commander Ivance and Lord Aeronson will not be pleased with their performance."

Prince Kent's s mouth twitched in amusement at his man's seriousness. "I do give you leave, Colonel. Having you investigate will give me relief on this matter."

"Very well, Highness."

By then, they had made the stable yard reserved for the king's militia. The place was quiet, as most of the men were out on rounds or taking naps for later patrols. The lack of activity suited the prince after a long ride. He dismounted with the rest of his party and led his horse to a hitching post. A sleepy stable hand came out to greet them and nearly fell over himself to oblige the royal heir once he was announced. They got their horses sorted out in the man's care and turned away to start the long walk through the city to the palace.

Their path followed a small lane between the stables, kennels, and aviary, as the animals of the crown were all kept together, for noise control, on the western outskirts. There were occasional yips and nickers along the path from beasts on the other side of the wall, but most of the animals were as subdued as the rest of the yard, lulled by the sunshine and calm. Only the aviary contained any commotion. The birds were squawking up a storm. There were only a few reasons for the birds to get so erratic, and one reason in particular had Prince Kent waving his men to stop and turn into the aviary: a messenger bird could have arrived.

Indeed, the aviary staff member was clutching a recently arrived carrier pigeon. The lad stroked the upset bird and cooed at it to calm down as he began to untie the missive from the pigeon's leg. Unencumbered, the lad set the bird in a cage. He was turning away from latching it when Prince Kent's party arrived.

"A missive has come?" Kent asked without formality.

The young man's eyes went wide at seeing the prince, he was quick to abase himself. "Aye, sir… ah, my prince. Ah, it looks like a seal from… Sealand?" He floundered to read the image.

"Sealand?" Prince Kent extended his hand for the missive. It was a royal seal from Sealand all right: the seal of Prince Par Fantill to be exact. The script on the outside of the paper was written in a beautiful cursive and indicated the letter was for the Golden crown. "Thank you…"

"Caddy, sir… ah, Highness."

"Thank you, Caddy. I'll take this missive to my father."

The lad bowed, yet Prince Kent had already turned away, occupied by the letter. One of Kent's men, Officer Keatten, made sure to pass a coin to Caddy for his service before following the rest of the group to a table, where the prince had stopped to read the missive.

The Golden heir's eyes were wide and growing wider as he read through the letter. By the time he was finished, his men were beyond curious about its contents. Something had to be amiss for Prince Kent to look so shocked.

"Highness?" Jared Deed asked for everyone.

"Men, our journey may not be over." Prince Kent finally looked up. "Prince Par Fantill and a handful of men are travelling from Goldview to the Aura Lakes at cavalry pace. He didn't even bother to ask ahead for our permission—he is in that much haste."

The colonel's eyes pinched at the news. "Why, sir?"

"Sunarian soldiers have been rescued from our enemy's hands. They are making haste to our borders from the Sunarian Command Front while, it is presumed, being pursued by the maunstorz. A message managed to reach Prince Par—he doesn't say how—but he writes that the Sunarians will need aid as soon as it can be made ready. He rides with all possible speed to reach their projected route. Currently, at his pace, he and his men could be one day's ride south of us. They will likely circumvent the capital for quieter roads and continue to the border. They hope to reach the Sunarian party in another five or six days—if everything goes well. As for the Sunarians, with Stars' luck, they will reach the border safely around the same time, if not before."

"Prince Par must be pushing his horses beyond their means to make up so much distance," Jared commented.

"That, or they're trading horses as they go. He mentions a Crystine commander rides with them. The Crystine are known to ride at a pace we in the South do not employ. Their cavalry pace is much quicker than ours."

"That would make sense."

Prince Kent bit his lip, thinking. "I can send a rider to intercept the prince's party and give them a token of my permission to travel Golden. They'll need it if they run into any of our militia, and they've chanced several days without it already."

"I will go, Highness," Officer Danver volunteered. "I do not mind a few extra days on the road for something important like this."

"Thank you." Prince Kent granted the leave. "Here's one of my personal seals to take to them. You have my permission for any supplies and money you may need."

"To a point on the coin, of course, Highness," Officer Danver teased as he accepted the seal.

"Of course. Stars' speed, Officer."

The man saluted his prince and turned heel to head back to the stables. Prince Kent had no doubts on his success at reaching the other royal's party. With one problem out of the way, he turned to other matters. "As for aiding Sunrise… I can't rightly call on Sardon. Ivance's men are too far away. And our men here—"

"May I suggest the small post of Quinton, Highness?" Colonel Deed cut in. "It's located southwest of the Aura Lake, at the edge of the Pika Mounts."

The town was tiny and the royal had never visited it. "Their forces are adequate?"

"Not large, sir, but an able militia of foot soldiers, archers, and a handful of knights. I was raised there, actually."

Prince Kent hadn't known that. "So, you know the area?"

"Of course. Beyond Quinton is a larger trading town, Cordova, near the border. Of all the towns near Sunrise, it could best handle an influx of refugees."

"Do you know the steward in charge?"

"Not well. I believe it's a Mayor Taylor Kite, but I am not certain of this."

"We'll need to check that in the registry—but that's easy enough to do." Prince Kent rose and indicated they continue into the city. "If we leave in two hours, we can make Clover by sundown."

"And leave without the king's permission?" Jared looked amused.

The royal heir snapped his fingers. "That's right. I knew I was forgetting something. Office Keatten." He motioned the man forward. "Can you take this missive to my father and tell his of our plans? He doesn't need to know my whereabouts, only that I've the mind to head out again and continue our diplomacy with other kingdoms."

"And if he asks, Highness?"

Kent made a face, knowing only a lie would keep his father from detaining them. "Say we plan to leave in the morning. For all haste, I can't have anything delayed over debates and counter-intrigue. Our allies in Sunrise depend on it."

"Right away, then, Highness. I will try to return to you as quickly as I am able."

§ §

Their party was making amazing time through Golden. Seven days from Goldview, and they had reached a small town called Songmarie, just twenty miles southwest of the kingdom's capital. Commander Matar rode ahead and made sure to find an acceptable inn and stable for the prince's party to spend the night. The others reached the town not long after and found the Crystine's horses tied outside the one large inn. Majestic, his white war charger, was hard to miss amid the scruffier horses of the townsfolk. The commander was quick to appear and wave them around the back to the small stable and pens available to the inn's guests. Commander Matar followed with Majestic. There was just enough room for the twenty-one horses they travelled with.

Following Commander Matar's suggestion, Prince Par Fantill and his party of seven guards, including Lord Gordar, each had three horses to rotate during the ride. The interesting configuration of riding horses and two ponied mounts had been effective in cutting down their time. On the forced trip, only two horses had needed to be traded for new mounts. Still, the number of horses along for only nine people had gotten them a few looks along the way—which, thankfully, were easily dissuaded by Sealand coin. This recent stop was no exception; it had taken a little convincing and more payment to secure the inn for their purposes.

"At this rate, my father's going to comment on my expenses," Prince Par commented as he was informed of the night's cost.

"I apologize, Highness," Matar replied. "I tried to talk the innkeeper down, but he wouldn't budge. He kept saying horses weren't cheap to feed."

"I'll bet it was the mention of the 'special' guest he has," Lord Gordar said.

"He didn't hear it from me that Prince Par was inquiring for rooms."

"No." Prince Par trusted Commander Matar to keep that a secret. "But Lord Gordar's banner can cause common folks' eyes to shine just as much. Everyone knows a lord lives fairly decently." They had decided to use his cousin's banners to keep attention from the royal. Still, most of the commons knew banners represented someone of higher standing and thus someone with money. It almost made the prince wish for sleeping on the roads. Yet, good food and comfortable beds meant they were better rested for the hard ride. Plus, if a horse or one of their party was injured, they had access to medical care. It had been a toss-up either way, but common sense and simple luxuries won out.

"Well, at least the inn is quiet right now. They had beds for all of us," Matar continued the conversation. "I've asked the innkeeper for a meal to be prepared. It should be ready about now."

"Good, I'm starving!" Prince Par stretched his aching frame after he distributed his horse's tack to the rails. "I'm all up for seeing if it's ready." The others agreed and started in for the warmth and comforts of the inn.

Lord Gordar paused on his way out of the pen area to look back and see that Commander Matar was still with his Crystal stallion. "You're not coming, Commander?"

Matar looked up from brushing Majestic's broad back. "I'll be along soon, Lord Farrylin… I just want to make sure Majestic here is cooled properly and sound." The white charger looked fit as a fiddle and had handled their travel like a veteran; however, Lord Gordar understood the commander's desire. His horse had traversed the whole span of Syre for five seasons and had fought in countless battles besides. Only a well-bred and well-cared-for mount could last such a grueling campaign. "I understand, sir. I'll have your dinner set aside and kept warm."

"My thanks."

Lord Gordar nodded and then followed where his prince and the other guards had disappeared to. His leaving left the stable yard quiet, a nice balm after a hard day in the saddle. Alone, the Crystine commander took to stretching his body. A particular stretch had him groaning. "We're getting too old for this, my friend," he said to Majestic as he straightened and held his aching back. "Someday, we're going to be forced to hang up our spurs." Yet, such a time seemed incomprehensible. Riding, commanding, and fighting were a life Matar knew better than one of leisure. As long as the maunstorz were still about harassing Syre, the commander had no intention of stopping. "Stars preserve me so that I live to see the day peace prevails in Syre."

Majestic bumped his owner, nearly toppling the distracted man. "Easy," Matar chided. "Food's coming." *And then rest. Stars know I need it!* The commander hurried to feed all their mounts—not trusting the innkeeper to feed them up appropriately—and made sure the water tanks were filled before heading in for his own dinner.

Commander Matar came in from the side door that emptied into the main foyer. The place was empty, save for the innkeeper and one guest: a Golden soldier, just arrived. The innkeeper saw the commander's arrival and waved him over. "Commander, sir. This man is looking for a party coming from Sealand. You gents were coming from there, right?"

"We were," Matar replied cautiously. He strode over with his nerves on high alert for trouble.

The soldier at the desk turned around and saluted him as Matar neared. "A commander you say?"

"Yes." He returned the salute. "I am Commander Matar of the Crystine but am travelling with men from Fortress Opal."

The man looked relieved. "Oh, thank goodness, I think I've found you at last! I am Officer Danver, guard to Prince Kent Argetlem. I was sent to meet with you by the prince."

Now that was news Matar liked to hear. "So, they received our report?"

"Yes, sir, hence why I'm here. Prince Kent thought you'd be in need of an escort and royal papers."

"That we are." Matar steered them away from the desk so the innkeeper could stop snooping in on their conversations. "Come. I'll introduce you to the rest."

He led the officer to the dining room, where the others had taken over the three tables. Introductions were made all around, and Officer Danver was shown a seat at Prince Par's table. The royal heir was relieved to hear his letter had been received and actions taken. "So, men are being deployed to the border?"

"Prince Par, I left before hearing word on that account." Danver looked contrite. "But I've no doubt Prince Kent will have a force sent to Sunrise's aid. He felt the urgency in your missive. By your account, I would assume he sent word to some of our forces eastward of the capital to move to Sunrise's aid. If I'm correct, we should angle toward the town of Cordova—as it is closest to the area you said their forces are headed for. I know those roads well enough and can lead you there."

"We are indebted to your assistance, Officer," Prince Par replied. "And we are grateful for your help on this matter. With your guidance, I hope to reach the border in time to save our allies."

"That is my hope, too, Highness. I will lead you as best I can."

"Tomorrow, then, we will leave before sunup. I offer coin for your stay tonight and for any additional horses you may need."

The Goldener looked shocked at the generous offer. "Thank you, Highness, but there is no need. I have been given—"

"There is need," Commander Matar interrupted. "We travel three horses to a rider. I'll go with you about the town after dinner to find decent mounts. Prepare yourself for the ride of your life, Officer. We won't stop until the next sunset."

Chapter Forty-Nine
§
The Gold Bracelet

Traversing northern Sunrise with worry of pursuit made the rescued band of men keep to the marching pace Zyanthena Sheev'arid ordered. About halfway across the grasslands, their path took them just over one hundred miles south of the Red Palace in Rubia and much too close to maunstorz presence to their east and north—or elsewhere as could also be the case.

Their party ventured past two villages, both containing frightened townspeople, and much open land between. Neither of the towns had much in the way of supplies to give, and Prince Rowin refused to take what he could not compensate them for. They ended up getting meager rations of barley and a salted pork shank from a mercantile family. The prince and his lord protector made the deal, leaving the rest of the men on the town's outskirts so as not to frighten the people. Upon their return he declared, "We may have to depend on wild game for the rest. The townsfolk have little food to live on and are scared out of their minds."

"With maunstorz roaming freely, I do not blame them," Loris Ravesbend replied. "Even if it looks as if these towns were not raided, there are enough stories about such atrocities in the Northern kingdoms to keep the populace worried."

"I'm surprised there aren't any raids," Yory Selèv commented, still faithfully beside his prince. "The maunstorz pillaged all over Rubia. Some towns were even razed to the ground."

"That is true. I wonder if the rest of Sunrise fares the same…" Zyanthena's brandy eyes glanced back over the town, looking for any signs of maunstorz damage. There wasn't any. Besides the stores being low—as was expected—there was no other reason for the townspeople to be hostile. "I think we should stay away from other towns until we cross to Golden."

"You've a bad feeling about something?" Lieutenant Dawson asked. He had been dividing the barley into smaller sacks to distribute between their company; without a pack horse, weight had to be evened out on various horses to not overburden them. He straightened from his duties to ask his question.

"Not a feeling per se, Lieutenant. Just... a sense of caution."

"We know better than to not trust your instincts," Lord Darshel agreed. "We will steer clear of other villages. If not for our sake, then theirs."

"Theirs?" Prince Derek asked.

The Shekmann nodded. "You're all fugitives now, wanted by the maunstorz who are controlling these lands—"

"With the king of Sunrise's permission," Prince Rowin added.

"Yes, that too."

"Which means the people could be threatened to reveal information about our whereabouts or for aiding us." The heir of Sunrise was quick to comprehend the problem. "Still, we will need enough food for another week or more."

"Leave that to me and the wolves," Zyanthena promised. "We'll find game to live off of. The rest of our needs will have to wait."

"Great," Prince Connel grumbled. "More sleeping in the cold and suffering the days with empty stomachs."

"Brother." Rowin bumped him with an elbow. "It's no worse than being in the cells of the Red Palace."

"Except now our meals aren't scheduled and the torture's self-inflicted."

It was a crude joke but did get the older Sunarian prince to smile. "Exactly."

"Well, at least we're all in the right mood for this," Prince Jace commented. "Let's get the food distributed and be on our way."

The others nodded and got to work. Shortly after, they were heading away again, angling off the established roads to avoid further towns, and picked up the trotting pace that the horses could handle for several more miles. In the calm of the day, their large group of riders seemed to be the only beings alive in Syre. The snow-covered plain stretched before them like a never-ending ocean. Its barrenness boded ill for game but promised relief from any pending attacks. If only it would last...

"Zyanthena," Prince Rowin called he cued his mount alongside Unrevealed.

"Highness." The warrioress had been adjusting her leather goggles that kept sand out of the eyes in the Aras Desert. Against the glare of the sun reflecting on the snow, the simple contraption gave her the best eyesight of them all. As the royal came up beside her, Zyanthena stopped fiddling with its strings to give the prince her full attention.

"Will you go in search of game now?"

"No. Hunter says there is no sign of anything in the area to hunt, though his pack is constantly on watch for food. They believe more prey will appear as we leave human territory."

"I hope so. We need more than what we have."

"We have enough to survive. As long as our pace stays consistent and we continue to outpace the enemy, everything will be well."

Prince Rowin sighed. "I wish I had your optimism, Tashek." He stretched his battered body, finding it protesting from old bruises and new alike. Riding in the elements after fighting for weeks was leaving him stiff in all the wrong places.

Zyanthena was giving him a careful stare; however, she averted her eyes to the horizon in an attempt to stay casual. "An interesting bracelet you own, Prince Sunrise. With such a valuable item, I'm surprised you didn't barter for better supplies."

The reminder had the Sunarian covering his wrist and looking around to make sure no one else had seen. "This isn't the kind of trinket that should be given away—even in such circumstances."

"One would ask why, especially when it looks to be pure gold."

"You're good at being pushy and polite at the same time."

The Tashek made a noise in her throat, refusing to agree or disagree. "Just remember, Prince, the Tashek are a practical people. Needs essential to survival are more important than material gains."

"This…" Prince Rowin hesitated but finally caved. "This bracelet is the only clue I have that my father could still be alive. It's a codex, of sorts, that may tell me of his whereabouts."

"May tell you?"

"Well, if I can decode it. It's written in three languages: a secret code my informant uses, Sunarian, and Tashek symbols. Aligned by the three sun symbols, they help piece together a message I was given with it. On the paper is written where my father's hideouts were, who he included in his inner circle, and why he left his throne in the first place."

Zyanthena raised her eyebrows in disbelief. "Such information on the former king of Sunrise is of incredible value."

"Yes."

"Too bad you don't have anyone with you who can read both Sunarian and Keshic or is good at puzzles."

His midnight-blue eyes rolled at her less-than-subtle hint. "You think you can crack it? I've tried, as light allowed, all those seasons locked in the dungeons of the Red Palace. It's not that easy."

"One doesn't know until they try."

Rowin chuckled and shook his head. "And one doesn't need to speak in third person to ask for a chance at the code."

He was rewarded with an innocent shrug. "Only if one isn't trying to be too pushy."

"So not subtle, Tashek." The prince looked away to check that they were still not being noticed; however, the rest of their group were preoccupied, the long hours in the saddle narrowing their focus to what was nearest to each of them. "Fine, I will let you look at it. But keep it concealed."

She tsked. "Just who do you think I am? Give me the time for the sun to reach its zenith, Highness, and I'll be able to read your paper."

Prince Rowin doubted that, but he slipped over the folded letter and bracelet under a handkerchief. He was curious to see how much Zyanthena Sheev'arid could decipher of the code he had gotten from the Madame Saida Newdõn, bawdy house owner, in Staria. Besides, they had nothing but time to kill as their party tracked toward Golden, and they might as well fill it with something useful.

§ §

At the appointed hour, Prince Rowin sidled his way back to the desert woman's side. "So?"

Zyanthena smirked. "Awfully impatient, Prince," she teased.

"So you didn't crack it, after all?" He made a face.

"I didn't say that." She looked away across the snow while she handed back his handkerchief. "I'm not sure what your informant told you when they handed over the bracelet and note, but they may have misled you."

Rowin frowned. "What do you mean?"

"The bracelet is the real code, written in Keshic, Sunarian, and Ancient Syrean—the third of which most do not know how to read. The person who etched the saying must have had only had a basic understanding of Syrean themselves, as the writing is crude. Still, I could make it out. As for the letter: it is coded, but in Keshic only, and the names mentioned seem to be code names themselves—I assume to protect the real identities of the contacts. Only your father would know these people—if he named them himself."

"She lied to me." The prince was distracted by that point. "But why?"

"I would think because your informant could not read the scripts and thought that you—being the king's son—would be able to."

Prince Rowin squeezed the gold bracelet in his palm until his knuckles were white. "I just don't understand. All this time, I thought this would help me. Instead, it is another dead end."

"Not exactly, Highness. Though you may not like the answer it presents."

"Answer?"

"Yes. I did say I could read the inscription." Zyanthena glanced the royal's way only until she had his attention, and then she looked away again to the horizon. "The Sunarian, I assume, you can read."

"Yes." The prince rolled the bracelet in his fingers as he read aloud the words he had memorized over weeks. "'I have forsaken my blood for that of another of greater importance.'"

"'The line of Kestral must be protected at the cost of all others,'" Zyanthena continued with the Keshic phrase and ended with the Syrean. "'And where the child is, there I will be also, as I have vowed to the woman I love.' It is signed with the mark of the Red Sun, used in the Syrean religious sects for the Red Star and its ruby Stone of Power."

"Why would my father write something like that?"

The Tashek sighed. "Certainly, you can't be so dense? King Richard made that bracelet as a vow and a reminder of that vow."

"But a vow to my mother, Sylvia? He would rather protect a child born of this 'line of Kestral' than continue his rule over Sunrise? He would rather abandon me for this child and give his brother this throne?!"

"The vow was not to your mother," Zyanthena countered.

The words startled the heir of Sunrise, who looked like he had been physically socked in the gut. "What?"

Her lips pursed, as Zyanthena debated on whether to tell the prince the truth; the knowledge would hurt him deeply. However, when he asked again for clarification, she gave it to him. "Kestral is the woman he refers to. Queen Kestral Xraxrain. The vow was to her."

"Queen Kestral? My father loved Queen Kestral?"

With her mother's soul trapped in the obsidian, Zyanthena knew the truth far more intimately than most. For just a moment, she wavered as Kestral imparted the memories of long ago. It seemed cruel for the prince to find out his father had left his throne for another woman—worse still, that King Richard had shared Kestral with another man, the king of Crystalynian. It was not unheard of for those of Tashek heritage to form such relationships as two men loving one woman or a woman two men; it was not common practice but was allowed as long as all parties stayed respectful of each other. Zyanthena sensed Kestral was leaving out a great deal—including why King Richard had left his wife, Sylvia, and given his throne to Raymond Sunrise—but she suspected it was for one reason: herself.

"Zy'ena? Sheev'arid, did you not hear me?"

"I heard, Highness." Zyanthena came back to herself, disconcerted by the facts her mother had laid out. She took in a breath. "Your father gave his vow to protect the princess of Crystalynian. The bracelet does not give a date, but it would have to be around the time of the kingdom's fall. A journal I read at Crystanian confirms such an action."

"The princess? The line of Kestral… but the child—?"

"Would be me, if you follow the logic to its conclusion." The Tashek felt Rowin's gaze upon her, shocked at the deduction she had led him to. There was confusion too, and anger, in that look—or so she guessed. Yet she dared not glance over to confirm it. "However, Prince Rowin, there is a problem with that message."

"What is it?" His voice came out steely.

"If your father was with the child—with me—he is no longer." She forced her brandy eyes to look at the royal. Zyanthena saw Rowin flinch at her words. "And I do not recall such a guardian in my memories as Zerra Starkindler." She motioned to the bracelet, forgotten in the prince's hand. "Your father vowed to be with me, to protect me, but I know no such man in my life. Your bracelet and codex of contacts has led you to the key to your father's disappearance, and yet I can give you no answer to his whereabouts. I am sorry, Highness. It is my fault for insisting I could read such a code. Instead, I give you such painful news."

Prince Rowin was quiet for a long time, and the clench of his jaw showed he was seething silently at this new information. Finally, he worked through his turmoiled thoughts enough to say to Zyanthena, "This is not your fault, Sheev'arid. It seems all these years I was mistaken over the kind of man my father was. I had hopes that his disappearance was for some better reason: illness, injury, or some kind of grand bravado." He choked on the words and clutched his father's bracelet tightly. "But I was wrong. He left his throne, his family, and his people for such ignoble reasons as a selfish love for a woman and child not his own. I've been chasing a ghost of a man who does not exist."

"That may be, Prince, or maybe not. I cannot tell you," Zyanthena replied. "But I do know someone who could provide more answers than me. A man who was around at the time all this happened." His eyes shone with hope—mixed with lingering anger—at the statement. "Commander Matar of the Crystine served the Starkindlers as far back as the time I was taken in by them. He may be able to tell us more about what happened around that time. Perhaps he even knows what happened to King Richard after delivering the princess and why he left her."

Prince Rowin scoffed. "Such tidbits of my father's past have been a lure to me all these years, but these new details…" He looked to the bracelet. "They have me reluctant to pursue such leads. Yet… I still feel such hope when I hear that information such as that exists. Only a child's desire keeps me clinging to such stupid notions."

"It's not stupid to wish to know one's parents and their reasons. Your father may seem selfish—now that you discovered this vow he made to Queen Xraxrain—but he was known as a just king, valiant and chivalrous. I believe there is a clear picture of his reasons for doing all he did. Do not let this one piece of your father be what defines him for you—at least not until you know the whole truth. There is much left for you to discover, Highness."

"If one was to have a Tashek's faith for in life, we'd all be steadfast against any qualms." The statement sounded sardonic to her ears.

"On the contrary, Prince of Sunrise, having such optimism does not come without any doubts. It is their duality that gives each of us the choice to choose to be courageous or cynical. I just choose to follow the former."

Prince Rowin's features softened at the wisdom, and he looked at his father's bracelet with more thoughtfulness. "Then I will choose to follow your advice and speak with the Crystine commander when next we see him."

"Which may be soon, Highness, if Matar got my message—and, knowing him, I have little doubt that he did. The truth about King Richard may be closer to your grasp than you think."

"I'll give a Star's hope that you are right, Tashek. I could use some better answers about my father right about now."

Chapter Fifty
§
Let It Rain Lightning

The thirteenth day of their grueling march dawned clear as far as the eye could see—which was to the looming Pika Mounts in the west. The natural rise of hills had many of the men coming to their feet with cheers of rejoice and revived spirits. The Pika Mounts signaled the Golden border; they were about twenty miles away from safety and a place to rest beyond maunstorz-controlled Sunrise.

The four princes were given the last of the coffee while the others took a watered-down tea of rosehips. The soldiers were quick to pack while the royals warmed up from the cold morning by sitting about the last of the fires. Only Prince Rowin, used to fending for his own equipment over all his years running around Syre undercover, found the idea selfish that the highnesses were doted on while the rest of their party made and broke down the camps. Of course, none of the other royals shared the sentiments. Still, the soldiers had firmly insisted that Prince Rowin keep himself from underfoot. They were anxious enough about it that the Sunarian had finally relented his duties to join his fellow royals in the daily, morning ritual of coffee about the fire.

"We've almost made it," Prince Jace said as his green eyes studied the dark rise of hills in the distance. "I am ready for real food and a decent bed."

"If the Goldeners will provide such," Prince Connel griped as he wrapped his cold hands around his metal mug to keep them warm. "They can be stingy."

"They will. They are our allies," said Prince Rowin.

The younger Sunarian rolled his eyes at his brother's comment. "There are few towns large enough to house refugees, and none have decent lodgings to begin with, only simple inns."

"Which will be enough," Rowin countered again. "And Zyanthena promised word was sent ahead of our need for aid. The Golden crown should be aware of our situation by now."

"You really trust that woman," Prince Jace jeered.

"Sheev'arid has done plenty for us all. Beyond rescuing us from the enemy, she's led us unerringly toward Golden and provided meat we'd otherwise not have. I would say we owe her a debt."

The Havener scoffed and gulped down the last of his coffee. "I agree with your brother. I won't hold my breath on Golden hospitality. Yet I'm all for a real bed after sleeping huddled on the frozen ground. Are you done?" Prince Jace motioned for Prince Derek's coffee mug. The pale Rubian was rarely one to talk in the morning, as he was too busy shivering. Upon being spoken to, the royal passed up his cup. The haughty heir of Blue Haven collected it with a shake of his head at Derek Chível's customary muteness. "I just hope getting this one into the warm indoors will bring some life back to him. It's like packing along a corpse."

"As if you'd fare any better being sick and barely clad in rags," Prince Rowin threw back. "And stop speaking as if he is not here."

"You do it too," Jace pointed out as he loaded the cups into his bag.

Prince Rowin tsked and passed over his cloak to Prince Derek. "I am sorry for that, Highness."

The Rubian eyed the cloak for a long moment before accepting it. "It's no problem. I'm more than used to being looked poorly upon because of my condition. I've learned to ignore such comments." Still, the sickly royal did look moderately improved with the extra layer of warmth. His bluish skin started to pink up. It was a relief to see the gesture had helped.

"We are ready to depart, Highnesses," Zyanthena Sheev'arid informed them, coming to the fire with snow to douse it.

"How does it seem?" Rowin asked as he rose to help with the task.

Brandy eyes flickered to the royal and then away, as they had begun to do since their private talk over the bracelet days before. Since learning she was the reason for King Richard's abandonment of his family and kingdom, the warrioress had given the royal heir a respectful berth to think over his feelings on the matter. Still, Zyanthena would speak candidly on matters of importance, when asked. "The land looks quiet and the way is clear. We should reach Golden by dusk."

"And the men?" Prince Rowin had learned the soldiers spoke more freely to the Tashek woman than to himself and the other princes. Her skills in getting them out of the Command Front so secretively had earned the men's trust as his own position as their heir had not.

"Are tired, hungry, and cold—as we all are—but spirits are high now that Golden is so near."

"That's good."

Zyanthena eyed the princes, assessing them as keenly as she had the soldiers. Everyone looked to be at their ropes' end. "I suggest we get a move on."

It was her usual phrase to the start of the morning. The Tashek had been a slave driver on their pace. Even being so close to their destination did not diminish her sense of caution. "We're on it."

The warrioress bowed and turned on a heel to disappear among the bodies of horses and men. Her leaving had Prince Jace scoffing as he came back over to collect the last of the items for the packs. "That woman doesn't relax for a second. If anything, she's more on edge today than when we started from the Command Front."

"I think it's a Tashek trait to be ever watchful. At least, I've never seen one that wasn't." That Prince Derek had spoken to the Havenese at all shocked the other three princes to a stunned silence; that he was so astute was another matter entirely. The Rubian ignored their stares as he stood and went to the horse he shared with Yory. When they were still eyeing him once he had mounted, finally prompted Derek to say more. "What? I was just making an observation."

"A good one," Rowin praised offhandedly as he too mounted up. "I would concur with your assessment. That we have one along gives me relief. Everyone will be less on guard because our destination is so near. That Zyanthena will be vigilant will keep us from any mistakes today." He motioned for his brother and Prince Jace to find their mounts—as everyone else was horseback. "You two coming?"

"As if you'd leave without us." Connel grabbed the reins of his mount. He swung aboard his black cavalry charger and settled the antsy horse with an experienced touch. "I'm all for getting to Golden today and not sleeping another night outside."

Prince Jace rolled his eyes at the Sunarians and swung his pack behind his horse's saddle to tie it down—correctly for once, as the days on the run had forced him to acquire the skill. "And Stars preserve me, I might actually get a break from all of you."

"Ah, come on, Prince Jace! You'd miss us after the weeks we've been through."

A dour look came to Prince Jace's face at the Rubian heir's teasing. Now that the sickly royal was warmer, he was lively with his words again—and an annoyance to the stuck-up Havener. "Hardly. I've had almost as much of this princely reunion to last a year."

"Now, now." Prince Derek grinned. "It's not the time for us to fight like children."

"We are not that." Prince Jace muttered back as he mounted. Aboard, he looked about for any signs that they were heading out. It served as a distraction from saying anything more the other prince. To his relief, the Lord Shekmann called out that everyone was to get a move on. They all formed up and headed westward as the last vestiges of dawn lit the sky.

§ §

Zyanthena and her wolves trailed their party. Now that they were so close to Golden, she could see the men were distracted by the lure of the Pika Mounts. It meant their flank was left wide open—a position any Tashek would worry over. It didn't help that Swift Hunter and the pack were restless of something approaching, though the landscape remained clear behind them. Knowing it was not the first time Zyanthena had heard of maunstorz catching up to riders, she asked her lupine companions to keep a wary eye out for any movements. Until there was cause to be concerned, however, she kept their news to herself, so as to not ruin the men's good spirits.

However, as high noon approached, the warrioress became more and more convinced that their good luck had run out. *Something*—a smell, unusual and fleeting—was in the air to make the wolves jittery.

Unassumingly as she could, Zyanthena angled Unrevealed around the group to Lord Darshel's side. The lord-governor of Kavahad was speaking with Loris Ravesbend about battle tactics as a means to pass the time. Still, he was quick to give the desert woman his attention as she appeared by his side. "Zy'ena. How does our rear flank look?"

"The landscape remains clear, My Lordship," she used his title in hopes of alerting the Shekmann to her concern. "But the pack is restless."

Lord Darshel frowned. "And what is it that you're not saying?"

"I think we need to send out scouts to our quadrants and have them use scopes to search beyond what our eyes can see."

"The enemy nears?" Commander Ravesbend asked.

Zyanthena shook her head. "Not that I or the wolves can sense—but that concerns me even more. I would like to be the one to backtrack our trail, just to be certain."

That the Tashek was acting so cautious had Darshel coming more to attention. "We'll organize immediately."

"Don't worry, Your Lordship, Sheev'arid," Commander Loris said, getting their attention. "I know which of my men to send out for a look-about. Leave this to me." The Sunarian man turned his horse aside and cantered away to tell the men. Six were quick to agree to the command and headed away north, west, and south.

"Take someone with you," Lord Darshel ordered of Zyanthena.

"I will take Dawson," she replied. "Keep the horses to a sedate trot. I will be back shortly."

The four scouting parties caught back up with the group in about twenty minutes. Not a one had seen anything of concern. The land was clear. Such news perturbed the Tashek woman—she still felt uneasy—but it soothed the fears of the others. Having the go-ahead that all looked fine, the party increased their pace again, while Zyanthena Sheev'arid took up her position at the rear. Still, there was no sign of life by the time the Senna River came into view. Once their party crossed over the wide river, they would be in Golden.

"There is a bridge about one mile to the south of here," Prince Rowin was telling Lord Shekmann as their group paused on the bank of the great river. The Senna River was wide and the current strong. Its cold depths looked very uninviting. "It's a trader's bridge. The road from it goes to Cordova, governed by Mayor Kite and his people. I have met with their administration before."

"Then we head south," Lord Shekmann agreed, eyeing the river with distaste. "I'm not sure any of us would fare well swimming across that."

The two Ravesbend soldiers were ordered to turn their horses about and yell out orders to the others. Tired men, some of whom had dismounted to ease their aching bodies, were slow to respond to the command. Everyone, horses included, were looking exhausted.

Which made them the perfect targets.

Zyanthena and her wolves were the first to sense the change in the air. That smell that had caused their restlessness earlier came on stronger than ever before, making many of the wolves whine. The Tashek was quick to respond to their warning, spinning Unrevealed around and asking him to canter up the slight hill that hid their view from the grasslands of Sunrise. At the top of the hill, the black stallion balked and reared at something in the disturbed grass beyond. A moment later, Zyanthena caught a shape just out of her vision: a large cat prowling, hunkered low.

Angling her head for a better look, Zyanthena tried to make it out, but the large feline—a snow leopard, she thought—blended into the white and brown landscape like a dream. The smell, however, was more distinguishable now that the Tashek was so close to the creature; it had a distinct tingle of majik mixed with the scent of pine and crude earth. "A snow leopard in Sunrise means only one thing…" she surmised. *Ravel is near.*

"Enemy!" Zyanthena yelled out just as the big cat came lunging from its hiding place. Unrevealed reared out of instinct and struck at the magical beast. The leopard's enraged snarl was loud enough to alert the wolves to its danger. The pack bounded up the hill to protect their master from the wild thing.

The men couldn't get a good look at what was attacking their Tashek scout, but her words had them all to action. The soldiers scrambled to get mounted while their commander and his son yelled for them to start a gallop south. "Hurry, hurry! South. Follow the river south!"

While the men hastened to comply, Zyanthena and her pack were still in the throes of attack with the snow leopard. Though the animal responded with screams of fury at the wolf bites, the unnatural creature was unfazed by the deep wounds. It confirmed to the warrioress: this was no ordinary cat but the animal companion to Ravel. Only majik would stop it. "Hunter, call them back. I must use Vauldin."

The large grey wolves jumped back immediately, giving their master room to call upon the obsidian's powers.

Unsheathing her *kora* blade, Zyanthena called for electricity. The blue-white charge sparked down her sword and continued beyond, licking its tendrils greedily at the magical animal. The power folded around the snow leopard and began to singe its beautiful fur. The creature screamed and writhed in agony before disappearing in a cloud of smoke.

In the wake of its dying screams, Zyanthena heard the distant sounds of armor jangling and heavy footsteps marching out a running pace. The maunstorz were nearing! "Hunter, Ember, we must go! Follow the others," she directed the pack and reined Unrevealed around to find the group had listened to her warning yell. A large swath of horse tracks followed the river's embankment south; everyone had gotten away cleanly. She asked the black charger and wolves to their fastest speeds as they followed in the wake of their party's horses.

Her quicker animals caught up with the group, and Zyanthena angled around the men until she was near the outside flank. If the enemy closed in on them, she wanted herself and Vauldin to be the first thing the maunstorz encountered...

Their group seemed to outrun the enemies—until the bridge of their salvation appeared ahead with a full mass of maunstorz fighters between it and them. They realized too late that their adversaries had created a diversionary attack to funnel them down to the real force. It was a brilliant pincer move.

"Halt!" Lord Darshel yelled, hearing Prince Rowin and the Ravesbends echo his order. Their horses were pulled up.

"They have us surrounded!" someone shouted.

Indeed, the enemies Zyanthena had heard pursuing could be seen behind them, while ahead lay the brunt of their problem.

"We should head back into Sunrise," a man suggested.

"No!" Zyanthena galloped forward to the head of their group. "We must reach Golden. Our only chance is getting to our allies."

"But these men are unarmed," Lord Darshel hissed. "Most will be slaughtered."

Brandy eyes flashed. "You have me, Darshel, and I have your faith. Get these men safely to Golden."

"But what—?"

However, she had spun Unrevealed away, signaling him for a charge at the enemy mass ahead of them. Alone, she and the black stallion galloped straight for the maunstorz blocking the way to the bridge.

Lord Darshel was stricken. "Zyen!!"

"Your Lordship, we must protect our rear!" Commander Ravesbend yelled at him. "All men with arms to our rear! Highnesses, to the inside! Soldiers, get ready to skirmish!"

But fight with what? Only thirteen men had any decent weapons along—all those Zyanthena and Darshel had brought from Crystanian. Those men so armed came to the outside to raise their weapons against what looked to be nearly one hundred and fifty maunstorz closing in from the south and northwest. It seemed a futile defense.

"Stars! What in the blazes it that?" One man then another yelled out. The words had everyone looking skyward to where the men pointed.

The formerly clear sky had darkened to an ominous grey while they had been scrambling into position. A bizarre rumbling, like thunder being boiled in a pot, came from the cloud. Its threatening mass had even the enemy maunstorz slowing their advance.

"You will let these people through!" a voice screamed, and the men realized it was Zyanthena Sheev'arid speaking, as if her voice was amplified by the dark cloud she had conjured. "Stand your men down, leader of the maunstorz, or *so help me*, I will bring down the full extent of Vauldin's fury!"

The desert warrioress had stopped Unrevealed in the distance between the main maunstorz force and the men she had rescued. Her hair and the black's were standing up wildly in the electric field she had called out of Vauldin; it made the pair look especially evocative and unearthly. The sight called all eyes to their location.

"I will not warn you again!" Zyanthena spoke once more and raised her arm in the air. "If you have witnessed the power of your own wielder's crystal, then you know I am not bluffing. I will have these men safely across to Golden, and you will leave this field today without attacking us."

The maunstorz shuffled, nervous at the unusual manner that they were being addressed, but the fact that they outnumbered their quarry three to one kept them confident enough not to lower their weapons. One of the enemies, bearing the rank marks of a general, stepped forward. The leader yelled something in their harsh tongue. His command made the fighters come to attention and ready their weapons; he planned to fight.

"So be it," Zyanthena murmured to herself and closed her eyes to feel the potential energy she had amassed in the cloud above her.

Calling on the powerful element from inside the accumulation of cloud, Zyanthena began to chant in Ancient Syrean a phrase that promised death and destruction. Just as she heard the sounds of enemies taking up a charge-chant, the Queen of the Black Star unleashed the untapped power stored in Vauldin over the past two weeks. In an astonishing display, the obsidian stone called out lightning from the grey cloud. Its wielder focused the harnessed energy on the enemies' weapons, feeling the ferocious element leap for them in gleeful abandon.

In a loud clap of thunder, the lightning came down in a spray of sparks and white-blue heat to char the maunstorz where they were. In an instant, more than two-thirds of the enemy lay in charcoaled heaps on the melted plain. The remaining maunstorz cowered back, chattering among themselves before choosing to turn tail and run. The enemies left the shaken Syreans behind.

The men Zyanthena had just saved were stunned to silence, rooted in place by their incomprehension and awe. All except for Lord Shekmann. Accustomed to the heir of Crystalynian's powers, he recovered enough to shout, "Zyen!" and cued Tano to race to where the Tashek and mount had stood just moments before. The warrioress had fallen from Unrevealed and lay by his front feet. The stallion stood over his charge like a silent guardian and almost didn't let the lord-governor near. "It's me, boy, and Tano. You know us. Please, I need to get to Zyen," Lord Darshel crooned as he approached the war charger. The Shekmann was finally allowed to the woman's side, where he gingerly rolled her over. "Zyen, Zy'ena!"

Just as she had during other immense invocations of power, she was knocked out cold. Around her neck, Vauldin still flashed with untapped power that seemed to sizzle and spark with a burst of lightning. The sight had the lord-governor backing off long enough for the stone to become dormant once more.

"How is she?" Prince Rowin asked, having been the first to recover from his shock and come after the lord-governor. His eyes were wide as he took in the aftermath of the majik. Concern tightened his features as he turned his focus to look over the condition of their savior. Had she sacrificed her life to save everyone?

"Alive and unconscious," Lord Darshel assured him as he touched the Tashek's beautiful face and tenderly put her hair back to rights. "And would probably be furious to find us not hurrying to the safety she secured us."

"I don't think we need to worry about that anymore," Prince Rowin replied. He lifted a hand to point westward. "Her display has called in the cavalry." Banners and horses were seen galloping up the road from Cordova. "Zyanthena single-handedly saved the day. There'll be nothing left for Golden to do but escort us into town."

Chapter Fifty-One
§
Observer

A safe distance from the rest of their force, Zeek Starkindler sat atop a Pika Mount on the Golden side of the Senna River and watched as the two forces made their stand by the Cordovan bridge. Not one to dispute his leader's forces, the prince had only done as much as Zephthaniel had bidden: observe how the Fifth general of the armies performed in recapturing their prisoners.

Exactly twelve days before, Zeek and the leader of the People of Xercon had made their usual rounds to the other camps—it was easy to travel with Ravel's powers. Their arrival at the Red Palace and Command Front had been met with humiliated bows, as both the great *seka'vlr*, Mansocan, and Chaenyeu, general of the Command Front, had been unable to keep their charges under lock and key.

The story was the same at both places: the prisoners had disappeared without a trace.

Disappointed in them, Zephthaniel had appointed Zeek to use his magic to search for traces of the Syreans. At the Red Palace, a faint signature had led to an old Estarian church, then disappeared; however, at Chaenyeu's post, Zeek's leopard led them across untouched snow to the Command Front's west until a track of hoofprints—enough to number the count of horses stolen—were found. The tactic was sneaky and disguised, which was how Zeek had come to realize what had happened. The prince reported back to Zephthaniel that a Stone of Power had to have been involved for such an elaborate cover-up. The talent of the wielder meant it was only one person (to his knowledge): Vauldin's heir.

Zeek had offered to track and recapture the escaped prisoners, but Zephthaniel had refused, saying his generals should take responsibility. *Seka'vlr* Mansocan, arrogant as usual, had refused to humble himself, saying he didn't need the three royals that had escaped. Besides, the *seka'vlr* had control of Sunrise and Rubia without need of the heirs. In the end, his logic had won Mansocan a short reprieve from punishment.

Chaenyeu, however, was much more subservient and vowed he would bring back all the prisoners. Promising everything would be handled, the Fifth and his *vsenk* had marched out at a run from the Command Front, following the trail of horse tracks. True to their word, the general's force caught up to the escapees just before they reached the Golden-Sunrise border. The effort was amusing to the prince, who had tracked them from a distance, watching and judging, with the sight of his animal companion.

The general's plans of pincering the Syreans and forcing them to flee south into a trap had been brilliant—until one, lone rider had galloped ahead of the runaway men and set herself as a barrier. Suspecting the rider to be the wielder of Vauldin—only someone with the means to be a terrifying buffer would have the balls to go forth alone before a great enemy force—gave the prince a new appreciation for the tenacity of the heir of Crystalynian. Zeek had shivered when the woman began to craft the dark cloud above herself and her horse and then warned Chaenyeu's forces to withdraw. The power she summoned upon their defiance was electrifying; even from his seat all the way across the river, Zeek felt its potent energy. He knew then that Chaenyeu's forces were done for—even before the blow was struck.

And what a blow it was! The rain of lightning the warrioress called from the cloud was incredible and deadly. Called to the metal in each *vsenk's* hand, it struck down the entire force in one definitive thunderclap. When it was all over, only charred pieces remained of two hundred eighty good fighters.

"Zephthaniel was right," Zeek whispered to himself, his body still shaking from the aftermath. "The obsidian stone is the most fearsome of the Stones of Power by far. That woman"—he couldn't bring himself to say *sister*—"is our greatest threat to the campaign." She would need to be dealt with if the people of Xercon were to take over Syre.

Without another glance, Zeek Starkindler teleported himself back to his *xercon'vlr*. The great leader would know how to handle this problem with the heir of Vauldin.

Chapter Fifty-Two
§
Reunion

Zyanthena came back to consciousness and found herself lying in a comfortable bed with a thick duvet. A strong arm was wrapped around her waist, holding her against the person's body. The sensation panicked her for a moment until Moon Ember's blue-and-gold eyes popped into view and the she-wolf informed her master to not worry over the Lord Shekmann's closeness; he had been with the Tashek since she had passed out six days before. When the Tashek hadn't woken, the lord-governor had refused to leave her bedside. According to Ember, it was the first, good sleep the Kavahadian had taken—and he had only climbed into bed as reassurance that Zyanthena was still alive.

The wolf's words were enough to calm her. Zyanthena sank back into Lord Darshel's chest and let his firmness ground her back into the world. "Tell me," she said near-inaudibly, knowing the grey wolf could hear, "what has happened since I used Vauldin?"

Moon Ember sat back on her haunches and proceeded to give the Crystalynian heir a detailed report on all the wolves had heard. First off, using Vauldin had saved everyone. The few remaining maunstorz had turned tail and run, though the knights from Cordova had made sure to hunt them down. Cordova was where Zyanthena was now. Prince Kent Argetlem had shown up to muster the Cordovan forces and to negotiate arrangements with the mayor. As luck would have it, one of the knights was well off and had volunteered his acreage and home for the refugees. Of course, the Golden crown promised to pay any costs for their lodging and health needs.

Among other news, another party had arrived, from Sealand: the royal heir, his lord protector, and bodyguards. One man, in particular, had come to see Zyanthena and had been distressed to find her unconscious.

"Commander Matar," she guessed. Moon Ember gave her best impression of a human nod. "Thank the Stars. I had hoped he would come..." The Tashek let out a sigh of relief.

Lord Darshel murmured in his sleep then, startling Zyanthena to silence as his arm spasmed around her waist. The Shekmann lord shifted and freed the Tashek from his grasp as he rolled over. Unencumbered,

Zyanthena rose to a seated position and studied the lord-governor long enough to know he was deep asleep before she slipped from the bed. She murmured thanks to Moon Ember as the she-wolf brought her the brocade dress she had worn. Fully dressed—including boots she found by the door—Zyanthena and Moon Ember exited the room, leaving His Lordship with the rest of the pack; everyone looked in need of sleep.

Alone in the hallway, Zyanthena stretched her body, groaning as it protested from being still so long. "Curses, Ember, if I keep blacking out from using Vauldin, I'm going to feel as if I'm eighty summers old!"

Moon Ember gave her a dubious stare and mouthed back that the Tashek should stop overdoing it with the silly thing.

Zyanthena tsked. "I see I'll get no sympathy from you." She motioned for the grey wolf to lead the way through the knight's keep—a full castle, it seemed, upon inspection from a window. "This knight has to be rich to afford all this."

Moon Ember answered her that the man was comfortable, but he had not let his money go to his head—being chivalrous and knightly and whatnot.

"You sound like you think he is a charmer," she teased and was rewarded with an irritated nip to her thigh; nothing painful, just a friendly reminder to behave. "I was just teasing you. Do you think you can find Commander Matar?"

The she-wolf huffed a *Who do you think I am?* and began to lead the way to the main floor of the castle. Following her wolf-nose, they headed outside to a small veranda set within a garden of roses. Even in the depths of Deepest Snows, the area was a lovely spot to relax and take in some sunshine. For its one occupant, a man used to the cold of the Crystal Kingdom, the day most likely seemed perfect.

Commander Matar was sitting with his back to the castle, reading a book and enjoying some tea. He looked well rested for someone who had just ridden from Sealand at cavalry pace. Still as fit as a fiddle, the Crystine leader could outpace men half his age. The thought that the commander had ridden that far and that hard, all because Zyanthena had asked him, gave the Tashek woman a greater appreciation for his friendship. Still, the warrioress couldn't help sneaking up behind the man, just for old time's sake.

"You know that doesn't work on me, right? My Night Fox." Commander Matar dropped his book to the table and stood to greet his

Tashek scout. She had been gone from his side for too long and he would not waste pleasantries on her.

"Master." Zyanthena's smile showed her deep affection for the Crystine man.

"Don't just give me that," Matar teased back and spread his arms to indicate he wished a hug. Zyanthena gave in and stepped into his fatherly embrace, relieved to finally have the opportunity to see him again. "Ah," Matar sighed. "Now that is better. All these seasons without you made this old man fret over what had become of you, but you look to be doing just fine."

"I apologize for giving you cause to worry."

The commander waved away the words. "I knew better. You're not one to get into trouble easily—at least, not without getting out if it just as well."

Zyanthena pretended offense. "I do believe you just said *I do* get into trouble—as in a lot."

"All in good fun, my Night Fox." Matar released her and waved the Tashek to the other chair beside his own. "I believe we have much to catch up on."

"A detail or two." Zyanthena settled and accepted a teacup. She found herself suddenly parched, now that drink was before her. The tea was downed in three good gulps.

"My, I should have brought a pitcher!"

"Sorry, Master. My first thought was of seeing you, not attending to other needs."

"Then, we shan't stay too long so that you can get proper food and hydration."

"I'm sure we could be here a while. You must have a bit to tell… you were in Sealand, or so the prince claimed."

"Yes, and that is a story. But you first, *Heir of Crystalynian*."

Zyanthena blushed at the title but knew better than to circumvent the commander's inquiries for her own. Of their two adventures, hers would definitely be more epic. Without further ado, she began a detailed report of all the happenings since leaving the commander at the Citadel of Light in Staria. It was quite the tale, hunting the maunstorz across Staria and Rubia only to realize an ambush had been set up near Carmine. How their party had been forced into the wilds of Crystalynian and then whittled down to small numbers. In the end, herself and Lord Shekmann had been pursued all the way to the ruins of Crystanian.

The parts of Vauldin's awakening she had to skim over as being in a coma had left her bereft of any awareness; however, the insights afterward and the heir's studies since filled in the lack of knowledge of those weeks.

"And using those old pillars. How did you figure that out?"

"I found an old compendium hidden away in the walls of Crystanian's library. You would be intrigued with all the people of the Second Age could do with contraptions and majiks. The use of the obelisks as well. The stones can activate the obelisks, but it's the ancient Syrean chants that call one obelisk to another."

Commander Matar gave the Tashek woman an odd stare, studying her far too critically. "Very few can read ancient Syrean script and none intelligently. You yourself were not too proficient, last time I checked."

Zyanthena held his gaze for a long moment as she analyzed the remark. It wasn't like the commander to sound suspicious. "Yes, well… I didn't just wake from my coma knowing it, if that's your concern. I had help learning to read and speak it."

"Help?"

"From two sources. The first was Queen Kestral."

Just the name had Matar frozen in shock. "Kestral," he whispered. "Kestral is—?"

"Not alive but not dead, either. Her soul is trapped inside Vauldin as penalty for using forbidden majik."

The commander looked stricken. "Such a penalty? No one should have to live an eternity in such a state."

Zyanthena pulled Vauldin from her bodice and held it aloft. Its obsidian facets glowed with a pulsing inner light, like flashes of lightning or the beat of a heart. It was beautiful in all its deadly power. "Kestral knows what her sentence is for and is willing to pay such a price. For all the horror you may think she endures, she would tell you it was worth seeing her daughter grown to womanhood."

Commander Matar looked torn by the answer. Reluctantly, he reached a hand out toward Vauldin yet paused before touching the Stone of Power.

His reaction was interesting for a Guardian of the Prism. It made her begin to wonder something… but the idea seemed ludicrous. "*Khataum?*"

Matar blinked and began to withdraw his hand. "Long have I wanted to see Vauldin again, but I'm afraid to touch such a volatile stone."

"It won't activate without my touch," Zyanthena assured him and set the obsidian between them. Without her contact, Vauldin went dark, seemed a plain stone once more. Without its flashing brilliance, the Crystine man finally reached for it and fingered its facets with nostalgia. His distant eyes made the Tashek say more. "You've seen it before, then? Vauldin and other stones?"

"Yes," the Khataum admitted. "Back when the Stones of Power were used in the Battle of Bil'cordys."

Bil'cordys, Zyanthena had learned in the Crystanian library, was a small town north of the Crystanian Palace. It had been just west of the field where Vauldin had activated its soul magic. The memory of all those souls flying around her were testament to how high the cost had been during that fight… and right after it was when Queen Kestral had used Vauldin to try to bring back King Trev'shel and Prince Verrin. Instead, the palace and its surrounding had been brought to ruin by earthshaking power.

"Then you knew my parents?" Like Rowin Sunrise, Zyanthena hadn't known about her father at all, except what Kestral said of the man; however, mother and daughter hadn't really explored that avenue much over the last seasons. The heir of Crystalynian had been more focused on getting proficient enough with Vauldin to counter Ravel's wielder, and Kestral had agreed with the need.

"Of course." Matar dropped his hands to the table, Vauldin still in his palms, to give his Tashek scout his full attention. "I can tell you anything you want to know."

"Are you *Jusoreen*, the man my father writes about in his journals?"

"*Jusoreen.*" The word was not spoken as a question. Matar knew the Keshic title of "a brave man or a man of great conviction." Still, it was obvious he was going to make Zyanthena fish for the details.

"Yes. *Jusoreen.* My father wrote of him often, but there is one poem, in particular, that makes we wonder about the man. Not many in Crystalynian spoke Keshic like Trev'shel. Even Kestral, a quarter

Sheev'anee herself, rarely spoke it from her accounts. Yet if you were known to them, *Khataum*, then you could be one to speak with him proficiently."

Matar's mouth twitched into a half smile. "You love your puzzles, my Night Fox," he said without really replying, Tashek fashion. "And what about this poem was so profound for you?"

Zyanthena stared back at the man she had served under for nearly three summers—a man who, in Princess Zerra's memories, was a competent protector of the Crystal crown. He was still a mystery to most around him, and Matar did not share his secrets readily. For this new look into his past, the commander was being especially stubborn. So, instead of replying directly, the warrioress spoke the words, now memorized from weeks imprisoned by the snows. "*E Jusoreen, al'ma, tenn'en sièd en noum, besh'en alm eín tân'shaumen. E Jusoreen, al'ma, si elen'een mai'ya auss'oum? Si tenn'alm saum etaul, e Jusoreen, ten'alma, ten'esh allauma?*"

The translation from Keshic was: "Oh, *Jusoreen*, my friend, when all is said and done, be'est mine until thy setting sun. Oh *Jusoreen*, my friend, can we share thee until thy end? Can we make our love last true, oh *Jusoreen*, our beloved, our dearest friend?"

The commander's eyes had closed when she spoke the Keshic. He seemed lost in the sweetness of the words. Only when silence had finally swept away the last of the sounds did he open them. "It's beautiful. Those words."

"And spoken to a man close to his heart. Kestral says that man was—"

"King Richard of Sunrise was referred to, sometimes, by the name *Jusoreen*, though only the king and queen of Crystalynian ever referred to him by that name."

Zyanthena's features looked flat at being interrupted. "Yes, well… that was my other suspicion." Still, she stared at the commander for a long moment, reaching into his gaze as if she could find his soul and read it. "The more I know of you, *Khataum*, the more I find you full of surprises. Still… you carry too many secrets in your heart. Or is it guilt, Master? Something most certainly weighs on you these days."

Matar gave a chuckle that grew to a nervous laugh as if trying to pass off how close his Tashek friend was getting to truths of yesteryear. For all their time together, Zyanthena had never pried and had trusted him implicitly. Now, however, transformed by magic and memories, the warrioress was not letting the past stay buried. "A soldier of Syre has plenty to weigh down his heart, especially when fighting has gone on since long before you were born."

"You know much of the past that is a mystery to those of us who fight today. Your insights can give us answers."

"Give the heir of Sunrise answers, you mean," Matar countered. He shuffled out a letter from a breast pocket. "I've been asked to speak with Rowin Sunrise once you are awake and to bring him 'candid converse' on topics of old. It seems you've told him I could provide insights to his father's past."

"Yes, and now I see you can do the same for me, Master. If you have it in you to humor wayfaring children about their parents."

"As if you feel so slighted, Zyen."

"No, I don't. You're right. But the prince of Sunrise does."

Matar played with the stone in his hand absently. "Many things should stay buried," he began. "Still, for you and what you've lost, Zy'ena, I will try to remember enough to piece things together. Just know that I've left a lot behind. It was easier that way."

The words were intriguing. So the commander really was carrying more in his heart than he let on. Peculiar, it seemed, for a man of such certitude on the field. "I can accept that, *ahnamen.*"

Matar sat back in his chair and stared away to the beauty of the garden. It seemed time he needed to forgive himself for promising to let go of secrets he had held on to for friends and rulers of long ago. Such a decision had to cut him deeply, and she gave him time to grieve. After some time had passed, Matar came back to himself and set the obsidian back before its wielder. By now, his features looked less pensive. "Come now, my Night Fox, I've let you get us so serious and off topic! Certainly, you were trying to make me forget that you've learned an ancient language that none can read but you."

Zyanthena stared at the Crystine man a moment longer and then resigned herself to being led back to the subject she had circumvented. That Matar could not only play the same game but also call her on it made her give into her own laughter at the matter. "Fine, yes, I guess I did. I almost had you there, Master. You must be getting rusty from not having me around for so long, if I can lead you into avenues you're reluctant to trod."

"That is definitely true," Matar agreed. He leaned forward and clasped his hands on the table. "So, how else did you learn to read ancient Syrean, besides from Queen Kestral?"

"A ghost."

"A…" Matar was taken aback. "A ghost?"

"I know Kestral doesn't approve—she never spoke to any even if she could see them. Too unnatural, she says. I, however, found this scholar quite charming, if not a little morbid about book rot and mice infestation. But that's another story. He says he was the officer in charge of keeping inventory on the king's library. You can only imagine his shock to learn Crystalynian was a dead kingdom and that seven others now make up Syre. He ranted about improprieties and the impudence of the younger generations for over a week."

"It seems you've had quite the talk with this fellow."

"All I had was time, thinking ourselves stuck all through the snows until Thaw, so I spent many an hour with the fellow. Only when I could read that book I found on the Second Age did I think another way was possible."

"Using the pillars, you mean."

"Yes. The book has numerous ideas you'd find impossible to create today."

Her commander sat back, still trying to wrap his head around the idea. "To travel in the same way as Ravel without the crystal is…"

"Not exactly the same. You must know your access and destination points and their names. There must be an obelisk at the ending points. Yet such a means to jumps to another place miles away in a breath is sensational—and useful."

"And it saved the lives of imprisoned allies and stopped the takeover of our Crystal by a third party. You've given us a great advantage we would long have lost by Snow Thaw."

"That was my thinking," she agreed, ever the battle tactician. "Once Prince Par Fantill said the princes of Sunrise were missing, I had to check out Rubia and Sunrise at the least."

"And Crystal. Thank you for putting a stop to that problem."

"Rast'enn was an obelisk I knew best—from memories as Zerra. I was there before I even knew what I was doing."

"Still, to have an ally use the excuse of my absence to take over the castle… it's unforgiveable."

"I'm under the impression that it was Prince Jace's idea—his wanting to prove himself by 'conquering more territory for Blue Haven.'"

Matar scoffed at that. "Arrogant upstart. He's a boy getting too big for his britches. I'm definitely having a word with him."

Zyanthena was very amused. "Yes, 'arrogant' does suit him. He was such a joy to lug around while I was out saving the world. I had wanted to leave him at Crystanian all winter—thinking some isolation would be good medicine for that inflated head of his—but Lord Shekmann persuaded me out of the notion."

"Probably best," Matar joked back. "He'd most likely think he owned the palace when you'd come to get him back."

"Oh, ghastly!" They shared a laugh. Just as Zyanthena was going to resume the conversation with, "So, Sealand—" Moon Ember startled them by sitting up and howling.

Commander Matar jumped at the sound. "Holy Stars above!" he whirled in his chair to look at the grey wolf. Finished speaking with her fellows, she blinked back at him innocently.

"Ember was just telling the pack I'm with you. Lord Darshel has awoken vexed that I left without warning again."

"Yes, well… unexpected howls aside, you had best get some food in you, in any case. Why don't we pick up my end over some soup?"

She nodded. "Ember, you can send Darshel to the kitchens."

Moon Ember howled again, and then the trio headed off in search of some sustenance.

Chapter Fifty-Three
§
Revelation

It was late morning, but the knight's staff kept a stew going for any of the residents off-schedule for mealtime. They were acquainted with the Crystine commander and bantered with him gaily while serving up bowls of venison stew with root vegetables and slices of fresh bread. They seemed equally pleased to finally get to meet the "sleeping woman on the second floor," as many a meal had been carried up for her constant guardian.

"That lord was certainly worried about you," one lady said, slipping Zyanthena an apple with a wink. "He'd barely give himself the time of day, using it all to sit at your bedside."

"Yes," Zyanthena had to agree. According to Ember, Lord Darshel had barely eaten or slept and not left their quarters since their arrival, he had been so anxious. "Well, thank you for your care of him and for feeding my wolves," she added at Ember's insistence. "It is appreciated." She gave the staff a bow.

The ladies giggled nervously. "Oh, so polite ye are, m'lady," the woman next to the first tried to beg of Zyanthena's kindness, as she was embarrassed by such praise.

"She's hardly a lady."

The words had the women stopping their chat to turn and find the handsome rogue of their discussion standing behind the desert woman. Lord Shekmann flashed his most charming smile and asked for his own bowl of soup. By the ladies' wide-eyed stares, they had not yet been properly introduced to the dashing lord-governor, who had stayed at an uncharacteristic distance from the womenfolk while Zyanthena had been in her unconscious state. They were practically drooling for the opportunity to get an up-close-and-personal hello.

"Ms. Zy'ena here is a Tashek warrioress and as crude as they come. She lacks the fine airs of ladies above such a station." Of course, the barb was about Zyanthena's leaving him again, but the staff didn't know that. They seemed flummoxed by the lord's smooth speech and smile but harsh words.

"And Lord Shekmann is the epitome of every lady's dream," the Tashek bantered back and made sure to set a piece of bread on his bowl with that daring twinkle in her eye. "These ladies would be grieved to have you dismiss them just because I am here."

"Oh! Oh, no we don't, Your Lordship," the ladies blushed and protested. However, Lord Darshel had gotten the hint. He turned his charm on them and thanked the staff laboriously for their service and assistance over the past week. By the time he finished to go sit with Zyanthena and her commander, all the kitchen ladies were swooning.

"Well, I hope you feel I've repaid them enough for their kindness," he said to Zyanthena as he set his bowl down. "As I'm sure to be swarmed all week."

But the Tashek looked pleased with his performance and their satisfaction. "A Shekmann is made for ladies' eyes or he is not a man. I think they've gotten their money's worth."

Lord Darshel huffed at that. "So cruel, my lady, for mine eyes have turned from all theirs, but yours have yet to stray."

"To all thy fair ladies' misery and yours as well," she sassed back.

The lord-governor just shook his head and turned his attention to their other seatmate. "Commander, good morning."

Matar rose and shared a handshake with the Kavahadian. If he had found their banter odd or too intimate, he didn't comment on it. "Lord Shekmann, I must thank you for your diligence over my Night Fox."

"I promised you no harm would come to her—less what she does to herself, of course. I intend to carry that promise to the end, sir." Compared to the last time the two leaders had met, this greeting seemed to hold mutual respect without any of its former resentments; Commander Matar seemed to trust the Kavahadian's sincerity.

"Well, I still extend my gratitude. Long had she been from my side. I only hope Zy'ena has continued to be of use to your force."

"The rest of my men are with yours at Wynward's Crossing. However, it is thanks to Zy'ena that we survived our time in Rubia and Crystalynian at all."

"As I have heard. Zyanthena was disturbed by the alliance with Southern soldiers and maunstorz. Your discovery has alerted us to problems in Rubia and Sunrise we had yet to be privy to."

"More Zyanthena and Aerrisson's discovery. Without the Tashek scouts, we would not have gotten the information we did."

"How is Re'shaird Aerrisson?" Zyanthena asked, now that his name had come up. They had had no news of him or Grant's forces.

Matar sobered. "Let me tell you of everything with our allies that you've missed."

It took over an hour to speak on everything the commander knew, from King Merretham Maushelik's death to Commander Grant's forces being rescued. He continued further with his own adventure from North Point to Fortress Opal to keep an eye on the activated Serein and the training of Prince Par Fantill. Matar ended with saying that all the main players from the Citadel seemed to be converging to their current location near Cordova—all sparked by Zyanthena's message. "You do not seem to realize the powers you hold yet," he chastised gently.

"Not my will but the Stars," she countered. "You do not find it *fated* that those who could be the eight stone wielders of Syre keep revolving around each other? That is Stars' destiny, not my power. But Syre needs us all coming together. The maunstorz are amassed in two of our kingdoms for certain and have rendered lands in pieces. We are weakened until we find our strength again. We need wielders and Stones of Power. We need Amun and Serein. We especially need Kevel, the Stone of War and creator of leaders. Without them, we are well behind our enemy come Snow Thaw."

"We have you, my Night Fox. And, judging from reports, you are quite proficient with Vauldin."

"Her blacking out notwithstanding," Lord Shekmann countered with a frown cast the desert woman's way. He would know all the times and ways Zyanthena had overdone it with magic.

Brandy eyes flicked across the lord-governor's face and then returned to her meal. "I would still feel more comfortable if there were other stones. Still, I am content to be the maunstorz's bane. Let them hammer away at me while others learn their majiks. I will be their shield."

"Kevel is the stone for shielding."

"But the heir of Sunrise doesn't have Kevel," she replied pointedly. "You wouldn't happen to know where the stone is, *Khataum*?"

Matar shared her stare, not intimidated in the least. "All will be revealed in its own time."

Zyanthena replied with a curse in Keshic.

"Now, now, my Night Fox, such profanities should be left to youthful brutes. You have a reputation to uphold." The commander stood.

Before he left, though, Matar said, "Oh, Zy'ena, now that you're up and about, we should have that private audience with Prince Sunrise. Tonight, perhaps?"

She nodded. "Yes, Master. He has waited long enough for information regarding his father's disappearance."

Matar sighed at her persistence. "If nothing else, I'll give that lad credit for being persistent. You too."

"There's nothing wrong with a son searching for his father."

"Or a daughter hers. However, sometimes answers dredge up a lot of pain."

"But still must be heard."

The Crystine man's mouth drew a hard line. "All that can be said will be, my Night Fox." It was a Tashek's promise, straightforward and allowing for only as much truth as a recipient could endure. "I have some other matters to attend to this afternoon. I will come for you after I am done."

"Very well, Master."

Matar studied his Tashek scout once more before giving a definitive nod. He said a last farewell in polite fashion before turning heel to set his dishes aside and exit the mess hall.

Lord Darshel and Zyanthena took their own leave once Matar had gone. By then, the dining area was becoming full for lunchtime, and it seemed best to not have a pair of wolves around to scare anyone. Upon the lord-governor's insistence, they returned to Zyanthena's quarters so she could "rest." Despite his manners in public, Lord Shekmann was ready for a full lecture on the warrioress's galivanting around without telling him. He looked ready to explode once the door was shut.

"Zy'ena, I swear you wish to be the death of me! When I awoke to find you gone—"

"And not without means of finding me." Zyanthena bobbed her head pointedly to the wolves. "That Ember was gone too should have told you I did not go without escort."

"And if you'd fallen, what good would that have done?" The look she returned had a hint of sardonicism to it. "True, Ember would have done something, but still—"

"But nothing. I can manage walking around without you."

The words seemed to deflate the Kavahadian lord, for his face fell to a dejected frown and he dropped to a seat on the bed. Forlornly, his emerald eyes cast to the side, where his hand fisted the blankets Zyanthena had slept under. "So then, I take it you will go back to your commander now?"

Zyanthena blinked at the question and quick turnaround in their conversation. "And would it make you feel better if I did? Don't you want to return to Kavahad and the people waiting for you?" The Shekmann's jaw clenched along with his hand on the sheets, but he did not reply. "And if not, then are your words spoken out of fear that I will go and leave you to such a choice?"

His gaze lifted at that—so it was more that possibility.

"Darshel." She came across the room from the mirror, where she had been undoing her braided hair. She came near and collected the lord-governor's hand so she could sit down beside him. Drawing in a breath, Zyanthena continued with, "You know me best when it comes to my being wielder of Vauldin. Others… do not know of my recklessness. For that, I would ask if you desire to stay by my side." She squeezed his hand. "I need you, Darshel. I need you to be my tether when I've forgotten the boundaries of this world."

Lord Darshel frowned. "I'm not sure I've been much help on that."

"Are you not? You've cautioned me to use less majik and rely on my own skills as a warrior. Without such words, I would be much worse off."

"You do have a way of throwing caution to the wind."

Zyanthena's soft smile held great affection for the lord-governor. "And who else would know such a thing?"

"I'm sure you could name plenty." Keen eyes stared back, begging to differ. Darshel sighed and ran his other hand over his face. "So you ask me to stay, but do you *want* me to?"

"Hm," she murmured. "Yes, that is the appropriate question."

"And?"

Zyanthena released his hand so she could spin herself to a knee before the Shekmann. She studied his face for many, long breaths before she was compelled to reach up to cup his face. She tilted his head forward until the Tashek could set a gentle kiss on his brow. Lord Darshel's eyelids fluttered closed as he soaked in the feathery-light touch on his skin. "I am willing to admit—*finally*—that I do want you."

Lord Darshel gulped at the confession. He seemed trapped between believing everything was over to hoping that their relationship would change for the better. They were on the precipice of either choice.

Zyanthena continued in the silence he allowed. "Darshel, I want you to stay, and I want you to keep telling me to stop when I've gone too far. If you're willing to be that for me, then I will do the same."

"I don't need you to tell me to pull my shots," he teased, trying to lighten the mood.

She tsked. "Then fill it in with what you want."

"You know what I want." His voice became huskier.

Zyanthena leaned back to take in the Shekmann's features, breathtakingly handsome and aristocratic. Right then, they were carefully crafted into a mask that gave him a more authoritarian look. It was cautious, that countenance. Zyanthena reflexively licked her lips, and his eyes centered there. "Yes… I do know what you want. You've made yourself very clear."

Under her fingertips, the lord-governor's pulse sped up. "Just as you have, Zyen. Two enemies thrown together by fate can still carry the enmity of their people."

"We are neither enemies nor following the ways of our ancestors. Fated, yes—and that carries such a weight."

"So… what does that mean?"

The Tashek rose, pulling the Shekmann with her. "It means I know when it's time to stop running against the current."

"Oh, that's encouraging," he replied sarcastically.

Her lips twitched. "Darshel," she protested, "I am trying here."

He cleared his throat. "I'll behave myself."

That got a smile growing across her beautiful features. "Appreciated." She paused, and Zyanthena's focus centered on the Kavahadian's well-toned chest at her eye level. He really was the greatest male specimen she had ever seen—it was understandable why so many ladies swooned over the Shekmann. "You and I have very different cultural views on such a proposition."

There was a slight growl of frustration at her statement. "Yes. I do know of your people's idea of a paramour. I understand it more now. Exclusivity and respect of each person's involvement, correct?"

She nodded. "And other such values."

"Zy'ena, after you, other women pale in comparison. My thoughts are filled with only you. My desires are for only you. Certainly, you can give me a chance to prove that?"

"Perhaps." It was a Tashek's way of saying *maybe.* "But—" There was a look that came to her eyes, sad and aggrieved. "You know of my history… that with Aerrisson, I mean."

"I do, Zyen, but *I am not him.*" Darshel shifted and put his hands on her shoulders. "I would not do to you as he has done. That I promise you. I'll do whatever you need of me to prove it. He was wrong to not keep his hold on you."

Zyanthena huffed at the phrase, not liking sounding like property. The sound made his hands tighten.

"I mean this, Zy'ena. You should be held and cherished, told every day how amazing you are. You are worth that."

The words had her features softening, but not enough to be totally convinced, so Darshel continued with a grave admission, "Zyen…" His voice became soft and compelling, as did his features. "Zy'ena, I… I've tried *so hard,* from first meeting you, to not have feelings for you. Desire, yes, but *feelings…*" He shook his head and choked on the words. The emotions he was holding in compelled him to turn away. "I've not felt like this for someone before. It's like wanting something… a connection... deeper and more concrete than I've ever had before. There's this *need* for it, just like the body needs breath. Without it… those times I've lost you, when you've fallen unconscious… I feel like there's this knife in my heart and I can't breathe! To think of letting you go… I-I just can't! This—"

"*Saum'mùl,*" Zyanthena interrupted, cutting his next sentence off. Lord Darshel stopped his pacing to look at her. "*Saum'mùl,* the act of 'adoration for another person true and wholly.' That is what you are feeling, Darshel. You would simply call it 'love.'"

It was as if the Shekmann lord had never heard of such a thing; he stood there flabbergasted.

Zyanthena chuckled. "His Lordship is without words."

Instead of replying, Lord Darshel marched back to the desert woman and swept her up into his arms. He paused just a hair's-breadth away from her lips as his emerald eyes cast about her countenance for any sign of dissent. When there was none, he bent her head up toward him and leaned in to capture a kiss. The first was hot and deep, full of his passion. It broke, and the one to follow was soft as he slowed to drink her in. The second kiss left them both lightheaded. "Zyen—"

"There is no more need for words, Darshel. There will be time for that later."

The Shekmann arched back enough to see the Tashek's features more clearly. He looked skeptical. "So that means…?"

"It means that, perhaps, this woman is wanting to know if you really are the lover you claim to be."

"O-oh! Now you've done it, *kyesh*. Just for that, I think I'll deny you the opportunity. Just until you ask me more appropriately."

"I—"

Lord Darshel cut her off by claiming that luscious mouth once more. It was enough to put a halt to any more words of protest. Satisfied, His Lordship pulled back from her and proposed something—almost—as appealing as bedding the ravishing woman: "Let's go to the practice yard and exchange a few blows. You know"—he winked—"just to make sure you've come to with all your senses intact."

"Your Lordship," Zyanthena growled.

He grinned. "Is that a no? Is the great Sheev'arid, *heir* of Crystalynian, and huntress of the North, turning down a chance to trounce my ass with her sword?"

"No." Still, there was a fire alight in her brandy eyes.

"Then take me up on the offer."

"Fine. I will." She turned on her heel and headed for the door. "Last one there has to do as the other orders for a week."

Lord Darshel laughed at the defiance and shared a look with the two alpha wolves who had listened in on their entire conversation. He gave them a grin and wink to show his victory before following the Tashek out to the hallway.

Despite not getting everything he desired of her, the Shekmann lord was happy. The final distance between Zyanthena and himself had been overcome. All that was left was to prove to the Tashek warrioress that she hadn't seen anything yet—and, for once, the Shekmann rogue wasn't thinking about anything beyond but how to make someone else enduringly happy.

§ §

Evening came with a knock to the door. Zyanthena disentangled herself from His Lordship's hold atop the bedspread, where they had both passed out in a companionable heap after their intense workout. She rose and hurried to the door to bid the visitor hello. As the warrioress had hoped, it was Commander Matar, come to collect her. The Crystine cavalryman gave her a once-over assessment of her disheveled clothing and said he would wait for her to be more appropriately attired for a meeting with the prince.

The Tashek turned away to her travel pack and pulled out her fighter's attire, being more comfortable in tunic, leggings, and a practical robe. Zyanthena tied back her wild hair with a beaded leather band and hurried into her boots. She was able to dress and leave without waking the Shekmann and exhausted wolf pack. To Moon Ember and Swift Hunter, her two astute guardians, she said, "I'll be with Prince Rowin of Sunrise. I do not know how long we will be." She finished by stroking their coats, knowing they enjoyed the gesture—though Hunter gruffly denied any pleasure—before taking her leave.

The hallways were quiet as commander and scout made their way to Prince Rowin's apartments. It seemed rude to talk much in the subdued atmosphere, so the two friends said nothing until they reached the prince's door. Before knocking, Matar turned Zyanthena to face him so he could say, "I'll let you take this lead, my Night Fox. You've spoken to the prince and know his desires."

"We spoke for only a short while, but I do know the subject of the matter." She took the bottle of wine her commander handed her. "Can I have your word that you'll tell the prince anything he needs to know?"

"And what makes you think I will know anything?"

"*Khataum.*" Zyanthena gave an exasperated look. "Enough with your secrets. Time for them has come and gone."

"As I said this morning: what can be said will be. Now, can you announce us to the prince?"

The Tashek sighed but turned to the door and set a fist to its surface. A moment later, the door was cracked and Lord Protector Rio Ravesbend's face popped out. "Lord Protector." Zyanthena bowed.

"Zy'ena." Rio grinned and pushed the door open. "My prince has been expecting you. Come, the fire is warm."

They were ushered into a small sitting room, with adjoining bedrooms seen exiting to the sides. Beyond was a bay door, its glass looking out onto the second-story balcony. Though only darkness could be seen without because of the time. Rio took their outer jackets and wine bottle and motioned them to the seating around the fireplace. The two Sunarian princes were already seated, nursing glasses of wine. Commander Matar seemed to balk at the sight of both brothers in attendance, but Zyanthena put a hand to his back and pushed him forward.

"Commander, Zy'ena." Prince Rowin rose to offer his hand. "Thank you for coming."

"Well, my Zyanthena is awake, as you see, so we could finally appeal to your request," Matar began. He took the seat offered to them and accepted the wine poured for him.

"Yes, I heard you had woken." Rowin turned his attention to Zyanthena. "Thank the Stars for that. You had us all worried—and after just saving us, no less!"

"I am sorry for the concern, Highness. I will try to not make a habit of it." Though it was looking more likely to be a common problem.

"After the display you gave," Prince Connel replied, "I think we can overlook a blackout or two. I, at least, am grateful to be saved from more imprisonment."

Zyanthena bowed her head at the praise. "I was not going to let any of you go back there, and I am glad it worked out."

"Worked out it may have," Rowin took over again, "but we have a long way to go to oust the maunstorz from Sunrise and Syre. I—we"—he indicated his brother—"have very little support to counter King Raymond. Even with allies' support, I fear we cannot overthrow the current regime in Sunrise. Now, more than ever, it's imperative for me to find my father and my birthright, the Ruby of Sunrise."

"We've seen the power of these mythical Stones firsthand," Connel continued. "A weapon like that would make the enemy think twice about messing with Sunrise."

It seemed astounding to have the two half-brothers agreeing. Had they not been imprisoned and tortured together, they certainly would never have seen eye-to-eye; however, the combined front was a relief.

"You do know that Kevel should never be seen as *just* a weapon."

Prince Connel began to object, but Rowin stopped him with a wave of his hand. The elder prince answered Commander Matar truthfully. "I know that it is more than just the Stone of War. It was rumored to have given my mother and I our shared abilities of telepathy. Beyond that, however, I know very little of the ruby. Still, I do not doubt that it can save Sunrise."

The Crystine man seemed to take in the royal, as if searching his soul for its integrity. Finally, he shifted and broke the stare shared with the elder Sunrise. "Zy'ena said you have something to show me?"

"Yes, something I got from an informant in Staria." Rowin reached for the handkerchief he had wrapped the gold bracelet in. "Zy'ena assures me it is a vow made by my father to the queen of Crystalynian. I thought it only a code to a letter that went with it." He held out the unwrapped bracelet. Matar stared at the bracelet for a long moment before taking it. As he held it up in the firelight, the commander's callused fingers ran over the etchings on the band. "The vow said my father would be with Princess Arrez, the heir of Crystalynian."

"But fate would be fickle over such a vow. The Stars separated the princess from her guardian."

Prince Rowin was shocked. "So, you know this piece and who owned it?"

"I know it. This bracelet was given away to protect someone."

"Who? The princess?"

"No. The owner's identity."

"My father, King Richard."

"Yes. At the time, the king thought it best to leave his past behind. It would protect all involved: the princess, her guardian family, the king's son, his brother, and the queen… Sylvia. There was too much at stake to leave such a history in the open."

"But—"

"The past is best not dug up, Highness! There's a lot you do not know of that time or of your family. Is it really worth digging through all that, *Prince?*"

"Yes. Yes, it is! If you know something, please, I want to hear it. I need to hear it! Sunrise's fate could rest in finding my father and the answers he knows."

Matar's features were wan. "*That* I doubt." His eyes shifted to Zyanthena. They shared a glance, and she nodded for him to continue. With a final hesitation, Commander Matar set aside the gold bracelet by his forgotten wineglass and reached into a secret pocket in his military jacket. "Just know… you were warned, Highness," he said as he held something aloft.

"Is that…?" The two princes shifted forward to see the red pendant hanging from the cavalry commander's hand. In the firelight, the stone's blood-red facets gleamed with raw potential.

"Yes, this is what you've been searching for: Kevel, the Ruby of Sunrise. I now give it to you… my son."

Acknowledgements

Whew! Book 2 just whipped itself right out of my fingers, like it had a life of its own. I hope all the readers who were anticipating book 2 got your money's worth! The characters and scenes had a hold of me right to the very end. I was excited to get this one out!

Thanks go, as always, to my family who continuously supports me; yes, I know these books take up a lot of space in my mind but thank you for giving me space to create! I love you all! My biggest thanks goes to my friend Kate Chouinard who, sadly, passed away shortly after this book's publication. I will greatly miss you! And take encouragement from your deep enjoyment of this series. Your memory keeps me going.

To the artist through SelfPubBookCovers.com/riafritz who made the cover of this book. Her artwork and design for the wording were what I used for all the Crystal books. Thank you, Ria, for having the balls to correct my designing. You made it look amazing! And lastly, to the authors who have come before who have been a reminder to me that if we all love to write we should share it with the world. Thank you!

Author Bio

Lindsey Cowherd is a Colorado native, acupuncturist, lover of fantasy and cowboy romance books, and an avid natural horsemanship devotee.

Despite being licensed as an acupuncturist since 2010, Lindsey still finds time for the small stuff: writing, watching almost anything Asian on streaming, singing and playing guitar, and especially enjoying time with her horses and dog.

She started writing as a young teen; the *Assassins' Guild* books being among the first full-length novels she ever thought up beyond her normal obsession with horses. Next, was her enthralling and detailed series the *Crystals of Syre*. Turning to a world immersed in martial arts, magic, and "places not of this world" has given her an outlet from everyday living and circumstances out of her control.

In 2019, Lindsey also delved into the genre of cowboy romances.

Connect with Lindsey at www.authorlindseycowherd.com
Also on Facebook, Instagram, Twitter, Good Reads!

www.ingramcontent.com/pod-product-compliance
Lightning Source LLC
LaVergne TN
LVHW040824090826
845145LV00001BA/29

* 9 7 8 1 7 3 4 5 6 9 1 0 0 *